I0656320

Checkmate

Book Seven

Mistress & Master
of
Restraint
Series

Checkmate

Wicked Reads
PO Box 29
Nelson, PA 16940

www.ericachilson.com/wicked-reads

Printed in the United States of America

First Printing, 2017

ISBN-13: 978-0-9979899-6-0
ISBN-10: 0-9979899-6-3

They call me Mrs. Whittenhower…

Readers have experienced the present through the points-of-view of Katya Waters, Dexter Hayes, and Dalton Fontaine. Now it's time to experience the events that took place during those installments through a different pair of eyes– Queen's. Checkmate parallels Restraint, Unleashed, Dexter, and Dalton. Questions will be answered through Regina Regal's perspective, and motives will sharpen into clarity.

Events aren't always as they may seem.

Regina uses self-restraint, when she'd rather go on an enraged rampage across Dominion, New York. She must choose self-preservation, where she surrenders to Maître du Jeu's extortion, rather than get even. Learning her enemy, while doing as they bid, Regina protects all she calls hers, at the cost of her pride and self-respect.

<u>Titles by Erica Chilson</u>

Mistress and Master of Restraint

Restraint
Unleashed
Dexter
Dalton
Queen Omnibus*
Jaded*
Queened*
Checkmate*
King
Faithless
The Hunter
Integrated

-Coming Soon-

Hero

BLENDED

Good Girl
Wildly Wedded Wife
Widow
Wanton
Warped

RUSTY KNOB

Rusty Knob
Tarnished
Stainless
Polished

Four & a half years until the present

Pre-Restraint

Chapter One

Screw it!

Queen sits around for no man, especially Whitt.

Playing pretend by living in denial, I only take the strength from my conversation with Jamie, leaving behind everything else that will completely debilitate me. Dragging in a deep breath, the force filling my lungs so quickly they burn, I let it out in a rush as I escape the Zeitler private room at Restraint.

Conversation flows down the hallway to reach my ears, so I step softly when what I truly want to do is stomp as I march into battle.

I never got a good look at the dungeon since I was blindfolded, then I was in a state of emotional shock. The shock has worn off, taking Jamie's words to heart.

What's done is done. What I do next is all on me.

Taking another page from– *don't go there, Regina* –Jamie's playbook, I linger at the head of the hallway, taking it all in while forming a battle plan before charging forward.

Shithole.

An emotionless wasteland of gray upon gray upon gray, no doubt Ezra's brainchild. The narcissistic, lunatic doctor is probably paying homage to the color of his own eyes. Cold, in both feel and temperature, the dungeon lives up to its name.

Radiating warmth in the cold with his darker skin and amber gaze, Marcus is so full of life, smiling blindingly at something his cousin says, but the humor doesn't reach his eyes– he doesn't belong in such a lifeless environment. I don't know Dexter well, but my impression is that he's a warm person whose tastes run even hotter. Tan and vivacious, Cortez is always the center of attention, and he deserves a better place to shine. Whitt– my sunshine shouldn't even be in here.

The only inhabitants fit for this desolated wasteland are Ezra and Faith, both paler than death, with Ezra's hair and eyes just as pale. Faith's fury runs red hot, and I have a feeling the man had a hand in turning the adorable child into the faithless Syn. There is a balance between the pair, as if they are connected and communicating even with distance and silence separating them.

I was meant to be here, to bring life into this cesspit of self-created and self-inflicted misery.

"Niel was showing off his armpit hair during our '*how to be a megalomaniac*' training yesterday afternoon, and I thought for sure Daniel would shit a brick." Animated, Whitt is telling Ezra a story about my son in a voice filled with pride and affectionate humor.

My gut clenches, twisting in on itself, because not only does Whitt know Niel inside and out, I have a feeling Ezra knows my son almost as well.

Soon– I'll give Whitt anything he wants as long as I get my son back.

Gracing us with a rare smile, Ezra goes from corpse to angel. "You don't know Daniel very well, Pretty Boy." Ezra shakes his head, white hair tumbling to brush along his forehead. "How is that even possible? Daniel is the one who helped tutor me through med school."

Shocked, Whitt gasps, "*My* Daniel?"

"Yes, *your* Daniel." Chuckling, Ezra sounds so much like Cortez, all heads whip in his direction. It's obvious to all, Ezra truly enjoys Whitt's company, almost as a centering force. Collectively, everyone relaxes and takes a deep breath, like Ezra's mood influence theirs. "Pay attention to the man, Whitt. He's a font of endless information, and a very good teacher."

"Daniel is an arctic blast in my home," Whitt mutters, expression glazing over with hurt. "Since it was Niel disrupting our lesson on the stock exchange to count his short-hairs, Daniel indulged him." Handsome face turning away, I can barely make out, "I would have gotten my fingers swatted with a ruler."

"Ah, good ol' Hillbrook punishments, alive and well in Misery Castle." Smiling broadly, Cortez insinuates himself into their conversation. "Does the carpet match the drapes?"

Head thrown back, Whitt is a glorious sight, but the sound of his laughter nearly brings me to my knees– Grant. Nodding his head up and down while laughing, he forces out, "Yes. The carpet is even redder than the drapes, and the dang kid announces every new hair on his body."

"Ah– he's just rubbing it in because you couldn't even grow a partial beard until last spring." Cort is being his usual snarky self.

"Ass," Whitt murmurs while wearing a fond smirk. "Niel will have a full beard in the next two years or so, mark my words."

"And you'll still be baby smooth," Cort taunts while patting Whitt's flushed cheek, causing Ezra to laugh. "I have no room to talk, and neither does he." Cort thrusts a finger in Ezra's direction. "Baby smooth for life."

"Whitney bought Niel a flannel shirt for his last birthday, and Prissy got him a shaving kit." Face a brilliant shade of red, Whitt looks so much like his father, to the point I'm thankful his voice is all his own. "They even managed to get Daniel to call Niel Lumberjack for the day."

Ezra and Cortez clasp their fists above their hearts, looking touched, and it confuses Whitt.

Deciding I've seen enough, I break away from my hidey hole. "The Ezes realize how Daniel meant it in a different way– Jackson," I announce. "Wild and crazy Jack. My son inherited his manliness from both sides of the family, even if Grant was smoother than a baby," I mutter wryly, realizing it doesn't hurt as badly as I thought it would. "No doubt testosterone bleeds from my son's pores."

"Hi!" Whitt chirps, looking beyond embarrassed, either because he was caught gossiping about the family I was excommunicated from, or because an hour ago he ordered me to fuck his friends…

"Um… this is awkward, Reg." Cortez has the decency to be ashamed of himself for earlier. "I– I don't know what to say, or how to say it."

"Bad position for a word-weaver to be," Ezra adds in, but he doesn't look ashamed or apologetic. Just business as usual for Dr. Ezra Holden Zeitler.

I ignore the billion elephants towering over us in the dungeon. "One question– does Daniel tutor Whitney and Prissy, or just you and my son?"

A collective breath is taken, almost as if they all thought I should punish them for my horrific initiation. I should– but I won't. As Jamie said, no one held a gun to our children's heads. I had a choice to stay and participate or leave, and I need to honor my choices' consequences.

I'm not allowed to play the victim or the hypocrite.

"Daniel is an asshole," Whitt snarls, lips curling aggressively to showcase his perfect teeth. The feral expression is at odds on his handsome face. "But he teaches us one-on-one, in groups, and all together. A Whittenhower is a Whittenhower is a Whittenhower. Katie said he had done the same with Grant, her, and Ade."

"And that makes him an asshole, why?" I coax, knowing Daniel is an asshole because he can't help himself, but I don't know where this animosity is coming from.

"Because Niel, Whitney, and Prissy were taught from birth, and Daniel ignored me. I wasn't taught lessons until he needed me to keep Niel focused, that's why."

"Grant didn't want this life for you, Sunshine." I reach for Whitt, but allow my hand to fall to my side. "That's why."

"And why should my dead *brother* get a say in my upbringing?" Whitt spits, causing all of us to jerk back, giving us the emotional equivalent of whiplash.

"About that– it's time to talk." This time when I reach for Whitt, he doesn't allow my indecision. His warm hand wraps around mine, then gives a reassuring clench. "Breakfast? I'm starving."

"I could eat." Whitt nods his head, humming to himself.

Our fellow Masters of Restraint look around at each other with unease, wondering if they are invited, or maybe they feel the discomfort wafting in the air like I do.

"Regina?" Marcus walks toward me slowly, as if waiting for me to faint like a delicate flower after the night I've had. "The rest… the rest of your initiation? My room? You and Whitt?"

"Nope." I pop the P. Eyes narrowing with defiance, I glare Marc's way. "Not happening, and I feel more than insulted that you actually thought it would."

"None of this was of my making," Marcus snarls, amber fire blazing my way. "If you want to disobey, it's not my problem."

"Getting soft, old man?" Ezra's words are light and humorous, but filled with barely suppressed rage. "Just because you've finally found a lover, doesn't mean Regina shouldn't be held to the same standards as the rest of us."

"Standards? Don't you mean warped perversions and cerebral torture?" I murmur, causing Cortez to snort.

"More like mind fucks," my partner-in-crime adds in. "Mixed with literal fucks."

"I didn't say Regina was my lover, did I?" Marc's careless words wound. "If I had, do you honestly think I would have allowed her to suck my cousin's dick and fuck my adopted son?"

"Harsh," Dexter breathes, sounding as pained as I feel. "Regina definitely owned it, though."

Allowing myself a half-second pity party, I close my eyes in a slow blink and release the breath I was holding. By the time I'm drawing in a fresh breath, I pretend I'm not bothered by Marc's dismissive attitude about the past eighteen months we've spent together.

"It's true." Marcus shrugs like it doesn't matter. "I wouldn't pass my lover around like a party favor."

"Judgmental, much?" Cortez jumps to my defense. "I don't know what game you fuckers are playing, but this dungeon is now neck-deep in bullshit. The stench is rank."

"Marcus, Maître du Jeu placed you in charge of Restraint's BDSM chapter, and it's your job to make sure all rules are adhered to. If Whitt and you negotiated for Regina's initiation, then all duties must be met."

"Ezra!" Syn barks loudly, like she's calling a dog to heel. "There is MdJ business, then there is family business–"

"Which is one in the same–"

"Ezra!" Syn stalks across the expanse of the dungeon to grip Ezra's arm, nails biting in. "You made use of Regina's body. I suggest you thank her for that and move on. She's not fucking Whitt in your room this morning."

"Then I'll have Pretty Boy ink in that M on Regina's hand, and we'll be done with this bullshit."

"Even you don't have *that* authority," Syn seethes, and Ezra's skin actually blanches paler than usual. Impressive. I assume either Syn has the authority, or knows who does.

Another puzzle piece slides into place, and the elephants in the room get harder and harder to ignore.

"Fine, *Master*." Ezra wrenches his arm out of Syn's grip. "Judge, Jury, and Executioner, *you* have Whitt ink in Regina's M. Then Marcus can go fuck his lover behind closed doors, just like our precious Grant always did. Let's be realistic. Their love nest is the brownstone, so she's probably fucking Jamie too, which means she knows who he is. Who here doesn't know Alex is Roman Alexander? Regina's bud from the hood? She's probably fucking him too. What about Stanton Green? Is Regina still in contact with Stanton?"

"Cort?" Syn addresses the last person she'd ever speak to. "Is Ez off his meds again?"

Yanking his partner to his side, Cortez looks about ready to pass the hell out. In a low voice, he warns, "Shut the fuck up, Ezra, before Faith kills you."

"Is Regina screwing Stanton too?" Ezra glares my way. "Let's fill the brownstone so Regina can fuck her way through MdJ."

"What?" Marcus and Dexter murmur slowly in unison, more confused than I am. If my brain wasn't spinning its wheels, I'd be launching myself at Ezra and clawing his perfect face to shreds.

"Jesus Christ!" Whitt tries to dislodge his hand from mine, no doubt envisioning wrapping his fingers around Ezra's throat. For a split-second, I almost allow it– I almost help. "Don't speak of Queen like that, Ezra. I thought we were friends."

"Daniel." Ezra releases a resigned sigh. "We'll be friends for life. What's one more fuck in Regina's long list of fucks?"

"Oh, my Lord." I groan, with Syn growling in the background. "I'm a grown fucking woman! A mother of two, and a business owner. I've had sex with two people until tonight, asshole. It's your fault I doubled that number because you can't shit or get off the pot by screwing your own partner."

"Way to take ownership in the state of your own vagina, Regina." Ezra does *not* like me.

"Since you obviously know Roman, I'll be sure to have him lecture you on the perils of slut-shaming, asshole. Your dick has been inside everyone in this room, or theirs inside your ass, except for Whitt. I bet given the chance, you'd bend over and beg him for it. Is that your problem? Are you jealous he's waiting to do me first?" Lips twisted in disgust, "You can have my sloppy seconds."

Whitt has the common decency not to comment on that, but his shudder speaks volumes.

"I'm not jealous." I thought Cortez was the pouting champion, but Ezra… Ezra wins hands down. "Whitt deserves what Whitt wants. We've all had to endure and adhere to ridiculous machinations." Ezra's voice is as cold as ice, and just as sharp. He speaks *at* me, not to me. "Why should Regina be any different?"

"Because anything that happened after the M was inked on my hand had nothing to do with my initiation, and you know it, Ezra." If he can use his asshole voice, then I can use my mom tone. "Because all of you warped motherfuckers may have thought Whitt and I were going to fuck, but Whitt and I knew it wasn't going to happen."

Facial expression twisted with indecision and confusion, Marcus gestures to Whitt. "You sure about that, Regina? All I've heard since young Daniel hit puberty was how you were going to be his first. I concealed your presence in the brownstone because I feared he'd cut my dick off for touching you first. He's under the impression you're Whittenhower property, but has since said I was okay since I was Grant's best friend."

A grumbling rolls through the dungeon, everyone in agreement, including the idiot holding my hand.

"Whitt was trying to humiliate me tonight, not get into my pants," I admit the painful truth.

"What?" Marcus is taken aback. "Regina, I've been going insane with fear and worry for the past two months. This was *not* about humiliation."

"Yeah, it was." Whitt has the balls to admit it. "I know Queen will eventually give in, but I knew it wouldn't be tonight, and I can't believe you all thought it would be. You don't know Regina very well if you thought differently."

"Why?" Ezra and Marcus say in unison, with Cortez looking sad, Syn confused, and Dexter enthralled with the drama.

"Just as Whitt seems to be the only person in this dungeon who truly knows me, I'm the only one who truly gets him. Whitt wanted to humiliate me because I'm a goddamn liar and a hypocrite of the highest order. Which is why I want to speak to Whitt in private, to put it all on the table once and for all, and then to apologize."

Whitt squeezes my hand, while every muscle in his body relaxes at once.

"All I know is if this is how this organization is run, by temper-tantrum-throwing children playacting adults, then it's no wonder this place is a shithole." I tug Whitt's arm, pulling him toward the nearest door. "I'll be back later tonight to get Restraint in working order, membership included."

Chapter Two

Walking hand-in-hand with Whitt is surreal. Neither of us speaks but it feels like the years melt away, like there was never a moment's separation. What is hard to wrap my mind around is how the man walking next to me is nearly the same age Grant was when we were together, looking like a perfect clone to his father. But instead of serenity and solace as we walk in silence, anticipation and veiled aggression flavor the air.

Whitt and Grant are not the same beast, and I'm unsure how to go forth, so I take Jamie's sage advice. The watcher knows us all best.

"Um… Obviously we have no car." I stumble over my words. "Unless you want to jack Ezra's ridiculously expensive SUV."

As we walk out the side door to Restraint and into the damp morning air, the rising sun casts an orange glow on the parking lot. Whitt turns to look at me with his eyebrow raised wryly. "I could call Albert, but…"

Whitt makes me feel uncomfortable, more so than when I was around Jackson and Daniel at the same time. I feel like a lost child again, one who knew nothing of the world, and I'll never learn the knowledge the man at my side possesses. It's the same feeling Marcus elicited in me when we first met. I hope this tension between Whitt and me dissolves quickly, before it gives him the advantage to bulldoze right over me.

"So… we can walk, or do you want to leave everyone stranded?

"Walk it is." Whitt's voice sounds like he holds all of my secrets and finds me cute. "Syn is a detail-oriented person, so I highly doubt she left Ezra's keys in the car. Unless you learned to hotwire in the hood."

"Ha-ha!"

This is so fucking bizarre on so many levels. Jesus Fuck, uncomfortable is an understatement. After fantasizing about our reunion for more than a decade, this is not how I envisioned it.

Feeling many eyes on me, I wonder who is hiding in the shadows. Ezra's Aaron and Roarke? Who watches Faith's back? I have no doubt Ezra and Faith are at the very top of Maître du Jeu's food chain– founders' council, not its BDSM front. Does Jamie have Roman and Kristal haunting our every step? Whitt is with me, so where is Albert, or even Martha? Is that how this enforcer business works?

Add paranoia to my discomfort.

"We could catch a cab and go home." Hope lingers in Whitt's voice, but I'm not ready.

"I can't, Sunshine." My stomach clenches as my feet take me to the sidewalk, with Whitt following at my side. "Daniel… I can't go back there, not after how I left things."

"Hey," Whitt breathes softly. "We need to talk, and I could eat, remember? So let's do breakfast and see where our conversation takes us. Plus, I long ago learned not to speak in public or private with so many listening ears, and I've often wondered how my private words were used against me in conversation when I uttered them when I was alone."

"Yeah, the first time I was in Cort's car, Marcus was listening to our every word, and I didn't know until afterward."

Marcus is one of the most intelligent creatures I've ever met, so I was a bit surprised at how shocked he appeared to be when I explained how easy it was to hijack his surveillance and use it against all of us.

Even our ears have ears, so maybe I'm not being paranoid after all.

"Fucking lovely," Whitt hisses, hand clenching around mine. "There is some bizarre shit going down, even Niel has noticed. We've tried to talk to Daniel about it, but he brings Diane in, and the pair of them tell us to leave it alone."

Testing the waters– always testing the waters… "Are they terrified or resigned when this happens?"

Whitt thinks about this for a block or two, and I have no idea where he's leading me. "Terrified is not an emotion Daniel ever exhibits. But I guess frazzled would be the best way to describe it, which is major for that man."

I mull that terrifying information over. "I doubt Daniel and Diane know exactly what's going on then, just that they know shit is going down like we do."

"I know more than most," Whitt admits, causing my steps to falter.

"You hate me," I blurt out. "I can tell you know the truth."

Pace slowing, Whitt whispers, "Do you ever feel like everyone in your life is betraying you by omission?"

I can barely swallow around the ball of guilt threatening to suffocate me. "Yeah, I do, and that answered my question, didn't it?"

Voice emotionless, "Yeah, it did," Whitt replies without hesitation.

Whispering softly, because to speak louder would make me choke on the words. "I believe you're the only person I know who has never betrayed me, Sunshine. Yet I betrayed you by omission, even if I didn't want to."

Swinging around, suddenly furious, Whitt drops my hand and faces me. I bite back laughter at how the Denny's sign illuminates his blond hair like an angelic halo. Eyes narrowed, muscles taut and coiled for attack, fists clenched, Whitt asks the question I've been asking myself.

"Why did you?"

Body slumping in defeat, "I don't know," flows from my lips like a coward. "Because I'm a mother, and the thought of someone going against my wishes with my children kills me, and I know this firsthand. For that reason alone, I kept Grant's wishes."

"My *father's* wishes?" Whitt challenges me.

"Yes, your father's wishes." Jamie's words ring in my head. *Own it*. "I won't apologize for not telling you when you were little. I was building a life with your father, trying to hold onto my own son with my fingertips, all the while trying to survive. I agreed with Grant's reasons, and I still do, even seeing the formidable young man you've grown to be."

"Why?" Whitt breathes, sounding just as defeated as I feel. "Why didn't he think I deserved *my* legacy? Why don't you think I deserve it?"

"No," I cry, reaching for Whitt. Tugging him roughly into my arms, I hold him, rocking back and forth while I tell the truth. "Your father wanted you to have the life he wasn't allowed to lead. A life of his own choosing."

"Was it because I'm gay?" Whitt sniffles against my neck, rubbing his cheek along my jawline.

"Partially," I admit, and Whitt jerks as if struck. "But not for the reasons you believe. His marriage to Cora, your conception, along with Niel's, it was all forced on Grant, and he didn't want you to live like that. Being gay, it would have made it even more of a nightmare, to be forced to marry, bed, and make children with a woman."

"I could do it." Pulling away, Whitt acts, sounds, and looks like the boy I'd grown to know and love. "I'm stronger than they think."

"I know, but you shouldn't *have* to do it." Hand moving on its own accord to cup his cheek, for a moment, I'm confused by touching and looking at a man who is Grant's doppelganger. It takes me ten seconds of blinking back tears to see Whitt instead of the man I lost.

"What your dad wanted for you, what your grandfathers wanted for you, your grandmother and your aunts and uncle, and what I wanted for you, is for you to grow into your own man, with your own passions, to find a man who will love this person we all love so dearly. *That* is why."

Whitt looks away from me, hiding the tears staining his cheeks, and my hand falls back to my side. "Okay, that makes sense in regard to why Daniel didn't shove his lessons down my throat before Niel and the girls were ready, but I guess it also explains why no one told me Grant was my dad."

Eyes scrunched in confusion, I try to get Whitt to explain. "What are you reasoning out?"

"Over breakfast– c'mon." Whitt grabs for my hand to tug me into Denny's of all places. "I feel eyes on me. There's a man over there by the bench watching us."

As Whitt pulls me into the diner, I check out the guy acting disinterested in us. Blank. Nondescript. Closely cropped brown hair, jeans and a leather jacket, with a cellphone in hand as if he doesn't even notice us. But I've seen him before– often.

"Have you seen Stanton Green recently?" I ask Whitt when we come to stop before the hostess station.

"No, why?" Whitt looks at me crosswise. "That's twice Dominion's lord of the underworld has been brought up, when I hadn't heard his name in ages. The last I remember of him was having forced playdates with Toddler."

"Toddler?" I snort at Whitt's insulting nickname for Binks. "Well, people age, but they tend to still look similar. That guy out there, I've seen him before. I don't know his name, but he was friends with Caleb Green before Stanton's little brother was shipped away to military school."

"That's disturbing. If you're one to keep tabs on people, you should know Caleb joined the Marines and is stationed somewhere playing GI Joe," Whitt murmurs, then turns on the charm for the hostess. "Hello, darling." The dimples pop and the crystalline blue eyes shine, and the fifty-something woman is about to swoon. "Could we have a booth with a front window, but away from the door? Please and thanks."

As Whitt's passenger, I trail behind him and the hostess, who has perfected the art of walking slowly, in case we get lost in the twenty feet from here to there.

"Thank you." Whitt's charm is still turned up to swoon, but if he adds flirting to the mix, I'm out of here.

Eyeing the man who utterly terrifies me, yet makes me want to pull him into my arms and never let him go, I slide into the booth. Flipping the well-used coffee mug over to signal I want some, I wait the hostess out as she lingers and bats her eyelashes at Whitt.

"Dear God," I groan. "There should be a warning label on your forehead." Laughing to myself, I shake my head back and forth. "So, if you haven't seen Stanton, then I guess you haven't seen Binks, either."

"Toddler?" Whitt visibly shudders. "Fuck no."

So much for that segue. Uncomfortable in the extreme, I pretend to look at the menu. "Um… so I should probably tell you–"

"That she's my sister?" Whitt fills in the blanks for me. Voice dry enough to catch fire, "I figured that out when I was six– thanks."

Hands stilling, I drop the menu to the tabletop with a loud clank to my coffee cup. "Why did you wait to confront me?"

"I thought you'd tell me when you were ready, I guess." Whitt's finger goes line-by-line on the menu. "I figured out Grant was my dad because my *sisters* didn't seem to take as much of an interest in me as he did. As my mother, Priscilla always deferred to Grant. If he wasn't my dad, then why would she?"

"PedoBear– holy fuck!" Covering my mouth with the back of my hand, my conversation with Kristal rears its ugly head. Laughing, I decide Kristal is a cunt of the highest order, but one with a warped sense of humor.

"What?" Whitt's eyebrows scrunch together in confusion, but his lips are twisted with amusement. "Grant was not like *that*.

I mean, I always thought Jackson's kissing on the mouth was a bit much, but I think that was to get a rise out of Daniel."

"Nail. Head." We're interrupted by a gobsmacked waitress who can't stop drooling over the young man seated across from me. Whitt, wearing expensive clothing like a second-skin, is a sight to behold in a diner of all places. "All-American Slam with white toast and coffee, please."

"Fit Slam and grapefruit juice," Pretty Boy requests, earning a sigh of pleasure from our waitress.

"For serious?" I volley across the table at the kid as soon as the girl shuffles away. "Fit Slam? Meanwhile, the middle-aged woman is eating enough to feed a horse."

"Middle-aged?" Whitt has the good sense to roll his eyes. "You're only thirty-one, right? Almost thirty-two? You seem to have forgotten that I've seen you naked, and even with being gay, I enjoyed the view." Noticing the flaming blush on my cheeks, he changes the subject before my attitude turns dicey. "As for the caloric mindfulness, Daniel has me on a double course load."

"So much for living your passions," I mumble underneath my breath. "Grant would be pissed." –I refuse to use present tense.

"Well, up until I reached the age of majority, Daniel was my governing authority." Animosity replaced by a softening of his features, Whitt's voice shifts to affectionate. "Double course load: business and art. Half for him, half for me."

Angry at myself, I voice my private thoughts. "I want to hate him, but I can't." Thankfully the waitress passing out our beverages saves me from explaining.

"I spend my days at the university. When I return to Misery Castle, Daniel forces me to sit at his desk with him– the old bastard pretends it's not for my company. Like I'm still in elementary school, he goes over my homework, while trying to override my professors. If the TA teaches one of my classes, Daniel calls up the Dean, saying he's going to pull Whittenhower funding."

"Good times?" I lift my coffee mug and clink Whitt's juice glass in a toast. "Same Daniel, different decade." Voice fond, but still holding a wealth of sadness, "At least you don't have Jackson going livid crazy on your professors with Grant trying to play interference."

"Daniel would embarrass you, too?" Whitt's laughter is a sucker-punch to the throat. All is not lost forever. "I have no life.

School. Daniel. Waiting for the kids to get home from school so Daniel can get his rocks off on teaching us whatever for the night. I sit on my ass, so that's why I avoid fatty foods."

"Jeesh. You're nineteen, Whitt– live a little." I wait a moment in the silence, then coax him to continue. "But don't stop talking. Gimme more."

All the charm Whitt had bestowed on the wait staff was pale in comparison to the high-wattage smile he flashes my way. Mouth drying up, breath hitching, all I can do is stare across the table as he indents his dimples.

"No one but the youngsters give a shit about what I'm doing unless I'm not doing as I was told." The sadness makes a reappearance by lurking in the depths of his eyes. "My favorite part of the week is when Prissy's trainer visits. Gymnastics. God, that guy is hotter than Hades. Straight. My gaydar is faulty, and I mistook his impressive bulge for a '*happy to see me*' showing."

Grinning, I chuckle underneath my breath at the crestfallen expression on our waitress's face as she delivers our breakfast platters. She doesn't even respond to Whitt's, "Thank you, darling."

"So much for Cinderella finding her Prince Charming at Denny's," I tease, doing my damnedest to hold back the laughter trying to escape.

"Prince?" Scoffing, Whitt looks more than mildly insulted. "Try KING, Queen."

"King Whittenhower." I try for teasing again, but it sounds like reality to me, which is terrifying. "So nothing fun besides ogling Prissy's trainer? How are your art classes? Do you tattoo often? How did you end up at Restraint?"

"Teddy– the trainer's name is Teddy. He is the highlight of my week for spank-bank material. Art class is still class, and I'm sick as fuck of formal education because I've been doing it since I was two, which is why I ended up tattooing in the first place. Not as often as I'd like, but Kristal and Syn humor me when I have a new design. Restraint–" Whitt's wicked grin is so wide I fear his lips will split in the center.

"There's a story behind that, I take it." Amazed, I can't look away from Whitt. Just sitting here, listening to him speak, is the highlight of my decade. I'm not even hungry, and I don't care that my food is getting cold.

"Daniel is boring, as you know." Whitt winks at me, the pisspot. "By the time I hit sixteen, I was getting angrier and angrier with every passing day. Daniel is also a weirdo, like he wasn't put off on my being gay. He would hand me books on things I'd rather experience than read." Voice warping until it's a facsimile of his grandfather's, "*You have to be safe, Daniel, and don't have sex with a woman unless you plan on procreating. Condoms are not infallible.*"

In between chuckling, I nosh on a piece of bacon. "*That* is the Daniel I remember."

"Yeah, well… it sucked having him quiz me on how I was feeling and why I was feeling it. Since I've never stopped chasing Ezra around–"

"Obviously," I mutter dramatically for effect.

"Ha-ha! On a whim, I told Daniel I wanted to train with Ezra, and he actually said yes. I was *flooooored*," Whitt draws out. "I ended up with Marcus, but Daniel was still proud of me, saying I was like Jackson." Whitt leans across the table and whispers conspiratorially, "What does that even mean? Jack wasn't gay, was he?"

"I would get so frustrated with Daniel and Jackson, where I'd war with myself over hating and loving them, to the point Grant would feed me juicy bits and pieces to keep me from killing the men. So unless you truly want to know, don't ask."

"Don't be a bitch, Queen." Smiling, Whitt points across the table at me. "I'm trying my damnedest not to be pissed at you, so if you've got the goods, you better produce 'em."

"Don't say I didn't warn you." I make Whitt suffer while I make a sandwich out of bacon, scrambled eggs, and toast. After a few bites, where the poor guy is practically vibrating with anticipation, I put him out of his misery.

"Jackson was a hellraiser in his time. Naughty, bisexual, and without morals, the man's worst nightmare was his heart meds, because they took away the use of his cock."

Empathizing, Whitt grunts in pain.

"Before I go on, I need to know if you know who Grant's father is."

"Jackson? Daniel?" Whitt doesn't even bat an eyelash at my question. "I was the little kid hiding in the draperies. If you don't think I saw Jackson and Priscilla making out, or Jackson hugging Daniel, and Daniel looking confused, like he was being boiled alive… I've asked Daniel more than a hundred times, and I even went to the source– Priscilla. But I always get a different answer each time."

"Really?" My wheels begin spinning again, giving me a migraine. "Grant always assumed it was Jackson. Anyway, since he couldn't get it up, Jackson found more cerebral pursuits."

"BDSM?"

"Yes, and I'm pretty sure Daniel's boiled alive expression was due to the fact that if he had let him, Jackson would have been more than happy to live a life of incest because it was the most perverse thing the dying man could do. As I said, Jackson was a hellraiser, living every moment on the edge, and that's about as far off the edge as one can get. Grant was always thankful Jack's cock didn't work, because he feared him manipulating Daniel in the bedroom."

"Manipulating Daniel?" Whitt sounds incredulous as all get out. "Pfft… yeah, right."

"Daniel is… a complicated man. A scholar thirsting for knowledge to make up for his lack of sex drive, which is why he asked the who/what/where/why/when/how about you being gay. Daniel is incapable of feeling arousal. While he loves Priscilla romantically, it's not sexual. So he's all mixed up in the head, finding affection to be a form of sexuality, which is how Jackson could have abused and manipulated him."

"What?" Whitt's jaw drops. "Come again?"

"Daniel is asexual."

"Dammit!" Whitt's fist hits the edge of the tabletop, never looking or sounding more like Jackson and Daniel. "Now it will be impossible to hate that man."

"I warned you," I remind Whitt, not even bothering to hide my smile at his befuddled reaction. "Grant told me via Jackson how a very bad man got a hold of Daniel when he was a boy, and it fucked him up. He had no sexual urges at all, and can't distinguish between affection and sex, so he doesn't do affection except with Priscilla because she's his wife and that's par for the course."

"Daniel doesn't like sex?" Poor kid looks faintly ill. "At all? I mean, that is life's greatest gift."

"No sex drive. No urge. No looking at a woman or man and getting hard. Daniel sees masturbation as another body function to be performed daily, and sex a duty you do with your wife. But

Grant assured me that Daniel enjoys the act itself, just doesn't have an on-switch to tell him to engage in it."

"The only time Daniel has ever touched me was the one time he slapped me." Whitt's revelation hurts my heart. "But like clockwork, about ten minutes before Niel gets out of school, Daniel is practically vibrating with need. He greets Whitney and Prissy, and looks genuinely happy to see them, but he acts like I have the plague. Niel– I've never wanted to be jealous of the most important person in my life, but when Daniel takes Niel into a huge hug and kisses his forehead, I die a little bit on the inside each time."

"Jesus," I whisper, eyes slipping shut from the pain etched across Whitt's Grant-like features, then realization strikes. "I don't even need to see my son to know he's growing up to look similar to Jackson. So while I find looking at you to be a comfort, I can't imagine how Daniel feels to look at you, or to look in the mirror and see what he's lost."

"Regina," Whitt cries out, and he hardly ever calls me by name. "That makes me feel worse. You suck in the comfort department."

"I wasn't finished." I reach for his hand, both of us forgetting the pretense of eating breakfast. "Jackson was Daniel's safe haven. But more so, the day Jackson died, Daniel and I had a conversation about good versus bad touch, and I taught him how to touch Niel. I had him hold Niel, using it to abate his grief. I gave Daniel permission to touch my son, and he took me at my word, and pushed all of the loneliness he must feel over Jackson and Grant into Niel."

"How am I to continue hating him?" Whitt hangs his head, looking sadder by the second. "The injustice kept me going."

"Hate Daniel on his actions, not for his inaction. As for you looking like Grant, it wasn't until Grant turned twenty-one that Daniel began touching him, realizing he was old enough and big enough to tell him no. Daniel's terrified he'll inadvertently violate one of you. You're not there yet, Whitt. So if you want Daniel's affection, then you have to stop looking at him like he's the Antichrist and just give him a hug."

"I don't… I don't think my balls are big enough yet." Whitt looks down at his hands. "Every day since you left, I've hated Daniel for making you leave. I was hiding in the draperies when Marcus told Daniel, and I was still in the study when you were told."

"That's–" sob lodged in my throat, I nearly suffocate until I choke it out. "That's how you found out your dad died?"

"Yeah, but see…" Whitt closes his eyes, unable to look at me. "You lost Grant that day, and had to give up Niel, but I lost my dad… and *you.* Daniel broke after Adelaide dragged you out. We all lost you both, and he couldn't handle it. He even begged Ade to bring you back, and had Albert looking all over Dominion for you. But you never came back, so I can't forgive Daniel, no matter how fucked up in the head he may be."

"Ade never– Fuck!" I suck in a large amount of air, filling my lungs to bursting, and then let the agony out with my exhalation. "I was in a bad place myself, truly believing Daniel was right about '*a son for a son*', to the point I doubt I would have come back if Ade had asked. Some days, I still think I'm punishing myself. Other days, I feel like I was never enough. For a few seconds a day, I feel like I lost the life I was meant to lead, and I'm just wandering aimlessly."

Whitt's laughter has my eyelids popping open. Quickly drying the tears on my cheeks, I begin to wonder over his sanity.

"I was raised in a motherfucking castle as the throwaway son, watching my *little* brother be treated like a pampered prince. Overlooked, my birthright was torn from me, and I'm so enraged I can barely breathe most days. Whittenhower Estates and all its holdings should have been mine. Jackson to Grant. With Grant's death, Daniel would have been a placeholder until I reached the age of majority. But with all these secrets and lies, my legacy is gone. Take that for aimless wandering."

Breathing through the pain, I slide the plates in front of me out of the way and to the side, then I slump forward with my forearms on the tabletop. "Did you want it in the first place?"

"Yes, goddamnit!" Whitt states with great passion. "We always want what we've been denied, especially when it was ours in the first place. So what if I'm gay? I don't need to make a kid when I can use the Whittenhower prince and princesses as my heirs. Jumping over me wasn't a way to avoid the inevitable, but a slap to the fucking face. Just as it was Jackson's decision to give the reigns to Daniel, it's mine for when Niel gets control."

"You need to ask yourself if you truly want the burden, if you're capable of shouldering it, or if you're just being spiteful because you were denied."

"My roots were torn out of the family tree, Regina. Do you get that? Imagine Curtis and Ella Regal without your name beneath theirs."

"Whitt, I understand that more than you could ever know." Resting my head on my forearms, I speak to the tabletop. "My own son isn't even *in* my family tree."

"Bullshit," Whitt spits. "I'm not going to do the '*who has it worse game*' with you, but I can assure you Niel's real birth certificate is in the safe in the study, and it has yours and Grant's names on it. When I was snooping for it, I found my own birth records instead. So I'm not going to debate whether I want or deserve what's mine, because it's rightfully mine, and that's all there is to say about it."

"Agreed," I mutter in defeat, unable to process all Whitt just said.

"As I said before, Niel is my favorite person on the planet, but it doesn't lessen the hurt that I was somehow deemed unfit at the age of five for my own legacy, while the very thought of a baby yet to be conceived was. It negates all the good I remember from Jackson and Grant, and highlights the cold relationship I have with the man who is legally my father. I just–"

After several long moments, I ask, "What?" assuming Whitt is waiting for me to coax him to continue.

"It's not about greed or power– I just want to prove I'm worthy. Then, when I'm ready, I'll pass the torch to a Whittenhower who is ready and willing, and it doesn't mean it has to be Niel, or my kid if I ever choose to have one. Hell, it could be Ella even. I don't believe in the way our family has been run so far, and that is what I want the most."

"The power to change our lives for the better?" I perk up, feeling the first stirrings of positivity in my belly, the addictive surge of power.

"Yes." Whitt's eyes glint as if succumbing to the same high I'm experiencing. "There is shit going on around us that I don't understand. There are more skeletons in Misery Castle than we have closets. Everything in my world is built on secrets and lies, and I want to tear it down to the very foundation and rebuild it again. But I need help– your help, Queen."

"What's your game plan on the Whittenhower front? Because I can help with some of the secrets and lies and the shit going on around us we don't understand."

"Thank you!" Not only is relief etched across Whitt's features, it's prominent in his voice. "I've been going through life alone, Queen. Other. I see Niel, Whitney, Prissy, and Ella as a group together, and the rest of my family in neat little boxes. But then there is just me. All alone."

Reaching across the table for Whitt's hand, I assuage his fears. "You're not alone anymore, Sunshine, and you never were. I promise."

"The heir to the Whittenhower throne matures at the age of twenty-four. Daniel believes he has another decade to rule from his brother's seat, not realizing I know who I am and where I came from. So that means I have a little over four years to take my legacy back, and I need your help."

"How?"

"I am the unknown heir apparent, and I need to become the guardian of the heir presumptive to ensure the welfare of every Whittenhower, those who are employed by us, and those who rely on us. I can't sit back and allow Daniel to take control, or my baby brother who is not ready by any stretch of the imagination. So I need you to help me become the guardian to my own heirs."

"What?" I slur. "I haven't been schooled in the finer points of primogeniture since I was in utero."

"You said Jackson, Daniel, and Grant bypassed me for your son because they wanted me to have a different sort of life. But what about what Prissy wants? Daniel is already looking at who to betroth to Whitney and Niel, and they've yet to reach fourteen. What about their lives and wants? What if Niel wants to sit in a dark room all day and write anime? Whitney is so serious, she could probably make a better politician than the asshat Daniel and Kent would try to marry her off to. She shouldn't be the first lady of anything, but *the* lady."

"I get that, and I'm on board with helping you so that every one of our family members can be who they should organically evolve into, not who they are predestined to become."

"Good, then I hope you won't tear my head off when you hear the solution."

"Out with it," I demand.

"By law of primogeniture, Jackson had three heirs: Me. Niel. Ella. If anything were to happen to us, the line moves to Daniel as Jackson's only brother. With no sons, the line would fall to Katie, leaving Whitney and Prissy to be the heirs. But that's neither here nor there since I still breathe, and I will fight to my last breath to make sure my brother and sister are healthy."

"Whitt," I warn. "Stop with the foreplay, and spit it out."

"I need to be the guardian of my own heirs, Regina." Eyes darting away, Whitt refuses to look at me. "If they were my children instead of my siblings… I found Niel's birth certificate, and I have it on my person to give back to you, to give you your son back. You are in possession of Ella. Technically Daniel has no hold over Niel, except for the fact that he is his grandfather, and would probably die without him."

"Daniel!" I use Whitt's given name to get him to get to the point.

"There's a method to my madness as to why I said you needed to have sex with me– why I kept guaranteeing you would." Taking a deep breath, Whitt finally drops the bombshell. "Because you'll have to consummate our marriage to make it legal. After we marry, after you allow me to adopt my brother and sister– my heirs –we will be King and Queen of the Whittenhowers, and no one will ever be forced to marry, or make children, or go into a profession that isn't their passion. We need to do this for the greater good of our family."

Heart beating out of my chest, a cold sweat beads along my spine. "Now I understand why Marcus was petrified of you." Slumping forward, I cover my face with my palms. "I… I'm at a loss for words, Whitt."

Leaning over the table, Whitt whispers so softly I have to struggle to hear. "I know Grant loved you, and I know you've been beside yourself with grief and loss. But Grant was far from perfect. He never treated you how you deserved."

"Whitt," I mutter weakly, heart breaking for a billion and one reasons, but mostly for the lie I've told myself for the past eighteen months, only because it hurts less to lie to myself than to accept the truth.

"My father was a coward. If I had been in his position, with you loving me as a man does a woman, I would have married you before God Himself, and every person I've ever come into contact with."

"Grant's not you," I try to remind him.

"I know– thank God. But I am not a coward, and I know you will never marry me as a woman does a man. But it doesn't matter, because I wouldn't be as proud to call you my wife as much as I would be to call myself your husband."

Chapter Three

On the verge of needing Wintercrest, I start talking to myself. "The one person I ever wanted to hear those words from abandoned me in the sickest fashion imaginable, while his son is now the one voicing it instead."

"Queen? Grant didn't abandon you– *he died*."

Insane laughter bubbles up my throat. "I– I can't go there with you, Whitt, not with all this shit hanging between us. I mean, I kept your paternity a secret, and I even know who your siblings are– your actual mother –and I know who the scary monsters are in our lives. I don't deserve you. I'm no better than Grant. A coward. There is a reason I didn't go to Daniel and take my son back. I believed the son for a son. I had a part of Grant through Ella, and I allowed Daniel to keep my son because I knew he needed him– because I wanted you and Niel to grow up as brothers… and I've never admitted that, even to myself, until this very moment."

"Thank you."

Not hearing Whitt, I keep up with my insane rambling. "I believe that's what Grant would have wanted. He purposefully made Niel for Daniel, whether he loved me or not, so I left my son there when Adelaide took me away. I didn't return because I couldn't look you or Niel in the eye, and I feared if I saw either of you, it would kill me not to keep you for myself. So it was easier not to see you or hear about you. Less torture."

"Regina? Didn't you hear me? I said *thank you*. Thank you, because you had no claim to me, so you left my brother behind to keep me centered, to keep Daniel sane. That is not cowardly– that is selfless. I've always known this because Daniel said it as fact, and it's been a comfort for me, hoping my mother did the same instead of just abandoning me."

"What?" I gasp, confusion and shock warring.

"Sometimes Daniel gets sad, and he'll talk about you because he misses you. It was two or three years ago when he told me exactly why you left and never came back, why he stopped trying to get Ade to bring you home. After sixteen years of thinking my mother despised me, this gave me hope– hope you just confirmed. Maybe Gwen didn't throw me away, but just selflessly felt I was where I belonged. Niel and I do belong in Misery Castle– it's ours."

"I–" at a loss, I change the subject. "I've never met your birth mother, but I know Priscilla is the best mother anyone could ever have, even if she's grandmothering instead of mothering. I try to think myself above envy and jealousy, but there is something about Gwendolyn Meyers that makes my blood boil. So as much as I'd like to think the worst of her, her son *should* think the best of her."

Filled with mixed emotions, Whitt stares down at his plate. "I… I've deduced who my siblings are by things Grant did in the past, and by how they treat me in the present. Boyd Spencer was the first. Before Grant even married Cora, Boyd was brought to Misery Castle to see me, and that's how Jackson and Daniel got it into their heads that Grant should marry Cora. Boyd and I didn't get along then, but do now. He's visited since I grew up, under the pretense to talk about him missing his sister– Cora. Who I guess wasn't actually his birth sister, was she?"

"No," I whisper, refusing to meet Whitt's eyes. "Henry adopted Boyd because he wanted a son. Yes, Boyd is your half-brother."

"I don't know him like I should, not like I know Niel. I want to know Boyd, but I'm not ready. Obviously I know about Toddler, because she is the only one Grant made me have playdates with. I have no idea what she's doing or where she even is, and a part of me doesn't care, but a larger part of me does."

"I know where Bianca is if you're curious. After babysitting her, and because she's your sister, I did keep tabs on her. She's a Prima Ballerina in a company in NYC, and was plagued by the founders forcing her into marriage with another founder's son. Do you want to know who your brother-in-law is?"

"I don't want to know–" Old rivalries die hard. When I met Dalton, after Marcus told me the kid's story and I found out he was gay, I looked into him and was shocked to learn his wife is Whitt's Toddler.

This will not end well.

"Then there was Fate, who was moved into Misery Castle to be near you, and then because her father lost their fortune. Only she would spend an afternoon a week, just me and her, and Albert didn't go with us. We'd go to the movies, take walks, go shopping or to museums, and this didn't end after you left. Still, once a week, she tells me about you and Ella and asks about my life."

"Yes, Fate is your half-sister."

"When I was a teenager, Faith– Syn, when she was transitioning into Syn while everyone was looking for Faith – would pop out of nowhere. She's the one who took me to my first tattoo parlor and found me a mentor to teach me. She's the one who I inked my first time, and my second… third… tenth. Last week. We don't talk about anything. Just my tattoo gun marking her flesh for all eternity."

"You're killing me, kid." Hiding my face against my forearm, I ignore the tears streaming down my cheeks.

"I don't know if there are any more siblings running around, but no one else goes out of their way to seek me out and connect with me, so I guess not. I have to drive past my mother's house at least four times a day, but I don't have the balls to pull up to her gate and talk to her."

"Your mother– Grant would get this look in his eye when he spoke of Gwen, likes she's broken, or maybe fragile, yet he gave off the impression she is utterly terrifying. I've never been able to wrap my head around it. She's not maternal from what I gather, but spends time with her children once they come of age and learn who she is. Fate spends countless hours with the woman, and she wants to share their stories with me, but I can't choke down my jealousy and fury long enough to allow it."

"It's kind of gross, but I'm glad you're on my side instead of my mother's." Whitt laughs without humor, and a disgusting thought has what little food I ate curdling in my stomach.

"Does my son feel about me the way you feel about your mother?"

"What, Queen? Oh, my God, no." Whitt reaches out to tug my hand away from my face so he can look at me. "Niel remembers you, loves you, and understands. Between Daniel and me, the kid knows you almost as well as I do. But he knows his place is in Misery Castle, and you don't feel yours is. He sees it as your sacrifice, not as abandonment. We'll find a compromise since you refuse to come home."

"I can't–" I finally admit the truth, while listening to what Whitt isn't saying. Misery Castle was my home, and it wasn't only Grant's loss that was felt. "I can't live there without him…"

"Queen." I hate the pity in Whitt's voice, because it makes me feel like the scum of the earth. "We get it. Daniel said just as much. It would be selfish of us to force you to come home, and he thought about using me and Niel to do it, just so we were comforted by your presence as if nothing had ever changed."

"Everything changed– *everything*." Gut-wrenching sobs try to bubble up my throat, but I swallow them down. "You're plan is flawed, Whitt. If we marry, what if you find someone you want before you turn twenty-four, and then our marriage will be a sacrifice for you to endure."

"I welcome meeting a man who makes me go fucking crazy." Whitt's skin turns a beautiful shade of pink, eyes glittering with delight. "But if he doesn't understand my need to lead my family in a healthy way, then he's not the right man for me. You'll be the only woman I ever marry, Queen. Your children are Whittenhowers, and you deserve the title as well. If, in the future, you or I find someone else we wish to marry, we'll divorce. But not until after I'm twenty-four and have control of everything Whittenhower."

"I have to admit something else." Shame, there is no other word for how I feel in this moment. "I'm in love with Marcus."

Whitt's lips quirk up in the corners, amusement warring with sadness. "I know. He's treated me like a son since birth, Regina. Marcus is a hard man not to love."

Staring at the tabletop, I murmur so quietly I can't even hear myself speak. "And Jamie."

"Oh… wow." Whitt's voice holds no judgment, only surprise. "I thought Ezra was talking out his ass."

"It's not how it sounds, but I can't explain." Clutching my stomach, I'm on the verge of throwing up. "I want to explain, but some secrets are not mine to tell. Shit! I'm going to be sick."

Charging through the diner, I ignore the odd looks patrons toss my way and our hovering waitress looking to swoop in to steal Whitt away from the crazy lady. Thankful the bathroom is unoccupied, I make it to the toilet with nary a second to spare. Retching up my guilt and shame, it's compounded by the fact that I'm clutching a disgusting toilet that's seen more filthy ass than a gay porn star.

"Ugh." I breathe deeply to settle my stomach, only managing to draw in the stench of my own vomit and the pissy, shitty smell of the disgusting bathroom. Bile rises, my gut twists in on itself, but there is nothing left to come back up.

Zombie. I crawl to my knees, then sway across the bathroom to the sink. After washing my hands to disinfect them, I use my palms to cup the metallic tasting water to my mouth. Spit. Rinse. Repeat.

Only wearing jeans, a t-shirt, and a jacket, I'm not like most moms or adult women. With no purse, I don't have the contents of an entire house plus the kitchen sink. The only thing I have is my cellphone.

Bent over the dingy vanity, refusing to meet my own gaze in the broken mirror, I'm dialing the phone before I can stop myself. The ringing stops, then dead silence.

"Tell me what to do, Jamie," I beg, voice rough from the burn of throwing up. "You must have known Whitt's plan, didn't you? What the fuck do I do?"

Hanging up, I slip back to the floor to sit on my heels, with my head in my hands. My cellphone is long forgotten to the sticky linoleum until it whistles sharply to gain my attention.

Jamie: *Do it.*

What? Is he on crack?

Mystified, I don't bother replying.

Jamie: *I've sacrificed everything to secure us because of Maître du Jeu, leaving Daniel in the dark to take care of our family. We can't have another generation, and another, and another of suppressed children turned broken adults. You have no idea the magnitude of destruction MdJ can bring down on our heads. Whitt can stop the cycle. Niel will stop the cycle. YOU have the power to stop the cycle so our children won't have to.*

–Do you have any idea what you're asking of me? Do you understand there is no going back once it's been done? What about you and me? I can't touch you after touching him. I can't love you if I have to marry him. Do you get that? DO YOU?!? It's too much to ask. TOO MUCH!!!

Jamie: *Regina, when you stop playing pretend, it's game over for anything you feel for me. I've known this all along, and I'll deserve it. Your self-respect won't allow you to love me. Your stubbornness will make you loathe me. I'm willing to ignore the truth for as long as you are, then I will repent. It's not that I won't step in and do what needs to be done. It's that I CAN'T. They won't let me. Do you get that, Regina? Do you? Do you get that MdJ knows you know too much?*

–I won't stop digging for answers, and I do understand and respect your loyalty to them.

Jamie: *Loyalty? Try complete and utter terror. If I fuck up AGAIN, Regina, they will take everything I hold dear away from YOU. Back the fuck off. Go home. Misery Castle was built as a fortification to protect its King and Queen from the very forces who built it. Go home!*

–I can't. Not without you.

Jamie: *Okay, fair enough. You're practical and pragmatic. Two of your strongest attributes, the very ones that made me fall in love with you in the first place. If you can't back off, at least protect yourself. More knowledge can be obtained by standing in the shadows and hearing what isn't said, than by your blunt-force-trauma approach.*

–I'll try. But this is your only warning. Not only do I feel like you've abandoned me, ignoring the fact that it's a punch to the gut like our children and I weren't good enough for you, now you're asking this of me. I don't know if I can ever forgive you for this. Ever. What you're asking of me, it's irreversible. Once done, it's done. I'll move on, no matter how much I may yearn for you, need you, love you... To ask this of me means I have to touch Whitt, and I can't touch you afterward. It's too sick to contemplate. Make your choice.

Jamie: *My choice will always be in my children's best interests, just as it will always be for you. I know I'm sacrificing my own happiness, and yours with it. I get it, Regina. I've known. Always known this is how it would play out. If you don't think that I'm not sobbing while wanting to murder everyone in MdJ* *right now, then you've got another think coming. Once again, I have to choose the welfare of everyone BUT me.*

–Last chance– are you sure?

Instinctively knowing his answer before he even sends it, I fall lax against the vanity with my head in my hands. The truth is battering at my psyche, but I'm too much of a coward to let it out, because it will implode my world as I know it. Also, because it's a truth best left unspoken. If I acknowledge it, James Atwater–Jamie –will be exposed, and no doubt that will endanger him once again.

Jamie: *I love you.*

Jamie: *I hope you'll forgive me.*

Jamie: *You're the bravest, most loyal, most loving woman and mother I've ever known.*

Jamie: *I will never stop loving you, no matter how much you loathe and resent me. Nothing I have done was ever to harm you, but done out of the purest of love because I needed to protect you.*

Shit!

–I love you. I hate you. Fuck you!

Jamie: *When you're ready, I'll be waiting for that ass-kicking. I look forward to it. Make me bleed.*

–I'll bleed you.

–This is a mistake– a big fucking mistake. But just like every other fucking mistake I've ever made in my life, I've made them all for you.

Jamie: *And you have Niel, and Ella, and now Whitt because of it.*

–But I don't have YOU!

Jamie: *Echo, you'll always have me. You just have to be silent enough to hear me.*

Chapter Four

Rage and heartbreak simmer in my blood. Loss, shock, and exhaustion have me swaying on my feet. In a fog of disbelief, I wind my way through Denny's knowing Whitt would never leave me.

Ever.

Steps faltering, I have to grip the back of the nearest seat, thankful there isn't a customer sitting in it. Marcus is sitting on my side of the booth, noshing on my bacon while chatting with an animated Whitt. Both men turn to me at once, smiling in welcome.

"I won't even bother asking how you knew where to find us." My voice was meant to sound surly, not as lifeless as death.

"Pretty Boy called me when you ran off to the bathroom to puke up your guts and have a panic attack." Marc's reply has me sliding into the booth next to him. Arm held out in invitation, without shame, I curl to his side with my face pressed against his chest. "But I tried to tell him that you were probably texting Jamie."

"Kill me," I mutter against Marc's shirt, causing his comforting scent to tickle my nostrils.

"I don't get… why Jamie?" Clearly Whitt has never came face-to-face with his own father. Knowing how sneaky the goddamn man is, it doesn't come as much of a surprise.

"I can't do this without releasing the truth–"

"You're not ready, Regina, and we both know it," Marcus warns.

"I hurt so much. I'm so angry, I want to tear things apart. He– he… he told me to do it, and I told him we were through if I did. Then he told me to do it anyway."

"As long as you don't issue me an ultimatum I'll never abide by, I'll take whatever you're willing to give me, and then take what you're not." Marcus shows his true colors, and it's so comforting I laugh. Chuckling with me, he leans down to kiss the tip of my nose.

"Hey! No kissing my wife," Whitt teases, causing me to stiffen in Marc's arms.

"Don't be a little shit, Pretty Boy." The possessive threat in Marc's voice has a shiver reverberating down my spine. "We've been over this for the past few months. Regina will be your wife in name only, and she and I are a packaged deal."

"Yeah, that's why you kept denying it back at Restraint." Whitt's eyes are narrowed with fury– fury in defense of me. Feeling another depth of agony and betrayal, I pull away from Marcus.

"Not counting my bullshit initiation, I've had two rejections and a proposal in one day." Flippant, I pretend my heart isn't fractured into three. "What's a woman to do?"

"A woman would realize Master Ez will become a pestilence should he realize how important she is to me. My son is not mentally stable, and has an odd code of balance, one you don't want to encounter."

"Do you want me to talk to Ezra?" Whitt's voice is hope-filled and helpful– naïve. "He really likes me."

"No!" Marcus and I issue our protest in unison. Marc's attention returns to my breakfast. Grabbing a fork, he stabs into my cold scrambled eggs, and then it disappears into the depths of his mouth.

"We need some ground rules." Marcus takes charge, only speaking when he's done chewing. "I've written up a prenup to protect both of your assets– and by that I mean your asses."

"Am I the only one who finds it hard to believe that my boyfriend is negotiating the terms of my marriage to the young man he's raised as his own son?"

"Yeah, you are." Whitt winks at me– the pisspot. "At least there will be love in our marriage, Queen. I've loved you since I met you."

"Aww…" Marcus croons, voice angry. "Shut the fuck up, Pretty Boy. To answer your question, Regina. No, I'm not good. Just as I wasn't good with what happened at your initiation. The thought of you consummating your marriage makes me want to stab the boy I raised as my own… with this fork."

"Well, just so we're all on the same page, I guess."

Flabbergasted, Whitt gestures to us with his hand. "It's not like you're ever going to marry her, you bastard. So stop acting like that. I'm the only one who respects Regina enough to make her an honest woman before trying to get her into my bed."

"Grow up." Marcus sneers. After one last bite off my plate, he produces a file from beside him on the bench. Flopping the file on the tabletop, he flips it open. "Read it and ignore us," he orders Whitt. "Regina and I need to discuss the personal terms to your marriage agreement."

"Sure." Whitt glows like he just won the lottery, and could give a shit less about what Marcus wants. Contract in hand, he settles against the back of the bench, and begins to read.

Arms enfold me, lips pressing to my ear. "We'll discuss Jamie in private, Regina. Not here. Not now. Not with Whitt. It's between you and me… and Jamie. This marriage has been discussed at length and it's the only option. On paper, that is. But obviously emotionally it is the hardest of choices for all of us to make. Well, not for Whitt. The kid is flying so high he could reach the moon."

"What's going to happen to us?" I murmur against the side of Marc's neck.

"The fact that you're not only speaking to me, but allowing me to comfort you after your initiation, learning I was keeping Whitt from you, and… Jamie. I guess whatever happens to us is in your hands. Because I'm here for *you* right now, not for any other reason."

"Do you think I should do this?"

"Yes," Marcus answers without hesitation. "But this is coming from a man who was betrothed for years before marrying when still a child. So perhaps my vision of reality is skewed. But from a financial and familial standpoint, this is about as secure as secure can get."

"All of this looks good," Whitt announces, dropping the contract on its folder.

Eyes narrowed, Marcus looks pissed. "Did you even read it?"

"I've been under Daniel's tutelage for nineteen years, Marcus. What do you think?" A pen materializes out of nowhere, and then Whitt is signing on the dotted line. "No matter what this says, when we finally divorce, Regina can have anything she wants. We're family. Divorced or not, my ultimate goal in life is to put her back in our home with our family. Nothing will ever change that. *No one*."

"Regina will never go back there without him," Marcus warns, showing he knows me better than I realized.

"Well, that's impossible, now isn't it?" Challenging, almost mocking, in the face of an alpha pissing contest, Whitt proves he can't be fucked with. "Regina's children, grandchildren, great-grandchildren will be inside Misery Castle, and I think that trumps my sperm donor any day."

"Daniel," Marcus cautions, voice tight with rage. "Don't push your luck. Never speak of him so disrespectfully."

"I can wait," Whitt promises while pressing the pen into my hand. "One day soon, Regina will see Grant for who he truly is, and his hold on her will fall away. I'd think you'd be counting the days until then too."

"You are insufferable." Marcus releases a litany of cursing in Hebrew I can't decipher. "If everyone is ready, I'll signal for Judge Nelson to join us."

"Judge Nelson?" I look around Denny's, eyes flitting from table to table. "Your opposition? The man you're trying to usurp?"

"The very one." Marcus turns smug while releasing a devastating laugh. "He owed me one. Not many would be willing to bind a union by only signing the license and walking away."

"In Denny's no less?" Eyes stinging with unshed tears, I want to ask if this is all they think I'm worth.

"Regina?" Marcus tightens his hold on me, while Whitt looks at me with sympathy etched across his face. "I can read your destructive thoughts. Why now? So you don't back out. Why here? Because some day you *will* marry the man of your dreams, and that wedding and the marriage after is the one that will count."

"Marcus doesn't want me to give his future wife a better wedding than he will provide, that's why we're doing it at Denny's."

"Shut up, Daniel," Marcus snaps, but he looks more embarrassed than anything. "None of us knows what the future holds, so let's not make a production out of something that *should* pale in comparison to the real thing."

"What was your marriage to Diane like?" Whitt and I ask at the same time.

Marcus crooks his finger, calling Judge Nelson over, even though I have no idea where the man is sitting. "Same procedure. Same judge. Shadow Haven's living room with only Cortez's mother– Celeste Hunter –Diane's sister– Pearl Hastings –Ezra, Cortez, Divina, and Dexter in attendance. After we signed on the dotted line, the grown women went off by themselves, leaving me, the new husband, to play with the kids because I was still a teenager."

"Still woe-is-me-ing your disastrous marriage, I see." Oh, yeah. Judge Nelson would have been obvious if I'd spotted him in the diner. Tall and imposing, the fifty-year-old man looks exactly like a judge should.

Whitt's biting his lip against a smirk trying to break free across his face. "Nice to see you again, sir." He shoves down to make room for the newcomer in our booth.

"Still whoring around in underground BDSM clubs and having me clean up your messes, I see," is Marc's comeback. "My companions should probably be told what price I paid for this little tête-à-tête."

"Feel free to embarrass me. But know you can't release the information to the public during our campaign, or I'll release what I know about *you*." Judge Nelson smiles at me lasciviously, as if I'm Marc's dirty little secret that will destroy his bid for the judge's seat. "Nice to meet you, Regina Regal– Dominion's richest woman."

"*Person*," I remind Judge Nelson. "Dominion's richest person, whether I have a vagina or a dick, no one has as much money as I do. Money I'm willing to exhaust to get Marcus what he wants– campaign-wise."

Clearly enjoying our exchange, Judge Nelson smiles broadly. "And soon to have the power of Dominion's oldest family to back it up."

"Robert, you're an asshole." Marcus tries and fails to keep the violence out of his voice. "The Whittenhowers and Zeitlers founded Dominion. At. The. Same. Damn. Time."

Clearly they like twisting each other's ball sacks for shits 'n' giggles.

"Yes, Marcus, I'm well aware of that. Perhaps we should give Ms. Regal more options. Like the Holdens, the Meyers, the Fontaines, the Spencers, the Greens, or the Simpsons instead, if you're one to split hairs on power. The lone, married Zeitler and the Whittenhowers are not the only seats of power in our great city."

"But Whittenhower blood flows in my children's veins, Judge Nelson," I remind him to shut this pissing contest down before it erupts into cock measuring. "That's all I give a shit about."

"Lucky families, all vying for your intelligence and money. Fucking one, marrying the other," Judge Nelson mutters dismissively– disrespectfully.

"If you speak of my wife like that one more time, you won't need to worry about what I'll do. Because Regina will find out whatever shit Marcus has on you, only she won't need Marcus to tell her. You forget what earned her those billions. Regina will hack into your network, one she created, I'm sure. Regina will learn all of your secrets, even the ones you lie to yourself about."

Whitt is glorious when he's livid. Even Marcus is staring gape-mouthed at the young man as he takes our presiding judge down like a lion felling a wounded antelope.

"Yeah, I wouldn't piss me off– I've had a bad day." I shift on the bench, utterly and completely in disbelief.

"It's only seven a.m., Ms. Regal. What the hell have you been up to when dawn just broke?"

"No doubt something you would've found titillating, Robert. May I call you Robert?" I don't wait for Judge Nelson to give me permission. "Could we get this show on the road? I have to check-in with my daughter– the one I had to fuck a Whittenhower to create –and then I have more money to make, so I can give it away. Perhaps a nap is in order before I pass the hell out."

"Wow…" Judge Nelson looks between Marcus, Whitt, and me, back and forth for several long moments. "I have no idea what the three of you are up to, but I'm glad I don't know. Perhaps I'll see you seated on the other side of my bench, and I don't mean as the prosecution."

"Do we look worried?" Marcus doesn't even flinch. He reaches over to squeeze my hand around the pen as a reminder.

I quickly sign the prenup, with Marcus and Judge Nelson signing it as witnesses. Without allowing the gravity of what I'm about to do to hit me, I sign the wedding license next.

Swallowing thickly, reality settles as I watch Whitt sign with fresh tears filling his eyes. Tears of victory. Tears of happiness. Tears that will turn to the deepest betrayal when he finally learns the last secret I hold back from him.

Chuckling without humor, Judge Nelson shakes his head back and forth as he signs the license next. "I just… you rich fuckers are bizarre, let me tell you. Word to the wise: don't fuck and you can get an annulment. Your only godsend is the fact you didn't get married in the church, because a Catholic annulment is not a road you want to go down."

"I'm not Catholic," I announce, confused.

"Yeah, but that boy is." Judge Nelson hitches his pen in Whitt's direction. "We go to church together several times a week, in case you're curious as to how we know each other."

"I'm gay," Whitt announces, not confused in the least. "My church has abandoned me, and I only go for Daniel– for Grant."

"If wonders never cease…" The signed license disappears into Judge Nelson's briefcase, and then he rises from the booth. "Congratulations, Mr. and Mrs. Daniel Whittenhower II. You're officially married by The State of New York."

"Holy shit," Whitt and I hiss in unison, while Marcus looks faint.

"Well, as entertaining as this has been…" Without a backward glance, Robert strides through Denny's, avoiding the questioning hostess, but slows enough to check out a waitress's ass.

"Do you have enough dirt on that asshole, or do you want more?" rumbles out my lips as I watch Judge Nelson get our waitress's number– the girl can't be a day over legal.

"Looks like our Cinderella is about to kiss a frog." Whitt watches Robert and the young girl with disgust.

Suddenly finding everything humorous, "I could always use more dirt on everyone," Marcus mutters wryly. "But as Dominion's District Attorney, I suggest you not tell me where you got said information, as I'm legally bound to report it."

"Dully noted," I deadpan. "In my future illegal endeavors, I'll be sure to keep you in the dark."

"You do that," Marcus teases me while taking out his wallet. "The wedding *feast* is on me." After flicking out a few large bills, he tucks the signed prenup into its folder. Raising to his feet, Marcus forces me to join him since I'm on the outside of the bench.

"I don't know what to do next." My voice doesn't accurately portray how utterly lost I feel in the moment. I fear the consequences of my actions, but I'm too numb to care at this point.

"Step one: leave Denny's." Marcus chuckles evilly, and my new husband joins in. "Step two: never come back."

Shuddering, Whitt is glowing with pride. "Unless it's on our anniversary."

"No, not even then, Pretty Boy," Marcus warns. "My gastrointestinal track is wicked pissed at you right now."

"That's so hot how the overeducated use big words to be polite, instead of just saying you're going to have diarrhea."

"Thanks for mortifying me, Regina." Marc settles his hand on the small of my back, effectively ushering me through the diner to the front door, only we walk at a faster clip than the hostess did. "I'm not going to be ill– *yet*."

"Marcus says ill instead of the shits." Whitt taunts, still engaging in their alpha male pissing contest. "Pompous ass."

"Child," Marcus taunts back.

"A child would call it the Hershey squirts." I come to Whitt's defense. "A grown man would call it the shits. A pompous ass would call it being ill."

"I don't want to fight," Marcus whines. "My belly hurts."

"No one forced it down your throat," I remind Marcus as we exit into the chill morning air. I take a deep breath, happy for some bizarre reason I'll never be able to explain.

Right or wrong, at least doing drastic shit makes me feel alive.

I love both of the idiots flanking me. Family. We're family, no matter what. Even secrets, lies, and betrayals will never tear us apart. We just may end up hating each other, but that can never erase the love. Which is why I long for Jamie to witness this ordinary exchange, maybe catch my eye and shake his head and roll his eyes at his son and best friend bantering back and forth. Swat Whitt upside the head for good measure.

Partners in crime.

Shuffling through emotions quicker than a bipolar person struggling with addiction, agony nearly brings me to my knees. "I need a few minutes to myself. Soon. I can't think if people are around me."

"Do you need to go to the brownstone?" Marcus offers as he leads me to the Spyder.

"No– I don't know," I mutter lamely.

"I–" Whitt looks between Marcus, me, and Albert leaning on the door of his Town Car. Whitt is stuck in indecision of where he belongs in the world, just as I am. "I'm going to go home and prepare Niel. I'll give you a few hours to do whatever you need to do, then Niel and I will meet you at your house."

My knees do buckle this time, and only Marc's arm hooking around my waist keeps me from landing on the filthy pavement. Breathing rapidly, nearly hyperventilating, my heart feels like it's going to burst.

Body shaking, "My son. You're going to bring me my son?"

Tears glistening in his crystalline eyes, Whitt knows his words will wound me. "All you ever had to do was ask, Queen. All you had to do was ask… But Niel and I aren't going to wait any longer. You're going to look us in the eye. You're going to spend time with us. Then, you're going to let us go home, knowing you'll see us again. If you don't want to be separated, then you need to swallow your pride and walk past the threshold of Misery Castle– to where you have always belonged."

Without allowing me to react, Whitt slips inside the Town Car, with Albert coming to life. With a fond smile and a nod, "Mr. Zeitler, a pleasure as always. Regina? Don't be a stranger, okay?"

"Okay," I mutter, sounding like a child as Albert slides into his seat.

Lost, I watch as if the miles and years of distance shrink down to nothing. I feel eighteen again. Left on the sidewalk in the shitty part of town, with a dying mother inside my apartment, no money in my pockets, and no food in the cupboards.

Back then, I was nothing but coping mechanisms and survival-instinct. Today, almost fourteen years later, I'm no different– stripped down to my baser form. More animal than human.

"I need silence, and I need someone to hold me." My words vibrate from my shaking lips. "Then I need someone to put me back together again, because I'm going to motherfucking break."

Chapter Five

Time slows yet moves quickly. Nearly despondent, Marcus had to carry me from the car, up to the red door with the cheery gargoyle knocker, where Roman let us in. Knowing what I needed, Marcus carried me to Jamie's bed.

Warm, floating in anti-reality, I have no idea how long I've laid with Jamie curled around my back, his tears streaming down my neck to dampen the collar of my t-shirt. Each drop an apology I can never accept, but the comfort and familiarity he offers is priceless.

The silence.

I needed his silence in order to think.

Thinking? What was I thinking? I hate thinking.

"I wonder if Marcus is ill." My voice sounds rough from disuse but loud in the quiet of Jamie's room. "Hershey Squirts? The shits? Montezuma's revenge?"

A precious gift. Jamie chuckles his monstrous sound, while shaking his head back and forth, and no doubt rolling his eyes at my poor attempt at refusing to be quiet long enough to be able to think.

"I'm not saying this as acknowledgement of you not being anyone but James Atwater… but do you realize you're now my father-in-law?"

Hands curled around my belly, Jamie's fingers bite in, while he makes a noise I can't decipher. Yelping in shock, I nearly come out of my skin when he sinks his teeth into the back of my neck in punishment for being a cunt.

"You'll always be my best friend, no matter what. Even if I hate you, even if I'm married to someone else, even if I'm with Marcus… you'll forever be my rock. The person who comforts, soothes, and anchors me. I'm only telling you this now because I'm feeling raw. But I'll deny this conversation ever took place later on, so I thought you better hear it now, because when I finally deal with this shit, I'll be screaming and tearing your head off instead."

Hands leaving my belly, my chin is tugged to the side until my face turns. Then scarred lips are pressing against mine. The kiss is a tender meeting of lips. An apology.

A goodbye.

He's releasing his hold on me, which is the most gut-wrenching thing of all, because it's not because he doesn't want me. It's because he does.

Our tears mingle as he pulls away. Elegant, thin fingers, hands I know better than my own, cradle my face like it's the most precious thing in all of creation. He's the only man who has ever made me feel beautiful where I believed him. Even though I can't see, I feel his eyes tracking over my features.

…And then it's over, as if it never begun.

Jamie curls back around my body, silent conversation over.

"We *will* talk," I promise, and he places a soft kiss to the back of my neck in affirmation. "I just… I can't admit it because that would mean losing this."

Squeezing me tightly, Jamie wraps himself around me as if he never wants to let go.

"It's not sexual." Even though there is the hardest of erections pressing against my ass, he would never ask. He would never take. He would wait with endless patience until I was willing to give by taking from him instead. "It's not platonic. It's not friendship. It's like… I know if I don't connect with you for years at a time, it won't matter. You'll never judge me. You'll guide me if I'm being stupid."

"It's intimacy, Regina." Marc's voice flows from the darkness when I never heard him enter the room. "True partnership. Something that takes a lifetime to build, but most marriages never achieve. A relationship free of judgement, jealousy, envy, and pride. You allow each other to grow and flourish, without having your own insecurities and selfishness stifle the other."

Jamie stiffens the closer Marc's voice comes, and then his arms turn to steel bands around my torso when Marcus sits on the edge of the bed.

"I won't lie. The connection the two of you share utterly terrifies me. It's what I thought Jamie and I possessed without the sex. But I see how wrong I was, and it's helped me deal and move on from my childhood notions of being in love with Jamie, when what I truly felt was partnership, pure love, and affection."

Marc's hand journeys across our bodies, and Jamie finally thaws. "I won't lie, I'd still do you both if you'd allow it, but that's just a fantasy reserved for the quiet hours in bed with my cock in hand, and that's good enough for me."

"Jesus," I hiss, shocked and annoyed that Marcus is making this moment about him, but at the same time I get it. Marc and I are too much alike not to *get* the other. I'm not ready for the moment, so he's taking the spotlight off me.

"Besides, reality will never live up to fantasy, so why ruin it." Marcus pecks my lips, no doubt sampling Jamie's taste lingering on my skin. "But see, I do know that the reality of Regina in my bed, in my life, and in my heart, is far better than any fantasy I've constructed that involves Jamie and me, and for that, I'll be eternally grateful."

"Do we all get how bizarre my life is right now?" Marcus ignores me, but Jamie laughs because he understands I came here for silence and to severe bonds that are holding me back. Meanwhile, Marcus Zeitler makes it about himself.

"I can hear your thoughts, Regina." A sharp slap reverberates the flesh of my thigh. "I'm trying to say I get it. I. Get. It."

"You get what?"

This time Jamie laughs scarily loud, the hollow sound echoing off the walls.

"I guess Jamie gets *it*."

"You're here to let him go, long enough to do what you need to do with Whitt." Marcus crawls on the bed, facing me, facing Jamie, but he doesn't move to infringe on our connection by insinuating himself in our embrace. "It's what I was doing for two months, fearing you'd never want anything to do with me again."

"Marcus." I sigh heavily. "As we've figured out, I'm great at pushing important matters under the rug so I can go about daily life without slitting my wrists. I enjoy your company, so I'm not going to kick you out of my life. If I'm pissed at you, I'll let you know. It's impossible to truly love someone if you are able remove them from your life without hurting yourself in the process… but you can hate their guts for the stupid shit they pull," I issue as a warning.

"I believe that was for you, Jamie." Marc's laugh is wicked ironic. "Being with you helped me let Jamie go. Now he's my friend all the time. Sometimes the friend I hate. Sometimes the friend I love. Always the friend I pretend isn't gorgeous and makes me hard because he's so ridiculous. But it's no longer an obsession. So I get it. I let him go so I could move on to you, and I enjoy all aspects of our relationship, Regina."

"Except the Whitt part, and the initiation part, and the part where we're not exclusive with any form of commitment."

"Yeah, there is that," Marcus mutters wryly. "And the fact that I occasionally fuck my own wife, like once every few years."

"What?" I gasp in shock, but Jamie is still lax around me, so it's old news to him. "And *now* is when you decide to tell me?"

"Well, being as how we are both now married to other people, people who we are obligated to bed every once and a while, I felt you'd understand and not pass judgment."

"Did you screw Diane while we were together?" Jealousy rears its ugly head. "Shit! Don't answer that. It's none of my business. It's not like I didn't mess around with Jamie, or cheat on him with you, or whatever you call it. Or my bullshit initiation. You're right. I'm officially a goddamn hypocrite."

"Regina is so adorable when she's flustered, isn't she?" Marcus and Jamie share a laugh at my expense. "Her jealousy is so cute, and highly flattering."

"Shut up!" I snap, causing them to laugh harder.

"When we met, it had been about six months since I'd been with Diane, and I didn't touch her until after our last time– maybe two, two and a half weeks ago. So it will be years before it happens again. Maybe we'll even divorce this time. Who knows? But I felt the need to share so we could empathize together. You will fuck Whitt. But not only that, you'll enjoy it, Regina."

"Thanks for being so rude and crude." Mortified, I want the mattress to swallow me. "Especially in Jamie's presence."

"Jamie is sexually enlightened and very adult, as you know by reading his books and fucking him. Did you know he has never fucked anyone but you and the whore cunt who needs to die?"

"Shut up!" I try again to get Marcus to stop, because any mention of Gwen has me acting like Marcus. "Turn off the possessive asshole you transform into. Now I can't distinguish if it's because of Jamie or me. Maybe both. We get it. You're the master of the goddamn universe. So please stop."

"My point hasn't been made, Regina. My mention of Gwen is because we both hate her for the same reasons."

"Does Gwen deserve to die because of it, though?"

"Yes," Marcus mutters flatly, causing both Jamie and me to snort at the ludicrousness. "As for your sexual exploits with the second most handsome man I know… there's too much Daniel in Jamie for him to get upset over you being with Whitt– unlike me, obviously. Jamie will want to examine every angle of Whitt's first time because he'll find it intriguing. Anyway, as I was saying. I get it. Which leads to this moment– here you are… trying to let him go just so you can function being around Whitt without '*slitting your wrists*' as you say."

"I'm just going to admit you get it so you'll stop, even if I don't agree with you, okay?" I turn in Jamie's arms to give Marcus my back. Try as I might, I can't see Jamie's features in the weak light, but somehow he can see me. Fingertips softly flutter against my cheeks, lips, even my eyelids.

White flashes, and I instinctively know Jamie's rolling his eyes at me over Marc's theatrics. I stare in the general vicinity where the white glows, trying to get across that I know Marcus is now punishing me for marrying Whitt, and will continue to do so while loving me. He's fucked up, but clearly so am I.

"It's why I'm able to deal with Whitt, feel proud of him yet want to kick his ass, because nothing compares to this." Marcus reaches down to where my hand is entwined with Jamie's. "But when we're all done playing pretend, when we stop acting as if Grant and Jamie are two separate entities, we'll see if this bond will stand the test of time."

"I'm going to fuck Whitt just to spite you now, Marcus. What do you think about that?" Jamie's proud laughter eclipses Marc's furious response. "You good with sloppy seconds? Especially since I didn't know I was eating from Diane's table."

"Behave, Regina." Knotting his fingers in my hair, Marcus wrenches my head backward. "I could tear your jeans off and fuck you right here and now, and Jamie would not only let me but get off on it. Then I'll send you home to *your* husband. How is that for sloppy seconds?"

The white glow is larger, meaning Jamie is not getting off on Marc's unacceptable behavior, and neither am I. "In another time and place, yes. But Whitt is my husband, not some other asshole, so be mindful of how you decide to insult him."

Done, I wrench my hair out of Marc's grasp, showcasing why I chopped it off in the first place. Then I kiss Jamie goodbye, lingering more for me than to upset Marcus. Both of the men are stunned, to the point they let me crawl from the bed without putting up a fuss.

“You two can bitch at each other like an old married couple, but I’ve got shit to do today and I refuse to put up with your tantrums.”

“Regina?” Marc’s voice is hurt, and I can’t fathom why. Then I get a clue.

“Get some rest, Marcus. I’ll see you tonight at some point. Okay?”

“Okay.” Sounding relieved, he murmurs, “Good.”

Not wanting to leave things negatively, because I have no idea what I’m walking into at home, I decide to let all the shit go.

“I’m going to have Roman drive me home. No doubt he’s going there anyway.” I turn to leave, with my hand on the doorknob. “Lord help me, but I love you both.” Then I leave them without looking back.

Chapter Six

The brownstone feels different the instant my foot hits the top step to go downstairs. The sound of a sport commentator flows up, so I follow it down to find the door to Roman's side of the house, not only unlocked but open.

My world rights itself on its axis. Roman Alexander is exactly who he used to be, only a smarter, more educated, and handsome version of his younger self.

I bite my lip against the smile trying to cross my face. Man cave. *This* is where they live and play, not the other side of the house. It's like Roman robbed an electronics store and kidnapped a leathersmith. A reclining leather sectional faces the world's biggest television– it's at least seventy inches and taking up an entire wall. The football players are life-size, with the ball more so.

Even with his back to me, Roman knows I'm here, just like the old days. "Grab me another beer from the fridge, and get one for yourself, then come on in, Reggie."

Shocked, I do as I'm told, the entire time wearing a goofy grin. Carrying my loot, I make my way back to my old friend, too scared to ask what changed.

"Thanks, Reg." Roman has to extract his hand from the Cool Ranch Doritos bag resting in his lap, but only long enough to pop the cap off his beer. "Sit with me for a bit, then we'll go to your house."

"Okay." I lower myself down slowly, terrified yet exhilarated in the change. The volume on the TV lowers and the closed captioning automatically pops on. Continuing to snack on his chips, drink his beer, and watch two teams battle over a pigskin, all of Roman's attention is actually centered on me.

I begin to sweat.

Ignoring the unsettling sensation, my eyes flick around the man cave, taking it all in. There's an entire bookshelf of James Atwater books, along with some I didn't even know existed, which is startling since I'm the one who runs his website.

Beneath those are half a shelf of Cortez Abernathy titles being bookended by an antique typewriter as decoration.

There are other signs of Jamie's habitation of this space, like the stack of journals and notebooks on the end table, anime graphic novels, and pilfered creations signed with DW II & III on the amateurish covers. But what is most startling is the past and current photographs of everyone we know, including my daughter and me.

Even though this is the first time I've ever entered this space, a part of me has always lingered here as long as Jamie has.

"You and I, Reggie, we're going to be real, like we used to be." Roman allows me to look around, but he plays commentator as I do. "After Edge Publishing was created for Cortez, Edge published the stuff Grant wrote when he was still a kid. As for the BDSM titles, I through IV were written while Grant was with you, with the profits of I through III buying this house."

"I would like to look at them more on another day when I'm feeling better," I whisper softly.

Roman is unrelenting in trying to remove my ignorance and denial. "Every book was dedicated to you." After rolling up his chip bag and placing his empty beer on the coffee table, he gets up and moves to the door. With the flick of his wrist, we're trapped inside the man cave. Then he sits back on the sofa, and turns up the volume.

"Ears– the digital kind." Roman explains, getting out his phone and opening a rudimentary app to do God knows what. "We're good. We only have to worry about Marc's nosy ears, and only those with Whittenhower blood are sneaky enough to go undetected when they walk or hide in the shadows. Since the resident Whittenhower is the one who told me to talk to you…"

"What?" Is anywhere safe anymore?

"Grant was in need of quick cash, and he's a genius, if you didn't already know that. So after the first three books were published, he contacted Olivia Fontaine, gifting her several hundred copies. If his plan had failed, he would have been out of thousands. But she owed him one after what she did to Marcus, and placed the books in her BDSM club."

"Um… not to be rude, or anything, but you're confusing the piss out of me, Roman."

"Olivia Fontaine is the head of the BDSM front of Maître du Jeu. She's *Master*. The first and founding club is her Kink. You've read the books. You know they are more nonfiction than fiction. After placing James Atwater's BDSM books on sale at Kink and passing them out to the ruling master of every club in their organization, the masters and members appreciated Grant's refreshing take on their realities, versus sexualizing and romanticizing BDSM. Sales exploded. There isn't a member of MdJ's global BDSM organization who doesn't own a copy of every book in the series."

"Holy shit," I mutter in appreciation.

"Grant's as self-made as you are, Regina. He's survived without a dime of Whittenhower money, and he donates almost as much as you do to Transcend. Grant *is* Transcend. When he's not writing, he's running the place."

"Are you trying to kill me? I'm sorry, but I can't deal with this yet. There was the Grant who died, and now there is Jamie." Slumping forward, my head hangs in my hands. "I just can't–"

"I know you're angry with me, how you don't understand what's going on, and how you're sticking your nose into things that will end up ruining our lives. I also know you're Grant's only weakness, even if he denies it. The bastard has two cellphones. The one he uses to talk to you is so encrypted, I doubt you could break into it."

"Wait a minute! Then how does Marcus commandeer it?"

"As I just said, Grant is probably smarter than you are," Roman states, not meaning it as an insult. "He has two phones, and he switches his SIM card back and forth. When he answers your questions he should never answer, it's on the Fort Knox phone. I can't crack it, and I bet he deletes your texts off of it. The rest of the time he uses the phone Marcus thinks is the only one in existence, and it has no passcode, and everyday conversations between you and Grant."

"*Jamie*," I stress.

"No, Regina. You and I, as I said, we're not going to play pretend. I won't coddle you like those two idiots upstairs. They say you're not ready, and I disagree. They're being selfish by keeping you to themselves." Roman points at his chest, then mine. "We're real, and I've never called Grant Jamie –and I'm not about to start doing it for you."

"You were…" Breathless, I can't even get the words out because they hurt too much. "Roman, you were *my* friend first," I grit out, emotions causing my voice to warble. "I should have come first with you."

“I was Stanton Green’s first, sweetheart, and you know it.” Roman sighs deeply, then pins me with his turquoise stare. “If Grant hadn’t stolen me because of you, I was destined to be Julio’s enforcer partner because Caleb had a higher calling. But since Grant and Stanton are master and puppet, I was given to Grant.”

“Master and puppet?” I scoff. “Grant is not as weak as he appears.”

“And what gave you the impression I was calling Grant the puppet?” Roman looks at me as if I’m the one who just insulted Grant. “Maître du Jeu is a bloody battlefield, and the founders ally with one another to survive. Everyone sees Grant as a cute, fuzzy kitten, and they leave him alone. Meanwhile, when Grant’s fangs come out, he whispers in Stan’s ear to get shit done.”

“I’m lost.” I fall back against the sofa, curling my feet beneath me. Grabbing for a puffy pillow to hug to my chest, I get a hit of scent that leaves me reeling. I’m in Jamie’s seat, holding his pillow, and I know this without asking.

Turning, Roman is not going to let me out of this room until he says his piece. “I’m a trained therapist, Regina. Addiction. Life skills. While my specialty is not mental illness, I still took the classes and hold the knowledge. There isn’t a cell in my body that can be swayed to let you leave until we’ve got this out. Not as your friend, or as Grant’s enforcer, or as a therapist. I can’t allow you to leave until I know you’ll be okay.”

“I’m fine!” I squeak, totally not fine at all.

“You’ve hated me since I came back into your life. Resented me to the point you won’t look me in the eye. You’ve written me as a villain in your private thoughts, and it’s all bullshit. We both know Kristal is my partner, in more ways than one. My partner for Grant– my partner in bed. So we’re going to start there first.”

“That isn’t where the animosity stems,” I remind Roman. “It’s how you failed to speak to me for over a year while I was in this house. I feel abandoned and rejected.”

“Not. By. Me.” Roman enunciates, teeth gleaming feral in the dim light cast from the TV. “You’re pushing your denial bullshit off onto me, instead of off onto the one person where it belongs. Let’s be honest, you’ve always had an idea… but we’ll play pretend on that front just so we can get through this conversation.”

“Get on with it– this has literally been the worst day of my life.”

"Bullshit," Roman says with affection, then he squeezes my knee. "Grant comes first for me, Regina, and since you come first for him, you come first for me. Kristal comes second, and not romantically."

With tears filling my voice, I ask the one question that's plagued me. "Why did you fuck her on my sofa?"

"Because Kristal comes second for me, and I needed you to help her so she won't destroy our lives. Yet you have not. We all have roles in this life, and her addiction is putting us at risk. I may be an addiction counselor, but I can't help her like you can. So I kept fucking her in your line of sight, knowing it was pissing you the hell off. I kept making sure Kristal would show her true, green colors around you, so you'd have it out with her and take her in hand… yet you have not."

"Fair enough."

"I'm going to start at the beginning, telling you all Grant wants you to know, and then I'm going to order you to back the hell off and leave it alone. You have to promise not to speak to Whitt for his own safety. But you also have to promise me you won't speak to Marcus, because MdJ is terrified of him, and they will hunt you down and take you out if you draw Marcus to their doorsteps."

"I–"

"And don't just agree so you can get the goods, then go tell both Whitt and Marcus. Because that's bullshit, Reggie. The girl I used to know never poked the hornet's nest. She walked down the street with her head down, not seeing the illegal shit going on around her because she had a survival instinct that screamed not to notice what others didn't want her to see. Got it?"

"I think I've played the ostrich for the past decade pretty dang well, don't you?"

"About the wrong shit, sure." Roman squeezes my knee again. "Albert wasn't supposed to explain anything to you, but he did. About the founders. Grant was never supposed to voice *anything* to you, but of course he did– still does. So I'll try to put it into terms you will understand."

"I'm not an idiot," I grumble, offended.

"Never said you were… let's see. Chess! That's perfect. Dominion's founders are our players. Each family has an elder and an heir. Each family has enforcers who have specific jobs. Grant is our chess player, but I'm the hand who moves the pieces while protecting our player. Kristal is our Knight, protecting our King and Queen. With the Bishops protecting the Pawns.

"Bishops and pawns? Who? What the fuck, Roman? We're human beings."

"All the chess pieces but the pawns know they're playing the game. The Knight lives with our Queen and hangs out with our King while he's at Restraint. The Bishops– Albert and Martha – dwell with all of our pawns, keeping them safe and happy, and keeping opposing players and their pieces away."

"Who's the Rook?"

"The heir. Grant doesn't believe in primogeniture, which is a point of contention in MdJ. Technically Whitt would have been our Rook, sitting beside his father with Kristal at his back, but there are extenuating circumstance that made that impossible."

"Like what?"

"Like the fact that you need to keep your piehole shut around your new husband. He's the safest person in the game, and he shouldn't even realize he's been playing since birth. Every family loves him. One elder is his father, one his mother, and several are his siblings. Ezra loves the kid like a baby brother. Then you have Olivia Fontaine and Stanton Green– Bianca's mother-in-law and father, and neither would harm a hair on her brother's head. Which means Grant couldn't play effectively enough to protect us and his allies if Whitt were to be seated next to him. Whitt wouldn't allow offensive or defensive plays against his birth family to keep us safe. It would remove the Whittenhowers right from the game, which was the point in the first place."

"Jesus Christ, is this how you live?"

"Every second of every fucking day, Regina." Exhaustion etches fine lines across Roman's face. "I thought being a mindless drug dealer was hard."

"Who's the fucking Rook, Roman?" Leaning to the side, I get into his face.

"The Rook will be joining the game once he's ready, and he's already been contacted by me, and given this same conversation. The Rook is excited, and that's all you need to know."

"Answer. The. Fucking. Question."

"The Rook has no ties in the game except to Grant, and has the ability to think clearly enough to protect us all."

Fed up, steam should be billowing from my ears. "Roman!"

Staring me dead-to-rights, Roman shows no shame or regret. “The Rook– or as everyone in MdJ calls him, The Prince –will be at your home in four hours to visit with his mother and sister.”

Chapter Seven

I walk home.

Every step is in silence, which means I have to think, which is a curse in and of itself.

I couldn't be around Roman for a second more. The truth was battering at my psyche, and I was three heartbeats away from charging up the staircase and pummeling Jamie to death, then I could actually call him Grant. I wasn't against making Marcus collateral damage either.

Roman understood this, because he stood in front of the staircase with his arms crossed over his chest, and then he let me leave without trying drive me home.

My home is quiet when I arrive, and for a moment I forget what day of the week it is, or how long I've been gone, or where everyone went. But then I remember Ade and Fate took Ella to Binghamton to the circus, and probably Katie and her girls joined them.

I miss Katie. I want to see her, but not as badly as I miss Whitney. I loved Whitney as much as my own son, spending every day of the first few years of their life together. I want to know her as a teenage girl, and I want to meet and learn to love her baby sister.

I even miss Daniel annoying me, and the cute, uncomfortable look he'd get on his face when Priscilla would tease him. I want to receive a mother-hug from Priscilla.

I want my family back.

But I'm too much of a coward to drive to Misery Castle and cross its threshold. Doing my damnedest to blank my mind, I go through the motions of taking a shower and dressing in yoga pants and a t-shirt. Creeping in the edges like Jamie in the shadows, I decide since I have no loud ladies distracting me, I'll work so I can't think.

In one of the tallest buildings in Dominion, across the street from Edge and beside Green, Empowerment stands proudly like a mark against my conscience, nineteen feet taller than

Whittenhower Enterprises. I didn't build it– I bought it when I needed a place of operations. The previous owners were a conglomeration, no doubt several founding families. Fate was the go-between, and I was so stuck in my grief that I didn't ask.

I didn't sell my soul, but I'm now one of those assholes whose status is shown by the height of their building and the zeros in their bank account. The only consolation is the fact that I have thousands of employees, whom I pay outrageously so their families can go to college and make the best of this life and generations to come. The innovated digital devices and apps we create help daily life instead of drain money from its purchasers. Profits go to organizations which help the greater good instead of line the pockets of the truly evil.

I don't go to Empowerment every day because seeing what I've built makes it real. I'm not a woman who ever wanted to be a part of big business, but that's exactly who I am. Even when I do go into work, I dress in street clothes.

I'll forever be Reggie from the block, no matter what I build. No matter how many businesses have been born from Empowerment. No matter how far our reach goes globally. I'll forever be an orphan with no money in my pockets or food in the cupboards, with a powerful brain in my skull as my only means of survival.

As a way to lie to myself, I work from home on small, tedious tasks like I'm a small-time coder in their computer lab cave. It's a comfort, like a warm blanket on a winter's night, or a hug from my daughter when I'm missing Grant and every other Whittenhower in existence so goddamn much my heart is fracturing in half.

I work to cope.

I have a contract with Edge Publishing to create templates for their editors, as well as create websites for any authors they shove my way. The work is monotonous, boring, and about as challenging as taking kindergarten classes.

It's not about money– I'll take all the work I can get to distract myself. My employees get furious with me when I try to do their work for them. The contract with Edge is with Regina Regal, not Empowerment.

Yet again, I lie to myself. Subconsciously I know I took the position with Edge publishing to be closer to James Atwater– to interact with him for the past decade.

I had refused to examine why I made sure James Atwater's website was the best out of all the authors who are signed with Edge Publishing, something Cort pouts about in daily email reminders requesting flashy bells and whistles.

If the idiot would write a good book, he wouldn't need gimmicks on his website. However, Jamie is so popular he has fanfiction dedicated to his works, which he showcases for download amongst his fans, along with a BDSM chatroom hosted on his site.

An email pops up in the middle of my screen, not that I was actually doing anything but staring off into space.

To: regina_regal@empowerment.com
From: author.cortez.abernathy@edgepublishing.com

Regina!

Why doesn't my website have that online poll thingy about which book my fans think is the best? I saw something like it on Facebook, and it bloated the author's ego. Their ego is not allowed to be larger than mine!

The font on Devastation's cover doesn't pop enough. Can you think of something that would look better and send it to my cover artist? Pretty please, with whips and chains, and a thick, juicy cock between your lips...

Love, your favorite author.

P.S. everyone is hosting giveaways. How do I do that?

To: author.cortez.abernathy@edgepublishing.com
From: regina_regal@empowerment.com

CORT!

For the last fucking time. I. AM. NOT. YOUR. BITCH.

Your ego is so big, your head is going to explode.

Those polls are arrogant and readers hate taking them.

You own an entire publishing company. You don't need my advice about anything.

I have better things to do– I'm not your personal web designer, where I drop everything to meet your whims. I employ freelance web designers for your use. If you have a problem, email Monica James, like I've told you a dozen times before. She knows how to get in contact with everyone Edge employs, as well as who I use. You hired her for fuck's sake. Do more than screw her for once.

How in the hell would I know how to host a giveaway, aside from passing out books on the street corner?

Are your books so bad that readers aren't willing to buy them, to the point you can't even give them away for free?

You're not my favorite author, but I love you anyway. Now leave me alone until you issue your next inane request I won't do for you.

Go away.

Sighing heavily, I lean back in my chair and stare out my home office window. Looking at my backyard, I try to remember who and what I wanted to be when I reached thirty and beyond.

Would my parents be proud of this version of Regina Regal?

I don't know– I truly don't.

A cold sweat trickles down my spine from the nape of my neck, and I fear I'm getting hot flashes a decade too soon. Panic. Existential panic. Swallowing it down, I shift my mind away from things best left ignored.

Avoiding my reflection in the half dozen computer screens glaring at me, I close my eyes to the fact that I can still see that eighteen-year-old jaded girl who thought she had the world at the end of her fingertips– the girl who thought she knew it all.

Almost fourteen years later… I'm the age my father was when he died, which means I'm the same age my mother was when she was diagnosed with terminal cancer. I don't think I have an ounce of my mother's strength, nor can I fault her choices now that I understand I know no more now than I did when I was a child.

The only difference is that the addictively fleeting feeling of invincibility has dissolved, leaving behind wisdom that is edged in ignorance. Every step I take is into the unknown. Only now, I actually realize I'm powerless and don't know shit about anything but what I've been taught or learned.

Now every mistake I make is premeditated, because I do know better. Oh, to be young again, when you have a license to be dumb.

"What the–?" Slowly lowing my chair until I'm seated upright, I stare at my bank of monitors. I was only using my laptop to email Cortez, but now an email popped up on every monitor in the network. "That's not from Cort."

With no address, it's not an email, but a message sent directly to me via my own server. Terrified, I rotate in my chair until I'm facing the largest monitor.

***Welcome to the game**, Mrs. Daniel Whittenhower II– formerly known as Regina Regal.*

*This is the only cease and desist warning you will receive. You have been fined **$1,000,000.00**, which has already been taken out of your personal account: Regina Regal via Dominion Bank & Trust. **Acct. #: xxxxxx3572**. The funds were transferred to Judge Robert Nelson's campaign fund, to help aid in his future battle with Marcus Zeitler.*

The loss of your money is not the punishment, as painful as it may be. However, having your name endorsing your lover's opponent was a fitting consequence for seeking information that was not yours to know. As an added extension to this punishment, every dollar you pledge to Marcus Zeitler will be matched in contribution to any opponent he may run against. Met by Maître du Jeu, as well as you, doubling District Attorney Zeitler's opponents' campaign funds.

Regina, that sounds painful, doesn't it?

Oui?

Non?

If you mention Maître du Jeu to Marcus Zeitler or Daniel Whittenhower II in any capacity, other than about our offshoot BDSM organization, you will be fined.

The entirety of your personal accounts AND Empowerment's accounts.

No fear on being late on your payments or having to cut such a large check. I will simply route your monies into Maître du Jeu's accounts.

Your contact in Maître du Jeu is Ezra Holden Zeitler. You are not to speak with anyone about our organization except for your contact. I suggest you do as you're told from here on out, Regina, because the monetary penalty won't be as severe as the emotional, mental, and physical consequences you and those you hold dear will endure. Your uncomfortable initiation from the wee hours of this morning will look like child's play.

This is your only warning.

***The Spencer. Boyd Spencer– Maître voleur extraordinaire**.*

"What?" I lean forward, reading the message several times, and it still doesn't sink in. "No," I issue in denial with my fingers poised over the keyboard. In less than a second, I'm logged into Dominion Bank & Trust. "Jesus Christ. How?"

Falling backward, my chair reclines, tilting me to the point I almost upset my balance. Confused, my eyes flick across my bank of monitors. "Boyd hacked the bank, or had someone hack the bank… but he somehow breached my firewalls to pop that message up in my network."

How?

For long minutes, my mind can't register the transfer of a million dollars out of my bank account into that jailbait fishing asshole's account. "Who do I kill first? Boyd had the audacity to call himself Master Thief Extraordinaire. Asshole."

I know Cortez has a huge ego, but maybe I do as well. I thought I was the biggest fish in Dominion– the richest, smartest, most powerful fish, gender be damned. But someone out there is better at my job than I am.

Moving quickly, "Jesus Christ," I hiss while lunging from my chair to the bedroom just off my office, which was converted to house my network server. It takes me a good ten minutes to disconnect all of the power sources and backup power sources, and remove it from the net.

"I don't know what to do!" Mouth agape, I stare in defeat. "I'm tired, and hungry, and stressed, and I've just been hacked, and a thief just stole a million dollars out of my pocket and could easily take it all, and only a disturbing sense of honor keeps him from doing so… and I got married today. I fucking got married today. My. God. I. Got. Married. Today."

Hyperventilating, I stagger to the kitchen. "My new brother-in-law just stole a million dollars from my federally secured bank account." Slumping into a stool at the kitchen island, I stare down at my hands. "If Boyd can do that, God help us all."

Lost.

My fingers wrap so tightly around my cellphone, my nails dig into the flesh of my palm. Hard. Harder. Harder still, I sink my fingernails into my palm. Blood wells up to clear my thoughts. Eyes popping open wide, no doubt resolve and fury are written across my face.

Whistle.

Joints stiff from the force I'm exacting, I unwrap my hand from around the vibrating device. Blood mars the touchscreen as I unlock it.

Jamie: *Are you okay?*

Huffing a maniacal laugh, I look around like a criminal, wondering where the cameras are stashed. Then I wonder if I'm being paranoid or realistic.

Jamie: *Boyd just showed up to gloat.*

Of course he did.

Jamie: *I tried to warn you. I tried to have Roman warn you. Then I warned you again and again. I was going to marry you, Regina. I was going to raise our children in the brownstone. I was going to fall asleep next to you every single night, and wake up beside you when the dawn broke. The ring and the proposal, that was real. My death was also real. Henry and Cora's deaths were real, and I won't burden you with the knowledge as how that came to be. MdJ demanded I marry Cora, and no matter how many times I petitioned for a divorce, they wouldn't allow it.*

Jamie: *They died, and I didn't. My punishment was losing you and our children. A self-inflicted punishment, because with an elder and heir dead, what would they do to someone who wasn't of our bloodlines? I became James Atwater to protect you. I let you go, and you fucking came back!*

I'm dialing while my phone is vibrating with new incoming text messages. "I get it. Okay? I fucking get it. You don't have to rub it in." Listless, I drop my phone to the countertop. Slumping forward, I rest my cheek in my upraised palm.

Whistle.

Jamie: *No matter what, Whitt is safe. Whether he knows the truth or not, my son is the safest person in Dominion. I thought if you were his wife, you'd be safe by extension. Regina, I'm so fucking sorry that I was wrong. Dead wrong.*

Jamie: *You can't tell Marcus– you cannot! Dexter knows, okay? Dexter knows, but we allow him to playact the ostrich with his head in the sand as long as he does as he's told. Just as you are now going to be treated, Dexter is treated. I am Dexter's contact. When MdJ makes a vote, and Dexter is our means to an end, I have to tell him to do it. In the beginning, after we lost his parents, he didn't want to participate. I know Marcus has told you about some of the torture he endured at the hands of the Fontaines... that was Dexter's punishment, with Spyder as the payment.*

Jamie: *Do you get it now, Regina?*

Jamie: *When Dominion was founded, it was Whittenhower, Holden, and Zeitler, with the others as laborers, indentured servants, and slaves. The Meyers bloodline has wanted to overpower all others to produce a* ***game over*** *since the inception of Dominion.*

Jamie: *Revenge.*

Jamie: *Just as Whitt being my heir would make the game unplayable for the Whittenhowers, the Fontaines wanted to have the Zeitler heir for power. Olivia wants to place her daughter in the empty Zeitler seat. Who would fight their own children? Their parents? Their siblings? It's why Gwen's grandfather and father forced her to seed every bloodline. Every bloodline has a Meyers save Zeitler and Fontaine. But Gwen has been working on it, and the others have been unwittingly playing into her hands.*

Jamie: *Meyers: Gwen Meyers.*

Jamie: *Whittenhower: Daniel Whittenhower II. Youngest son of Gwen Meyers.*

Jamie: *Holden: Zane Zeitler. Grandson of Gwen Meyers.*

Jamie: *Spencer: Boyd Spencer. Eldest son of Gwen Meyers.*

Jamie: *Simpson: Fate Simpson. Eldest daughter of Gwen Meyers.*

Jamie: *Green: Bianca Green. Youngest daughter of Gwen Meyers.*

Jamie: *Fontaine: Dalton Fontaine, husband of Bianca Green, son-in-law to Gwen Meyers. Non-player, refusing to procreate to forge the bloodlines.*

Jamie: *Zeitler: Dexter Hayes. Childless. Marcus Zeitler. Spyder Zeitler, daughter of Olivia Fontaine. Destined to marry into the endless supply of Meyers' blood.*

Jamie: *Maître du Jeu: Literally our Master of the Game– Faith Simpson, middle daughter of Gwen Meyers.*

Jamie: *We– I!– need this to happen. I want off this horrific carnival ride from Hell. Whitt cannot play the game at my side, which is why I will be bringing Niel into MdJ in the next few years. As it is now, we can barely torture one another, which makes the attacks that much more pointed and vicious. But one day, when the Meyers' blood has finally infected every line, there will be no one left to attack. If not my generation, then our children's generation.*

Jamie: *I can't take it anymore, Regina. For this very reason you can say no more to Marcus. If Marcus knew, he'd destroy the very structure MdJ has constructed. They realize this, and it has them running scared. A council of scared, sociopathic founders is not a pretty sight to behold.*

Jamie: *You have to do as Ezra says, but you have to stay the hell away from him. Ezra is the worst of the worst, because he's not sane. Ezra breeds victims. Whereas the rest are very sane, they have absolutely no moral compass. They– we spent our entire childhoods being tortured by our bloodline's opponents, then we were warped and forced to fuck for the sake of breeding Meyers blood, which has turned into spending our entire adulthoods making their children pay for their evil deeds.*

Jamie: *I nearly suffocate on the things I've seen and done in the name of survival. That is why I couldn't look you in the eye, Regina. You can hate me when you finally come to terms with* *who I am and with what I've done, because I deserve it. I don't deserve you, and I never have.*

Numb, I redial and press speakerphone. "What am I supposed to do? What if Ezra asks impossible things of me? How exactly do you plan on finishing this bullshit soon? I just… I can't. Who knows? Do you ever plan on being you again?"

Thumb jabbing end, all I can do is wait for his reply. Listless, I slip off the stool, cellphone in hand, and drag myself to the sofa. It's an eternity as I wait for the whistle signaling Jamie's reply.

Jamie: *What are you supposed to do? Obey Ezra. What if Ezra asks something impossible of you? Welcome to my world, Regina. Do it. Regret it. Let me get even because of it. That is how it is, and how it will always be, until the evil game meets its conclusion.*

Jamie: *How will it meet its conclusion? Stanton sacrificed his own daughter to protect us all, only to learn Dalton is gay. Push Whitt at Dalton. Push him hard. Dalton is intelligent, gorgeous, and my son's perfect balance. Hope and pray they grow together organically, because Faith, Stanton, and I are willing to force it if it doesn't happen in due time. Game over = a child created from Dalton and Bianca and Whitt and Spyder. A pair of partners who can't bear each other's children, will undoubtedly look to their female counterpart for surrogacy.*

Jamie: *When I play, Regina, I play the long game. In this, you will help me. I promise I will reveal myself prior to our Whittenhower King and Queen taking their throne in Misery Castle. You and I, we will go home together.*

Jamie: *From here on out, you need to concentrate on securing your financial institutions and completely reconfiguring your network server. I suggest debugging your home on a daily basis, perhaps twice per day if you have anyone other than Whittenhowers in your space, Fate not included. Put all of your energy into rebuilding your relationship with Whitt and Niel. No matter what happens with MdJ, whether we end up at each other's throats, we are family. Take care of our family first, make the sacrifices necessary, and try to enjoy the small things in life. Take nothing for granted. Shed your stubbornness, hypocrisy,* *and pride, because those attributes will put a target on your back, and make you so arrogant you won't think they will be able to get to you. Always remember Boyd's first lesson. They can get you anywhere, everywhere, and even trump you at your own game.*

Jamie: *Echo. Echo. Your life always parallels mine in delay. Good luck being in love with someone whom you can't confide in, in fear they will be harmed. When the time comes, when you decide to loathe me, think of how you feel looking Marcus in the eye, making love to him, and trying to build a life with the man, all the while lying by omission. Remember this when dealing with Fate and Kris as well. You are strong enough, good enough, deserving enough, and powerful enough to survive* Maître *du Jeu. No matter what happens, I love you, Echo.*

Chapter Eight

"Mom!" Ella's voice jars me out of my sedation. Trying and failing to appear animated, my arms open automatically to enclose my baby girl. Squeezing tightly, I bury my face against her downy hair, praying my tears don't seep through to dampen her skin.

"I've missed you so, so much." My daughter is a big girl, but I pull her into my lap as I sit on the sofa. If I could, I would absorb her back into my body to protect her. "Did you have fun? Did Aunt Kate and the girls go with you?"

It's sick, but I pretend I know what's going on in my daughter's life. Even though Ade never once mentioned her sister and nieces, I can trust that she would go behind my back and do such a thing.

"Yeah!" Voice pitched high with excitement, Ella pulls away to retrieve her cellphone from her tiny, girly purse. I've never used a purse in my life, but once a ten-year-old starts her monthly visitor, you have to find a solution to the annoyance.

More girl that I'll ever be, the pink designer handbag is filled with cosmetics, lady bit protection, and her purple, glittery cellphone. Peering inside as she fishes around, I notice a few candy bars, a Happy Meal My Little Pony Pegasus, and a Nintendo DS.

"Is there a kitchen sink in there somewhere, too?" I tease, pretending my world didn't ignite at my feet since the early morning hours.

"Mom–" Ella's laugh is purely Grant. The glorious sound will only be amplified when I finally get us all together again. I won't have to wait long before I get to hear Ella and Whitt laughing together. "So my favorite part of the circus was the elephants, but Prissy was terrified."

Devious as all get out, my daughter scrolls through her pictures until she finds one of a teeny, tiny girl screaming her head off. No more than seventy pounds and only four feet tall, the ten-year-old has bright, crystalline eyes and a blonde ponytail.

Priscilla Preston is all Whittenhower.

"Prissy's gorgeous," I murmur underneath my breath, pretending tears aren't staining my cheeks. "Silly girl. I hear she loves gymnastics. Did she freak for the acrobats?"

Eyes glinting with pure pleasure, Ella slides off my lap to sit on the sofa, giving me a view of Fate and Ade. Fate looks terrified, while Ade looks confused. "Prissy couldn't see– ya know, 'cuz she's so short. So she stood up the entire time the acrobats were in the ring." Snickering evilly, "But people yelled at her."

"So what'd she do?"

"Look–" Ella thrusts her phone into my hand. On the screen is a young woman with dirty blond hair with brown highlights. There's movement to the image because her ponytail is whipping in an arc. Standing, facing the crowd instead of the ring, Whitney's face is twisted with ferocity as she points in some grown man's face.

Whitney is thirteen and a half going on forty. Now I understand Whitt's comment about how she shouldn't be some politician's first lady, because she'll be *the* lady.

I don't even have to ask, I just know Whitney Preston is the type of person who will protest against injustice and stand up for what she believes in. A female Daniel made better by the gift and drive of passion.

"So why did you love the elephants so much?" Being snoopy, I continue to scroll through the images, releasing genuine laughter. "I'll be sure to grab some of these and have them printed. Fate eating a mountain of cotton candy needs to be commemorated. Ade, this one of you bartering with the dude selling glow stick necklaces is really good. Ah… Kate looks nothing like I would have ever imagined."

"How so?" Ella retrieves her phone, tilting her head sideways to get a good look at her aunt. Hair cut into a reasonable bob, with a flower patterned blouse and khakis, Katie is at least a size twenty, when I expected her to be skin and bones, bleached, augmented, and botoxed to look good on camera during campaigns.

"Kate looks like a mom instead of the plastic doll Reg thought Kent would make her out to be." Ade's voice is stiff, thinking I was judging her older sister and brother-in-law.

"Smarmy politician or not, their love for each other is real, Reg. Good or bad, they deal."

"I don't get it?" Ella's squinting, trying to see what's wrong.

"Baby girl?" I reach forward to thumb her phone to sleep. "Nothing's wrong with Aunt Katie. She's perfect, and I'm proud of her for not bending to societal standards and misogyny."

"But what if Aunt Kate wanted to look like a plastic doll?" Ella's still staring at me, and I can hear her father calling me out for being a hypocrite. I may not have seen the expression on Jamie's face when he typed those texts, but I don't need to because it's written across my daughter's features.

"Nothing– nothing at all." I shrug. "It's only wrong if a woman feels pressured to look a certain way to fit in, or because she thinks that's the only way you can find or keep the love of a man. If Katie wanted to look like a plastic doll, more power to her. If she wants to look as nature sees fit, good for her. The point is to own it because it's what you want, not what someone expects from you."

I know I always come off as preachy, but my daughter is destined to be a size eighteen, maybe bigger. A beautiful woman who will forever hear, *if only you were thinner, you'd be so pretty*. At ten, twenty, thirty, forty, I want my daughter to accept herself as she is, and realize size and beauty have nothing to do with being a good, productive human being. If she wants to make a change because she doesn't feel comfortable in her own skin, it should be because of how she feels about herself, not because of how others make her feel.

Ella's big because of how she is structured and built, not because of the candy stash in her purse. We exercise and eat healthy, and nothing besides starvation and surgery is going to change it. She's a ten-year-old in a grown woman's body, surrounded by other ten-year-old bullies and older kids who will see her as prey.

"Why did you like the elephants so much?" I tug a strand of Ella's hair to get her undivided attention.

Pink cheeks blushing red, Ella tries to put her thoughts into words. "Because they look so sad, like they're trapped. Since they can't roam in Africa or wherever, I wanted them to know I appreciate their captivity."

"Damn," Ade breathes out as she flees the living room. "I gotta pee. I'm not getting sappy in my old age, dammit!" Floats down from the hallway. "I just drove three hours with a stop at Starbucks."

"Does she really have to pee?" I mutter in Fate's direction.

Smirking, Fate looks like she knows a secret. "Yeah, Ade bitched the whole way home, refusing to use any rest stops."

"Diva," Ella, Fate, and I say in unison. Then I add, "Go get changed into your comfy clothes. Our highly anticipated visitors are due any minute."

"Visitors? Oh, I *love* visitors!" Ella hops up, not even bothering to ask who is coming over, chattering to herself the whole way to her bedroom.

"I have absolutely no idea how the two most introverted people I know had an extroverted child."

"Ella's my happy pill." I don't comment on Fate finally using the present tense, instead of playing pretend with me. Someone in Maître du Jeu must have put out a memo to their sneaky snake members.

"Let's glue her to your side then, eh?" Sheepish and worried, Fate has the balls to approach me from where I'm seated on the sofa. I try to remind myself of the resurrection secret I'm keeping from my children and Whitt, and the world-ending secret I'm forced to keep from Marcus.

Don't be a hypocrite, Regina.

I can't pick and choose who I'm mad at when I'm doing the same damn thing to others. This makes rational sense, but emotionally it doesn't compute.

"I'm sorry, Regina." Fate stands before me, so short we're nearly the same height with me seated. "I can't say anything other than that. Sorry for keeping you in the dark about… Jamie. We were all in keep-Regina-alive-mode for so long, and the truth would have harmed you more than the lie. You get that, right?"

"I'm not– I'm not ready to go there with you, or anyone for that matter. I just can't. Not right now with what happened to me today. I have to prioritize. Initiation. Marriage. Extortion. Accepting apologies and offering forgiveness I don't feel isn't that important to me right now."

"Understood." Fate reaches for me, and I allow it. Curling her small body around mine, she tries to comfort me in the only way she knows how. "What Boyd did, I want you to know that I wasn't privy to it. He waited until I was out of town to call the meeting. It happened while you were with Whitt this morning, and Team Regina was out-voted."

"So Boyd knew when I was with Whitt and Marc– Jamie and Roman?" I'm feeling sicker by the second. Heart-sick.

"Mom called me while I was gone, and she gave me a play-by-play." Fate shifts to sit next to me on the sofa, getting so close we look like we're cuddling when she's only trying to speak so softly no one else will overhear.

"I shouldn't be telling you any of this. If you were anyone else, I would just roll with it. No one, and I mean *no one* speaks about what happens outside of the meeting with anyone but those who are invited to said meeting. They could have my head for this– literally."

"But you're not worried because you're just like Whitt, where everyone is your relative?"

"Sorta." Fate twists up her face. "But I'm not adorable and charming, or male. Don't be mad at Boyd, because he was actually on your side. Yes, he voted for you to be punished, as a way to draw you in so you could actively participate. But it was Ezra who called the vote. It was Ezra who wanted a far worse punishment. It was Ezra who compromised on the laxest punishment in order to be named your contact."

"A million dollars, hacking my network, and a threat was lax?" My voice pitches high with an upward inflection.

"Regina, Grant *died.* That was a punishment gone awry. My dad is dead." Fate's voice wavers. "My mom– Lara –she didn't commit suicide. People die. Worse, they are sexually, mentally, physically, and emotionally abused. If you don't play the game, and learn to play it well, you either lose yourself to the plays, or they break you down until you resemble someone you didn't know existed. So, yes, a million dollars wasn't even a slap on the wrist. It was Maître du Jeu's version of a *NO!*"

"Does everyone else who has a Maître du Jeu contact speak as we are?"

"Fuck no!" Eyes enlarged, face paling, Fate looks petrified. "No, Regina. No crosstalk whatsoever. You do as you're told, or you suffer the consequences. Most just assume they are being blackmailed."

"Christ." I scrub my hand over my face.

"This is the last time I will speak to you like this, Regina. I… I– I can't handle what would happen if I did." The doorbell chiming interrupts Fate but has my heart beating out of my chest. "Ready?"

“Fuck no,” I cry, voice warbling with fear and excitement. “I want to run to the door so quickly I fear I’ll land on my face.”

Smiling beatifically, “Then I’ll help drag you to your feet. C’mon, clumsy.”

Together, holding hands, Fate lends me strength. My knees are knocking, I’m shaking so badly. With a deep breath, I twist the doorknob.

“Oh,” I huff in disappointment. “It’s just you guys.”

“How rude,” Kris pouts, genuinely looking hurt. Gorgeous as ever, though. Short and curvy, tan and inked, she dressed demurely today instead of in fetish wear with her perfect tits on display.

I have no idea why Kristal is envious over me. I’d trade bodies in a heartbeat– nothing else, though.

“Who’s watching the mute?” I ask of Roman and Kristal, not liking Jamie being alone with the likes of Boyd and his ilk running around.

“Marcus–” Roman pauses, glancing in the living room to see Ella haunting the kitchen beyond. “Marcus and Jamie are taking a much-needed nap.” He won’t call him Jamie for me, but for my daughter…

“My God, they were so fucking crabby.” Pinching her fingertips together, “I was *this close* to putting Benadryl in their warm milk.” Kris pushes me a bit. “You gonna let me in the house, or what?”

“Or what?” I mimic her. “I’m just wondering if you ever dosed my daughter with that concoction when she was a toddler.” I step to the side, holding my arm out dramatically. “Why are you knocking on the front door? Just open it and come on in. Don’t be a pouty stranger when you live here.”

“Threshold ban, remember? Too much sex in communal rooms.” Kris walks right on by me. “Hey, baby Chica. Whatcha cooking?”

“Mom said we’re having visitors, so I’m making snacks.” Ella’s excitement is palpable. “I don’t know who, but I want to be a gracious hostess. What should we make? Are you hungry?”

“I could always eat, Ella. Let’s search the fridge.” Kris is good with my daughter, and that’s why I’m going to help her later tonight.

“You should think about getting some mother/daughter cooking classes, or something.” Roman rubs my shoulder as he passes by. “We’ve been discussing doing a few down at

Transcend. Not many people are doing home-cooked meals, and prepared is so much more expensive– not that that's a problem for you."

"Minus the million bucks jacked from my account this afternoon," I mutter snottily as I peer out into my driveway. Seeing no Roadster, I shut the door. "But I think that's an amazing idea. Let me know what you need, and I'll provide it. Everybody in this house loves to cook because we love to eat."

Roman sits on the sofa he's yet to soil, with Fate scurrying off to the kitchen to make sure Kris doesn't unorganized her cupboards. "It's early yet, but is culinary school in the future?"

"I have no idea." I sit next to Roman, ignoring the fact that I need a goddamn hug, reassuring words, and some comfort, and I don't care who gives them to me. "Truth be told, Ella reminds me so much of my mother. Maternal. Loving and caring. I don't give two shits what Ella wants to do with her life. She's smarter than hell, but if she wants to get married and have ten kids, more power to her. Just as long as the guy loves her for who she is and isn't a douche, I see stay-at-home-mom in her future."

"Hey! Why don't we have any WiFi?" Ella shouts from the kitchen. "I need to look up a recipe."

"Use 4G," I shout back. "I have to rebuild our server."

"Oh, okay!" Ella sounds confused but perky. "Have fun with that."

Voice filled with challenge, smugness, and anticipation, "You know I will."

I'm coming for your geeky ass, Boyd. Your sister living in this house changes nothing. You tagged me, now I'm it.

"Cookie baker?" Roman smiles like he's proud of me, having no clue of my revenge-filled private thoughts. "Feminist Regina Regal with a 1950s housewife for a daughter. Progress. I like it. Party planner? Pastry chef? Daycare provider? I'm totally buying Ella an apron. I'm sure Priscilla passes out sets of Whittenhower pearls as party favors."

Swatting Roman in the center of the chest playfully, I laugh out, "Jackass," just as the doorbell rings.

This time, without hesitation, I run like a madwoman– and I don't trip.

Chapter Nine

Heart beating out of my chest, I fling the door open because I can't wait a second longer. My thirteen-year-old son is on the other side of the door, after a ten-year separation, and nothing is going to stop me from seeing him.

Behind me I hear the commotion of Adelaide seeing past me, of my daughter's, "*Oh, my God! I should have made cupcakes!*" and Roman calming the situation. I don't even care that the door hit me in the shoulder with the rebound.

My eyes are locked in on its target.

Whitt stands behind Niel with his hands on my son's shoulders. I want to run up and engulf Niel in a momma hug, but I don't want to frighten him. Eyes the exact same shade of green as mine glisten with tears. Full lips, just like his father's, quiver as he tries not to cry. Worry and awe are etched across features, which represent every member of the Regal-Whittenhower family tree. I drink in every aspect of my son's appearance and catalog it into categories.

Grant– so much Grant. Me from all the features I passed down from my parents. My godawful hair the color of my dad's and my mother's eyebrows. Jackson's build with my father's stout height contributing. Daniel's elegance and composure. Priscilla's love shining from Niel's eyes. The same mischievous glint Ella often wears, as does Whitt– as does the rat-bastard hiding out across town missing this moment. But he'll have this too, sooner rather than later, if I have any say in it.

Time is not a distance. I see each of us in Niel, and I instantly know my son because he's a vital part of me.

Aching with each reverberation, my heart pounds inside of my chest. My palms sweat as my fingers clench and loosen. It takes everything in me not to lunge forward and touch my son.

My son.

"HI!" I chirp, voice breaking.

"Hi," Whitt's soothing voice interrupts my examination of Niel. My eyes instantly flick up to connect to Whitt's, and the comforting relief is like taking a toke off of an intoxicating drug. "I'll give you both a moment out here alone." He moves past my son, who's frozen into place and looking at me with haunting eyes and a quivering mouth.

Whitt breathes into my ear, "Wife," and then softly kisses me on my jawline.

If it was anyone but Whitt, I would say he was gloating. But he's just that sure of himself. I try to stifle the tremor that betrays my body's reaction to my husband. I flush for so many reasons that I don't want to examine too closely, and Whitt chuckles at me. He likes that I turn into a bashful girl around him. I think I'm the only one who's met the true Daniel Whittenhower II. If they had, they'd tremor too.

"Ladies," Whitt politely greets everyone in the living room. "Gentleman," he says to Roman.

"What are you doing here?" Ade issues in a panicked tone.

"No worries, *sister*." The resentment runs deep, but quickly changes to charm. "Ella, come give me a hug."

I turn to watch as big brother and baby sister meet, maybe for the first time, but I have no idea if Ade has been taking Ella to Misery Castle enough for her to be well acquainted with Whitt already. Curious, I want to watch their body language to find out, but Whitt pushes the door shut before I can witness their reunion.

"Hi," I say again, voice warbling with uncertainty. I want to call Whitt back because I'm terrified of the reception I'll receive from my son.

With a fortifying breath, I slump down to the porch to sit on the top step. I do all I can to look harmless and less guilty. Niel's a few feet away on the sidewalk because he had backed up when Whitt walked into the house. I don't blame Niel– his behavior reminds me of me when I met Marc and I kept trying to back away.

"I'm glad you came." Voice barely above a whisper, I realize I'm acting like a coward. I raise my gaze to stare my son in the eyes. "I'd understand if you hate me. I hate me, too."

A tear hits my arm.

I hadn't known I was crying.

My son's big for his age– tall for now, but will no doubt be shorter like Grant and my father. He's brawny like Jackson and my dad, and he already has reddish-blond peach fuzz on his cheeks. He's so unlike his father in looks, who is slightly feminine, but the vibe my son releases is all Grant. Calm, soothing, no doubt with a playful side hidden beneath the somber exterior.

Niel is built just like me– hardy. I watch as his thick forearms cord as he clenches his fists, working his manly fingers. Is he angry at me? Or is he feeling as I am, frustrated and confused by the need to reach out and steal a hug?

Lame, but I have no other segue offered. "Do you work out? I was mature for my age, too. So is Ella." I try to sound calming and not betray my eagerness to hear his voice.

"Yeah," Niel murmurs shyly with his eyes cast to the sidewalk.

Jesus, all is not lost. A sound I never thought I'd hear again flows from my son's lips, drawing tears to blur my vision. Niel's voice is an exact replica of his father's– soft and calming, a little deep with a rasp at the end. It makes a person lean closer to hear better while gooseflesh beads along their skin from the pleasurable notes. It's at complete odds with his appearance. Niel looks like he could break you into two, but his demeanor and tone would have you thank him while you cried.

"Grandfather doesn't approve, because it's not a gentleman's sport. But if I don't lift, I get into trouble." He smoothly flows to the sidewalk to sit crossed-legged in front of me. "Batting tennis balls or swinging at golf balls does nothing for me. He wouldn't give in with Rugby, saying I'd get hurt. Grandfather and I play billiards, but… weights and the heavy bag help– can't explain it."

"We all need an outlet for our emotions," I mutter bashfully, mind unable to come to terms with how this is reality. I'm actually holding a conversation with my son. We're sitting face-to-face on my front sidewalk, and hellfire isn't raining down upon us.

Thoroughly intrigued, my eyes study every inch of Niel while we chat, and his eyes are doing the same routine to me, concentrating on my face while looking at me with his head cocked to the side.

"What do you do?" Niel blushes and looks at his hands.

Ah– he's adorable. The rough-and-tumble mixed with Grant's demeanor will draw woman like flies. My son could be poorer than dirt, and everyone would still love him. Added to the fact that he's the heir to two powerful dynasties… we need to invest in a cock-block before someone takes advantage of him like Gwen did his father.

Jesus Christ, Grant was only a year and a half older than Niel when Gwen moved into Misery Castle. That puts our life into perspective, and why it was so important that I did what I did this morning.

"I work– nonstop. I just recently found out swimming helps." I laugh, remembering the mini-fight I had with Kristal back in September. She was teasing me for being frivolous for having a glass enclosure built to connect to the back of the house, covering the pool and patio, so we could swim and relax year-round. It wasn't so much a fight, as it was me being embarrassed. I didn't like how Kristal thought I was being cute for finally spending my own money.

"Grandfather suggested building an indoor pool off the solarium. He had a hot tub installed for Grandmother last winter, but I secretly think he wanted it for himself. It's Grandfather's zone-out area."

"The pool in the center of the back lawn isn't really ideal with Upstate New York's ever-changing seasons."

"It's actually a bribe." Niel's lips curl into a private smile, and he tries to hide it. "For you– we heard you swim, so it's in anticipation for when you come home. Yours is just a pool, and Grandfather and I wanted to give you an Olympic-sized one so you can really do laps."

"Niel," I sigh out my son's name, unsure how to respond.

"It's okay." That smile gets wider, filling more and more with Grant's mischievousness, but it's laced with Jackson's essence. "Whitt will eventually get what he wants, right? Even if what he wants is my own mother? You *will* come home. It's just a matter of timing and getting around your stubbornness."

"I– I have no idea how to respond to that, Niel." I prop my elbows on my knees and just stare at my child.

My dad, Grant, Daniel, Jackson, and Whitt stare back at me, and it's terrifying to note all the strongest parts of their personalities are reflected in my son. Niel has no weak spots that I can discern– Jackson and Daniel's genetic engineering was perfect.

"There is no response to a proven fact." Eyes so very much like my own level on me, but they see me more clearly than if I were looking in a mirror. "We have no secrets, Mom. I thought I should get that out of the way so we could… I don't know. *Transcend* it."

Head bowing, I just chuckle underneath my breath, hearing my mother tell me how much she and my father were terrified of me because I didn't think nor act like a child– ever. Ella. Ella has always acted her age, even if her body is far more mature. Niel, I don't know how it's humanly possible, but the boy is more mature than Whitt was. A soul-deep maturity that can't be taught nor learned. It's inherent.

Voice filled with wonder, "You are Daniel's pride and joy," I say without a shadow of a doubt. "Mine too. Do you have any passions? I know you like to write anime with Whitt illustrating for you. Grant– your dad, he was a writer–"

"*Is*," Niel stresses, drawing me up short. "Dad *is* a writer." Raising a hand to ward me off, Niel's voice is as soothing as his actions. "Before you freak out, Grandmother told me a long time ago. I have no idea if she told Whitt or not. But she just said a mother can feel her son. I don't know if this was bullshit she told herself, or if she was trying to comfort me. Is this true? Could you feel me all these years?"

"God, yes!" Fist resting over my heart, my voice warbles with suppressed emotions. "Always, Niel. You were always with me, the driving force to keep me putting one foot in front of the other during times when I didn't want to get out of bed."

"Grandmother started getting out of bed, and that was when I figured out she actually came face-to-face with Dad. Then she smiled again, spending all of her time at Transcend. I saw the back of him there, just a split-second before a Native American dude hid him from sight– that guy in your living room."

"His name is Roman Alexander, and he works at Transcend," I admit, not denying the rest of my son's claim. "I suspect you'll be hearing more from him."

"Yeah, a few weeks ago, actually." Turning sheepish, Niel tugs at his frayed jeans. "I can feel Dad, and I can feel you too. Whitt thought Grandmother and I were hallucinating, saying psychic shit is fake. But he was just jealous because we could feel you and he couldn't– I tried to tell him it was because we didn't feel empty, not that we could actually *feel* you and Dad."

Lips shaking, I try to sound reasonably calm. "I get it– it's not bullshit. When my dad died, I just knew it. I wanted to rally against the world and deny it, but deep down I felt the absence. I was with my mom when she passed, and I felt the moment she slipped away. The void can't be filled– it only makes more space to house more people."

"See!" Niel smiles at me conspiratorially. "Whitt says I'm full of shit. Like I have premonitions, and how I said you were okay. I even told him Dad was still alive, and that only pissed him off more. Whitt can be a dummy– he says his private thoughts are like wishes, and they are granted, no matter the consequences." Laughing ironically, Niel sounds too much like Grant– not the laugh itself, but the tone of it. "We're like an Urban Fantasy novel."

"Let's try to make sure it's not a tragic one."

Humor still written across his face, Niel's serious voice tells another story. "We can try."

"Do you remember us?" I ask quickly before I change my mind. "Not from pictures or stories told, but *actually* remember us in true memories?"

"Yeah," Niel shakes his head and his out-of-control hair falls into his eyes. He brushes it away, but doesn't seem annoyed by it.

"I remember you both. Real memories. Then Whitt makes sure I don't forget anything else, even if I want to." He pauses and shuffles a couple feet closer. "I didn't want to forget. I wrote everything down that I remembered and I add to it when something else pops into my head. Plus, I write down all the stories Grandfather and Whitt tell me. Grandmother and Aunt Kate talk about you, too. Whitney– she's the only one I let read my journal so she would remember you when she sees you again."

Touched beyond measure, my eyes sting with tears and my chest feels tight. "I remember everything, too, even when it hurts to remember." I whisper to my son. "Especially the memories that hurt."

I close my eyes for a moment, trying to push the pain of the past away. Feeling a tentative touch on my bare foot, I open my arms for Niel and wait for rejection.

My son flies into my arms and his weight pushes the wooden riser into my back. It'll bruise, but it will be worth it. I squeeze him tightly, marveling at how big he is– solid, firm, and in my arms. He has to weigh almost as much as I do. I inhale his scent. He doesn't smell as I remember. He's no longer a child. The manly aroma makes me simultaneously feel sad and proud.

My hand seeks his hair. It feels just like mine- wiry. It's blond, but with more reddish highlights than mine holds, no doubt darkening as he ages. My dad had bright red hair, and he lives on inside my son, just as Grant does.

We don't speak. We mutually weep and hold on tightly. Niel's tears dampen my t-shirt as he hiccups and breathes deeply. I rock him and pat his hair in a gesture that's as natural as breathing– a gesture that he felt for the first four years of his life.

A light touch brushes my hair back, fingers too elegant to belong to my son. I hadn't heard Whitt come onto the porch since I was so absorbed with Niel. "I thought maybe you'd like to see your children interact– we won't pretend they don't know each other, but this is different than being at Hillbrook." Whitt adds softly, not wanting to ruin our moment, "I closed the door so we have privacy."

Whitt helps Niel and me stand, both of us wobbling on shaky legs from sitting in an awkward position for too long. I glance back at my daughter. Sensing how important this is for me, Ella's clear, blue eyes water and her tiny bottom lip quivers just as her brother's does. It's so precious that I can't help but smile.

They awkwardly stare at each other, looking so much alike yet so very different at the same time, but no one would ever doubt that they're siblings. Eyes cutting to the side, I glance at Whitt– yeah, they wouldn't doubt him being the big brother, either.

I've never been so proud in my life. My family is standing on my porch, together for the very first time in our lives– someday soon, I'll drag Jamie's ass out of the brownstone, forcing him to complete our family.

Swallowing down the bitter rejection, feelings of abandonment, and slowly simmering rage, I'm overcome with emotions I can't name. Instead of wallowing in the negative, I appreciate the positive.

All is not lost– this is a new beginning.

I want to laugh, cry, and rejoice.

Feeling faint, as if this moment can't be part of reality, I wonder if I'm dreaming. If I am, then I never want to wake up again. Try as I might, I can't force Grant to manifest on my porch, so apparently this truly is reality.

I look Whitt in the eyes and his lips twitch until his cheeks dent. He quickly wipes a stray tear away and extends his hand for me to take. I take what he offers– strength and support –and hold on for dear life. We stand hand-in-hand as Niel and Ella mirror each other.

They both shuffle on their feet– unsure, wide-eyed, and trembling. “Hey.” Niel juts his hand out to shake. “This is so bizarre.”

I chuckle underneath my breath– you don’t greet a ten-year-old like that in the world Ella’s grown up in, but you do if you’re a Whittenhower. She looks at her brother’s hand in confusion, scrunching her tiny blonde brows.

Whitt smacks Niel upside the head and says, “Hug her, dipshit.”

Hiding my face against Whitt’s shoulder, I silently sob while choking on delighted laughter. This is surreal. Grant used to do that to Whitt constantly when he was being a dipshit. I always wondered if Whitt’s head was misshapen from the constant thumping.

How is it humanly possible to miss Grant this much, while simultaneously despising him?

With awkward movements, Niel embraces Ella for all of two seconds, patting her on the back. Her face barely reaches his chest with the difference in their heights. He steps back and stares at her.

“I-I-I– I don’t know what to do or say,” Niel admits, whispering underneath his breath. “It’s bizarre how you look just like Dad and Whitt.”

Face transforming from uncertainty to acceptance, Niel yanks Ella back into his arms and gives her a real hug. He finally acknowledges that she’s part of his matched set– the only person on this earth that is his complete counterpart with both the same mother and father.

Noticing me lilting to the side, Whitt’s arms surround my waist to hold me up. Seeing my children hugging and smiling was something I never thought I’d experience. I had come to terms with my fate. I believed that the universe was punishing me for a heinous crime I must have committed in another lifetime, and I was thankful to have Ella while sacrificing Niel for Daniel’s happiness and the Whittenhower’s legacy.

“I can’t believe you’re here.” Ella’s soft voice giggles. “I’ve been asking everyone about you. Prissy tells me all sorts of stuff.” She blushes. “But it felt like I had to stalk you around school.”

"Yeah, they separate us pretty well," Niel mutters, eyes cutting in my direction. "I knew Mom didn't want us interacting, so I stayed away."

"Oh," Ella whispers. "I always wondered why you weren't home when Auntie Ade brought me to visit our grandparents."

Betrayal thrumming in my veins, Ade and Grant are two asshole peas in a pod, aren't they?

Eyes flicking up to meet Whitt's, I ask a silent question.

"No, I wasn't home, either," Whitt answers my unspoken question. "Ade came around when Niel and I weren't there, probably knowing we'd rat her ass out to you, given the chance."

"I-I-I–" I'm such a hypocrite for being furious with Adelaide when I hold back devastating secrets from Whitt. But that doesn't lessen the level of betrayal I feel in the moment. Unable to face the truth about Jamie, I know I'm transferring all of that betrayal and abandonment onto Adelaide, but I can't help it.

Emotionally distraught, I truly don't know up from down anymore.

"We need to finalize what we did this morning. I heard about this last week, and that is one of the reasons I was in a hurry. Do you understand?" Whitt asks me, but with Daniel lurking in the depths of his eyes. He's in dominance-mode. "There are too many people who have access to my heirs, and I don't trust them."

Terrified, my voice shakes. "Okay," is all I can muster. There is something about Whitt that makes me submit. I have no idea why. He's not manipulating me in any way.

With Grant, we met each other head-on. Trust was the foundation, where we took the lead when we knew what we were doing. Trust– pfftt!

With Marcus, I loathe it when he tries to dominate me, doing everything I can to assert my own power.

With Whitt, is this a form of manipulation I am too blind to see or feel? Or do I feel so guilty, I'll allow him anything he asks as repentance? The 'why' doesn't truly matter, because I can't stop myself from following Whitt's lead.

"I don't like Whitney," I catch the tail end of what my daughter is saying. "She bosses me around, so I tell her she's not actually a Whittenhower– she's a Preston."

"Ella," Whitt says sharply, eyes cutting quickly to gaze at Niel. "Whitney is older, and you need to listen to her. She has your best interests at heart. With the last name Preston or not, Prissy and Whitney are as much a Whittenhower as you are."

Whitt schools his little sister, and she looks at him in indignation. "You're not my Dad." Ella turns defiant, "I'll do what I want."

Ella has never had a male figure in her life, with three women raising her and an aunt influencing her negatively. Whitt and I did the right thing this morning– I have no doubts or reservations now.

"You'll listen to whomever I tell you to, Ella," I chastise her. "I raised Whitney for as long as I raised your brother. She's a good girl, even if you don't agree with her."

"You don't know her," Ella snaps. "She tries to boss me around!"

Like mother, like daughter. Ella may have the propensity to nest like a momma bird with chicks, but she will be the one in charge of her household. Lately, she's tried to tell me what to do, already bulldozing over Fate with great confidence. No doubt, Whitney is ten times more formidable, and Ella resents it.

Whitt flows to his knees to crouch in front of Ella. He takes her hands in his and looks her deep in the eyes. Surprisingly, Ella stills immediately.

"I know this is difficult for you since you've never had to put up with anyone but your mom telling you what to do. You haven't grown up in a household where there is a hierarchy. Even though I'm a decade older than you, you see us as equals because I'm your brother."

With rapt attention, Ella gazes at Whitt like I do. There is a commanding air emanating from the man that will not be ignored. No matter how much we loathe obeying anyone else, we can't seem to not fall under Whitt's spell.

"Ella, I am *not* your equal. This is something Niel has understood from the start. The older we get, the more brotherly we become, but I'll always be his father-figure. From this moment on, you will look to me as a father and Niel as an older brother. You can fight it, but it will be futile. In the end, you'll just anger and upset your mother. Do you understand, Ella?"

"Yes," she whimpers.

Ella isn't used to men in general. This house is filled with women, with the exception of Roman being around when he shows up during daylight hours. She's appropriately intimidated by Whitt and Niel, so I know she'll do as she's told.

“Good,” Whitt smiles grandly, showing off his dimples. “I’m really nice, just ask your brother. Niel practically gets away with murder. But I will not tolerate discord within the family. I know you and Prissy are best friends, but it’s more than that– you’re cousins. Whitney is your blood too, and family always comes first. You don’t have to put up with Whitney’s crap, but don’t antagonize her either. Understood?”

“Yes, sir,” Ella says, but her voice warbles. I still see that stormy light in her eyes– challenge.

“Don’t call me, sir. I’m either Whitt or Dad to you.” Choosing to ignore instead of squash the challenging air emanating from Ella, Whitt kisses her forehead, and then rises.

“Ella, formally introduce your brother to the rest of your household,” Whitt orders, expecting to be obeyed. “I need a moment alone with your mother.”

Ella surprises me– she doesn’t look to me for confirmation; she simply does as she’s told. Outside of our daily routine, I usually have to beg her, and she doesn’t listen to Fate at all. Ella truly needed a masculine presence in her life.

Chapter Ten

Wordlessly, Whitt pulls me back into his embrace and holds me so tight I can barely breathe. Burying my face into the crook of his neck, a sense of comfort and rightness descends. Whether I can meet the challenge head-on on my own, it doesn't matter, because Whitt will be fighting alongside me.

"We'll get through this. It'll feel like a long time before we can live under one roof. But after the past decade, it will seem like an instant."

"I can't go back there," I mutter, for what feels like the billionth time today. "I can't."

"We'll discuss an arrangement, where Niel and Ella can go between their homes, if you're that dead-set against going home."

"I sound so selfish," I whisper against the crook of Whitt's neck, voice warbling. "But I'm just not ready to face Daniel again. I can't– not yet."

"I understand," flutters against the top of my head, and I believe him. "I need to thank you for trusting me enough to go along with my plan." The reverent tone in Whitt's voice warms me as much as it scares the shit out of me. "No matter how much time we spent apart, I still know you, Queen– inside and out."

Whitt flutters a kiss to my cheek, and then the hollow beneath my earlobe. Unbidden, my body lights up, and I curse it for betraying me. I don't understand why Whitt affects me this way, but he does. I'm sure as hell not going to admit it– that's a path only leading to misery.

Guilt. Love. Terror. Abandonment. Rejection. Fury. Sadness. Fear. A grown man who looks like Grant, but doesn't sound like him– a man who utterly terrifies me yet enlivens me, touches me in an inappropriate way, and I let him because I'm incapable of saying stop.

I don't know if I want him to stop– I need Whitt, and I fear rejecting him will take his support away.

My girls have lied to me every day that I've known them.

Marcus has lied to me, yet we are in the same boat when it comes to Maître du Jeu.

Grant lied while telling the truth– Jamie tells more truths than I can handle.

Whitt– I'm the one who has lied to him, and if he wants to kiss me, then I'll let him. I'll let him do whatever the hell he wants, because he deserves it, and I deserve the consequences.

I've never understood Grant more than I do right this second. You love the person you are betraying, because the secrets you hold are not yours to tell, even if they directly affect the ones you love.

I'm a hypocritical bitch, who deserves to be made to feel like a whore, as her husband kisses her exposed flesh… whore, because this is a boy I thought I'd raise as a son, my own children's brother.

Grant's son.

That spineless asshole abandoned me, betrayed me, lied to me, and threw me away, both a decade ago and this morning.

Whitt deserves anything he wants, and Jamie deserves any pain that will undoubtedly come his way from it. But I'm the one who will be hurt the most. My pride. My self-respect. Most importantly, my sense of self-worth will be torn to shreds and tossed into the gutter from whence I came.

Grant is dead to me.

That self-worth that's floating in the gutter should demand I loathe Jamie, but the most powerful part of my being refuses to let go of the threads holding us together. Love conquers all, but my rage is battering in from all sides, gaining momentum with every kiss from my new husband.

I hate myself– I hate myself because there is a part of every girl who needs validation from a man, who is needy and wanting. That part is ecstatic in Whitt's presence.

"Daniel?" I sigh involuntarily– mind, heart, and body warring. "This isn't a good idea. I'm practically your mother."

Laughing as if the water I tried to douse his fire with was actually gasoline, Whitt terrifies me more. "Never my mother, Queen. I might have been a small child, but I was waiting to grow up to be your partner."

The fact that I don't say no is a silent invitation. Whitt kisses his way along my jawline, toward my lips. Try as I might, I try to push him away with a palm to his chest, but it's futile. Whitt just clasps my hand, pressing my palm firmly until I can feel his heart beating rapidly beneath.

My body breaks out in goosebumps, and my hair stands on end, as Whitt's lips descend on mine. I whimper against his mouth, equally terrified and enlivened. It's like a drug– you know it's not good for you, but you can't stop yourself from having a taste. The more you imbibe, the stronger the need, until it's a full-blown addiction.

Whitt kisses me with expert precision– slow and smoldering. All-consuming.

"We could go to your room," he mutters breathlessly against my lips, then pulls away so I can answer. Kiss traveling down the column of my throat, he's unrelenting.

"No," I'm proud to have the ability to deny him. "We have to go chat with everyone in the living room." I don't sound convinced, even to my own ears. "I'd like to see my son– watch how my children interact."

Typical man, sounding way too much like his father for my liking. "I only need a few minutes," he teases, showcasing a horny, one-track mind. "I'm so amped up, one touch would have me popping."

"Maybe I need more than that?" I tease Whitt back, hoping that douses the fire.

"My apologies, of course." The lust dies down, but the flame is still strong. "Queen, I just ache so much." He whines while pressing and releasing an impressive bulge against my hip, like it's my duty as his wife to take care of it.

Fifty years ago, it would have been my duty, and everyone everywhere would have ridiculed me for thinking otherwise. As a feminist, I want to wrench Whitt's balls for thinking the way he does. I may have been his father's whore, but I'm not his.

Thoroughly disgusted, that needy, desperate for validation, little girl dwelling deep inside me is secretly pleased Whitt wants me as much as he does, which makes me hate myself all the more.

Gay or not, clearly Whitt has developed some sort of Regina Regal fetish. Even as a kid, he was in competition with his own father, trying to prove he was more Whittenhower, and it's transcended his natural sexual leanings. There is no disguising lust, passion, and need, and this kid has it in spades– for me. It's not flattering, simply because Whitt's brain rewired itself to steal me from his father for stealing his legacy away.

"We can't do it like this," I protest weakly as Whitt pushes me against the outside wall of the house with a thump. I worry the neighbors will see, but it's a screened-in porch. More importantly, I fear everyone in the living room heard the loud sound we made on impact with the wall.

Lost to lust, "I ache," Whitt groans, all of his manipulative powers on display. What Whitt wants, he gets. "Kissing you during your initiation, feeling you naked against me, watching people touching you…"

Whitt trails off as his hands glide down my thighs to grip the backs of my knees. Displaying his strength, Whitt lifts me until I'm forced to relent by wrapping my legs around his hips. He circles in an instinctive wavelike motion, grinding into me.

A low moan pours from my lips. "We can't do this." My gasp turns to a hiss when his bulge hits my sweet spot. Riding along the hard ridge of Whitt's cock, I lose sanity. "It'll be obvious to everyone in the living room," I warn, trying to come to my senses.

My body flashes with sweat when I realize I'm on my porch with my husband dry-humping me like a horny teenager. Uh–yeah, Whitt's still a teenager for a handful of months.

Sinking to an all-new low, I realize just how fucking depraved I truly am. I deserve whatever bullshit comes my way. Maybe Boyd can tax me again, or Ezra will just murder my soul with whatever Maître du Jeu demands he'll make. I'll do it, and I'll deserve it.

"We can, and we are." Whitt growls, dominant nature erupting. With force, he gives a few more grinding pumps to accentuate his words. "If we can't go to your room, we're doing this right here."

As I give into Whitt, my head hits the wall with a heavy thwack. I'm coming to realize, no one can say no to Whitt. Just hold on and enjoy the ride. He goes from polite Whitt to a crazed master in a split-second. Warm hands yank my shirt out of the way, exposing my bra. Intent palms squeeze my breasts until I gasp in pain. Lips crash against mine forcefully, leaving behind a punishing sting.

Same album, different song. Whitt wants to hate me but can't, just as I feel for Jamie. Until all the cards are on the table and indiscretions are forgiven, every interaction between us will be the push-pull between fury and absolution.

Right now, I'm Whitt's Jamie. This mind fuck makes it impossible for me to hate the man who abandoned me and our children, while stoking the flame of my rage, because the betrayal I dealt Whitt, the betrayal I'm paying for right this instant, was not by my own hand.

Never giving into anyone, I yield to Marcus on my own terms because I'm his equal. But for some indescribable reason, I turn passive for Whitt. Instinctually knowing he'll do anything and everything in his power to protect me. I will come first, not because I was Grant's mistress, or the mother of the Whittenhower heirs– simply because Whitt has an unnatural attachment to me, one that should be severed, no matter how much I need it.

I allow Whitt to take his pleasure from my body in a debt of gratitude that is gratifying in the moment, but debilitating in actuality.

Within seconds, we're groaning into one another's mouths, fighting to suck on the other's tongue. My fingers dig into Whitt's back, inches above where my heels bite into his hips. I rock into him as he rolls his hips against mine. Fire courses through my body and coalesces in my core, erupting from my throat in a deep moan.

After sucking down my moan to silence it, Whitt bites my lip as he hisses out his own release. We stop moving. We stop breathing. We remain still and silent as his bulge pulses and beats against my quivering flesh.

Rolling my glazed eyes, I meet Whitt's heavily-hooded, satisfied peepers. "You're going to be the death of me," I murmur.

"Never," Whitt says reverently. "We're each other's salvation."

Lost in the faith I place in Whitt, I'm passive as he places my feet on the floor and straightens my shirt.

Unable to voice what I meant, I think it instead. I had meant how one day Whitt will find the love of his life, and then he'll leave me heartbroken. Less than twenty-four hours back into my life, and I worry about the next time he'll leave me again.

"Told you so." I try to hide my terror, but some seeps through as I glance at the huge wet spot blooming on the front of Whitt's trousers. "They'll know."

"Ha! It's not all mine," Whitt teases while untucking his shirt to cover the growing spot. "You're my MILF, what can I say?" His infectious grin spreads across his face.

Shaking my head at Whitt, I mutter, "You're incorrigible. Really, I don't want you to think this is the type of woman I am… after all you've seen today. Until my initiation, I'd only been with your dad and Marcus, which was pre-approved by your dad. But don't expect me to explain that one, because I won't."

The shame-filled tone of my voice erases Whitt's grin, and I wish I hadn't voiced what I just did. "Queen, you're my wife, remember?" Cupping my cheek, Whitt proves how mature he truly is. "Even a religious fanatic couldn't fault me for wanting to touch you and for you caving in. But, even if we weren't married, sex is not wrong."

"Unless it makes you feel bad about yourself," I mutter underneath my breath, and Whitt pretends not to hear it.

"I know you didn't want them to know, but I'm not ashamed." Standing before me, hair mussed up while wearing cum-stained pants, Whitt is entirely shameless. "Um… your lips are a dead giveaway, though."

My fingers immediately seek them out, and I wince. "Shit! They're swelled up to the proportions of a Botox addict."

I'm not stupid– I realize Whitt was marking me, placing his 'mine' stamp on my ass. I would feel angry if I didn't understand it. Even mild-mannered Grant possessed this urge. After nearly two years under the insane tutelage of Marcus Zeitler, I understand the undeniable need to brand that which you deem as yours, which was why Marcus has been going batshit crazy for the past few months.

I get it, but I don't have to like it.

"The adults won't give a shit, and the kids might actually be happy that their mom has a man," Whitt tries to reassure me.

"Yeah, their *brother*," I grumble incredulously, suddenly feeling sick to my stomach with deviancy. "As for the adults, I look like a cradle-robbing cougar."

"Kristal will be so proud." The humor in Whitt's voice is washed away quickly. "This afternoon, I'm petitioning adoption for both Niel and Ella." As quickly as he became serious, it shifts again. This time his expression changes to teasing. "I should get the benefits of their mother's bed, don't you think?" Whitt blue eyes shine with mischief and he smirks his dimple-inducing grin.

"Yeah," I snort, a vital part of me dying while another one blooms to life. That fucking girly part of me, Mom was positive existed, is enthralled– the part Mom said needed to be nourished, while I threw it back in her face how cuddles don't put a roof over your head or food in your belly.

"How are we hiding this?" I gesture to Whitt and me, and the fact that our marriage and the children's adoption will be public knowledge.

"If Daniel doesn't think to look, then he won't know where to look. Money can hide anything, and we only need a few years." Cupping my cheek, Whitt whispers his thumb across my swollen lips. "I don't care if he knows, because Niel will tell him. The only thing I care about is securing my legacy and controlling my heirs. I never want another Whittenhower to be placed in the situations my grandparents and dad had to live. The way you had to live."

"Twice." I remind Whitt how first Daniel and Jackson did this to me with Grant, and now he's doing it to me too. "And now you."

"Mine was by choice– forced or not, Grant celebrated his time with you." Mistaking my look of guilt as grief, "Trust me, Queen," Whitt begs, not only with his words, but with the tone of his voice, the look in his eyes, and the expression on his face.

"I do. Let's go get into some trouble." I open the front door, knowing my walk of shame will be nothing compared to the legendary one I'm doing inside my own head.

Chapter Eleven

Ella's high voice is chattering away about school with a captive audience. I try to slip around the outside of the room so no one takes notice. Niel sees me first. He scrunches his eyebrows and looks confused until his eyes light on a smug Whitt ghosting behind me.

Men, no matter how young or old, they just 'get' it. Smirking with wry amusement and, oddly, satisfaction, Niel shakes his head. No doubt my little bastard sent his big brother my way, thinking Grant's doppelganger would lure Ella and me back to Misery Castle, where everyone thinks we belong. Closing in on fourteen going on forty, more and more every single day, Niel still thinks exactly like Daniel. Unbeknownst to Whitt, Daniel probably set all of this shit into motion, knowing what countermoves Whitt would make, all of it drawing us back together again. I never discount Daniel's machinations.

Face flushed as red as a stoplight, my son's reaction draws everyone's attention my way. Kristal looks amused yet mildly jealous. Fate blushes and looks fascinated by Whitt, when she should be pissed that I just scandalized her baby brother on our front porch– *Jesus Christ, Fate's my sister-in-law.*

I grab for the nearest object to keep my ass from smashing to the floor– the wall. Staring everywhere but at anyone with a pulse, I refuse to look at Roman because everything he sees, Jamie sees, and I completely avoid Ade.

"How about some snacks?" I offer in a cheery voice, trying to hide how my heart is beating in my throat. Jamie's now my goddamn father-in-law. Holy Christ, I'm going to keel over. "I'll fix us something."

I'm a Whittenhower…

A. Goddamn. Whittenhower.

Rushing to the kitchen, I refuse to look anyone in the eye while ignoring my daughter's protests about how she's the hostess of our demonic little gathering.

I don't know why I feel so guilty.

Innocent Regina meekly says from the depths of my conscience, "B*ecause you're a grown woman over thirty, and Whitt hasn't even reached twenty yet! He's Grant's son, Regina! Stop before you regret it."*

Jaded Queen happily supplies, *"Whitt's your husband– fuck him already. It will serve the spineless cocksucker right."*

But Jamie doesn't suck cock.

"Who said I was talking about Grant? Marcus should have stopped this insanity if he was really in love with you and wanted to claim you, but he didn't. Grant didn't. They let you get away, and Whitt snapped you up, and he's fucking ecstatic to have you too. Even cold as ice Daniel wants you in the family. Own who you are, Mrs. Daniel Whittenhower II. Fuck your new husband to spite everyone, and seal the deal before someone or something takes it away. Celebrate! Be proud of the cougar you are, ya lucky bitch!"

I don't like Jaded Queen, because she sounds too much like the side of me I'm trying so desperately to suppress. My mind keeps spinning rapidly. In the middle of the night, I was initiated into Maître du Jeu, going way beyond BDSM involvement. By early morning, I was married to a Whittenhower. By afternoon, said Whittenhower wants to adopt his siblings.

"Grant lost all claim to his brats when he orchestrated his own death and led you to believe he was dead for over a decade, all the while living beneath your nose like a goddamn rat. Play pretend all ya want, but we know the truth. Fuck your husband and rub it into his face, then send him a copy of his children's birth certificates with his own fucking son's name listed where his used to be. If you deserve whatever Whitt throws at you, whatever Maître du Jeu forces you to do, then Grant deserves no less than losing everything he so freely abandoned and gave away– you included!"

"Shut up, Queen!" I mock-scream, voice barely audible. "I can't listen to any more of your shit."

"You mean the truth? Fine! Live in denial, until you bloody snap and kill yourself or someone else."

"Bloody? Am I British now? I thought for sure you'd turn French after this morning's extortion."

"Make friends with your new brother-in-law, because it seems Boyd has some hidden talents you need to learn. You're no longer the best in Dominion– best woman? Sure. But is that really good enough for you, Regina? The opposing team has

better players, and you've never strove to be anything but the very best of the best. Marcus would be disappointed in you. You're now on the 'B' team. Arrogant and totally complacent–"

"Shut up!" Palms covering my face, I pledge to drown out the vindictive, revenge-seeking side of myself, because that will do no one any good.

"You look weak right now, Regina. WEAK! Compassion is great, until you realize everyone in your life is using you as a pawn. Everyone in your living room should be your enemies, because friends don't betray friends. Your daughter has been lying to you for how long? How long has Ella been visiting Misery Castle? Blame Ade all ya want, but Ella lied by omission to ensure she could go back, time and time again."

"Stop!"

"Even Whitt's using you. Your son, do you honestly believe he's not making Daniel's plays for him? Plays against you and Whitt, to maneuver you where they want you? That spawn of yours, you made him and Daniel honed him. He looks like the shifty type, so innocent on the outside, but playing all the angles from the inside. Remember how your mind worked at his age? Scary, huh? Can you even trust your own children, Regina?"

Trying to silence the voices arguing in my psyche, I dip my head in the sink and turn on the faucet, allowing the frigid water to clear the rage-fueled lust fog from my mind. Since the initiation, Queen's been trying to take over. I don't have multiple personalities; I'm just no longer able to play pretend.

While my mind roils, I contemplate putting the stopper in and filling the sink with icy water, and then holding my breath until all my troubles fade away.

From behind me, "How could you?" Adelaide accuses, voice tight with suppressed fury, managing to be heard over the spray of water.

I can't hate Jamie. I refuse to be angry with Whitt for using me like the rest of his family has. My inability to hate Adelaide's family members makes her the perfect target.

"Haven't you figured it out yet, Ade? There's a Whittenhower gene that makes you all want to fuck me," I mutter snidely, but the water muffles my sarcasm. "Except Daniel, since he's incapable. I'm just thankful the rat-bastard didn't want me to sire his progenies– probably scared he'd make more girls. He only had granddaughters, too."

"What are you talking about?" Ade demands, having heard way too much over the rush of the water.

"Oops– my bad. Having secrets from you."

"I'm at a loss right now." Ade's voice fades, but not because she leaves the kitchen. "You just insinuated something major about my family."

"*Our* family. Need I remind you, none of this was of my doing?" Reaching forward, I shut off the water. "I was more than happy to go about my business, go to school, and live a life of my choosing. The Whittenhowers stepped in and derailed me, not that I would change a thing because of my love of Grant and our children. But fourteen years later… another generation of Whittenhowers want more than I'm willing to give."

Blotting my short hair with a kitchen towel, I glare Adelaide down. Queen was crowned early this morning in more ways than one. "Seems I'm destined to always give the Whittenhowers what they want, even if it hurts me."

Flashing an arrogant, baiting smirk at Ade, it's either that or punch her in the throat.

"Did you have to fuck my baby brother?" Voice lost, Ade looks torn between compassion, jealousy, and anger.

"HA! Is that what you think is happening?" Incredulity is so thick in my voice, I nearly choke on it. "I haven't fucked your baby *brother*, yet. But under the circumstances, it's unavoidable."

In response, Ade glares at me, causing me to bark a sharp laugh.

"We've already established that Whitt was mine a long time ago, didn't we? I'd get out of my sight if I were you, you treacherous bitch. I don't even want to look at you right now."

"What the fuck did I do?" Voice horrified, Ade looks offended, but I can see the guilt lurking in the depths of her eyes.

"It seems the second I left Whittenhower Estates, you told the man who broke my collar bone with his precious Steuben paperweight that I was pregnant. Then you've proceeded to tell him all about Ella on every occasion he asked. He's known everything about me since day one– where we live, where we work, who is in our lives. You've been taking my daughter to see someone who has been my enemy."

"Regina– Daddy isn't your enemy. It only made you feel better to hate him, so he allowed it. There was no son for a son. If you would have come home, he would have let you back in."

"All of which you failed to tell me," I remind Ade. "I'm not a mind reader. But we both know I'm not the groveling type, when I shouldn't have to grovel. Did pride keep me away from my son? No. Honestly, I don't hate Daniel at all. I think he needed Niel more than I did, and I think my son needed him too. We could have made an arrangement, where I could have at least seen him on weekends. But do you know what I didn't need? One more person lying to me with every breath they take, forcing my daughter to do the same."

"Reg, it wasn't like that," Ade tries and fails at defending herself.

"Just give me some space. At least leave the kitchen. I can't deal with this on top of everything else. I do so much to save you and your family, and you have my own daughter betray me– your own niece. But you probably didn't see it as a betrayal, since no matter what, you'd have unlimited access to Ella."

"Daddy was no threat to you, Regina. He never once wanted to take Ella away. He just wanted to know her as well as he knows the girls."

"It wasn't a chance I was willing to take when the man already had my son." Voice breaking with emotion, I suffocate on the agony I've felt for the past decade and then some. "*I* would've been the one torn from yet another person I created when I have no family to speak of. You selfishly used me and my children, and even Whitt to secure yourself with your father. I should just let you rot in Wintercrest. It would serve as a righteous punishment. But I'm too loyal to ruin you in such a way."

"Regina," Ade gasps, more shock than outrage reverberating her voice.

"I need space. Then I need an apology. But, most importantly, I need to not see you right now, Adelaide." Forcefully, yet quietly, I grit out, "Just go."

Moving quickly, I dunk my head back into the sink to stifle the sound of my cries. Releasing all the agony of betrayal and abandonment. Over the years, I've lost all that I thought I'd gained.

Fate. Kristal. Adelaide. Jamie. Roman. It was all an illusion. Even Marcus has let me down, showing me his weak points, leaving me to not trust nor respect him.

Whitt, I know deep down he isn't playing me. He may or may not be Daniel's puppet, but only because he doesn't realize it. Even Daniel is someone else's puppet.

Aren't we all?

I'm the one who is betraying Whitt by keeping secrets, secrets that aren't mine to tell. The misguided loyalty runs so deep, Marc's weakness is mine too.

Grant.

I must have faith in myself to soldier on when all I want to do is curl up in a ball and weep.

Startling me, a hand rubs soothing circles in the center of my back. At first, I don't recognize the touch. But once I do, I'm slightly surprised at who it is.

"Hey," I breathe to Roman. Pulling away, I pat my hair with the towel again, hoping the droplets cover up my leaking eyes.

"Are you okay?" Roman's voice is soothing– the old Roman, saying the words Jamie would utter if he had a voice. The young man I used to know peeks out at me, turquoise eyes ensnaring mine.

"I want my friend back," I whine to Roman. "But I know it's not possible."

"You don't like who I've become?" he teases with calculation, and I have a light bulb moment. "I thought for sure you'd feel pride over an educated, community-minded Roman Alexander."

"Ah– you don't like who *I've* become." I lean against the counter and smirk at the sneaky asshole. "I know there's no way you and I can ever be in that place we used to be in. I get that your loyalties lie elsewhere, but I don't want you to walk around on eggshells anymore, either."

"Back at the brownstone, when I had to stop you from confronting Grant–" that singular word has my eyes slipping shut in pure, unadulterated agony. "All bets were off. I miss the old Regina. The Regina who lived at Misery Castle was the same as Reggie from the block. But this creature," Roman gestures at me. "Is a fucking stranger to me, and I don't know how to deal with it."

Eyes watering, I mutter a truth I'm too proud to say to anyone but Roman. "I'm about to break."

"Oh, sweetheart," Roman cries, sounding as if my words cut him deep.

"You're right– you're goddamn right. The girl who lived with Grant, she would have acknowledged the world around her in a heartbeat. She was placed in an impossible situation, but she made the most of it. This woman I am today, I don't recognize her either."

Reaching out to cup my jaw, Roman rocks my world with the simplicity of his solution. "So find her– fuck everything else. Find our Reggie and reclaim her as your own."

"To do that, though." I have to look away from the raw honesty Roman is shining upon me. "To find that version of myself is to give up the stronger version."

"Reggie?" Roman tilts his head, getting into my line of sight. "There is a difference between numb and strong, and weak and vulnerable. To open yourself up to how you feel, to own why you feel it… being vulnerable is not weak– it's human."

"To feel–" my voice cracks so hard, I fear I'll never speak again. "To feel is to hate him."

"Oh, Reg…" Roman tugs me into his arms, holding me so tight I'm able to breathe instead of suffocate on my biggest fear.

"I can't lose him again– even if I only have a small piece of him." Face pressed tightly to Roman's neck, I've never needed support more than I do now.

"You're going to have to hate Grant in order to forgive him. That's the natural order of things."

"Maybe I don't want to move on, Roman." A sound flows from my throat, a cross between a whimper, a whine, and a sob.

"Who said anything about moving on? How about moving forward instead?" Pulling away, Roman forces me to look into his eyes. "I don't know what the future holds, but I do know what our present looks like. It will be bleak as shit if you don't pull it together and stop being dead inside and out. We need our Regina back. We need a new voice– a different perspective. As long as you stick your head in the sand and playact a martyr, which, by the way, is not your natural state-of-being, we'll all be stuck in stasis."

"You asked who said anything about moving on? I'd say what I did this morning was pretty fucking permanent, and unforgivable. A man would never forgive a woman for marrying his son, and having to go to bed with him too."

"Grant will never have to forgive you anything, Regina. You know him better than I do, and I've lived with him for a decade.

Get your shit in order, then go see him. Look Grant in the eye, even if it's only to punch him in the face."

"I'm in love with two different men, and married to a third. I have liars coming out of the woodwork, and I just lost a million bucks this morning. Now I have to defer to Ezra for whatever the fuck that may be. I'm pretty sure I'm the opposite of having my shit in order."

"The Regina I remember would take three friggin' minutes and figure out a plan of action, then she'd kick ass while taking names." Gripping my shoulders tightly, Roman leaves fingertip bruises. Then he shakes me swiftly three times, causing my head to snap back and forth on my neck.

"Be *that* Regina. Do it! Do whatever you have to do in order to survive, and make no apologies for it."

"Okay," I murmur breathlessly, an odd energy infusing me. "I will."

"Good." Roman releases me in an instant, and I slump to the counter at the loss of his support. "Just never tell me or anyone else what your plans are, or I'll be forced to report it to the powers that be."

"Voldemort," I tease.

"There's my Regina." Roman cuffs my chin while grinning. "I'll give you a few minutes to get your head on straight, and then you should spend some time with your son."

All energy fleeing me, I slide down the cabinet to ass-plant to the floor. Resting my head on my knees, I try not to think, even though thoughts are swirling though my head like a swarm of angry bees.

Be *that* Regina, Roman had said.

One: I'll deal with Jamie later. I honestly need him in order to go to sleep at night. Once the other shit has been handled, I'll make moving forward a priority.

Two: Boyd. He robbed me blind. After I secure my server, I'll steal my money back.

Three: Whitt. Give Whitt whatever the fuck he wants, because making him happy will make me happy. My guilt is lessened purely on the knowledge that I will share all of the secrets I hold very shortly, as soon as I deal with the first item on my list.

Four: No matter what Jamie and Boyd said, I will never play this divided loyalty game again. The fear keeps us beholden to Maître du Jeu. There are no secrets between Marcus and me, not anymore, and there never will be. Grant was the ferret who kept us in the dark and apart by telling us different secrets. Marcus got Jamie's identity, while I was told the truth about Maître du Jeu. I will not keep quiet, no matter what they may threaten.

Five: the girls– all of them. Ella will never lie to me like this again. I will meet and get to know my nieces. Fate is Fate. Kristal has a punishment coming, because Roman is right. I'm the one who has to administer it, because the secrets Kristal has been keeping from me have been eating her alive, and ruining our friendship in the process. Ade– I can't deal with her yet, not until after I deal with Grant.

Six: Ezra. Whatever may happen, I will not sit around waiting for an edict to come down from on high. The fear of potential blackmailing would be a constant cloud of misery I refuse to live under. Ezra may have Marcus wrapped around his little finger, and the whole of Dominion's founders at his back, but I will never be Ezra Holden Zeitler's bitch.

Tonight, Restraint is mine.

Chapter Twelve

Walking from the kitchen to the living room in a daze, I find everyone staring at me strangely. Shit! I went for snacks and come back empty-handed.

"Kid–" I snap my fingers at my son. "Follow me." Moving down the hallway, I sense Niel is following me. Standing to the side, I push my office door open, then gesture for my son to go in first.

"Holy shit!" Niel murmurs in awe, green eyes flicking over every surface. "This is where you work?"

Chuckling underneath my breath, I pull my chair out and plunk Niel's rear into it. "We don't get any visitors, so your reaction is the first I've gotten to enjoy." Looking around my space, I take it in with fresh eyes. "It's all the monitors, isn't it? That's what you find impressive?"

"It's like the Batcave, or something from a science fiction movie." Niel rambles on about how awesome my work station is while I shut and lock the door. "Grandfather kept your office at home exactly as you left it, and it looked nothing like this."

"Technology has changed a lot in the past decade," I remind the boy, trying to ignore the fact that everything in my old office is exactly as I left it. "I spend the majority of my time in here," I admit while I type a few keys on my main keyboard. "Everyone will say I tend to get depressed, which I won't deny. At the worst of times, I never leave the house, emailing those who are a cog in the company machine. When I'm feeling good, I'll go into Empowerment."

After waiting a heartbeat to see if Niel would respond, I slowly bring up the classical music level until we won't be disturbed or overheard.

"Shostakovich?" Niel sounds surprised, but a pleased smile twists lips that are a replica of Grant's. "Did you mean for it to be ironic how Empowerment is based in downtown Dominion in the Meyers building?"

"Meyers?" I squeak out, hip coming to rest on the edge of my desk. "Come again? The building Fate acquired for me was her own?"

Niel snorts, one shoulder shrugging elegantly. "Now that's not common knowledge, Mom." My son *tsk-tsks* me. "The irony of Dad's second mistress buying the original's building doesn't escape my notice. I'm sure Dad got a kick out of it."

"Wow…" I breathe in a mix of awe and terror. "You're one scary motherfucker, aren't you? How you must make your grandfather proud."

"I am his most coveted possession, favorite person, and comfort object. So, yes, I make Grandfather exponentially proud."

Fingers shaking, I turn the volume up a notch, realizing there will be no getting to know one another through small talk between my son and me. Slumping in defeat, I fold to the floor.

Turning in my swivel chair, Niel looks me dead-to-rights. "Out on the porch, we agreed to be honest with one another. I'm showing you my dark side, knowing you were trying to control your own while you were in the kitchen."

Too terrified to ask, yet I can't stop myself from doing so. "Dark side?"

"You know, the part of you that is capable of doing very bad things because you see the weakest point in a person? The part that sees right and wrong as very black and white, and wants to punish the wrong doers? But the good in us overpowers our need to be the justice-seeker, so the masses are safe to rest in their hypocritical beds."

"How old are you, again?" I mutter in disbelief, eyes tracking over my son's features. So manly, but his elegant affect belies the strength shown.

"Whitt was never a kid," is Niel's answer. Swiveling, he faces my bank of monitors. Fingers lighting on the keys, he speaks while typing. "He doesn't have that 'kid' side to him. Since Whitt never forgave Whitney for stealing his name, she's tried to emulate him. Prissy, she's more childish than her age, but it's sweet instead of annoying. My sister is both young and old, like I am."

"Like you are?" I mutter incredulously, because right now Niel's acting older than I am.

"Mm… hmm…" Niel murmurs while typing in code. What the actual fuck? "I act my age, ya know? I like to play video games and goof off with my friends. There are girls I like, even if Grandfather doesn't approve. I indulge Prissy, with Whitney getting huffy in the background. For fun, I make Grandfather do things he never would have otherwise."

"For real?"

"Obviously Grandfather is very reserved, but he never used to play billiards or get in the hot tub. I manipulated him into taking Grandmother to the Virgin Islands for a few weeks–during school, so we all could have an excuse to stay home." Niel laughs at some memory remembered. "Grandmother was over the moon for months when they got back. From then on, Grandfather told me I was to remind him to treat her right."

"Yeah, Daniel's incapable of romance," I mutter underneath my breath.

"Grandfather has told me extensively about his asexuality, so there is no need to hide it from me, Mom," my son chastises me. "He thinks Jackson's spirit entered mine upon his death."

"That's not very Catholic of Daniel," I mutter wryly.

Niel's snort turns to sinister laughter. "I found Dad's tower." My son shocks me to my very core. "Whitt used to joke about how everyone thought there was no 'tower' Dad ran off to for hours, sometimes days at a time. He of little faith thought Dad was cheating on you. But I found it, and it was on Whittenhower Estates' grounds."

"I… I'm at a loss for words, Niel."

"It wasn't twenty minutes later, as I was reading one of hundreds of journals, that Roman was walking in to extract me." Chuckling, Niel actually looks pleased with himself, peachy skin turning crimson. "Now *that* got Dad's attention."

Intrigued, I lean forward, knowing no one will ever know Grant, not really. Even with access to every single one of his written words, there would be lifetimes of thoughts never released.

"What did you find?"

"It must have been an old stone fortification from when Misery Castle was being built. Dad's tower is out in the woods, miles from the main building. No power or heat, in the attic space was a desk, leather chair, and mountains and mountains of journals. Most of which were Jackson's. I'm guessing it was Jackson's tower first. Maybe even Wilhelm's."

"Jesus Christ," I hiss in wonder. "What I wouldn't give to read those."

"Come home," Niel demands, knowing even that won't entice me. "It doesn't matter anyway, because somehow Dad has the area triggered. Two more times, I've gone back there. Now I'm unable to get inside the building, but just walking the perimeter brings Roman around."

"How?" I breathe, intrigued.

"Beats me," Niel mutters with a shrug. "I was given a consolation prize– two, actually."

"Kid, don't be this way," I warn. "Just spit it out."

"Ha! Grandfather said I have your personality."

"And here I thought you acted like Daniel."

"Precisely," Niel mutters while wearing a smug smirk. Pointing to my sound system, "This is Grandfather's favorite piece– mine too. And yours, it seems. I was told you and Grandfather didn't get along because you act too much alike."

"Kill me."

"No, not before I give you the lowdown on what Roman gave me." Swiveling in his chair, Niel presents all of my monitors, each featuring a different picture of Grant. With the touch of his fingertip, Grant's tower is shown. Tall and ominous, but shorter than the trees towering around it, the stone structure is exactly as I envisioned Grant's space. "I snapped a few pics with my cell before Roman scurried in like a rat."

"I call your father a rat," is out of my mouth before I can stop it. "Shit! I didn't say that– forget you heard that."

"I love you, Mom." Niel flashes me a bright smile filled with pleasure, and my heart fills with joy. After a few keystrokes, more images fill my monitors– images from the recent past at Whittenhower Estates, even pictures of Daniel and Priscilla on vacation to Saint Thomas. "I hooked you up to my cloud."

"Thank you," I say with all sincerity, beyond touched at the gesture.

"I've learned a lot from Whitt, only I've taken it a step further. People only see the kid, not the mind inside the kid's head. See, Whitt was incapable of acting his age, so people still feared him. Me? I am a kid. I act like a kid. But I think like an adult."

"But they don't know that, do they?" Nodding, I get it. "Daniel must, though."

"Grandfather doesn't know everything, no. But he does know me inside and out, but only the things I allow him to see. So I'm the harmless, feckless kid who will someday run everything Whittenhower. Meanwhile, Whitt's the brooding one who was shoved from his rightful place. It's all very maudlin."

"You..." voice airy, all I can do is shake my head in awe as I find my son more fascinating than terrifying. "Blow my mind."

"Listen?" Niel turns his head to the side, ear closest to the sound. "Whitney learned this section on the violin– it's beautiful."

"Yet disturbing," I add. "Haunting and desolate."

"So very apropos to fill Misery Castle's hallowed halls," Niel fills in. "I have the best of both worlds. Grandfather knew you'd kill him if I wasn't allowed to grow organically, so I'm allowed to do whatever I want. He was thrilled with my aptitude with the business and how much I truly do respect and adore the cold bastard. I exercise my freedom constantly."

"Explain," I demand.

"Easy– I'm a free agent." Niel swivels the chair back around, staring at the monitors I'm trying to ignore. Fifteen different images of Grant appear in varying growth stages. "One day, you and I are going to beat the living shit out of this man. Believe it or not, Whitt will probably kill him."

"Then why not tell Whitt the truth?" I ask, having asked myself that same question dozens of times today alone.

"Why should I?" Niel says as if he doesn't grasp the concept of scruples or ethics, but maybe he doesn't. "I'm a free agent. I know things Whitt doesn't. Things Daniel will never learn. Things you shouldn't know, but Dad was a very bad boy for telling you."

"How do you know these things?"

"Free agent– it's like I'm on everyone's side." Niel winks at me. "Mom, you really shouldn't know of Maître du Jeu's existence. Like Diane and Grandfather, they believe they're merely being blackmailed by their lifelong friend, Olivia Fontaine. Olivia is their contact, similar as to how Ezra will be yours. They don't know anything about the inner workings, so that's why Dad was a bad boy. It's why you should keep your mouth shut, even though we both know you won't."

"And you know this how?"

"Marcus will know everything you know before the next dawn, but you'll save Whitt by keeping him from the truth." Swiveling around abruptly, Niel faces me. "I know because it's what I've been doing. Meanwhile, Diane and Grandfather have been striking up an offense, with Whitt running around like a chicken with its head cut off, and I'm just sitting back gathering knowledge."

"Lovely," flows with disgust.

"Mom," Niel says sharply to gain my attention. "I'm not going to show my hand until I get to sit at the table. It won't be long, and I'll meet Dad face-to-face while attending my very first founders meeting. It would be stupid of me to spoil it before I know anything, wouldn't it? I can do more good by knowing what Grandfather and Diane are doing, while influencing Dad and his allies to vote a certain way to protect us all. A free agent isn't without ethics. Don't you watch Survivor?"

"You utterly terrify me," I whisper, voice breaking. "Yes, I watch Survivor. It's your dad's favorite show. Marcus and I watch it religiously, with Jamie in the background."

"We should watch it together, discussing how their ploys went wrong. Grandfather, Whitney, and I watch it, and then do a replay with an intensive discussion."

"You want me to watch Survivor with Daniel?" I repeat, as if I just heard Niel wrong. "With Marcus *and* Jamie?"

"Trust me– it will happen eventually." My eyes are drawn to the easy way Niel makes keystrokes on my board. An instant later, two leather-bound books are shown on every one of my monitors. "These are my consolation prizes via Roman from Dad."

"It just dawned on me, but I shut my server down. How the fuck are you pulling up these images." Crawling to my knees, I lean my elbows on my desk.

"I'm hot-spotting my cellphone, Mom." The kid rolls his eyes like I'm a moron when it comes to all things digital. "I was told to give the one journal to Grandfather."

"Why?" I breathe, leaning in closer to inspect their covers. A snort is pulled from me when I notice how they're bound exactly the same as all of James Atwater's novels.

"After telling me he'd cut my nuts off if I read it, Roman said to feed Grandfather a story about how I found it in the study behind some books. It was a peace-offering from Dad, though. It was a journal written by Jackson, with every story featuring Grandfather."

"You read it, didn't you?" I whisper conspiratorially with my son.

"Of course," Niel says without shame. "I just downloaded the digital file I made to your computer. Grandfather was a *bad* boy."

"I thought that was Jackson's role in the family?" I tease.

"Let's just say I learned more from that journal than I have from anything else in my entire life." Niel shudders in either revulsion or delight.

"I'll have a hard time looking at Daniel without envisioning what is no doubt inside that journal," I mutter in wry amusement. "After knowing Jackson, and seeing him and Daniel interact, I don't fault them for whatever deviancy they were up to since it was most certainly based in the purest form of love."

"Yeah, I can guess what you think is in the journal, and it is… but the rest is not what you think." Tapping on a monitor, "Read it, and you'll see what I mean. My respect for Grandfather went through the roof after I read it."

"Ugh, I don't have time today, and I really, really want to," I whine, causing Niel to chuckle.

"I also downloaded the contents of the other journal to your computer, and I hid both in a folder with a passcode– the day of the month each of the Whittenhower heirs were born, in chronological order."

"Damn, you most certainly are my child." Unable to help myself, my lips quickly press to Niel's smooth forehead. "Proud of my devious baby boy."

"Thank God, or else I would've had to delete the folder," Niel teases me, blushing bright red while looking pleased beyond words. "The second journal was written by Wilhelm, with additions made by Jackson, and hundreds of pages added by Dad. There is blank space for me too."

Eyes scrunching in confusion, I stare at the monitor, as if I can read what's hidden beneath the image of the leather-bound journal. "What is it?"

"It's the Whittenhower Heir's Guide to Maître du Jeu," Niel rocks my world. "And you now have access to it. There is also one titled the Whittenhower Elder's Guide to Maître du Jeu, which clearly is in Dad's possession."

"Holy fuck, batman," I mutter in awe.

"I know, right?" Niel looks at me conspiratorially, as if we're partners in crime. "Wilhelm never mentioned succession. But Jackson wrote of how to become the elder– by death or by stepping down. There was a bunch of private notes written between Jackson and Dad that tore me up– some funny, sweet, but mostly intense. Wanting the same between us, Dad actually wrote me a note about how he will step down with no fuss when he thinks I'm ready. But if I try to kill him for anything other than abandonment, you'll kill me instead."

"I'm at a loss for words."

"Mom." Niel looks me dead-to-rights. "This is only for you to read, okay? You can share whatever you think is important with Marcus, but don't show him the actual pages. Please? It's Whittenhower's history, and Jackson's words are precious, no matter how blood-thirsty they sounded. No matter Dad's faults, I won't betray him when he's such a private man."

"Your dad knew you'd give this to me," I point out.

"Roman told me not to show you, saying Dad told him to relay that as a message, which clearly sounded like, "*Make sure Regina reads this word for word.*"

"You have no idea how creepy you sound right now, Niel– your dad's voice is flowing out your mouth. I…" stammering, I get choked up emotionally.

"I got the voice, but Whitt got the laugh and looks. Which is probably a good thing with what he wants from you. Obviously Dad was your type–"

"We will not be discussing *that*," I state firmly, causing Niel to blush. "No doubt Daniel has given you a dozen medical journals in lieu of the sex talk, and Whitt is the best source for a real conversation. So you and I, we're going to be a dead-zone when it comes to anything sexual until you come of age."

"Plus, we really don't know each other, so it does come off as creepy." Niel smirks, baiting me.

"Up!" I tug my man-sized child from my chair. "We're going to rectify that starting now. No more talk of intrigue. I want your personal details, hopes and dreams, and how you view the world."

"Tit for tat?" Niel arches an eyebrow, looking freakishly like me. "If I have to answer, so do you."

"Tit for tat," I agree, and for the next few hours, Niel and I get to know each other.

We'll never have a mother/son relationship, because that ship has sailed. My son is too mature of the mind to accept mothering from me. But we begin the type of relationship most parents fail at once their child becomes an adult.

We don't become friends– we become allies, partners, sharing information and trusting on faith that the other knows what they're talking about. I give advice, and Niel not only listens, he files it away for when he'll need it.

After witnessing the dark side of my son that he suppresses around everyone but me, Niel allows his child-self to erupt. For a few stolen hours, I get the simplistic joy of listening to a sweet, introverted boy prattle on about a lifetime of words he wished to share with me.

The dark side and the looks come straight from the Regal branch of the family tree, with a little help from Jackson and Daniel. But deep down, Niel's personality mirrors Grant's so closely I find myself swallowing back tears the entire time.

Tears because Grant should be here with us. Tears of sadness, but ultimately tears of silent rage for the abandonment I feel that was also dealt to our children. The death of a loved one can't be erased, but to be abandoned writes on the very fabric of who you are as a human being. Whitt, Niel, and I have infinite wounds which thankfully never cut Ella too deeply.

In the end, we end up talking about family and memories shared, because that is ultimately the ties that bind.

Blood or not, without shared experiences, respect, and love, no family or friendship can survive without a stable foundation. Niel and I are starting from scratch. It's bittersweet, but it fills me with hope I didn't think I'd ever feel.

I swallow my rage, because not only do I have my son back in my life, miracles do happen, even if they come at a steep price I'm unsure I can survive paying.

Chapter Thirteen

After spending a few minutes to compose myself, I ended up texting both Jamie and Marcus for advice on a few of the steps on my to-do list. Jamie agreed that I had to head Ezra off at the pass, and to not bother speaking with Marcus about it because of his ties to Ezra. He also gave me a heads-up that Roman would be entering Restraint shortly, bypassing the training and initiation. Both Jamie and Marcus felt I needed an ally inside and out of the dungeon– one who is neither a friend nor foe to Ezra, but a true equal in the secret world hidden by Dominion's founders.

As I was ending my texting marathon with Marcus and Jamie, I received a group message from Ezra, which terrified me to open. Almost like he has a sixth sense, Ezra got to me first, but with Restraint business. He called a Masters of Restraint meeting this evening at eight o'clock. With Jamie's and Marc's advice, I planned Kristal's punishment and guilt-letting to commence after the meeting.

Beyond exhausted, I snuggle down on the sofa in between Whitt and Niel, then release a sigh of contentment. They both smell so familiar and comforting, I simply close my eyes and listen to Niel and Ella chat about mutual acquaintances from school.

"Kris, are you working tonight?" I ask, keeping my voice as casual as possible. I don't wish for her to catch on how she will be made an example of this evening as my very first scene in public at Restraint.

"Yeah?" Kris answers with an upward inflection, as if she's worried it's a loaded question. She should be worried.

Shit! I'm out of a babysitter.

"Fate, we have something we have to do tonight." Whitt strings tight with tension, of which variety I haven't a clue. No doubt he received the same group message, but obviously Fate isn't invited to *that*. "You should go get ready." I give her ample notice, as the girl takes forever and a day to primp. "We're going back to Restraint tonight."

After a quick glance at a shocked Kristal, Fate answers me with a question, voice trembling. "We're finally going back there?"

So tired, my eyes continuously slip shut, only to slide back open to get a read on Fate's body language. As an adrenaline junkie, she's thrumming with anticipation. But Fate's a scaredy-cat too. This will make for an interesting evening.

I nod my head at Fate in answer, and she hops up and leaves the room in a flurry of excitement.

"This will not end well," Kris predicts, but I'm unsure if she's speaking of Fate or herself. The leery expression on her gorgeous face screams she knows she's in for it, but is smart enough to know not to ask.

"Roman, since Marcus is spending the rest of the day and night with the mute, can you keep an eye on Ella this evening?"

"Depends." Roman smirks, holding out just to be a piss-pot. "Give me the details."

"Ezra called a meeting, but I want to show Fate off tonight too. So it'll only be for a few hours. Ella can get herself ready for bed, and you can do whatever you normally do in the evening. Just don't leave the property."

"Sure." Roman winks at me. "I have a movie I've been meaning to watch."

"I don't need a babysitter!" Ella protests, not liking the influx of alpha males in her life. Just wait until she meets Marcus. HA!

"This isn't up for debate, Ella," is my reply, while Roman, Whitt, and Niel all agree with me. My kid gets the hint that her surge of independence will not be tolerated when even Kristal agrees with me.

My eyes drift shut again as exhaustion presses down on me. I didn't get any sleep last night, or the night before, or the night before that either.

"In the future, I'll be at Restraint every second you are," Roman confirms my suspicions. "So maybe Fate going there will be reserved for special occasions, so she can be here with Ella."

"You're right– Ella won't see it as being babysat, just being at home as usual."

"I can hear you, you know?" The teenage bullshit seems to be coming early with my daughter.

Lovely.

"Remember when I said there was a hierarchy to how I was raised?" Niel murmurs softly to take the sting out of it. "Your freedom is over, sister."

A sinister snicker flows from between my parted lips. "You've yet to meet Marcus." The adults and Niel join in my laughter. "Roman babysitting you will be like having an overgrown kid on the premises. If you don't want to be babysat, I can always make you go stay the night with your grandfather."

"Home's perfect– thanks!" My daughter's attitude adjusts mighty quickly. I'll have to remember Daniel is a good threat to curtail bad behavior.

Surfing the gray area between wake and sleep, I rest my head on the back of the sofa and allow my eyes to drift shut.

"You need a nap," is whispered into my ear, followed by a lingering kiss tickling my neck. Try as I might, I can't stifle the sigh of pleasure in my weakened emotional state.

"Ella, please show your brother your room. I bet he'd like to see if you still have the graphic novels we made." Whitt's smooth voice lulls me further into sleep, to the point I don't mind him bossing my daughter around.

"Yeah, I kept them all." I crack my eyelids and laugh at my daughter's excitement. "C'mon!" Ella yanks Niel up off the couch, then pulls him down the hallway. Niel better watch out, or she'll be telling him what to do next.

"Kris, you should probably get ready for work," Whitt demands, brooking no room for argument after mastering the submissive for more than a year. "You have to be at Restraint earlier than we do."

"I don't remember you being so bossy," Kris whines. "What's happening tonight, anyway?"

"Starting tomorrow, we're opening the dungeon to the public. Marc, Dexter, and Ezra were told to do it by Master Fontaine from Vegas."

"Wow, the head bitch is passing out edicts?" I don't miss the way Kristal's voice warbles, because I happen to know there is a distinction between Maître du Jeu the BDSM group, and Maître du Jeu, the playground for our sadistic founders. No doubt the founders are playing a game at Restraint, one Dexter and Marcus know nothing about, but surely Ezra does.

"Marcus and Dexter wanted nothing to do with it, but Ezra persuaded them to comply." Whitt confirms my suspicions. "So tonight, Ezra's passing out jobs for each of us, demanding our presence at Restraint every night. The Masters are meeting, and then Ezra's meeting with us individually."

"Well, aren't you buddy-buddy with Ezra all of a sudden," I murmur underneath my breath, jealous that Marcus didn't give me those details. But maybe Marcus didn't have them to give.

"Whoa…" Kristal whispers in awe as she leaves the room. My eyes follow her out the back door, across the lawn, and until she disappears into the guesthouse.

Once it's just the three of us, Whitt lights into Roman. "Whatever you hear in this house, doesn't leave this house." Whitt uses his Master Daniel voice on Roman, and I simultaneously suppress a shiver and a chuckle.

"Kid, seems like you'd figure out nowhere is secure enough to hold a conversation, especially this house. But I won't get into that with you, as that road leads to being silenced."

"This impacts everyone's future." Whitt's face turns deadly, and I never imagined that his soft, blue eyes could turn so cold, or that the dimples in his cheeks could harden into anger.

"If you don't think I've heard this speech before, you're sadly mistaken. I even had to read it from Jamie's flying fingers."

"Why would Jamie give two shits about what happens to us?" Whitt's voice breaks with confusion, but not enough to hide the resentment lying beneath.

"Just go take a nap." Roman changes the subject. "You both need one. I'll watch the kids. Ella already knows me, and Niel and I have some getting to know one another to do." Choosing to ignore us, Roman pulls a paperback from the back pocket of his jeans, flips to a dog-eared page, and then begins reading.

Is this the real Roman? He reminds me of the man I used to know. Roman just back-talked Whitt while Whitt was displaying his master voice– didn't even flinch.

As if hearing my thoughts, Roman looks up at me and winks playfully.

Smiling to myself, I notice whose book Roman is reading– Nocturnal Silence by Cortez Abernathy. The spine has been bent repeatedly until you can't read the title. Either Roman's a bad book owner, or he's read it a million times.

Tapping Roman's book to gain his attention, "I'm sure Cort would give you a new copy." I take note of the yellow highlights and the ink marking the spine. Roman has very precise but slanted handwriting.

"You've seen the shelves in my living room," Roman reminds me. "Cort gave me an entire set of signed hardcovers. But I'd rather carry this around." Roman nonchalantly shrugs his shoulders, then tucks his inky hair behind his ear. "I can't hurt this paperback, and it fits in my back pocket."

"How many times have your read this?" I'm curious since this is Cort's only horror novel. It's about a sociopathic serial killer who has an insatiable craving for raping whores. After using and abusing them, he murders them slowly, then either dumps the bodies in a lake or has his younger, reluctant partner-in-crime clean up after him. It's written from the perspective of the cleanup guy. It was eerily realistic, showing the bond forged between the two men, not the killer versus his victims. Cort dabbles in all the genres, but this is the only book he's written of this type.

Nocturnal Silence doesn't seem like something Roman would like. But then again, I don't know this Roman.

"A lot– I'm trying to figure out if it's autobiographical without actually asking." Before I can interrupt and ask if Ezra, Cortez, and Aaron's captor was the serial rapist, Roman cuts me off. "Now go do whatever it is that newly married couples do when they say they're taking a nap. Whitt looks like his pressure release valve is going to burst."

Whitt blushes a beautiful shade of pink, and it warms me to see he's still innocent in some ways. Whitt's blush fuels my own. Even Roman isn't unaffected. Looking up from the book, he's momentarily dopey-eyed.

Whitt is– words cannot accurately describe how beautiful my husband is. Angelic is the only thing that even comes close. I will never admit this out loud, because I don't know if the absence makes it stronger, but Grant was so otherworldly, just looking at him made my heart stop.

Lost in Roman's expression, I don't see Whitt move until I'm slung over his shoulder. Reminiscent of the wee hours of this morning, but only in reverse, Whitt's palm smacks my ass as he strides down the hallway toward my bedroom.

Chapter Fourteen

"Thanks, I could use a nap," flows sarcastically as I'm unceremoniously dumped on the bed. Dragging my pillow over, I curl around it. My eyes begin to flutter shut, but immediately jolt open when I hear the telltale click as the lock on my door is engaged.

"No!" I yelp in fear, knowing I'm too weakened to avoid Whitt's influence and manipulations– I'll give him whatever he wants but regret it later. "No, don't be doing that." I watch in horror as Whitt's deft fingertips unbutton his shirt– one button at a time.

Pop…

Pop…

Pop.

Fuck!

"I won't remain a virgin forever, Queen," is said in a quiet voice, as if I'm the one acting like a virgin on her wedding night.

Those gracefully long fingers unhook platinum cufflinks embossed with a DW, then gingerly place them on my nightstand.

"No one's asking you to." Hiding my face against my pillow, I try to swallow around the bubble of anxiety lodged in my throat. "Go find a cute dude with a hot, tight ass, and bang the ever-loving hell outta him."

"I want my wife to be my first," Whitt announces without a hint of shame or regret. "Regardless of whether or not I'm a virgin, we still have to consummate our marriage, and I'd rather have it mean something. Not some drunken hookup because you want to get it over with, and no lies that it happened when it didn't. *I'll* know it didn't happen."

Masculinity rings in Whitt's tone as I try to wrap my mind around Whitt being a grown man with grown man needs, even if they're disturbing and involve me.

Jamie was right– I've been stuck more than a decade in the past, sitting in stasis, neither evolving nor devolving while everyone around me has changed.

Rolling to my side, I try to look at Whitt with fresh eyes– the eyes of a wife. There is no ignoring Whitt's sculpted chest– no hair, scars, or marks, just the lean expanse of pale perfection.

Whitt's body looks like a pleasure playground, and I'm not sure I'm mature enough to handle admittance.

A disgustedly expensive shirt is draped over my lampshade.

"I'm not ready," I blurt out, nervousness ringing loudly.

"I'm beyond ready," Whitt says with great confidence, when with someone else it would sound like a cocky air. He's not being arrogant– he's really that goddamn special, and we all accept it as a known fact.

Deft fingers pluck at Whitt's belt, slowly drawing it through the loops. My heart beats against my ribcage frantically as every inch of leather is pulled free.

What does he plan on doing with that belt?

"I want to know you as a man first, Whitt." I swallow audibly in the resounding silence. "This is too soon– too much."

"I understand." Belt looped in hand, Whitt stares down at me without a shred of disappointment. "It's been a long day for you, and it's nowhere near over. You and I need to get reacquainted as adults first. But just know this, I am a grown man, Queen. A. Grown. Man."

"I–" '*beg to differ*' tries to flee from my lips, but it gets cut off before I can continue, simply by the power of Whitt's stare.

"When you were my age, you were treated as the mistress of Misery Castle, and I mean that as the lady of the manor sense of the word. You were working freelance, already a mother, and living in a committed relationship with my father, while giving Daniel a run for his money. Don't even try to say I'm a child, or I'll call you a hypocrite."

"Fair enough." Shifting on the bed, there is no comfort to be had during this uncomfortable conversation. "But I'm not ready– *today*. Give me some time to wrap my head around it. Okay?"

"Okay, but when? Name a date," Whitt commands.

I rush to obey, but no words manifest on my lips.

"Do you have any idea how insane I've felt after watching you give Dexter a blowjob? My all-time favorite hobby is getting my dick sucked. Judging by your enthusiasm, you make sucking cock an art form."

"Wow…" eyes bugging from my skull, I'm in awe over how nonchalantly that rolled off Whitt's tongue. "Did I get transported to an alternate universe? Did you really just say that to me?"

Ignoring me, Whitt continues. "Then you fucked my friends– I could tell you were uncomfortable, and the only thing I wanted to do was make it better."

"It was by *your* doing!" I shout, aghast.

Whitt has the common decency to shrug, but he ruins it with what he says next. "If you can't tell me when, then I'll take what's mine." He doesn't threaten– he promises.

Snap… Zip… Whisper of fabric…

"I'm sorry," I mutter in a panic, knowing how fragile male egos can be when it comes to sex, and the entitled, misogynistic, misguided concept of how my vagina belongs to every male in my life, but not me. "I only, sort of, enjoyed Dexter. Ezra and Cort... I don't even want to think about that ever again." My voice breaks with shame. "I didn't want you to see me like that."

"I didn't say I didn't *enjoy* watching– you were incredible. I want you to explain why not me. Do you find me lacking?" Whitt sounds unsure for the first time since I've met him as an adult.

I look at Whitt, *really* look at him.

Standing at the foot of my bed in a pair of silky navy boxers, Whitt's chest and strong thighs are marble perfection. My eyes seek the path of the deep V of his abdomen, then they're drawn to the freckling of sandy hair that paves the way to the bulge barely contained by his boxers. Hissing in shock at my body's reaction, I clench my thighs around my pillow.

Eyes relighting on Whitt's face, I follow along his strong jaw, finding his cleft chin at odds with his button nose, sensual lips, and dimples. Wispy blond hair flutters against his sarcastically-arched eyebrows. Beneath are a pair of devastating clear blue eyes, which are open with honesty and purely wicked.

I swallow, nearly choking on my rising lust.

"You have no idea the effect you have on me, Whitt. I don't have adequate words to describe you. Nor do I want to admit how much it frightens me to want you." Growling deep in my throat, I make Whitt's trademark, frustrated sound.

Cocking his head to the side, Whitt not only looks at me, he sees *into* me. "Then why?"

"I'm scared, okay? I'm an old lady, and here is a young man who wants me to pop his cherry, all so he can go to Restraint and fuck with wild abandon. Then one day, when I least expect it, you'll find a man and leave me all over again. Don't you see how much pressure you're putting me under, when I'm already drowning from the weight of stress?"

"There's so much wrong with your statement, Queen. I'll never leave you." Whitt thumps his clenched fist over his heart as a silent vow, no doubt truly believing it when I don't. A nineteen-year-old can't make that kind of promise, even if he means it in the heat of the moment. Proof-positive, Whitt's father left me when he was twenty-seven.

"I haven't been a child since the day I was born, and you damn well know it. What's between us isn't about sexual orientation. I'm gay, so what?"

Staring at me in defiance, challenging me to disagree, Whitt stands at the foot of my bed with his hands framing the bulge in his boxers as proof that it doesn't matter whether or not he's gay when it comes to me.

Right this instant, I remember Regina Regal is a realist. This is no fictitious gay-for-you situation that you read in a romance novel. I'm not so goddamn irresistible that my hotness transcends sexual orientation. This isn't a love affair so intense Whitt can overlook my girly bits.

My new husband, who basically was my stepson long ago, he's got some freak-ass, mommy kink at the very least, or a way to stick it to his dad because he's got daddy issues. Either way, it's not truly about me, but some psychosis with his abandoning parents who are a match made in Maître du Jeu hell.

If it's the last thing I do, I'll get this boy laid by another boy, if only to show Whitt how much better sex can be with someone you desire, not someone you're doing out of obligation or perversion.

"I'm a woman!" I cry out the obvious, trying to get past his mommy issues. "I don't have a dick for you to suck, and I sure as hell won't let you screw my ass because you don't want pussy."

"You're more of a man than most I've ever met!" Composure cracking, demanding Whitt makes an appearance. "If you don't think that makes me want to fuck you, then you're insane."

"I don't have a dick!"

"It's not about having a dick. It's not about anything you think it's about. Jesus, Queen." Whitt growls his noise of frustration.

"Then what's it about?" I mutter underneath my breath.

Flying across the bed, Whitt lands on me heavily with a strained grunt. Face bright red in anger, his chest is pumping as he pulls in air rapidly. Frozen in shock, all I can do is stare into Whitt's eyes as his fingers grip my arms, clenching to the point of bruising.

"You don't get it, do you?" Whitt shakes me forcefully. "I'm in love with you, Regina." He abruptly lets go, and then sits on my thighs.

"You don't know me well enough to say you're in love with me. It doesn't work that way. There's lust and infatuation, then the love of family and friends. To be in love with someone takes time. It takes shared experiences. To say you're in love with someone you haven't seen in a decade… I call bullshit. You can just straight-up love me, but you don't know me enough to be *in* love with me."

"The fuck I don't!" Whitt shakes me again, like he can somehow force what he believes into me. He's crazed with frustration and uncontrollable emotions, and it's terrifying to see him break.

"Regina," Whitt uses my given name to get my undivided attention. "The moment you stepped from the car in front of Misery Castle, I knew you would be pivotal to my existence."

"*That*, I believe," I murmur to calm Whitt down. "I felt it too."

"That was the first time I hated Grant, all because he was a man and he could have you. I wanted you as my wife, but this same mind I'm using right now was stuck in a child's body. As I watched Niel grow in your belly, I pretended he was mine. When Niel was born, I wanted him as my son. Do you have any idea the guilt I feel?"

"Guilt and I aren't strangers."

"Not this type of guilt– I always get what I want, no matter the consequences. It's a fucking curse. My jealousy took my dad away from us. Grant's gone because of me. I wished for you and Niel, and now I have you. You're my Mrs. Whittenhower and Niel will legally be my son, and I feel sick with joy over it."

Shoulders curling, Whitt sobs frantically into his palms, and I'm stunned into silence. I didn't have a clue. This is what Marcus was warning me about– how we never know how someone secretly feels. The burdens they carry may be heavier than our own.

Rubbing Whitt's thighs in soothingly circles, I know he doesn't feel my touch because he's lost in his misery.

"It's not your fault, because no one can help but feel what they feel. A self-fulfilling prophesy only works on *self*, not everyone else." Taking a deep breath, I can't listen to Whitt's sobs without telling him the truth.

What kind of cunt would I be to keep this secret? Someone I couldn't respect is who I'd be.

With a deep breath, I mutter the truth, even if it's ambiguous. "I think you need to pay a visit to the brownstone, Daniel. Do it."

"I'm *me*, Regina!" Whitt lashes out like a wounded animal. "Do you honestly believe I didn't snoop around the instant I was told I couldn't meet Jamie face-to-face?"

"Jesus Christ," I wheeze, overcome with a pain so intense it robs my breath.

"When I say I hate Grant, I fucking mean it," Whitt snarls. "I could see you struggling this morning, struggling to not only admit it to me, but to yourself. We're in this together– I *do* love you." Whitt's hands slip from his face to land on his thighs where I'm touching him. Clenches my fingers, he tries to center himself.

"I know. I believe you." I believe Whitt *believes* he's in love with me, even if I don't. "I love you, too. Always have, always will, no matter what."

"I know." Looking coy, but it's not an act, Whitt's lips curl up into a devastating smile.

"I need to know something. What do you plan on doing after you lose your virginity? What have you been doing now?"

"I've just been doing oral and hands, and I'm always safe. My powers of manipulation only run so deep, and I'm sure Marcus will de-nut me if I touch you more than a few times… so I'll be with Kristal afterward."

"Kristal?" No jealousy rings in my tone, just utter shock. "How about we find you a hottie with a dick and a tight little asshole instead? A guy your age who loves art, is into BDSM, and has a filthy mind."

Chuckling underneath his breath, Whitt apparently finds me cute. "It's not that I want Kristal– it's because she understands my needs. Her preference is two guys, so I have something to look at while we play." Whitt blushes so brightly his skin feels warm to the touch. "I can't afford to get involved with a guy, unless he's the one, ya know?"

"Yeah, I guess," I mutter incredulously. "You're afraid he'll use your heart against you, and then blackmail the family."

"Exactly– no matter how hot the sex could be, nothing is worth that."

"But won't it be difficult for you to be with me? I mean, I'm not Kristal. There won't be another guy in the mix for you to get your rocks off with."

Staring down at me with a twisted smirk, Whitt laughs like I'm being ridiculous. "How many times do I have to say it's not about sex between us? I'm attracted to *you* the person. Did you forget the porch in your old age? It was only a few hours ago."

"Jackass." I hit Whitt upside the head for old time's sake.

"I want you, okay? I… uh…um…" Whitt stutters, face blazing crimson red. "Yeah… I…um… watching you nurse Niel was when I had my first–"

"Ooooohhhh," I drawl out in shock.

"I'm not a pervert, even though I can tell you think I am one. It just unleashed something in me, so I followed you around after that… and other stuff." Suddenly bashful, Whitt won't look me in the eyes. "Now you know what a huge freak I am."

"Your birthday," blurts out without thought, because I'd do anything to take Whitt's discomfort away.

I remember a cryptic conversation Marc had with me after I met *PB*. He said it wasn't uncommon for Pretty Boy to identify sexually with me– something about coming into his sexuality. I assume Whitt spoke to Marcus about this.

"What?" Whitt's eyes are bright, so I know he understands.

"Your birthday is in a couple months, and we'll consummate our marriage as my gift to you. At least you won't be a teenager anymore, because that just creeps me out. Plus, it'll give me some time to get to know the man you've become."

Nodding with enthusiasm, Whitt mutters, "Okay," very quickly, like he's terrified I'm going to renege. His lips spread from a smirk to a huge shit-eating grin as he tries not to look excited over the prospect of me agreeing to pop his cherry.

"Doesn't it bother you that it won't be the man of your dreams?"

"Nah– there are different kinds of virginity." Whitt acts like it's no big deal, but I'm not buying his nonchalance. "First kiss. Handjob. Oral, giving and receiving with both cock and pussy. Sex with a woman. Anal with another man– both giving and receiving."

"Wow, way to overthink a natural act." I roll my eyes at the idiot who's practically vibrating with lust.

"And here I could've been your first teenager," Whitt teases shamelessly.

"Jackass," I laugh as I smack him in the chest.

Suddenly serious, Whitt grabs my fingers and gazes at me with lust-filled eyes. My breath hitches in my throat, knowing I'm about to fall off the edge and pass the point of no return. I don't even recognize who I am anymore.

Pulling my hand, Whitt positions me until I'm sitting upright with him straddling my lap. Needing to be the one in charge, the one who takes the initiative, I tilt my head up and kiss him.

Immediately, Whitt tries to take over the kiss and dominate me, but I won't allow it. Nipping at his upper lip, when he gasps in surprise, I impale his mouth with my tongue. Thrusting sharply in a rapid rhythm, imitating the act Whitt wishes I was preforming, I take charge. Fighting for control, Whitt thrusts his tongue against mine, but I capture it between my lips and suck.

Moaning, Whitt grinds his hardness into the softness of my belly. Fingertips biting into his hips, I pull until I can feel the entire outline of his cock impressed against my stomach. I saw a glimpse of it in the dim lighting of the dungeon at Restraint. Long, rosy perfection, but not too long. It was thick, but not too thick. Its curve was created to rub against my g-spot or a guy's gland. Whimpering and moaning, I flex and clench my thigh muscles.

Needing to be in control, Whitt tries to take over the kiss again. Laughing, I punish him with a sharp bite to his tongue. Dominant and not having it, Whitt's fingers wrap around my hair, then give a sharp yank.

Whitt isn't playing anymore– we're two masters dueling for who's in control. Biting him wherever I can reach, I scratch his back. My nails find purchase in his flesh, forcing a pain-filled grunt to erupt from his throat.

Gravity changing, I'm flipped to my stomach with Whitt sitting on my ass. Before I can react, my wrists are clasped at the small of my back by one of his hands. With mindboggling speed, my t-shirt is wrenched up to my neck until it's between my clenched teeth. Restraining me, my shirt traps my arms while silencing my pleas.

"I was trained longer than you, Queen, and my specialty is restraints," Whitt warns in an ominous tone. "Unlike in life, in bed, I'm in charge, whether it's with another man or a woman." After hissing menacingly in my ear, Whitt bites the nape of my neck as he shifts his weight.

Trust.

Instead of allowing the panic to overpower me, I reign it in by submitting. Mind spinning, never in my life have I felt this level of release. The immense weight is lifted from my shoulders by someone stronger and more capable than me.

With Marcus, who demands I submit, all I feel is resentment for him not respecting me or seeing me as who I am.

With Whitt, I'm not fighting for control. I'm in awe of the man he's grown up to be, the innate power he harnesses, and I want to see what other tricks he has in his arsenal.

Held captive by my shirt and the hand at my wrists, my heartbeat slows and my muscles relax. Reading my body language as a sign of my surrender, the shirt is tugged until the hand that holds my wrists encloses it, effectively yet effortlessly restraining me.

With measured movements, my phone is pulled from my back pocket and placed safely on the nightstand. Whitt controls me with one hand while his free hand methodically lifts my hips until I'm on my knees. Deft fingertips slide my yoga pants down my hips, past my behind, working them free of my body.

In the near silence, the only sound is our labored breath. Our bodies communicate where words cannot. Whitt is shouldering my burdens, proving he is dominant enough to take care of me. By submitting, I acknowledge this as fact.

Body falling lax at once, that glorious cock grinds into me from behind with only silk boxers and a thong separating our flesh. I whimper in need, then cry out when Whitt rubs his length over my most sensitive spot.

Panting roughly into my ear, "Beg," Whitt orders…

… And I obey. "Please," I plead in a forceful rasp, but it's muffled by my t-shirt.

I have no clue what Whitt has me begging for, but I do know I want it.

"More," the word vibrates down my spine, peaking my nipples and engorging my clit.

"Please, Daniel," I beg in a tone that doesn't sound like my own, nor does it sound like Queen. It's the girl I never allowed myself to be. "Fuck me."

Freezing still, I'm shocked senseless. Did I just say that? In the heat of the moment, they say our words are never truer. I come to terms with the fact that I want Whitt inside of me, how I need him inside of me, even if it's toxic for the both of us.

I know it's so wrong, but I repeat it again. "Fuck me," is rasped roughly, barely heard through my makeshift gag.

Whitt's sensual, satisfied laughter rumbles against my back. "No," he whispers, sounding shocked to have said it himself.

Taken aback, rejection slices through me. Whitt said no? Did I hear that correctly? Disbelief and disappointment war inside my mind.

Insane with want, I start to beg in earnest. "Pleeessseee, Daniel… fuck me. I need to know what you'd feel like inside me. I beg of you."

"No," Whitt murmurs even softer than before, the single word reverberating down my spine with the intensity of a punch.

Fingers bunch in the front of my thong, and then tug down sharply. The snap of the fabric renting is deafening. Whitt pulls my panties away slowly, making sure the seat rubs against my aching pussy as he pulls them free. Whimpering in delight, I'm so sensitive, the feel of air fluttering against my flesh nearly brings my climax.

"Marcus demands that we immediately submit, but I believe in earning your submission." Leaning down over my back, Whitt presses his lips to the shell of my ear, issuing a demand. "Say it."

Whimpering like a wounded animal, my body flushes until I'm soaked between my thighs. A muffled cry escapes my gag when Whitt rubs the length of his cock down my soaked slit. The only barrier between us is his boxers. The silk is immediately saturated by my wetness, and it sticks to him like a second-skin, outlining his cock.

"Fuck me– make me your wife!" Groveling, when I didn't think myself capable of this level of acquiescence, "I submit. Please!"

"What am I?" Whitt breathes directly into my ear, sounding more mature than I'll ever be.

Jerking from the sensation, my movements press Whitt's cock against my aching flesh. Amazed yet shocked, an orgasm flows through me in an instant. Sobbing out my release, it's muffled by my t-shirt. Writhing against Whitt, my knees grow weak as I tremble and quiver under his control.

"My husband," I mumble, hoping that's the answer to what Whitt's asking. My mind has now taken a permanent vacation.

"What am I?" Whitt asks in a dark voice that's as frightening as it is arousing.

Fingers clutching the front of my bra between my breasts, with a rough movement, Whitt rips it from my body. A sharp gasp of shock rushes out between my parted lips. No doubt, my back will be bruised from the force.

Inertia, my heavy breasts swing like pendulums, rubbing my nipples against the duvet. Sparks ignite throughout my body from the sensation radiating from my nipples to my core. A vicious aftershock rolls through me, clenching my pussy and forcing me to throb against the length of him, as if my body is physically trying to pull his cock into me to satisfy the ache.

The perversion makes the intensity that much stronger– the toxicity heightens the addiction.

"A man!" Shouting, I force the words through the fabric of my t-shirt. "You're a man!"

"And don't you ever forget that," Whitt demands– his manipulative powers know no bounds, and I hold no immunity to the effects.

After releasing me from the t-shirt, Whitt throws it across the room. Plucking me from my knees, I'm rolled over to rest on my back. Melting into my mattress, my arms and legs writhe on the bed involuntarily, twisting in the blankets and sheet as I groan from how incredible it feels. My nerves are alive with pleasure. The air on my skin feels glorious. Whitt's eyes on my body ignite me.

Cherishing the sensation of pure bliss flowing through my veins, I know it will soon flee, leaving me more confused and empty than ever. But for now, I hold onto it in order to survive.

My lips curve into a victorious smile as Whitt kisses me, knowing I'll soon get what I want. Not allowing me to take charge, Whitt kisses me his way– overpowering with possession and all-consuming.

“No,” Whitt breathes against the side of my neck, running the tip of his nose down the column. “You said my birthday, and my birthday it will be.”

Settling between my thighs, Whitt embraces me. My legs part and my hips thrust against him in silent invitation. My fingers inch their way underneath the silk of Whitt’s boxers to clench the firm globes of his ass. Wrapping my legs around his hips, I use my heels to pull away the fabric acting as an annoying barrier between us. After a dozen or so times of my trying to pry Whitt’s boxers down with my heels, he starts to chuckle.

“Tenacious, aren’t you?” Releasing a toe-curling laugh of pure satisfaction, Whitt puts me out of my misery by yanking his boxers off.

Impatient, I wait for Whitt to lower himself down to me, and when he doesn’t, that frustrated noise erupts from my chest.

“Do you want me to take the ache away?” Whitt murmurs in a voice you use on a child. “Does my wife hurt?”

“Yes.” Voice bitchy, I sound none too pleased.

“You regret your bargain now, don’t you?” He says sweetly, calculation shining down at me from his crystalline eyes.

“You bastard,” I growl, knowing the asshole is teaching me a lesson, doing exactly as I’d do.

“Next time, you will discuss matters with me instead of picking a date out of thin air. We will think it through. You will tell me your grievances. You will be honest with your husband and yourself.” Whitt schools me with a frustrated master’s voice. It’s deep and resonating, if not a little frightening, yet hotter than hell. More moisture spills from my cunny to pool between my ass cheeks.

“Yes, Daniel.” I agree, even if my dominant side is silently snarling.

“Did you learn your lesson?” The back of Whitt’s hand flutters down my abdomen. I concentrate on his movements and not his words. I’m too far gone to pay attention.

“Uh–” words fail me.

Arching off the bed, I groan deep from my chest and immediately start to come as Whitt taps the velvety, bulbous head of his cock against my engorged clit. Fingernails digging into his ass, I try to press him closer. But I can’t budge him, even as he grunts in pain as I draw the crimson kiss of blood.

Rocking my head back and forth in agony, it feels so good it hurts. My toes curl up to greet the backs of my feet as nonsensical sounds spew from my throat.

Unable to hold back, I combust when Whitt rests his cockhead against my opening. Doing everything I can, I try to force him to breach me. Flexing my hips, I use my fingers and heels to push him deeper into me. When Whitt doesn't give me what I want, I threaten him with words of torture.

Half-crazed blue eyes ensnare mine, no force on this planet will push Whitt to enter me. He's teaching me a lesson. But more importantly, he's silently screaming that nothing will make him go back on his word, even if we both want it. If I hadn't already respected Whitt, this would have done it.

Spiraling into him, I never want to crawl back out. "I love you," I whisper hoarsely, the honesty leaving me feeling emotionally raw.

Eyes bulging in shock, as if Whitt can't believe this is reality after wanting it for so long. His neck muscles flex as he plants a heavy palm firmly on my stomach to keep me still. I'm pushed into the mattress as he comes. Never wanting Whitt to go back on his word, I don't fight for control, or try to force him to enter me.

Holding his cockhead to my opening, none of his flesh entering me, Whitt's fiery release shoots inside of me from the force of his orgasm. Ever the man, Whitt's seed marks me as his wife, while tainting us both with the toxicity of our relationship.

Laughing manically, Whitt curls his spent body around mine, never voicing private thoughts that no doubt mirror mine.

"I'm surprised to learn you're a brutal Master, Daniel." I whisper against his hair. "Mad props."

"I told you how no one sees me– how I walk around cheerful and polite." Whitt manages to pull away, but connects with me nevertheless. "I hide behind my gentlemanly demeanor, but I demand total submission. My kink is control– total control. I know what I'm capable of and how demanding I can be, and you just felt how strong I am. No one but you has ever seen it. They think me weak like my sire."

"Grant's not weak." I defend the one person I should hate most on this earth, truly seeing his visible weaknesses as strengths.

"Never defend that spineless coward around me again, Regina." Whitt's tone is a cutting chastisement as he pulls away from me, putting both physical and emotional distance between us. "I'll never voice how my view of you has changed because you're not as angry as I am. I don't care if you still love him or not– he's dead to me."

Instead of fighting with him, I allow Whitt to feel what he feels. Grant's abandonment and all the lies affect Whitt the most. I was just the mistress, and I truly believe Grant learned to love me. But Whitt– Whitt was Grant's oldest son, the one who's legacy was torn away by lies, only to have his father leave him alone in this world.

Grant's priority should have been Whitt, just as mine should have been Niel. I left Niel for his own good, left him where he belonged and I didn't. It would be hypocritical of me not to see Grant's point-of-view when it comes to Whitt. But as one of the people who was left behind, I also understand the rage Whitt is barely keeping in check, and the emotional wounds Grant left behind on our souls.

Those wounds can never be forgiven, nor will they ever heal. But I won't make them fester by poking them until they bleed.

"What's your goal after you take your family back?" I change the subject for sanity's sake. "How do you see yourself in the future? Just sitting at Daniel's desk at night, after lording over everyone at Whittenhower Enterprises during the day?"

"Regina, I'm not completely phony, you know. I *am* polite and friendly– it's not an act."

"I know." Then I whisper the truth, "You're frustrated by how your grandfathers and father treated you. You feel abandoned by both of your parents, and the pain is eating you alive. I lost my entire family, then I left my son after Grant abandoned us to Daniel. I understand because I've been on both sides of the pain. But any idiot can see how special you are– intelligent, loyal, giving and caring."

"Stop!" Whitt presses his palm over my mouth, silencing me, but he's blushing a beautiful shade of pink. "Besides, I'd rather have everyone underestimate me. I love my family and friends, and I'll do everything in my considerable power to help them. But if you're asking me about how I see our life in the future–"

I interrupt Whitt, wanting to get to the heart of the matter. "You don't have to give me the reasons why you want to take control of your legacy. That's not what I'm asking. What do you want in the future?"

"I want us to be happy. I see you with lovers of your own choosing. God willing, I see me with my own too. At least until this mess is over and our family is secure, then we'll be free to marry for real. But I'll never abandon you, Queen."

"I know," I whisper, voice breaking. "You and I aren't built to leave people behind, not after knowing how much it hurts."

"Exactly. No matter what, I see us as family. I want everyone I know and love to be healthy and happy, to find their own dreams. I want to live without fear, without limitations and restrictions placed on me by people who should have no say."

"I fear we're not going to like ourselves when we finally reach our destination– but I'm willing to take one for the team to secure us all."

Whitt looks at me, truly looks at me, trying to steal my secrets. No way in hell am I ever going to tell him about Ezra being my contact. Whitt would step in, seeing Ezra as his childhood crush. Whitt would defend me, which would put him into the position Grant sacrificed his life to prevent.

If Grant is strong enough to sacrifice himself for the greater good, then so am I. The only difference is I will never be content to be Maître du Jeu's pawn, even if I was in a position of power. I'll do as I'm told while keeping my eyes and ears open, and I'll plan while no one is looking.

I just hope when it's all said and done, I can live with my choices. But it won't matter, as long as everyone is safe, happy, and healthy. It will be worth it. Unlike how Grant feels, when everything he's tried to prevent is happening anyway.

"I know you think I'll find some prince and leave you, but you're wrong. That prince will either fit into our kingdom, or I won't have him. This goes for your lovers as well. Marcus does have our best interests at heart, but I won't lie by saying you being with Grant isn't a kick to the teeth."

"I call him Jamie," I breathe as if it's a secret. "To admit Jamie is Grant, truly admit it, is to destroy whatever sanity I'm holding onto. I need him right now– he lends me strength. I know you don't get it, and I understand. Once the walls come crashing down, I don't think I'll be able to survive the emotional fallout. I need Jamie– I *need* him. Don't hate me because of it."

"Queen, I could never hate you, nor will I ever leave you. No matter what, even loving that rat, I'll always love you."

"I'll take nothing short of unconditional from you," forces out of a throat clenched to keep the sobs at bay.

Praying to a god I'm not sure I believe in, I hope Whitt's dreams are realized. If Whitt is correct, truly believing all he has to do is wish and the thought brings it into fruition, then I want him to wish harder than he's ever wished for anything.

"Wish us happiness, Whitt– wish for happiness."

Chapter Fifteen

"Nervous?" I smirk at Fate, finding her excitement contagious and cute as all get out.

Fate tries not to smile back, but after a few seconds, a grin spreads her lips. "Yeah. But you have to stick by me, okay? This is only fun if I don't have to worry about anything." Her melodious voice quivers, betraying her nervousness. I nod that I have her back.

Fate's practically bouncing on the balls of her feet as we walk toward the front of the waiting line at Restraint. People groan and complain as we walk by. One guy screams, '*get to the end of the line!*' like we're line-cutters, not summoned by the owners. I glower back at the dude, and he shrinks into the crowd.

"Just the man I was looking for," I say to the bruiser guarding the door. "How ya doing, Aaron?"

Am I a good actress? I have no idea. Fate and I have it all on the table, but I also know I can't ask in-depth questions without bringing harm to her. So to say it's difficult to look at Aaron and smile, while wondering if he was at the Maître du Jeu founders' meeting this morning, where a vote was held on 'fining' me a million bucks as the lesser of punishments.

It's also hard to swallow as Fate smiles sweetly at Aaron, and the man smiles back like he hasn't known her his entire life.

I'd move if it wasn't for my children and the men I love. I seriously want to throat-punch every single person I come into direct contact with for making me feel like a paranoid mess. What if I think someone's guilty and they're not? It's not my fault–they're the ones who made me a paranoid wreck, and this moment was probably orchestrated as well.

Anger aside, Aaron looks like the sweet boy-next-door type. It's hard to believe, but he's more adorable than he was two years ago. Manliness is filling out his feature, and it suits him. He's still shaving his hair close to the scalp– pity.

"Do you remember us, Aaron, because I remember you?" I cover my resentment with a flirty tone I tell myself I picked up from Kris, when in actuality it was the tone I used when bantering with Grant.

"Queen," Aaron's tone holds great respect, and I begin to wonder about his acting chops. After a suspended moment, he turns to smile at Fate. With a teasing tone one uses on a child, "Angel, are you behaving this evening? I see your master made sure you wore flats this time."

Fate blushes. I've been around her when she's gone after spineless fuckboys, and she was relentless in her pursuits. But if you place Fate around a real man, she turns shy. Using my body language reading skills, I can tell Fate is not only terrified of who Aaron is and what he's capable of, she respects him too.

"We've had an attitude adjustment since we were here last time, I assure you." I smirk down at a trembling Fate, and the three of us share a smile. We are all so full of shit. Aaron knows there's a monologue playing out inside my head, and he no doubt finds it hilarious.

"Ladies, may I?" Aaron pulls the stamper out– there has to be a better way. "Boss is waiting for you near the bar."

I want to ask why Ezra isn't wherever the meeting is being held, but I don't dare. "Thanks," I reply, then pull Fate behind me as she drags her feet.

Something's up if Fate would rather be around Aaron than Ezra. "No boogiemen, I assure you. I'm right with you." I murmur my reassurances, but I don't think Fate buys it.

"I'm not worried about myself," is Fate's cryptic reply. "Watch your back, Reg." Eyes slipping shut, she scares the piss out of me. "Please stay away from Ezra. Reg, I'm warning you. Just do as he asks of you, then keep your distance."

"Duly noted," I mumble, realizing everyone who knows what's going on has said the same thing. Whitt sees Ezra as the boy he's had a lifelong crush on. Marcus loves Ezra unconditionally, flaws and all, and I haven't had time to tell him about the million bucks and the edict from on high. Jamie… Grant is terrified for me. Kristal gave me a hug and told me to watch my back, even knowing I plan on punishing her tonight in the dungeon. Now there is Fate.

What the fuck does Ezra have in store for me? What am I missing here?

Well, Regina, I think to myself. *In a world where a million dollars is a slap on the wrist, one should be utterly terrified.*

Aaron's older, bigger doppelganger opens the door for us. Looking the man in the eyes, "Hello, Roarke," I acknowledge his existence. "We'll be working closely together soon."

Fate has the common decency not to play pretend. "Hey, big guy!" Just as she was with Aaron, there is respect in her tone. But she's more relaxed around the ex-cop, enough so she rubs his gigantic bicep as a way to stroke his ego.

"Be careful this evening, Ms. Simpson," Roarke's voice is deep and resonating. "Mrs. Whittenhower–" news travels fast, and now I know Roarke and Aaron were witnesses to the meeting that was all about little ol' me. "Find me immediately should you run into any problems. I'll even protect you from Ezra."

Ah, that's why Fate is more comfortable around Roarke–he's not drinking Ezra's Kool-Aid like Aaron must be. There are zealot enforcers, then there are ones like Albert, whose job is to protect everyone from their founder, and the founder from himself.

"Thank you," I murmur with all sincerity while placing my hand on Roarke's chest… because, why not? The guys is built like a Mack Truck. Patting once or twice, I appreciate his body, but I make sure he knows it's out of respect, not lust.

"You're welcome, and I do look forward to your help running this place. It's in sore need of a strong hand. Restraint's success was a bit of a shock to us. Ezra's always in his own head, and Aaron's struggling because he doesn't know where to begin. So you'll be working with Aaron, and I presume Elder Whittenhower will be sending Roman your way, even if it puts him at risk with both of his enforcers on site."

"Shit," I hiss. "So we're not going to pretend I'm ignorant, I guess."

"You are no Diane Holden or the two eldest Daniel Whittenhowers. You were originally vetted as an enforcer by our late Mrs. Zeitler, thinking you would be a good companion to her grandsons. Just keep your eyes and ears shut, like you use to in your old neighborhood. You know nothing, see nothing, and hear nothing. Do as you're told, and should Ezra go off the rails, above and beyond what duty calls, contact me and I'll rein him in. I suggest you don't get the Whittenhowers or the Zeitlers involved, if you catch my drift. Rationality versus emotion."

"I've got nothing to say to that," tumbles from between my numb lips. "Rebekah singled me out for this?"

"You were intelligent and stable, yet destined for a shitty life. I'd say Mrs. Zeitler was correct in her estimations."

"I–" I look to Fate, and notice she is and isn't surprised.

"I thought they wanted you as Grant's enforcer," Fate explains. "So color me shocked, but the truth makes more sense. Our freshman year, Dexter and Marc were with us at Hillbrook, with Grant a freshman at college."

"You'll find Ezra at the bar." Roarke gestures, making my surroundings come into sharp focus. Sound hits with the force of a tsunami to the face– the music is louder than my last visit, more tribal. Its hedonistic beat lures me to the dance floor, beckoning me to join the mass of gyrating bodies.

"I suggest you take care of business and personal first, and play later," Roarke warns, and I finally notice Ezra sitting at the bar while wearing his ridiculous hood.

"See ya around, Roarke." I pat his chest again before stepping out of his orbit. "I have a feeling we'll get along well."

"Same here," Roarke says with a brisk nod. "Watch your back."

"From now on," I draw Fate's attention from our surroundings. "Unless you'll get punished by your sadistic founder members, you have to tell me what I need to know."

"That's a fine line you draw, Reg." Fate slips her hand in mine, then squeezes a few times. "There is nothing you don't need to know. Just as there are things I'm not privy to on purpose. We all know different things, taking counsel with our allies. So I can tell you nothing."

"Lovely," I grumble, annoyed.

"Exactly– welcome to the world I was born into."

There are noticeable differences at Restraint since my initial visit almost two years ago. Basically, it's no longer a shithole. The floor is glossy black and the walls are gray concrete, giving off an industrial feel. There are twice as many booths and seating areas– the red velvet seating is filled to capacity with patrons of every age, sex, and creed.

In her pissed off, angsty glory, Syn is leaning against the back wall by the entrance to the dungeon. Her hair is purple this evening with razor-cut bangs. She's wearing leather pants and a matching shirt that covers her from neck to wrists. The only skin visible is her hands and face. Not only does Syn look like a sadist, she looks nothing like the Faith I used to know.

Fate worries her bottom lip between her teeth as she stares at the sadist as if she's a complete stranger. The look screams fear, as if Fate is scared of Faith.

It's a complete role reversal. Fate looks the part of baby sister, wearing a flowing, light blue dress and ballet flats. Innocence radiates off of Fate, and its scent captures those closest to us. Hell, it even has Syn looking back at us with eyes held wide with fear because my faux submissive is master bait.

A hooded figure waits for us by the bar, and I can tell it's Ezra by the tension riding his shoulders. Cort's more relaxed, easily going with the flow. Ezra is one of the most serious people I've ever met. Leaning against the bar, he surveys his club. While it looks like a relaxed pose, every muscle is taut and at the ready.

Treading lightly, I try for a dutiful tone. "Boss, you requested my presence?"

Turning slowly, Ezra's gunmetal eyes pin me mid-step. Fury emanates in waves, directed toward me. I'd like to think Ezra's having a bad night, but I can tell all of his rage is directed at me.

On instinct, I drag Fate behind me in a protective stance.

"You're late," Ezra mutters underneath his breath, but I can hear it over the pound of the music. No doubt everyone heard the venom in his hiss.

"Ezra?" I quickly retrieve my phone to check the time. "You said eight o'clock, and it's seven fifty-nine." Glaring, Ezra's look could literally kill someone with less fortitude than me. "What did I do to earn such ire?"

"Later," Ezra grunts– his tone the sound of glass grating on glass. "Come with me," he demands, fingers enclosing my wrist. With a sharp pull, I'm jerked forward. "Fate stays here."

"Wait!" I dig my heel in as Ezra tows me from the bar. "Fate can't stay alone," I protest in a panic. Men and women alike are hovering like sharks in the water scenting fresh blood.

Snapping his fingers, "Kristal, watch her," Ezra orders impatiently.

"Go behind the bar and help, Kris." I quickly rub Fate's shoulder, not wanting to let her out of my sight. "You'll be just fine. Chat up the hot guys while pouring their drinks."

Fate does as she's told, listening to me, not Ezra. A few hovering people back off in disappointment, but the rest belly up to the bar, trying to gain Fate's attention.

"You watch her." Leaning on my palms, I bend over the top of the bar, getting into Kristal's face. "If anyone touches Fate, it's your funeral. I mean it, Kris. You already have a punishment coming. Earn my trust back, watch out for our girl."

"I promise," Kristal replies in a serious voice I didn't think her capable. She pulls Fate underneath her arm, cradling the more fragile woman to her side. "We'll be here, collecting tips we don't need, all because the furious one doesn't trust outside help."

I mull Kristal's words over while Ezra pulls me though the club like an angry parent. When we reach the entrance to the dungeon, Syn quickly types in a code at the door, then we march right through. Syn follows us with the same energy as a building storm cloud.

I want to get a good look at the dungeon, but the lights are off as Ezra pulls me toward the back hallway. Bypassing several doors that have name plaques, I'm yanked into a long room that's dominated by a conference table and chairs. Seated around the table are all of the Masters of Restraint, including Dalton who has yet to be initiated. I don't have time to acknowledge anyone before Ezra's slamming me into a chair hard enough that my tailbone smashes into the seat.

That's going to leave a bruise.

"Ezra? Behave," Marcus warns, looking more lost and sad than angry.

"Don't!" Ezra points at Marcus as he sits to his left. They stare at each other for a few suspended moments in time. A sigh of relief escapes me because I'm no longer the object of Ezra's agitation.

I quickly look around, noting Marcus is at the head of the table having a stare-down with Ezra on his left. On his right is Dexter. Next to Dexter sits Cortez. Syn glares at Cort from directly across the table. He smirks back at Syn in a taunting manner, but his eyes are on his partner and Marcus. In between Cort and me is Whitt, and he's staring at the silent fight, too.

My husband is too engrossed in the standoff to acknowledge me, but I let it go, because to examine it too closely would mean my feelings would get bent.

The sides of the table aren't balanced, and it's driving me to distraction. On my side, no one sits across from Whitt, me, nor across from Dalton. Basically, only Ezra and Syn are on one side of the table, with Dexter, Cortez, Whitt, me, and Dalton on this side. I find this contemplation a worthy distraction from the silent standoff occurring at the head of the table.

The creepy factor flows up my spine to light into my psyche. My lover sits at the head of the table, with his adoptive son glaring at me. The man to my left is my husband, making everyone else in the room related to me. Syn is my sister-in-law. Being that grown up Bianca is also my sister-in-law, and she's now married to the fellow on my right, Dalton is also my brother-in-law.

Mind blown– like seriously fucking blown.

Adopted by Marcus, Ezra is related to Dalton in a roundabout way, since they share a sister– Spyder.

Now I appreciate Maître du Jeu's meddling with who marries and creates children with whom. Too many would accidently dip their toes into their own family trees, creating six-fingered children. No wonder they outsource with the likes of me. With their need to keep all the money and power in the families, someone needs to be on top of that shit, or else incest will run rampant.

"Why aren't you next to Syn?" I tilt my head in Dalton's direction.

"Syn punched me earlier," Dalton mutters with pride. Sure enough, he has a small red spot on his chin. "I'm not a Master of Restraint yet, even if I was born and raised by Maître du Jeu's Maître." The real Dalton rears its gorgeous head in the way his lilting tone caresses the French as if it's his native tongue– maybe it is. "Syn didn't think I should be at this meeting, but Ezra vetoed her bitchiness."

Snorting, it turns into an uncomfortable laugh. For some reason, I highly doubt, after being raised in Vegas, Dalton knows it's actually a secret society of assholes running Dominion, not just a BDSM group. His mother may be in charge of the deviants, but I doubt she's the one running the founder's freak show.

"I'm never going to get used to the redundancy of saying The Game Master's master." Sarcasm is so thick in my tone, you could choke on it. "Talk about egotistical."

"Master of the Game," Dalton gives a different interpretation. "Not the Game Master's master. The person in charge *is* Maître du Jeu."

Covering her mouth with an upraised palm, Syn softly coughs but it sounds more like a sadistic giggle. Cort joins in with her, leaving half of the room confused, with Marcus and Ezra too busy bickering in hushed voices to notice.

Loathing one another, Syn and Cortez find common ground with an inside joke, which means Dexter, Whitt, Dalton, and I don't know shit about anything, and probably Marcus doesn't either. That's comforting in a bad way.

"What did you say to Syn to get her to punch you?" I ask Dalton underneath my breath, hoping not to be overheard. Having sonic hearing, Whitt's chest quivers as he tries to suppress his laughter.

"Usually it doesn't take much to anger her, but it takes a lot for me to get underneath her skin for some reason." Smiling evilly, "You don't want to know what I had to say to earn this bruise." I can tell the guy wants to be a little prick, and his act intrigues me.

I'm assuming Syn's reluctance to strike Dalton would be the same as mine. Both of us know Dalton is our brother-in-law, but he's kept in the dark.

"Maybe I wanna know," I muse underneath my breath, wanting to get to know the young man.

Dalton laughs quietly while shaking his head no, brown hair flopping around his ears. Could he have chosen an uglier wig?

Adding yet another dimension of creepy, Ezra finally pulls the hood off his head. With fury etched across his aristocratic features, Ezra finger-combs his short white-blond hair, then runs his elegant hands over his face.

"What's your malfunction, Ezra?" Marcus tone of voice is astonished– I guess this isn't Ezra's usual behavior.

"I don't like being told what to do!" Ezra barks. "I'm the goddamn man who envisioned Restraint, from conception to reality. The reason there is a line around the block is because of me, and I don't appreciate being told what to do."

"Is the irony failing to escape anyone else's notice?" I mumble, causing a few snickers to erupt.

"Shut your fucking mouth!" Ezra stabs a finger in my direction while glaring daggers.

"Ezra!" flows in unison from Marcus and Whitt.

"No, I don't want to hear another word from any of you. This afternoon Master Fontaine demanded I open Restraint to the public at large, which will bring about an entirely different set of problems our way. I wanted to say no, but I couldn't."

"Ah, there's the irony!" flows from my lips before I can stop it.

"Regina," Marcus chastises, and it rubs me all sorts of wrong. "You're not helping."

"Really?" The bitchiness in my tone is surprising, but it doesn't cause me to hesitate. "I was initiated in the wee hours of this morning, with no say in anything I did. I fucked half of the people in this room when I didn't want to. So excuse me if Ezra's having a bad day because Olivia Fontaine has his nuts in a vise."

"Regina!" Marcus tries again to get me in hand, which makes me spew more.

"I was initiated, then married, then extorted as a punishment, then ordered to come here. I can safely say that we're all dominants at this table, and not a goddamn one of us likes to be told what to do. But you don't see me lying down and dying over it. Deal, Ezra– just deal."

"You're my problem, too!" Ezra screams. "Not only does Olivia have me by the balls, I was outvoted in my own club. Because of you!"

"What the fuck did I ever do to you?" I bellow back, ignoring my cellphone vibrating.

"What?" Ezra squawks. "You have my father wrapped around your finger."

"Jealous because that position is reserved for only you?" I volley back.

"Cunt," Ezra snarls to the background noise of Cortez laughing like a loon. "Restraint was my creation, but I needed help from Marcus and Dexter. Minutes after Olivia sunk her claws in me, Marcus and Dexter say they voted for you to manage my club. My dungeon. Mine!"

The definition of irony. While shouting about Restraint, Ezra is screaming mine while pointing at Marcus. Freudian slip of epic proportions.

I shut up because there is no winning against a lunatic, there is no negotiating with terrorists, and dealing with Ezra requires both.

While Ezra calms himself, I sneak a peek at the text I just received.

MdJ: *Just a friendly piece of advice. Don't purposefully anger your contact, especially when that person is Ezra, unless you have a death wish. Use self-preservation, Regina.*

Eyes flicking up, I go from person to person, reading their body language. Most people are starring at Ezra as he calms down, but my eyes connect with Syn and hold. She tilts her head to the side, toward Ezra, silently communicating that by baiting Ezra on his own turf, I was dragging myself off to slaughter.

MdJ? Ah! Now I get the inside joke. While Olivia Fontaine may be the head bitch of the BDSM community, Syn is clearly the Master of the Game on Dominion soil. Which explains why she emits the same dark energy as Ezra, but is a billion times more emotionally controlled and mentally stable.

Wow. What turns us into who we ultimately become? The little girl from Rusty Knob, West Virginia, who used to wear her blonde hair in girly pigtails and played Barbies is the nexus of evil.

"Obviously Restraint has some major changes occurring, with Regina taking over the helm and Olivia demanding our dungeon admit the public. So I called you here to discuss how your duties will change."

"Before you bitch–" Marcus cuts us off at the pass. "None of us wanted this. But to borrow Regina's turn of phrase, we have to deal. Since you pledged yourself to Maître du Jeu, you've got to buck up or shut up."

"Enough of the idiotic phrases," Ezra grumbles, rolling his eyes. "After Marcus is finished entertaining us, I will be meeting with you individually to hand out your duties."

"Okay," Marc draws out, staring to the side at his son. "Tomorrow evening, we will allow patrons to apply for membership to the dungeon. There will be an application, with certain restrictions, before any approval will be granted."

"That will be *my* job," Ezra directs pointedly at me. "I have *all* the say in who and who doesn't set foot into *my* dungeon."

Marcus ignores Ezra's outburst. "What we need from you is to monitor the membership, and to make sure everyone is safe, both inside and outside of the dungeon. With Restraint's popularity, we're encountering safety issues. Until we have proper protocols in place, only members of Restraint and their guests have access to the dungeon. Those who abuse their position will have their membership revoked. We will try this out for a while and see how it goes. We may expand or close, depending on how this works out."

"Or we may find other means to get Master Fontaine off our asses," Ezra purrs, clearly lost in thought on how to stick it to

Dalton's mom– the lady who held Marcus captive for a year and stole his billionaire juice to make Spyder.

"As you see, Dalton is among us without an initiation. I'm training both Alex and Dalton at the same time, and Aaron on my off-time. After suffering through Regina's initiation in the wee hours of this morning, I will not torture our three newest masters, especially when we don't have a balanced male to female ratio with blooded relatives in the mix. I draw the line at rape and incest to satisfy the rules of initiation."

Ezra's face whips to the side "Do you, now?" he mutters snidely. "Nice of you to change the rules for the newest members, yet you subjected the rest of us to a much worse fate. Rape and incest, he says… hmm…"

"Oh, hush!" Dexter interjects. "Whitt's initiation was a blast. You and I, our initiation was bullshitting around the poker table. Anything bad that happened at Cortez and Syn's initiation was *your* fault– nothing that hadn't happened in the past, I might add. As Regina said, you should have just dealt with it and got over it. Instead, you made it worse. Besides, I don't want my dick anywhere near Aaron, Dalton, or Alex."

"You will be the last person to talk down to me," Ezra threatens in a cold voice, which elicits a shiver out of our membership.

"Ezra will pass out your duties," Marcus ignores how Ezra keeps blinking repeatedly, like he's warring himself in his own head. "I'm sorry to ask for more of your free time, but it's a necessary evil, which can't be avoided."

"Dexter– my room!" Ezra commands, standing so abruptly his chair hits the wall. All I can hope for is that Ezra calms down before it's my turn, especially since he's blaming me in the first place for how powerless he feels.

As soon as Ezra follows Dexter from the meeting room, a collective breath is released. Ezra's tension was suffocating.

"What the fuck?" I ask anyone who will answer.

"I haven't a clue what crawled up Ezra's ass," Marc mutters, just as confused as the rest of us, but he doesn't seem surprised by the tantrum. After scrubbing his palms over his face, he sighs deeply.

People begin filing out into the hallway, softly talking amongst themselves, until it's just Marcus, Whitt, and me left, which makes it all the more awkward.

Whitt leans over to whisper into my ear, voice somber. "Sorry about what you'll probably see tonight– I have to act as I always do."

"I know," I mutter quietly in reply. "It's fine."

A sardonic snort fills the room– Marcus. The sound changes to a growl when Whitt leans to the side to kiss me softly. My new husband's lips dance over mine, and the awkward level reaches an all-time high.

Noticing how I refuse to become his passenger, especially in front of Marcus when I want to be respected, Whitt pulls away to look into my eyes. "If it bothers you, we will figure something out."

"I. Will. Be. Fine." I enunciate each word. I have to be fine. This is how my life will be from now on. Whitt getting his dick sucked is the least of my worries. We may be married, but we'll never be a couple. It's a sad reality, but nonetheless true.

I'm nothing if not pragmatic.

Ezra, on the other hand, is going to be a motherfucking huge thorn in my side, I can feel it more strongly than a premonition.

"Okay, if you're not…" Whitt laughs at my vexed expression. "We'll revisit this conversation if you're not okay with what you see in the dungeon. I never want you to feel disrespected by me. Remember what happened when you wouldn't talk to me earlier?" Voice light and teasing, Whitt's threat is hidden beneath.

Whitt's gaze holds a wealth of remembrance and a ton of scorching heat, to the point I turn into a girly idiot like I'm the innocent one. Looking away, I try to hide my blush.

"Oh, I learned that lesson, Daniel." Voice husky with reluctant lust and a bit of anger, "We won't have a repeat."

"Hmm… my birthday feels ages away." Whitt kisses my cheek, while huffing naughty laughter beneath his breath. "Well, I guess I'll go hunting while Ezra rakes everyone over the coals."

"Make sure you pick a girl with strong jaw muscles." I taunt, as if this isn't one of the most bizarre conversations I've ever had. "Or you could do yourself a favor and find a guy to apply the suction to your cock. Just saying…"

Marcus shuts the door after Whitt leaves, silencing the riotous laughter. Falling backward, Marcus leans against the door while gazing at me with amber eyes so intense I can't help but squirm.

Standing abruptly, I start to pace the small meeting room, needing to burn off excess energy.

"You really don't know what's wrong with Ezra?" I count the chairs as I walk around the table. We have a lot of room for expansion. I wonder who'll join us next.

"No." Marcus heaves a heavy sigh, sounding defeated. "There's no reasoning out why Ezra is behaving a certain way. It just is what it is."

As I make a pass in front of Marcus, he snags my arm to draw me into a tight embrace. "I need comfort, as do you." Tugging gently, he pulls us to his chair, cuddling me on his lap.

We don't speak as he rhythmically rubs my shoulders and neck.

The calm before the storm

Focused on the soft yet deep sound of Marc's breathing, I can hear muffled conversation out in the hallway. Dexter's deep voice is angry, then Syn shouts, "*Oh, hell no!*" I want to know what's going on, but I wouldn't miss this comfort for the world.

"Are you alright after your initiation and Whitt?" Marcus breathes against my throat.

"No," I admit for the first time, getting choked up about it. "There are a few more things we need to discuss, but I can't get into it right now. I have to deal with Ezra first, then I'm taking Kristal in hand. I decided to be practical. So instead of stressing over what I've done, I'll deal with what needs to be done instead."

Enflamed with hurt and rejection, I want to scream how Marcus gave me away. Grant gave me to Marcus, and then Marcus and Jamie both gave me to Whitt, like I'm a baton meant to be passed during the relay race we call life.

If Marcus truly loved me, why didn't he have the balls to declare us a couple at my initiation? Instead, he outright denied it, and then demanded I suck his cousin's cock and screw his adopted son.

Am I destined to deal with these broken men who need to grow the fuck up? That's the major reason I can't accept the fact that Jamie is Grant. I need Jamie, the grown up, mature version of the man I used to know. I need his stability, patience, and sound advice, but it's at the cost of my self-respect and self-worth.

To truly be empowered, I have to let them all go, without apologies or explanations, and I don't know if I'll ever be ready. A person with self-respect and self-worth would never accept the injustices dealt. I've made major mistakes, and I'm no hypocrite. I don't know if it's worth it– I honestly don't know if *I'm* worth it.

I love Whitt, but it's not the same as I feel for the man whose arms surround me. Marc's scent fills my nostrils, like a potent narcotic thrumming through my veins. If I ignore the bad, I can admit I'm addicted to how Marcus makes me feel, just as I get a hit off Jamie with every conversation exchanged.

After two seconds in Marc's arms, I can finally relax, as if the constrictive fist clutching my lungs has loosened and I can take a deep breath. If I had a choice– were forced to make a choice –Marcus is who I would pick as my lover, and I'd be happy for the rest of my life. Not as a consolation because Grant abandoned us all and Jamie doesn't want either of us. I genuinely love Marcus, and I've accepted it as fact. If you can accept someone's faults, and they accept yours in return, they're the one.

I'm terrified one isn't enough, always craving the one I'm not with, worried that means I don't truly love either one of them enough.

Maybe it's because I'm a woman without faith.

My husband and his father are Catholic, with Jamie being highly devout, while my lover is Jewish. They all marry for life, which means I'm truly and royally fucked because I'm wed to the wrong man.

Whitt deserves more than this, but maybe I do too…

"I don't regret marrying Whitt," I admit to cover up what I'm truly thinking about. Pipe dreams that will never be realized. I married Whitt, Marcus is married to Diane, and Jamie is married to his cowardice.

That's about as final as final can get. What I can give is partnership, trust, and loyalty, but only if it's equally given back in return.

"After seeing my children hug, laugh, and chat while I watched, nothing could make me think it wasn't the best idea in the world. But that doesn't mean I'm not having a hard time coming to terms with the arrangement. It's the type of marriage I said I'd never have. It may be based on love, but not the kind a husband feels for a wife, or a wife for a husband. This will either work flawlessly, or it'll decimate me."

Left speechless, Marc pull me tighter to his chest, fingers clenching on my arms. The reassurance keeps the words flowing from between my lips, even if they shouldn't.

"Whitt wouldn't have been my choice of a life partner. But, then again, that choice was ripped from me."

"I know you see him as two individuals– Grant died and Jamie was resurrected, and they aren't the same entity." Two years ago, Marcus was jealous of my connection to Grant, loving the man as much as I did, and in the same exact way. But after the sting was soothed, Marc realized Grant hurt us both.

Voice tight with suppressed tears, "I'm truly sorry you lost Grant."

I want to say, *"I didn't lose Grant– he left me,"* but what flows instead is a shock to both of us.

"Who said I was speaking of Grant?" Queen's rough, deep voice erupts from my throat.

Marcus gasps and clenches me tightly, knowing I'm insinuating he was the one I would have chosen as my life partner, because he's the one who wants to be here as much as I want him to be.

Grant may have chosen Marcus for me, but at some point, he's going to lose us both when we decide to move on without him. At least that's what I tell myself in the quiet hours at night, as a way to comfort me with the terrifying sting of reality. In fantasy, Jamie choses me, or he chooses Marcus after deciding his sexuality is fluid. In reality, I can't lose Jamie, because I never had him. But I could lose Marcus if we don't stick by each other's sides.

"This afternoon, I told Whitt that I loved him, and I meant it. But not in the way I wished I did." Sighing, I bury my face against the side of Marc's neck, trying to fortify myself for what I have to say next.

"I told Whitt I'd consummate our marriage on his birthday, and I meant it. If I had a choice, I wouldn't do it. But since I don't regret marrying Whitt, I have to commit to what that truly entails."

"Oh, Regina." A heavy palm rests on the top of my head, fingers clenching in a rhythmic massage. "This is what I tried to prevent, but Whitt is a formidable opponent when it comes to negotiations."

"To be honest, I do and I don't blame you," I admit with surprising ease, not caring that Marcus flinches in pain. "Does my marriage make me a bad person? I'm in love with two people, neither my husband. Someone I can't have and someone who doesn't want me."

"That's not true." Marcus will forever defend himself and Jamie. "I give you as much of me as I possibly can– more than I give anyone else. But I do know it's not enough. As for Jamie–"

"It's entirely Jamie's responsibility to express his feelings," I caution, basically telling Marcus to shut up. "Instead of curling into a ball and feeling nothing, I feel alive. Organized religion dictates how I shouldn't want anyone but my husband. The moment I signed that license, my brain should shut my body down. But since my marriage didn't erase my feelings for you and Jamie, I'm an immoral person. So maybe I wasn't meant to be in a traditional marriage. Perhaps I'm a different breed of human who can't live by society's standards, or maybe I'm just fucked in the head."

"Or maybe you have finally found where you belong." Marcus kisses the top of my head. "I've only known this type of living. I don't know how regular people live. I was young when I lost my parents, and they weren't a love match– I assume it was arranged by our founders. I was lucky because my grandmother was an incredible woman, grounded."

My mind spins back to when Roarke informed me Marc's grandmother was trying to shape me into her grandsons' enforcer. My scholarships weren't altruistic on her part. She was no doubt in the thick of MdJ's bullshit. My guess, with her husband's untimely death, Dexter's mother became the Zeitler elder, with Marc's father as the heir. Since the boys were too young, with the death of their parents, the responsibility fell on their grandmother's shoulders. At least she tried not to pass the torch to Dexter and Marcus, or maybe that was just Dexter's ethics holding him back.

I feel like a shit heel, because as my mind took a mini-vacation, Marcus continued to pour out his heart.

"Where I failed was when I married my wife. But it wasn't like I had a choice. My grandmother dropped me off when I was still a minor and going to school. I don't regret it for the same reasons you don't regret Whitt. I love Ezra and Cortez with every fiber of my being. I love Aaron and Divina as well."

"Kids change everything," I mutter in understanding, knowing Marcus is devoutly loyal to Ezra and Cortez, and Aaron and Divina by association.

"Whitt loves you, don't think otherwise. But let me tell you, he loves the kids more. I don't say that to upset you, or make light of what you feel for one another." Marcus coaxes to soften the verbal blow. "But isn't that true for you, too?"

"It's because they can't take care of themselves yet." I agree with Marcus wholeheartedly.

"Ah– perhaps. But the need to be a caretaker never fades. Yes, what Cort and I do is inappropriate on some levels. Cortez isn't my son, and he's a grown man. It's just the dynamic we have, where I have to meet his needs, and in turn he meets mine."

"I don't know what my needs are because they're all over the place," I finally admit.

"Regina, it takes a lifetime to learn what your needs are. They evolve as you grow and change as a person. With every new experience, they lessen or strengthen. It will take a lifetime to figure out your needs, and just as long to overcome them. It's just the tip of the iceberg at our age– imagine how lost and confused Whitt must feel."

"Which is my struggle, because I have no idea if I'm harming Whitt by giving into his manipulations."

For a few minutes, we contemplate my predicament. Marc's arms continuously clench around me, until we're fused as close together as humanly possible.

Voice beyond sad, "I'm sorry," Marcus says after a while.

"For what?" My heart flutters in my chest. Is Marcus sorry he loves me? Sorry I love him? Sorry I married Whitt because he didn't speak up and stop it? Sorry about what?

"Regina, it's better left unsaid, don't you think? Because once it's released into the world, you can never take it back."

What the hell does that mean? Seriously, Marcus is making me go full-blown idiot girl. Does he want to take back his feelings for me? Wish them away, ignore them? Tears prickle my eyes, to the point I have to hold them wide open to halt the betraying moisture from escaping.

"You want to take it back?" My voice quivers, breaking with a croak. "You want to take back how we feel for one another?"

"Not the words or the emotions, Regina. I love you, and nothing will change that. Fuck that, I'm *in* love with you,"

Marcus says with great conviction, causing my heart to flutter with hope for our future.

But then Marcus goes and deflates my joy. "It's the feeling of hope the unspoken words would elicit. Someday, I'd love to express all of my feelings for you, for everyone and anyone in particular. I'd love to share my past, and have you be my future. This is why I don't want you or I to say anything we may regret later. Especially with you refusing to acknowledge the truth about Grant."

"Actions speak louder than words, Marcus." I throw his own words right back at him.

"I know. That's why there's no need to profess anything, Regina."

Raising my face to his, I notice Marc's full lips are parted on a breath, and his eyes are heavily lidded. Flushed with need, I want to kiss Marcus so badly I ache. It's not sexual in nature– pure intimacy and the need to connect on a higher level.

I don't mean to compare, but I can't help it. Whitt is thrilling and exciting, yet he fills me with peace. But Marcus enflames my soul and challenges me– completes me.

A loud voice in my head shouts, *"But where does that leave Jamie?"*

Shut up!

Fingers clenching against my back, Marcus appears to have stopped breathing as he wars with himself. "I promised myself I'd leave you alone until after you and Whitt have found a rhythm to your marriage. But–"

Marc's face lowers, and I eagerly tilt mine upward in silent invitation.

"Regina," a voice sounding like fingernails scratching down a chalkboard interrupts our moment. "It's your turn. My room. Now."

Ezra glares at us as if I'm the Whore of Babylon, Marcus is his husband, and we were just caught cheating together. The tension radiating off the man is terrifying, even if his body language doesn't express it.

We weren't even kissing, nor were we sitting in a salacious manner. It's the drugged expression on our faces that makes our involvement beyond obvious. No matter Marc's protests to the contrary during my initiation, if Ezra had any doubts about whether or not we'd been lovers, he doesn't now.

The enraged expression on Ezra's hardened face screams how he's always known Marcus and I were a couple. For his mother, maybe even a little bit for himself, I feel my pain riding in the air. Ezra will get his retribution for me touching that which is his, and for sneaking in from the outside to take control of Restraint.

Since Ezra can't take his feeling of powerlessness out on his adoptive father, he's going to punish me to punish us all.

As I slowly rise from Marc's lap with trepidation, his warning call stops me. "Ezra, your actions have consequences."

Ezra's lips twitch and his eyes go cold as a silent signal I can't interpret. Marc's fingers grip my wrist, not wanting to leave me alone with his son, as if he can sense the violence promised.

Fuck it.

Rock meet hard place.

I can't *not* go with Ezra, not when he holds my leash thanks to Maître du Jeu. If I don't do as I'm told, the ramifications affect everyone in our lives.

No matter what Jamie warned, the first chance I get, I'm spilling every detail to Marcus.

Leaning down to kiss the corner of Marc's mouth, I never take my eyes from Ezra. It doesn't matter what I do, he's going to play with me anyway. I could be respectful or disobedient, and he would give me the same treatment.

I have no idea what happened since early this morning to have changed how Ezra views me, since I heard no complaints while I was taking one for the team with his dick lodged in my asshole. When Ezra had the chance to truly bring the pain, he took me softly and with great care.

I'd bet, if Ezra could have a do-over, he would literally rip me a new asshole.

Chapter Sixteen

A forceful palm on the back of my head smashes me face-first into the wall. Crying out as cold cement digs into my cheek, my arms hang limply at my sides. Gravity displaced, the sum of my weight is on my face and feet. Teetering precariously, Ezra holds me in place.

Everything occurs in mere seconds, leaving me stunned frozen in disbelief. I left the meeting room with Ezra in tow, and as soon as I entered the Zeitler room, he shut the door– with *my* face.

The background noise to my shock is the repetitive beeping sound of Marcus tapping the security code into the door, trying to get in to stop Ezra. With quick movements, a bar is slid between my belly and the door, securing us inside, with no one getting in or out. I can't hear anything in the hallway, reasoning out that this room has been soundproofed.

In slow-motion, it's been no more than ten seconds as I've been frozen in shock, a boot knocks against the inside of my left ankle, then my right, until my legs are spread as if Ezra pulled my puppet strings.

Echoing in the silence, flows a scream so primal it sounds subhuman. My ears ring from the agony released. Mind and body on a delay, Ezra's on his third thrust before I register the violation. Pushing his length where he wasn't invited, he feels large and thick inside my unprepared body.

Whimpering from a myriad of pains, moisture rushes to the source to pave the way. Shame overpowers disbelief over how my body immediately accepts Ezra's invasion– relishes the total abandonment of power.

Shock– not the bullshit type that signifies awe, but the physiological response to a mental, emotional, and physical trauma. In shock, the only thought that courses through my mind is that I wished I'd worn pants so I would've at least had advanced warning.

I'm wearing a corseted dress– the bottom is overlapping panels of purple iridescent sheer fabric. The corset is black, laced with purple ribbon. I have no underthings on– no protection.

Is this really happening?

Am I being raped?

I should have worn pants.

I shouldn't have angered Ezra– everyone had warned me.

Regina, it's not your fucking fault! You could have worn armor, and this sociopath would have used the bolt cutters hanging on the wall to get what he wanted. You did nothing wrong!

But it's my fault for putting myself in this situation.

NO!

Ezra didn't seem interested in me this morning.

This is NOT about sex!

Mind reeling between warring thoughts, I didn't have time to fight back, let alone react. It couldn't have been more than twenty seconds. There was a level of complacency, never expecting Ezra to do this to me, even if he was pissed off.

Women shouldn't have to fear being raped, Regina!

But it's our reality. We can't go walking around unaware, in spots that are known to be dangerous. It's called self-preservation.

There is self-preservation, then there is blaming yourself because a man feels he has a right to do whatever he wants to you, without permission. You should be able to walk around naked with your fingers up your pussy, and a man shouldn't touch you unless he's invited. You don't go dropping to your knees to suck a dick just because you find the guy hot. Imagine that scenario. Ludicrous, right? And not because society pretends women don't have sex drives.

Maybe if I hadn't worn this dress. Did Ezra see a flash of my ass when I got up off of Marc's lap?

Yeah, because that ass is so irresistible it drives men to rape. Seriously, are you listening to yourself? It's gross that you truly believe what you're thinking, the one who says she's empowered. Mothers need to teach their sons how to treat women as humans instead of property. None of that bullshit about treating a woman how you'd like your mother, sister, or daughter to be treated. As if our only value is in direct correlation to a specific man. Treat us how you'd treat a fellow human.

Men and women think differently.

No, it's bred into them. Women could cover every square inch of their bodies and never speak a single word, and a rapist would still rape them. It's not about lust– it's about control. There is inborn, human instincts wrought through hormones and the drive to mate. Every male animal doesn't mate with every female it comes into contact with. Humans have something Ezra seems to lack– higher reasoning skills and self-restraint. This is all male ego. We have failed as a society.

Not all men are rapists.

No, but all little boys grow up with a sense of entitlement they never grow out of. No matter what, the one with the dick rules. Every man has crossed the line with someone, even if it's something disrespectful said out of anger, or manipulations used on the wife, or liberties taken with a date who had too much to drink, or private thoughts as if women aren't their equal. It starts small, and when not checked, the violations gradually worsen, depending on the personality of the man.

I'm a mother of a son.

Then you best make sure Niel knows what Ezra is doing isn't right. Do I believe Ezra needs to be shot over it? No. Reformed, yes.

How?

I think we need to stop treating our little darling boys like they're something special, and getting jealous when another girl gets their attention. Your grandmother hated your mother, remember? Why? Because Ella stole Curtis from her, because only men matter. Women fight each other over men, while the men simultaneously weaken us to that fact. There are billions of people on this planet, having a dick doesn't make them a special snowflake.

Jesus, I'm not like that.

Truly, deep down, every woman secretly craves being validated by a man, even if he's not worthy. For an empowered woman, you've let all the men in your life walk all over you. Most girls hear, "It's just a handjob." "I bought your burger." "I'll just put the tip in." "One more drink and we'll loosen up your frigidness." "You stay at home with the kids all day while I work. If it wasn't for me, you'd starve. Show your appreciation with your mouth and get to sucking, bitch!" "Just roll over and go back to sleep, baby. I'll be done shortly." Think about how men see us as whoring ourselves out for their benefit with every action they make.

My God, Queen. You hate men, don't you? You hate the institution of marriage?

I have you as the example, don't I? Are you not being raped by a man right now?

STOP!

Regina Regal always goes for broke. "It's just a kid." "It's just another kid." "Seal it with a handshake? No, we seal it with body fluids." "It's your initiation, so you do as your told, even if it's sucking off one guy, then fucking two others, with an audience." "We're married, so now it's your duty to take my virginity, even though I know you don't want to." "I fucked you in the ass, so now you're fair game for life– you can't say no, and I don't give a shit if you actually say yes."

Shut up!

No! You need to listen, now that I have you as a captive audience since you're playing turtle and refusing to acknowledge that Ezra is raping you. His dick hurts, doesn't it? It's rubbing your vag raw, Regina. FEEL IT!

Go away, Queen!

You've been raped in every possible way. THAT is why you've been in stasis. Apathetic. THAT is why you're making stupid decisions and getting in over your head. GRANT IS JAMIE! You've always known but couldn't handle it. James Atwater for shit's sake– Grant's pretentious double middle name. Take it out on Grant instead of yourself. That coward abandoning you doesn't mean a goddamn thing about your worth– it's a smudge against GRANT'S! Now Ezra's dick is in you without an invitation... which is Grant's fault too. What are you going to do about it? Huh?

I should have fought back before Ezra crossed the line.

How? When?

Shame descends, lowering me to less than human. If I speak up, everyone will ask why I didn't fight back, when Regina Regal is a born fighter. They'll want to know why I was so stupid.

Jamie– Marcus.

I can't say anything because Marcus will be torn between his loyalty to Ezra and his love for me. Jamie might do something stupid at the next founders meeting.

You're such a tragic wench. You get that, right? This little piece of misogyny I do believe. If you disrespect yourself, men won't respect you. You fucked Ezra eighteen hours ago, and Marcus didn't stop it then, nor did he seem to care. So what makes you think he'll care now? What? C'mon, hit me with some romantic bullshit you don't truly believe. I'm sure he'll care, maybe even hold you while you cry, but he won't actually do a damn thing about it.

Yanked from my mind by a brutal thrust, my stomach cramps. "Welcome back," Ezra rasps roughly into my ear, slowing his pace until it's no longer violence personified. "That gray area in your mind, it's similar to floating in subspace. I've seen it many times."

Baffled, distressed laughter spills from my throat as Ezra holds a cordial conversation with me about the state-of-being rape victims experience as a defense-mechanism. Meanwhile, my mind backs up, leaving me to mull over the finer details. Like when did Ezra pull his dick out of his trousers? It must have been as he was walking behind me to this room.

"Ezra's very angry with you," he cautions in the third-person.

No longer pounding into me, Ezra simply rotates his hips in a circular motion, stretching me to accommodate his girth and length. When he no longer meets resistance, he pushes harder, and I hiccup a breath with every thrust. Panting roughly in my ear, Ezra's smoky scent seeps into my skin.

Still in shock, I remain passive and don't fight back. Hell, my lips can't even form a protest of no.

"Marcus mouth-fucks my partner, so I'll fuck his. That seems fair and balanced."

"Jesus Christ," is a grunt torn from my throat.

"You were classmates with Ezra, and I know you don't believe in Jesus Christ as your Lord and Savior, any more than Ezra does. We can agree to disagree that Jesus was a man, but he wasn't the Second Coming of Christ. If you're looking for faith as a comfort and guide, I suggest you join Marcus in his teachings."

"Are you for serious?" Stammering, I can't wrap my mind around a single fucking word out of Ezra's mouth. "Are you soliciting me for conversion right now? While raping me?"

"With your love of cheesesteaks, meat-lovers pizza, and Italian subs, I ought to tell you how Marcus doesn't force us to abide by dietary laws–"

"Or any laws. This is madness!"

"If you tell a soul about this, I will be forced to inform Ezra's mother about how you're fucking her husband. She wouldn't take too kindly to that knowledge. Diane wouldn't hurt Marcus, but she would harm you– I like you. You do know the reason why Marcus says you're a lesbian is so that Diane would never suspect you as his lover," Ezra reveals in a voice devoid of any emotion.

"What?" rolls off my stunned tongue. "You just went from Judaism to extortion without missing a single thrust."

Not one to be derailed, "If you love Marcus, you'll keep your mouth shut." Ezra's voice is no longer the glass-on-glass grating sound, flowing into purring a smoky cadence that arouses instead of repels.

After adjusting the angle on my hips to get deeper, Ezra releases the hand pressing my face into the door, then he rubs my cheek until the marks diminish.

"Why?" I whimper, voice sluggish with shock.

"Because Ezra was angry with you and I wanted you… Because Ezra knows what Marcus has been doing to Cortez. I've had enough. Today Cortez came home and could barely speak, and it was your fault. Ezra kissed Cort, but he tried to get away. Try as I might to shelter Ezra from the truth, I knew why. Ezra finally got a taste– a taste of Marcus on Cortez's tongue. Then he reached inside Cort's pants, finding them saturated from the half a dozen times Cortez came while he was being violently skull-fucked by Marcus. Ezra is not a fool!" he shouts while thrusting upward with enraged violence.

A garbled grunt is forced from my chest as Ezra's thrusts strengthen with his fury. Gripping my hips, he pumps upward at a sharp angle. The nails sinking into my flesh to draw blood don't hurt as much as the fiery hot cock searing me from the inside out.

"Call me Master Ez, Regina. You're to defer to Ezra or me for all things MdJ, and you will do as we say." The words are menacing and forceful, but they're spoken with a soft tongue.

As the only logical reply, "Yes, Master Ez," is grunted out in quick succession from three fast, powerful thrusts.

Mind unable to interpret my emotions, I choose shame to focus on. I feel sick inside because a pressure I'm trying so desperately to suppress is building inside of me. Whimpers pass my lips as Ezra shifts to hit that swelling, traitorous spot deep inside of my body. The orgasm from my g-spot always hurts with its intensity. I don't want to have an orgasm while Ezra rapes me, as if it cancels out the violation. But the added humiliation of having *that* type would be far worse.

If I could, I would curse Ezra for having a curved penis.

"The rape was for taking the management of Restraint out of Ezra's hands," Master Ez explains. "In the future, every time Marcus skull-fucks Cort's mouth, I will fuck you– a partner for a partner."

"How fair," I mutter sarcastically, my breath leaving a damp spot on the cold, metal door.

"Balance," Master Ez says in a creepy voice, as if I paid him a compliment. "This time it's rape as punishment for causing Marcus to skull-fuck Cortez today, as well as taking Restraint. It's not the first time I've raped."

"How many?" voice trembling to match the quivering flowing up my legs. If it wasn't for Master Ez pressing me to the door, I'd fall to the ground.

"You're my third, but you will be the last. From this moment, it will be your choice. You either let me fuck you, or I will drag you to Diane, where she will ruin both yours and Marc's lives."

"That's not really a choice, is it?" Knowing Master Ez is all about balance, I add. "That's not fair."

But he chooses to ignore me. "Your only option is to keep Marcus de-stressed, to the point he will leave Cortez alone. I like you as a person, Queen. This isn't about you, and for that I'm sorry. Regardless, don't attempt to warn Marcus not to fuck Cort's face. If you do, I'll take you to Diane. The choice will always be whatever I suggest versus Diane's wrath."

"That really isn't a choice, Master Ez, and you know it." I grunt as he thrusts with my every word. "It's called blackmail."

"Good, I'm glad we understand each other," Master Ez says with dark humor.

"Never negotiate with terrorists is the first rule, Master Ez. What if I just go to Diane myself?"

"Never forget how Grant died and Jamie was resurrected. That was Maître du Jeu's doing because Grant needed to be silenced. Again, your fault. Those who talk are rendered mute. I don't threaten, Queen. I give you a choice between what I want from you and the consequences if you don't give it to me."

"Black and white, give me the rules," I issue as a demand.

"I respect you, Queen," Master Ez purrs while swiveling his hips. "Keep Marcus happy and away from Cortez to ensure Ezra is happy. If not, I fuck you. If you don't let me fuck you, then I will go to Diane. If you go to Diane, then I go to MdJ. If you don't abide by the edicts passed down from MdJ, and whatever else I decide, I'll go to MdJ. Remember how Grant is dead– never forget who put him in the grave."

"Maître du Jeu."

"No," Master Ez whispers in my ear. "You."

That singular word, with all its implications, snaps me out of the anti-reality I've been suspended in with Master Ez. Sensations bombard me from all directions, but I still can't believe that he's doing this to me.

This morning, I willingly allowed Ezra into my body as a way for him to connect with Cortez. I didn't do it out of sexual gratification, and now he's repaying me by raping me against a cold door as if my body is just a powerful vessel he is draining to fill himself.

This morning, he was Ezra. Tonight, he's Master Ez. Do they coexist, having knowledge of what the one manning the body is doing with said body? Or does one half flicker out into nothingness while the other controls everything?

I cannot imagine Ezra behaving this way, nor can I fathom him raping me.

"The first time I raped, I didn't realize it was rape. I was fifteen years old, and I was ordered by Diane to help her with a problem she was having. He was kind enough not to say anything, allowing me to keep my dignity. A year later, I learned what I'd done was wrong. The look of horror on his face as he awakened informed me he hadn't called for me. He wasn't mean to me, but he asked why. I told him how Diane said he wanted me to do it. Later that night, Diane screamed at me, saying I was a rapist because I was a product of rape. Diane only speaks to me in public, blaming me for what my father did to her."

Gut-wrenching sobs flow out of me in abject horror, but not for the acts Master Ez is inflicting upon me. The act he's describing, and who he violated by his mother's request, I weep for the child and the man, both then and now.

"I thought you should know more about Marcus. Now you can understand him better when he holds you at arm's length. Instead of blaming Ezra, Marcus blames Diane for what happened to him, for what she made Ezra do. Marcus couldn't save us from Ezra's birth father, though. I will never speak of the horrors Cortez endured, for what Ezra had to do was pale in comparison. Ray made Ezra rape an innocent girl who was walking on a trail. Since then, I've been good until you. You will be my last victim– I can't do this anymore."

"Katya Waters?" voice quivering with terror, too much is making sense, to the point I can't absorb it all.

Without hesitation, "Yes, Katya will become *my* wife," Master Ez says matter-of-factly.

"Why me?" I ask again. "Why target me? Marcus and Katya weren't your fault. This–" I struggle to get away from Master Ez in explanation, but he's stronger than he appears. "This is your fault– you're doing this to *me*!"

"Marcus wouldn't touch Ezra. He always looked at Ezra as his son, yet he looked at Cort like a lover– a confidant. Cort and Ezra have to share every experience, and Ezra doesn't understand what's wrong with him that Marcus doesn't want him. Cort took Ezra's place by Marc's side. Since the abduction, Cort won't touch Ezra, but he'll swallow Marc's cock, loving every disgusting second of it. You even the score. Balance. Every time Marcus takes Cort, I will take you. Because we're all fucked up and I'm trying to fix it!"

Master Ez howls a primal scream while thrusting violently. Stomach cramping, it hurts as much as it feels exceptional. Willing myself back into that gray area in my mind, I try to shut myself off and not feel how the intense pressure builds. My choice is to either embrace my release, or suffer through it.

"Master Ez?" I calmly call, causing him to still as I speak.

"Yes, Queen," Master Ez says softly against the back of my neck, breath fluttering my short hair.

"Does Ezra see you doing this right now?" I ask just as softly.

"Ezra's but a passenger– he thinks and watches, but he cannot stop us without effort. His pain doesn't want us to stop." Master Ez explains how he and Ezra are not the same entity.

Master Ez calls me Queen. Ezra, the boy I met when he was fourteen, only calls me Regina. As soon as I confirmed how he's two different personalities, he no longer pretends to be Ezra while speaking in the third person. His demeanor changes, even the way he touches me.

“Master Ez? You were born in the woods of rural Pennsylvania, weren’t you?”

“No, I made a brief appearance when Ezra was very young, then I laid dormant for years. I solidified after the abduction, when Cort and Aaron showed up. I protect Ezra from unpleasantness and mete out the punishments he can’t stomach but desires. I helped Ezra deal with the ordeal with Katya, but he was the one driving us.” Master Ez speaks calmly, as if he isn’t speaking of every facet of rape. “Ezra wanted Katya all to himself– he didn’t even want to share with the half of him that enjoys women.”

“Why are you trusting me?” It’s an odd question, considering he’s raping me and will be blackmailing me every time Marcus and Cortez are together, added to whatever the hell the founders want from me. All that aside, I need to know why the one who protects Ezra is placing his faith in me.

“We know that if Marcus trusts you enough to love you as his partner, then we must as well,” Master Ez replies without hesitation.

“I’m not Marc’s partner,” I stammer in denial.

“Yes, you are.” Master Ez’s reply is firm. “We also behave around Marc’s Jamie– your Grant. We keep our distance. We don’t punish Elder Whittenhower, but we do vote against him if Marcus makes us angry. But we’re lenient, because Ezra would never harm someone Pretty Boy loves.”

“You’re raping me right now,” I point out. “Someone Marcus, Jamie, and Whitt loves. I’m *Pretty Boy’s* wife, for fuck’s sake. I should have been a person who was untouchable to you.”

“I’m not physically harming you, Queen, and this isn’t the first time we had sex.” Just as I suspected. If you fuck a sociopath once, they believe they have an all-access pass to your body for life.

Since Master Ez is the chatty sort, I decide to keep him talking, like one talks down a wild animal. Maybe the more he sees me as human, the least likely he is to physically harm me. Mentally and emotionally? That ship has sailed.

“How come you picked me?”

“I wanted you.” Now that the Master Ez cat is out of the bag, he freely gropes me as a straight man would. Cupping my tits, he squeezes. A pleased sound rumbles up his throat and his cock jerks inside of me. Yeah, Master Ez is bizarrely straight while his counterpart is gay. The passenger of this freak show must be miserable while the driver gets his rocks off.

"Queen, you are equalizing. Ezra feels the justice in what we're doing, even though he's screaming at me to stop, to shut up and pull out. Ezra is gay, but I am not. I was created to help Ezra through times when he would need to bed a woman."

"What does that even mean?"

"Being one of the youngest elders didn't make Ezra immune to the seeding the bloodline game the founders play. I would assist Ezra when he had to mate his intended."

"Adelaide?"

"Yes and no," Master Ez mutters cryptically. "Yes, I was the one who had sex with Adelaide, happily so. Starting earlier in Ezra's teen years, I would override his natural persuasion. Each elder must create an heir. Ezra was an elder before he ever reached the age of sixteen."

"Jesus Christ," I snarl, infuriated. The founders create their own worst enemies, out of their own children. Then those children grow up to repeat the cycle of abuse. Which is exactly why we have enforcers like Roarke and Albert.

"We've discussed that blasphemous term already, Queen," Master Ez cautions. "My adult life has been a game of watching Ezra lure Cortez into our bed, or touching those he shouldn't. I wanted to have someone to make *me* feel good for once. This morning, while the lovers were using you, I wanted to please you but they didn't notice."

"Nuclear fallout would have gone without notice," I murmur snidely.

"I was pissed at Ezra for neglecting my needs by ignoring yours. Adelaide was cold in bed. This was the first time I could enjoy a woman who enjoyed men, and Ezra ruined it. I'm so sick of waiting to have my needs met, when all I do is for Ezra. He wouldn't even give me a small taste."

"So this is you rebelling against the one you protect," I muse, baffled at the complexity of mental illness. I may war with my emotions, but Ezra is literally split into at least two personalities. How do you blame the whole man, when only half is violating you?

Mind fuck.

"It will be awhile before we have Katya. She's perfect for us– I prefer women and Ezra has a confusing connection to her.

Katya was *his* only victim. Since Cort can't figure out what the hell he wants, Katya will please Ezra, Cortez, and myself. We'll be mutually happy," immense pleasure laces Master Ez's tone. "Balance."

Getting a better understanding, I decide to fight fire with fire and place Ezra in the passenger seat. "Ezra wants you to leave right now so he can put a stop to this, doesn't he? You said you protect him and do as he says, then why not stop if you're causing Ezra mental and emotional distress?"

"No, I'd rather stay." Horny man outweighs the reason for his creation. "Queen, you're aching inside– I can feel it. Let me ease you. I promise to allow Ezra to rise if you come for me first."

Master Ez is the owner of the velvety seductive voice that lulls you into compliance. When he's pissed, it's scratching glass on glass or fingernails down a chalkboard.

Ezra's voice is smooth and calm– always.

"I don't want to come for you, Master Ez," I mutter defiantly. "I didn't consent to this, and I'd stop if you'd allow it."

"You lie to yourself. You enjoy the loss of power, even though you think you shouldn't. You feel shame because you feel alive right now."

"Bullshit," I snarl, more enraged than ever. "That's a lie you tell yourself to erase the fact that you're sexually assaulting me. If you were anyone else, I'd go to the police in a heartbeat, and your ass would be in a prison cell next to your serial rapist of a sire."

"No need to get nasty, Queen," Master Ez sounds hurt.

"Are you shitting me?"

"I can feel you inside, how tight you are rubbing against my dick– you're so swollen that you must be in pain. Let go."

"No, I don't want you," I grit out between clenched teeth, my jaw aching from the tension.

"The only reason this is force is because I needed you to know I was serious about our arrangement. I'm not harming you, I offer you choices, and I give you pleasure, so stop being nasty to me."

"You need some fucking help," I mutter, at a complete and total loss. You can't reason with an insane person– you just can't.

"You already took Ezra into your body– it's the same dick, just a different personality who enjoys a different hole. I prefer a warm, wet pussy, when obviously Ezra's an ass man," he says this matter-of-factly without a trace of humor.

"Just come– I won't tell your rapist friends you failed. I won't come to lessen Ezra's guilt over what you're doing to me. Coming doesn't negate rape."

"You already won't tell anyone, Queen," Master Ez politely reminds me. "But this will go on until you get relief. We will chat while I keep my dick in you– I won't relent. Every time we're together, you'll orgasm for me. We will go forever if that is what it takes," Master Ez issues as the most sadistic of warnings.

Motherfucking dominants and their power-trips. The fact that Master Ez is a product of Ezra's personality adds cerebral fuckage to the arsenal. The unholy union between a rapist and a cunt, created a sociopathic psychiatrist with multiple personalities. Just my luck that one half took an instant dislike to me, while the other took a shine to me.

Giving up, I decide self-preservation is more important than shame. "Fine, get to working. Standing here having a conversation while my feet fall asleep isn't going to get me off."

Mind swirling in utter chaos, there isn't a fiber of my being that wants to enjoy this experience. Out of every tragic event I've suffered through, this fucked up situation will leave the biggest scar.

I don't want to understand this figment of Ezra. Master Ez is the part of Ezra that helps him deal with pain and loss. He's incapable of seeing this from my perspective, unable to feel the emotions of a normal person. Ezra feels everything, while Master Ez feels nothing. Master Ez is a sociopath who sees rape as a viable option as long as you both have release.

Shocked crying transforms into gut-wrenching sobs, Master Ez has to hold me up because I lose the ability to stand on my own. Every few seconds, I hiccup, with snot running down my chin. The metal door has condensation beaded on it from my labored breath, and the sticky residue from my nostrils combines with my falling tears.

Confused at the distress I'm displaying, Master Ez stands behind me, still inside me, but he doesn't take sexual gratification from it.

Decision made, Master Ez shifts to yank his dress shirt off. Following that, he pulls off his undershirt. With the t-shirt, he goes into caregiver-mode. After all, Ezra created him for that reason. After gently cleaning my face with his undershirt, he hands it to me.

Taking account of my dead legs, Master Ez shifts his hips around, arches my back downward, popping my ass out, and then brings my legs together until his are on the outside. Once I'm in the position where he can violate me easier, Master Ez pushes a few test thrusts to see if it's where he wants me. After a few adjustments, a thrust hits its target, causing me to hiss from the ache building.

"Keep the shirt– I don't want you to ruin this gorgeous dress." Compliments while raping me. Should I thank him like a good girl should? Should I feel special because he's taking care of me?

Fuck you, Master Ez!

"Press it to your cunny to catch the flow– you're going to gush for me, Queen. Someone has kept you primed all day and didn't give you relief. Damned fools. It probably started with those blubbering lovers. You need to find release with a cock." Noticing I'm not following his direction, "I said press the shirt against your pussy," Master Ez repeats when I don't immediately comply.

It's a surreal experience. I stand frozen like a stunned animal because my mind and body no longer communicate.

A heavy sigh ricochets through the room– another Master Ez trait. He slides the shirt from my loose hands, then covers me, holding the shirt between my clenched thighs.

Moaning a deviant song of pleasure into my ear, Master Ez rolls his hips in a rhythm he finds gratifying. "You're such a good girl, Queen. Even after two kids, you're tight. I'm pleased you haven't had many lovers, and that Marc's mammoth cock hasn't stretched you out."

Another disturbing compliment. Am I to thank him for finding my cunt tight while he rapes it?

Groaning, Master Ez speeds up his thrusts. Clenching my teeth until my jaw aches, I whimper because the building pressure hurts so badly. Not wanting to do it, I start to cry again. With every pass of his cock, the pressure builds and builds. Avoiding shame, it takes all of my control to stay my release. Right now, I hate how I can have a g-spot orgasm– it's embarrassing and too powerful. The pressure is excruciating, adding to the need to release. One moment you feel like you're going to have an accident, then the next the floor floods with your ejaculation.

"Queen, let go. Let me ease your ache. You're upsetting Ezra," he manipulates me like a master.

"We can't have Ezra upset, now can we?" I mutter sarcastically.

"No, we cannot," Master Ez replies in all seriousness.

Fuck!

Master Ez was created to ensure Ezra never got upset, and I know I won't get off this crazy train until I give in.

Powerless. Humiliated. Debased.

Closing my eyes, I concentrate on the smooth slide of Master Ez's cock gliding over that engorged spot. My body's primed, already releasing an overflow of moisture to flood the t-shirt. Marrying my breathing with Master Ez's, his chest moves rapidly against my back with every grunt. I equalize myself with his rhythm.

I huff several breaths in time with his thrusts. Every muscle in my body flexes, nearly cramping. Turning to jelly, my legs lose all function. Master Ez holds me up with his hands on my hips and his cock impaling my cunt.

"Out! Pull! Out!" I shout in a panic. "I can't if you're in there."

As soon as Master Ez pulls back, dick sliding free from my clenching channel, I flood the shirt. Fabric absorbing my fluid as a sponge until it can hold no more, it drips warmly between my fingers.

Tremors wrack my body, teeth chattering, from the force of every nerve in my body firing at once. Without giving me a break from the assault, Master Ez presses his dick back inside, anchoring me or I'd fall to the floor.

Grunts, one right after another, erupt from my chest as I seize. Eyes rolling back, I almost bite my tongue. I never want to do this again. It's horrific in its intensity. It's the strongest, most powerful orgasm of my existence. But it's not pleasurable– my soul bleeds shame and powerlessness.

Master Ez releases inside of me, doing the very thing I despise most. His cries ring out loudly, but I'm too far gone to acknowledge it or experience it.

The man behind me holds his body in a softer manner, but it's taut with tension. Silently sobbing, the tears flow hot but quickly cool beneath his breath fluttering against my neck. *Ezra* holds me, kisses my neck in apology.

Master Ez doesn't kiss.

Master Ez doesn't cry.

Ezra's tears aren't apology enough for the injustice he just dealt.

Either Master Ez is a hit and run bastard, or his orgasm lessened his hold on being in control, allowing Ezra to erupt from the depths of their shared mind.

"I guess I should feel honored over the fact that you trust me enough to reveal your split identity. Beware, many of your secrets were revealed as your counterpart raped me. I should be honored, but I'm not. However, I will keep our bargain. Master Ez will protect you to the death, and frankly, I want to live."

"No harm will come to you," Ezra forces out, sounding tortured.

"Your definition of harm doesn't quite match up with mine. You need help, Ezra, and I'm going to make sure you get it– if only so I can protect myself from you."

Hand releasing, I drop the soiled t-shirt to the floor. Splatting with the weight of my release and the force of gravity, my legs get drenched. The puddle on the floor is impressive by any standards.

"Inform Master Ez how that was the most painful orgasm I've ever had, and I'll be prepared for it next time." I turn and look at Ezra, finding a broken man who looks like a little boy that has lost his way.

"If you speak to me, you speak to him," Ezra mutters sheepishly, refusing to look at me.

"Ezra, I'm going to need a referral from a colleague to get through the aftermath of what I just endured."

"I'm sorry," he whispers through his incessant sobbing.

"We're not going to play the blame game, as that would mean we have to go back to the origin of the problem. Your mother, but then she could probably blame her parents or your father. You're not to blame for what happened to your mother, or how she manipulated you into harming Marcus. You're not to blame for what your father forced you to do to Katya. However, you must take responsibility for your actions, starting with what you just did to me. I don't give a fuck if you have twenty personalities– if one fucks up, you all fuck up. It's still your cock violating me and your seed on my thighs."

"No one ever blames me," Ezra has the audacity to say.

"Maybe they ought to, so you'd actually get help, instead of enabling you. If we played the blame game, they're just as responsible for you raping me as you are. But I don't play games, Ezra. Your dick– *your* fault."

"You don't understand," he whines, no doubt this bullshit works on everyone else.

Using the last of my physical and emotional energy reserves, "I get it, Ezra. You have daddy and mommy issues. A lesser woman would be drawn into fixing the bad boy. It strokes their ego to think they can tame the beast, as if their love and pussy are more magical than the next woman's. I don't have Stockholm syndrome. I'm not going to fix you– I'm going to get us both help."

"My *professional* opinion. If I wasn't gay, I'd have that type of woman flocking around me. The fixer– they don't see the man as a person. A project they fix to get a hit on their own self-esteem. It's a parasitic relationship."

"The aristocratic looks and the money override your insanity, but not for me," I mutter in disgust. "If I ever see Diane face-to-face again, you won't have to worry about Master Ez telling her our secret. After what she's done to both you and Marcus, she deserves a worse fate than I've had. I understand why you had a sociopath manifest inside your mind, but that doesn't mean you're not responsible for your actions."

"I couldn't handle knowing–" Ezra sniffles, then clears his throat. "I couldn't handle knowing that Cort was with Marcus. It angered Master Ez how broken I felt. We agreed you would be the balance, because it would be the same as what they're doing to us. Plus, Master Ez wants you. The added bonus was that I knew you were strong enough to live through it and stay sane."

"I don't see what Marcus and Cortez do together as cheating. They were doing it long before I was in the picture."

"Then you do need therapy, Regina," Ezra deadpans. "The constant denial you live under must be suffocating."

My legs still won't fully support me, but I can't have Ezra's hands on me for another moment. Hands outstretched before me, I use the wall as a guide while I stumble to the bathroom.

Moving slowly, my vision clears and I gaze forward. Appalled, my fingers are pressed against a wall of torture. Restraints hang from the ceiling and devices sit on the floor. I'm touching some kind of object that I don't want to examine too closely. I try not to wipe my filthy hands on my already soiled dress.

"You're perfect for Marcus," Ezra calls out from behind me, trailing me as a ghost would. "The part you're trying to use self-righteous indignation to suppress– the part you're burying deep inside your psyche, while shouting how what we did was rape, and your body had a physiological response to pleasurable stimuli. I'm not saying that isn't the case. But the shame born over by the door, that wasn't about rape– it's about how enlivened the rape made you feel."

Stumbling, I try my damnedest to shuffle toward the bathroom– freedom, security, and cleanliness.

"The part you're not welcoming is the counterpart that will satisfy Marc's needs. My actions do have consequences, but I didn't pay the price. I made Marcus the way he is, just as I've now made you the way you are. You know what I've done, don't you?"

If Ezra sounded smug, I wouldn't answer him. But he sounds nothing but contrite. "I could guess, but I don't want to even contemplate it. It was your mother who fucked you up, and it was your mother who used you to fuck Marcus up. Your dick– your fault. Her son, her command– Diane's fault."

"If only one person does the deed, that person is solely to blame," Ezra tries to counsel me.

"No," I mutter firmly. "Just as how the entirety of Dominion's founders are to blame for every single atrocity their membership wreaks. Diane probably couldn't handle what happened to her– misery loves company."

Reaching my destination, I step into the bathroom with my hand on the doorknob. "Piece of unsolicited advice. I don't think I'd trust Diane's account on anything." I do to Ezra what he did to me earlier. Destroy the way he views the world. "You know your mother is fucking your fiancée, right?"

Utterly crestfallen, "No, I did not," Ezra mutters in defeat.

"And now you do. Consider it payback for the rape. Don't be in here when I come back out." I shut the bathroom door on Ezra's response.

Chapter Seventeen

"Regina?" Exiting the bathroom in a fog of determination, I try to pretend I don't hear Marc's voice, or see his silhouette, or smell his comforting scent. I keep walking as if I'm alone.

"Regina, what happened?" Marc's concern stops my feet, but my mind screams for them to keep moving forward. There's no looking back, as you can't change the past. There's no pausing in the present, because your past will catch up with you. The only thing you can do is move forward as quickly as possible to escape the past while ensuring the same mistakes are never played on repeat.

Voice hollow, I reply, "You know what happened," while staring at the purple nail polish on my toes.

"Tell me," Marcus tries to persuade me– to coax instead of make demands.

Amber fire is burning into my forehead, Marc's way of begging me to look at him without verbalizing it. He knows what happened, which is why he's taking a backseat and making no demands.

I can't.

I can't look at Marcus because I'm dead-eyed. The mirrors of my eyes reflect the torture in my soul. Upon meeting me, Marcus had said to me how for someone so young, I had a tortured soul. That was two years ago. I just aged a decade in the last twenty-four hours. I can only guess what his eyes would see if he gazed into my soul today versus back then on the sidewalk in front of the brownstone, back when my world was deliriously numb.

At the time, Marcus had also said he'd have fun breaking me– his adopted son just beat him to it. Does that please Marcus, or does it anger him how he lost the chance to someone else?

"I can't," I mutter weakly. "If I look at you, you'll have your answer."

I *need* to unburden myself, to crawl into Marc's lap and sink into his warmth. I want him to hold me together as I break apart.

Choking on a sob, my mind conjures up Marcus holding me together while Jamie's silence fortifies my strength to persevere.

I can't– I can't stop, even for a moment. I must forge ahead to escape the sad reality of my truth.

"Yes, you can. Come sit with me." The tight control is evident in Marc's voice, by the way he's trying to sound calm and reassuring. I have little doubt that he was outside the door the entire time, envisioning what was happening inside this room. While I had to experience it firsthand, I can't imagine the devastating sense of powerlessness Marcus must have endured. I know it's not the same as how I felt, but I'm empathetic enough not to be an ass and blame him.

I wonder where that twisted fucker ran off to. Ezra probably put that ridiculous hood back on and is playing hide-and-go-seek with the customers. Which is he right now? Ezra, or Master Ez? I wonder if it's Master Ez who chokes Cort. If it is, I bet Ezra cheers from the sidelines.

"Marcus, I can't– I just can't," I mutter in defeat. "Not right now. I need a sense of control. I need a purpose. I'm doing this for me, because I can't make you feel better right now by opening up to you by bleeding tears."

"Regina, I am not a selfish piece of shit," Marcus bites out, rage sparking beneath the patience in his tone. "Not only do I wish I could erase what happened, I blame myself for not preventing it. But I'm smart enough to know this isn't about me, so we don't get to talk about it. I just want you to know I'm here for you should you need me."

"Marcus, I trust you without fail. Just as it is with Jamie–" my eyes slide upward, but they still don't connect with Marc. "We don't need to rehash the same shit over and over again for me to believe it. I know what you're feeling right now, without you actually saying it. But it would be easier on me to take a few hours to process without getting into it."

"Okay," Marcus whispers. "You need to feel in control and productive, so what does that entail? I'll help if you need it."

"Kristal– Jamie gave me some advice."

"I'm well aware what your plans are for Kristal this evening. I just thought… I just thought after your ordeal, you wouldn't be up for the task and what it entails. But I underestimated your need to charge forward. But, Regina, promise me something. Promise me you will let it out."

"Eventually." Stepping forward a few paces, I lean against the side of the sofa. Gathering courage, my eyes flick up to take in Marcus sitting in an armchair. "The past twenty-four hours changed me, and not for the better. There will be fallout in the aftermath that I'm not sure I can handle. I'm not sure you can, either."

"I would like to at least try." With tears thick in his voice, I know Marcus worries I'm blaming him, just as he worried I'd leave him after I learned of all the secrets he was keeping.

"I'm not talking about us right now. You're married to Diane, and I'm married to Whitt. But we're both emotionally dependent on Jamie. Now is not the time for that conversation. Nothing has changed between us."

"Nothing?" Marcus sounds skeptical, and I envision him raising his eyebrow high.

"What I meant by handling the fallout– I think I need to find a therapist Ezra has never came in direct contact with. I need to work through this denial that is holding back the rage. I need to work through what has happened in my life since I was fourteen years old. I just…"

Shaking my head from side to side, I'm at a loss how to put it into words, so I go for broke. "We all need to grow up. My son is closing in on adulthood, and we're all reacting instead of acting. We all need therapy, we need to stop the scourge on this town, and we need to stop enabling Ezra."

"So you *do* blame me," Marcus stresses, voice breaking.

"Goddamnit, Marcus! This isn't about you, got it?" With a hundred reasons I can't look at him, rage has me glaring in his direction. "We need to grow up, think of other people first and foremost, and get help. If my arm was broken, I'd go to a doctor. If my spirit is broken, I should either visit a religious head or a therapist."

"There are four clinical psychiatrists who are currently treating Ezra, so that route hasn't helped my son. But I do believe in counsel. I go the faith route, but I can understand why you'd chose a therapist instead."

Slumping, my ass hits the sofa cushion. "After what I learned from Jamie and Niel today, after being subjected to Voldemort… while we were sitting in the meeting room, I just took one look at what we've all become. When I met Ezra and Cortez, they were innocent with so much potential. Now Cortez is clearly sexually confused and needs therapy after his time with Ray, and Ezra should by all rights either be in prison or Wintercrest. Syn– how did Faith turn into Syn?

"I won't go down that path, and I already feel myself changing for the worse. The people in my life have been warping me, twisting me up until I don't recognize myself. But it stops tonight. No more. It's on my terms or not at all, even when dealing with extortion."

"Extortion?" Marcus leans forward, doing his damnedest to get close enough to touch me, but I don't allow it.

"I have no idea if this is a safe place to speak or not, so I won't. Don't you just get sick of it? I don't want to join their merry gang of sociopaths, nor do I want to become the puppet to their master. Why do we allow it? Why do you?"

"I don't know," Marcus gives as an answer, and I accept it because I can tell he's not pushing me away. He truly doesn't know, and neither do I, but that's okay since we'll figure it out together eventually.

"I honestly don't know either, which is why I'm going to concentrate on the shit I do know while I figure out the rest."

"Did Ezra do what I think he did?" Marcus sounds utterly hopeless.

"What do you think Ezra did?"

"I'd rather not say in case I'm wrong." Marcus knows he's right. I can hear it in the hopeless quality of his voice. But there is a tinge of fear– fear that Ezra isn't fit to be roaming Dominion.

"And I'd rather not say in case you're right," I volley back. "I'm not confirming, nor am I denying your suspicions, because I will not be the cause of the fissure forming between you and Ezra. I've already been accused of being the one who killed Grant. The reason Jamie stays away. The reason you get frustrated and seek out other sexual outlets. I won't be the reason Jamie attacks Ezra, nor why you and Ezra have a falling out. I won't be the scape goat anymore."

"Christ," Marcus snarls, falling lax against the chair cushion. "If there is one thing Ezra excels at, it would be passing the buck off onto other people. Combining that talent with manipulating a situation or event until the outcome is in his favor and not yours. You are not to blame for any of that shit– you're not to blame for anything, Regina, and I fucking mean it!"

Scrubbing a hand over my face, I'm surprised to find no tears staining my cheeks. I haven't cried since I entered the bathroom, not even while I was douching Ezra from my vagina. When the shock finally wears off, I hope I'm not alone.

"Well, I found the tip of the iceberg tonight, and I don't like what I found. Maybe it was Ezra manipulating the outcome in his favor– probably, actually. But Ezra weaseled his way into my brain and rewired it until I feel nothing but shame. Shame for not fighting back. Shame for physiological responses to stimuli. But now that the monster has been unchained, I can't lock it back up. I'm never going to be able to turn it off again. Even now, after only an hour since the need was last fed, it's already creeping on me," I hollowly admit.

The truth making me bold, I finally look at Marcus.

Eyes soft yet sad, the beautiful amber glows with a wild light. Marcus is relaxed because he's exhausted. Fine lines bracket his eyes, caused by stress instead of laughter. I know exactly how those lax lips feel kissing my temple– a kiss I'll forever crave. Hair wild, the curls threaten to spiral since Marcus is a few weeks overdo on a haircut.

I appreciate this side of Marcus. Wild and untamed– unkempt. Passion suits Marcus better than the ethical, uptight lawyer he pretends to be.

I love the man he is– the man Marcus hides. We've been dead inside, fighting wars that aren't our own. Jackson Whittenhower and I are of a like mind now. The Spyder was meant for high-speed, reckless driving at three a.m., not sitting in a protective garage. Our bodies were meant for freezing cold swims at the lake, not sitting in an office twenty hours a day.

Mom warned how my computer programs wouldn't keep me warm at night– money can't give hugs and dry tears. I was ignorant and arrogant, thinking Mom was wrong and I was right, when all along it was a lesson I had yet to learn. I said hugs wouldn't put a roof over my head and food in my belly. I have money, and it sure as fuck can't give me a hug or dry the tears it causes.

I want to *live* my life. Not only do I want to live it, I want to build one with the people I love. Our time on earth is too short to do anything less.

I just want Marcus so bad that I'll finally admit it. I want him for me, and for no other reason. The waterworks start all over again. Not bawling, snot blowing sobs– just a gentle fall of tears. If I had a choice, I would have wanted Marcus as my husband,

and it hurts me to realize this on so many levels. I loved Grant, and I love Jamie more, but neither was loyal enough to stick around. Whitt is an incredible man, and I've repeated over and over again how I'd never regret my decision to marry him. But deep in my soul, a place where I can be honest with myself despite the pain, I do regret it.

I'd marry Whitt a thousand times over to secure a stable future for my children. But on the thousandth-and-first time, I'd beg Marcus to be mine.

Our children grow and move on. If I don't carve a life of my own, then what will I have when they're off to create a life of their own making? They will have careers, spouses, and children– they will still be the epicenter of my world, but I'll only be on the orbit of theirs.

"Would you like to play pretend?" Marcus flinches when the eerie quality of my tone hits his hypersensitive ears. "In the land of make-believe, where if we don't say it, it isn't true– it didn't really happen. It didn't irrevocably change us. Shall we play that game?"

Defeated, Marcus nods his head in reply, unable to put a voice to what he's thinking.

"We can pretend I'm not in love with you, how I don't want you as my husband. We can pretend that you're not in love with me, too. We can pretend that life hasn't fucked us every day since we were kids. We can pretend that your son and his sociopathic alter ego didn't just rape me. Hell, I could continue to pretend that the violation didn't unleash something monstrous in me."

Sigh silent, Marc's eyes slip shut, and from the corners, several droplets of moisture fall. I just confirmed his suspicions, effectively counteracting my game of pretend until it becomes the game of reality.

"The huge puddle on the floor over by the door–" I point in the general direction. "We can first pretend it doesn't exist, then we can pretend you probably didn't step in it on your way in here. We can pretend that Master Ez didn't demand an orgasm so Ezra wouldn't feel guilty for yet another rape."

Ignoring Marc's sharp intake of breath, I go for broke. "We can pretend that Master Ez didn't tell me some scary-assed shit. Things I wish I could scrub from my brain permanently– things that make me want to smuggle an innocent woman to safety. Things that make me want to drive to Shadow Haven with a shotgun and shoot your wife in the face. Hell, I'd like to kill

Diane just because she has the honor of being your wife in the first place– the rest is just icing on the shit-frosted, insanity-cake.

"Our very real realities are make-believe, simply because I added pretend in front of them. The earth doesn't stop spinning on its axis when I cry. The sun will still rise in the east come morning, whether I'm angry, sad, or in denial. The moon will still control the tides if I whisper I love you in your ear. No matter how narcissistic we may be, we're not the masters of the universe. Our actions do *not* affect everything, Marcus. But our responsibilities will not wait for you to get your head out of your ass."

"I–"

"No," I warn. "You've ignored Ezra's problems since you met him. You've sat passively by while Diane abused you through Ezra. Those actions broke Ezra into two, when back then it would have been a simple fix. You allowed the problem to fester until it became my very real problem. Just as I'm now allowing all my problems to fester, because I would rather play pretend instead of facing the cruel reality of the world we live in."

Marcus moves to stand from his chair, and out of reflex alone, I shove him back with a palm landing firmly on his chest.

"I have a submissive who needs to be taken in hand. I ignored the problem that was under my nose. Kristal is a ball of guilt over divided loyalties, no different than a drug addict chasing the pain away. Tonight, I will exorcise her demons, then at a later date, we will solve the emotional ramifications. When I walk out of the dungeon tonight, no one will doubt that I can run this place like a well-oiled machine."

"I've never doubted you," Marcus tries to interject, but I'm done listening to what he has to say.

"No worries, Marcus. Someone has to keep an eye on the membership, since your son sure as fuck can't. So you go wander off to play your game with your wife, allow the mother of your daughter to keep her away from you, have Cort suck your dick knowing how it harms Ezra's mental health, and continue to allow Jamie to keep your nuts in his back pocket. While you're too busy to take care of your own business, I will make sure everyone behaves here at Restraint. You needed a partner, and now you have one, whether you like it or not."

Managing to feel empowered after being debased, I stride over to where Marcus sits in stunned silence. Lips parted, brown eyes blazing with amber fire, I want Marcus. Kissing him aggressively, I don't allow him to return the kiss. I'm in control, even if it's just for these few minutes as the adrenaline of the past twenty-four hours turns me into goddamn superhero.

"I love you, Marcus," I whisper in his ear and the moon doesn't implode in the night sky. "I love you so much that every cell in my body aches to be with you. I will forever be yours, no matter who I have sex with. I'm not conflicted– we're both in love with Jamie, and I accept that as fact. But somewhere on this journey, my love for you has strengthened to the point it can survive anything and everything that tries to destroy it. It even survived Grant's ghost and our dependency on Jamie. Have some goddamn faith in us, Marcus."

Pulling away from him, I hold Marc's gaze while his chest rises and falls in rapid succession. He tries to formulate words, but I've scrambled his mind.

"I need you tonight. Not for sex unless I initiate it. I need you to hold me while I cry. I need you to hold me while I come to terms with the fact that your son violated me, turned me into a shame-filled creature, and forced me to listen to his confessions.

"Marcus, I need you to whisper pretty lies into my ear, telling me I'm not to blame, that none of it was my fault, and how I'm not a fucking freak. If you aren't in my bed when I get home, after I've spent the night taking care of your membership, don't ever try to get into my bed again," I threaten, and I mean it.

Queen's voice– *my* voice is low and scary. Marcus knows I don't mean my literal bed. If he isn't waiting for me, I will rip him out of my heart. Not only that, he will lose my trust and respect. This isn't about an affair– it's about mutual responsibilities. Marcus needs to take care of the fallout his son created, which means he's someone who should help me heal.

"I'm giving you the choice I was never given. The choice Grant wasn't given. The chance to be decisive instead of a coward. You can chose us– you can choose to have faith in us while we mutually meet each other's needs. There will be no abandonment after keeping my heart on a string. The choice is *us*, or get the fuck out of my life."

Quitting while I'm ahead, I don't wait around for Marcus to formulate a response filled with excuses and denials. I move forward, checking important tasks off my to-do list. Still burning off my superhero energy, I'm on a mission and her name is Kristal.

Chapter Eighteen

Slanted eyebrows pierced with metal rings greet me, but it's the sneer that has my heart stuttering. "You shouldn't have egged Ezra on," Syn chastises me as soon as I enter the hallway. Numb, I just stare back at the woman with a gobsmacked expression on my face.

Insulted and taken aback, words flow when I wish they wouldn't. "Do you know what Ezra did to me?"

"You should've behaved like we all told you to do. But you didn't, now Ezra is torn up about what he did." Hands fisted on her tiny hips, the bitch has the audacity to blame me for not only getting raped, but for Ezra being upset about his actions. "Piece of advice, I'd suggest you just do as you're told, or you will be held accountable for Ezra going off the deep end."

"Fuck. You." There is no other reply to such horseshit.

Stalking into the meeting room, I collide with Dalton. Expecting the same treatment, I flinch back as if preparing for a strike. But I'm rendered speechless for another reason. The tiny young man in middle-age garb wraps his arms around my neck like a child would, giving me a hug.

"I-I-I–" If anyone could keep the tears at bay, they must be dead inside. Of all the people to offer me comfort, it's Restraint's antagonist. "Does everyone know?" My worst fear is everyone seeing me as weak because I allowed Ezra to get the best of me, which is why Syn will never respect me.

"Since I live upstairs, I was hiding out in here–" Dalton gestures around the meeting room. "Ezra and Syn didn't know I could hear them arguing." Extracting himself from the hug, Dalton pats my shoulder. "Deep breaths. Put one foot in front of the other. Once this happens, the odds are exponentially higher for a repeat."

"Especially with Ezra," I grumble, face crimson with the kiss of shame. "I just…"

"Queen?" my title curves with an upward inflection, making it sound like a question, all because Dalton's French accent refuses to be subtle. "You're still the same person you were last week, yesterday, and thirty seconds before you were violated."

Suffocating on a sob that won't release, for a few seconds, I think I'm dying.

"Just breathe," Dalton reminds me. "Syn doesn't understand because she's never been raped. I've been here for a few months, and I've never met a more narcissistic person in my entire life."

"Vegas isn't exactly Sunnybrook Farms," I tease, trying to get my emotions in check.

"Exactly. Syn reminds me of my mother, and that isn't a compliment. Only my mother would probably respect you after what you just suffered. Anyone with compassion would."

"I owe you one." Awkwardly, I pat Dalton's shoulder, noticing how he has at least three shirts on to create bulk. "Thank you."

As quickly as he appeared, Dalton disappears into the hallway. Odd boy, that one.

Duty calls. Dragging a chair from the meeting room, I allow the metal feet to scrape on the floor as I walk into the dungeon. All members are in attendance and all eyes are on me. The room is cavernous with a few people milling around. The lights are bright, in total contrast to what I would find comforting. But the dungeon isn't about comfort. There isn't a single seat in the room. I notice a few of its inhabitants are using the BDSM devices as benches.

The long room looks narrow in comparison to its length, but in reality it's wide. Apparatuses line the wall, most I'm familiar with from my time at the brownstone. Spanking benches and horses, several St. Andrew's crosses, and framework to restrain your victim into submission line the long walls. I raise my eyebrows at the pet crate, and I can't help but grin at the gigantic birdcage. The rear wall is lined with implements for impact play, tools that bite and sting, ropes and restraints of varying types, and toys. The toys are for sex, and apparently someone here likes roleplay. Children's toys? I shake my head at that. Who here is our resident toddler?

The walls are cement with large sheets of shiny metal riveted in no discernible pattern. The industrial-height ceiling is decorated with ductwork and random poles, with chains hanging from them. Several bars are on pulley systems, allowing them to pivot, raise, and lower. The floors are slate tile the exact shade of Ezra and Cortez's eyes. It would be good for easy cleanup.

The center of the dungeon is an open space with a single bare bulb hanging above it. Yes, I remember this spot well. Was it really only eighteen hours ago?

All-in-all, Restraint has the bones of a well thought-out dungeon. It puts the nightclub area to shame. No doubt it will be an uphill battle, but with some comfort items and dim the lighting, the dungeon could be one of the best in the state. No one wants to play under the high-wattage lights of a sports stadium at midnight. It would feel like an examination room in a hospital, or an interrogation room of hostile terrorists.

I'm sure there's a kink out there for that, but it should be majority rules in the dungeon. No squeaky wheel gets the grease syndrome. There must be extra space in this building for rentable private rooms featuring specific wants and needs.

Body running on autopilot, my mind is creating to-do lists to transform Restraint and its dungeon into a place I'd be proud to call my own.

I plunk the chair under the naked bulb, then turn my attentions to the inhabitants gazing at me with curiosity and one with guilt. The Masters of Restraint are all here, with the exception of our leader, since Marcus has to remain anonymous and refuses to wear a ridiculous hood, which now adorns Ezra and Cortez's heads. A large amount of people I've never met are here as well. I assume many of them are submissives our masters use to play reindeer games.

Whitt's standing frozen in shock with his cock in Kristal's mouth. Guilt etches across his handsome features, like a kid with his hand stuck in the cookie jar, seconds after momma said no sweets.

Another thing that needs to change– Kristal is giving herself to Whitt, working his cock like a pro, and what thanks does she get? She gets to kneel on a cold, hard tiles for as long as the job takes. Submissive or not, show some goddamn respect for the ones servicing you.

In my early thirties, I'm neither young nor old, but the thought of my bones mashing into the tile… I already had to do that during my initiation, and I thought the cold discomfort was part of the hazing.

The Masters of Restraint are entitled asshats and a female sadist.

I don't feel anger at my husband, which is rational with my way of thinking, but probably not to him. No doubt it's an ego destroyer how I don't care. Besides, Whitt looks amazing and virile with his perfect flesh parting Kristal's luscious lips. If I were a man, I'd want to fuck that mouth, too.

No more fun and games, because Kristal has a punishment coming.

Several ladies watch me from their position next to my husband and roommate. One is Fate, who's perfectly fine, and obviously looking everywhere than at the blowjob.

I smile at Fate with immense relief. I'd worried about Kristal's impending death if a hair on Fate's head was misplaced.

Three more ladies join their group: A pretty, ginger-haired lovely with soft, peachy flesh. A beautifully pink, girl-next-door, with blonde hair and the largest natural breasts I've ever seen on someone so petite. The last is a hard-eyed woman glaring at me with tight lips. She's a rail-thin brunette with a sour expression on her puss. There's a story there, and it makes me wonder if this is the elusive Monica James I email back and forth with for Edge Publishing projects.

I walk over to Fate, and touch her hand with a fingertip. "How are you doing?" I whisper into her ear. "You good?"

"I'm okay," Fate stammers a reply, blushing an unholy shade of red. "It's been good so far. I helped Kris tend bar, and then we came in here. But I don't want to see that–" voice frightened, Fate gestures to where Whitt is frozen still, as is Kristal.

No doubt my housemates are terrified I'll go postal because Whitt is my husband, as well as the discomfort Fate must be feeling over the fact that Whitt is her baby brother. For fuck's sake, what was Kristal thinking?

She wasn't, that's what Kristal was thinking– everything is about her.

I pat Fate's hand to let her know it's okay. I'm not going to cut off Whitt's cock.

Eyes rolling heavenward, I mutter, "You guys so need me." Reaching down, I tug Kristal to her feet. "Upsy daisy, little Miss Dyson."

"I'm–" Kristal has nothing else to say.

"Nah-uh." I shake my head at the cocksucktress. "Time to learn some self-respect, Chica. You go sit in that chair over there," I command. "And don't move unless and until I tell you to." Relief crossing her expression, Kris scurries away to sit in the chair.

Whitt starts to speak, but I silence him with a finger. Yes, my middle finger.

"What's your name, hun?" The buxom blonde blushes invitingly underneath my gaze.

"Kayla," she says in a tone bleeding innocence and shyness.

"Are you allowed to play, Kayla?"

"I–um… I don't know?" Kayla ends it with an upward inflection, asking me the question, when I'm the one who needs the answer.

Go to the source, I guess, since Kayla doesn't know. "Do you have a master?" I'd forgotten the lesson Marcus had taught me about how literal you must be because submissives are very evasive in nature.

"Yes," Kayla replies.

OH, MY GOD! For the love of all that is holy, I'm going to throttle Kayla. Another item on my steadily growing to-do list, I need practice in submissive speak.

"Who, Kayla?" I fail to hide my impatience. "Who is your master?"

"Master Ez," Kayla replies without hesitation.

Oh, good Lord. Save this precious child from that sociopath. I'm a grown woman, a mother, business owner, and a trained dominant, and that lunatic was still able to get the best of me… this submissive woman-child's sweet nature is going to be destroyed.

"Thank you, Kayla." I turn to address her companions. "Ladies, give me your name and the name of your master." I get straight to the point, being as black and white as possible.

Gingy and the brunette, who I assume is Monica, look like they've been around this block at least a dozen times before. They don't play coy like Kayla, though my intuition screams Kayla wasn't playing.

"I'm Heidi," the red-head answers first, sounding confident yet polite. Somewhere near the range of thirty, there's an air about the woman, like she's in charge of her life. Maybe she's a natural caregiver, so that makes her submissive in nature. Submissive doesn't mean you don't know what you want, or how to get it. "I need no master, but I play with Dexter."

Peachy skin blushing, Heidi is comfortable in her own skin– I like this chick.

"It's nice to meet you, Heidi. You may call me Queen." Projecting my voice, I say it loud enough, so everyone who's paying attention knows to call me Queen instead of Mistress. Since I hold everyone's curious gazes, the message was received loud and clear.

"Call me Queen, and nothing but when I'm on the premises," I warn the membership. "Starting tonight, this is *my* dungeon, just as that is *my* club. You will come to me first, and I will defer to those in charge. Do I make myself clear?"

The rumbling begins as the crowd looks around at their fellow members. The noise level increases, to the point the confusion echoes off the dungeon walls. I leave them to their conjecture, not explaining how I'm saving their behinds. No one should have to deal with Ezra, because the man is not safe. Since I'm already under his thumb, I may as well protect the masses while I suffer.

I give my attention to the brunette, ignoring everyone else. "You're Monica, correct? From Edge Publishing?"

"Yeah," Monica looks at me askew, not trusting me. "How did you know?"

Leaning into her personal space, even though I'm positive Monica isn't comfortable with that, I whisper for only her to hear. "We correspond a few times a week about projects I'm doing for your company. I'm Regina Regal. No need to tell me whether or not you have a master, because I know which asswipe put that bitchy scowl on your face, and I don't blame you after he strung you along for two years."

Reaching forward to shake my hand, Monica gains some confidence from our exchange. "I'm happy to finally put a face with the name. It's nice to meet you, Queen."

"I have some fun planned for you, but you can say no." Stepping away, I toss out over my shoulder. "I'll be right back, ladies– don't move."

Taking Fate's hand within mine, I lead her over to the outside wall, to where she'll have a view should she want to look, but she'll be out of harm's way. Settling Fate on a spanking bench, I decide tonight will be the last time I bring her here until I get the place straightened out. I can't worry about Fate while trying to do my job, while also watching my back and protecting my virtue.

Leaving Fate to sit and observe, I locate Dexter. Standing in the exact same way when I first met him almost two years ago, arms crossed over his bare chest, only wearing a pair of leathers and no shoes. The man's ringlets obscure his gaze, making him look disinterested.

After being on my knees on this hard floor, the sadist owes me.

"May I borrow your submissive?" I infuse my tone with respect. "While Heidi said she's a free-agent, I don't want to step on your toes."

"Okay…" Dexter draws out, confused. "Why?" Eyebrow quirking high, I note how his eyes are just as expressive as Marc's, the same color too– it's unnerving.

"I need to teach Kristal a few lessons tonight," I explain. "I am in need of willing participants."

"Kristal's a menace," is all Dexter says. Must be the subtle nuances of conversation are also lost on seasoned dominants, because I have to be black and white literal with Dexter as well.

"Do you mind if I use Heidi in my example?"

"I have no claim on Heidi," Dexter finally responds after several long moments. "Ask her before you pair her with someone. She's straightforward in her needs and wants, and will tell you if she's uncomfortable. She's a masochist, but enjoys sensual playing if no pain is to be dealt."

"Good– thanks for the information." Unexpectedly, I smile at Dexter, and he looks surprised. Running his fingertips though his curls, he smirks back at me with good-natured camaraderie.

I look around to find the guilty-eyed, hooded bastard. I'm a firm believer in charging into battle, but being fully prepared first. Ezra is my present and near future, and now I know what insanity I'm dealing with. So I swallow my pride, and will cry in private.

The partners are standing close together, off to the side. I can tell by the way Cortez is chatting animatedly that he doesn't know what Ezra had been doing an hour ago. I wonder how many secrets they keep from one another.

Marcus may keep secrets from me. Lord knows, Jamie does. But that says more about them than it does about me. Moving forward, I'm going to be an open book with them.

Sensing how I need to speak with him, Ezra starts to stride toward me. Taking my power back, I won't wait for him, nor will I go to him, but I'm willing to meet him halfway.

"I need to speak to your dominant side," I say cryptically, trying to hide the fissure of fear creeping into my voice.

I may look like a brave yet stupid bitch for speaking to my assailant, but that doesn't mean I'm not vibrating with terror and rage.

Ezra's lips twitch in the mouth-slit of his ridiculous hood. "Regina, we're one in the same." He keeps his composure for less than ten seconds, then the smug smile spreads to showcase feral teeth.

"You could have fooled me," I mutter underneath my breath, causing Ezra to chuckle.

A mix of guilt and lust shines out at me, confusing me further. Ezra isn't lying about how he is Master Ez. I know they are one in the same, but how does that work?

"I need to borrow Kayla. Does she play with anyone in particular? Or is she just for Master Ez's amusement?"

"I'm Kayla's master, Regina, but she's for only one man. I have never touched her– not even once."

"Does your other half, who also happens to be you, use his influence on Kayla?"

Frustrated, a long-suffering sigh hits my ears– Hello, Master Ez.

"Queen, we are one in the same," Master Ez repeats in a different voice– yeah, because that's going to convince me that Ezra is in control of himself at all times. I've seen more of Master Ez than I ever have of Ezra. I'm guessing if you share a brain while the other drives the body, it wouldn't be too hard to pretend to be the other half.

I could even see Ezra blaming Master Ez for actions he made, simply to escape the consequences. *"I didn't do it, so don't punish me!"*

"Kayla is for Aaron's rehabilitation. Cortez plays with her occasionally." His answer is blunt and to the point, as is Master Ez's way. "Since Cortez has sworn off the other submissives, in light of Katya coming home, Cortez rewards Kayla when Aaron cannot."

"What do you mean by *'when Aaron cannot'*?" I ask, but Master Ez doesn't answer.

A gaze warms my face. Looking up quickly, I catch Aaron staring at me with curiosity. He has taken the spot where Ezra had been standing, right next to Cortez. I hadn't noticed Aaron with the suffocating presence of Ezra and Cortez eclipsing him.

"May I borrow Aaron too?" I nod toward the brawny cutie, deciding it wouldn't be fair to use his woman on anyone but him. Aaron and Kayla, both young, blond, and blue-eyed, what an adorable couple they make.

"Whatever for?" A blond brow pops in curiosity.

"Kristal's going to be forced to orgasm repeatedly, then when she's most vulnerable, she and I will have a private chat. Since she's a highly visual creature, I need a few couples engaging in sex acts to keep her primed."

"Forced orgasming– I approve of your methods, Queen." Master Ez nods his head, the hood covers and reveals the line of skin above his collar with every movement. "Sex is sex, and should be done for pleasure."

Scoffing, "Do you see the irony behind your statement?"

"Hence why I insisted you orgasmed." Master Ez lifts his hand to clear the air, and I swear this is Ezra pretending to be Master Ez, as the intensity he releases is nowhere near the same level as it had been. "That's neither here, nor there, and not a part of our discussion. Kristal was using sex as an outlet for her pain and guilt, until it became an addiction. She was chasing the high it offered, but it was taking more and more sex, to the point of orgies, to feel the smallest of buzzes."

"How do you know this?"

"Why do you think Cortez was cut off from the stable of submissives he was fucking nightly, including the same orgies Kristal attended? These few months have been a sexual detox, in anticipation of Katya coming home… Kayla may suck Aaron, but he'll need my support to get through it."

"Never mind then–"

"Yes, it's part of the process. I know what I'm doing, Regina." See, I knew it was Ezra masquerading as Master Ez! "I'm a psychiatrist, after all."

"Irony."

"I'm not pretending." Ezra takes the insult in the spirit in which it was given. "If you see me blink several times in quick succession, it's me fighting for control. You wanted to speak to

Master Ez, so I let go. Out of respect for you, I had to cut him off when he brought up your orgasm."

"Shit!" Hand out to ward Ezra off, I walk away. I don't run, but I walk away very, very quickly.

"Kristal?" I call loudly. "Do you know why you're sitting here? No need to catalog the huge list of offenses since we don't have all night."

Kristal grins at that– bitch.

"I'm a compulsive liar and a sex addict. I broke the sister-code. Repeatedly. I can't be trusted."

As I stand before Kristal, the crowd closes up to circle around us. Their contagious excitement and curiosity cloud the air.

Eyes flicking from member to member, I'm surprised to see a few submissive males. Not that I think they're like unicorns. But other than Syn, most of the masters use female submissives. After questioning Marcus and Cortez, I know Syn only deals pain, never sex. So perhaps Dexter doesn't mind either gender, as long as they're a masochist.

"In a way, this is a test for me too. I've lived in Dominion my entire life, and some of you I've known since I was a teenager. A few others, I met when I started my training, which was closer to two years ago than a year. But in that time, I've never performed in this dungeon. If I'm strong enough to lead you, then I better be good enough to entertain you."

While the membership murmurs to one another, I turn my attention back to the curvy spitfire who's in need of direction. Tonight Kris is wearing a black corset, which squishes her impressive assets up to her chin. A tiny, black thong peeks from between her thighs, and the inch of fabric barely covers the split of her hairless folds.

"Kristal, this isn't a punishment." I announce, and the crowd vocalizes Kristal's surprise. "I love you. More importantly, I actually like you as a person. I want to respect you, but I want you to respect yourself even more."

"I–" Kristal tries to interrupt, and I know she's testing my fortitude, not sure if I'm strong enough to tame her.

"Sex means many different things to many people. I met you an hour before I lost my virginity." Kristal and I share a smirk while people in the crowd gasp in awe. "You gave me sex advice like a mother on her daughter's wedding day. Then I got advice from my new lover. Somewhere in the years since, you've gone off the rails."

Expression open, seeming to be receptive to what I'm trying to accomplish, Kristal speaks to me, and I allow it. "What did he tell you?" She cocks her head to the side, inspecting me.

I know when Kristal's and my relationship became strained. It's not her fault, nor is it mine. I'm empathetic and compassionate enough to realize how much it must have destroyed her to watch me grieve. To tell me the truth would have been to break loyalties she forged long before she formed ties with me.

"I know you were damned if you do, damned if you don't," I admit softly, no doubt making most of the people wonder what we're speaking about. "Either way, I would have been destroyed. So instead of hurting me, you suffered instead."

Tears staining her cheeks, Kristal looks away from me, trying to hide from all the eyes on her.

"On the night I lost my virginity, I learned a valuable lesson. Sex should only ever be used as a connection. There's passion and the need for pleasure– those are minor to intimacy. Since that lesson was taught, I've seen many miserable people use sex as a weapon, not only to hurt others, but to hurt themselves.

"I've been harmed by sex. I've been violated, debased, and extorted. I've been treated like a whore, as if the only value I have is between my thighs. I can't control what others do, even if they're doing it to me. I can only control how I react. But do you know what I've never done?"

Question rhetorical, deafening silence descends on the dungeon.

"Sex can be used as a connection, or it can be used as a weapon. But it's a weapon I've never leveled at myself. That's why we're here tonight, Kristal. You are disrespecting yourself by using sex as a toxic drug. You don't do it because it feels good. You do it because the high you get feeds into the dark well of insecurity you have. The more you fuck, the worse you feel about yourself. So you fuck even more and more and more, needing proof that you're worthless and only the sum of what's between your thighs."

Moving forward, I cup Kristal's gorgeous cheek. "I saw something in you when you were fifteen years old. I may have helped, but it was *you* who studied, learned the lessons, passed the classes, and graduated with honors. I may have built an empire, but not without your help. You do your job, just as you do your job here. You are a pivotal part of my household, helping me survive a decade of apathy, reminding me to do the small things with my daughter. I still see in you what I saw that first day. I wouldn't allow anyone to harm you, so why should I stand by while you harm yourself?"

"I-I-I– I can't stop myself," Kris sputters, tears spilling rapidly down her cheeks. "It's a compulsion."

"No, it's a toxic addiction. I will continue to see in you, what you don't see in yourself, until you finally see it too."

"I think you're as blind as a bat," Kris teases, laughter warping into a sob. "I've been horrible to you."

"Consider this last hoorah your intervention. As you orgasm, imagine it as all of your insecurities and dark feelings bleeding out of you. Then you will go into a sexual detox for an entire month. No intercourse. No oral. No self or mutual masturbation. No Kissing. You may hug the members of our household for reassurance and comfort. No Alex."

Several gasps of shock radiate around the circle. While I need them to see me as badass, I'm not doing this to gain their favor or scare them. This is between Kristal and me, and it's been a long time coming.

"After your month has concluded, you will only be allowed to have sexual contact with Alex in a romantic relationship setting. If you wish to feed your BDSM needs, you must ask permission from either me or Whitt. You no longer need to worry about making decisions, because you will have, not one, but two masters to rely on."

Whitt's, "Holy Shit!" has a smirk pulling at my lips.

"My cousin and I made the right decision," Dexter interjects. "The current bosses need to concentrate on their careers and family."

Cort's snort echoes around the dungeon. "Don't you mean Queen is more capable of running Restraint than we are?"

"Yes, but I was trying to be diplomatic." Dexter tries to insult Ezra and Cortez, but ends up making our resident asswipe giggle like a little bitch. "The two of you have corrupted what my cousin and I tried to build. Between you fucking anything with a pulse, and Master Ez sabotaging everything, no one could do any worse than the pair of you. At least Queen is lucid, has business sense, and has our best interests at heart."

"I will concede on this, and only this," Ezra interrupts, but he sounds terrifyingly like Master Ez. "I reserve the right to veto power."

"Restraint and its membership and clientele need a protector, and I am it. With the bosses yielding to my leadership, next up is helping our sex addict. My apologies to the dozens of you who liked to fuck Kristal without a care of what it was doing to her."

Gazing around at the membership, knowing we will be expanding under Master Fontaine's orders, I make them a promise. "No one will ever take advantage of anyone under my watch, even if it's as simple as exploiting insecurities. Respect is at the cornerstone of BDSM, and that includes self-respect."

"You think having sex means I don't have self-respect?" The addict is talking, struggling to exist, because if Kristal heals, the addiction dies.

"For fuck's sake, Kris!" Cort steps in. "Don't pull that goddamn slut-shaming bullshit Alex is always using to cover up the fact that you put out a welcome mat at the entrance to your pussy. We all know Queen means you don't give a shit who you welcome, and that's the problem."

I try for levity by changing the subject. "My dad used to laugh as he swatted my ass." I pull a few chuckles from the crowd. "Dad would say, '*this is hurting me more than it's hurting you*'. Dad didn't spank me hard, but I'd cry like I was dying. All the while, Dad laughed. I finally understand what he was going through."

Do I pull a rabbit out of a hat? Nah, but I pull it out of my corset. Well, not a rabbit– a butterfly. I found this purple butterfly toy in the Zeitler room, housed in one of the many drawers in the apothecary table. It's in its original packaging, or else I wouldn't have taken it.

"This is going to hurt me more than it's going to hurt you, simply because I have to hold the responsibility of administering tough love, and then the guilt as I watch you struggle to understand why we're doing what we're doing. *You* are the only one getting all the benefits."

Orgasm torture.

Kristal's eyes widen slightly and her lips part. As a sex addict, she's excited to experience the high. But rationally she knows this will be the end of that recklessly toxic lifestyle.

"I'm so sorry," Kristal sobs, and sorry she sounds.

Every enabler knows that the addict does feel sorry in the moment. They mean what they say when they promise never to use again. But then they cave to their demons, time and time again. The cycle continues until another force steps in its path. Willpower isn't the answer. The hormones released during the high alter the wiring in the brain. Kristal has to change her view of the world and herself, not just her view on sex.

"There's nothing for me to forgive," I reply with all honesty, not allowing Kristal to use me as an excuse to abuse herself. "The only thing I want from you is to alter your path. You need to become the best version of yourself– the version I've always known you could be."

Butterfly clutched in one hand, I pull a vibrator out of my corset with the other. Who needs pockets when you have large breasts? They created ample space for storage inside my corset. Lastly, I retrieve a small butt-plug and a vial of lubricant.

"Whatever you do, don't move from this chair. You can beg. You can cry. You can scream. But the one thing you cannot do is leave."

With a clinical air, I kneel between Kristal's feet, humming to myself as I work. As I gently roll her panties down her legs and off her feet, I massage the path until she relaxes beneath my touch. Using gentle pressure with my fingertips on her inner thighs, Kristal opens for me.

Kristal's a tiny thing with a pretty, pink cunny. Her hairless folds hide nothing of her swollen lips and the moisture trickling south.

I saturate Kristal's area with lubricant because I don't want to harm her in any way. This entire exercise is meant to teach her how there's such a thing as too much of a good thing.

An intensity fills the dungeon, causing my captive audience to breathe audibly. If I were to sniff, it's almost as if I could scent their lust riding the air.

Eager for the attention, Kristal turns helpful as I slide the butterfly's elastic anchoring over her legs to settle the vibrating toy at the nexus of her thighs. With the press of a hidden button, it buzzes to life. I move it around until Kristal's mouth forms an O, letting me know I hit the yummy spot. I tighten the straps to keep it in place, and let it do its thing until the fresh batteries die.

Going back to work between her legs with clinical ease, I slide the butt plug around in the slick lube, preparing it for entrance into her pucker. A heavy moan erupts from Kristal's throat as the toy slips past the ring of muscle.

The intoxicating cadence of Kristal's moans ignites the libidos of our gathered watchers. The whisper of clothing as they shift and step from foot-to-foot reverberates loudly in my sensitive ears.

Kristal has her first orgasm before I'm even finished. She thrashes around, and I wait for it to subside. She loves the plug, just like I knew she would. I don't judge. One of my most intense sexual experiences was when Marc was deep inside my pussy and Jamie was buried to the hilt in my ass.

A shiver of remembrance works its way along my spine.

After Kristal calms, I slide the vibrator inside her core, meeting absolutely no resistance after her orgasm. She's still clenching erratically, but it goes in easily. She isn't very tight from her addiction, but that isn't necessarily a bad thing. If a woman is too tight, a guy will blame her because he turns into a one-pump chump. At least the guys will last long enough to make sure Kristal gets off too. Being too tight removes all other forms of fun that would render it painful.

Setting the vibrator in place deep inside Kristal, I turn the base until it roars to life on the highest setting. This will also remain in place until the fresh batteries run dry.

Kristal's already on the edge of her second orgasm, so I pat the butterfly covering her clit and coo tauntingly. Screaming my name, Kristal comes for me. She didn't shout Queen, which I found annoyingly disrespectful– *Regina*. I don't fault Kris, because after fourteen years of calling me Regina, it's a hard habit to break.

As Kristal thrashes around in painful ecstasy, I pull the last of my tricks from my corset. Her pink nipples pebble for attention, with her corset riding down to expose her breasts. Perfectly round globes, ones that no doubt overflow a man's hand, heave invitingly with her every breath.

After rolling the nubs between my fingertips to harden them to stiff peaks, I slip the vibrating nipple clamps on. They're not too tight, as I don't want to restrict blood flow. I just want the vibration to keep Kristal on the edge. These won't be taken off until the batteries die too.

Riding toward her third orgasm, worry clouds Kristal's features. A puddle grows on the seat of her chair as moisture flows from around the slim vibrator. I know for a fact she's never had a g-spot orgasm, so I'm unsure if she's unable to hold her bladder because of the intense vibrations. There's fear in her eyes, so maybe this is a first for her.

I know that look– Kristal is definitely having a g-spot orgasm. It's isn't as explosive as my first was with Marc, or as earth shattering as my second was with Master Ez, but that small taste frightens her, realizing this will not end soon.

"Queen… please…" I said Kristal could beg, and beg she does. "No more– can't take anymore."

"Kristal, I'm showing you how much I love you by taking care of you." I coddle her with no intention of stopping her torture. "I'm giving you a lesson you'll never forget."

"If you love me… you'll stop this." Kristal's voice quivers as another orgasm strikes her. Writhing, groaning as if in agony, her fingertips clench the air, finding no purchase on her imaginary handholds. The pool widens– finally a real amount was released.

"You will endure this because you need to learn. If you loved and respect yourself, you wouldn't do the things you do. Having lovers is one thing, coming close to a thousand is insanity."

Multi-colored hair whipping around in an arc to stick to her sweat-slickened forehead, Kristal looks demonically possessed. Lips peeling back, she bares her pearly teeth in a snarl. "You're trying to shame me!" The addict rears its ugly head, being defensive and obtuse in a way to end this. If this ends, the addict survives.

"No shame in sex. It's how the sex makes you feel and why you have it. Sex isn't a weapon, not to hurt yourself or others. Your lover shouldn't be responsible for fighting your demons. It shouldn't be about power and control, or marking your territory. It shouldn't be a means of holding onto someone, or to heal, or to get what you want. If it's for anything other than connecting with another human being through pleasure, then it's toxic. Same goes with making children. If children were made for any other reason than through a connection, then those children will be raised in a toxic environment by broken, immature parents. This is not about shaming you– it's to show how you need help. Grow the fuck up, Chica!"

"How long?" Kristal mutters, terror causing her voice to break.

"Until the batteries die, Chica," I warn, voice more than mildly threatening. "And everything was brand new with fresh batteries, so be prepared for a long journey to enlightenment," I taunt in a voice gone husky from power and lust.

Kristal's cries go unheard– it's a form of manipulation forgiven with children. Hungry, tired, in need of comfort or entertainment, wanting to be held, a baby cries because they can't vocalize it, nor do they understand what they need.

The cry is so startling, the parent drops everything to care for the baby. But as a baby matures into a child, they begin to ask for their needs to be met. Whether they crawl in your lap and demand a story, or say they're hungry. This is when they learn patience as well, as their non-pressing needs can wait until they align with the rest of the family. Later in life, that compromise made for the family transcends into fitting into society.

Kristal is a grown woman who has always whined to get her needs met, or threw a bitch-fit because she didn't know what she needed. Everyone around Kristal caved, because it was easier to shut off the bitchiness, crying, and manipulations by giving in immediately– from birth to nearly thirty. This was a disservice done on Kristal's behalf. Her parents need their asses kicked for creating a woman like Kristal– I see women like her everywhere.

Instant gratification. Kristal's scared, crying to gain comfort from me. If she vocalized that, I would have comforted her– on my own terms. She can ask, but that doesn't mean she'll receive. Kristal is not a baby or toddler, and she's not in mortal danger. We wouldn't be in this mess if she'd learned to express her emotions and ask for her needs to be met.

Be an adult.

Walking away, I turn to the entertainment portion of our evening. I know eventually the vibrations will numb Kristal, but she's also an addict. I believe watching others perform will keep her primed.

Smiling, I pick my next victims. Marc said how at our age, it's just the tip of the iceberg for our needs. So far I've learned two things tonight, both complementing each other– cancelling out their effects.

One: feeling shame and self-loathing, Master Ez is my outlet in that arena. I understand Kristal because of what happened earlier– the terrifying facet Master Ez revealed. Intellectually, I know it was my body's way of turning the mental and emotional trauma into a physiological response. But I fear once the switch has been flipped, there is no turning it off.

Two: playing puppet master. A sense of power descends, bringing a soaring high with it. I have an entire dungeon under my control, and I hope I can keep my ethics in check, knowing power corrupts.

Since I've had enough Master Ez for the night, playing puppet master sounds amazing.

Kayla is standing between Ezra and Cortez. It's a humorous sight to see a pink-skinned, petite yet voluptuous girl being flanked by two identically shaped men in expensive business suits and creepy hoods. Kayla looks like a virginal lamb to the slaughter, and they're the zealots escorting her to the altar of their pagan god.

As I pull Kayla away, Cort mouths to me, "*Jesus, Regina. I'm impressed.*" I smirk at Cort, because I'm nowhere near finished.

I find the happy bruiser on the other side of Ezra– I look to the eyes, noting Master Ez is riding shotgun again. Thank God.

Asking in a calm, tentative tone, "Aaron, would it be okay if Kayla pleasured you?"

Aaron's body tightens, and not in a good way. Ezra's hand immediately seeks the nape of Aaron's neck, then he gently massages the tension away.

Fingers fumbling with his zipper, I'm about to call it off, but then Aaron pops his cock out the fly of his jeans. Aroused to the point of pain– the bulbous head of Aaron's circumcised cock is nearly purple.

Without hesitation, Kayla drops to her knees, emitting a loud clack on the tiles. Eager, she licks Aaron from balls to tip. As a result, Aaron's cock pulses and flexes, and I worry he's about to pop.

Standing behind the nervous man, Cortez pulls Aaron's back to his chest. Holding the bigger man's weight, Cortez rubs Aaron's shoulders and chest in a soothing manner. Ezra joins Cort in their quest to relax Aaron.

Speaking volumes, Kayla thinks nothing of this interaction.

I've never seen the three of them together at the same time, let alone interacting. Actually, I've barely seen Ezra and Cort together. The bond they'd forged through growing up together, their abduction, and the aftermath, is a humbling experience to witness.

Aaron must still have hang-ups regarding sex, and no doubt Ezra and Cortez blame themselves. They're trying to help Aaron through Kayla. Judging by the way Aaron's cock behaves, he punishes himself with abstinence.

I can't stand by and watch, because I feel as if I'm intruding on a very private moment.

In the background, Kristal's crying out while in the throes of yet another orgasm, and it gains my undivided attention. The pool at her feet is enormous, and the vibrator is starting to slip from her body on the tide.

With an elbow to the ribs, Syn nudges Dexter, then points in the general vicinity of where the vibrator is wiggling free. Smirking, he reaches forward to push the vibrator back inside Kristal's depths. He gives it a few more twists, then pumps the vibrator in and out a few times until Kristal's high-pitched scream warps into his name.

I allow Dexter to display his sadistic tendencies, especially since he's grinning from ear-to-ear at Syn's appalled expression. It's not like she didn't prompt him to do it, only getting more than she bargained for. Looking away, Syn's air is that she's above it all.

Moving on, I gesture at a few of the people I've never met– I can only assume they're submissives since they aren't training to become masters. The men look on the verge of fainting from blood loss, which is drawing the women's attention southward.

"Handsies." I twirl my finger, then pump in the universal sign of jerking off. "Boys and girls, feel free to relieve the pressure."

Arms crossed over their chests, my next victims are standing awkwardly side-by-side, trying to hide their reactions behind grumpy expressions– Whitt and Dalton.

Overhearing as I approach, Monica whispers to Heidi how she never wants me to top her. A bubble of laughter flows from my lips, causing Monica to take a step back in fear. She catches herself mid-step, and it pisses her off. Meanwhile, Heidi looks anticipatory, like she sees the possibilities. Taking their hands, I lead them to the grumpy master and the grumpy master-in-training.

Dalton look scared shitless and sick to his stomach, so I change my trajectory slightly to calm his nerves. Whitt looks curious, intrigued about the level of deviancy his wife is displaying. He's trying very hard not to smirk, but failing spectacularly.

"Put those dimples away, Master Daniel," I tease in a flirty tone, knowing Whitt will adore the extra attention.

"I'll try, Queen." Whitt tries to sound serious, but then he ruins it by snickering instead. "Well, what do we have here?"

"A gift– after all, it's your favorite hobby."

I push both ladies to their knees in front of my husband– the ultimate of wedding gifts since I refuse to give him a wedding night. Understanding, Whitt's head hitches backward, opening his throat for the naughtiest laughter that's ever graced my ears. Pretty sure the entire dungeon became aroused from the seductive sound.

Raising an eyebrow that is far too dark to match that shit-brown wig he wears, Dalton shuffles to the side, trying to get closer for a better view. He even moves his neck, tiny chin curving down, making sure he misses nothing.

"These beautiful ladies would like to service you, Master Daniel," I announce in a tone tinged with amusement.

Without hesitation, Whitt responds by unzipping his trousers, dropping both his pants and boxers to his ankles. Clearly the boy has no issues with insecurity. Marble skin flushed pink, with his cock jutting upward toward the ceiling, Whitt looks at me in challenge.

The wideness of his eyes informs me how Whitt's shocked that I'm doing this. Oh, he more than wants it, especially since I'm not only going to witness it– I'm orchestrating it. Hard cock desperately trying to hug his belly, with pounding force, it pulses with desire.

Dalton's huge eyes bug out, front teeth sinking into a pouty bottom lip. When he releases the bite, I notice how his lips are stained red. It takes me a moment to realize Dalton covers his lips with foundation, meaning that ruby-kissed shade is his natural color.

Marcus said it was a pity that Dalton had to be in disguise, because the young man is a devastatingly exotic creature. Marc also said that someday Dalton would make a man very happy.

Laughing with joy, I hope more promises are kept. The devious sound has Whitt scrunching his eyes at me in confusion. I'm going to get my husband laid, proving to him that a mouth is not just a mouth– the body attached to it sure as hell matters.

Impatient, Heidi palms my husband's cock, trying to bring it down to her lips. But Whitt's too hard, so his cock won't give way and bend. I watch in amusement as two women negotiate on the best way to go about this situation.

They settle with Monica bent at the waist over Whitt's dick, with Heidi crouched between his legs, working his sack.

Watching in sick fascination, I gasp as Whitt's length disappears down Monica's throat. She's a pro-cocksucktress. Judging by the grunts emanating from Whitt's chest, she has been previously acquainted with his cock.

Whitt proves he's had the pleasure of both of them– probably the majority of the warm, wet mouths attached to female submissives in this dungeon. Hand palming the back of Heidi's head, Whitt pushes her tight against him at a sharp angle, suggesting she's feasting at his taint.

A loud moan draws everyone's attention. Our heads whip to the side in unison to find Aaron climaxing into Kayla's mouth.

Ezra presses his palm over the bulge in his pants and openly stares at me. No doubt Master Ez has buried Ezra deep and is piloting the bus. The lunatic fucking winks at me, then laughs when I stare gape-mouthed at his audacity.

Turning away quickly, I realize I was the only one who was captivated for more than a glance. The atmosphere in the dungeon has changed– no one is in control anymore. The submissives are openly masturbating, some screwing each other.

Probably lovers off and on, Dexter's kneeling in the center of Kristal's cum puddle, tormenting her with the vibrator. Dexter's hand moves rapidly as he draws more fluid from Kristal's depths. Sharpening into focus, I gasp in shock when I see what Dexter is doing.

Kneeling, Dexter rubs the head of his mega-cock around the cum puddle. He's jacking off while swirling around in Kristal's release. All the while, Kristal's tormented pleas are feeding into Dexter's darkness. In an endless cycle, Kristal cries, causing Dexter to release sadistic laughter, with the laughter egging her on to cry more.

Dexter's not hurting Kristal, but I still can't watch, even though she's earned this. If I stop it, Kristal will never learn her lesson and she'll revert back to her destructive ways.

It's hurting me more than it's hurting you is a lesson I'm learning today.

Turning my attention back to the ladies servicing my husband, I find them servicing themselves too. Their tiny hands are moving quickly underneath the clothing covering their pussies.

Both men flushed, Whitt stares at Dalton's mouth as Dalton stares at Whitt's cock.

Standing behind Whitt, I support him. With an evil giggle, I whisper into his ear. "Dalton's pouty mouth sure does look fuckable, doesn't it?"

Whitt grunts, hips jerking in answer.

"I know what Dalton really looks like," I tease, teeth nipping at his earlobe. "Do you see how red and juicy his mouth looks? Mmm… with that strong jaw, I bet he has some good suction action."

Leaning the bulk of his weight into me, Whitt makes that frustrated sound deep in his throat.

Voice a purr in Whitt's ear, "I bet you'd like me to tell you what he looks like, wouldn't you?"

"Please," he breathes, voice catching.

"As you watch Dalton's mouth, he watches your cock. It's not Monica's lips he's dreaming are wrapped around his dick." Slowly enunciating each word, I draw out Whitt's torments. "In Dalton's fantasies, it's his lips wrapped around *your* rosy cock."

Whitt groans pitifully, eyes following the line of Dalton's gaze. He groans again and looks at the man's face. Dalton's gaze flicks to Whitt's for a split-second in confusion, then returns to watching the action. It takes less than a heartbeat for Whitt's gaze to latch onto the humongous bulge tenting those hideously baggy pants Dalton wears.

"Jesus, how big do you think that is?" I muse into Whitt's ear, voice taunt yet coaxing. "Don't you wish he'd take it out and show us? I'm wicked curious. Ten inches at least. Wow!"

Huffing an amazed laugh, Whitt turns his face to mine. Tongue peeking out, he quickly licks my lips to be a shit. Snickering at the irritated noise I make, he looks back over to Dalton.

"I have a secret," I taunt Whitt. "Dalton isn't quite a year older than you."

While kissing the shell of Whitt's ear, every muscle in his body turns bowstring tight, and I can sense he's close to coming.

I feel no jealousy as two women suck Whitt off– I'm happy Whitt's enjoying himself. I feel no jealousy as he watches the man next to us, no doubt envisioning those ruby-kissed lips swallowing him whole– I'm proud of Whitt for knowing what he desires.

"I have a secret," I taunt Whitt again.

I can tell Whitt's holding on by a thread. Both of us playing a game where no rules were given, he knows not to come until I allow it.

Pressing my lips tightly to Whitt's ear, I breathe permission. "Dalton's gay."

Whitt explodes. Monica chokes on his release, while a sensual keen echoes around the dungeon. I hold Whitt up as he spasms, witnessing his eyes locked tight on the man standing next to us, all the while spewing garbled, nonsensical words.

Curiosity has me watching Dalton instead of my husband and the submissives servicing him. I need to know if I should maneuver the two of them together. It would be the gift of a lifetime if I found Whitt a lover in every sense of the word.

Dalton whimpers, pale skin flushing crimson. A wet spot on the front of his jeans is spreading, so I yank him behind me so he can have his privacy. Everyone is too absorbed by Whitt, Monica, and Heidi to notice.

I know a little thing about shame. Wearing a disguise, hiding his face behind makeup, eyes behind contacts, and his hair behind a wig, Dalton would feel shame if attention were drawn to him. Dalton has respected me since the second we met. In return, I will help him keep his self-respect.

Holding Whitt up as he regains his composure, I kiss his cheek and whisper, "I love you, Sunshine," directly into his ear. Once he's stable on his feet, I turn quickly, facing Dalton.

With a yank, I have Dalton's shirt pulled out of his pants. He starts to protest by flicking my hands away, but he quickly catches on. Adjusting his shirt, Dalton covers the cum-stain, and then walks to the side with a stiff nod of thanks.

Knowing Whitt is in good hands, I stride to an exhausted Kristal. Slumped in her chair, Kristal is panting. Instead of terrorizing her, Dexter's softly talking about accounting. Huh– sadist and sex-fiend accountants.

Sliding the chair to the side, out of the way of the mess Kristal made, I kneel beside her. Gently, I pull the plug from her body, moving onto the vibrator, which the batteries had died. Dexter was fair enough to stop when the vibrator did.

The butterfly is also dead, so I don't bother being careful with the elastic bands. Ripping it from Kristal's thighs, I'll try to remember to buy a new butterfly, plug, vibrator, and nipple clamps to replace the ones I took. One nipple clamp is dead, so I remove it. But the other is still slightly buzzing. I could go easy on Kristal, but I don't. I leave it on.

"Submissive boys and girls!" I call out, expecting to be obeyed.

A gaggle of about ten men and women stand around me, all wearing different versions of the same expression– worry. Monica and Heidi look ready to go home and veg, while Kayla steps from foot-to-foot. The rest of them, I'll learn their details tomorrow night when I take over.

"You will clean the dungeon before you go home. These toys get thrown away. The chair is to be disinfected, then placed back into the meeting room. The floor needs to be scrubbed. If you work together, it won't take longer than fifteen minutes."

They grumble unfavorable things about me to each other, but do as they're told, so I don't bitch them out.

After picking Kristal up as if she were a small child, cradling her to my chest, I walk from the dungeon, down the hallway, to enter my new private room, with Fate following dutifully behind.

"I'll get us some comfort items," I promise my girls. "And have keys made up for each of us." Settling Kristal on the toilet seat, I continue rambling. "I'm just thankful for the serviceable bathroom."

After stripping my dress, I remove Kristal's corset from her torso. The nipple clamp has finally died, so I toss it in the trash.

I pull us into a warm shower, refusing to think of why I took my last shower. The only thing keeping me strong, holding me together, is the fact that Kristal and Fate need me to be their rock.

With hot water cascading over us, I hold Kristal to my chest while she cries. But the most disturbing yet pride inducing phrase I've ever heard in my life is uttered in a reverent voice on repeat.

"Thank you, Master… Thank you, Master… Thank you, Master… I'll make you proud, Master."

Gazing out of the shower enclosure, I watch Fate as she sits with endless patience on the tile floor.

They both need a keeper… and now I'm their master.

Chapter Nineteen

After depositing my girls in Fate's bedroom and checking to make sure Ella was in one piece, I finally step into my bedroom, ready to fracture. What I find instead draws me up short.

Feet slightly hesitate, then I continue on my path like I'm unfazed. "Hey!" I smile privately as I walk to my closet. "Have you been here long?" I breathe a sigh of relief, but deep down I knew Marcus would be here like I demanded.

"A couple hours," Marcus mutters bashfully. His tone makes me look at him, and I find a blushing Marcus resting on my bed in a pair of plaid pajama bottoms and a white t-shirt. His ankles are crossed and he's typing on his cellphone.

Marcus Zeitler is in my bedroom, and I think I like it.

Heart hammering, I pretend sweat isn't beading at the nape of my neck. "Bored?" I tip my head in the direction of his cellphone.

"No," Marcus grins broadly. "I'm pestering Jamie."

I'd rather banter than turn into an emotional mess. After helping Kris through two hours of sobbing, I don't have the energy for my turn.

"Is Jamie bored?"

Eyes flicking back and forth, Marcus keeps looking me over as I undress, but he's trying to be covert about it, like he fears the sensual attention will break me. The thought of Marcus worrying actually puts me at ease as I pull on a pair of shorts and a tank top.

"Jamie's working." Marc's eyes shine with mischief, but it's just a façade. He's playing pretend, waiting me out. "He's *trying* to work, but I'm having fun bugging him."

"Talking about me, are ya?" I tease, knowing damn well that's what's up.

"Always," Marc's reply is serious, but he instantly changes his tone back to light and playful. "I just started texting him. Mini-Grant loves attention, and she finally went to bed about a half hour ago."

"What?" I mutter in shock. "Ella was asleep when I left–*five* hours ago."

"Kids have radar for when the babysitter is still awake. I learned that quickly when I had four kids roaming around Shadow Haven. I was their plaything." Marcus laughs at some memory I'll never experience.

"I bet they saw you as a big kid," I tease back.

"I was still a kid..." A haunted look crosses Marc's expression. "Anyway, I came here after I left Restraint. I knew Jamie was trying to work, so I left him alone. Everyone was at Restraint except for Roman. Poor Roman." Laughing the world's most intoxicating song, Marcus shakes his head.

"What?" I notice Marcus is in an exceptional mood after the events of the past twenty-four hours. Needing something I can't name, I crawl onto the bed and sit astride Marc's thighs. Blinking, he quickly hides his look of shock. "Poor Roman?" I remind Marc, since he looks gobsmacked.

I feel better sitting higher than Marcus, able to look down at him, while being on top so I'm in control of the situation. He can't move unless I allow it. Most importantly, I have the upper-hand. I'll only allow his touch if I want it. The door may be to my back, but I know Marcus literally has my back.

After blinking the surprise away, Marcus regains his composure. "I walked in expecting Roman to be napping or reading, instead I found him on the couch with curlers in his long hair and eye-shadow being applied liberally." Releasing another laugh, Marcus has never looked happier.

Who knew this man longed to be domesticated.

"Ella needs to learn some man stuff. There's too much estrogen in this house." Marcus snickers at Roman's plight.

"No way did my daughter let you go unscathed." I would pay good money to turn back the clock and be here when Ella and Marcus met for the first time. It would have been a cherished memory. But, then again, maybe my interference would've been a detriment, both more concerned with me than getting to know one another.

"I had my nails painted." The mischievous twinkle in Marc's eye tells me he loves kids. Wiggling his fingers, he displays how they're shiny– clear, thank God. But when he wiggles his toes, I bust a gut– a rainbow of ten colors.

"At least Ella's painting *inside* the nails now. It could have been much worse."

With my attention on his toenails, Marcus pushes a book toward me with his foot– #14.

"Holy fuck!" I exclaim, excited to see whether or not any of the incidents from my training made it into the book. "Did you bring this?" I arch an eyebrow in demand.

"Nope, the James Atwater first edition was here when I sat down." As innocent as a newborn babe, Marcus clasps his hands over his chest.

"Sure it was," I mutter sarcastically. "You're a poor liar. If you didn't, then Roman."

"Wrong again!" Marcus laughs sardonically, reaching out as if he wants to touch me, but he drops his hand before he makes contact. "I didn't bring it. Roman didn't bring it. But you should see the inscription."

"I seriously need to get some self-worth, self-respect, and my head shrunk," I mutter with disgust, but the giddy smile never leaves my face. While hugging the heavy book to my chest like a lover, I run my fingers over the embossed number. The grain of the Cordovan leather skips beneath my fingertips.

After taking a deep breath, I crack the book open, then I begin leafing through the pages.

For our Regal Queen– they call her Mrs. Whittenhower.

A gasping wheeze nearly suffocates me– a ball of pure emotion I'm not sure I can survive.

"Shh…" Marcus uses his tone to soothe me, still afraid his touch isn't welcome. "I know– I understand how painful it must be to read those words."

"Regina Regal– they call me Mrs. Whittenhower," I murmur words from my private thoughts. "The name isn't foreign to me. It feels right, but it's the wrong husband."

"But to say that out loud means, not only do you disrespect your husband, knowing if he found out he would be gutted, you lose a bit of yourself. You feel that admitting you wish you were Grant's wife means you have no self-respect."

"Exactly."

"Regina?" Marc's bravery knows no bounds– resting his palms on my thighs, he squeezes to comfort me. "Self-respect is about how you feel about yourself. Someday, be it tonight, or four years from now, or a decade… you'll realize loving Grant, wishing you were his wife, it will never change your worth."

"Marcus." I level him with a frank stare. "If a man cheats on a woman, she needs to leave him, because he obviously doesn't respect their relationship, or her, or himself."

"Circumstance is pivotal to what you're trying to accomplish with your argument." Marcus, as a lawyer, he's forever a debater. "People change. They drift apart. But sometimes they see the error of their ways, grow up, and drift back together again. Besides, Grant has never cheated on you– not in life, or death, or rebirth. Only you."

"Marcus, Grant didn't cheat on me– he *abandoned* me and our children. If I had an ounce of self-worth, it would dictate I never forgive him, let alone love him."

"Love isn't a choice you make, Regina," Marcus chastises. "Nor can it be willed away because you're angry. As I said, in the future, when you finally grow up, you'll understand how happiness overpowers conviction. I wish I lived in a world where I could have been Mr. Whittenhower, where Jamie loved me back. He could have abandoned me, and I still would have taken him back."

"You're insane," I snarl, understanding what Marcus is saying, but refusing to give in and agree. "I can't go there, Marc. I can't."

"I don't want to fight about Jamie," Marcus murmurs, a plethora of emotions written within his tone. "I only wanted you to know I understand how you're feeling… about everything."

Since Marcus is treading carefully, I don't bitch at him. I don't want to have Marcus revert back to the man who would try to bulldoze over me, tell me what to do, and disrespect me. Since we sat in the car before my initiation, a new connection has forged between us.

Leaning to the side, I struggle to tuck the book underneath my mattress. James Atwater's books are hidden from impressionable eyes. No daughter should have such an intimate gaze into her father's mind.

Sitting upright, still astride Marc's thighs, I sigh heavily. "I'm not okay– I'm not stupid enough to say I am, nor will I insult your intelligence by saying I am." Reaching up, Marcus wipes stray tears off my cheeks with a fingertip, when I hadn't realized I was crying.

"Marcus, I can't dwell on it. I have to keep putting one foot in front of the other, marching forward. The only thing I can change is our future. I can make a difference. Tomorrow, I'll get up and go into Empowerment, where I'll secure our servers and database. During the afternoon, I'll spend time with my children. Tomorrow night, I'll go to Restraint and begin a new chapter of my life, knowing that puts me at risk with Ezra."

"Regina, you don't have to." This time, it's tears flowing down Marc's cheeks. My voice had been level, my words inspiring and positive, therefore it's his demons playing out inside his head.

"Yeah, I do actually– Jamie challenged me this morning. First he told me not to share my knowledge with you, then he said it was my turn to experience the agony of keeping secrets from my loved ones. I never thought I'd see the day where he didn't know me." I toss my cellphone on Marc's chest. "Read it. My integrity comes first, because I refuse to negotiate with terrorists."

Laughing that intoxicating sound that drugs me, Marcus shakes his head left and right. "Regina, Jamie knows your reactions to everything better than I do. He's always accurate. If he said that to you, he did so knowing you'd share with me."

"Goddammit!" I reach for my phone, refusing to play games anymore.

"Mine!" Marcus bats my hand away, then opens up the text message I shared with Jamie. Curious to his thoughts, I watch as emotions flit across his features.

"Boyd? I *liked* him. Asshole. I know every single person Jamie lists in these messages, most of them are close to me." Voice gutted, Marcus closes his eyes for a heartbeat. When they open, there're tears clinging to his lashes. "Wait!"

Marcus shows me the phone, pointing out a specific part. "This doesn't make any sense. I was confused as I was putting two and two together when I learned of Dalton Fontaine and Bianca Green being forced to marry. See?" He points again. "Where Jamie is describing how the Meyers family has a vendetta, wishing to have their bloodline running through all the families."

"I understood it when I read it– I mean, it made sense. Imagine being their bitch, then gaining enough power but never truly being treated as an equal. So if their family sat in a position of power within every family, Dominion would belong to the Meyers bloodline. But there is no Meyers' blood flowing through Holden, Fontaine or Zeitler veins."

“Powerless. That explains why my bloodline was weakened to a single heir, and we’re not sitting on the council… Which is why they suggested hooking up Dalton and Whitt, which machinations aside, is a spectacular idea.”

“They’re actually feeling one another,” I murmur, feeling like a matchmaker. “If I didn’t place Whitt’s happiness above everything else, I’d steer him clear, because I don’t want that Gwen cunt getting her wish.”

“Gwen,” Marcus snarls, looking like he smells shit. Jealousy. I hate Gwen because she seduced a child– Stanton was too young too. But Marc hates her because Jamie is his. “Since no Meyers is getting in my pants or Dexter’s…”

“Spyder,” I grit out, feeling disgusted. “I’m so sorry, Marcus.”

“Well, I’m not. At least they’re going the surrogacy route–” I glare down at Marcus, and he laughs over my tortured past. “Actual surrogacy, with *Whitt*,” he stresses how that’s the best outcome any father could want from the founders. “As for Dalton, his dick is not going anywhere near Bianca again. Trust me on that.”

“Eww.” Shuddering, I think of the precious little girl I used to babysit, and my stomach twists.

“It looks like another surrogacy plan. A gay couple with their sisters gifting the use of their womb and an egg so their genetics will mingle. Calculating, but still sweet.”

“It’s probably the sweetest thing they’ve ever contemplated, the sick fucks. It must have something to do with how Whitt’s either related to everyone, or loved by them. So they’re being nice by giving him someone he could want and love, while gifting children in an appropriate fashion.”

“Probably. I’m impressed by their long game, since my daughter is only fourteen. So it’s at least four or more years out. Anyway, that marriage was unnecessary, as there’s already a Meyers/Fontaine union.”

“Excuse me?”

“Faith is Gwen Meyers’ middle daughter, and she’s been with Olivia Fontaine’s oldest son since she was sixteen.”

“Come again?” I croak out. “Faith– I mean, Syn. She has a partner? Wow,” I breathe out in mystification. “That explains the no-sex rule she has at Restraint. Maybe she can’t have kids.”

“Faith can,” Marcus says without hesitation. “Why do you think Jamie listed a Meyers in the Holden bloodline?”

Leaning forward, I stare at the text message, wondering how I missed that the first time. "Who's Zane?"

Marcus hesitates for a second, choosing his words wisely, no doubt. "My grandson."

"What?" I squawk. "What the actual fuck?"

Marc ignores me. "So they plan on using Spyder, which is probably why I was held captive and milked in the first place. They don't need this bullshit between Dalton and Bianca. Unless Levi can't have kids–"

"Whoa… whoa… whoa… back the fuck up, buddy!" I tear the phone out Marc's hand to gain his undivided attention. "First, you can't just drop that bombshell and not ante up. Second, isn't Levi the guy who literally *milked* you?"

"One in the same, yes," Marcus says, no shame in his tone whatsoever, clearly not blaming this Levi fella. "There will be a story portion of this evening, *after* we get this sorted out."

"Okay, but answer my questions first," I demand, seated in my power position above Marcus.

"I didn't learn about my grandson until Faith and Cort's initiation. Which is why it will be described as hell on earth for all eternity. If you want to know where the animosity stems from, imagine dating a girl who gets knocked up by your partner. My guess, it was on founders' orders, and Cort was out of the loop. The shit said that night makes so much more sense now."

"That's why Faith disappeared?" I guess. "It had nothing to do with Cort nabbing Fate's v-card?"

"Oh, *that* happened, but probably in retaliation for whatever was happening with Faith and Ezra. You know how Cort operates."

"He gets even," I murmur in appreciation. "No wonder Cort got so upset when everyone blamed him for everything." Heart clenching, I want to find the asswipe and give him a big hug.

"I got to know Faith well while she was dating Cortez, like another kid roaming around Shadow Haven. So when she up and disappeared, I was beside myself. Jamie put me out of my misery by telling me how Faith was staying with Stanton. Which makes sense now, since Faith was probably helping to raise her baby sister."

"It also explains why Jamie knows everything about everyone… I won't go digging about your grandson, because I can tell you're not ready, so explain Levi."

"Have you read Nocturnal Silence?" Marcus treads lightly once again.

"Yeah, why?" I mutter, seeing Roman's copy in my head.

"Levi is the narrator," Marcus breathes.

"Holy shit!" I shout. "Roman was right."

"You probably met him before, but never knew his name. Levi was tight with Caleb Green. When he was in Dominion, they were fused at the hip. I heard Caleb this and Caleb that while I was in captivity."

"I saw him outside of Denny's!" Fist clenched, it lands too hard on Marc's belly. "One look at the guy, and Whitt and I ended up talking about Caleb. Why?"

"Well, according to these text messages, Levi was making a report prior to the '*make Regina pay*' meeting."

"They're all despicable people," I snarl.

"Hey, I like Levi. He's practical and efficient as an adult. He's raised my grandson as his own since Faith became pregnant. Ah– I bet he's sterile. Hence the need to get his baby brother to knock up a Meyers."

"Syn and this Levi fella must be a terrifying power couple," I mutter in awe.

"Levi is actually playful and funny when he's relaxed." Marcus smiles, reliving moments I'll never experience but hope he'll share. "He made my stay in Vegas livable. The lifetime of nightmares was the heavy cost– for both of us."

"I'm sorry, Marcus." Voice filled with tears, I've never felt more connected to Marcus than I do now. "Master Ez said some things, where if I read between the lines…"

"I know how you feel right now, Regina." Marc's fingers twitch, then he gains courage enough to twine them with mine. "I can see you holding it together by concentrating on everything else but fixing the issue."

"I–"

"There is no fix," Marcus admits, voice cracking. "You're looking for answers, trying to figure out who to blame. There are no answers and no one to blame. Unless there are answers and someone who's responsible, your mind can't wrap around it. You could blame Diane, but then you'd have to blame her parents, and her parents' parents. You could blame the founders, even. You can't blame Ezra, because blaming someone with a mental illness is incomprehensible for a person as ethical and compassionate as you."

"How did you…" I trail off, not sure if I'm ready for that answer.

"You could blame me, saying I'm an enabler for not getting Ezra help. But you can't, not only because you love me, but because I've done nothing but help him since I was seventeen years old.

"That kid had a stable of therapists before I met him. The summer Ezra turned thirteen, he was catatonic in bed for nearly a week. Diane was ready to sign commitment papers. But he awoke with Ez as his passenger. There are three of them, Regina. Ezra, Ez, and Master Ez."

"Shit!"

"And I love all three. Ezra is when Ez and Master Ez form into one entire personality," Marcus rambles off like it's no big deal.

"Then the man everyone sees is Ez, but the man I see is Master Ez, and no one sees Ezra?"

"Occasionally Ezra is revealed. Not often, no."

"No wonder Syn was so angry with me." I see that entire exchange in a different light. I will defend Grant to everyone until the day I die. Syn was defending the father of her son, worried about him going off the rails with guilt.

"Ah– you should see your face right now, Regina. Since you can't blame the person who raped you, you look for ways to blame yourself. Had I not let my guard down around him when we were alone? Had I been inappropriate around him? Did he somehow perceive an action of mine as permission? Since I didn't fight back, it can't be called rape. Shamed, debased, when at your lowest point, you felt connected to your rapist, enough to find the pleasure he was offering as a way to survive the ordeal. Then it awakened a sickness in you, a form of self-loathing so evil, you're not sure how to handle it."

Chest split wide open, as if my soul is bleeding, all I can do is stare at Marcus with tears streaming down my cheeks. Silent sobs cause my body to shudder, every muscle quivering with the need to do… something. Anything to escape the truth.

"So when you tried to ask me how I knew how you felt in the moment," Marcus brings up my aborted question. "I've been there. I know exactly how you feel about it all. Those weren't your thoughts I was just expressing. They were *my* own."

The flood unleashes.

Falling forward, I curl into Marc's open arms. I've had to be so strong for everyone else with no one as my rock. Not only is Marc offering to be that person, he knows exactly how I feel because he's walked in my footsteps.

"I love Ezra, Regina," Marcus whispers against the top of my head, fingers carding through my hair. "I feel like admitting that is somehow a betrayal between you and me."

"That was… that was one of my fears. I didn't want to put you in the middle, and I didn't want Jamie to strike out at the founders. I'm not like most women, and I know that makes me sound illogical. It's a foolish, romantic gesture if I were to demand you cut ties with Ezra, especially when he's mentally ill with the pressure of Maître du Jeu riding him. I'm not a catty person– you don't need to prove your love for me. It's not a pass or fail test, because I just know you love me."

"Oh, Regina." Marcus squeeze me so tightly, I cease to breathe. After a few heartbeats, he lessens his hold. "I've never shared this with anyone but Jamie. There was never a need to talk about myself, because those who were with me understood. All of my agony was shared. What had happened between Ezra and me, Diane and me, and everything in Vegas versus me, it was always shared pain."

"Tell me," I command, and Marcus obeys.

"I was a sheltered kid. The Zeitlers lived at Lake Serenity. My grandfather died, and my parents and aunt and uncle were greedy assholes. Grandmother forced them to live elsewhere in Dominion, leaving Dexter and me behind with her. We had an entire mountain and lake at our disposal, but not much human interaction. We had private tutors in every major subject. Our only friend was Jamie. He always arrived with his mother on a daily basis, right after our classes concluded. There was a generational gap between my grandmother and Priscilla, because they were mentor and student when it came to philanthropy.

"I've discussed with my therapist at length, how this no doubt bred my attraction to Jamie. He was the only person I knew who wasn't a blood relation as I came into my sexuality. This is why I knew how Whitt felt about you."

"Wow," is a short burst of air expelling from my lungs. "That's all I got. Wow."

"We left Lake Serenity only to attend Hebrew School or charity functions. My parents and aunt and uncle intervened when it came time to go to Hillbrook. Obviously Grandmother was sickened at the prospect of her sweet, sheltered, Jewish boys attending a Catholic school where they'd be an outcast. But I'm sure she knew the truth of it. Hillbrook was a requirement from the founders, no doubt. Freshman orientation."

"How the hell did you survive?" I gasp in awe, pulling away to retake my seat on his thighs, so I can look him in the eyes as he speaks.

"How did you?" Marcus murmurs wryly, shrugging one shoulder. "My dream was to get married, have kids, and live on a big estate, where my family would be safe and secure, and we wouldn't allow anyone into our lives who didn't need to be there. Then one day, the bottom dropped out of my world view."

"I'm so sorry– I know exactly how debilitating that feeling is."

"It truly is," Marcus whispers. "Grandmother and Priscilla were busy at Transcend, and told us three stooges to sit outside of their office on a bench. We were teenage boys, being teenage boys, in a community center filled with teenage girls."

"Ah," I drawl out, smiling. "I wish I'd gotten to know teenage Marcus."

"Teenage Marcus had no game." Marc flashes me a naughty smirk. "Teenage Marcus was religious and conservative, and had spent three years getting the shit beat out of him at school– cerebrally mostly."

"Yeah, until you filled out, with Dexter being so short–"

"Let's not forget about pacifist Jamie, who had too many divided loyalties. He couldn't exactly beat up the kids who would help him lead one day, you know?"

"Holy fuck. I miss living in a world where my actions only affected *my* future."

"Anyway, idealist Marcus was hanging out with his boys, eyeing girls and laughing up a storm. Being an idiot basically. This knobby-kneed girl was walking down the hall toward us, and I wanted to call dibs. See, that's what boys do. We call dibs. Jamie saw her first, and dibs flowed out before Dexter and I even knew what was happening."

"Did you get into a fight?" I can't help but smile.

"Elbow fight." Marcus laughs, the sound pure music to my ears. "We were sitting on a bench, elbowing each other in the ribs. The closer she got, the farther my mouth dropped. Dexter was like, '*Don't be such a prick, Jamie. Look at Marc's face– he wants to go talk to her.*' But Jamie just looked at me and whispered, '*I'm so sorry.*' Then my world crashed."

"What? How?"

"My guess, Jamie knew how later that day I'd be dropped off at Shadow Haven, when I never even knew I was betrothed. Where I'd spend the rest of my life."

"What?!" I shout in outrage. "Your grandmother didn't explain?"

"My parents and aunt and uncle dragged me there, with my grandmother screaming obscenities the entire way. Grandmother didn't know, either… so Jamie called dibs to save me from disappointment. But now, as I read over your texts to him, I'd guess it was also because the girl was meant for Dexter."

"Come again?" flows out between numb lips, heart battering the inside of my ribcage.

"This fourteen-year-old eighth-grader, with her wild hair and knobby knees, I saw her the same day I met Ezra and Cortez for the first time. So I forgot about her because I had that wife and family I'd longed to have. Readymade, with an older woman I truly grew to love as a husband does a wife. Then the nightmare became reality.

"My wife was a lesbian. My son was mentally unstable, and his cousin was a flirty bastard."

"Cousin? Divina is Ezra's cousin," I remind Marcus, thinking he's losing it. "Bastard is the wrong pronoun for that sweet lady."

"Celeste Hunter lived with the Holdens, with her little boy–Cortez Hunter. Diane was good friends with a pair of twins, Celeste and Raymond Hunter. One twin became her constant companion, while the other *allegedly* raped her. Flirty bastard–Cortez."

"Ezra and Cortez are cousins?" Eyes held wide, all I can do is stare at Marcus in horror. "Blooded first cousins?"

"Why do you think so many incest jokes are thrown around–it's not a private joke by the sneaky snakes hiding in our midst. It's common knowledge. Ezra became catatonic when he found out, withholding the information from Cortez for six years. The abduction let the cat out of the bag. Cort was a minor, but it still said Raymond Hunter was Ezra's father in the papers. Which is hard to ignore when your name is Cortez Hunter."

"Which is when the pseudonym of Cortez Abernathy was born."

"Exactly. Julian Abernathy was some name Celeste tossed out as Cort's supposed father… and that's the real reason why Cortez struggles to be intimate with Ezra."

"Oh. My. God."

"Yes, Regina. *Oh, my fucking God* would be more appropriate. My life has been a goddamn living nightmare since the day I was dropped off at Shadow Haven at the tender age of seventeen. From Idyllic Lake Serenity, with the pure life I'd led, to being dropped into a hedonistic den of secrets."

"Kinda like going from the hood to a fucking castle," I mutter more to myself.

Huffing a laugh, Marcus doesn't want to be amused by me, but he is. "You're making me lose my train of thought," he chastises. "So, for the next few years of my ended childhood, I bonded with the residents of Shadow Haven, graduated Hillbrook, then Celeste was losing her fight with cancer just after Diane and I got married."

"How was married life in the beginning? Sorry to interrupt, but I'm just curious, seeing as how I'm newly married myself."

"Newly married, yet spending your wedding night with the likes of me," Marcus murmurs wryly with a wink. "Good, actually. Diane is a very cerebral person, so our relationship was solid from the start. She treated me as a grown man, and spoke to me while she grieved Celeste and dealt with Ezra's illness. At first, the no sex wasn't an issue."

"What about the sex?" blurts out before I can stop it–curiosity kills the cat.

Eyes slipping shut, Marc's face manages to pale then go crimson in a split-second. "I-I-I… I had never even masturbated before. Shush!" Marcus stops me before I get started. My jaw is wide open, catching flies, so I snap it shut.

"Cuddle and tug buddies, remember? I was a married man, thinking his wife was leaving him alone because he was too young and naïve to pleasure her. The kids in the house were screwing like rabbits. No joke. The flirty bastard and the creepy bastard, they liked to freak the fuck out of their religious yet impressionable mentor."

"Wait!" I hold my palm up to ward off Marc's complaint. "You *must* explain that in *great* detail before you move along with story time."

"Pervert," Marcus mutters with affection, blushing. "It wasn't long after I moved in, the pubescent boys started screwing each other. Of course, I was outraged, but Diane just shrugged it off after Ezra's breakdown. Diane is an enabler. Anyway, Cort would flirt, and Ezra acted like I was insulting him because I didn't want to touch him inappropriately. They would figure out where I was going to be at any given time, so I'd walk in and catch them fucking. Like Ezra bent over the sofa arm with Cort inside him, when all I wanted to do was watch television."

Shaking my head over and over again, "That– I've got nothing."

"I didn't acclimate to Shadow Haven well, Regina. I was of the line of thinking that you only had relations with your spouse, and here were the kids who were supposed to be my kids, fucking each other as a way to get highly negative attention from me.

"Even after my stay in Vegas, I couldn't deal with it. Never having had consensual sex in my life, I had to witness the boys getting a three-way on with Faith when they were only sixteen. I was *livid.* Marching up and down the hallway, screaming for Diane to intervene."

"If my son–" trails off, as I envision tearing my own child's sack from his body.

"Backing up some. The boys are almost six years younger than me, but they were more mature than I was at that age. *Sheltered*," Marcus stresses. "I held off, not pressuring Diane until after we got married. I was twenty, almost twenty-one. I needed advice, or an outlet at least. That's how Jamie got involved."

"Cuddle and tug?" I tease. "I know you didn't have ulterior motives, but I'm sure it was no great labor for you to play with him."

It amazes me how a man with such a dark complexion can turn such a brilliant shade of red. "I was too innocent, Regina. I'd never masturbated– I'm not lying. Jamie was experienced in my eyes, after Gwen and making a kid. Plus, he has a lot of Daniel in him."

"The cerebral side. The scholar."

"Precisely… Jamie and I had held each other for a long time– years. It felt nice, and I knew without a shadow of a doubt I felt romantic love for him, not just attraction. Jamie was the only person I trusted enough to help me. He demonstrated, then allowed me to join him from then on."

"Until you tried to help him?" Reaching forward, I cup Marc's cheek, because he looks on the edge of tears.

"I don't know what I am, okay?" Marcus blurts out, cheek warbling beneath my palm. "I'll never lie to you. I get aroused looking at people. Only natural. But mostly, I can appreciate their beauty– every person has those qualities as long as you look."

"But you don't want to fuck them?"

"No, I don't," Marcus admits solemnly. "I knew I was in love with Jamie, and I thought I was in love with Diane, and I wanted both of them sexually. Insanely wanted in them. But my religious teachings kept me away from touching Jamie, let alone myself. Then Diane wouldn't touch me at all."

"I'd say Diane is an idiot, but it's not her fault she likes what Ade's selling." Marcus narrows his eyes on me interrupting him again. With my fingers twisted in front of my lips, I pretend to zip my mouth shut.

"When we cuddle, it feels so warm and safe and happy. I never want it to end. So of course I get aroused. No doubt Jamie has fibbed to you a bit. Sure, he was pissed when I grabbed his dick, but he has no issue sleeping naked with me. Or being half asleep and rutting around–"

"Oh. My. God!" Palms covering my eyes, as if I can actually see it. "I'm… speechless." Coughing a few times, I try to get control over my rampant thoughts. "Holy fuck, batman… mind took a vacation, and probably not where it ought to go."

Marcus chuckles a laugh that can only be described as pure sex. "Why do you think I still hold out hope? The guy freaked out on me, but still would cuddle naked and jerk off together. Then would move around in his sleep, leaving me covered in Whittenhower's finest."

"No!" I put my hand out in a stop motion. "Move along. Can't listen to any more, or I won't digest anything else you say from here on out. I want your story, Marc. So get to spewing."

"Yes, ma'am." Sarcasm thick in his voice, Marcus rolls his eyes at my transparency. "Jamie still cuddles with me, but no nudity or tugging," he pouts, murdering my fantasies. "Married, way older than the idiots getting some, I started begging my wife."

"Bitch." My upper lip curls into a snarl.

"Proactive is a better term," Marcus mutters begrudgingly. "As you've deduced, Ezra feels slighted by me sexually, which made him easily manipulated. Before you go off on a tangent," Marcus stops me. "Diane has issues, all I'm well aware of, so I get it. I just don't like it. My first sexual experience outside of mutual masturbation was waking to lips wrapped around my cock. My first thought was that it was Diane. So I was way into it. My second thought was how I assumed I must be dreaming. My third thought was while I was coming. My eyes snapped open and connected with gunmetal gray eyes. But then I realized the white hair was short instead of long."

"Oh, Marc," I cry out, clutching at my heart, having no idea how he must have felt in that moment. "I'm so sorry. So sorry that happened to you."

"I don't– I don't know if I can put this into words," Marcus falters, eyes turning glossy. "I had felt so guilty, worrying that I was cheating on Diane with Jamie– I spoke to my Rabbi. This world… so imagine how I felt when I realized what happened with Ezra? In my heart, he was my son. In my head, I knew it was a form of rape. But I played the blame game– the blame *myself* game."

"Earlier…" I can't say it out loud. "I had a constant stream of consciousness during, to the point I didn't experience most of it. I have a feeling we thought similar thoughts."

"No doubt, Regina," Marcus whispers. "No doubt. I did what you're doing. I didn't talk about it. I pretended it didn't happen. I couldn't look my wife in the eye, or Cortez. Because not only did my rape equate cheating on Diane, even if it wasn't my choice, Ezra cheated on Cortez."

"That's why–"

"Cort always retaliates, even if it hurts him… and me." Voice lost, Marcus has a faraway expression etched across his face. "What Cortez and I do is most certainly a direct result of things Ezra has done, even if we can't blame him."

"Can't, or won't?"

"*Can't*," Marc stresses. "Can't. The next time… it was a few months later. I was going to college, concentrating on my studies while trying to find a path in life. My parents and aunt and uncle died– intentional plane crash. So I was obviously distracted. It happened again, but worse. So much, much worse… and it broke me."

As I sit on Marc's thighs, I stare down at him as he tries to control his facial expressions, as emotion after emotion scrolls on by. Giving up, he covers his face with his palms, barely stifling a sob. Chest quivering, I have no idea how to make it better, because I don't know how to help myself.

I cry for us both.

"I snapped, and I can't say what happened next. Not can't– I *won't*," Marc stresses the opposite of before, voice raw with agony. "I broke, fearing I broke both Ezra and Diane. But hindsight is twenty-twenty, and Diane broke because she broke me. She honestly thought she was doing the right thing– as twisted as it may have been. So I found myself carried away by Pearl's security team– her enforcers. Aaron and Roarke's fathers. When I came out of my state of shock, I was being carried from a private jet by meaty thugs."

"Wow…" Sitting back farther, I marvel. "From sheltered, to twisted, to criminal empire. Marcus Zeitler knows how to become jaded."

Snorting through his tears, Marcus smiles at me in thanks for lightening the dark mood. "Bait and switch, Regina. Bait and switch. I *loved* Sin City at first. After I got my shit together, I made some friends. We gambled, took in the sights, then we began training beneath Master Fontaine. I had a private suite in a brothel."

"High roller, ya big pimp," I tease, grinning from the fond tone in Marc's voice.

"My only friends were family mandated, even Jamie. I met this guy about the same age as me. I was only twenty at the time, turned twenty-one in Vegas. Devlin– we were fast friends. Gorgeous black man. Artists should sculpt Dev. I'm not saying that in a creepy, I want to fuck him way, either. That's not how I roll," Marcus steals my turn of phrase.

"Devlin was fascinating to watch, but more so to speak to. We trained together and played together. My first *real* friend– no shared emotional baggage. I met Olivia's kids and husband. They presented a united front, so I thought they were solid. Levi was fifteen at the time, almost sixteen, and Dalton was six. I really liked Olivia."

"Why?" I drawl out, trying to hide the note of jealousy tinging my voice.

"Olivia was strict and firm, yet had a gentle way of instruction. She was fair and compassionate to her working girls. Olivia's husband was a mafia movie cliché, so I found him hilarious. I felt out of my element, but I wasn't in Dominion, so that was okay. At Shadow Haven, which was my new home, I should've never felt uncomfortable. Sin City? No one should feel comfortable."

"What changed?" I fear asking, but I can't stop myself.

"About three or four months into my stay, Olivia changed. She would flirt with me, and I wouldn't respond. Did I find her attractive? God, yes," Marc's voice breaks, and I swear to God, I'm murdering Olivia with my thoughts. I have no idea where this jealousy is coming from, but I hate it.

"Olivia aroused me, but that's not how I function." Scrunching his eyebrows, I fear Marcus sees the jealousy written in my mind, but he's lost in his own thoughts. "I'm not built like everyone else. I need to be emotionally attached to someone. I can find them attractive, appreciate their attributes, even become aroused, but… my upbringing rears its ugly head."

"Marcus," I caution. "We were strangers when you touched me–*fucked* me."

"I met you before I met Diane, Ezra, and Cortez," Marcus confirms my thoughts. "If you honestly believe I didn't know you almost as well as Jamie did, you're nuts. Jamie shared everything with me– *everything*."

"I don't know how take that, Marc," I murmur, voice sounding lost. "I truly don't."

"We both know what Jamie was angling for, feeling guilty for not wanting me when I wanted him, feeling guilty for how you two came to be, while feeling insecure that he wasn't enough for you. Jamie was sharing, giving me something to hold onto."

"Shit!" I hiss with feeling.

"Back to our regularly scheduled program," Marcus teases. "Olivia has an ego on her, the likes of which you've never seen," Marcus warns. "One night, she groped me, and I didn't get hard for her. She couldn't handle that. Then she arrived in my bedroom, slipping into my bed while I was asleep. Cheating… I couldn't get hard."

"Ego?" I gasp out, realizing Marcus was tortured because he didn't want Olivia.

"*Mirror, mirror on the wall, who's the fairest of them all?*" Marcus recites. "The Evil Queen. The Black Widow. Olivia Fontaine. Whores came next, getting a similar reaction. So Olivia was mollified. Then male whores came after, confusing Olivia when I didn't respond. Knowing my shame, Olivia delivered her son."

"Oh, my God! NO!" I shout, palm covering my mouth in disgust.

"Yes. I was free to roam Olivia's domain during the day. I was allowed to train. Then I realized my new friend was actually my captor. Devlin kept me in line– reluctantly, as the friendship was real, but it tainted it. At night, the doors to my suite were locked, and only opened when I had unwanted visitors. Visitors who would grope or suck on my flaccid cock."

Eyes flitting back and forth, heart fluttering, my mind spins, unable to grasp what Marcus had to live through. My ten minutes with Master Ez, a guy I'd previously allowed to have sex with me… as wrong as it was, I can't complain in the face of Marc's tortured past.

"Levi started coming around– only keeping me company. Sometimes Dalton would wander in, wanting me to read to him. Dalton was a sweet kid, while Levi acted like an abused pet. Levi's demeanor had us cuddling. Not cuddle and tug. Simply the sympathetic need to connect."

"I'm glad you had that comfort, Marcus– truly."

"It was a double-edged sword, though. Levi spoke of his grandfathers and their friends, and of how he and Caleb would hold one another *after*… so he was receptive to being held. Men have an involuntary reaction to feeling safe and warm and loved. Levi was holding me for once, and Olivia walked in, immediately noting the state my body was in."

"Oh, no."

"I have never seen such a rage in my entire life, and Ezra has had some legendary fits." Body shaking beneath mine, I try to soothe Marcus by rubbing his tummy. "I felt like a pervert, but it had nothing to do with Levi. *At all*. I already knew that if I'd gotten hard for one of her working girls, Olivia would have murdered them."

"For real?"

"For real," Marcus stresses. "So here I was, being held by her son– Levi does and doesn't look anything like Olivia. But the only thing that saved us was the fact that he was a guy. Olivia now assumes I'm gay, when I'm not. I have to be romantically and emotionally connected to someone, while physically attracted to them. There is no casual with me. I have no name for what I am. But that was why I couldn't get hard for Olivia or anyone she sent for me."

"What did she do?"

"Since I could get and stay hard around her son, Olivia demanded he extract my semen," Marcus says this in an emotionless voice. "We were given privacy, so I jerked off into the condom while Levi kept his back to me… until his grandfathers got involved, and I will never, *ever* breathe a single word of our shared nightmare, even upon threat of death."

Dark skin turning deathly pale, I fear Marcus is going into shock, so I reach forward to rub anything I can reach to get the blood flowing. I don't know what to say, and I have a feeling whatever I'm imagining isn't brutal enough.

"I–" Marcus sounds like he's talking through a straw. "I wasn't the same after that– *ever* again. It was at the end of my stay, and I finally learned why Levi had that look in his eyes, a look I now wear. Getting what she wanted, Olivia sent me home. The first thing I did was locate Levi's dad and stepmom– they were living an ordinary life in Dominion after escaping the life we live. Levi was doing joint visitation between Dominion and Vegas. I inadvertently changed a boy's life for the worse."

"What?" I gasp in shock. "What can be worse than being molested by your grandfathers?"

"I didn't understand at the time, but I do now. Levi was given to Raymond Hunter as an enforcer partner. Olivia's ego is huge, so my guess is she has no heir, so Levi was given another position. The Levi I met was only wounded, but the one I've seen in the years since is broken. It took me about three pages into Nocturnal Silence to figure out Levi was the narrator. Now I know Cortez is involved in Maître du Jeu, because Levi is always shadowing him."

"Shit!" I hiss. "I honestly thought Cortez wasn't involved because Ezra has who he needs."

"I have a feeling Cortez and Levi are a matched set, similar to Aaron and Roarke– for who, I have no idea. After Raymond was arrested, they probably took a vulnerable Cortez to fill the family position. I've been thinking nonstop about the past and how every move made was to maneuver us into positions far into the future."

"A past you want to forget," I murmur, completely understanding.

"Exactly. After I came back, it was an eventful few years. The boys were hanging out with Faith, then they stopped and were abducted. They were never the same, nor was I. Then Jamie did what he did, and my world became very narrow, only worrying about Jamie's welfare and concentrating on finishing my degree and my career, because that's all I had control over."

"Then I showed up and made you see the light," I tease to lighten the subject matter.

"We woke each other up," Marcus agrees. "You felt apathetic in your mourning, knowing damn well your Grant was James Atwater. You don't have to admit it, but c'mon… I get it. I was living it. You were apathetic, as was I. My behavior has reflected yours, which I think is actually amusing Jamie to no end."

"Cowardly bastard," I snarl, bitter resentment and rage leaking through.

"I suggest you turn the light out," Marcus says abruptly.

"What?" Eyebrows knitted together in the center of my forehead, I try to wrap my head around the subject change.

"Unless you want to deal with reality, I suggest you turn the lamp off," Marcus mutters, eyes never moving from a spot over my left shoulder.

Hairs raising on the nape of my neck, I reach to turn the light off.

Chapter Twenty

Husky yet shaky, my voice sounds loud in the darkness. "What are you doing here? How did you get in here?" Knowing neither question can be answered audibly, they're directed to Marcus. "How long has he been listening?"

"Regina," calm and soothing, Marcus tries to talk me down from the fit I'm about to have. "With what happened tonight, do you honestly believe Jamie wouldn't need to see you in person."

Silent, even in his movements, I can feel Jamie ghosting closer, causing every nerve in my body to alight in pleasure and shame– shame because I should hate him, but can't.

Hesitating near me, I can practically feel Jamie thinking, wondering if he's wanted or not. Of course, I'm a sucker for his insecurity. Goddamn him!

"Jamie came with me, Regina. Roman let him in through your bedroom French doors while I entertained Jamie's mini-me. He's been working in your office. I said he was working– I didn't say where."

"How long have you been listening?" I include Jamie, because I couldn't deal with people talking about me as if I wasn't in the room. "Yeah, I guess I should learn sign language and start looking you in the eye. Kinda hard to read your hands if it's dark."

A rough huffing sound curls my lips. Taking my answering laugh as permission, Jamie kisses the nape of my neck, then begins rubbing my back.

"We need to have a sit-down with our children," I warn Jamie. "Sooner rather than later." He nods against my skin, then kisses me again. "I'll give you three months. If you don't arrange it, I *will*."

O K is written against my back with a fingertip. **Jamie**. I try to read between the lines, but come up short.

"I don't speak Jamie's shorthand," I direct toward Marcus. "What does it mean when he says Jamie?"

"Best guess, Jamie needs to stay as James Atwater, at least for a while."

2 4 is pressed into my skin next.

"Until Whitt gains control over Whittenhower Enterprises? Why?"

M I N E. Fingertip pauses. **N O**. Pauses. **H I S.**

"Mine. No. His. Marcus?" I call out, confused.

"Everything Whittenhower belongs to Grant Whittenhower, but he doesn't want it. Until the heir reaches twenty-four, Daniel is taking care of business. Should Grant be resurrected, it'll be his." Tone turning sardonic, "Which, let's face it, would piss Whitt off something fierce."

"You'd give it to Whitt anyway," I murmur, even more confused.

"The corporation's bylaws would probably need to be changed, which would take time. Daniel is doing a great job, and Whitt will be a good figurehead. Jamie would hate that life. Let him be free, Regina."

"Jesus Christ," I snarl, enraged. Jamie's hands leave my body in a second, worried I'll strike out at him. "I'm not mad at you," I grumble to mollify Jamie. "I mean, I am furious as all get out. But this anger isn't directed at you. *Right now*," I add, so he knows I'll probably always be angry with him.

"Regina." Marcus reaches out, resting his hands on my thighs to calm me. "I'd love to have a partner, build a house on Lake Serenity, and live the rest of my days without this stress. But that isn't going to happen without ending this bullshit. So I'd suggest you get with the program. Jamie stays Jamie, even after you guys have a huge knockdown, drag-out with your kids. After Whitt is comfortable in his new role, Grant *will* be resurrected."

A growl echoes around my bedroom, Jamie evidently doesn't want to be who he was born to be.

"Should Jamie even be telling us what he's told us?"

Movement surrounds me, and I can see shadow figures from the light being cast from the French doors. Marcus doesn't move, still lying beneath me. But now Jamie is at the side of the bed, Marc's hand in his. He's manipulating Marc's fingers, somehow communicating with him.

"Jamie's forming what he wants to say on my hand," Marcus mutters, distracted by what Jamie is telling him. A sharp snort flows from Marc's throat, then a chuckle. "He says he's already been silenced, then killed. What more can they do to him? Now they're attacking you, which is exactly why he's sharing the wealth. Ah– he wants to know if his son delivered the journals to you."

"Yeah, but I haven't had time to read through them."

"He says all we need to know is in the journals. He's not drawing Whitt into this. Same reason Jackson kept Daniel innocent. The Whittenhower figurehead must be protected at all costs. Niel will be the go-between. Ha! Yeah, your kid is pretty dang crafty."

"What are you laughing about?" I demand.

"Jamie's terrified of Niel, while he's terrified *for* the kid. Insanely proud, though. Niel has been instigating Diane and Daniel to do their own shit, while creating his own chaos with Whitt and Whitney. Now he's playing his mother. The kid bounces all over the place, making everyone think he's on their side."

"Survivor," I mutter, impressed. "Our reunion was not how I envisioned it over the years. I didn't think I'd be talking about intrigue with my thirteen-year-old son."

Marcus and Jamie share a snort. "Every generation of Whittenhowers has a more cerebral kid. Jamie wanted to be free. Katie was just a normal girl. Yet Ade was warped in the head. Then there is Whitt, who feels like an outsider. Niel is a combination of all of you. Ella probably acts a bit like Katie. Whitney is Daniel Jr. while Prissy is the most childlike of them all."

Deep breaths, Regina. Deep. Breaths.

You are not a coward.

Do it while they're distracted.

They're in your home, in your bedroom.

Deep breaths.

You can do this.

Take your power back.

Deep breaths.

Be Queen.

Moving so quickly, there is no room for hesitation, my fingers twist the knob on the lamp resting on my nightstand.

Stunned immobile, silence descends as my eyes drink in reality.

Huffing in a deep lungful of air, followed by another, and another, I can't blink. Nothing could possibly force my eyes to close.

I've known it was true. Just as Niel said, I knew the difference. I felt the loss of my father, then the loss of my mother. Even Jackson left a void behind in my heart. But I could feel Grant throbbing like a phantom limb, refusing to be ignored.

As soon as I was contacted to work on James Atwater's website, the grief and depression worsened because I felt unworthy. Abandoned. Left behind because I wasn't good enough– our children weren't worthy of Grant's love, affection, and attention, not even his proximity.

The abandonment is what had the grief turn everlasting.

Everyone Regina Regal loves abandons her. By default, they abandon her children too.

I lost Whitt and Niel the same day I lost Grant. He knew it would happen, and didn't think me worthy of his sons, or else he would have stayed, instead of leaving them to Daniel with me thrown out of Misery Castle.

I haven't allowed Marcus to take root in my life, holding him at arm's length, fearing the same. Marcus was safer, simply because he was married. I married Whitt within hours of Marcus admitting he loved me, because nothing was tying him to Diane anymore.

If the most loyal and gentle person I've ever known could leave me, anybody can.

Knowing, refusing to look Grant in the eyes, I could rationalize how Grant and Jamie were the same human being, but not the same person. Grant is dead– Jamie was reborn. If they weren't the same individual, then I couldn't blame Jamie for Grant's sins.

A part of me has hated Roman simply because he uses Grant's name, while Marcus has always called him Jamie. One wouldn't allow me to play pretend, while the other needed to pretend with me.

Standing before me isn't the man I loved and lost– the man who asked me to be his Mrs. Whittenhower. No, Jamie is silent. Jamie is scarred. Jamie told me to be someone else's Mrs. Whittenhower because he doesn't want me.

Grant wanted me, but he died. Jamie wants to be near me, speak to me, touch me, but he doesn't want to be *with* me.

Petrified crystalline blue eyes connect with my gaze. "Grant," is wrenched out of my chest, a hallow sound of mourning.

Jamie *is* Grant.

Grant *is* Jamie.

There is no either/or. They are one and the same.

Grant committed the sins. Grant abandoned me. Jamie committed the sins. Jamie abandoned me. Grant's actions and Jamie's actions are the same.

Illogically, I want to murder whoever carved his beautiful face. It's too difficult to see this man as anyone but Jamie. This is not the Grant I used to know.

A monstrous sound is torn from Jamie's chest, then his fingers begin to fly. Unable to understand, I can't watch. Looking away, I stare at his body instead, ignoring the endless stream of agony pouring out of my throat.

Those are Grant's pajama bottoms, worn thin with love.

"Regina!" Marcus shakes me, leaving a bruise to mingle with the ones his son left on my flesh, while leaving another invisible bruise on the ever-growing pile in my psyche. "Stop whatever insanity is playing out inside your head. Reason it out." Fingertips bite into my shoulders, shaking me with brutal force. "Did you want to endure what happened tonight? Did you? Do you want to deal with Ezra on a daily basis? Do you? Do you honestly believe Jamie would leave you if he had a choice?"

"Grant left me. He died. Which is all a bullshit lie to help me sleep at night, because the reality is that Grant abandoned me." I mutter in a listless voice to the background soundtrack of agonized keening.

The noise is coming from me.

"Jamie *is* Grant," Marcus points out, as if I'm too stupid to realize it. "I've called him Jamie since we met as toddlers. Grant Atwater was still alive. Just as how we can't call all three Daniels Daniel, Grant was called Jamie by his friends."

Refusing to look at the man in question, I gaze directly into Marc's pitying gaze and release the truth of it all. "*Your* Jamie didn't abandon me like *my* Grant did– he just doesn't want me enough to claim me."

"Regina–" Marc's protest is cut off by me being thrown on the bed, my position reversed. Only this time, it's Jamie looming over me. Blond eyebrows knitted in the center of his forehead, one bisected by a wicked scar that extends down his cheek, cutting his lips in half.

God, even disfigured, Jamie is still the most beautiful man I've ever seen. Instead of the artist devaluing Grant's beauty, they turned Jamie into a masterpiece. Breath catching in my throat, all I can do is stare wide-eyed in awe.

My memories didn't do Grant justice.

Sick to my stomach, I see now how wrong I was to see Whitt only as his father's son. Whitt is his own man, because the man glaring down at me is most definitely his own man now.

Grant is here. With me. With Marcus. Right now. Alive and well. No matter how furious I am, I take a moment to accept the gift that is being given, even if it makes me a total head-case because of it.

Movements jerky, Jamie gestures to his face, as if he's carving up his own flesh with a fingertip. Then he sharply points at me.

Message received. Excuse not accepted. The gift bubble bursts until only the anger remains.

Defiant, gutted, refusing to be controlled or manipulated after the last day I've lived, words flow from the depths of my being– words I've always held but refused to acknowledge. "I could warp all of this bullshit until none of us are accountable for our actions– our *inaction*."

With Jamie– Grant gazing down at me with love and patience, I can't… I just can't. Eyes clenched shut so tightly, a migraine is on the horizon. I let it all out in a stream of verbal vomit I can't take back, even if I wish I could the instant it flees my tongue.

"This isn't a romance novel, Grant!" Head whipping to the side, I glare at Marcus, including him in the horseshit. "This isn't an epic love triangle. Our reality is not some lifelong love affair where time and circumstance held us apart. The brooding artist, his muse, and the orphan who loves the one who can't love him back, so he takes the muse as a consolation prize."

Jamie's growl reverberates along his arms, down his fingers, to flood where our flesh meets, and all it does is instigate the violence that is begging to erupt from my throat.

"This isn't fiction! There isn't some reader's heart breaking for us!" I snarl in Jamie's face, and I'm impressed how he doesn't flinch in the face of my rage. "There isn't a reader who is screaming for me to kick one of your asses to the curb and forgive the other. There are no fangirls clenching their Kindles, chanting Team-Grant or Team-Marcus from the safety of their sofas."

"Regina?" Marcus talks down to me like I'm losing it, but I have to inject a hefty dose of reality into this anti-climactic reunion.

Jamie's weight shifts, until it's only his presence holding me on the mattress, which fuels the silent rage storming in the pits of my soul.

"This angst was *self-created.* By you!" My scream warps as my head whips to the side, voice projecting to include both Jamie and Marcus. "There is no '*who will Regina Regal–* excuse me – *who will Regina Whittenhower choose?* Grant? The man who turned an innocent girl into a jaded woman then abandoned her. Marcus? The man who showed her how the jadedness was actually numbness, but strung her along and lied to her every step of the way while secretly using her to get closer to the one he truly wants. Jamie? The man who passed no judgment, who seemed to get Regina the most, but was betraying her more than Grant ever did– *could.* Because Jamie knows Regina better than Grant ever did, better than Regina knows herself."

"Hey." Marcus tries to soothe me by resting a hand on my shoulder, but I don't let up until I pour it out. "Please, no third-person bullshit. It reminds me of Ezra, which is terrifying."

"I've never been saner," I spit out. "We live in this place called reality, which seems to be a foreign concept for the writer in you, Grant." The truth in my words is the reality-check we need. "Fuck Maître du Jeu, and all they stand for– it's a fantasy world created solely to do bad things while using excuses for enjoying it."

"Christ," Marcus hisses, voicing the singular word etched across Jamie's twisted features.

"I've been without you longer than I've been with you. I've loved the concept of you far longer than I've loved the reality of you– if I've ever known the reality of you."

Eyes flicking, Jamie seeks out Marcus, and the effect is like jet fuel poured onto an inferno.

"NO!" I bellow, not giving a shit if I alert everyone in my household. "MdJ is a motherfucking excuse, *Jamie,*" I sneer. "Let's face it, the only thing that's kept us apart is *you*!"

"*Regina,*" Jamie mouths, tears streaming down his mutilated face, the dampness following the groove of a harsh scar bisecting his cheek. Before I can even think to do it, he anticipates it. Gripping my chin between his elegant fingertips, Jamie refuses to allow me to hide by looking away. I'm too distraught to simply close my eyes, not after being deprived of the sight of the only person I thought I'd ever give myself to totally and completely without hesitation.

Guilt. My rage is merely hiding the guilt I feel.

Breaking when I already thought I was broken, "I know I was the reason Grant died!" I shout into Jamie's face, the force so violent the veins in my forehead throb and pressure builds behind my eyeballs. "It's my fault you died! It's my fault you can't speak! It's my fault your face is scarred!" Breaking down completely, my last words barely escape my throat. "It's my fault for being alone with Ezra!"

Crushed in more ways than one, I'm silenced by the fierce press of a mouth over mine. Screaming, Jamie eats my sound. We're not kissing– it's a primal melding of agony. Without hesitation, my arms are wrapped around Jamie's back, with my fingers biting into his flesh. My legs clutch him to me, feet digging into his rear, refusing to ever let him go again.

Sobbing, great wails of pain echo around the room, but I'm too far gone to worry about my household overhearing.

"Shh…" is spoken silently against my lips. "Regina. Shh…" Pulling away, Jamie looks down at me, hot tears dripping down to splatter against my cheek and chin. Vivid blue eyes track across my features, reading me like an open book.

Satisfied I won't behave like a wild animal, Jamie's hands slide forward to cup my face, thumbs brushing in a soothing, rhythmic pattern along my jawline. The silence should be thick, but it's comforting– it's when Grant and I communicated the loudest.

"Grant," I try again, because I will have to say this on repeat for life to wrap my mind around it. It's safer for me to forget about Grant, let the past die, and to move forward with Jamie as if he's a different human being. But that's not fair to Grant's memory, or to Jamie, because those memories belong to him, or to me and our children.

Right now, I'm not ready. This man is Jamie, and I fear he always will be.

Resting his forehead against mine, Jamie allows tears to spill down to cover my face in a wash of remorse. He's not apologizing– he's revealing his emotion. Bare and raw.

"Are you okay?" Jamie mouths, expression filled with compassion.

Laughing, my eyes flick to see what time it is, wondering if it's one a.m. because that's the line Jamie uses to start all of our text conversations.

Mind reeling, I remember one of the first notes Grant had ever written me, back before my mother had even died. A note left behind in a garbage heap outside of my old apartment. A note Roman and Julio found, along with the others, and delivered them safely to Misery Castle. A note left behind when Grant died. A note Adelaide retrieved, along with all the others. A note echoing the pain of my abandonment from the depths of my wall-safe.

"Are you okay?" I ask in return, knowing no one ever asks the silent one. "After what happened to me tonight, I think it was probably worse for you and Marcus to know it was happening, or had happened, than having experienced it myself." Looking to Marcus, I repeat the question to him too.

Shaking his head no, causing tears to fly all around, Jamie surprises me with a smile. "No," he mouths, then he lifts off of me. Bereft at the loss of his weight, I understand when his fingers begin to fly.

Long, elegant fingers communicate words Grant was always too reserved to speak. Jamie has found his voice in the silence.

Snorting in amazement, Marcus begins shaking his head. He doesn't translate until he finishes crawling to sit on his behind with his back to the headboard.

"Jamie's giving orders, Regina," Marcus murmurs wryly. "This is the side you never got to appreciate with Grant. When Jamie finally speaks, he demands he be heard."

Hands stilling, Jamie narrows his eyes at Marcus, then he makes a stabbing motion at Marcus, then me, with a single finger.

"I can figure out what that means. He wants you to tell me what he said, doesn't he?" Jamie nods in confirmation, then his fingers are moving again.

"Fine– so dramatic." Marcus rolls his eyes, always acting younger when Jamie is around. Less stifled. Happy. "Word for word, after apologizing to me for having to say this. Never give into Ezra. The elders our parents and grandparents' age, they were a different lot, who agreed with sexual exploitation and abuse of power. This generation was their victims, so they don't abide by it. Particularly with Faith behind the helm."

"I was right on that!" I mutter with excitement.

"If Ezra tries to use sex against you, immediately state how you will contact Faith. I'm to tell Diane about our relationship, and Jamie is stressing how I should get a divorce, because he feels I'm denigrating you to the position of mistress, and that's not fair."

Growling, I glare at Jamie. "You did that to me!" I remind him, earning a bunch of finger movement in reply.

Laughing, Marcus stares at Jamie's hands while speaking to me. "Glad you're coming to terms with how Grant and Jamie are the same person, Regina. I was worried I'd have to send you to Wintercrest. Jamie says he was young, stupid, and cowardly. By the time his tenure as Grant Whittenhower ended, he was changing how he treated you. A decade later, I should know better."

Making a funny noise, Jamie crosses his arms over his chest and nods his head once in agreement, blond hair flopping to cover the scar on his forehead.

"You had me marry your son!" I point out the hypocrisy, and earn a growl and a chuckle for my efforts.

"I'm to tell Diane the truth and stop touching Cortez, so Ezra will have no fuel. But since it's Ezra, Jamie says you're to use Faith against him. You must do what Maître du Jeu tells him to tell you to do. If the cost is not high, just do it. If the cost is too high, meaning sexual favors, physical or mental assault, run." Marcus glares at Jamie. "You don't think very highly of my son."

"Marcus, he raped me tonight– don't fucking go there," I warn. "I want to forget about it."

"Well, Jamie isn't going to forget about it. Faith is on a rampage, and Jamie is deciding on how best to punish Ezra. Punish him? Really?"

Eyes holding glacial fire, with his teeth bared, Jamie's snarl is frightening.

"I know more than anyone about how it feels to be raped by Ezra," Marcus snarls back. "Twice. He's mentally unstable. Adding fuel to that fire is fucking moronic. Think logically, Jamie."

Ah– anyone with a brain knows what Jamie's next gesture means.

"I've tried, but you won't let me," Marcus mutters sardonically. "I'd even bend over for it."

"Don't fight." Voice filled with the mental, emotional, and physical exhaustion I feel, I fall to the mattress, hitting my elbow on Marc's knee. "Marcus, if Ezra had learned as a child, he wouldn't be doing this shit as an adult. As long as no one gets hurt, doses of medicine need to be administered… oh, that's goddamn awesome." My purr of pleasure warps into a moan when strong fingers locate my foot and begin to massage. "Don't stop."

"One thing has never changed." Marcus doesn't look jealous, more amused than anything. "Jamie will forever try to meet your needs."

Laughing, it doesn't take knowledge of sign language to figure out what Jamie says next. "He said he meets yours too, didn't he?" I tease. "Stop talking– more rubbing."

"Yeah, Jamie said that, but not very nicely," Marcus pouts as he fishes around the bedding to locate my phone. "Are the journals uploaded onto your phone?"

"Shared file in the cloud– passcode birth dates of the Whittenhower heirs," I ramble off mindlessly. After the past few days– past twenty years –I'm going to take advantage of the comfort and pleasure that is so freely being given.

Old times melding with recent events, Marcus, Jamie, and I act as usual, only this time it's in the light. "I missed you both for the past few months," I admit, acting girly and emotional. "It hurt worse than before. I can't explain it. It's like you gave me what I needed, only to take it away."

Marcus doesn't speak, but reaches out to hold my hand while he thumbs through documents on my cellphone. We'd said everything we needed to say in Ezra's SUV before my initiation, and every time we've spoken since.

Jamie can't speak, but he does respond. Scarred lips twisted in a sad smile, Jamie kisses my big toe, then continues on massaging. He's trying to connect with me through touch– I know that. But he's also trying to take the pain away, even if it's not possible.

It would be so easy to play pretend, forget the past, and think of Jamie as a person I met almost two years ago. I could start a relationship with him, erasing the sins of the past, but I fear that would hurt more than it would help.

As Jamie's touch ventures from my feet, every new spot he hesitates, as if he's asking for permission to continue. This isn't only because of what Ezra did to me, where he took my power away, this is a total Grant move. It took years before Grant would initiate. I can tell, this more mature version of the man I used to love, once permission is given, Jamie will take that as a resolute yes until a no is given.

"There isn't an inch of me you can't touch– inside or out – and I don't just mean physically." Voice raspy, I admit the truth, because tonight I don't have the energy to feel the rejection, abandonment, and rage I should be feeling.

Trust– taking me at my word, Jamie moves toward my knees, hitting all the right spots to get me to groan and wiggle around the mattress. Marcus laughs that masculine sound that is pure sex– Half naughty. Half evil. All sex.

"Added bonus when your masseuse knows your body better than you do… Jackson was a hoot!" Marcus laughs again, more comical than lusty as he reads on my cellphone. Thumb rubbing my wrist, he speaks absentmindedly. "His private thoughts are even better than the bizarre shit he would say aloud."

"There are days I don't think of my parents, but Jackson always finds a way to be heard from every single day. Usually it's a sarcastic comment I knew he'd struggle to suppress."

Fingers curled to his palm, Jamie pats his chest, directly over his heart, while wearing a soft expression. Universal, anyone could interpret what he's saying. Just by his facial expression alone, I know it pleases Jamie how we appreciated and understood Jackson as much as he did. Our thoughts keep his father alive.

"Daniel pops into my head from time to time too," I muse. "Does he know about you?" I point my toe, touching Jamie's thigh as he kneels on my bed.

In reply, Jamie shakes his head, blond hair covering his eyebrows. Grant's hair was perfect, never a strand out of place. Jamie isn't unkempt, just laidback.

Free.

Jamie is free.

Leaning forward, Jamie tweaks Marc's toe to get his attention, then they hold a conversation without me. First thing in the morning, I'm figuring out what I have to do to learn sign language.

"I know. You know. Niel knows. All of Maître du Jeu knows. Priscilla knows. Daniel will be told as soon as Jamie speaks to Whitt and Ella. Then he will tell the rest of his family when he's ready to be Grant again." Laughing sardonically, "Which would literally be never if we didn't press for it. Not the telling his family, but being Grant Whittenhower."

"I'm sorry," I murmur, but instantly feel stupid for being compassionate about something that ruined me for over a decade. Marcus laughs and Jamie pointedly rolls his eyes at me.

With just a look, Jamie speaks volumes, then he goes back to massaging me. Not only because I need it, but because he wants to do it. Unlike someone like Marcus, Jamie's touch is without the expectation of repayment. Not that having expectations is a bad thing, but it's nice to not feel the pressure around him when I'm pressured by everyone everywhere.

Marc's and my personalities are too demanding, while Jamie's is giving to the point of not having his needs met because he doesn't ask. But he's more stubborn than we are, because he's only going to give to those he chooses, and only when he feels like giving it.

Tugging at my leg, Jamie asks me to roll over onto my belly. Getting settled, Marcus moves almost absentmindedly to pull me across his lap with my cheek resting on his belly and my torso resting on his thighs. After some wiggling, we get comfortable with his soft bulge cushioning my breasts. Marc hums to himself as he thumbs through the journals on my cellphone, with his fingers feathering through my shorn locks.

Lost in the sensation of Jamie's and Marc's hands on me, I float, allowing my mind to wander and my emotions to even out. *This*. I missed this. I can lie to myself every moment of the day but this very instance. There is no way I didn't recognize Jamie as being Grant as soon as he stepped near me during my first trip to the brownstone. Just the feel of his eyes had me lighting on fire, pouring life back into my veins.

For nearly two years, the three of us hung out at the brownstone, and I felt complete. Happy. Content. I didn't need anything because I had everything I knew I'd ever need.

Once Marcus pulled away from me in preparation for Whitt coming back into my life, I lost my center of gravity. I don't blame Marcus, even if I should, because he did what he felt was right. Instead of being jealous, possessive, and controlling, he stepped away so I could clear my mind, find myself, and make my own decisions. Marcus respected me, even if it hurt, and I respect him for it.

Jamie is an entirely different beast, and I have no idea how to handle it. I can't lie to myself anymore, but I'm not ready for the fallout just yet. I don't know if I could survive the loss of Jamie in order to satisfy my need for self-respect.

My company is called Empowerment, for shit's sake. I must lead by example, for my girls, my daughter, and my employees. As a feminist, equality and respect are at the cornerstone of my belief system. Yet, for the life of me, I can't quit Jamie. I don't want to, no matter how much he's hurt me. I'm waiting for the self-righteous indignation to kick in, allowing the rage to fuel my ability to cut Jamie out of my life.

Always on edge, always stressed, Jamie's soothing, silent presence is my drug of choice, and I can't give him up just yet.

"Jackson had a wicked mind." Hearing while feeling the vibration through his belly, Marc's words are laced with humor and loss. "Motherfucking twisted, entertaining, he saw the world through a lens no one else ever has. Are there more journals?"

Fingertips leaving where they were dimpling the back of my thighs, I don't need to look over my shoulder to know Jamie is communicating with Marcus. It's not like I have a clue what he's saying anyway.

With the scars, lack of voice, and the total personality overhaul, it's no wonder I view this man touching me as the confident James Atwater and no longer the stifled Grant Whittenhower. I almost feel as if I'm dishonoring Grant's memory and cheating on him because I prefer the more mature version.

Perfectly content, happy even, Marc's smiling privately as he watches Jamie's fingers fly. I wait patiently, because I'm too exhausted otherwise to feel left out of the conversation.

Marc plays interpreter by responding and leaving me to deduce what Jamie said. "You definitely got your love of words from Jackson then." After a brief pause, a chuckle laced with sex flows from Marc's lips. "I feel like I'm getting a peek into your mind, Jamie, instead of Jackson's. If it wasn't for the events being described, I swear it was you writing this."

A ghastly laugh fills the air, and it soothes me instead of frightens me. Then the questing fingertips are back, attacking the knotted muscles in the back of my thighs with expert precision.

"Yeah, you're right," Marcus answers whatever had accompanied that sardonic laugh. "Jackson was willing to get his hands dirty, where you say you're not." Sighing, fingers leaving my hair to pull through his tight ringlets, Marcus shows that while he's content, there is silent but deadly discontent roiling beneath the surface. "After a lifetime together, sometimes I don't think I know the real you at all."

"Mirroring my thoughts exactly," I murmur against Marc's belly, rubbing my face on his t-shirt. "I thought I knew Grant, but I didn't. Mature woman that I am, I *know* I don't know Jamie. At all."

"Yeah…" Another sigh, but this time Marc's fingers return to comb through my hair. "He knows us inside and out, from our best to our worst, yet he only shows us what he wishes us to see."

Growling, a hand whips out to grab for my cellphone. Rhythmic tapping is replaced with the device being lowered into my line of sight. Eyelid popping open, I peer up to read what Jamie had typed into my notebook app.

Don't speak of me as if I'm not right HERE! I shared those journals with you both and Niel because I want you to know me– the real me –even knowing there are mortal consequences for my actions.

"Master of guilt," Marcus grumbles, sounding like the man I met on the first two trips to the brownstone– the man who was resentful of Jamie, causing Jamie to smash glassware to get him to stop.

It was never a pissing contest over me. It wasn't Marcus upset that Jamie didn't love him the way he wished he did. It wasn't the secrets and lies. It's how Jamie doesn't let anyone in, doesn't allow anyone to know the real person while making it beyond easy for us to open up to him and show the dark corners of our deepest fears.

"I concede on speaking as if you aren't here– my apologies." Marcus reaches out to take the cellphone back, allowing his fingers to brush Jamie's with intimate affection. "But that doesn't change the truth of my words."

An indescribable noise erupts from Jamie's chest, but it's not aggressive– more deflated, or perhaps frustrated. As with everything, we ignore the problems. Marcus begins reading the journal again, and Jamie goes back to rubbing me.

"Someday we'll have to act like adults," I murmur against Marc's belly, causing him to squirm underneath me.

"Your breath is tickling me." Marc bops me on the tip of the nose with my phone. "Someday is not tonight," he schools me. "So close your eyes and enjoy how Jamie always coddles you."

"He does *not* coddle me," I snarl, causing Marcus and Jamie to laugh at my expense. "Fine," I concede, sounding grumpy. "But I earned some coddling after what I've been put through for the likes of both of you."

"Instead of apologizing, or saying thank you…" Marcus trails off, shifting beneath me until he's able to bend down to kiss my forehead. "I'm going to try to give you the respect you deserve and treat you differently. Partners," he says pointedly, and I'm impressed how he doesn't glance over my shoulder at Jamie. "We can't survive how we've been living."

World shifting beneath my feet as my axis realigns with my new reality, I realize Marcus and I truly are equals now, and I don't know where that leaves Jamie in our equation. Hell, I don't even know if Jamie wants to be in our equation. He'll probably run off to his tower, happy to be rid of us.

Isn't that why Grant drew Marcus and me together in the first place? So we'd have each other and leave him the hell alone.

"Hey!" I yelp sharply as teeth sink into the back of my thigh, with scarred tongue following to soothe the sting. "Shutting my brain off now," I promise, because Jamie knows me better than I know myself. "Ugh!" is a grunt of pure pleasure as fingers go back to kneading a path up to my ass cheeks. "Yeah, right there," flows huskily from my throat.

The soft bulge cushioning my breasts is no longer comfortable as it hardens. Marc's squirming for several reasons now, not just because my hot breath is tickling his taut stomach. Eyes no longer focused on the cellphone screen, my reactions to Jamie's expert touch hold Marc's undivided attention.

Going boneless, my back arches until I'm resting on my knees, elbows planted on the bed beside Marc's hips, with my head hanging limply over his torso. Joining the fun, my cellphone is tossed to the mattress, then fingers seek the tense muscles of my neck. All the while Jamie rolls his palms over my ass, with his fingers pressing into the small of my back.

"Jesus," is a purr of pure pleasure. "Feels so good."

Roving from my back to my front, confident hands venture north, slipping beneath the bottom of my tank top, then skate along my belly. Fingertips tickle my ribs, setting my senses on fire. Breathing rapidly, mind shutting down until I can't think about anything but the feel of their hands on me, a soft moan is pulled from my parted lips.

Marc's animalistic grunt echoes my moan, with Jamie playing a dangerous game that's going to raze our reality and turn us to nothing but satisfied ash.

Releasing primal laughter of sexual intent, Jamie palms both of my breasts, with his knuckles no doubt whispering over the bulge growing harder and harder in Marc's pajama pants.

Eyes flicking up, I watch as Marcus stares at Jamie, handsome face torn with indecision. "Don't go there," Marcus warns in a voice tight with need. "Don't go there unless you plan on delivering." Shocked, Marcus is leery of Jamie's intentions, as am I.

Why now?

Why touch both of us at the same time, even if it looks accidental?

Jamie does nothing on accident.

Every time we were together, Jamie was the observer while Marcus was the aggressor, with me as their passenger. When I shared my body with them at the same time, Jamie was totally against touching Marcus in a sexual manner.

"What game are you playing?" I echo Marc's thoughts, no doubt.

Hands moving on my tits, I close my eyes, envisioning Jamie shrugging in response. Marc's eyes narrow, then widen with another purposeful graze of Jamie's knuckles dragging across his bulge. Warring with himself, I watch as Marcus moves away as far as the mattress will allow, instead of jerking his hips forward to meet Jamie halfway.

Voice thick with a need that draws tears to my eyes, "I don't trust this," Marcus murmurs, eyes closing in defeat.

In answer, Jamie retreats, settling to kneel between my legs with his hands resting on my hips. Then the massage resumes, excluding Marcus from his touch.

Ignoring the elephant in the room, I fall into the rhythm of Jamie's strong hands on my body, of mine wandering Marc's sides, and of Marc's addictive caresses lulling me into compliance.

A deep moan echoes around my bedroom, being swallowed by Marc's sharp protest. "What the fuck are you doing, Jamie?" Marc bolts upright, almost yanking us off the bed, a split-second after I registered Jamie's warm mouth coming into contact with my lady bits.

While they have a standoff, eyes silently communicating, I marvel over how Jamie managed to slip my shorts off my hips and Marc had pulled my tank top up to my shoulders without me noticing.

Another lick has a shudder rolling along my spine. Eyes slipping shut, I close out the world and stop my mind from spinning out of control.

I don't want to think.

I just want to be.

I need to feel safe, and loved, and cherished, and forget the outside world for five fucking seconds. My problems will still be there once the orgasm fades.

But Marc isn't going to let it go, and it isn't jealousy pushing him forward. "That is inappropriate after what happened this evening," he chastises Jamie in a voice tight with suppressed violence. "You have no idea how powerless rape makes you feel, and here you are taking without asking. It's so unlike you, Jamie."

In response, Jamie leans down and buries his entire face between my legs, mouth working like a starving man at a feast.

Head falling forward to Marc's belly, my ass raises up in invitation. Shameless, all I can do is allow Jamie to do whatever the hell he wants to do, including spearing my cunt with his tongue and sucking on my pussy lips.

Marcus is gearing up for an epic temper tantrum, but my burst of insane laughter dries it up before it's released. Laughter– part shock, part pleasure, all wonder.

This man– I know *this* man. This is the Grant I knew and loved, when I felt Jamie was high above it. A man who is fine sharing me with the one person who loves him as much as I do. The cerebral man who thinks himself above petty jealousy and possession– he's the man devouring my pussy because what happened over the course of the last twenty-four hours has unhinged him as much as it has Marcus and me.

Grant can abandon me all he wants, but nothing will ever convince me the man doesn't want me.

With a laugh stuck in my throat and mirth riding my eyes, tears slip down my cheeks as I gaze up to Marcus. "I need this," I admit without hesitation. "Jamie knows me more than anyone, so trust that he knows what he's doing."

Marcus reaches down to grip my chin, not allowing me to hide against his t-shirt. "Why? Explain." Tan face paling, "I can't imagine allowing someone to touch me like this afterward. I just can't…"

Jamie's moving behind me, mouth possessing me– owning me. The silent one is making a lot of wet slurping noises and primal grunting. Every nerve in my body is firing pure pleasure, without the fight or flight response switching on. It just feels *right*.

"The first few times we had sex," I remind Marcus, "I had no say in it, remember? Permission was assumed."

Face turning a putrid shade, Marcus looks on the verge of being sick. "I can't apologize enough, Regina. I was wrong, so very wrong."

"Jamie– *Grant* –whatever," I mutter, annoyed yet close to combusting by Jamie's expert skills. Marcus is not a fan of foreplay, and my neglected pussy is rejoicing that her man is back. "After years of waiting for permission, he knows permission is assumed–"

"I know your pussy belongs to Jamie," Marcus snarls, the furious edge is definitely jealousy.

"As I was saying… Jamie knows he has permission, permission he granted to you long ago. Permission you used without asking me every time we had sex."

"I-I…" Marcus trails off, and Jamie stops feasting until we get this settled. Marcus can be very insecure at times.

"You've fucked me nonstop for the greater part of two years, Marcus." Amusement is thick in my voice, but so is impatience. "Now, after what happened tonight, I appreciate that you're trying to respect me by waiting for me to initiate. But it feels a helluva lot like pity, not respect. You pity me for what happened, see me as weaker. Jamie doesn't. He's pissed. He's reclaiming what's his."

"Of course– what's *his*," Marcus mutters snidely.

"You'd think your insecurity of Grant getting in me first would've dissolved after you planted your flag on my ass for the past few years."

Appreciating my sarcasm, Jamie rumbles his disturbing laughter. Marcus, not so much– eyes rolling heavenward, he misses what Jamie's doing behind me. My grunt is soft, because I knew what was coming next, but it's still a shock.

"Jesus Christ, Jamie!" Marcus whisper shouts, head tilted to the side in utter confusion. "You're really going to fuck Regina?"

"Yes," is a whisper pulled from between my lips as Jamie seats himself to the hilt inside my willing body. "You of all people must know how I need my power back," I murmur to Marcus.

"God, Regina." Marc's eyes are held wide in silent horror, instinctively knowing every emotion and disturbing thought playing on repeat inside my mind.

"Ezra– he… he was *inside* me, and I didn't want him there– *in* me. I was powerless." Voice breaking, I have to swallow a few times before I'm able to continue. Marcus stares at me with sympathy, but it's Jamie's silent rage wafting around the room that has my words spilling.

"Powerless, as if my body didn't belong to me. Dehumanized." Watery eyes flicking up to meet Marc's, I feel no shame over having Jamie penetrating me. "I need *this*," I stress. "I need this. I need to feel in control. I need to erase that Ezra was ever inside me– inside my body, inside my mind, inside my *hell*."

Marcus responds with tears, respecting that I should be the only one with a voice– the only one to have a say in what happens to me, without passing judgment.

"My body was taken from me, so easily and without a fight." Learning forward, I rest my forehead on Marc's stomach, hiding my face from view and allowing his t-shirt to absorb the agony spilling from my eyes. "God… I'm a woman bigger than most men, and it was so easy for Ezra."

Jamie shifts, pulling free from my body, and I'm immediately bereft at the loss. Jamie was lending me the strength to face this right now. Not later. Not never. *Right now*.

Manhandling me without issue, after peeling my clothing off, Jamie moves not only me but Marcus too. We don't put up a fight, allowing Jamie to arrange us until we're lying on our sides. Marcus and I are face-to-face, bodies barely touching, with Jamie spooning me from behind, connected in every way possible.

Jamie gives me the courage to speak the words Marcus needs to hear, the words Jamie already knows are inside of me, needing to come out.

"A woman like me should never feel vulnerable. Strong mentally, physically, emotionally, and financially, I should be close to invincible. But from birth, girls are taught what not to do to mitigate the chances of their power being taken away. We're always alert to the possibility of being violated. But that isn't control over our bodies. That's fear– that fear means we never own our bodies from the moment we're born."

"Fear saves lives," Marcus speaks with hesitancy, worried I'll be insulted.

"Fear doesn't save lives, instinct does," I say pointedly to Jamie, not knowing if it's fear that has him hiding, or if it's truly how he wishes to live. "Living in fear is not living at all, and I'm done. We know who the boogeymen are. We know they do whatever they want, without consequence, and without a reason. There is no anticipating it. Reading Jackson's journal should teach you how to live life to the fullest. I'm done. I'm done not living."

"Regina?" Marc's amber gaze squints, confused as he tries to reason out why I'm saying what I'm saying. Reaching up, he cups my cheek– his touch as intimate and connecting as Jamie's inside me.

"We can't erase what's happened. We can't rewind. I learned how everyone we know and love has been tainted, and it's time to purify us all. I don't care how long it takes, or what we endure, this must come to an end. We have to unify– for our children's sakes. But, tonight, I don't give a shit. This isn't about anyone but me."

Understanding, Jamie's arms surround me from behind, one palm coming to a rest on my breast, fingers dimpling my flesh. Mouth latching onto the side of my neck, Jamie kisses me with a passion Marcus can't fathom.

This is where I would be judged. Wanting sex to regain my power– to have a choice in who enters my body. Marcus is stuck in the horror of what he endured, unable to come to terms with wanting to use sex to erase rape, because he believes rape is about sex.

Besides the commonality of mashing body parts, sex and rape are a power-exchange. One is given freely, and the other is stolen.

"You're thinking of how you reacted to your rape, Marcus," I point out. "I'm not you. We're not talking about what happened to you right now. This is about me– right here, right now. The wound is still raw and fresh, and I need you inside me to help fix it."

"I can't…" Marcus trails off, expression warped. "I was nearly catatonic, then rage-filled. It took me a long time to want sex– until you," he gestures toward Jamie and me.

"I'm not you," I remind Marcus again. "If you can't, I understand. But don't judge Jamie and me because we can." Turning my head slightly, I draw Jamie down to my mouth by wrapping my palm around the back of his neck.

Losing myself to the feel of Jamie's scarred lips, the feel of his aroused body moving within mine, and the warmth of Marcus even if he isn't participating, I don't forget. I cry the entire time, cry for what I've lost. The feeling of invincibility– my freedom from the fear.

Marcus is crying, and it's hard to ignore with the sound of agony ringing in my ears, the sight burning into my eyes, and the sensation of it washing down my breasts in a cooling wave of tears.

I always saw Grant as weaker because he was the caregiver, the submissive individual. Marcus and I were in control, in charge– we had all the power. Jamie proves how very wrong I am, showing me how caregiving means he's in control, because you can't steal love, empathy, or sympathy. It must be freely given.

While I suffer in my selfish need to heal, and Marcus wallows in past wounds, Jamie selflessly gives us what we both need, even though it costs him more than he's probably willing to give.

Unable to be aroused in the sight of my pain while suffering through his own, no doubt Marc's confidence takes a billion hits. Jamie gives me what I need by being inside me, but he gives Marcus more.

Hand leaving my body, Jamie reaches into Marc's pajama pants, taking him in hand. "What are you doing?" Marcus bats at Jamie's hand in a panic, voice breaking, but his wonder-filled eyes tell another story. "Don't go there if you're not willing to go *there*," Marcus warns.

But Jamie doesn't let up, arm moving up and down as he tugs at Marc's cock with firm strokes. Eyes forced shut, Marcus grits his teeth as if he's in misery, but it's obvious how aroused Jamie is making him. Chest heaving, breath panting across my face, Marc's body is flushed crimson red, with his cock the hardest I've ever seen it.

Marcus has always confused me. Sexuality in general always has. It's not a black and white entity. I learned from Daniel how it's a fluid thing that can change when love is introduced.

There isn't a fiber in Jamie who is aroused by Marcus, but that doesn't mean he's turned off by him either. Jamie loves Marcus, always has and always will, and I've long suspected it isn't the love you'd have for a brother. Maybe it's not the love you'd have for a lover, but it's definitely a love you have for your partner.

Just because you're straight doesn't mean your own gender repulses you. I'm proof positive of this. Obviously I'm all about cock, but I was able to touch my girls without issue because they needed it. Because they needed it, I enjoyed it. I didn't suddenly turn bisexual after going down on Fate– I was as straight as ever. My view of my sexuality has never changed, because mine is not a fluid thing.

I understand how Whitt operates, and why he wants to have sex with me, even if he doesn't want me sexually. I get how a guy in his sexual prime is turned on by the prospect of the pleasure to come, not the person who is servicing him. Whitt wants his dick sucked dry, and he hasn't ventured to the need of emotional connection. Instead, he's going to get it from the submissives at Restraint, and try to get his emotional needs fed by me. I won't be Whitt's crutch, but I will keep my word about his birthday present.

Then there is Marcus– the sheltered, religious little boy whose world view didn't match what his body and mind needed to feel fulfilled. I've witnessed his arousal and interest in both sexes, but I also know his *on* switch doesn't turn on unless he's emotionally attached.

Making another sacrifice, the one he's held onto his entire adult life, Jamie's love for Marcus and me is greater than his reluctance to touch another cock.

"Why?" Marcus bats at Jamie's hand, putting forth no real effort to dislodge him. "I want Regina– I don't need you to be my fluffer. I just needed to get out of my own head." The next time he bats at Jamie's hand, it's to press closer.

Tears renewing, Marcus looks betrayed and hurt. I put him out of his misery with the truth, because insecurity and I are not strangers. It took a lot of soul-searching before I realized Grant wanted me regardless of a contract we signed. Jamie wants me, even if he won't step forward and claim me. Jamie probably wants Marcus too, but there is a selfish, cowardly part of Jamie who won't give himself to anyone. I have no idea why, and maybe I never will.

Inside me, Jamie flexes and throbs as if we're hardcore fucking when we're at rest. Just as he's always been, Jamie pours precum like he's ejaculating. "Believe it or not, Jamie is harder now that he's touching you, and I'd know…" trailing off, I gesture behind me to bring levity to the dark mood descending.

Jamie is the brooder. Marcus is the sinister one. Then there is me, who is either apathetic or destructive. We can't go *there* tonight without turning it into a suicide pack.

"You lie," Marcus accuses, but he quickly forgets the insult as Jamie twists the head of his cock. "If you stop, I'm going to kill you." Tendons in his neck straining, Marc arches in a mix of pleasure and pain. "You've teased me since I was eighteen, goddamn you!"

Jamie stops.

Jamie's hand jerks out of Marc's pajama pants, and I can't help but laugh at how Marcus goes postal with rage– a rage I doubt I'll ever shed.

"Goddamn you, *Grant!*" Marcus pulls out the big guns, calling his Jamie the name he never speaks. "What the fuck game are you playing?" Warring with himself, Marcus looks between my face and Jamie's, simultaneously wanting to bolt but not wanting to leave me.

Laughing his beastly sound, Jamie reaches forward to tug Marc's pants down. Marc's so far gone in his fury he doesn't even react. Huge cock revealed, looking angry and thicker than I've ever seen it.

The night I lost my virginity, Grant was proud of his length, but self-deprecating about it. *"I'm bigger than your curling iron."* I never understood, because he was above average. Then I met his best friends– conquered both of their scarily huge motherfucking cocks, and it all snapped into place.

If it had been Marcus to take my virginity, I would have run like a bat out of hell, straight to a convent. After sucking Dexter off, if Mrs. Zeitler had managed the feat of matchmaking Dexter with me as his enforcer… I don't think that thing could fit.

Tonight, after Jamie played fluffer, I'm curious to see if I can conquer Marcus at his worst. "Jesus Christ, I'm salivating," I mutter shamelessly in a voice that solely belongs to Queen, eyes glued with lust to the purple object of my desires.

My outburst shocks Marcus out of his fit and causes Jamie to laugh even louder. As freakishly terrifying as the sound is, it's a pleasure to actually *hear* Jamie.

Blushing, Marc grunts when Jamie wraps his hand around the wicked dick. "I guess you weren't stopping after all," Marcus mutters, embarrassed by his bitch-fit.

Axis shifting yet again, witnessing Jamie's pale, elegant hand wrapped around Marc's thick, veiny cock is a sight I hope I never forget. Yet again playing puppet master, Jamie maneuvers me around, hitching my thigh over his hip. While spooning me, he scoots me closer to Marcus. Then Jamie's cock slips free of my body, only to be replaced with Marc's.

Our breath hitches in unison at the sensation of Jamie guiding Marcus inside of me. Eyes slipping shut on a moan, the perversion of knowing it's Jamie's pre-cum gliding the way for Marc's cock has me shuddering.

Forgetting his malfunction from earlier, Marcus tries to take over, going into pile-driving-mode, where he decimates my pussy with his Coke-can-sized cock. But it's Jamie who's in charge tonight, and Marcus only gets a few thrusts in before a hand is wrapping around his length, tugging him out of me.

"Hey!" Marcus shouts, frustration getting the best of him. But I miss what he says next, because Jamie is back inside me, only taking one thrust. Then it's Marc's turn, where he tries to steal more than one thrust, and has his cock swatted in punishment.

I'm lost in confusion and Marcus is lost in frustration, so it takes about a dozen times of Jamie's silent instruction before we get with the program. Spooned from behind by Jamie and face-to-face with Marcus, they each take a thrust in turn before pulling out and allowing the other the pleasure.

The juxtaposition of a thick cock being replaced by a long cock, one from the front, then one from the back, is an epic mind fuck, leaving me a quivering mess.

"I don't…" Marcus stumbles over his words, having a hard time speaking because it's his turn again. "I don't get it."

"Just a guess," I pant breathlessly, leaning into Marcus to control the depth Jamie is taking. "This is author James Atwater with us tonight. Not *my* Grant, nor *your* Jamie. The silent observer wants to be heard. What do you expect from the guy who writes BDSM for a living? He's obviously up to something wicked."

"I'm being punished because I refuse to do foreplay with the world's slowest sex," Marcus muses sarcastically. "Consolation prize is the fact that I have Jamie's juice slicking my cock."

"Ha!" Laughing like I should have an express pass to Wintercrest, "I thought the same fucking thing." Marcus joins in with my amusement, and it pisses Jamie off, to the point he stops fucking us altogether.

After some fumbling, my cellphone is thrust between Marc's and my face.

All you do is fuck. No foreplay. Just straight to fucking– both of you. I'm showing you how to make love to each other, idiots! If you love Regina as much as you say you do, I suggest you get over yourself. Regina has a line forming behind her, and I'm sure one of them will lick her pussy instead of tearing it up.

"That suspiciously makes this sound like a one-off," Marc mutters with great disappointment, earning a growl for his response. "Like Jamie's taking one for the team, then leaving us with what he's taught."

"A line?" Wrenching my head to the side, I glare back at Jamie. "Two men does not a line make. A gay rapist and a gay kid? Who exactly is into pussy licking?"

Glaring back, Jamie sticks his scarred tongue out, then flicks the tip in invitation. "Jesus Christ," I hiss, pussy clenching around Marc's cock, forcing a grumbled sound from his throat. "Will you lick me now?"

"God, yes! Please." Marcus practically goes into convulsions, imagining Jamie's tongue near his dick. "Now?"

After rolling his eyes at us like we're being children, Jamie laughs. While we're stunned stupid, he switches up who's inside of me. Gripping Marc's dick, much to the man's delight, Jamie then rubs the head on my engorged clit, much to mine.

"So close," I murmur, loving the feel of Jamie gliding inside of me and Marc's thick head drawing me to the edge of orgasm. Shuddering, pleasure works its way down my spine to form a ball of pressure in my belly.

Minutes pass where I'm suspended on the nexus to climax, where Jamie slowly rolls into me, with one hand masturbating both Marcus and me, and the other groping my tits. Marcus feasts at my lips, while Jamie sucks a necklace of hickeys down the column of my throat.

Marcus and I groan in frustration when Jamie switches up again. With Marcus throbbing deep inside me and Jamie's slick cock dampening my ass crack, there's no more clit-action.

After completing a thrust to the hilt, Jamie stops Marcus from retreating by gripping his ass. Which, I have to say is the hottest sight of my life– the possibilities whirl through my mind, even knowing they will never come to fruition. But it's fucking hot to fantasize. Poor Marcus, also imagining, then hoping, but knowing it's not going to happen, all in the span of a split-second.

My heart breaks as I watch the emotions warp across Marc's face, ending with the resentment and fury I don't allow myself to feel.

"You touched my dick, and you used it on Regina. Don't touch my ass unless you plan on using it," Marcus growls, turning surly with sexual frustration, then his voice turns as dry as ash. "I can't see how Regina could possibly make use of my ass. You know why no one touches me there. *No one*," Marcus stresses, but the hope in his eyes tells another story.

Blushing beautifully, Jamie pats Marc's behind in an apology, deflating two-thirds of the occupants in my bed. Then he mouths, "*Don't move*," and it's the first time I find his muteness a difficulty, as I wish he could communicate with me easier. After I learn sign language, it will be better. But what happens when we're in the dark and I can't see to *hear* him?

"I don't remember sex with you being so mechanical," I mutter with wry amusement, causing Jamie to laugh. God, sometimes we fucked for days straight. Jamie is at total odds with how Marc pounds me in the ground in under five minutes flat. To have them both in my bed… "Why are you moving me around again?" I ask of why Jamie's directing me to wrap my arms around Marc's back and hooking my leg around Marc's hip.

"*Don't move*," is mouthed in our direction again, with a flash of fear crossing Jamie's mutilated features.

The warm weight of Jamie's body aligns with the back of mine again, as I lay still in Marc's arms. The only part of Marc's body moving is the slow, impatient beat of his cock inside me and his eyes flicking around, trying to communicate with the silent man at my back.

"What?" Marc and I grunt in unison at the feel of Jamie's cock blindly poking where we're joined. My, "What's going on?" gets eclipsed by Marc's, "You better not be fucking with my head. Don't go there unless you plan on delivering, and for shit's sake, don't hurt her."

"Huh?" is my response, because I have no idea what's going on.

Shaking with anticipation, or maybe even with a bit of fear, Marcus answers my grunted question. "You said you wanted both of us in you tonight," Marc's words hold many meanings. "I suggest you grin and bear it, and try to relax, because Jamie's about to try a feat I've only read about in his books."

Grunt warping in my mouth to form an O of surprise, every muscle in my body contracts at once. Fear. Real fear of pain that may be inflicted. Both men are above average, one in length, one in girth, and they are both struggling to enter a place where only one should go.

Marcus holds me as tightly as I hold him, both of us leaving fingertip bruises behind. But we're panting for two very different reasons. Marcus, because Jamie's cock is rubbing against his, fighting to fit inside of me. Me, because Jamie's cock is fighting to fit inside of me, and the painful stretch burns as if I'm being sacrificed on a pyre.

A switch flips inside my psyche, letting everything go, allowing my mind to shut down and my body to awaken. This is Jamie. This is Marcus. They may burn and sting and stretch me to my limits, but neither will harm me. Releasing the stress, I revel in the discomfort, because it means I've survived the hellish life I've led since my father passed and my mother was diagnosed with cancer. Every day has been a fight to survive, whether I was young or old, or poor or rich.

For a suspended moment in time, it feels like forever, but not nearly long enough to last a lifetime. Marcus, Jamie, and I hang in the balance where we forget where one of us begins and another ends. My belly is cramping, my pussy is on fire, but the sensation of hands and mouths soothing me with their reassurance makes it all worth it.

Poor Marcus is releasing a string of grunts, groans, and moans, mind and heart unable to deal with the fact that Jamie is freely touching him, kissing him probably for the first time, with heat Jamie may or may not feel for the man.

We're all but a passenger to the passion. Mouths seeking a mate, cocks slipping and sliding together inside of me, and hands gripping and tugging with passion, yet adding soothing caresses of affectionate intimacy.

Grant and I had always made love, even when we were hardcore fucking.

No matter what, Marcus and I were never able to truly let go during the act, always making it more of a battleground of repressed aggression and resentment.

Jamie lowers our emotional shields to one another, allowing us to truly connect for the very first time– shields we need to survive whatever fallout Grant created.

Chapter Twenty-One

Stretching and rolling around on the mattress, my hand blindly seeks my cellphone hidden in the sheets. "God, is it morning already?" I growl, not ready to face the day while simultaneously needing to extend the events that occurred during the middle of the night.

"I didn't think you were a heavy sleeper," Marcus murmurs wryly, locating my cellphone first. With the flick of his thumb, he's silencing my alarm. "I think a car alarm is quieter than your '*wakey, wakey, it's day breaky*'?" he teases me for what I've named my alarm.

"It's from Fable," I explain. Popping open an eyelid, I realize Marcus is drawing a blank. "The video game."

"You play?" Marc sounds baffled.

Chuckling underneath my breath, "Marcus, what I do for a living pretty much demands it. I do leave the house on occasion– there would be no surviving an IT convention. They'd look at me like a hydra with one head if I didn't play."

Laughing some more, I realize I never asked Niel if he enjoys playing video games. I'll ask him that today. Smiling widely, I realize I can call my son up at any time and ask him tiny, ridiculously inane questions to satisfy my curiosity.

Wow.

Marcus is staring at me like he thinks me cute. "Okay, so that explains the name of your alarm, but why is it so loud?"

"Yeah… well…" Arms stretched overhead, I grip the headboard to elongate my torso. Groaning, I realize I hurt pretty much every-fucking-where, especially between my thighs. "Insomniacs tend to really conk out, and it would take an apocalypse to wake us."

"You need to sleep more often," Marcus reminds me, and I warm at the affectionate tone he takes with me this morning. Somewhere between sitting in the car before my initiation, getting hitched, being assaulted, and then Jamie's appearance, Marcus changed the way he views me, and I like it.

"This girl's far too busy for sleep," I mutter flippantly, scrubbing the sleep from my face with both palms.

"Do you have a lot going on today?" Marcus reaches over to wipe my eye with the corner of the sheet, removing embarrassing eye-gunk. I'd forgotten what it was like to wake up the morning after.

"Way too much." Groaning in frustration, I sit up in bed with my back to the headboard. "I have to go into work today to check our online security, then I have to get this house back online. I'd like to share a meal with both of my children at the same time, maybe invite Whitt along. Tonight I have to go to Restraint to clean up Ezra's mess, so I'll need to meet with Aaron and Roman at some point today."

Chuckling warmly, Marcus can't seem to stop staring at me like he's never seen me before. "If you had a cock, you'd be hard right now describing your heavy schedule– workaholic."

"What's on your agenda for the day?" I grab for my cellphone to check the time, wanting to give Marcus some attention before I totally blow him off until tomorrow or the next day, especially since he's never woke in a lover's bed before, which is probably why he looks moony-eyed yet sad at the same time.

"Let's see…" Marcus locates his phone off my nightstand. "I should probably make my way to Shadow Haven and make sure everyone is still breathing." A funny look warps Marc's face, and I don't understand it. Eyes darting everywhere, he looks as if he's trying to spot ghosts hiding in the corners. "Hmm… anyway. Jury selection at eleven. I'm supposed to carve out some time for a meal with Dexter. Then I'll probably hole up in my office and prepare for trial. I'm sure my co-counsel is worried I'll be a no-show, so I better give Tanner all of my attention for the next few weeks so we don't lose our case. "

Marcus doesn't mention his wife, his lunatic son, or the man who services him, perhaps because they are a given and would rub my already frayed nerves raw. But the most important person of all is absent from Marc's schedule.

"No Jamie?" My eyebrow hitches high, knowing Marcus can't go a few hours without him. Codependency is a real thing.

"No," Marcus mutters firmly, if not coldly. "Absolutely no Jamie."

"Okay… so this is probably going to insult you, where no insult was meant." I tread lightly, finally realizing the Master of the Universe does have insecurities, and I seem to be the cause of some of them, with the rest belonging to Jamie. "I'm happy it's you with me right now, but where the hell did our cowardly mute go?"

Rolling to the side, Marcus reaches down to the floor to pick something up. My heart rattles inside my chest when he comes back up with a few sheets of lose notebook paper that was scavenged from my desk.

Self-explanatory, Marcus doesn't need to answer my question.

Just like Grant, Jamie is gone.

With shaking fingertips, I take the letter when I'm too frightened to read it. Marcus settles a soothing hand to my shoulder, lending me the strength I can't seem to muster.

"I feel so emotionally raw right now, it ain't even funny." I try to laugh it off, voice warbling.

Marc murmurs sympathetically, "I know."

Echo & Antithesis,

We cannot go down this path...

While you both have been in stasis, I've been growing as a human being by examining my mistakes. I am not the person you think I am. You both see me as I was, but not clearly now.

A selfish man would take what is so freely being given, burying old pain beneath new pain. But I am not that selfish man anymore. I will not build the foundation of a new relationship on the remains of the old. Until we work out what has happened in the past, dealt with what's happening in the present, I cannot in good conscience build a future with either of you.

One day, if we don't repair what has been broken –what I've broken –one of you could tear my soul free of my body, and I couldn't survive it. The anger, the resentment, the need for justice, it would taint every word we speak. I can't love either of you freely, not when I'm waiting for the other shoe to drop.

The ultimate in payback would be to begin a real life with one of you, only to have you pull back. Sike! Hurts, don't it?

The guilt... the guilt is eating me alive, and I'm doing my damnedest to alleviate it for the sake of all of us. Thinking. Endless self-reflection. Therapy. Confession. Counsel with my priest. Airing my mistakes, on purposes, indiscretions, and on accidents for those who it affects to hear and see. Reconnecting to those I've abandoned, slighted, and harmed in the past.

Not unlike working the twelve steps, the Serenity Prayer is always playing out inside my head.

God, grant me the serenity to accept the things I cannot change, courage to change the things I can, and wisdom to know the difference.

Marcus, my antithesis–

We've shared a special bond since the day we met. A connection that I knew could never be severed. The version of me who died, he exploited this connection. You ought to be angry with me, but you're not, which means you have not dealt with the pain I've caused you to suffer.

I promise I am making reparations, as I couldn't go on without righting my wrongs.

Marcus, I love you. I truly love you. It's a pure form of love that may be able to transcend the fact that it's not romantic or sexual in nature. I've seen it work with my fathers– the ability is inborn in me. If we are able to grow up and heal, I can promise I will try in the future.

You need help. Yes, I listened to your entire conversation from the moment Regina entered her bedroom, none of the revelations new to me. You need professional help. You need to leave Cortez alone, give Ezra boundaries, develop a relationship with your blooded daughter, and divorce Diane.

You love Regina in exactly the same way you love me. It's why I've never worried. Regina is a special human being, and even my complete and total opposite in all things would fall for her.

Regina has her own problems, which makes it okay that you're still touching those you shouldn't while still married to another. Out of respect for Regina, I'm going to demand you cease your ridiculous behavior before I give my blessing for the two of you to be together.

Go ahead and be immature, use each other to forget the truth... I won't have either one of you if you won't grow up. Rome wasn't built in a day– it's taken me ten years to find myself, and I'm still soldiering forth. You guys must at least try.

Marcus, remember that man you used to be– the conservative, religious man who wanted a happy family, living a stress-free life at Serenity Lake. That isn't a fairytale. It's a possibility if you'd only get out of your own way.

Get help!

Echo–

First things first. I did NOT abandon you. I didn't want to leave. I was protecting you. But I hear you, Echo… I hear your pain, the guilt, the shame, the mourning, and I want to take it all away. It would be so easy to fall into you, as we were before. But I'm not that man anymore, and you're not that same young girl who hadn't been jaded yet.

Second, nothing has ever been your fault. The truth is all about the perception. Your truth. My truth. You are not to blame in either truth. Don't play the blame game, simply gather facts. Be rational. Be Regina.

Third, I want you. Don't try to create insecurities that should never exist. You know I want you. Marcus knows I want you. The whole of the world knows I want you. But that doesn't mean I deserve you, or should have you.

We're not there yet, Echo. We're not. I wish we were. But to touch as we did last night… once the rage explodes, it would destroy whatever we're trying to rebuild. I want this too much to jeopardize it with instant gratification.

Our children, arrange a meeting for us tomorrow. The venue is of your choosing. I expect it to be an uncomfortable affair, so I understand if you don't want to taint a location with the memory of our meeting.

Not only do I wish to be their father, I am their father, forevermore. Whether you and I are together, or not, that doesn't change the genetics. I am their father, but I want to be their dad.

This is not about abandonment, which I accept as if you all see it that way. What I mean, for me to wish to be with my children, that doesn't take away how I feel about you. I'm giving you the power here, Regina. Choose to use it wisely.

Do I regret not making you my Mrs. Whittenhower? My private thoughts are a toxic stew of misery I cannot escape. Do I believe I deserved to be your Mr. Whittenhower? No. Fuck no! I gave my son his wish at the expense of my own happiness. I will not jeopardize whatever I try to build with you or him by touching my son's wife.

Last night was not a mistake. It was a goodbye to who we used to be and who we are now. But it was a promise to who we will become.

After all the work I've done on healing, I will not revert. I will not touch another man's wife, nor another woman's husband. Nor will I couple with someone who will touch others as a form of self-harm.

You both are toxic to me right now. I will help you. I will listen. I will hold you when you cry, and try to be your anchor. But I cannot be your lover.

I'm not selfish anymore, to the point I am stepping away, knowing you may never let me back in. You have to examine what I've done to you and others before you can give me forgiveness. I understand how forgiveness isn't absolute. As long as you hear me, I can survive, even if you never forgive me.

Hear me.

If, in the end, when the ashes of our past lives have been swept away, if you find yourself unable to forgive me, I will truly understand. If you're still madly in love with each other, I will freely give my blessing, even if that means neither of you love me anymore. But, know this, even if we aren't together, I will never allow either of you to cut me from your life, even if it means sitting in silence.

My body on Earth is temporary, while my soul is for all eternity. When I go, it will be with a cleared conscience. Only God can truly forgive, but I need you both to hear me.

–J.

Pages flutter from shaking hands, "Jamie doesn't want us," I cry out, fury lighting in my veins to take root. "After last night, how could he reject us?" The letter falls to the mattress, one page landing on the floor.

"Turn the last page over," Marcus mutters wryly, a little grin flirting with his lips, so I bend down to retrieve it.

Reggie from the block–

If you said I don't want you, then you're not hearing what I'm trying to say.

I love you.

Open up your mind... have a listen.

–J.

"Regina, don't even attempt to form an argument about how Jamie doesn't know you," Marcus mutters wryly, eyes glinting with tears that refuse to fall. Now I understand the bizarre mood he's been in since I woke.

"That motherfucker," rumbles past my lips. "I can't believe… I just can't." Visibly shaking with fury, even my teeth begin to chatter. "If Jamie was in this room right now, I'd fucking punch the motherfucker."

"I'd hold him down for you if you'd let me take a turn." Head jerking to the side, Marcus refuses to look at me. He grabs for a pillow, clutching it to his chest like a teddy bear.

"I feel judged," I snarl, upper lip baring my teeth. "Judged by this enlightened creature who says he's not judging us. A part of me wants to do the opposite of everything he told us to do, simply to prove he doesn't know us."

A laugh of pure misery flows up from Marc's throat. "I know, right?" Amber eyes pin me, refusing to shed the tears threatening to fall. After last night, our shields are finally going back up. But instead of forming a solid burier around our broken hearts, it's bringing us closer together. The walls are down between us, completely. But we're erecting walls to keep Jamie out– the cowardly rat-bastard.

With a thump, Marcus punches my pillow. "It's like a game to him, when he says he plays no games. I know Jamie meant every word he wrote, and truly believes them. But now I'm left wondering, did he say that shit knowing I'd do A? Or did he say to do A, knowing full well we'd do B to spite him?"

"I'm doing B, because I don't have time to arrange a meeting with our children today, at the last minute." Jumping from the bed with purpose, "I've got too much shit to do to indulge his needs and wants."

"Jamie waited a decade," Marcus mutters snidely. "He can wait another for all I care. The rat should have to arrange the meeting himself, not let it fall into your lap." Squeezing the life out of my pillow, "I want to murder him, and no doubt he's anticipating that."

"He knows us too well." I pick out my clothing for the day, not giving two shits that I'm naked with dried cum making my thighs tacky. Office-wear at Empowerment is whatever the hell you feel like wearing. I grab for a pair of jeans and a softball t-shirt listing Empowerment as one of the sponsors.

"That's the problem with the quiet types." Marcus laughs at his own joke. "Always watching, their silence lulling you into spilling your deepest and darkest. You get so comfortable, you don't realize they now know all of your secrets, and you know nothing of theirs."

"Exactly!" is a call of victory as I locate my favorite pair of flip-flops, not giving two shits that it's still winter in the Mid-Atlantic. I have slippers resting beneath my desks in all of my offices. Stepping back out of my closet, I muse more to myself than to Marcus. "Do you think he'll come back to us?"

"Probably." Marcus steps from the bed, naked as the day he was born. The bite mark on his shoulder is too delicate to be from me, and it had to be near impossible for Marc to have managed to cum-splatter his own shoulder. Those scratches on his ass are not from me either, and there's no way I was the only one to bruise those luscious lips. "But I'm not waiting around for Jamie to decide we're worthy of him– goddamn him!"

"I love you, you know that, right?" With my clothing clasped to my chest, I feel more vulnerable than ever. "You're not my consolation prize." My unasked question doesn't go unnoticed.

Grabbing for his overnight bag, Marcus freezes. Eyes connecting with mine, "I love you too," and I know he's saying I'm not his consolation prize either. Neither of us can fill Jamie's absence, but after the past few years, Jamie can't fill ours either.

"Shower with me?" I ask, gesturing to Marc's bag. "We can eat breakfast with Ella afterward."

"I can…" Marcus turns slightly, refusing to meet my gaze. "I can use the guest bathroom– I know how you want privacy while you–" pointing at my thighs with his shame wafting in the air "–douche."

Tilting my head to the side, trying to understand Marcus, "Why would I douche?"

"Because I'm in there, even if Jamie is too." Marcus tugs on his pajama pants, then begins hunting around for his t-shirt so he's presentable during his walk of shame to my guest bathroom.

"Marcus?" I call, stilling him. "I'm not the same person I was decade ago, or even last year. I'm definitely not the same person I was the day before yesterday."

Marcus nods in understanding, ringlets bobbing around his head because he's way past due for a haircut. I hope he never cuts it again– I love unkempt Marcus Zeitler. But, the thing is, he doesn't understand.

"You're right, I am going to douche." Walking up to Marcus, I pull the strap of his leather weekender bag off his shoulder. "I'm going to douche Jamie away, because he doesn't deserve it after the shit he just pulled."

Marc's gasp of surprise has me smiling.

Taking his bag with me, I make sure Marcus follows me into my en suite bathroom, or else he gets to do the walk of shame in his pajamas. "Feel free to refill me as we wash."

"Holy shit, you are really pissed at him, aren't you?" Marcus beats me into my own bathroom, eager.

Dropping our clothing off on the vanity, I lay it all out. "We have to keep moving forward, Marcus. We have shit we need to do, and we have to stop worrying about Jamie. If he wants us, he knows where to find us. I won't play hide and seek any longer. I have to deal with Ezra, both for Restraint and as my MdJ contact, and I can't be emotionally weakened around him."

"Words cannot express how deeply sorry I am." Marcus caresses my shoulder, and I've never believed him more. "I'm going to talk to him, and I know that sounds stupid, but it ought to help."

Reaching into the shower, I adjust the water temperature. "Jamie gave me away to you, then he gave me away to Whitt for marriage. Actions speak louder than words. I can't deny how hurt and furious I am right now, but displaying that is a luxury I can't afford. You and I, we have to do what we have to do to survive."

"Life goes on, even without him." Marcus steps into my shower, then he softly tugs me to join him. "I always thought it tragically romantic, how Jamie hid away in the brownstone, secretly pining away after you."

"Bullshit," I snarl. "Total bullshit. I said we aren't living in a novel, and I meant it." I grab for a loofah to scrub all traces of Jamie off my skin– off Marcus too. "Jamie has had no problem telling us things we shouldn't know over the past few months, then giving us those journals. Jamie put me on MdJ's radar and got me in trouble. If he wanted me, he would've been with me. If he wanted to be with our children, he would've been. It was all a choice he made with an agenda behind it."

"Maybe Jamie is trying to repent." Marcus takes the loofah out of my hands, then begins washing my back. Proof that Marcus is more in love with Jamie than I've ever been. "Like he said in his letter."

"Maybe he is. Maybe he isn't." I flip around to look in Marc's eyes. "I don't give a shit either way. Jamie has gotten off on the tragedy of our lives together, playing the victim and martyr, and I won't be a two-bit player in his story anymore."

"You and me?" Marcus smiles tentatively. "You and me against the world?" Gazing at the water swirling down the drain, he suddenly looks shy– coy even. "I don't trust Jamie anymore. I don't trust his motives, because he knows us inside and out and we know nothing of him. So whatever he wants us to do in his letter, I'm going to do it on my own terms, on my own time. Because cutting off Cortez will not help matters."

"The man told me to marry his own son, made love to me on my wedding night, then had the gall to judge you for still being married while touching him and me. Divorcing Diane would make her free to have Adelaide, which I suspect has something to do with it. Jamie's suggestions are not as altruistic as he would like to lead us to believe."

"Agreed." My loofah hits the shower wall with a violent splat. "I want to strangle him," Marcus snarls.

"We have to see him in the next few days, and we can't go down for murder. Plus, we'd feel bad about it later," I mutter wryly while leaning out of the shower to grab the reusable douche bottle hiding nearby. "How about some vengeance-filled hate-fucking after I wash away what the cowardly rat-bastard left behind?"

Marcus stares at me in awe, amber eyes shifting with lust, pupils blown. Swallowing audibly, he takes the douche bottle from my hand. "This is my cunt now, right? It's no longer Jamie's?"

Head hitching backward to hit the tile wall, laughter spills freely. "Sure, Mr. Possessive. You can make use of *my* cunt all you want, but it will always belong to me."

Chapter Twenty-Two

Proactive, my name is Regina Regal. *Shit!* I mean, Regina Whittenhower– never going to get used to that. I'll visit the courthouse in a few days to officially change it to make Whitt happy. Somebody ought to be happy. Too bad I'll derive sick satisfaction in it because I'm Daniel Whittenhower II's wife, and not Grant James Atwater Whittenhower's.

Fuck him– the rat.

Today was a day of new beginnings, where I was too busy to dwell on the fact that Jamie has yet again rejected and abandoned me. Okay, I lie. I thought about Jamie all day, with rage simmering just beneath the surface and a few trips to the bathroom to dry my tears. My employees kept commenting on how red my eyes were, so I used the excuse of seasonal allergies, which they bought lock, stock, and barrel. Fate's assistant, Kym, went as far as to make me a get-better-soon basket of goodies.

I swear to God, when I see Jamie's mutilated face next, I'm going to throat-punch him.

Since I can't control if someone wants me, loves me, or wishes to be with me, I worked on the problems I could solve. My home and the guest house are now back on the network, with Dominion's branch of Empowerment as secure as I could make it. Running all the security checks was a cold dash of reality, thinking about how talented Boyd is and how easily he knocked me off my pedestal. Empowerment has a global reach, and I have my IT team going crazy all over the world to batten down the hatches.

I invited Aaron and Roman over to discuss what changes we should make at Restraint while I worked on my home network server. It took the better part of an hour before Aaron stopped acting so sheepish over what Ezra had done to me. I'm assuming Ezra told him, because I don't want that mortifying knowledge spread around. I could tell Roman knew too, by the way his hands were curled into fists every time Ezra's name was brought up in conversation, which was a lot since we were discussing Restraint.

As soon as they left, I made an appointment with a therapist– I can't go this alone, and I can't truly talk over my feelings with anyone else, because we're all too intertwined.

All hope of having a sit-down dinner with my children and husband were dashed. Ella had a spelling bee, and the entire Whittenhower family was attending a political fundraiser for Kent Preston up in Albany.

I did manage to fit in a call to both Whitt and Niel, leaving it up to them for when we descend on Jamie and call him Grant again. I couldn't bring myself to explain it to Ella– I will just before we meet him as a family. Ella's ten, but death is just a theory to her after never having lost anyone close to her. Her father was gone before she was born, and with him coming back into her life, I don't want her to think resurrection is reality. Cowardly rat of a father is reality.

Death is final.

I hope Ella tells her father how much fun she had eating breakfast with Marcus. How amazing Marcus is with kids. How Dad was missing out on so much by fleeing in the wee hours of the morning like a cockroach escaping the light.

Me, bitter? Nah.

"Hey!" Kris calls out to me as I stomp my way through Restraint, with the crowd parting by my fury alone. "What's gotten into you guys?" I don't ask who 'you guys' are, because I don't want to know. Kristal obviously had to check-in with Jamie a few times today.

Going into boss-mode, "Keep up the good work, Chica– let me know if you need anything." Then I disappear down the back hallway to Ezra's office, our soon-to-be shared office. Nothing like sharing a space with your rapist every night– in a room with a lockable door.

Breathing through the panic, I think of the positives. The fact that I don't have to wait in line or walk in the front door to enter Restraint was pretty convenient. There's an *employees only* door Roarke mans when we're coming in and out. Oh, and I'm in charge now, just when I need it the most– to hold power over Ezra.

To take my stolen power back.

Lies. All lies. Even with therapy, I'm never going to be right in the head again, and I did nothing to deserve how my view of the world has changed. The injustice of it all, and my new-found fear and vulnerability.

Rationally, I know I've been channeling all of my rage over Ezra into Jamie, and so is Marcus. I truly believe everything Jamie had said in his letter had value. But right now, I know Jamie will allow me to make him a target, because I can't get my pound of flesh out of Ezra, not when he has me by the balls thanks to Maître du Jeu.

Jamie owes me for every day I've suffered since I turned eighteen years old. He'll just have to deal with paying for Ezra's sins– sins Ezra wouldn't have committed had it not been for Marcus. But who's keeping score, anyway?

Feet stilling, I rest my forehead on the wall just outside of Ezra's office. Blunt fingernails digging to find purchase in the cinderblock wall, my mouth opens up into a silent, primal scream of pure agony and terror.

"Ezra Zeitler is just a boy you met at Hillbrook. He's your lover's adopted son. He's your best friend's intended. He's your husband's version of a wet dream. He's now your partner in running Restraint. He has no power over you, unless you let him."

For a good minute or two, Queen whispers empowering, pretty lies, allowing me to garner courage to knock on the door an inch to my right.

I was having a productive day, where I forgot about my reality for all of two seconds at a time, until I received a demanding text message from Ezra just as I was sitting down to dinner. Without reading the message, just seeing his name on my lock-screen produced a visceral reaction. Kristal's homemade enchiladas fermented in my belly, and I was thankful it was just Kris and me sharing a meal at the kitchen island. Because I ended up vomiting all over the floor on my way to the kitchen sink.

Kris asked if I was pregnant, not realizing I had been raped. We aren't the friends we used to be, so I didn't feel the need to totally wreck myself emotionally by relaying the torturous details. Besides, I'm sure it will come up at the next founder's meeting, where the psychopaths will deposit my shame into their deviant spank-banks for later use.

Feeling like Jamie, all cowardly, silent, and lurking, I pull out my cellphone. Empathizing, I wonder if Jamie has a reason for his erratic behavior, as I do now.

Dr. Lunatic: *My office. 9 o'clock sharp. I need your computer expertise. –Master Ez*

I'm not sure why Ezra doesn't just ask Boyd, but maybe this is personal instead of MdJ business. Staring at the time on my cellphone, with my hand on the doorknob, I remember how deranged Ezra acted last night when he said I was late.

At exactly nine, I knock. My heart beats louder than the sound of my fist on the metal security door. Hell, I can hear the chug-a-lug in my ears over the pound of the bass flowing down the hallway.

I knock again– louder this time, my sweat leaving a damp mark on the door.

Three ladies giggle as they leave the women's bathroom across the wide hallway from me. "Sarah!" A tall blonde pats her friend on the butt in response to whatever was said. "Behave." They all share a private laugh, swaying down the hallway toward the dance floor with only having a good time on their minds.

My body shivers with trepidation, envy, and sadness. Those young ladies deserve to have a good time– to be free. Trepidation, because the odds of that freedom turning into a nightmare is too high. Envy, because I know I'll never be carefree like they are now. Sadness, because I doubt I ever had that joyous freedom, after a lifetime of being in survival-mode.

Meeping like a toddler, I jump a foot in the air when a heavy palm lands on my shoulder. Smiling politely, like he's trying hard not to laugh, Aaron reaches past me to unlock Ezra's office door. Without speaking a word, after turning the knob in demonstration, Aaron strolls back down the hallway to stand sentry at the front door.

After quickly wiping the sweat from my brow, I run my hands down my thighs. Swearing beneath my breath over how ridiculous I'm being. Because leather is not absorbent, I use my t-shirt instead.

Armor.

I'm wearing armor tonight.

I refuse to put my body on display, leaving an opening for an asshole to use it against me as a defense for taking what isn't freely given. Ezra was able to catch me unawares and use my clothing against me last night. Without a knife, or the coercion tactics to make me remove my leather pants, there is no way Ezra's dick is entering my vagina. I'd seriously thought of ways to protect my mouth from intrusion, and came up short. *Teeth.* As for the rest of me, to be ironic, I'm wearing the novelty t-shirt patrons buy with Restraint's logo on the back.

I enter, because I'm not scared of Master Ez.

With immense relief, I lean against the door with my eyes shut, slowly trying to even my breathing. Why did Ezra ask me here if he wasn't going to be waiting?

"You look gorgeous," a silky voice purrs, and I jump out of my skin again.

"I thought you weren't here. Why did Aaron let me in?" My voice quivers in fear– let's be fucking real for a nanosecond. I'm motherfucking terrified of Master Ez. "I'm wearing pants and a t-shirt. Save the false flattery on someone who gives two shits."

Surrounding me, the office doesn't get a second of my notice. All I see is my innocent rapist. Master Ez sits at his desk like a fallen angel. Thankfully, he doesn't get up, but he smirks at me lasciviously. Steel eyes glowing in the nondescript, dim room, Ezra tries to command me to look at him… so I look an inch above his shoulder to prove I can.

"I ask the questions, Regina." The cadence is smooth, but there is an undercurrent of threat.

Regina. Ez calls me Regina. Master Ez calls me Queen. The true Ezra is a combination of both– an integrated personality. The whole Ezra is the one talking to me.

But why is *HE* looking at me like that?

"I don't understand that look, Ezra," I mumble, stomach threatening to eject the few sips of water I took before heading in here.

"As I've said over and over, we are one in the same– Master Ez and I." He sighs like he gets sick of pointing out that fact.

"Um– yeah…" croaking on my words, I'll never live it down how terrified Ezra makes me feel. Rationally, I know what he did was wrong. But why am I reacting as if he fucked me with a chainsaw, not a harmless cock I'd previously had inside my body?

Because Ezra took from you, Queen interjects as I try to formulate a coherent reply.

"Ezra, you say you and Master Ez are one in the same, yet he wants ladies and they're missing an appendage for you to enjoy." I tease, because anything else would scare the shit out of me.

"Regina. Regina." The bastard laughs a disturbing sound– disturbing because the purity of it is beautiful, coming from an angelic looking man who commits sins without consequence.

"The Ezra I used to be liked boys. That changed– quickly and against my will," he says pointedly, because I would know all about against my will.

To a twisted bastard like Ezra, he probably sees what he did to me as an induction ceremony all of its own. I was initiated as a Master of Restraint, but Ezra inducted me into Dominion's secret sect of sociopaths and their victims. I'm terrified to ask if there are any members who have not raped or been raped among their ranks. Power-hungry narcissists.

"Master Ez only likes girls. Doesn't it seem likely that if who I used to be liked boys, and who manifested liked woman, that perhaps I enjoy both now? If we are to cohabitate in peace, we have certain concessions to make."

"Okay, so your other personality is straight, you're gay… I don't think being bisexual is how it works. What happens if one day you are mentally healthy again? What are you then?"

Smirking a nasty little smirk, Ezra shrugs one shoulder, pulling his expensive suit across his chest.

Looking everywhere but at Ezra, I take in the room with one hand gripping the doorknob for dear life. It's just an office, not a scary lair where Ezra takes his intended rape victims. Gray walls, gray flooring, gray furnishings. Narcissist. A serviceable desk is holding many monitors and laptops, much like the one I have at home. Several filing cabinets line the rear wall, and two cushiony chairs face the desk.

Nothing to write home about, but the minimalistic efficiency of the office is a comfort. It's a place to get work done, and nothing more.

"What do you want me to call you– this you?" I point at Ezra, waving my hand about, trying to be respectful of his mental health issues.

"If we are in the dungeon, regardless of who I am, you will call me Master Ez and I will call you Queen. In private, we are Ezra and Regina. In Restraint, we are the Boss and Queen."

Testing, Ezra looks at me expectantly, waiting for me to call him the appropriate name.

It's like a riddle. We're in Restraint, but in private. He keeps calling me Regina, but that doesn't matter. The bastard is probably tricking me.

"Boss, what do you need of me this evening?" I murmur with an appropriate level of condescension.

Lips twisting, Ezra admits defeat. "Well played. Come around my desk. Come to me," he tries to lure me with a soft, coaxing tone.

Leery, I walk slowly, trying to figure out what sort of game Ezra's playing, because he's always playing a game. He does have three laptops running on his desk, so perhaps he did need my help. The anticipatory look on his face is frightening as all hell, though. His eyes are darker than before and tracking my every move.

"What the fuck?!" I shout, enraged at the sight before me. "Put that fucking thing away, you goddamn pervert." Snarling while pointing at Ezra's erect cock being displayed through the open fly of his trousers, I'm no longer sick to my stomach. "A deal's a deal– a deal I didn't make, nor was it broken," I remind him.

"I know Cortez's mouth hasn't had Marc's cock lodged in it since we last spoke." Ezra doesn't play by his own rules. If I hadn't worn my armor, he would've gotten me unawares again, dick cocked and at the ready.

"Is this about Marcus?" I accuse, and judging by the wince, I'm right. "Take it up with Cortez if you don't want him sucking dick. Better yet, let him suck yours, which I'm positive is the root of the problem."

"*You bitch*," Ezra snarls, pale face turning a wicked shade of red. "Marcus lied to me when I asked you both outright whether or not you were lovers. Lied!" he shouts, veins in his forehead visibly throbbing.

"I wonder why," I muse dramatically, hand waving at his leaking cock. "Look at you! Look how you're behaving."

"I won't lower myself by calling you a home-wrecker," Ezra speaks down to me like I'm street trash. "It's hard to argue and lie about cold, hard facts. There's only one Spyder in the Tri-State area, and it was parked in your driveway for sixteen hours," he professes in disbelief.

"How do you know that?" I accuse, already thinking of ways to secure my home.

"I've learned from the very best," Ezra mutters arrogantly, leaning back in his chair to display his cock like the threat it truly is. "Marcus thinks he has secrets. Cort thinks he has secrets. You think you have secrets. You all have none. Marcus taps us, so don't you believe I might do it as well?"

“You guys are fucking lunatics,” I snarl at Ezra, furious at the prisoner I’ve become.

“Welcome to the family, *Mom,*” Ezra mutters snidely. “My daddy issues mean I will make it my mommy’s issue,” he taunts, cock jerking with excitement, dribbling pre-cum onto his starched, white shirt.

I may be terrified, but my voice is strong. “You will never touch me without permission. Ever. Again.”

“I relived our time together a thousand times last night.” Since Ezra can’t screw me, he’s cerebrally fucking me instead. Gripping his dick, he gives a few pumps of his wrist. “I’m nearly rubbed raw.”

“There is nothing you can do to surprise me– I’ve seen your dick three times in the past forty-eight hours. You’ve fucked my ass, raped my vagina, and now you’re masturbating to visions of my rape. That screams you’re a sick puppy.”

I show no fear in the face of Ezra’s lunacy, even if a dribble of pee is escaping to dampen my underwear.

Leaning forward, hand still enclosing his cock, Ezra is wafting menace. “You are knowingly engaging in a sexual relationship with the man who is married to my mother, while cheating on your new husband, who happens to be one of my closest friends. The man you take into your body also happens to be cheating with my partner. Excuse me if I’m…” Taking a deep breath to center himself, Ezra keeps blinking. “Enraged,” he whispers softly, at odds with the violence of the singular word’s meaning.

“Are you sure Dominion’s founders didn’t emigrate from Syn’s hometown of Rusty Knob, West Virginia, with all the incest you’ve got going on? You’re a cousin-fucking, daddy-wanting rapist. It’s a fortunate thing you have no blooded siblings. Your family tree is so twisted, you made a kid on-demand because they feared a city full of six-fingered inbred, sociopathic, one-percent-ers ruling our country into destruction.”

Stunned stupid, Ezra just stares up at me, hand frozen on his cock, mouth gaping wide open. Clearly no one has ever dished Ezra’s shit back to him.

“Who are you to judge me, *Mom?*” The evil glint in Ezra’s eye promises vengeance for my out-of-line commentary. “Your kids were made the same way I was– the same way my son was.” Snickering with his face warped into a snarl, “You married your own stepson.”

"Emphasis on *step*– but even that's a technicality, seeing as how Grant and I never married. It's not like we are first cousins, or anything." With the roll of my eyes, "Take your malfunctions up with your batshit-crazy, lesbian mother who's cheating with your fiancée, the adoptive father you want to screw, and your cousin-partner, and leave me the hell out of it." I applaud myself for my composure. "I refuse to be a cast member in your deviant soap opera."

Readying to lunge across his desk and choke me to death, Ezra's about to lose his shit. "Stop saying that about Cortez! How would you feel if one of your children was in the same situation that Cortez and I are in?"

Voice warbling, I change the subject– Syn did teach me not to poke the hornet's nest last night. "See, I'm here for two reasons. One, we have to work together here at Restraint, because I believe in what you've built."

Pausing, I decide on the fly whether or not I should voice the other reason. Everyone else sticks their head in the sand if they aren't one of Dominion's monsters. They allow themselves to be blackmailed, forced to do horrible things to the people they love and respect, and gift their children to whomever is the highest bidder. The pawns never fight back out of fear of the unknown, because of the punishments they've suffered.

I'm not a goddamn pawn– I'm the motherfucking Queen.

"The second reason is because Voldemort demands I attend your every whim. I'm not going to pretend I don't know what's going on, who's involved, or why it's happening. I will admit I have no desire to know what I know, but I refuse to pretend I don't know it. So I will do as I'm told, accepting the edicts passed down by Maître du Jeu, but what I will not do is allow you to rape me because you think you can. My body is off limits to your temper-tantruming lunacy. If you touch me, I will go straight to every single person in MdJ, and then I will tell their pawns exactly what's happening."

Gun-metal gray eyes held wide, Ezra's silence is deafening. He looks at me in utter terror– terrified of me and for me.

Realizing his heinous behavior will push his plaything to the brink, to the point his peers will take it from him and destroy it, Ezra takes a deep breath and releases it on a sigh of defeat.

"I suggest you toe the party line– you know nothing, hear nothing, see nothing, and only do as you are instructed. I will never utter a word of what you just said, because I love and respect those who would be devastated by your loss." Voice ominous, hands visibly shaking, "You have a lot to offer this world, so please exercise some self-preservation."

"I will if you exercise self-restraint," I warn, but it's more of a negotiation.

"Duly noted– my apology for my behavior last night is the fact that I'm not turning in the very person who has the power to destroy us all." Shifting, Ezra zips up his pants, then places his hands on the blotter on top of the desk like a good boy.

Ezra never planned on taking me by force tonight– he was using it as a threat if I didn't comply.

We both know where the other stands now.

"Let's get to work." Ezra reaches over to snag another rolling desk chair, placing it next to his.

With great hesitancy, I take a seat, rolling as close to the desk as I can get, so I'll be able to access the keyboards. I ignore Ezra's lusty stench tainting the air. Two of the laptops and a desktop monitor have live security feeds on them– nine boxes of black and white video each.

Taken aback, my eyes widen in awe. I recognize the rooms in the brownstone– private rooms I've only just been allowed entrance. Restraint's main club and dungeon are loaded onto the desktop monitor, usual for any place of business. One of the laptops features several cookie-cutter offices somewhere, and a bunch of rooms in Lord knows whose houses.

Examining the tiny video feeds closer, I'm a heartbeat away from bashing Ezra's skull into the desk.

"Oh, c'mon," Ezra mutters with great impatience, yanking me back into my seat. "I'll hook you up with the links to these feeds if you'll help me. It helps me sleep at night, so I don't have to go every-fucking-where to locate my loved ones. I doubt you would've appreciated me crashing your cuddle party in the middle of the night."

"What the fuck are you talking about?" I snarl, glaring down at the sight of my bedroom on the monitor.

"I have PTSD–"

"No shit!" Furious, I'm examining the angle so I can locate the camera when I get home. "You're giving *me* PTSD!"

Jesus, why didn't MdJ grant me someone else as my contact? Anyone else but Dr. Lunatic.

"–DID and OCD, and a bunch of other disorders." Ezra sighs, looking away from me as he speaks. "I was kidnapped from my bed, then Cortez and Aaron were taken. I can't get five minutes of peace unless I know everyone is sleeping soundly. Last night, I was freaking the fuck out when I came home to Shadow Haven to find Marcus not sleeping in his bed. I grabbed my laptop to find out he wasn't in Grant's bed either."

Body shaking with rage, I remember Marc's odd behavior this morning. Was he thinking of how Ezra keeps tabs on him at night? "When exactly did you put the camera in my bedroom?"

Ezra has the decency to blush, which is quite impressive on his very pale face. "I sat in your driveway early this morning, staring at the Spyder, terrified something was wrong with Marcus because I couldn't see him– I had to see him with my own two eyes. Grant saved me from myself when he exited your house."

"That motherfucker better not have–"

"Regina, no," Ezra stops me before there is bloodshed. "I had Aaron do it today." Knocking my hand away from the monitor, "I'd suggest leaving it where it lies, as I'll just barge into your bedroom next time if I can't lay eyes on Marcus to know he's safe and sound."

"You are *sick*," I hiss.

"No one will debate that fact," Ezra murmurs without shame. "I would think you'd appreciate me watching out for everyone. All safe and sound, tucked in their beds every night." Sounding beyond proud of himself, he segues into another uncomfortable topic. "I've been speaking to Katya Waters on the web as two separate personalities."

"Oh, how that must be incredibly difficult for you to do," I mutter sarcastically.

"It's surprisingly easy." Ezra's deep, hardy laugh suggests he didn't catch my sarcasm. "Katya is ignoring me. No matter how many times I ping her, she will not respond."

"How frustrating that must be for you when your victim refuses to be stalked…"

Ezra rolls his eyes at that, apparently immune to sarcasm. "One of the personalities is Kimber, a survivor of violence. The other is Dr. Jeannine– Katya's court-appointed therapist."

"How the fuck did you manage that feat?" Head cocked to the side, I stare at Ezra's tranquil face. The crazy ones always look like angels. "Never mind– if Boyd can take a million bucks out of a federally secured banking institution, then you can pay a judge off to appoint a victim's rapist as their therapist."

"My sperm-donor was the one convicted of raping Katya. Don't be so crude– stop calling me a rapist." Affronted, Ezra glances at me with sad puppy dog eyes. Seriously? "I'm being purely altruistic with Katya. She isn't getting any help whatsoever. She's in denial and it's stifling her life. I hoped it would help if I counseled Katya, because I do know the details she's refusing to acknowledge."

Baffled beyond measure, while shaking my head in disgust, I murmur, "That's disturbing on so many levels."

Ignoring reality, Ezra speaks over me. "But I do worry that it's become obvious how I'm not who I say I am. Dr. Jeannine is easy to play– female or not, a therapist never speaks about anything private. Kimber is the issue. I have the victim perfected since I'm using my own experiences to draw from, but it's the girly chatting I can't do. Katya wishes for friendship, and I have nothing to draw from that's female. I can't tell Katya what I do on a daily basis because it would utterly terrify her."

"Let me get this straight– you want me to be this Kimber person to snare an innocent woman for you." Turning to face Ezra, I glare until he'll look at me. "A woman your family has destroyed. A woman you've been stalking in the most intimate of situations, playing her therapist. Is that what you are saying?"

Jesus Christ, are ethics dead?

I always ask myself if my parents would be proud of me for my actions, even if they're used as a means of survival. A resounding **NO** echoes in my psyche. My parents are rolling over in their graves.

"Yes and no," Ezra lies flawlessly, but I can see right through his bullshit. "I'll give you the logs of our previous chats. You're a true lady, believing in female empowerment and feminism, and Katya needs someone to help her rise up. Plus, you understand girly stuff."

"Girly stuff? If by that you mean I have a vagina and tits, sure." Slumping forward, I rest my elbows on the top of the desk. "Katya isn't super girly, is she? Not that anything's wrong with that, but that's not exactly my forte. Look at me."

"I like how you look," Ezra's immediate reply sounds sincere. "I don't expect you to talk about makeup and hairstyles. I don't know what women go through," Ezra whines.

"I have no say in this at all, do I?"

"No, absolutely none," he mutters matter-of-factly.

"I have a condition," I negotiate.

"Name it." Ezra's entire demeanor changes now that he knows he's going to get his own way.

"You can't force Katya Waters to do anything. Ever. I mean *anything.* Do you understand?"

"Regina, contrary to my abysmal behavior I've displayed with you, I do have Katya's best interests at heart. I want to know her, and I want her to live a full life outside of the fear my father instilled in her. I feel responsible, guilty, and ashamed, and I'm trying to do the right thing here."

"Okay," I quickly mutter to shut Ezra up, because he's blinking uncontrollably again, and usually terrifying things happen afterward. "Just so we are both clear then. If you force Katya Waters to do anything, I will cut your dick off and stuff it down your throat."

"Crude," Ezra chastises, looking like he's sucking on a sour lemon.

"Truth," I mimic his tone. "Everything will be Katya's choice and on her timeline. You will not pull creepy shit, then play the victim when you're caught. If anything happens to her–" I reach over to grab the appendage that turned me into a victim last night. "–gone." Squeezing as hard as I can without leaving lasting injuries, I swallow down my disgust and bizarre lust as Ezra hardens in my hand.

"While I'm playing Kimber, I know I'll get attached to Katya, and I'll feel responsible should any harm befall her. You've already done the worst thing you could do to me."

"Oh, there are far worse things than having sex with me without your consent, after I'd already been inside your body," Ezra says haughtily. "Trust me on that, Regina. Worse. So much worse."

"Ezra," I growl out of frustration, because he's turning playful and that's even creepier than the stoic lunatic routine.

"I want you to feel protective of Katya." Ezra smiles serenely at me, so I know I'm in for it. "Especially since one day you may become Katya's mother-in-law."

I smack the bastard's chest, and his delighted laughter is a result.

Jesus Christ, Ezra is fucking creepy hot in the most disturbing of ways.

"It could happen," he assures. "Besides, you'd be better for the job than my mother is." Playful tone warping into something serious, Ezra holds my gaze and makes a vow. "I will not force Katya sexually. In fact, I will not have sex with her until she comes to terms with who I am to her. I will make Katya come to Dominion willingly, and she will stay willingly, and anything that happens between us will be by her choice. I make this vow, and I promise whomever is driving my body will abide by it."

Sometimes I wonder if the dissociative identity disorder is merely a coping mechanism Ezra has learned over the years. Is he a whole person, inside and out, and using this as an excuse like a child blames the dog for eating his homework, yet on a grander scale?

Noticing how I've checked out, Ezra tries to regain my attention. "Is that fair? I said you were the last of my victims, and I meant it."

"How chivalrous of you, Ezra." I swallow down the need to grab a pen off his desk and shove it into the side of his neck. "Too bad you didn't stop with your last victim."

"We're talking about my last victim right now, Regina," Ezra mutters conversationally, as if he doesn't sound fucking warped. "I promise to make up for what I did to you in the future."

"God, imagine how stress-free it would be if you didn't assault people, and then take years to make amends. Just imagine…" flows sarcastically.

"I can't have a personality transplant." Ezra shrugs, looking confused yet innocent. "I am who I am."

"Irony– says the man who may or may not have multiple personalities."

"I will do the creepy shit, as you call it, because I need the surveillance for my own peace of mind. If I don't have it, I may resort to nastier measures," he threatens.

"Jesus Christ," I hiss out of fear. "This conversation will be revisited. *Often.* I'll watch your mental state, Ezra. I mean it. Katya was hurt once, *by you*, even if your father took all the blame. Katya may not have the strength to survive a second time."

"Regina, I realize this better than anyone, which is why I'm doing it in the first place," Ezra murmurs softly, sounding contrite yet sympathetic. "This is for Katya's own good, so force her to respond, or whatever you have to do to get the message to her. We've been speaking for three years, and she's stopped responding. I'm worried, and I miss her." Voice quivering, his next order is filled with nervousness and desperation. "Find her."

Eyeing Ezra like you would a wild animal, I pull a pile of papers over, then begin reading through the chat logs Dr. Jeannine and Kimber had with Katya. Ezra was surprisingly sane and gentle with the woman, and I recognize a lot of truth in his words.

"What are your real intentions?" I ask without looking up from the conversation logs.

"Marriage and a family, and as normal a life as we can have." Ezra actually sounds earnest in his needs and wants. I wonder where that leaves Cortez in the equation.

"What of Restraint?" I mutter absentmindedly.

"Katya needs and wants BDSM, Regina. I've been talking to her for over three years. Restraint was just an idea we were toying with as Marcus taught me BDSM as a discipline and practice to work through my issues. I was almost finished with my training when I started speaking with Katya. Believe it or not, she's the one who brought it up."

"How did that conversation come about?" I quickly scan the sheets in front of me, looking for keywords to pop out at me, to make sure Ezra is being honest.

Ezra seems hesitant to answer, which piques my curiosity. "Katya said James Atwater's Roman Numeral books helped her come to terms with her needs."

"Jesus Christ, of course I can't escape him, even here."

Ezra's eyebrow raises at that, but he doesn't ask what my malfunction is– maybe he doesn't care. "The idea of Restraint became reality because I wanted Katya to have a place to explore who she is at her core."

"I have the say of when Katya comes to Restraint, Ezra," I warn, brooking no room for argument. "Kimber will persuade her."

"Fair enough," Ezra breathes, but there is a calculating bent to his tone.

"I'm changing the login and password on this account," I warn, deciding preventative measures are necessary. "I promise not to out how you're actually Dr. Jeannine, but Kimber will be me and me alone. No interference."

"May I at least sit with you while you chat with Katya?" Funny how elegant, polite, reserved, compassionate, and composed Ezra can be when he's not acting insane. I almost don't recognize this man from the one who brutally raped me, yet wanted me to seek pleasure in the violation. Ezra is a walking contradiction– maybe he truly does have multiple personalities riding him.

"Tonight, if I can get Katya to answer, but not all of the time." The thought of Ezra shoved up my ass so he can sit with me while I speak to Katya at all hours of the day and night is utterly terrifying. "I'll print out the chat logs, and deliver them daily."

"Okay." Grinning beatifically, the bastard looks angelic and innocent. Pure. Boy, how appearances can be deceiving.

"What's your plan to coax Katya Waters to Dominion?"

"A position at Edge Publishing has just unexpectedly opened up." Ezra makes a hand gesture, voice giddy. "Katya will be with us within a month or two, no longer. Her apartment is already ready."

"This is yours?" I tap the security feed. It's a modern designed living room. Even on the black and white live feed, I instinctively know it's gray. Plus, the living room is outfitted in the same microfiber chairs that are in this office– the same ones that are used in the Zeitler private room here at Restraint. Ezra must need the consistency to stay sane.

I recognize Cort's leather jacket hanging on the arm of the sofa, with a few notebooks and a laptop resting on the coffee table. That is definitely Cortez and Ezra's apartment. One of them is a binge-eater, because there are a few empty chip bags, boxes of cookies, and Coke cans scattered around the laptop.

"This is Katya's new apartment, I bet." I tap the adjacent screen. The apartment has the same layout, right down to the same major pieces of furniture, but there are more comfort items– decorative pillows, throws, and candles. There's a bookcase with empty photo frames and small knickknacks. There's a set of coasters and a runner on the coffee table. Items a man would stereotypically predict a woman would enjoy.

"Nice, isn't it?" Ezra seeks my approval, looking like a little boy wanting me to pat him on the back. Motherfucking bizarre. "Katya told Kimber what she enjoyed, and Kimber's *very* generous." Ezra giggles softly underneath his breath.

"Well played, Dr. Lunatic." I snort. I can't help but laugh with him– *at* him.

After cataloging who Ezra is spying on and where he's doing it– so I can avoid those places like the plague –I notice the third laptop has a web browser running. Pushing closer to the desk, I get to work. After five minutes of typing in commands with the IP addresses Katya uses most often, I'm able to track her movements. Then I start pinging her.

"The Lunatic, really?" I shake my head at the screen-name he chose for Kimber. "How apropos." Reading over the chat logs… "You picked me because I'm the biggest feminist you know, didn't you?"

"Um…" Ezra has the common decency to look embarrassed. "Technically the biggest, simply because the other feminist in my life is the smallest female I've ever met." Syn. "But I feared her tough-love approach, versus your friendly and compassionate demeanor."

I file that information away for later use. Ezra is terrified of Syn– good to know.

Lunatic: *Here Kitty, Kitty. Come out and chat…*

"Regina, you make me proud." Smiling, Ezra moves to pat my back, but is smart enough to let his hand drop before he makes contact with my body. "You're as diabolical as Marcus. You two will be excellent together." Ezra says this without the tone of disapproval and jealousy that is usually present.

Part of Ezra wants Marcus to be happy, while the other part wants Marcus for himself.

"I was under the impression that you didn't like the idea of Marcus being my lover, seeing as how you took to sexually assaulting me for shits 'n' giggles."

"Oh–" Ezra waves his hand, like he's clearing the air, because what he did to me was no big deal. "Balance. We were righting a wrong, and now it's all balanced. The fact that Marcus has been sharing my partner, it was only fair he shared his too."

"Sure, if said partner gets a say in it," I remind Ezra.

"You and I, I know we'll fuck again. Remember the epic orgasm?" Ezra has the balls to smile sweetly at me. "Your choice, of course."

"Of course," I sneer in disgust. "Are you going to share Katya when she gets here?" I try to get Ezra to see reason, how his logic is fatally flawed. "Do you think Katya is the type of woman who would be okay with you assaulting your father's lover? Is she going to be okay with the obsession you have for Cortez, and how you have daddy issues?"

Ezra's expression twists with silent contemplation. After a moment, he nods, arrogantly sure of himself. "If Katya wishes to share with other people, then yes, I will share her. I'm possessive– all dominants are. I guess it depends on who I'm sharing with. Cortez? As long as I'm included, and Katya wants me more and loves me best…"

"Yeah, that's gonna work out for ya, buddy." I pat Ezra's shoulder, knowing he doesn't realize I'm being sarcastic, when he thinks me supportive.

KitKat411: *Kimber?*

"Woohoo!" I clap loudly with an odd burst of adrenaline.

Lunatic: *Hey! KitKat, long time no see!*

"Enough with the exclamation points," Ezra mutters dryly. "Cortez and Grant would have your head for that. It's as distracting as it is annoying."

"There's your Ivy League education rearing its expensive head." I don't bother to turn away as I roll my eyes. "The reason you were failing with Katya was because Kimber sounded like she had a stick up her bum and a silver spoon shoved in her mouth. Kimber suspiciously sounded exactly like the overeducated, pedigreed Dr. Jeannine. A.k.a. Dr. Zeitler."

"Point taken, Regina," Ezra concedes gracefully while plotting what he will do next.

KitKat411: *I'd love to talk, but I'm on my way out to dinner with my family. Can we set up a time to chat? Sorry I've been so busy lately. I have a bunch of stuff I'm getting settled. I just found out I got a new job this afternoon.*

Lunatic: *Congratulations!!! Name the time and I will log-on. You know I'm never far from the virtual world.*

I used extra exclamation points just to piss Ezra off, who is sighing like I'm slowly killing him with my low-rent punctuation.

KitKat411: *Tomorrow evening? How about 9-ish?*

Lunatic: *That's perfect! I'll see you then. & Kat, congrats!*

KitKat411: *Thank you, Kimber. G'night.*

"Was that good?" I look at Ezra, anticipating a bitch-fest, but what I find is a man clearly infatuated with Katya Waters. Ezra's cold eyes are heated, glazed from just the thought that Katya was on the other side of a computer screen talking to us for no more than thirty seconds.

Snapping out of his frozen state, Ezra sparks back to life. "Excellent, Regina. But I can't join you tomorrow evening. My mother is dragging us to a charity function." Ezra releases a menacing growl of pure frustration.

Before I can respond to that, the door opening has me jumping in my seat.

"You didn't?" Cortez enters swiftly, fury etched across his features, but it's the betrayal and disappointment wafting from the man that has me flinching.

"Do what?" Ezra murmurs ever so innocently as he shuts the lids to all the laptops, leaving only Restraint's security cameras open on display. Hmm… interesting. "I thought you were writing this evening."

That explains the binge-food and cans of caffeine on the coffee table in their apartment.

"Why does it smell like sex in here?" Stomping forward, Cort's standing in front of the desk before I can even blink. Eyes roving up and down, taking in every inch of my body, "You didn't harm Regina again, did you?"

"Again? You know." Ezra's eyes drift shut, and his pale skin turns a putrid shade of green. Evidentially the man can feel shame.

"Goddamn you, Ezra," Cortez snarls, coming around the desk to pull me from my seat. Hands rubbing up and down my arms, he checks me over to make sure I'm healthy and hale. After reassuring himself that I haven't been violated this evening, he pulls me into a tight hug.

Eyes drifting shut, I press my face into the side of Cort's neck, needing any bit of affection and support I can find. I hadn't realized how on edge I'd been all night until someone offered to hold me upright. Cortez smells like Marcus, and I take comfort in that, even if that means Ezra will go off the rails.

Queen may not need a white knight to come to her rescue, but sometimes I do.

"I can understand why Regina didn't tell me. I get why *you* wouldn't," Cortez levels at Ezra, voice tight with rage. "I ate dinner with Dexter, Marcus, and Jamie, and not a single one of them had the balls to tell me what you'd done."

"How did you find out?" Ezra shifts in his seat, appearing as if his ass is being held over a fire. "Perhaps we're having a breakdown in communication, and you heard wrong."

"Shut the fuck up!" Cortez bellows, pointing in Ezra's face while holding me tight to his chest with his other hand, as if he can protect me from what's already come to pass. "Dalton, of all people, chased me down at Edge. Then I had Syn light into me on my way in here."

"Cort–"

"Just don't," Cortez warns Ezra in a vicious tone filled with violence. "I'm sick of your bullshit. Don't come home." Releasing me, he steps away, closer to the door and farther away from his partner. "Regina's between a rock and a hard place right now, so I don't fault her for being here with you when she had no other choice. But if you take advantage of Regina again, I'll gut you in your fucking sleep."

As quickly as Cortez arrived, he vanishes.

Here I was using threats about snitching on MdJ, or how I was going to go to Syn, when all I had to do was call my buddy, Cortez. Because Ezra looks a breath or two away from christening the desk with his shame.

"I'd suggest locating your wastebasket before you destroy the electronics."

Insane laughter bubbles up Ezra's throat instead of vomit. "Cortez knows I don't sleep," is his bizarre reply to the premeditated murder warning.

"Always looking on the bright side of things, aren't you, Mr. Optimistic? It can't be much fun to live in that apartment together when you both act like bitter, vindictive bitches who are stuck in the past. Grow up– you're a psychiatrist for shit's sake."

"Sometimes you're too close to the problem to solve it," is Ezra's genius reply.

"So step back, dumbass. You said Katya will be here in a month or two, yet you're adding fuel to the fire between you and Cortez instead of dousing it. Whatever Cort does sexually, he's been doing it forever. He stopped with the submissives here at Restraint. You may have raped me last night, but you cheated on Cortez. No doubt he saw that as a double betrayal since he and I are friends."

Ezra reaches for the wastebasket, but nothing comes up.

"Is this the type of united front you want to show Katya?" Stalking forward, I use my height to intimidate Ezra as I lean over his chair and get directly into his aristocratic face. "Is. It?"

Ezra scowls and sulks for a few moments as I stand over him. I start to feel like a bully, because clearly the guy is broken. I have no idea what's playing out in that disturbed head of his, but I know what I need to do. I need Ezra and Cort together for many reasons. The main one is that I don't want to draw an innocent woman into our fucked up web. Plus, if Ezra is happy with Cort, and hopefully with Katya, Cortez should leave Marc's cock alone.

This is where I have an enlightened inner monologue about how I'm above monogamy, and mature enough to handle its absence. Total bullshit, that. Deep down, I want a partnership, where my partner puts me first. My parents were happy and in love, and they stayed by each other's sides no matter what. They fought, and they made up, but they didn't go fuck other people to avoid their problems.

Sure, there are mature polygamous people out there. Do I think I'm capable of being one of them? Doubtful. Not with how dominant and possessive Queen is. I also don't believe Ezra, Marcus, and Cortez are mature enough to handle the toxic games they're playing– a game they keep dragging my ass into.

None of this is about being mature and enjoying sex– all of it is a power struggle between broken individuals who have been victimized, who are now going around creating new victims instead of dealing with their issues.

I need Ezra and Cortez in relationship bliss, so maybe my lover will stop obsessing about their lives and Cort's mouth.

Jamie was right about a few things, even if I don't want to accept them. He shouldn't lead Marcus on, not when Marc's life is a pile of shit. Jamie shouldn't touch me, not when I have so many men having a power struggle over my vagina.

From now on– my vagina, my choice. Even if it's the wrong choice, it will still be a choice *I* made.

Peering up at me, practically begging for my help, "How?" Ezra murmurs shyly, so sweet and innocent, and broken. "How do I fix it?"

"I must have Stockholm Syndrome," I mutter to myself, finally understanding why smart girls fall for the broken bad boy they believe only they can fix. No, I can't fix Ezra, but I have to help. It's not in my nature to turn anyone away.

"No, Regina." Ezra looks up at me, holding my gaze. "You realize I'm a human who makes mistakes. Even though I hurt you, that doesn't make me a monster."

"Jury's still out on that," I mumble underneath my breath.

Eyes darting to the side, Ezra breaks our connection. "I didn't mean it. Master Ez thought it was the perfect balance. I do agree with him, though." Voice soft, barely a whisper, I have to struggle to hear Ezra. "I lied earlier– about my dick. I'm not chaffed from jerking off to the sick memory of our coupling. It was from scrubbing myself raw. The reason I couldn't vomit wasn't because I wasn't sickened with myself. It was because everything I've ate and drank since last night immediately leaves my body and I'm empty. So very empty of everything but shame."

"Good Lord, please tell me this isn't you manipulating me." Fingers curling into fists at my sides, I understand why Marcus treats Ezra as he does– why everyone treats him as they do. "Goddamn you, Ezra."

"It's true." Gray eyes rolling up to connect with mine, Ezra's voice pitches high with hope that I believe him. "I was so scared and hurt for you while Master Ez was doing what he was doing to you last night." Blinking repeatedly, he fights to stay in control. "I've been where you were, Regina. I've seen so much…"

Flopping down into my chair at the desk, I snarl and roll my eyes, furious with myself for buying the crap Ezra is selling.

"I was powerless to stop it, but I understood why Master Ez was doing it. It's wrong what Marcus and Cortez do. The two people who should love me more than anyone on the planet– the two people who should never betray me, they betray me with each other. I know it doesn't make what I do wrong right, but it still hurts. I can't stop it– I feel so violated after they protect and avenge me."

Proving he's not a sociopath, Ezra clutches his chest, showing where it hurts. Breath coming in a pant, eyes glistening with tears, I believe this is the elusive Ezra– the integrated personality who seems ashamed of what figments of his personality do to his body when he's powerless to stop it.

"Jesus Christ." I grip his hand, realizing Ezra isn't speaking of rape in the form of a dick in his body against his will. But, rather, when your mind takes over your body to protect you, but ends up violating you instead. The whole Ezra has to take responsibility, even if he was the powerless passenger in the act.

"I just–" Ezra's fingers clench mine tight, until our knuckles turn white. "A monster turned parts of me into a monster, and I don't know how to handle it. My therapists said this is why I won't fully integrate, because then I'll have to deal with the fallout. I'm trying, Regina," Ezra stresses. "I'm about to let Cortez go if he won't change with me. I want to be whole for Katya– she deserves this person."

Ezra's pointing at himself while blinking furiously, and I realize this is his way of screaming out for help. I'm such a goddamn sucker.

"For the past three years, I've been making changes." Looking at me again, trying to get me to understand. "Something snapped in me when Cortez and I were with you. It made me furious that we had to use you like that because Cortez won't give us what we both need. He constantly punishes me– what he does with Marcus is my punishment. A big, fat '*fuck you, Ezra!*' I snapped and hurt you to hurt both of them, and that's not fair. But that's why Master Ez did it. I'm so sorry, Regina."

This is the point in my life when I begin to contemplate my own sanity. Here I sit, acting as my rapist's confessor, and I'm crying for him.

"Well, the first step in forming a united front with Cortez would be to apologize. I get that Cortez is just as wrong as you. Whatever wrongs you committed doesn't give him license to commit wrongs in retaliation."

"Cort does that." Head hanging in his hands, Ezra's voice is nearly a whisper. "It's all cause and effect between us, and I don't know how to stop the cycle. But I've been trying."

"At some point, you either have to wipe the slate clean and start again, or admit you can't and move on."

"That's where I am. Right. Now." Ezra sits up straighter, showing determination. "I told Cortez that Katya was coming home, and I was trying to get my life turned around. Either Cort forgives me for the billion times I've apologized, or he leaves with his self-righteous indignation intact. Cortez and I aren't even together, so don't go saying I'm cheating on him with you, or with Katya when she arrives."

"I think I understand that more than you realize," I muse to myself, thinking of Marcus, and Jamie, and Whitt, and now Ezra. On paper, I sound like such a slut. In reality, my worth isn't dictated by the number of dicks my vagina has taken. "You can't cheat on Cortez if you're not in a committed relationship. Just as Marcus can't cheat on me, and I can't cheat on Whitt."

"We can tell ourselves that…" Ezra commiserates, knowing damn well how much it hurts, how lonely it feels, and how our sense of worth is diminished because we don't come first in the lives of the people we love most.

"Cort bullies me until I force him to submit– on purpose, so he has no responsibility in the act. He'll tell me he loves me, makes love to me, then wakes the next morning and it's all erased, only I'm left being blamed. We've only been intimate a few times since we were eighteen, but he fucks anyone he wants while I'm to remain celibate or it's cheating… what Cortez is doing with my father–"

Blinking, voice raising, I stop Ezra's tantrum in its tracks before someone else starts driving the bus. "What do you do when you get home at night?" I prompt.

"If Cort gets home before me, we fight. There's no letting it go for him. The instant Cort lays eyes on me, he's gearing up for battle. It's so stressful– I'm always on edge, never feeling at peace, and it doesn't help my mental state."

"For fuck's sake." I love Cortez. He's one of my best buddies, but even I will agree with Ezra at this point. Now I understand Syn's '*don't poke the hornet's nest*' text. We don't need to walk around on eggshells, but Cortez ought to not instigate every waking moment.

Over the past two years, Cortez has whined to me about how Ezra is the biggest cheater for touching Adelaide, and Dexter once years and years ago when they weren't even together. I was baffled then, because she was Ezra's fiancée and they were only together a handful of times. Meanwhile, I know for a fact Cortez had screwed at least a hundred people in that time frame, including having his mouth fucked by Marcus.

Everyone has a breaking point– it's too bad I was on the receiving end of Ezra's.

Jesus Christ, am I actually rationalizing why it was okay for Ezra to rape me?

"Why do I feel like you and Cortez are Ross and Rachel from Friends?" I mutter sarcastically.

"*We were on a break!*" Ezra proves he was merely ignoring my prior injections of sarcasm while displaying his playful side. It's nice to know Ezra does other things beside plot global domination. "At least I'm Ross in the equation. Rachel was dead wrong."

I go in for the kill. "Well, I guess this is why you don't fall in love and fuck your family–"

"You're a cold bitch, Regina," Ezra mutters with appreciation. "Yeah, there is no escaping Cortez, even if we're on a break. He'll forever be a part of me, especially when I hardly have any family to speak of. It's why I allow him to treat me the way he does."

"It's done. It's over. It can't be erased or forgotten. But it can be forgiven and overcome." I chant, voicing the thoughts that got me through today, making it so I don't despise Jamie with every cell in my body. "What happens if you get home first?"

"If Cortez isn't home, I take a shower and try to relax, all the while shoring up my defenses. Then when Cortez finally comes home, he instigates a fight before he closes the door at his back." Ezra practically spits the words. "His self-righteous indignation knows no bounds, while calling me a cheater from a decade or two ago, after he just got done sucking my adopted father's dick."

"Have to say, there are always two sides of the story, and now I have both." Jesus Christ, am I truly empathizing with this bastard. Apparently, I am.

"Cortez never touches me unless it's in anger. Basically, we resent each other and our friendship is nonexistent, which is why I gave him the ultimatum and decided to see if I could find happiness with Katya instead. We seem more compatible, to be honest. Katya is an easy person to love."

"Wow," I murmur in awe.

"Yeah, wow… Katya will probably forgive me quicker for what my father did to her, while Cortez will take it to the grave, even if he had responsibility in it. Ray Hunter is Cort's uncle, not just my father, and what happened was about the both of us, not just me."

"Wow," I release again, mystified. "This is what you need to do. When Cortez tries to fight with you, ignore him. When he calms down, start a conversation that doesn't include a trigger-warning."

"What do we talk about?" Ezra gazes at me like I hold the secrets of the universe. It's amazing how a singular look can make a person feel powerful and alive. Validation supposedly comes from within, but I've yet to get the memo.

"How about Katya?" I offer up as a conversationally safe topic. "You could share what you learn about her, and share what your plans are. Bond through Katya, and it may help you move on from your past."

"I'll try," voice laced with hope, Ezra sits up straighter in determination. "If I can get Cortez to stop bitching at me for a few seconds, I may be able to get his attention with Katya news."

"Every night, why don't you try to touch Cortez with comforting affection? A hand on his arm, or any simple, nonsexual touch." As I speak I put a hand on Ezra's arm to show him what I mean. Just as I thought, he relaxes underneath my touch, though I get the feeling Ezra is a highly reserved person who doesn't allow anyone but a select few to touch him.

"Cortez won't allow me." Ezra scowls in defeat, eyes swirling like storm clouds.

"Then be relentless, Ezra– I know you can be," I mutter wryly. "If you want something bad enough, you'll get it. This is Cortez we are talking about. You'd die or kill for him, but for some bizarre reason, you won't swallow your pride by trying to connect with him."

Shifting in his seat, Ezra looks decidedly uncomfortable, like he's upset that he's not the smartest, most intuitive person in the room. "You have a point."

"Maybe try to hold Cort's hand while you chat. If he pushes your hand away, then back off and don't get angry or emotional.

Try again the next day, and then the next, and the next, until Cort will hold your hand back."

"Cortez doesn't want my touch!" The grown man whines, and I want to smack the shit out of him because of it. I don't know if I'm still speaking to the same identity as I was a minute ago. Even his voice has pitched higher, like a prepubescent boy.

"Just try. What do you have to lose? After a few times of holding Cort's hand, add something else, like maybe a kiss on the cheek before bed. It has to always be in comfort and affection–no sexual connotations –and eventually you'll bond together through touch, comfort, and familiarity. Like how it used to be. Don't you want to offer Katya a safe, happy home?"

"More than anything." Ezra sighs in frustration, scrubbing at his face with upraised palms. "Even if Katya wasn't to join us, I'd want to repair the damage between Cortez and me. I can admit that I'm at fault. Cortez is culpable for what he's doing with Marcus, but the rest is all on me."

"Ezra?" I call softly, because now he's acting like a little boy hiding his face in his hands. "I can rationalize why you did what you did to me. But what I don't get is why you did it when you knew it would make the divide between Cortez and you that much wider. You would've been better off a few days ago…" I trail off, allowing Ezra to take away from that what he will.

"It was the right thing to do." The hands drop and Ezra's angelic face reappears. "It's like when we discipline our submissives. If you do wrong and you're punished, it's over. The actions may not be erased, but they are forgiven. I don't have that with Cortez. There is no balance. No amount of rights will remove a singular wrong when it comes to him. But this isn't just about Cortez. Marcus. Marcus understands, even if he doesn't like it. Balance. With balance, there is no more guilt and shame."

I don't interrupt Ezra, but I have a sneaking suspicion this balance thing is important to his mental health, probably how his personalities need to balance each other out. The black and white, right and wrong, would be a comfort to a mind always erupting in pure chaos.

"Cort and Marcus did the wrong thing, and I'm disciplining them so they'll learn their lesson. Whereas, they've been punishing me every time they're together. We can tell someone until we're blue in the face about how something makes us feel, but they won't understand how painful it is until it happens to them. I didn't want them to hurt, but I needed them to stop hurting me."

"Yeah, what about me? I didn't do a damned thing wrong," I seethe between clenched teeth.

"I apologized, and I said I would make it up to you," Ezra offers innocently, as if he didn't hurt me beyond measure. "But do you know what hurts the worst, Regina?"

"What?" I mutter flatly, because everything pretty much hurts.

Sighing, Ezra turns to face me with tears in his eyes, as if he truly doesn't want to hurt me, but he knows his words will. "After seeing the pain and fear you experienced last night… after Cortez found me puking my guts up and scrubbing myself with bleach… after learning why… they still did it anyway."

"What?" I squawk, mind unable to allow my emotions to take me where they wish to go, which makes me feel like Ezra must all the time.

"I gave Cortez and Marcus a taste of their own medicine. I forced Marcus to feel how I feel every time he takes Cort's mouth. I know it's their decision, but it still impacts me. My actions hurt both of us, and I thought it would hurt them too. But Cortez wraps his self-righteous indignation around him like a warm blanket, and Marcus just didn't seem to care."

"Don't say shit like that," I warn, suddenly furious because I feel the gut-wrenching need to cry.

"If Marcus had felt as horrible as I felt, experiencing the torment of his lover being taken by another, then he would've never touched Cortez again. But I could smell Marc's stench wafting off Cortez when he walked in here, and I know you did too."

Ezra lunges from his seat to begin pacing the office, all the while blinking furiously to control his identities. Meanwhile, I'm blinking away the emotions threatening to spill from my eyes. Feeling sick, I hug the wastebasket, but thankfully nothing comes up.

"I know you have an inner monologue that somehow makes what Marcus and Cortez are doing okay because they were doing it before you were in the picture. How you say to yourself that you've touched Grant, fooled around a little bit with Pretty Boy, and was taken by me, so you don't deserve loyalty and faithfulness or exclusivity. But your actions do not erase Marc's inaction and reactions."

"You're right," I murmur, remembering my thoughts on being mature, and how I wasn't *that* mature. "When I'm away from them, it hurts. When I'm with them, it makes sense. It seems natural for them to touch, not a perversion or betrayal… just natural."

"CORTEZ WON'T FUCKING TOUCH ME!" Ezra bellows in torment, causing the paintings on the wall to vibrate and the pen cup to tip over.

Tears streaming down his rage-reddened cheeks, Ezra looks on the verge of a complete and total mental breakdown. Flinching back, I freeze at the sight of Ezra's agonized fury.

Calming slightly, voice breaking from the strain yelling placed on his vocal cords, "Cortez touches Marcus– cuddles with him. Cortez gives Marcus what he refuses to give me. They love each other." Bending at the waist, Ezra doubles over, sobbing violently.

"They aren't in love with each other like you and Marcus are, but it doesn't matter. It's not even about the blowjobs anymore. Their needs feed one another. But it's gotten to the point in their codependency where the blowjobs are just foreplay for something far greater they both refuse to acknowledge."

"I can't– I can't do this, Ezra," I stammer, terrified as my emotions threaten to drown me while Ezra's drain me dry. "I'm your ally, because you want Cortez and I want Marcus. But I don't want them like this. I want Marcus to choose me, and not by default. I'm already struggling against the ghost of Grant being Jamie. I accept your apology, but all you've done is ruin something I was feeling good about when I got up this morning."

"What?" Ezra's head cocks to the side, like a hawk sighting prey, as if happiness is a foreign concept. "What did you feel good about?"

"After Jamie left us, I knew he was no longer someone dividing Marcus and me. I felt closer to Marc than ever. Now, while I listen to your problems, they're turning into mine. Because even without Jamie tearing our goddamn hearts out, I have Cortez to worry about now."

"You should be worried, Regina." Ezra slowly approaches me, then retakes his seat. "I know I am."

"I was feeling good, outside of what you'd done to me, Jamie abandoning me once again, and dealing with MdJ, all because Marcus was my equal partner. But you had to point out how Marc fucked Cort's face tonight, not giving a shit how that would make you or I feel."

"The truth hurts," is Ezra's answer, but I'm finished with him for the night.

I storm out of our shared office, door clanking shut behind me. I need some fucking support after playing therapist to the twisted sonofabitch, Dr. Zeitler.

Chapter Twenty-Three

Running blindly, I make it two feet down the hallway before I run head-long into a tiny yet solid person. Palms pressed against my chest, holding me steady, for a split-second I hope Syn will comfort me. But the enraged expression on her face has me drawing back.

"Regina," Syn says curtly, gazing up at me from nearly a foot below, but somehow it feels like the younger, shorter, smaller woman is looking down her nose at me. "We need to talk."

"Why do I feel like a husband right now, when his wife says that the instant he comes in the door after working late?"

"Cut the sarcasm." Staring me down, Syn folds her latex-enclosed arms over her chest. My mind cannot rationalize how this woman, covered in black from head-to-toe, with piercings all over her face, tattoos peeking out at me from the collar of her shirt, and blonde hair dyed inky black is the same girl I used to know.

Whatever happened to Faith Simpson that turned her into the sadist Syn, I don't want it to happen to me too.

"You need to make better choices, Regina," Syn chastises me– ironic, considering I was just mulling over her decisions. "Especially now that you're working here at Restraint," and '*being MdJ's bitch*' goes without saying. "Whatever is going on with you and Ezra must remain even-keeled."

Head cranking backward as if struck, "Are you fucking shitting me?" I blurt out, stunned beyond measure. "Like seriously, what the actual fuck? It's none of your goddamn business, but Ezra and I made amends."

"Good." With a quick glance down the hallway, Syn shifts on her feet, then looks back up at me, obviously uncomfortable. "I don't know how to tell you this, okay?"

Heart beating out of my chest, the need to run back into the office and grab the wastebasket is upon me. "What?" I squeak out.

“Listen, I’m not a bitch. Okay?” Syn looks up at me earnestly. “I do care about you, Regina. I’ve done my best to protect you, and a lot of people have done the same. We left you alone to your own devices as long as you stayed out of our hair. We will continue to do so–”

“As long as I continue to do whatever you ask,” I interrupt, pissing an already volatile woman off.

“We offer you more respect than the others,” Syn points out. “But I refuse to treat you all girly-girly, where we do lunch and be giddy sisters-in-law.”

“No shit,” I mutter bluntly, eyeing the woman like she’s a cold-blooded killer. I can’t see Syn even eating at a table, let alone in a restaurant. She probably kills her own food, skins it for her leather outfits, and then eats it raw.

“Your actions impact your children, Regina.” Syn steps forward, getting into my personal space, but it’s so we won’t be overheard by a group of women passing by to enter the ladies room. “You need some self-respect. Do you want Ella to mirror your behavior? Do you want her to think it’s okay for men to treat her the way they do you?”

“The. Fuck?” I squawk, then curl my body down to Syn’s, proving I’m older, taller, smarter, and stronger. “Listen here, bitch. You don’t even know my daughter.”

“If someone farts in Dominion, I smell its stench,” Syn snarls, baring perfectly blunt teeth, when one would expect them chiseled to points by body modifying artists. “I know every detail of your downward spiral over the past few days.”

“Then you know it’s not my fault,” my voice quivers with rage and injustice.

“Bullshit!” Syn snaps, looking like she just ate shit. “Take responsibility for your actions, for once. Don’t go around saying how strong you are, yet allowing everyone to lead you around by your vagina.”

“Says the woman who was dating Cortez?” I throw Syn’s dirty laundry back in her face. “While fucking Ezra– made his spawn. Your son must be evil incarnate.”

Not even breaking a sweat, this woman has a serious set of steel balls and an iron-clad sense of self. “I was sixteen, Regina. I was a child, an orphan. By eighteen, I didn’t have a choice. I’ve made mistakes and I learned from them.”

“So get off your high-horse and quit calling out mine,” I mutter venomously into Syn’s heart-shaped face.

"My mistakes were in the past– yours are in the present. You've fucked more people in the last seventy-two hours than I have in my entire life."

"I bet we share those same notches on our bed posts, little girl," I hiss with arrogance lacing my voice. "I only count Marcus and Grant. That shit with Cortez and Ezra… besides, who I fuck doesn't change who I am."

"I'm not even talking about Cortez and Ezra." Syn tries and fails to keep the smirk off her face, but it's the look of pity that follows that has me falling backward to prop up against the hallway wall. "Your recent choices are lunacy. We all know we can't trust Cortez and Ezra–"

"I hear a but in there somewhere," I mutter, all energy fleeing me, sensing my world is going to shift on its axis again. "Just say what you came here to say, because clearly hurting me is on your agenda tonight, when I've been bitch-slapped nonstop for the past few days. Just kick me in the kidneys while I'm down."

Sighing, the girl I used to know peeks out of Syn's badass persona for a split-second. Reaching forward, she rubs my forearm to comfort me, which means the news is bad. Very bad.

"I understand everything with Whitt, okay? I don't blame you. No one does. It's even admirable how you're making him wait until his birthday. I honestly believe you are a very moral and ethical person, and I'm sorry you have been put through things that are outside of your control. But you need to get some goddamn self-respect, because you have a son and daughter to raise by example."

"Explain," I order. "Cut the foreplay. Explain. Now."

"I've known Grant since I ran away. He's helped me through many bad times– I won't even go there. I've known him since he was with you, and I've known him the entire time he's been James Atwater. Okay?"

"Hurry up," I snarl, heart beating so fast I'm about to faint.

"You're better than all of this, Regina. You should be angry, for yourself and your children. What Marcus and you did with Grant last night should've never happened. It was wrong– for *you.* Neither of those men deserve you, and the fact that you think you deserve their maltreatment is the problem."

"A man won't respect you unless you respect yourself," I utter words of advice my mother had told me, words I've passed onto Ella and my girls. "If they aren't held accountable for their disrespect, they will always disrespect you."

"Exactly." Syn rubs my arm in solidarity. "I've been with my partner since I met him at fifteen. He's raised Zane as his own. We have our problems, which I won't discuss with you. But I do understand how lines get blurred and multiple partners are necessary for the exorcising of ancient demons– like with Marcus and Cortez."

"I'm being shamed by you because I don't have a reliable man?" I mutter incredulously.

"No." Syn shakes her head, inky strands getting caught on her piercings. "For loving unreliable, unavailable men whose actions belie their words. No one came to your rescue after what Ezra did, don't you find that odd?"

"Cut me deep while you're back there." I gesture to my back. "Thanks for calling me unlovable."

"Women fuck men because they think that will keep them around. Grant left early this morning–"

"We're going through some shit," I mutter, wondering if that's the truth. "Some women fuck men because they enjoy sex with that person. If we feminists believe who a woman has sex with doesn't define her, then you can't judge her for who she's been with. That's hypocritical, *Faith.*"

"How many times does that man have to reject you, Regina?" Syn cocks her head to the side in a practiced move that Ezra used earlier. Ezra and Syn are like a one-two-punch of demoralization. "If a man wants to be with you, he'll be with you. If he doesn't, he'll leave you. *Twice.*"

"You cunt," I seethe through gritted teeth.

"Men should earn the right to enter a woman, because it feeds their primal urges to hunt and capture. You don't run, you don't lie down and let them catch you– you throw yourself in their path, and then cry because they don't think you tasty enough to capture and kill."

Visibly shaking, even my teeth chatter. "You. You are a piece of work, you know that?"

"Grant runs off, and you let him come by for a booty-call. You want a partner, a housemate, a lover who will do foreplay and make love, right?"

"Don't most people?" I shrug, confused. "Don't say you don't. It's not that odd of a request."

"But you settle for less than that, when an empowered woman wouldn't." Syn twists the knife deeper in my emotional wound. "Marcus won't let you suck his cock, tells you he loves you after pounding your crotch with little care to your enjoyment, then goes to the one he really wants to suck his dick. Remember, if a man–"

"I get it, okay?" Voice cracking, I feel ashamed of myself on so many levels, I want the floor to swallow me whole. "This isn't some angsty romance novel between too many star-crossed lovers. Marcus is married, which is a great excuse to avoid commitment with me. He tosses Whitt at me, ensuring I can't commit to him for at least the next four years of my life. Jamie tells me he's on a quest to find himself, then runs off again, leaving all of his shit in my lap. Marcus says we're partners, then goes and has needs I can fulfill met by another, when I'm more than willing to feed that need. Then he refuses to fill my needs. I. Get. It. Faith. *I get it.*"

"Then I suggest you get some self-respect," Syn demands. "Show your daughter how women don't wait around for a man to mistreat them. Be that empowered woman you are meant to be."

"Did you just use the same poetic pentameter as the Be All You Can Be in the Army?"

Syn looks at me, fights a laugh, then gets pissed off more so than before. The piercing in her lip is about to jump off her face and stab me in the eye.

"Seriously, stay away from Ezra." Syn shakes her head, trying so very hard to remain angry when she wants to laugh. "Your personality is like candy to him."

"You and I are nothing alike, accept from our varying approaches to feminism."

"Exactly. Cortez had a thing for me because I sound like Ezra." Raising a perfectly manicured and dyed midnight eyebrow, "You sound like Cortez."

"Shit!"

"As I was saying before you so rudely interrupted me." Syn stares down at me again, from almost a foot below me. "If you're ready for a partner, one you wish to be a part of your daughter's life, perhaps the man getting his dick sucked by his son's partner is not a good fit for you. Grant–"

"I can't take anymore," I mutter, hand out to stop Syn from speaking any further. Stride cutting down the hallway toward the club proper, I leave her by Ezra's office door. "Leave me alone."

"Regina?" Syn calls after me. "Queen wouldn't pine for the man who was arriving at my mother's house as I was leaving."

Feet stilling, my head twists to the side like I'm in The Exorcist. I stare Syn down, and all I see reflected back at me is pity.

Syn's next words have me on the edge between puking and murder. "Perhaps Grant's quest to find himself took him to Gwen's front door."

Bedroom. Syn meant her mother's bedroom.

Gwen. The original Whittenhower Mistress. Whitt's mother. The one Grant loved and lost. Jamie didn't leave me to go find himself, waiting for me to find myself too. He left after getting a goodbye fuck to go find Gwen.

Gut twisting, I nearly fall to my knees in agony, but Syn's next words are the final nail in my coffin. "Reality check. Actions speak louder than words, Regina. There aren't any obstacles keeping you and Grant, or even you and Marcus, apart. Nothing is keeping Grant and Marcus apart, as they spent the day together. Grant only broke it off with *you*."

Closing my eyes in defeat, I lean against the wall for support. Fuck my world tilting on its axis. The motherfucking axis broke off and is floating in outer space somewhere.

"It's not you, Regina. It's their dicks wanting in other people, because your pussy isn't made of gold and the sex is mediocre at best. They all either want to be deep inside or have a dick deep inside their assholes, because women aren't good enough for them."

"You are disturbed," I mutter, feeling Syn's self-loathing emanating from her all the way at the mouth of the hallway. Mind lighting on the things Marcus said about Levi Wilson and their time trapped together in Vegas, I come to a conclusion. "Is this about me, or your partner? Are *you* not good enough for Levi?"

"Grant was only with you as his cum-dumpster. After he fulfilled his duty to beget heirs, he ran away and hid from you, had his friends and family hide him from you as you grieved. It's not that they think you don't need their love and support, because you're strong enough to survive without it– it's because they don't think you deserve it. They can't respect a woman who acts like you do, pretending to be all strong when you're actually weak and needy. It *is* your fault– all of it, for not standing up for yourself and telling them to fuck off. You should have fought back!"

"You are a sadist," I breathe, tears threatening to burst if I blink. "An arrogant, sadistic, judgmental bitch, who clearly has a score to settle with me."

"I'm a realist who has protected myself since I was sixteen, with no help from anyone. If I could do it, surely a billionaire genius who is two hundred pounds and six foot tall should have been able to do the same."

"You just got lucky, little girl," I whisper in a dead voice. "You just got lucky."

"It's not luck– it's called not being a fucking idiot, Regina. They aren't *your* men. First you tried with Roman. Then Grant. Even Stanton and Julio. Jackson and Daniel. Whitt. Marcus. Back to *your* precious Jamie and Alex. Lately it's been Cortez. Now Ezra. Stand on your own goddamn two feet and support yourself. You don't own all the men in Dominion."

"What? Are you jealous?" I mock Syn. "Don't you rely on your partner? Or are you taking your problems with him out on me?"

"Even after suffering as I have, I still managed to raise my son by myself, and my nephew too. You abandoned your own child."

"And your mother abandoned you," I remind Syn. "Gwen the Whore abandoned all of her *many* children."

"Grant apparently has a type– gross how you lowered yourself to achieve it." Syn stares me dead in the eyes, fury warring with pity. "They aren't yours– they belong to other people, and you belong to no one."

"Fucking cunt," I snarl over my shoulder as I stalk into the club. Taking one look at the horror and violence etched across my face, patrons *run* to get out of my path. My eyes seek the bar, finding Kris having a good time, and all I can think to do is take a bottle and get pass-out drunk.

Feet taking me in that direction, my eyes light on another option, wrenching me because my feet point one way and my head another. Copacetic, my system syncs back up, and I find myself striding across the club to a booth where Roman and Dexter are having a drink and a good laugh.

"Hey, Reggie–" Roman's smile freezes on his face as he takes in my expression. I have no idea what I look like right now, but judging from Dexter's wide-eyed expression, it's not good. "What's wrong? Did something happen? Ezra?"

Dexter is sliding from the booth, readying to avenge my honor, which unfreezes me slightly. Here is a sadist who manages to be compassionate and protective, and we're practically strangers. I guess Syn would have me feeling ashamed of myself, seeing as how a smaller man is trying to protect my mammoth ass when I should be doing it myself.

"Ezra and I aired our grievances." I wave my hand in the air. "It's not forgotten or forgiven, but it will be worked out with my therapist at a later date," I mutter in a dead voice. "Hook me up with some weed," I order Roman.

Choking on his drink, Roman covers his mouth with his palm, sputtering beer all over the booth's tabletop. Dexter laughs, then slides back into his seat, always waiting for the next airing of the Mistress & Master of Restraint drama played out live before him nightly.

"Reg, you know I don't deal anymore." Roman's eyes flick toward an uncontrollably guffawing Dexter.

"Bullshit– ante up, Mr. Mellow."

Roman thinks I'm joking, but one glance at my take-no-prisoners expression has him doing a double-take. "Regina?" Roman leans in closer to me, whispering. "I'm a drug and alcohol counselor and a life couch. I don't deal or do drugs."

"Again, I shall repeat. Bull-*fucking*-shit. I wondered what the major difference was between Grant and Jamie–" Dexter and Roman flinch at the vicious tone in my voice. "He's sky high and mellowed out, and I need some."

"Why?" Roman demands, reaching for my wrist.

I yank my arm out of Roman's reach before he makes contact with my flesh. Yet again, I feel betrayed by him. Roman was supposed to be my friend. He spent the afternoon with me, watching me suffer over the loss of Jamie, and he never once told me what Syn just did. Syn told me to be a cunt. Roman should have told me so I could guard my heart against this agony I'm suffering right now.

"You and I," I mock Roman. "We were supposed to be real to each other, true?"

“Yeah?” Roman replies hesitantly, ending on an upward inflection of confusion, making his answer sound like a question. “Regina, you’re scaring me.”

“Either give me something to mellow me out, or I’m going over to the bar and telling Kris to hand me an unopened bottle. Both will impair my judgement. One will relax me, but the other will depress me. Your choice.”

“Why?” Dexter looks at me from head to toe, and I’m ready for him to find me lacking as usual. But this time he sees something he hadn’t before, and smiles at me faintly.

“It’s either forget my own name, or murder half the population of Dominion to protect the other half,” I answer in all honesty. “One is possession and a hundred dollar fine. The other is life in prison for a premeditated murder crime-spree.”

“Going after Ezra, are ya?” Roman laughs that goddamn, condescending laugh men make when they think a woman is either being cute or fucking stupid. Every woman on the planet has heard it too many times to count. Dexter doesn’t join him.

“No, but I’m sure Ezra will ride shotgun if I ask him,” I deadpan, not a single muscle in my body twitching. “Something tells me we could bond over bloodshed. Maybe paint our faces crimson and fuck in the spilt blood afterward, since no one gives two shits if Ezra shoves his dick in me or not.”

Dexter crawls over the top of the booth, hand reaching to pull something out of the front pocket of Roman’s jeans. Once he’s seated again, rolling papers materialize out of nowhere, which he’s filling from the Altoid can he commandeered from Roman.

Lickity split, Dexter rolls a joint right on the table in the middle of Restraint, before God Himself, completely without shame or judgement.

Clearly Dexter imbibes, and Roman is his dealer– they probably toke up together. Roman never used his product– the hardcore drugs were more in demand, but I remember Roman not looking at pot the same way.

All of Maître du Jeu ought to light up and refrain from torturing one another. Someone should hold Syn down and force a special brownie or two down her gullet– maybe Levi would screw her then, so she’d leave my sex life alone. The little girl needs to fucking chill out.

"Don't smoke this until you get home," Dexter warns in a sympathetic voice as the joint passes from his fingertips to mine. "I get where you're coming from, Queen. If you need anything at all, you know where to find me."

Yeah, but if I ask for help, I'll be judged by Syn for doing so. She'll add Dexter to my list of damsel-in-distress saving men– a list she liked to imply I've fucked as repayment for services rendered.

Nodding my thanks, I tuck the joint into my bra. Then I gaze at a gobsmacked Roman. "I don't give a fuck, buddy. Go over to the bar and tell Kristal how off the rails I'm being. Don't bother with your mute, because he doesn't care either way."

"What's up with you?" Roman just stares at me with confusion and a little bit of hurt. "What happened?"

"What hasn't happened?" My answer amuses Dexter, and I realize he got most of the sense of humor gene in the Zeitler family. "Everywhere I look, people are lying, betraying, judgmental, self-righteous, hypocritical assholes."

"Yeah, I think Queen's answer sums that up," Dexter mutters wryly, trying hard not to crack a smile.

Sure, I'd love to think Dexter's on my side, but he did have dinner with four assholes on my shit-list. Jamie. Marcus. Cortez. Roman. So, nah– I'm going to err on the side of caution and just not trust Dexter.

"Let's just say, I was given a reality check, and leave it at that."

"Reg–" Roman reaches for me again, but I step away. "Do you want me to drive you home?"

"I don't need anything from anybody for any reason ever again," is my answer as I walk away.

"I think that was Regina's polite way of saying *no thank you*," Dexter's voice follows me. "Or maybe she meant *fuck off*."

Chapter Twenty-Four

Thankfully I make it home, by the sheer grace of God, before I took my frustrations out on innocent pedestrians for simply existing. Clutching my steering wheel, I imagine the satisfying crunch of metal-on-metal if I were to floor it as I enter my driveway and plow straight into Fate's sporty car.

I don't– but I want to.

Slamming the front door shut behind me, I speak into the living room, in case anyone is in the vicinity. "I need to be alone."

Movement registers as Fate breezes down the hallway toward my daughter's bedroom. It's a good thing I didn't look at my best friend's face, seeing as how her baby sister is her doppelganger. In this fit of rage, I may end up pounding Fate's face simply because it reminds me of Syn.

I bet every goddamn one of them look like Gwen the Whore.

Now my inner voice suspiciously sounds like Marcus.

I wonder if this is what it's like for Ezra every minute of his life. This consumable, uncontrollable urge to do *something*, because it's like bees are stinging your brain and you hope your actions will make it stop.

With how I feel right now, knowing I have the strength and ability to do real damage to those I love, I can sympathize with what Ezra did to me. I don't like that I was the one who took the brunt of the pain, but I *get* it now.

Stalking toward the dining room table, I wonder if I'm a piss-poor excuse of a mother. Would my mother be proud of how I'm raising Ella? Syn made it sound as if I've had a revolving door of men coming and going from my home. When it was only this morning with Marcus– ever.

I've kept parts of me separate to remove any undue influence on my daughter, but maybe it wasn't good enough. How much of a saint do I need to be to please someone with such exacting standards as Syn? I was celibate for nearly a decade, during my twenties no less. In the eighteen months since, I'm only counting Marcus and the repeats with Grant turned Jamie.

A woman my age to have loved and fucked only two men is a unicorn. What does Syn want from me? I know for a fact she has more notches on her bedpost. What a hypocrite, calling herself a feminist, buying into the stereotypes that men can't help themselves but to rape, that the more women they sleep with the better, and the number a woman has had sex with determines her worth. Too many and she's worthless. Not enough and she's unwanted and unlovable. Value increased or decreased because a man shoved a dick into a woman's body, whether she wanted him to or not. Yeah, that sounds fair. I wasn't aware Syn was the sex police, determining what is right and wrong for everyone about everything.

I've always known I wasn't a good enough, strong enough mother to raise Niel. Sure, I sound sexist because I felt I was a better fit to raise Ella. Niel belongs where he is, even if that makes me feel guilty, as if I abandoned my son on the same night Grant abandoned us all.

Fuck– I am a piss-poor excuse of a mother. Syn's right.

As I pass by the table, my hand snatches up the candle lighter, then I make my way through the French doors and out onto the enclosed back patio and pool area. Slumping down on a chaise, I put my feet up and kick off my flip-flops.

"Hmm…" I hum, rolling the joint between my thumb and index finger while staring at it with utter fascination. "What does a girl do when she finds out not one, but two, of her lovers are cheating on her?"

Staring at the joint, I contemplate how I really feel. "Worthless. Powerless. Not good enough. Ugly. Too tall. Too fat. Too strong yet not strong enough. Too much woman for some men, yet not enough for others. Too smart, yet too stupid for the likes of Boyd. Gullible yet jaded. Powerful yet weak. Intimidating yet socially awkward. Lonely yet smothered. A slut yet sexually inept. Mediocre."

Placing the joint between my lips, with the press of my finger, the lighter ignites to kiss flame to the tip. Drawing in a deep inhale, my truth rolls out my mouth along with the intoxicating smoke.

"Unlovable."

As I methodically inhale and exhale, waiting for the buzz of the enraged hornet's nest in my mind to settle, my eyes drift shut to close out the view before me. The pool reminds me too much of why I enclosed it in the first place. For months, Marcus ignored me. The loneliness was suffocating, debilitating. I swam to escape the inescapable.

Syn said if a man wants you, he'll come after you.

In those months after I left the brownstone, no one came after me.

No one.

Only the possession Marcus felt, knowing he was handing me off to Whitt, drew him to me. While sitting in the car at Restraint, just before my initiation, my life as I knew it began to change. Hard to believe, Marcus and Jamie were only back in my life for just over forty-eight-hours. Sure, a lot happened in that timeframe, and I've changed at a cellular level, but that doesn't mean *they've* changed.

This morning, Marcus left a happily ignorant Regina who thought we were equals. I thought we were going to deal with our pain over Jamie together. Marcus was angry at Jamie for abandoning us, but then he ran off to join the rat this evening, instead of being there for me when I needed him the most... of course, Marcus had to have Cort suck him off, since apparently I'm too shitty of a lover to perform that sex act.

Even Whitt got what he wanted from me, then left to go do his own shit.

From one inhale to the next, my legs are drawn up to my chest with my arms locked around my knees. Then the sobs come, flowing out of my throat in a primal song of grief and shame.

Is Syn right? Am I too needy? A damsel in distress? Right now, I'd love to call out for help, have someone comfort me, because why should I suffer alone if I don't have to? I suffered for a goddamn decade, longing for someone who didn't want me.

Because I'm a glutton for punishment, I test Syn's theory, even knowing it will hurt when I find out she's right.

Cellphone in hand, I call Jamie first, knowing he'll text me back immediately as always. If he doesn't, then he truly has cut me out of his life for being a toxic train wreck.

"Hey– it's me. I just..." a heavy sigh escapes me as I contemplate what to say. "I just feel so alone and worthless right now, guilty and *asha*–" voicemail cuts me off from finishing.

Ashamed.

I regret my message instantly, realizing I'm acting exactly as Syn said I would. Needy, clingy, chasing the man instead of having him come to me. But how is he to know I need him unless I tell him in the first place?

In the past, when Jamie was Grant, he would become livid when I waited to tell him I was upset. He'd say I was being stubborn, how everyone needed a support system, and I was cutting his balls off because I wouldn't let him help shoulder my burdens.

But that version of Grant no longer exists, and Jamie didn't text me back… just as Syn said he wouldn't.

As soon as I dial Whitt's number, I'm sent directly to voicemail, which means he pressed *ignore*.

"Hey, Sunshine," I quickly whisper into the phone, now knowing how long of a message I can make. "Tell Kent I wish him luck with the campaign, and take a selfie with Niel for me, would ya? Bye."

Ringing and ringing in my ear, my heart breaks with every passing second.

This is Marcus. If I wanted you to know where I was, you'd already be there, so just leave a message.

"I just wanted to hear your voice," I ramble inaudibly. "I guess I'll see ya when I see ya."

Phone in hand, I contemplate calling my son, but I don't want to be a bother. We just reacquainted ourselves, and I don't want to smoother Niel to the point he dreads when I call him.

They aren't yours– they belong to other people, and you belong to no one.

I'll probably have Syn's voice whispering negativity in my ears for the rest of my life. Crawling from the chaise, I palm the ground to gain leverage to stand, and then I listlessly lean against the house, making my way to the French doors leading to my bedroom.

A ghostly apparition appears before me, hair a white halo in the moonlight. I don't even startle– pot is a glorious thing.

"I wasn't aware marijuana contained hallucinogenic properties," I mutter sarcastically to my unwanted yet welcomed guest. "What are you doing here, Ezra, stalking outside my bedroom door?"

Earlier tonight, I would have literally been pissing my pants should this event came to pass. Now… I leave the door open for Ezra to follow. Of course, when I catch a faint whiff of Marc's and Jamie's combined scent wafting in the air, the gut-wrenching sobs renew.

“I was worried about you.” Ezra pats my shoulder in a platonic gesture of comfort. “I heard what Syn said, so I followed you after I gave her a piece of my mind.”

Cries ceasing, “She make you feel like shit too?”

“Yeah, but I have psychotropic drugs for that, so I don’t have to bum pot off Roman via Dexter.” Ezra shows his sarcastic side. Nice.

Falling to land ass-first at the foot of my bed, I rest my head in my hands. “Why are you here?” I ask my question again, using different words, hoping for the truth.

“Because I know how you feel right now.” Ezra sits next to me, but doesn’t move to touch me. “You’re gutted over what Syn revealed, while Marcus is off doing whatever he’s doing–”

“He’s doing Cortez,” I interrupt.

“He is,” Ezra agrees, voice cracking. “I have a live security feed to prove it.”

“Jesus Christ, whatever you do, don’t show me.” Shuddering, I wrap my arms around myself, trying to get a hug anywhere I can get it. “I don’t think I could survive watching.”

“Not right now, no,” Ezra agrees– he’s being too agreeable. “So you’re feeling gutted while Marcus is doing Cortez, completely dismissive to your pain. I’m in the same boat, different port.”

“Oh, my fucking Lord!” I shout, completely floored. “You just made a joke!”

“Regina,” Ezra’s hoity toity tone is back in action, but he’s teasing me. “Do you have to exclaim when you speak? I thought we covered this earlier.”

“I wish I’d known you before you…” I trail off. “I think I may have liked you.”

“Well, I am a man who is rather hard to ignore.” Ezra shoulder bumps me. “I’m just a man, Regina. I’m not a monster– I promise not to hurt you. I honestly wish I could self-harm to take the guilt away, but my meds erase the urge.”

“Damn those pharmaceutical companies for finally getting something right.” I grin at Ezra, realizing the benefits of the pot have finally kicked in. “I don’t know if I’ve been this down before, not even when my parents died– after Grant was a blur.”

“I did come here for a reason.” Ezra stands from the bed, too curious to sit when he could explore my private possessions. The man even cracks open my dresser drawers. “I’m going to put your mind at ease, because I need help getting my partner away from yours. Then, if you're agreeable, I'll show you something."

"To be honest, that petrifies me."

"It should." Ezra disappears into my closet, coming out with a t-shirt clutched in his hands. "Cort would love this." He holds up my Kings of Leon concert t-shirt.

"Put it back," I order, pointing, and Ezra pouts better than most babies.

Next Ezra returns with a pair of suspenders, completely baffled as to why I own a pair. "I've known Faith since forever, but we became friends at sixteen, then mutual prisoners by our families, then parents at age eighteen. If you're in the trenches with someone, you learn how they tick."

"That's how I feel about my girls." High or not, nothing is as amusing as watching Dr. Lunatic trying on my suspenders.

"Faith is judgmental– a right-fighter, only seeing things from her point-of-view." Running his fingertips along the suspenders, Ezra rocks back on his heels. Clearly his meds aren't working enough. "Faith is literally the judge, jury, and executioner, but she's grown more arrogant and narrow-minded over the years. I may be nuts, but I understand being a fuckup and the valuable lessons you learn from it. While Faith believes you should've never fucked up in the first place."

"Yeah, I gathered that." Shame seeps in, and it vaguely sounds like Syn.

"How can you learn and evolve without a past to propel you forward?" After unsnapping the suspenders, Ezra runs them along his palm. "While Faith is right from her perspective, she's wrong from yours. Since Faith wasn't talking about herself, her perspective doesn't matter. She doesn't get a vote on how you feel, act, or react. That is inherent in your emotional makeup, and can't be altered. It has to be from your perspective, from Marc's, from Grant's. Do you understand?"

Color me shocked, but I can't believe the words are flowing from my mouth. "You're actually a proficient and caring psychiatrist, aren't you?"

Pale skin blushing, Ezra looks pleased with himself. "You really helped me earlier when I needed you, even though by all rights you should have cut my dick off. I appreciate that, so I'm returning the favor. But, yes, I do an amazing job for my patients, because I've been *there*. I can empathize with them. It's why I want Katya here, because I can help her."

"If you help Katya, you'll feel better about the past, won't you?"

"It will be a major burden lifted off my shoulders, even if all I do is give the woman a job and a fresh start at having a life outside of fear." Ezra returns my suspenders to my closet, then comes back out with a belt. Bizarre.

"Faith was only seeing from the outside looking in, so her view is skewed. Yes, Marcus is with Cortez, and I hate it. But I'll demonstrate why later, if you let me. Yes, Marcus ran off to see Grant today. Syn made it sound salacious, when it was a family dinner they have on a weekly basis." Pouting again, "One I'm excluded from attending."

"They don't invite you?" I blurt out, awed.

"No." Ezra folds my belt in two, then snaps his own thigh. Ouch. "If I get near Dexter, Cortez loses his shit. So *I* was the one excluded." He draws out, then he says in a hurry. "And Grant, Roman, and Cortez are usually furious at me because of–"

"Voldemort?"

"Exactly." Ezra smiles brightly. "Enemy camps at the dinner table make for uncomfortable conversation."

"Christmas must be a blast." I fall back on my mattress, relaxed– high.

"Jewish." Ezra points at his chest. "The enemy camps are divided during Jesus' birthday celebrations to maintain peace on Earth and goodwill toward men, and all that Christianity bullshit."

Giggling, I roll around on my mattress. I'm never smoking weed again. I don't giggle.

"Gwen–" my animalistic growl gives Ezra pause. "I don't know if Grant is fucking her or not. I'd venture on the side of not."

"Why was he at her house then?" I challenge.

"Hell, Regina, *I* was at Meyers' Manor today. It's the… central location, and I'll leave it at that. But just know, while everyone jokes by calling her Gwen the Whore, I can read people pretty well. I've never been within ten feet of the woman since I was a child, even while inside her house during a meeting– Gwen's a walking trigger warning."

"Did Syn purposefully mislead me?" I struggle to sit up on my bed, heavy ass sinking into the mattress.

“No. As I said, it’s about perspective.” Ezra gingerly sits on the bed next to me. “I told you earlier why I chose you instead of Faith to act as Kimber, and you just learned the painful lesson of why. I fear Faith will be horrible to Katya, but in a meaning well sort of way. My son sucked all the empathy out of his mother in utero.”

“Ha. Ha. Ha.” The giggles are coming uncontrollably.

“You laugh, but I’m not kidding.” Ezra arches an eyebrow, then waggles it. “Would you shower with me?”

“Naked?” I squawk in shock.

“No, fully clothed in a snowsuit and skis.” Rolling his eyes, Ezra demonstrates he has a master’s in sarcasm. “I’ve seen you naked. I’ve been in your ass and pussy. I suggest we try a new *port* of entry.”

Good humor dissolving from my features, I grumble, “That joke’s been played out.”

“You said you had both sides of the story earlier, where it came to Cortez and me,” Ezra reminds me. “But that’s not true. I’ll use Faith’s lesson in perspective to prove my point. On the surface, depending on which one of us is venting, and to whom, the other would look to blame. But we both are.”

“Explain,” I order, intrigued. I like this philosophical side to Ezra. Logic mixed with emotion.

“Marcus has issues that have him exorcising his demons through oral. Cortez is Marc’s perfect counterpart. Then there is me, the one who doesn’t have the stomach to do what Cortez needs me to do. I’ve tried, but I freak out and fear I’m harming him. Which is why I never put my foot down with an ultimatum to Marcus. I’m trying to be selfless and compassionate, even if it’s killing me slowly. I’ve sat many a night as you have this evening, filled with loneliness because Cort’s not with me, worthlessness because I can’t meet his needs, and suicidal thoughts because of it.”

“No wonder you want Katya here. The bullshit between you is less complicated than the chaos surrounding you and Cortez.” Slumping forward, I rest my head in my palms. “I–”

“What I’m about to ask will make you think me a monster for suggesting it, yet I believe it will offer not only a sense of balance for us both, but will be the start to healing the wound I created in you.”

“You’re being awfully calm right now,” I point out, suspicious.

"When I'm helping others, I'm even-keeled. It's through discipline and focus, which is why I look forward to going to work every day, as I get to be wholly me while I'm there."

Refusing to delve too deeply into that, I change the subject back to the matter at hand. "What did you want to ask me?"

"Would you allow me to skull-fuck you?"

Mouth agape, all I can do is stare at Ezra in silent horror, watching a crimson blush flood up his neck and into his cheeks.

"I know, Regina." I can tell Ezra is in therapist mode, and wishes to pat my arm in comfort. "I need to show you why Marcus and Cortez seek each other out, because I can't fill that need in Cortez. You need to see if you're able to fill it in Marcus. But know, Marcus may be avoiding it with you for the simple fact he wants love between you, not his demons."

"If you hadn't– after what happened– I don't think it's a good idea for me to touch you like that," stammering, I stumble over my words, heart beating a rapid tattoo on the inside of my chest.

I simultaneously want to say yes and no, for the simple fact I felt alive during the assault. I didn't like it. I didn't want it. But I didn't feel dead inside for a few moments. There was this floating clarity, where I was able to detach from my fears and worries, and just exist. Everything else was someone else's problem. I wanted that from the pot, but it didn't happen.

"I think it would help with that," Ezra pauses as if he's reading my private thoughts. "I'd be doing this for you, Regina."

With narrowed eyes, I flash Ezra a loaded look.

"Yes, I will orgasm," Ezra says as if it's too crude to voice. "I wouldn't ask you for a regular blowjob, even if it's my preference. Trust me when I say I loathe doing this, and I usually go limp a few seconds into it with Cortez. So this will be a mild exploration of what our partners are doing to each other, or I wouldn't be able to be hard enough to show you."

Staring at Ezra, really looking at him, I can see the sincerity in his expression and hear it in his tone of voice. Ezra wants to help, and instead of telling me, he thinks showing me is the answer.

"I'm scared," I whisper like a small child would after a nightmare. "This wouldn't be about sex or connection, and I can't grasp that… not after–"

"It's therapy, "Ezra answers my hesitation. "You and I will bond during it, and I'm hoping that helps remove the fear over what I did to you. It can't erase it, and apologizing won't fix it." Sighing deeply, gunmetal gray eyes seek to connect with me. "I love Marcus, Regina. I want him to be happy, and I think he could be with you. I fucked up, help me fix it for all of us."

"I don't trust you," I admit without hesitation.

"You shouldn't," Ezra's replying before I even finish speaking. "But you can trust Marcus. You need to come to terms with what he's doing with Cortez, so the betrayal doesn't hurt as much. Maybe move him toward getting help, so there is a conclusion to this behavior."

Head dropping in hands, Ezra looks utterly defeated. "I can't live a lifetime with Marc's dick in Cortez's mouth. I can't suffer through it, especially when Cort gives me nothing but grief in return."

Is this a sob story, or is this real? Fuck if I know– I can't tell anymore. My instincts are shot.

"I understand how you're feeling right now, Regina– how you've felt in the past. Cortez has cuckolded me since I was a twelve-year-old. The few intimate moments we've shared in our adult lives are tainted with violence and resentment. I was young when I begged Dexter to touch me, to feel… *something*."

Stockholm syndrome can be the only explanation as to why I'm empathizing with the man who raped me early last night. I'm losing my mind– I have to be.

"I was forced to touch Faith, so I used Cort in order to get through it, even though he didn't realize it at the time. The cousin thing, that isn't our issue. Everything else is our issue. My adult life, I've been manipulated and demanded to perform sexually, even if it's only been a handful of times. I've been basically celibate, while watching my partner screw a swath through Dominion and suck my adoptive father off on a daily basis. What I did with you…"

Ezra looks me dead in the eyes, and I know he's wholly himself and being open, honest, and genuine. This *is* Ezra. "What happened between me and Marcus when I was a kid, I take my responsibility. But the guilt isn't as bad because it wasn't my hand that forced it. Faith and I were forced, be we did it on our own terms. Ade and I… my terms, even if Master Ez had to perform for me."

"Dexter? Cortez?" I request after Ezra stops speaking for a few minutes, just staring off into space. I don't want a part of his personality right now– I need all of him. I use a singular name to snap him out of it. "Katya?"

Laughing sardonically, Ezra comes back to life, like someone flipped his switch back on after changing his batteries. "Katya and I were mutual." Looking away, he whispers as if it was a secret. "Non-consensual for the both of us, and it's haunted me ever since."

"I'm so very sorry," I utter with absolute compassion.

"You wound me, Regina." Ezra palms his chest over his heart. "I don't deserve your understanding because of what I did to you, even if what I did doesn't erase what happened to me."

Snorting out a puff of air, I laugh, knowing exactly what Ezra means and how he feels. Been there, done that, have the participation t-shirt.

"Dexter? Dexter is intelligent, compassionate, loyal and trustworthy. Patient. It helped that his hotness tied into my daddy issues." Ironic laughter flutters from both our lips, because to fuck Dexter is to pretend he's Marcus. "Sure, Dexter didn't want me in the way I wanted him, but he gave me what I needed because that's what a dominant does for their submissive. That's what training was like– I was learning through the position of submissive, and Dexter knew cutting off my sexuality was slowly killing me, as in suicidal thoughts."

In a voice filled with such longing, I ach for Ezra, "The skin-hunger." Sighing, he pins me in his stare. "The need to be touched by someone I trusted, someone I wanted, someone who would give me what I needed instead of take–"

"Jesus Christ," I hiss in pain, never feeling closer to anyone in my life.

"Right or wrong, I *needed* Dexter, and he gave it to me." Voice warping with rage and resentment, "Then Cortez came in, played the goddamn victim, and made it about him. We weren't together. He hadn't touched me in *years!*"

As Ezra speaks, I realize I owe Grant– Jamie, whatever –I owe him *nothing*. I owe Jamie no guilt or shame over who touches me. He needn't give me permission to do a goddamn thing. Some of what Syn said was accurate. I've tampered with my self-respect as a way to continue to be dependent on how

Jamie makes me feel, even if how he makes me feel is false. His actions are louder than his silent words.

Cortez and Jamie are good friends, and they are a lot alike. I love Cortez, but he is a selfish fucker. Everything I've heard was from Cort's point-of-view up until tonight, and now I understand Ezra's lecture on perspective.

"I haven't–" Ezra starts and stops, closes his eyes, then sighs. "I haven't truly had a real sexual connection with another human being, one that wasn't tainted, in my entire life. Not truly. As an adult, what little contact I've had with others, it was toxic. Which is why I believe Marcus won't allow you to participate in his skull-fucking. Also why I want Katya here with me, as I will never allow her to see the depths I've gone in the past."

Motherfuck, I'm going to hand Katya Waters to Ezra on a platter, and a part of me will blame her if it blows up. Now I get Syn being mad at me over what Ezra did to me. Is Ezra infecting me with his insanity?

"I want a baseline, Regina." Ezra reaches over to squeeze my hand, just a comforting, connecting touch of skin-on-skin. "Katya will be my baseline, so I can stay even all the time. Balanced. Like how I feel when I'm offering therapy to my clients."

"Why the shower?" I blurt out, confusing Ezra with my swift subject change. "You asked me to take a shower with you?" Deciding I'll just rip the Band-Aid off, "Do Marcus and Cortez do it in the shower?"

Perfect mouth hanging open, Ezra just stares at me for a suspended moment, then the blush rises on his pale skin, getting darker and darker. I'd like to think he's playing coy, but I have a feeling this innocent embarrassment is the real Ezra. That's a scary thought.

"I um…" Ezra uses his palms to scrub at his face as an excuse not to look at me. "I've worked all day with clients, then I came straight to Restraint." He levels me with a potent look–all male, eyes liquid silver. "You deserve a spotless dick in your mouth, should you honor me with the pleasure of showing you how Marcus and Cort behave, all the while helping you past a hurdle I created."

"Oh– wow," is my stupid reply. I'd love to blame the pot for being daft, but my heart is beating so quickly, moving oxygen in my blood supply, my brain is feeling light and fuzzy.

Alive. What I feel is a release of potent endorphins, which makes me feel alive.

"Unlike Marcus and Cortez, we will be naked, whereas Marc only pulls his cock out of his fly. For your comfort and mine, I won't touch anything of yours below your neck, and you won't touch anything but my genitals. We'll also have a safeword, which they do not use."

"Safeword?" Shit just got motherfucking real.

Nodding, Ezra levels me with a very serious look. "This is about trust, Regina– power-exchange. I won't go as far as Cort requires of me, where he wants to be suffocated on my cock, nearly passing out. I may say some dirty things I won't enjoy. But I'll give you a snapshot of what they do together."

"I can't trust you after…" Stumbling over my words, I actually fear hurting Ezra's feelings. Talk about a mind-fuck. "After last time."

Ezra rises to his feet, jutting his hand out for me to take. "You shouldn't trust me to be a mind-reader, which is why we'll use the safeword. Since this activity will impeded your speech, we'll also use a backup precaution."

Laughing, I take Ezra's hand, and his fingers immediately wrap around mine. "You know, I never really contemplated what a safeword entailed, other than it being a *full stop*."

"Just because there is trust between two people, just because we are a dominant, that doesn't mean we know what's going on inside someone's head, even with body language and physiological responses. It's a backup for when we miss something. Our partner has to take responsibility for their own welfare as well, and not blame us for our inability to use clairvoyance to help them with what they themselves don't understand."

"Around a lot of blamers?" I tease, knowing Ezra's speaking of Cortez. "I must be losing my goddamn mind," murmurs from between my parted lips as I drag Ezra into my en suite bathroom. "This is so wrong."

"For the right reasons," Ezra whispers, looking around my bathroom with an appraising eye. "The safeword is Chrysalis."

"Why?" comes as a grunt as I adjust the water spray.

"You'll soon come to understand." Ezra smirks privately. "If you're unable to speak, pinch my flesh three times in quick succession, and I will stop immediately."

"Too bad I didn't use those techniques earlier," I mutter begrudgingly.

Fingers poised to undo his buttons, "Regina?" Ezra calls softly to gain my attention. "At some point, Master Ez may erupt, because of how this activity makes me feel–"

"Then we won't do it!" Hands flying up, I begin to rebutton Ezra's dress shirt.

"But," Ezra cautions, fingers settling over mine to stop my nervous fretting. "Master Ez will abide by the safeword and pinching, as he is governed by black and white rules. So don't fear. He may be rough in his skull-fuckery, but it will still pale in comparison to Marcus and Cortez."

"Why?" flows without thought as I examine what Ezra could possibly mean by that.

Blushing, elegant fingers fly over the buttons, then Ezra drapes his shirt on the hook on the back of the bathroom door. "My physique is leaner than Marc's, less muscular strength."

After training with Marcus, with his gorgeous bronze skin, and Cortez with his golden tan flesh, seeing Roman's comforting russet tone, my children and all of Gwen the whore's offspring are best described as healthy pink, and Kristal's the epitome of warmth– the juxtaposition of Ezra's flesh is mind-boggling. Their warmth to his cold. There is something intriguing, forbidden about a man so pale you fear for his health, yet Ezra is probably one of the healthiest specimens I've ever laid eyes upon. Strong, yet lean, his muscle definition is eye-catching, leading me to look where I probably shouldn't.

A shudder of fear and anticipation rolls down my spine as Ezra's fingers pluck the button on his trousers, then begins to lower his fly. I can't look away, but I should want to, right?

I can't hate Grant. I can't hate Ezra. What the fuck is broken inside my brain? Do I have no sense of self-respect or preservation?

Knowing what is being revealed, my eyes light on Ezra's nipples instead. I've been with a few men, seen most of them naked in the past few days, all have tan or darker nipples– Marc's are dark brown. There's only a kiss of pink dotting Ezra's chest– feeling the attention of my gaze, they bead but don't flush darker.

No wonder when the man blushes, there's no hiding it.

Voice shy, I know it's still Ezra driving the bus. "My mother is pale, as is my father," is his explanation to my sick fascination with his skin tone. "As is Zane– he has better hair than any of us." He chuckles with obvious pride. "But he's jealous of his cousin, because he doesn't like being called the albino at school."

I'm a ruddy mess thanks to my dad's contribution to my genetics. Pale with splotchy red and brown freckles. Ezra is flawless, colorless, seriously looking like an innocent angel I'm forcing to fall.

"His cousin?" I remember Syn shouting how she is even raising her nephew.

"Boyd's son, Torian. He's mixed– very pretty boy." Ezra smirks at me privately, like he's sharing a secret. "Zane's jealous, especially because the boy has the Wilson husky eyes. Intoxicating combination."

"Why isn't Boyd raising his own dang kid?" I don't realize I've spoken aloud until Ezra's sinister laughter hits my ears.

"Forget your time with Faith already, have you?" The irony is thick in Ezra's voice. "Syn felt she could do a better job raising Torian, so she refused to give him back after a playdate."

"Let me guess, Syn simultaneously says his mother abandoned him while ignoring requests to give him back."

"Bingo!" Ezra points at me while shaking his head in disgust. "Faith's always right, and has my balls in a vice because of my son. Fun times. What's the most ironic, Tori's mom is an elementary school teacher, for Christ's sake. But Faith and Gretchen loathe one another, with Torian and Boyd caught in the middle."

"Jesus fuck," I snarl, fingers curling into claws.

"That's what happens when two sets of siblings come together. Boyd and Faith hooked up with Levi and Gretchen, and the lines of loyalty are blurred. Which explains the predicament you find yourself in currently."

"No shit." Unable to help myself, my eyes flick downward. It takes less than a blink of an eye for a slight flush to work its way up Ezra's body, all because I'm staring at his flaccid cock. Ignoring my attention, he continues to strip, then politely hangs his clothing on the back of my bathroom door.

Even Ezra's cock is pale, with thick blue veins. I wonder if it flushes with life once aroused. Grant's is almost red with want, and Marc's is nearly purple. It's baffling seeing someone who is cleaner looking and shines brighter than my bathroom tile.

Insanity spews from my mouth as Ezra steps into my shower. "When you converted–" my hand waves in the general vicinity of his cock. I've been acquainted with the piece of flesh, once in my ass and once in my vagina, but I've never really *looked* at it.

Laughing carefree as he grabs for my body poof and the shower gel, like we're friends now and he can let his guard down. "At the hospital, after my birth," Ezra mutters wryly. "Same with Cortez… and most of the population. The Whittenhowers are uncut to send a message of superiority to the people of my faith."

"Yeah, because the extra foreskin flesh actually means something," I mutter underneath my breath while watching Ezra soap himself up. There is something inherently erotic and intimate about watching someone wash themselves– private.

I absolutely shouldn't be enjoying the view, but I can't help but watch, lingering on the best bits of Ezra's flesh, covered in my lemon-scented body wash.

"You may leave your unmentionables on, for your own comfort." Ezra beckons me to join him.

I can't let that go. "If I use exclamations, you're too fucking polite."

I wait for it…

"Don't be vulgar, Regina." Ezra turns his back to me, insulted. Pouting.

It's no wonder Master Ez is a foul-mouthed deviant– Ezra's so restricted, he formed another personality to let it out. I will eventually break Ezra of his pompous-ass-ness. Katya is from small-town Pennsylvania. It will drive her batshit to be chastised for her diction. Those chat logs with Kimber showed a woman who loved to swear– my kind of girl.

"Just curious…" I trail off as I remove my t-shirt and jeans, leaving on my bra and underwear. Ezra's right– it is a comfort, even if wet cotton is uncomfortable. I'm not taking a shower to wash. I'll be kneeling on the tile, getting my throat fucked.

Tilting my head to the side, I home in on the object in question. "If you showered in front of Cortez, or just showed him your perfect specimen of an ass, he couldn't resist you."

Chuckling with his back to me, I watch as a blush draws life to his flesh. "I thought you said I was to work on building intimacy with Cortez, Regina? Shouldn't seduction be an expert course when we're stuck at novice?"

"Jesus, learn to take a compliment, why don't ya?" Grumbling, I squeeze into my shower.

"You are so high right now." Grinning Ezra looks proud of me. "It's wearing off, but you're freer than you've been in a long time. It's nice."

"That was the first and last time," I promise myself.

"Good." Swallowing thickly, I watch as Ezra's Adam's apple bobs with nervousness. This is the man who used courtesy when he slowly worked himself into my ass, not the man who violated me up against a steel door.

So why am I hoping Master Ez appears as a cock slips between my lips?

I'm fucking disturbed.

Taking in my expression, Ezra blinks once, and then everything goes to hell.

Shoved abruptly to the shower floor, I fall but don't catch myself because I didn't expect it. Slipping and sliding, trying to stand, I marvel in horror at how quickly Master Ez roared through Ezra– it's the eyes. You can tell by looking at Ezra's eyes. Gray storm clouds turn to the churning of a thunderous sea.

Slipping and sliding around on the sudsy tile, I try to gain leverage in order to stand, but Master Ez holds me down with merely a hand on my shoulder, exerting no pressure. Master Ez uses the shower to his advantage.

"You don't get to manipulate Ezra by playing with his emotions." Yelping in a sharp burst of burning pain, Master Ez has as much of my hair as he can grab wrapped in his fist. "Ezra has been, and always will be, a lonely kid who longs for friends. You'll only hurt him."

Floundering, my ankle hits the side of the glass shower surround, instantly bruising me. My hands lash out for anything they can reach, accidently brushing against an erection. Eyes wide in horror, I can't not look. What was pale and hanging loosely is now a promise instead of a threat– red and angry looking, Master Ez is painfully aroused.

Hands yanks me roughly until I'm facing Master Ez while resting on my shins and knees. One of his fists is in my hair and the other is wrapped around his angry cock. Staring, I watch as it throbs to its own beat. Then Master Ez begins to jerk himself off before my very eyes, ending with a twisting stroke to the head.

This was the cock and the man who violated me. Terror roars through my veins, and I freeze, forgetting both the safeword and the gesture. Pee dampens my underwear to flow down my inner thigh, then swirls down the drain with the flow of water.

Blinking rapidly, Master Ez takes in my terror, tastes it on the back of his tongue, then digests it. With a whiplash effect,

Ezra is looking down at his hands, as if they don't belong to him, or maybe wondering how his fingers became tangled in my hair.

"I... um– shit!" Ezra hisses with feeling, a red wash of mortification enveloping his entire body. "If it's any consolation, Master Ez knows Marcus is rougher than that with Cort."

Eyes flicking everywhere, not lighting on any one spot, I try to calm my racing heartbeat. "He is?" I murmur in shock, shock over how alive I feel in the moment– free.

"Um…yeah, he is." Ezra won't look me in the eye– he just keeps swallowing while blinking. "This won't be as bad for you as it is with Cortez. As I said, I'm not as strong as Marcus, but I'm also not as…"

Ashamed, Ezra's hands fall away from my hair and his cock, then I figure out where he keeps going with the Marcus comparison. Marc's cock is as thick as a Coke can, whereas Ezra's is longer and thicker than average but not suffocate-me-sized. On a girl like Katya? Yes, Ezra could inflict damage. But I'm a bigger framed person, with proportionate features.

I realize two things simultaneously. One, if Cortez needs this, Ezra can't give it to him. Two, I don't want Ezra's cock in my mouth.

"No offense, Ezra, but I want to be your friend, and you can't do this." It's bizarre to feel in charge while kneeling on the shower floor, with a softening cock a whisper from my cheek. "I need to know what they do."

"I don't understand." Ezra steps back, almost butted up against the far wall of the shower. "I want to be your friend too."

Staring up at Ezra, I pant in a mix of fear and anticipation. "Master Ez, fuck my face–"

Neck jarred back roughly, two hands are palming my skull, fingers biting into my flesh. "Suck it," Master Ez demands in a cold voice, using his leverage to move my body.

Lips pressed together tightly, I shake my head no out of reflex, and the movement snaps off a few hairs. Wincing in pain, I realize my error as Master Ez tightens his hold on my skull. The more I struggle, the harder Master Ez grips, and the more moisture beads out the slit of his angry cock.

Master Ez wants me to fight– wants me to be his prey.

I cease my struggle because I won't let him win– Master Ez chuckles lightly, like he anticipated my reaction three moves ahead of me. No doubt he did.

Fingers gripping with bruising force, my head is wrenched forward. My knees grind into the wet tile floor, offering me no leverage but a helluva lot of pain. "Suck it! Suck it down!" His warped demands cause his voice to go deeper with lust. "It's just flesh– it won't hurt you unless you don't give in and take it."

Giving in, letting go, finding that white space where I'm not in charge and being held accountable for life-altering decisions, I make the choice to better understand Marcus and Cortez, to understand Ezra. To understand myself.

Dexter's cock was a lot bigger. I can do this. I can do more than do this– I can revel in it.

Salivating for a taste of an activity I've gone far too long without, I don't even care whose cock I suck down. Mouth opening, I prepare to slowly work Master Ez's length in. With a tentative lick to the weeping slit, I tongue his opening. Underestimating my partner, the bulbous head of Master Ez's cock hits my gag-reflex before I can even react. Choking, sputtering, the burn awakens me as I struggle to breathe through my nostrils.

Grunting in pleasure, Master Ez gazes down at me, locking his eyes with mine. The hot yet cold, calculating man is as intriguing as he is terrifying, and I find myself wanting to experience the worst he has to offer.

Am I punishing myself? Fuck if I know. All I know is I want it to hurt, to make me feel alive and outside of my head.

Fingertips denting into my skull, Master Ez's animalistic grunts are in time with his thrusts. Knees sliding on the title flooring, I latch onto Master Ez's hips for leverage, fingernails biting into his flesh to stop the violent onslaught. With pounding force, my eyeballs reverberate in my skull, causing flashes of light to nearly blind me.

I am but my vicious captor's passenger. I am a vessel used for his pleasure. It goes on for what feels like hours. Tears drip down my cheeks, but not nearly as rapidly as saliva pours from the corners of my lips. The spray of the shower washes all the evidence away.

Harder. Harder still. With every thrust in, Master Ez's cock pounds the back of my throat before forcing entry downward, cutting off my air supply. Pulling out, I'm unable to control the speed, depth, or force used in my mouth, causing my teeth to graze his flesh.

Wincing, Master Ez grips my skull tighter, fingers splaying across the back of my head to the nape of my neck. As punishment, he snaps his hips forward with so much force I nearly vomit.

Suffocating, Master Ez doesn't draw back out. Three seconds turns to fifteen, as we stay in a holding pattern with a dick lodged down my esophagus, blocking my airway. Gray blurs along the edges of my vision, a threat of what's to come if I don't get a gasp of air. Twenty seconds turns into forty-five, as Master Ez uses the fight my throat is giving him as the stimulation he seeks.

"You're a filthy little mouth slut, aren't you? Always open and ready for a juicy cock to slide in, but no one will give you what you seek. Swallow around my cock, Regina. Swallow."

Pinch.

Pinch.

I can't force myself to pinch a third time. Harder still, Master Ez presses into me, purposefully trying to push me into pinching him one last time, so he can prove himself worthy of my trust.

Refusing to give in, but knowing I won't stay conscious long enough to work Master Ez to completion, my hands move on their own accord. Subconsciously, my mind must supply an answer I can't hear, but my hands instinctively know what to do.

Forgetting all about the cock burning my throat and the tears of terror spilling down my cheeks, I go into survival-mode. Nearly hairless pale balls rest on the inside of my left wrist, tickling me just as three fingers sink deep into Master Ez's tight ass.

"Regina!" Ezra bellows so loudly it echoes off the walls in the shower and the bedroom beyond. Unable to take more than a few more second before I pass out, I experience his cock fluttering like a hummingbird's wings against my tongue.

The calm before the storm. Pulling out slightly so I can breathe, Ezra explodes in a rush, pumping shot after shot of cum down my throat. All the while I keep fucking Ezra's ass with my fingers and rubbing his balls against the inside of my wrist.

As I swallow and swallow, it hits me out of nowhere.

My eyes roll back in my head as every nerve in my body fires at once. My skin tightens and tingles, and muscle after muscle flexes and relaxes, as if I was hit with an electrical current.

I climax without touch. My mind releases pleasure as endorphins flood my system. Moisture floods down my thighs to mingle with the water cascading down from the showerheads.

"Oh, my God!" Ezra laughs in a burst of amazement. He is Ezra right now– has been since I inserted my fingers into his flawless ass. Voice filled with a wealth of awe and pride, "Did you just come from sucking my cock? Maybe you'll have no problem satisfying Marcus after all."

After slipping my fingers from Ezra's behind, I crawl on my hands and knees to the wall, then lean against it, not caring how uncomfortable and restrictive the wet cotton of my bra and underwear is. Tilting my face in the direction of the closest showerhead, mouth open, I allow it to wash my shame and tears away.

Shame, not for doing what I just did, but shame for getting off on it. In a moment when I should have been terrified, I was electrified, and it disturbs me on a level I can't comprehend.

"Shh…" The shower cuts off, then elegant hands are swathing me in a towel– so much for hiding my tears. "It's okay. I knew this would happen. You've had so much going on, I've been waiting for you to break. But you never seem to hit rock bottom. I thought subspace would be a welcome vacation from reality."

"It was," I mutter, rubbing my face against the soft terrycloth. "But I'm back on Earth again, and it's worse than ever, here in reality." Gathering some strength, I hit Ezra where it hurts. "You helped rape me… at the end. It was you who was concerned with me getting off. You pretended to be Master Ez, why?"

"Shit!" Ezra hisses, sounding almost pained. "It was too late when I was able to grab control, so I tried to gift you with honesty about Marcus and me, then make sure you were pleasured instead of pained. You were already in subspace, so stopping would've had you dropping. I brought you down as gently as possible. It's why I wrestled control back a few minutes ago when you pinched me."

"I feel like I should thank you." I wrap the towel around me tighter.

"Don't, Regina– don't." Ezra flows to his feet fluidly, grabs a towel for himself, and then begins drying. "I'll try to do right by you, but I can't always promise I will. I'll fuck up, because I always do, but try to remember how I was tonight. That's the real me."

"No promises, but thanks for showing me what Marcus and Cortez do– I don't understand it. I don't like it. But I'll ignore it until we figure out how to stop it."

"Thank you for calling a cease-fire truce with me, Regina." Ezra bends down to kiss the top of my head, then his hand is slowly tugging me to my feet. Voice turning shy, "And for the epic orgasm. It's been a long time since anyone pushed my button, if you know what I mean."

Chapter Twenty-Five

After a pat to my shoulder and a sympathetic smile, Ezra left without as much as a backward glance, ghosting away as silently as he had arrived. It's bizarre, sharing intimate details and body parts, yet never kissing or even feeling the urge to kiss. It gives a different perspective on sex for me, how it can just be an act performed.

While sitting on wet tile while wearing saturated *unmentionables,* my mind drifts to Grant. Is that how he felt when he was with me? Did he go into auto-pilot and do what needed to be done? Or is that my insecurities mixed with Syn's revelations?

Actions speak louder than words, I wholeheartedly believe. In the moment with Grant, then Jamie, it felt real, but the running away and hiding tell a different tale.

A decision made in anger, resentment, rationality, and with great care, I decide I am the one in charge. Niel is my son, Ella my daughter, and Whitt my absentee husband. Other than Grant, I am the common denominator. I'm sick of living a lie and being made to lie, while living on other people's timelines.

Tomorrow is the day.

It makes me livid that I have to do what needs to be done. I envision Curtis Regal walking away from my mother and me, then my mother having to tell me he didn't die. A small part of me rejoices, but the logical part of my brain supplies the image of my stocky father lying dead in the morgue when he was in his prime. A real man, broken by happenstance. Dad abandoned me too, but not by choice. He never would've wanted me to see him like that, to identify his remains, to become Mom's caregiver instead of daughter, and watch both of them die on me.

Abandoning me.

I try– try as I might to examine how Whitt, Niel, and Ella will feel meeting Jamie face-to-face after he abandoned them. Then I realize that's impossible, because my dad loved me more than life itself– he loved my mother, and was loyal.

Dad and Mom didn't abandon me– they *died.* Given the choice, they would still be by my side. Grant was given the choice, then chose to pretend to die just to get away from me and our children.

The more I think about how my daughter will feel come tomorrow, the bottomless pit of despair is filled with hatred and rage. This wasn't just about me, no matter what Syn said about how I sucked in bed or was unlovable. Grant left us all behind.

All of us.

Then Grant cherry-picked who was deserving enough to know of his existence, leaving me to be one of the last to know. So why the hell should I give a fuck what Grant thinks, what day and time he wants to tell the truth, or whether or not he wanted me in the first place?

That doesn't stop those thoughts from spiraling out of control inside my head as I scrub shame from my skin. I'm not ashamed of what Ezra and I did earlier. Ezra and I were equals, even with Master Ez riding shotgun– there was mutual respect there. I felt alive for a few moments, able to see clarity.

Shame, because if I had learned my mother knew of my father's continued existence after he abandoned us both, yet continued to see him afterward, allowed him to disrespect her with every breath he took, I'd hate her more than I hated him.

Grant's actions were blatant, no matter the circumstances. Black and white disgusting. Mine? It's subtle, the betrayal. As the closest person in my daughter's life, her caregiver and teacher, mentor and leader… I failed.

Tomorrow, I get the horrific task of sitting Ella down and telling her the truth. That is my punishment for withholding the truth. Even if I'd told Ella the day I had figured it out, it would have still been my punishment. Punishment for not choosing wiser, for allowing Jackson, with the backing of Maître du Jeu, to force my hand.

Niel was the heir. Ella was *my* choice, a choice I made out of emotion instead of logic. I loved Grant when I shouldn't have. Delusional, only wishing to see what I needed to see, rather than the reality of the situation.

Undying love is more palatable when speaking to your children about their creation, versus the reality that they were brought into this world with either a purpose or as a sleight-of-hand to distract me from reality.

Have another kid, Regina. Let me ask you to marry me, Regina. While you bask in the glow of my bullshit lies, excuse me while I sneak out the backdoor and never come back. Allowing you to believe me to be dead, grieve endlessly for me, then come back and tell you to pick up the pieces.

"Fuck you, Grant!" I snarl as I stalk out of my bedroom, dripping dry on my way. I yank on a robe, allowing it to wick away the rest of the moisture. Eyes flicking around my bedroom, I wonder what it's going to take to let this all-consuming rage go.

Almost twenty-four hours later, I can still smell Jamie and Marc's mingling scent, and it turns my stomach. What we shared, what should have been a beautiful moment, was yet again Grant playacting to distract us, then he runs away.

Stalking back into my bathroom, I grab a washcloth and the spray disinfectant from beneath the sink. After tearing the bedding off the mattress, creating a large mountain near the French door, I scrub down the bedframe, the side tables, even my dresser, and the walls with the disinfectant.

Not caring that it's in the dead of winter in Upstate New York, I wrench open the double French doors to air the stench of sex and men. But I have to go a step further, opening up the door from the pool area to the fresh air beyond.

The spray bottle of fabric refresher is up next, with the mattress getting doused, along with every other piece of fabric in my bedroom.

Panting, chest heaving, it's not enough because I can still smell them. As long as I can smell them, I can see it vividly playing out inside my mind. As long as I see the visage of the three of us tangled up in my sheets in this bedroom, making love and speaking silent words with our bodies, the rage-fueled wasp nest is still buzzing and stinging my brain.

There isn't enough pot on the face of this planet to quiet the beast. Instead of going down the destructive path of bad decisions, I decide to incinerate the smell until it's nothing but ash.

Reaching down, I bear-hug the huge bundle of sheets, pillows, even the duvet, then nearly trip as I stride out the French doors to the enclosed pool area. After struggling through the door to the backyard, with a sheet wrapped around my left ankle, I chuckle in victory.

After unceremoniously dumping the wadded up bedding in the center of the backyard, I trudge back inside the pool area to grab the candle lighter I left by the chaise lounge during my earlier exploits.

Laughing manically, it takes three tries to draw flame with the lighter. I try the sheet first with no results. Then the duvet. Finally the pillows. The goddamn shit won't burn because of the frozen ground and the threat of snow riding the air.

Cinching my bathrobe tighter, I angry jog around the pool, nearly falling in, then pop out into the dining room.

My mother used to say, *"Regina, if you go out one door and come in another, we're going to get visitors."* Dad and I were introverts, so we didn't like visitors.

There are two sets of French doors on the back of this house, both leading out to what used to be the patio and pool area, which I had enclosed. Does it count if I keep going in one door and out the other, since they both lead to the singular door to the backyard?

Mom, what do you think?"

Acting on autopilot, I instinctively know there is a bottle of nail polish remover on the coffee table. There isn't a day that goes by that Fate and Ella aren't changing the color of their fingers and toes.

My feet don't even still as my hand reaches out to latch onto the narrow bottle. Zipping around the living room, I snag yesterday's newspaper off the kitchen island. Then back out through the dining room I go.

Ignoring the fact that there are now lights on in the guest house, I just hope and pray Roman is doing something shady for the rat in the wee hours of the morning, instead of stalking me from across the lawn with his spitfire partner-in-crime.

Humming an empowering song by Lesley Gore, I walk in a circle around my bedding, creating a pyre, all the while dousing it with nail polish remover.

"You don't own me. I'm not just one of your many toys. You don't own me. Don't say I can't go with other boys... And don't tell me what to do. Don't tell me what to say... and please, when I go out with you, don't put me on display... 'cause you don't own me. Don't try to change me in any way. You don't own me. Don't tie me down, 'cause I'd never stay."

Smiling while singing lightly, I toss the newspaper on top of the pile, then take a step backward. Eyes riveted, the lighter flicks to life on the first press, which I use to ignite a rolled up section of the front page. Taking another step back, I toss the flaming piece of paper onto the pile.

"*I don't tell you what to say. I don't tell you what to do. So just let me be myself. That's all I ask of you.*"

For good measure, I pitch the lighter on top of the pile. After a split-second, the violent *whoosh* fills the air, warming my face and toes, while blowing my hair back off my forehead.

"Mom was right," I mutter as the fire licks at my purple and white duvet, singeing it brown before it consumes the blanket like a hungry beast. "Go out one door, come in another, you'll get visitors." I'm not commenting on the pair of heads staring at me from across the lawn, or Fate grasping the door casing to the pool area.

"How long have you been here?" I don't bother looking over my shoulder– I simply sense his presence with me now that my earlier high has worn off. Not the weed…

Rage.

But it's still simmering beneath the surface, preparing to erupt whenever it fucking feels like it.

"I hope and pray this display isn't because of something I've done." Marcus steps up to me, shoulder brushing mine, then reaches into his jacket.

With avid fascination, I watch as Marc's hand, cast orange from the fiery light, pulls out a piece of gum from his inner pocket. After popping it into his mouth, Marcus slowly works the gum with his teeth. Then he contributes to the fire with his wrapper– a receipt quickly following.

"I left my phone in the Spyder." Marc's eyes flick in my direction, but he doesn't turn to face me, too engrossed with my pyre. "Had it been in my possession, I would've been here earlier."

I believe Marcus. None of my rage was directed at him tonight. I'd channeled it to know Marc better, but it was never out for his blood.

"Have you spoken to anyone since you met up with Cortez?" Marcus has the common decency to flinch in guilt, as if he was caught cheating. But that's not why I asked. I need to know Marcus came to me on his own.

"No." Fingers trail down the inside of my arm, along my wrist, then slide between mine. Squeezing tightly to reassure himself, Marcus seeks a connection with me. "After a late lunch/early dinner, whatever you want to call it, I worked late on my current case. Then I met Cortez in the living room at Shadow Haven."

"Ah!" comes out unbidden, like I solved a clue, which Marcus takes totally the wrong way. His hand freezes in mine, when previously his thumb had been rubbing soothing circles into the back of my hand. "I take it the living room was the point of origin, and you visit it when you're most stressed?"

Eyes nearly the same color as the fire are held wide, then Marcus slowly turns to face me. "I… you know me better than I realized. I thought you were furious with me, and it took me by surprise, like it was out of nowhere."

"The fire has nothing to do with you," I admit without hesitation, but don't elaborate.

"It wasn't a wild leap." Marcus chuckles so lightly I barely hear it. "Seeing as how I was the last person who slept in those sheets."

Squeezing Marc's hand tightly, it takes everything in me to wrench my eyes from the fire. "Marcus, I take you as you are," is all I say.

With Ezra's help, after a lot of soul-searching, I realize I will never fit into anyone's tiny, labeled boxes. Whatever was going on with Syn tonight, it wasn't about me. I was just a convenient target for her frustrations. I may understand, but it still wounded.

It's Marc's turn to go, "Ah!" But he adds an, "I see. Jamie."

"Syn, actually," I mutter wryly. "But the root of it is about Grant."

My use of Jamie's birth name takes Marcus aback. He may have always called Grant Jamie, but the problems I'm having with the man stem from over fourteen years ago until now. Grant will take ownership of it.

Yes, I compartmentalize Grant versus Jamie. I can't help it.

"Jamie may know us inside and out, with us not truly knowing him, but he's judging us, even if he says he isn't. I've always taken him at face-value, not wishing him to change." Syn's outlandish behavior was just an exaggeration on what Jamie's goodbye letter stood for– judgment. "I'm happy for him if he's truly seeking his own path. He can judge mine all he wants, but it won't change how I see myself."

"I've felt off all damned day." Sighing deeply, a shudder rolls down Marc's spine. "Words cannot express how it felt to sit with Jamie at dinner, and pretend last night didn't happen– to pretend Jamie wasn't judging me for my involvement with the man who was entertaining us with constant chatter as we ate."

No matter how Syn spun her perception of Marc's time spent with Jamie today, I never doubted it wasn't as Marcus is saying now. Syn wasn't with us last night– she didn't see the lost look in Marc's eyes this morning. She doesn't know Marcus and I take each other's faults, spouses, and fucked up fuck-buddies, and all, because we *get* each other as equals.

"Then the bastard had the gall to hug me…" Marc trails off, and I know that's the trigger that had him in Shadow Haven's living room with his cock shoved down Cort's throat.

"Not a competition, or anything," because I refuse to play that game with the man I see as my partner. We're in this together. "But at least the rat contacted you. Didn't text me back, nor did Jamie text at one a.m. like he has for nearly two fucking years, every damn night."

"He didn't?" The upward inflection in Marc's voice guts me. "I just–"

"Want to swim?" I murmur in Marc's direction, eyes watching the waning fire. It can't spread because the ground is frozen, and the threat of snow will descend as dawn breaks.

"I– what?" Jerking back, I've totally confused Marcus, because I'm switching conversation threads quicker than Ezra and Master Ez.

"I got the creepy crawlies underneath my skin." I don't mention how it's rage. Just thinking and speaking of Grant makes me want to drive across town and throat-punch him. "I have to move to release it."

"Like the fire? Like the song? Like the compulsive cleaning of your bedroom?" Marcus follows my lead as I tug him into the heated pool area. Thankfully my nosy housemates retreated to their bedrooms. "Like Ezra being here?"

"Shit!" I hiss with feeling, realizing Marcus has been here for a long time indeed. "I'll explain after our swim."

"Well, your tone of voice and body language inform me Ezra didn't harm you, so whatever did happen, I'm okay with it. Not that I have a choice."

No doubt my song is stuck in Marc's head.

"You don't get a say in what I do, but you are more than welcome to feel whatever you feel about it. Emotions are inherent." Reaching up, I slip my hands beneath Marc's jacket, then slowly peel it down his arms. "I understand why you and Cort seek one another out. Between what Cortez learned of what occurred between Ezra and me, and what happened between us and Jamie, I understand how you both must have needed that release."

"Understanding it doesn't equate to your feelings over it, does it?" Marcus murmurs wryly, understanding me because I understand him.

Fingertips plucking at the buttons on Marc's shirt, "Exactly," I murmur with a smile, but it freezes on my face when I see the marks from last night's adventures. Jamie's marks. Swallowing down the rage, I continue to unbutton Marc's shirt, trying my damnedest to ignore the suck and bite marks, ones that are identical to those on my body.

When I reach for the fly of Marc's trousers, his fingers bracelet my wrist, stopping me. "I can't perform tonight, Regina," he warns, voice sheepish. "I don't want you to think I don't want you."

Eyes flicking between my fingertips as they hold the zipper pull, and up to Marc's concerned gaze, I infallibly trust him in a way I never have with Grant. It's called maturity. We've all matured, and I know how to read the signs.

"I'm creeping closer to forty every dang day," Marcus murmurs self-deprecatingly, which causes me to laugh.

"You just turned thirty-five." I try and fail to hold my amusement. "But don't worry, I'm not trying to seduce you right now. I meant what I said in my voicemail. I wanted to hear your voice, just be near you."

"I know." Marcus releases his grip on my wrist, then helps me tug his zipper down. "I'm just explaining how after last night's epic sex-fest, the stress, and the aborted skull-fuck because I couldn't get off, my dick might not be in functioning order, and I don't want you to see it as rejection."

"Wow– Cort couldn't get you off?" That gives me pause, because Marcus is even more upset than I realized. "Was this the first time?"

"No," Marcus admits without shame, shaking his head to accentuate his point. "Many times. It's part of the–"

"Part of the intense therapy session?" Kneeling down, I untie Marc's spiffy leather shoes, then slip them off his feet, silk socks following in their wake.

"That's an apt description, Regina." Marcus smiles, and it actually reaches the corners of his eyes. "I can't skinny dip in your pool."

"I can." My robe falls to the wayside as I draw to my feet.

"What about… What about Ella?" Hesitant, Marc's gaze lights on the fact that there are no lights on in the guest house. Easier for them to watch us this way.

"Well," I drawl out, tiptoeing to the pool steps. "Ella came out of my vagina, Marcus." A sharp burst of laughter flows from my lips. "We're a household of four women. My nudity is seen as just being *me*, not in a sexual nature."

Slipping into the pool, the warm water slowly caresses my body as I sink lower and lower. I needed this. For some reason, it helps me connect with myself. "The water's amazing," I beckon. "Keep your shorts on, Marc– no different than swim trunks."

"Yeah, just don't sprout wood," Marcus grumbles to himself, kicking off his pants.

"The risk assessment says that's pretty low, since we've already established how your cock is hibernating."

Looking all around him, as if fearful one of my girls will appear out of nowhere, Marc adjusts the waistband on his navy boxer briefs. "I didn't have my naked girlfriend floating around in a body of water earlier– your risk assessment is flawed."

"My daughter sleeps like the dead," is cut off as I go under water to swim the length of the pool. The displacement of the water signals Marcus joins me.

For however long, Marcus and I swim laps, then take breaks to play like little kids. After we're finished, we make our way back to my bedroom, where we work as a team to make up the bed, which we promptly fall into.

Evidently our shields are still down between us, because we talk about how our day went, all the while touching one another in the way I tried to explain to Ezra that was missing between him and Cortez.

Marc's emotions are all over the place as I speak of my experiences. He seethes about Syn. Laughs over Dexter stealing Roman's weed, yet is slightly concerned over the fact that I smoked it. Is awed that I allowed Ezra to connect with me in such a manner in order to understand how he ticks.

Somewhere in the middle of the night, where we're both covering up the marks Jamie left behind with our own, we bridge a gap we've always avoided. We touch and kiss and suck for connection, with no thought to our destination. Marcus allows me to go down on him in the exploratory way I favor, and he gives as good as he gets.

The orgasm isn't an overpowering rush. It's more like a soft brushstroke to our flesh, leaving us sated.

When I was growing up, watching how my parents interacted with one another, listening to my mother's advice on love, I never in a million years could contemplate the ability to love one man so completely, while equally loving and loathing another.

In the wee hours of the morning, as fingertips trail down my spine in a loving caress, I still can't wrap my mind around it, and I'm now in my early thirties. But my lack of understanding doesn't make it any less true.

Marcus and I, we fit together. He's married, but so am I, and it's not to each other. If I were to go by Syn's rules for *my* life, it would be a sign we don't fit, even though we most certainly do. Someday we may be together by society's standards, but maybe we won't. I'm not going to cut off the best part of my life because it doesn't fit into someone else's tiny box of normality.

Marcus and I agreed how his involvement with Cortez is toxic, even if we understand the need. He admitted it hurts him to know Ezra and I have somehow struck a similar connection, even though he can rationalize the need.

With Ezra's help, Marcus and I will get Cortez and Ezra back together in a healthy manner, even if that means Katya Waters is collateral damage. Otherwise, they may destroy the relationship we're trying to build.

We agreed Jamie can't harm our partnership, for the simple fact our emotions mirror each other when it comes to him. Whatever decision we make in regards to Jamie, the other will find it impossible not to follow. But Cortez and Ezra, their lunacy does have the power to tear us apart.

"Stop thinking," Marcus murmurs against my shoulder, lips curling into a private smile. "It's so loud I can't think."

"Ha. Ha." I mock laugh. "When we're old and gray–"

"I'm already old," Marcus teases himself.

"Ha!" I snort this time. "When we're old and gray, we'll be lying in bed just like this, our thinking keeping the other awake."

The certainty in my voice takes my breath away, and I know Marcus senses it too.

"I guess I have a lifetime ahead of me where I have to fuck you into oblivion just so I can get some rest." Moving quickly, Marcus has me pressed beneath him, cock already returning home. "I love you, Regina."

"I love you too," flows like water from my tongue.

"Jamie did text you back." Marcus crash-lands me into reality. "So I texted him with a time and place for tomorrow."

Marc's thoughtful gesture has, "I love so goddamn much," spilling from my lips, tone conveying how much it means to me that he took the time to take care of something that will be unbelievably difficult for me.

"I'll also round up everyone, leaving all your attention with Ella." Fingertips brush the hair off my forehead, as eyes bore into mine. "Feel whatever you're feeling, Regina. Be human."

Chapter Twenty-Six

"I talked to Katya Waters today," I say conversationally as I pull into the underground parking garage beneath The Edge Building. I'd rather concentrate on things I can change, other than the nightmare I'd just gone through, and the one to come.

Marcus was nice enough and smart enough to arrange a mutual location, one that had no sentimental value to any of the Whittenhowers or me. Ezra easily offered up an unoccupied, smaller meeting room on the first floor of Edge, directly across from his office.

"Really?" Marcus turns to face me as far as the seatbelt allows. In the dim light, I can see shock written across his features. "You said you were now Kimber, but I wasn't sure you'd go through with it."

While I park in a reserved spot near the elevator, with the Roadster filled with Whitt and my children parked next to us, my mind drifts back to earlier today.

"Ella, come sit with me for a minute." Tugging at my daughter's hand, I draw her to the dining room table. I'd made sure no one else was home during our conversation. "I need to tell you something."

Ever-trusting, my daughter sits at the table while using a fingernail to push down the cuticle on her thumbnail. I quickly remove the brand new nail polish remover from the table before she begins giving herself a manicure.

"I need all of your attention, okay?" Reaching back, I toss the bottle on the buffet table, because seeing it reminds me of what I did in the wee hours of this morning. "This is important."

"Okay." Sitting up straight, with her shoulders back and her hands folded on top of the table, Ella waits patiently.

My daughter has never looked more like her father than she does right now, which makes this conversation all the more difficult.

Deep breath, no easing into it. "Your father is alive."

"Duh!" Ella laughs, pink skin coming to life with a blush. "Whitt made Niel and me write a note to the judge this morning for our adoption hearing. Whitt wants me to call him Dad, even though he's my big brother. I don't know– I'll probably just let him boss me around but still call him Whitt."

"No, sweetie." Deep breath, hold it in, then release it as words. "Not Whitt. Yes, Whitt's adopting you." Fuck! Heart racing, I'm not sure I have the ability to explain this properly. "Grant James Atwater Whittenhower– the man who is your biological father is alive."

"But..." Tiny blond eyebrows knit in the center of my daughter's forehead– watching her reason this out is killing me. "So Whitt won't be adopting us?"

Stay strong, Regina. Stay strong.

I go with facts, staying away from any emotion I'm feeling. "No, Ella. Whitt is still adopting you– the hearing is next week."

"Oh, so Dad doesn't know about us?" Shifting in her seat, Ella gets closer to the table, blue eyes filled with hope. "Did he have amnesia or something? Was Dad kidnapped? Did he just remember and contact you? Was that why you went nuts last night and burnt your bedding? Is this like on General Hospital?"

The little girl, who is obsessed with Harry Potter and Vampire Academy, is going in the direction I feared she would take, making this all the harder on me. Since I can't explain MdJ to a ten-year-old girl, the only other conclusion is going to hurt us both.

I interrupt Ella's romance-inspired ramblings, and make a note to stop Fate from sharing her favorite shows with my daughter. "Your father doesn't have amnesia, nor was he kidnapped. In fact, he has lived across town your entire life."

The man Ella has idolized, where she had spent years drilling Adelaide for stories, just so she could be closer to a dead man... pouty bottom lip quivering, Ella is too smart not to get the implications, which is why I hate Grant's guts right now.

"Dad didn't want me?" Ella's voice pitches high, turning into a tween girl shriek. Blue eyes turning cold, my daughter can't handle the fact that her father abandoned her, so now I'm a convenient target.

"What did you do to make Dad leave?" Ella accuses, and I try so very hard not to allow it to affect me. Judging by the way my heart aches and my eyes burn, that's a bullshit lie. "Didn't Dad love you enough to stick around? What did you do?"

When I replay this conversation to those who ask, I will erase this from what I'm willing to share. But nothing will erase the way my daughter is looking at me with hatred, as if I ruined the very thing she's always wanted most– to have a father.

Ignoring the accusation, "Grant died, and that's all I was told, okay?" Ella's not okay with it– never will be, and neither will I. "I had suspected for some time that James Atwater was your father, but I wasn't sure. It's not exactly something you can just come out and ask without looking delusional."

"What about Whitt and Niel? Did Dad love them? Did he see them? Was there something wrong with me because I remind him of you?"

"Remind him of me?" I mutter wryly. "You are your father's daughter."

Closing my eyes, I command them not to release the tears threatening to fall. Ella is ten. She doesn't realize what she's saying. She can't wrap her mind around it, and neither can I. I lied to myself for a decade, rather believing Grant dead than being abandoned on purpose.

Ella's blaming me, asking the same questions I continually ask myself, because she knows the unconditional love of a mother, and to blame Grant means she will never know the love of her father. I get it, but it motherfucking hurts.

"Your father has contacted Niel recently, but they have not met face-to-face. Whitt knows your father is alive, but hasn't seen him. A few nights ago, I finally looked Grant in the eyes for the first time in over a decade. Since then, I have been trying to set up a time for all of you to meet, which is why I'm telling you now."

"You should have told me then." Ella shows her Regal side, with the same passion and vehemence I possess. Leaning across the table, there is no other way to describe how my daughter looks.

Betrayed.

Not abandoned or betrayed by Grant– betrayed by me.

In a calm belying the storm raging in my belly, I manage to get out the words. "I'm telling you now, because we're going to see your father today, and I needed you to be prepared."

"You should have told me last night, so I had time to pick out something nice to wear– Dad needs to see that I'm a good

daughter!" Gulping rapidly, I manage not to vomit on the dining room table as Ella shouts at me.

"Your father loves you no matter what," I mutter, wishing I truly believed it.

"Dad would've loved me more if it hadn't been for you!" Scrambling to her feet, Ella slams her chair as she pushes it back in. Then she storms from the room, shouting over her shoulder, "You had to have done something to him!"

Men always come between women. We say we're independent, empowered, and equal, yet we're the ones who hinge our value on a man. The men don't do it– we women do. Whether men want us or love us more than other women determines our worth. Father. Grandfather. Brother. Uncle. Teachers. Guy friends. Husbands. Boyfriends. Boss. A strange man down the street. Women need them to say we are worthy of their attention or affection.

Treat her how you'd treat your mother, or your daughter, or your sister, we always hear other men saying to each other, as if our value is in the comparison to other females. You're not like any other woman I've ever met before, many women hear dates say, as if that means they are somehow more special than the last date. To elevate one of us is to lower another. The disgusting fact is that we preen when we hear this, how we're a unique snowflake in a landscape of nagging vapid women who can't keep a man because they're too high maintenance. Because being like a man makes you a better woman in their estimation, as long as you have big tits and a small waist at the same time.

A man will tell you how amazing it is that you watch sports with him, drink beer, and play video games because you're not like any other woman he's ever met before. At the same time, a woman in heels and a designer dress will turn his head. This is the same guy wearing a filthy t-shirt stained by pizza sauce with beer-breath-infused compliments, like his opinion of you has any bearing on your true worth. The guy doesn't even put in an effort to keep the girl– it's her insane need to keep the guy away from other women that has her trying so hard to fit his mold.

All moments must accompany the phrase '*for a girl*'. You kicked ass on that video game for a girl. You're an amazing programmer for a girl. You're tall for a girl. That's a killer throw for a girl. You have a lot of money for a girl.

No one ever says '*for a guy*' to a man.

Our pride and achievements must be handicapped by the fact that we have a uterus. Our ultimate quest is to make men proud by battling other women like they're the prize, so they will want to keep us and stick around and give us scraps from their table. We women have to earn their affections, while they take us for granted and assume we'll be where they left us when they return. Ever the faithful bitch.

If a man cheats on a woman, it's her fault, or the other woman's fault, but never the man's. No. Never. She stole him from you, not that he voluntarily left after looking elsewhere. Men don't think or say this shit– women do. It's what our inner monologues scream, and it's what other women say about their betrayed friend or loved one. *She should have tried harder to keep him.*

After preaching these tenets to my daughter from the moment she was born when the examples presented themselves, even in the eyes of a child who was raised by a feminist and my two female friends, it's my fault Grant left us– I wasn't enough for him, and by default Ella was too much like me so he left, when she hadn't even been born yet. Not that Grant was the problem– no, it had to be one of us women who pushed him away. This is the irrational thinking of a ten-year-old child, yet it mirrors my own unspoken thoughts. It's disgusting how women are born with this sense of needing a man to validate us, even when we work so hard to dispel this toxic notion.

In the face of my daughter's irrational reaction, I've finally come to terms and accept that I have no fault in what Grant did to me and our children. I didn't push him away– he left and stayed gone, until the situation to come back fit an agenda he was pushing.

Syn's attack makes sense now more than ever, even if she didn't realize she too was affected by this plague of who belongs to which man, which man wants which woman more. It's not about not having a golden vagina, or being unlovable, or being around men who enjoy a man's company more than mine. There is no odometer counting the dick strokes in a pussy, where low mileage makes you unworthy and high mileage makes you worthless. Syn was pretty much saying men do it better than women.

While Syn's version of feminism is deeply flawed, she was right about one thing. It's not whether I deserve Grant's love and attention, or Marc's, or anyone else's for that matter. If they don't treat me right, they don't deserve *my* attention. It's not whether or not I'm better than another woman, or should be treated how a man treats his own family, or whether or not I can do it as well as a man can– it's how I should be treated with the common decency of a human being to another human being.

False words are heard by those who live in a fantasy world, but actions scream so loud I can't ignore the sick reality of the situation.

You either fit together, or you don't, and you can't force it to work.

Not realizing it, nor understanding it, my daughter will forever blame me, be jealous of me in regards to Grant. This will be a wedge between Ella and me, unless and until I can show her how her worth is in her mind, her behavior, her contribution to life and those around her, not in a man's opinion of her. It's up to Grant to prove how there are different types of love when it comes to daughters, sisters, mothers, versus wives and lovers. I can't explain how a father should love his daughter unconditionally, no matter how many other women are in his life– Grant has to.

After Ella tore my heart out and stomped on everything I've ever taught her about being a woman, I had given myself twenty minutes to break down in my bathroom. I spent that time screaming my injustice into a pillow as my daughter prettied herself up for a man who doesn't deserve her.

I was proud that I didn't defend my actions to my daughter, because she would've only seen it as an admission of guilt. If I had told the truth, I would've hurt Ella far worse. If I had told her how much her words hurt me, when the time comes and she finally sees the truth, the guilt would have eaten her alive.

I had put on a blank face, walked to the car, and now I find myself sitting next to Marcus, talking about everything and anything other than what is slowly murdering me inside. My daughter wouldn't even ride with me– she'd called Whitt immediately and demanded he take her instead.

I can feel Whitt's pity wafting from the Roadster next to us.

"I talked to Katya for about two hours today," I explain to Marcus, who is being patient, no doubt gauging my true emotions. "Syn showed up at Empowerment– just appeared out of nowhere like a tyrannical ninja."

I laugh without humor, but don't say the rest of what happened aloud. Syn thanked me for whatever I'd done with Ezra to make him seem more even-keeled. Then she informed me how Ezra will randomly give me tasks to complete, but my main goal is to keep Ezra balanced. If I fail to keep the insane sane, MdJ will punish me.

My life depends on Katya Waters falling in love with Ezra, then taking him off my hands. Should I fail a direct order from MdJ, not only do I ruin Katya's life, I ruin my own and all those I hold near and dear.

Message received. Fuck my ethics, and fuck what Katya Waters needs and wants out of life.

I've had a horrific day, to be quite honest.

"I really like Kat. She seems grounded, so I think she'll do Ezra some good." Chuckling, I think back to our chat, realizing it was the highlight of my day. "Kat's the opposite of Cortez in a lot of ways. She's proud when she can afford a pair of jeans at Target instead of Walmart. She gloats over finding expensive purses at the Salvation Army for next to nothing."

"Ezra is going to destroy that poor woman," Marcus murmurs in abject horror.

Yup, and I get to deliver Katya to her destruction on a silver platter.

"Maybe you shouldn't help him." Marcus takes off his seatbelt, then turns to look at me. Reaching out, he takes my hand, since I was white-knuckling the steering wheel. "Maybe Ms. Waters would be better off where she is."

Snorting, I just shake my head in defeat. "Katya can't come to Dominion yet. She told me she needed until summer break because of the school year."

"What's that about?" Marcus sounds as confused as I feel.

"Katya is a very private person, so she wouldn't say. It was important enough that she couldn't leave, even if it meant losing her job. I didn't push. I told her to write Edge Publishing a note. Then I hacked into their email account and sent her a reply with a start-date at the end of June."

"Ezra didn't take that well, did he?" Marcus mutters wryly.

"Surprisingly well, actually." Flicking off my seatbelt, I open my car door. "Ezra seemed glad I was on his team, called me proficient and everything. Ceded control of Restraint to me because of it, only retaining veto power should he not like my decisions."

"Fuck," Marcus mumbles as he gets out of the car.

Staring at each other over the top of my car, "Exactly," is the only reply I can formulate. "Ready to get this shit-show started?"

Face crumpling with a combination of agony and sympathy, Marcus flashes me a sad smile. "I'll be here for you afterward, Regina. Anything you need, I promise I'll be here for you."

My, "Thank you," dries up as Albert pulls the Whittenhower Town Car into the spot next to mine. Eyes flicking in Whitt's direction, we both share in our confusion.

"Everyone I invited is already with us," Marcus murmurs, head tilted to the side, trying to get a look inside the car.

"What the–" Whitt charges around my car, getting to the back passenger side of the Whittenhower Town Car before Albert can reach it. "Daniel," is a growl from deep in Whitt's throat as the door swings open. "Were you following us?"

Albert looks directly at me, addressing no one else. "I felt it was time, don't you?"

Whitt is still tearing Daniel a new asshole, not even allowing the man out of the car. "What are you doing here? How did you find out? Have you always known? Jesus, Father, why didn't you tell me?"

"Your daughter snitched, didn't she?" Our Chica is upstairs in the meeting room with Roman and the rat. The slight tilt of Albert's chin is answer enough. All it takes is a tight hold on Whitt's arm to get the man to back off and let Daniel out of the car.

Albert has always been in charge of the Whittenhower men–his wife, Martha, leads the women with her caring touch, tough love, and chocolate cake. Kristal is the perfect melding of her parents, guilt and sex addiction aside.

Whitt steps out of the way, waiting for his answers.

Not needing to answer any of Whitt's questions, the answers are evident by the way the Daniel carries himself in defeat. Blond hair streaked with white at the temples, handsome face twisted in agony, blue eyes rimmed in red from holding back tears.

"It's good to see you again, Daniel," I go for polite. We may be oil and water, but mutual agony transcends petty differences in the past.

Grant abandoned his father, leaving him to take care of an entire empire alone. After sharing the task first with Jackson, then with Grant, Daniel is the type of man who needs partnership. If it hadn't been for Niel, I don't know what state Daniel would be in today.

"Grandfather," Niel speaks softly, walking around a stunned Whitt to get near the man. "I know it's a shock." With affection, respect, and a bit of reverence, Niel wraps his arm around Daniel's shoulder and leads him over to where I'm standing.

"Are you going to be okay?" I swear to God, I'm getting more mind-fucked by the hour. First I empathize with Ezra, and now I'm worried about Daniel. "I get to hit him first."

Not one to show emotion, the always stoic Daniel twitches his lips, fighting back a smile, then he looks on the verge of bawling. "Albert said we were going to meet Whitt and your children for dinner, but he pulled into Edge's garage instead. He literally just told me what's happening as he parked the car."

Life sucking out of me, "Jesus fuck," I hiss in pain, not caring if my kids hear me or not.

Niel acts quickly, pulling his grandfather into a tight hug– my son's brawny body is evidently a comfort to hold. I notice Whitt out of the corner of my eye, looking away, but not before I see the flash of jealousy first.

"Do it." I yank at Whitt's sleeve. "Imagine how he's feeling right now. Just do it."

"Nah-uh…" Whitt shakes his head, grumbling, all the while I keep nodding.

"You're a grown man, Whitt. Act like it. Daniel needs you– Do it," I hiss, sounding like a snake. "Now."

"Fine," Whitt mutters begrudgingly, stepping toward his brother and grandfather. Hovering awkwardly near them, it takes Niel backing away and thrusting Daniel at Whitt before the hug occurs. Surprisingly, it's not nearly as uncomfortable as I imagined, because Daniel immediately latches on as if he's hugging Grant instead.

Sniffling, I look away. The hug was more for Whitt than Daniel. Some healing needed to be done today, since we'll be poking our wounds until they bleed in a few minutes.

Ella may still be wicked pissed at me, but the gravity of the situation is finally hitting her with its full force. Gripping the back of my sweater, Ella tries to hide behind me.

Refusing to accept Ella behaving like her father– cowardly –I put her in the center of everything. "Daniel?" I call out, tugging on his suit jacket. "I'd like to formally introduce you to your granddaughter. I know you've met many times without my knowledge, but I thought you'd like to give her a hug too."

I have no idea why I became the permission giver. With Daniel, he only hugs grown adults who he feels are physically capable of protecting themselves against unwanted advances, no doubt because of his past. With my children, and apparently Whitt, I have to grant Daniel my permission. I need to pass this information onto Katie for her daughters' sakes as well.

"Hello, Ella." Daniel sounds shy as he tries to hide his emotions, but he's smiling down at his granddaughter with pride and a glistening of unshed tears showing his pain. "When I look at you, all I see is your father." Eyes flicking up to mine– "And the determination and intelligence of your mother."

Unable to watch the family reunion unfolding, I pretend I'm not running away like the rat. But I have a good excuse– I need thirty seconds alone with said rat. "I'm going to hitch a ride on the elevator. Come on up when you're ready." Then I bolt for the elevator on the right before they try to follow me en masse.

Obviously Marcus squeezes in with me before the doors shut. "Nice diversion, Regina," he whispers with pride, but hard emotions are riding him as well. "Devious."

"I needed five second to compose myself, and I couldn't do it with Grant's posse of Whittenhower clones."

Marcus moves to hold me, trying to support me the best he can, but the elevator door opening interrupts us. "Wish we would've been going to the penthouse," I grumble as I step out of the elevator.

"Short ride to the first floor," Marc teases, reaching for my hand to pull me from the bank of elevators at the left side of the building. "I'll lead the way since you don't know where to go."

"Of course," blurts out as a distraction as we cross the glossy tiles, walking toward the security guard posted at the reception desk. "Gray. Everything has to be gray in The Edge Building." As an intimidating welcome, the titles form a gigantic silver **E** in front of the six double doors at the front. At the top of the arc is **The Edge Building**, with the lower arc screaming **Holden Zeitler**. "That's pretty snazzy," I mutter with begrudging respect.

The Edge Building is truly edgy, industrialized, with a lot of light flooding the first floor thanks to the windows having less tint. Ezra's touch is obvious in his building, whereas I just slapped an Empowerment label on my building and left it as it was, deciding to only maintain it. Now that I realize I bought my building from both sides of my business partner's family, Fate probably had a hand in designing the warm and welcoming look before I bought it. Most of the tallest buildings in Dominion are shared between several families. Empowerment used to belong to the Meyers, Spencer, and Simpson families.

Only three buildings belong to a singular family. Empowerment. Whittenhower Enterprises. The Green Building. Even Ezra shares his dark beauty with his birth family and adopted family. Edge is the tallest, largest, and most impressive by all standards, so it makes sense to share the costs from an economic standpoint.

Marc's laughter is light, causing a tight ball of nervousness inside my belly to unravel. "There's fresh flowers in vibrant colors," he points out, waving to the security guard, who just gives us a welcoming smile, not forcing us to check-in. "Shadow Haven was decorated by Diane and Pearl's mother, so it's much warmer than what Ezra would like."

"This is half your building," I remind Marcus. "Don't you get a vote?"

"A quarter my building– a quarter Dexter's. Ezra has control of the other half because Divina gave her quarter to Ezra as an '*I'm sorry I'm marrying your partner*' consolation prize to pull him out of a rage-influenced catatonic state. She also signed over Shadow Haven to him."

"Jesus," I hiss in disbelief as I'm drawn toward a hallway at a right angle to the front doors.

"Ezra had to be sedated through the entirety of Cortez and Divina's honeymoon." Nightmares haunt Marc's expression. "And there are no Christian symbols in this building," he reminds me, getting annoyed as I turn into a blasphemer.

Normally Marcus lets it go, but emotions are running high right now. Not that Marcus cares whether I'm a Christian or not. Hearing Jesus reminds him of his uncomfortable education at Hillbrook's Catholic school, where he was bullied for being Jewish.

"What the–" tumbles out between my numb lips when I catch sight of who's walking ahead of us. "Speak of the devil and he shall appear."

Hearing me, Ezra flips around and stops dead in his tracks. Flashing me a shit-eating grin, Ezra's posse looks sedate at his back. “The enemy is camped in my conference room.” Ezra chuckles to himself, not sharing why with the class. It must be some inside joke, because Aaron blushes bright red and Roarke’s guffaws echo down the hallway.

“Are you taking your meds?” Marcus goes on the attack, striding down the hallway at a fast clip to get to Ezra. Must be Ezra being in a happy state is impossible if his medication is working properly.

“It’s been a fabulous day.” Ezra’s smile is blinding, making him look more than ever like an angel descending.

“One of my worst,” I grumble, reaching the gathering of men in the middle of the hallway.

Laughing hardily with his pale arms spread like wings, “Witness the resurrection!” Ezra points at the door to my right, still laughing. “Take him to Hell, Regina– the coward deserves it.”

Joining in their boss’s celebration, a laughing Roarke and Aaron part, revealing another guest.

“Holy shit!” Head cocked to the side, I peer down at the smaller man. “Boyd?” Not much taller than his dinky sisters, Boyd looks like he ought to be over at Empowerment, either hiding in the coding cave or behind a desk doing the accounting. With muddy brown hair and drab, messy clothing, Boyd’s only remarkable feature is his crystalline blue eyes– eyes all of Gwen’s children have.

Eyes narrowed, Boyd looks angry at himself because he took a step backward, like he was going to hide behind Roarke for protection– from *me*.

“Regina,” Boyd mutters curtly, voice not betraying how his fisted hands shake.

Striding up to Boyd, “I bow down to the master,” I mutter with good humor and respect. This time he does take a step backward, but then he realizes I’m going in to shake his hand. “You have some tricks you need to teach me, buddy boy.”

Boyd smiles in relief because I’m not going to kick his ass. Then he laughs a melodious sound, causing Boyd to go from unremarkable to a man worthy of being Gwen’s kid. I can see parts of Fate, Faith, Whitt, and Bianca shining from Boyd’s face. Head tilting toward the closed door at my back, “I don’t know, Regina– you’re here to join our enemies.”

“I take it Boyd’s not here for therapy,” I tease, anger simmer in my blood. “Ezra,” I caution in a disappointed voice. “You better not be plotting while the Whittenhowers deal with something beyond painful."

"Oh, wouldn't dream of it." Smirking, Ezra has the audacity to wink at me. "Pretty Boy! Daniel!" he calls out, genuinely looking pleased to see them, notifying us that the rest of our party has arrived. Albert's name turns into a sneer, though.

I gather Ezra doesn't like Grant and the Whittenhower enforcers, but enjoys the rest of the family. Makes sense, considering Ezra's mother is Daniel's closest confidant.

Leaning into Marcus, I whisper into his ear, "Why is Ezra so pleased with himself?"

"Because he's up to no good, that's why," he whispers back. Firm hand cupping my elbow, he directs me to the conference room. "Let's get in there while Ezra distracts everyone."

"Ezra and Boyd are friends?" I mutter in confusion as my hand presses the lever down on the door. "That's a fucking unholy alliance, if I've ever seen one."

"I've been watching everyone," Marcus says ominously, causing me to pause with the door inched open. "Trying to get a read on how all this shit works. Those born within a few years of each other, they're either allies or mortal enemies. I'll use Jamie and Stanton versus Ezra and Boyd as example. I'm guessing Fate is a swing vote, and Faith is a singular entity who takes no sides."

"More like judge, jury, and executioner," I breathe the words Ezra used last night for Faith as I enter the room, ignoring the happy chatter at my back. Ezra genuinely sounds happy to see my family. It's no wonder Whitt turns into a besotted fool around him.

Eyes barely registering the movement, my breath hitches in my throat as Grant turns to face the door as it opens. A smile tugs at the scar tissue bisecting his lips all the way to his eyebrow.

Starvation.

Gut-wrenching starvation.

The hunger to drink in Grant is a compulsion I can't resist. Eyes darting quickly, I take in almost six feet of his body in less than an instant. The agony of seeing what I've gone so long without twists my guts and threatens to spew out my mouth.

Hands fisted, eyes burning with unshed tears, rage nearly blinding me, my body moves without a directive from my mind. The reverberation of flesh hitting flesh reaches my ears before the stinging in my hand manifests.

In a fog, I recognize loyalties are being tested. Roman and Kristal move in tandem to stop me from harming the head of the Whittenhower family. *My* friends would stop me– the betrayal mixes with the rage and abandonment to form a toxic stew.

Grant laughs a monstrous sound from deep within his belly. His bizarre amusement stops Roman and Kristal in their tracks just as their hands reach out to me. With a handprint blooming on the flawless side of his face, Grant looks more alive now than he ever had.

Red.

My eyes wash with the crimson color of unleashed rage, and this time I feel my fingers clenching to form a bone-breaking fist. Elegant fingers snare my wrist before I make contact, causing my eyes to first flick to Roman then to Kris. Shock etches across my face as I note neither one of them stopped me from punching Grant.

Kristal looks torn, heart-shaped face twisted with indecision. While Roman looks determined to protect me from myself.

Smiling beatifically, chuckling that ghastly sound, Grant's fingers loosen from my wrist, then slowly flow up my arm to my neck, thumb finding the hidden bite mark Marcus tried so desperately to cover with his own.

No longer the coy boy I met when I was eighteen, or the unsure young man I lost, Grant is a confident grown man– the man who made love to Marcus and me, then left without so much as a backward glance after we dozed off in the wee hours of the morning.

Expression turning serious, Grant allows me to stare at him in shock and awe, accurately reading all the emotions crossing my face. Blanking out, I come back to reality at the feel of scarred lips brushing against mine– the affectionate touch more of a question than an answer.

"You left me, remember?" I spit out between clenched lips, words vibrating against Grant's mouth. "Twice."

Fury crashes into my heart, shattering it into a billion pieces of broken hopes and dreams and a future never to be realized. "You don't get to kiss me like that anymore," I warn, the rage weaving its way through my body, rewriting on the very fabric of who I am. The warning turned threat becomes a promise as Grant's head hitches to the right at a painful angle.

Rage burns from my eyes, melding into the stinging on the back of my hand. The scarred side of Grant's face now matches the reddening perfect side thanks to the back-handed hit I just delivered.

A look of pure pride crosses Grant's face at the same time shame and horror slam into me. I just hit someone– *hit Grant.*

"I'm sorry," I mutter in shock. "You're allowed to do whatever you do, and I have no say in it. If I don't agree, I don't get to hit you because of it." Face burning with shame, I try to look away from his knowing eyes. "I can't force you to love me, to stay with me. But my self-respect will make sure you never hurt me again. I apologize for hitting you."

Long fingers wrap around my throat, and I don't move to protect myself from being strangled. A meep of surprise floods Grant's mouth after escaping mine. Instead of strangling me, Grant kisses me. Instead of kissing me with questioning affection, he ravages my mouth like a starving man at a buffet.

The rage rebuilds, with passion and lust riding in the passenger seat. My fingers clench those wrapped around my throat, nails digging in so Grant can't pull away. No longer needing oxygen to breath, I part my lips, needing Grant's taste to survive.

A vision of blood and semen floods my mind, showing me a fantasy of riding Grant's prone form, fists smashing into his face as I cum on his cock. Startled, I fear for my mental health as I reevaluate who I am as a person.

The moment I realize I need to cross the hall and sit on Dr. Lunatic's sofa is the moment I realize I am fucked in the head.

Chuckling a lusty sound, as if he can hear my disturbing private thoughts, Grant pulls away, raspy tongue slicking along mine as he parts. A shiver works its way down my spine, lighting in my lower belly, causing my pussy to clench as tightly as my fists.

I don't know whether I want to fuck Grant, or murder him, or perhaps a combination of both.

Stunned, with my shoulders slumped forward, my head hangs on my neck in defeat. My emotions run the gamut, to the point I can't accurately describe how I feel, let alone understand it. I drop into the nearest seat at the conference table, elbows hitting the tabletop with a loud thunk. I'm not the one running this shit-show, so I stay quiet, even if my children are involved. This is Grant's problem.

"Well, Ella... I guess that answers every question you lobbed at me during the car ride over here." Whitt's voice flows from the open doorway, blooming shame to cross my cheeks. "Some things never change," he mutters begrudgingly, voice tight with jealousy. "Whether Grant's dead or alive, that magnetic connection between your parents will never die."

Unable to look at my children or new husband, my eyes seek out Marcus to give a silent apology. Instead of jealousy and anger, I find Marcus shaking his head back and forth, making that sexual sound all men release when they're thinking thoughts they shouldn't.

After mock-punching his Jamie in the shoulder, Marcus takes the seat next to me. Putting me out of my embarrassed misery, Marc palms the back of my skull, forcing me to hide my face against his shoulder.

"Just breathe," Marcus whispers into my ear, compassion and sympathy lacing his voice. The hug he shared with Jamie yesterday no doubt had a similar effect on Marc as this kiss did on me. "Everything will be okay, but I can't promise this won't hurt."

After nodding in assent, I take a deep breath and pull away. Eyes rising, I take in the tableau happening around me. If agony was a tangible substance, it would be visibly weaving in the air, slowly sucking up all the oxygen in the room until we're left to either breathe it in and accept it or suffocate.

With the table separating them, Grant stays frozen yet animated, allowing his children and father to look him over. He has no need to study them, because he's been watching from the shadows during his death.

Marcus and I share a look of surprise, realizing we can read Grant better than we thought. It's obvious that Grant is terrified to join the land of the living as himself, happy yet apprehensive. Fingers twitching at his sides, Grant will do anything to hang onto the anonymity of the James Atwater name.

Fingers flying, scarred face twisted with a silent apology, Grant tries to communicate but falls short. Niel comes to the rescue, because I'm too wounded to speak and I have no idea how to read sign language. Marcus, Roman, and Kristal remain silent, with Albert standing in the doorway, because this is between Grant and his family.

"Hi, Dad." Niel is a brave boy, who looks like me but has many of his father's personality quirks– quirks I adored but now miss. There's a shy confidence my son exudes that has an addictive quality. "Do you want me to translate?"

The only movement in the room is Grant's eyes flicking to the tablet resting on the tabletop.

"Okay…" Niel looks uncomfortable, but I can't muster the strength to help him. I'm a bad mother who is forcing the father to step up and do his duty. But Grant can't even do that, letting the responsibility fall to his youngest son.

Reaching back, Niel grabs his sister's hand, tugging her forward. "This is obviously Ella." He laughs sardonically, because my daughter is the female version of her father.

Sparking to life, Grant flows smoothly around the table, eyes sighted in on our daughter. Watching the wonderment written across Ella's face, with Grant's back to me, I don't know what gesture he makes next. Whatever it is, permission is granted by the huge smile gracing my daughter's face.

Shaking hands cup chubby cheeks, molding over the features Grant genetically gifted his only daughter. Neither speaks– one muted by tragedy and one by wonder. A sob is torn from my throat as Grant's back bows forward, lips pressing sweetly to our daughter's forehead.

Heart breaking and mending, then breaking and mending, over and over again, I'm unable to witness it and keep my sanity. Unbidden, my head falls forward with my arms wrapping tightly around it to shield me. I barely register Marcus rubbing soothing circles in my back with Kristal and Roman massaging my shoulders as if it's a group effort to keep me from breaking apart.

Refusing to make this about me, I gather the courage to glance up. With one hand still touching his daughter, with Niel smiling at his back for support, Grant tries and fails to get Whitt to accept him.

"You won't take my legacy from me," Whitt grits out from between clenched teeth, blue eyes throwing sparks of hatred. I know exactly how Whitt is feeling in this moment. Leaning down, the son is several inches taller than his father, Whitt gets into Grant's face. "This family will be my responsibility on my twenty-fourth birthday, and neither you nor Daniel will take what's rightfully mine. *Mine*. You don't deserve us!" is shouted in a voice that instantly draws tears to flow down my cheeks.

The son thrusts a finger into his father's face, a hairsbreadth from injuring Grant. "Vow. Mine. You cowardly bastard, even though I know you have no honor, I want your solemn vow that you won't come back and take my legacy away."

Without words, Grant communicates by fisting his chest directly above his heart while bowing his head in supplication. The sincerity can be felt riding the air, but it's not good enough for Whitt. Because Whitt has something I don't– self-respect.

"That's all I ask of you," Whitt seethes. "Back off. Let me lead this family after you tried to take it away from me by giving it to my baby brother. Give me what should have been rightfully mine." Finger pressing into the fist still clenched at Grant's heart, Whitt demands, "Stay dead, asshole. Stay dead, because I'm angry enough to make it happen for real."

Turning to flee, Whitt makes it two feet before Albert is manhandling him in the doorway. Age is not a factor for the Whittenhower enforcer after a lifetime of wrangling Whitt. In less than three seconds, Whitt finds himself sitting on the opposite side of the table from me, a pout of frustration pulling at his lips.

"I understand," is gulped out from between my numb lips as I reach across the table to take Whitt's hand. "Trust me, you're not the only one in this room entertaining murder fantasies. But you wouldn't want to visit mine."

"Yeah," Whitt growls, refusing to look at me but his fingers wrap around mine. "It didn't take much imagination to figure out what you were thinking when I walked in here." Unable to help himself, a knowing smirk flirts with his perfect lips. "My murder fantasy began when I saw his hands on you, and it became bloodier as I realized you weren't letting him go."

"I won't apologize for how I feel," I whisper for only Whitt to hear, knowing full and well everyone is listening. "And no one expects you to either. Grant deserves whatever we give him."

"At least you're calling the asshole Grant." Whitt finally looks at me, rage and amusement warring in his eyes. "If I had to hear you call him Jamie one more time, I was going to gut him."

"I'm trying," is all I can say.

Not even pretending, Grant listens to Whitt's and my conversation with great interest. Upon noticing that it's met its conclusion, Grant turns his attention elsewhere.

Daniel.

We're all feeling something else.

Albert, Roman, Kristal, and Marcus have always known, long ago coming to terms with who Grant wished to be. I've known long enough for it to hurt, but seeing is harder than believing. Whitt is physically vibrating with rage. Judging by the ease in which Niel holds himself near his father, Grant and Niel have met, meaning Niel has lied to me already to protect his father. Ella is silent in her awe, eyes never leaving her father's face.

But then there is Daniel, who has had about twenty minutes to deal with the blow. Leaning against the wall near the door, because Albert isn't allowing anyone to leave, Daniel looks lost in the agony, as if he's experiencing not only Grant's death, but being transported back to Jackson's as well.

The level of betrayal Daniel is feeling mirrors that of Whitt's and mine. I don't want to empathize with a man who made my life a living nightmare, then wounded me seconds before throwing me out of our home, but it's hard not to in the face of his agony.

Father is devoid of sound, but it reaches every ear as we read the singular, emotional word shaping Grant's deformed lips.

Sucking back a sob, I try to get a read on Grant instead of concentrating on Daniel, because the look on Daniel's face is no less devastating then the one I witnessed the moment Jackson left this world.

Shock is written across Grant's face, like he didn't expect to miss Daniel as much as he did, and didn't expect to be ecstatic to be near him again. Magnetic. Not asking for permission, Grant launches himself across the space to tug Daniel away from the wall.

Just a fraction of a thought sparks in my mind, and I find Marc's eyes, knowing the same thought hit him too.

Who the hell is really Grant's biological father?

Grant is a mature man now, his genetics no longer hidden by his youth. Forehead to forehead, arms wrapped around each other, Grant and Daniel are the carbon copies of one another with only a generational divide between them.

Identical.

No trace of Jackson to be found in Grant. Jackson's spirit shines from my son's eyes as Niel watches his father and grandfather reconnect, while wearing an expression only Jackson could muster.

"Someone's got some explaining to do," Marcus murmurs into my ear, evidently hearing my thoughts.

Marc's words connect with Whitt, and he turns to look at us, thinking the same thing we are. "I've asked every day for a decade, and get a different answer every time," Whitt mutters in our direction, eyes going back to stare in disbelief at Daniel being emotional.

Jackson was a fiery presence. Wild. Unbridled. Bigger than life could contain. Jackson's booming voice, brawny body, and uncontrollable hair matched his personality.

Jackson was Wilhelm Whittenhower's first born in all ways, with Daniel taking after their mother. Reserved, introspective, and cerebral. Beautiful. Fair of hair and skin. Soft and small, with creamy skin.

"Grant's branch looks like it's connected to the wrong limb on the tree," I mutter, looking from Whitt, to my daughter, to Daniel and Grant embracing, then back to Niel– the only one who looks remotely like Jackson in the room. But looks are deceiving, because my father bore those same wild attributes. As do I, which is why Jackson chose me to carry the Whittenhower heir.

Standing with his arms folded over his chest in the doorway, "Let it go," Albert warns, threat more of a promise.

Yeah, because threatening us makes me not want to dig deeper.

Whitt rolls his eyes at me and Marcus chuckles as if my private thoughts were broadcast to their minds as well.

Arm curved around his older doppelganger, Grant directs Daniel to a chair– Niel immediately sits next to Daniel. Smiling sweetly, Grant rubs our daughter's back after helping her into the seat between her brothers. Then Grant sits next to me, farthest away from Whitt as he can get, directly across from a gobsmacked Daniel.

Moving in tandem, the Whittenhower enforcers do their duty. Albert shuts the door, then leans against it with his arms folded over his chest. Kris and Roman flank the back of Grant's chair, with Kristal more behind me than Grant.

Shivering next to me, Grant's nervousness is visible as he pulls the electronic tablet in front of him. A stylus appears out of nowhere. Trying to concentrate, it feels like a million years for Grant to write something– anything.

With a deep breath, Grant presents the tablet.

Hi!

We breathe out as a singular entity– the relief palpable.

In less than a heartbeat, I'm at the door. Not only does Albert not stop me, he opens the goddamn door for me.

Chapter Twenty-Seven

Blanking out, I find myself butted up against the wall across the hallway, with my head tucked to my knees and my arms hugging my legs. Eyes closed against the spilling tears, I try to self-comfort, because this isn't about me.

I can't… I know everyone in that room will buy the shit Grant's selling. Their hearts are hurt, but not enough that they won't drink the Kool-Aid Grant's serving. I refuse to be a thirsty plant seeking Grant as if he's my sun.

Grant hurt me, hurt us all, and he won't have to pay for it. No vengeance dealt, not even a dish of justice.

Sure, after my foray with Maître du Jeu, I'm positive there are scary reasons for whatever Grant's done, but I don't give a shit anymore. The reasons don't matter. Now does. It's too little, too late.

It's not about me, but I can't help but wish someone would give a shit about what Grant's put me through. Forced me into a relationship, impregnated me with two kids, then asked me to marry him after nearly five years, disappearing an hour later for a decade. Yes, these were choices I made, choices made based on false promises and emotions. All the time I grieved, Grant was across town, content to know we were okay, to check up on us from the shadows, not offering us the same comfort.

Our chemistry may be magnetic, and he can tell me he loves me until he's blue in the face, but Grant's actions scream like a banshee. I don't require him to treat me with dignity and respect–I sold myself and my children, and forever I'll be relegated as the woman who survives off his scraps.

A letter.

A text.

A glimpse.

A kiss.

A false I love you.

Grant was content with me being an orbiting satellite around his life, but never truly including me. Now, he's not *in* my life either. Grant checks in when he wants, not when I need. The connection I developed with Jamie was Grant's way of seeking redemption, where he didn't let me into his life while trying to alleviate his own guilt by helping me in mine.

This isn't about me– I'm not Grant's family. I'm the woman who had his children, children that should be his sole focus. I not only accept this as fact, but welcome it. Grant needs to put all of his focus on his children, because I survived life before I knew him and after he abandoned me.

Four years is a drop in the bucket out of the thirty years I've been on this planet. I've lived longer than both of my parents, and I sure as shit can live another three or four decades with Grant as a satellite orbiting our children's lives, as long as he stays out of my path.

After all, I'm not the only woman to give Grant a child– doing so doesn't make me special.

It makes me fucking stupid.

"Hey." Whitt's voice draws me from my inner turmoil like a ray of sunshine on the darkest of nights. A hand appears in my line of sight. "Let's go for a drive."

Voice warbling after crying, I only manage a weak, "What?"

Expression serious, Whitt's eyes glint with calculation. "C'mon. Let's take the Roadster out for a wild ride down the highway at breakneck speeds like old times."

Not waiting for a reply, Whitt grips my wrist and tugs me to my feet. Mind spinning, I'm on autopilot during the walk down the hallway, through the vestibule, and the short ride down the elevator to the underground parking garage.

Whitt has to stop me before I wander to his car. One hand holding mine, the other grips my chin to make sure I check in with reality.

"I could be a total dick, but I don't want to be like my dad." Eyes earnest, Whitt waits until I mull over what he's trying to explain. When he notices that I'm not getting it, he explains. "I could lie, and you'd be hurt. I could evade, and you'd be hurt. I could tell the truth, and then I'd have to share you. Since I'm placing your interests above mine, I'm choosing your happiness over my pride."

Mind suddenly catching up, "You're going to tell me why you're with me and not Marcus, considering this meeting was for *your* benefit."

Emotions cross Whitt's features at warp speed. Sadness. Fury. Compassion. Jealousy. Love.

"Everyone but Marc and I were enthralled by the Second Coming of Christ. So while you were in the hallway having a conflict of conscience, Marc and I were engaging in a text battle over which one of us could escape."

"Why not both?" The heavy weight surrounding my heart lessens, and I'm able to smile and tease.

"I'm a good negotiator," Whitt mutters smugly, all confidence, not arrogance.

"Marcus is a litigator by profession," I remind him, suddenly terrified if this young man can take Marcus on and win.

"I have my ways." A private smile quirks Whitt's lips, then he releases the truth. "Tonight, Marcus and I are on the same team, putting you first." Fingers clench against mine, offering affection and support. "We decided this has to be a one-on-one situation, with the other left behind so he can tell you everything you missed. Even if you don't believe you want to know, you may regret that later."

"So why did you leave and Marcus stay?" I stress, getting the feeling Whitt is talking around something that will break my heart.

Eyebrows scrunching in the center of his forehead, looking more like pity than confusion, Whitt puts me out of my misery. "It's not what you think, which is exactly why we were battling it out. Marcus isn't sticking around because he's obsessed with his Jamie more than he is with you. He bowed out, wanting to look like the hero."

Eye roll.

"So maybe that's my take on the situation." Whitt releases a funny little laugh, making fun of himself. "Marcus was being the bigger guy, knowing you and I feel the same way and we need each other right now, because I couldn't sit in there any more than you could."

"Why?" I blurt out, needing to know Whitt actually feels as I do, versus him assuming he does.

"Because Grant did this to us!" Whitt growls, fisting his chest. "I'm so furious right now I can barely think. That goddamn man is sitting up there, with his faithful followers soaking up his attention, like he didn't tear our hearts out of our chests and piss in the wound. He doesn't deserve the ability to tell me why he did what he did, because he hasn't earned it. I don't forgive him, and nothing he has to say to me will make me forgive him, no matter how much I love and miss him."

"Loving and missing Grant makes the betrayal worse– the abandonment. The grief even if he still breathes, because we lost him no matter what," I say in all honesty.

"Get your ass in the car, Queen." With a hard tug, my feet are moving. "It's my turn to show you I can drive."

Chuckling underneath my breath, I crawl into the Roadster, mind going back more than a decade and a half to when I learned to drive in this very car, with Grant, and sometimes Jackson, in the passenger seat holding Whitt on their lap.

Those driving lessons felt like freedom, and I mourn the loss for Whitt not having Grant and Jackson teach him how to drive this wicked car.

We sit in silent contemplation while Whitt traverses through downtown Dominion traffic, then exits the nearest ramp to the highway. Gazing out the windows at the lights speeding by, I wish it wasn't winter so we could have the top down.

"Daniel." Whitt's voice spooks me out of my thoughts, feeling intimate in the quiet darkness of the car.

"Daniel?" I mutter, feeling like I missed something.

"Daniel taught me how to drive." A private smile curls Whitt's lips. "I could tell you were reminiscing about when you learned to drive, and were feeling pity that I didn't have the same experience. Daniel taught me how to drive, squeezed into the passenger seat with Niel's big ass hogging all the room."

Laughing while shaking my head left and right in astonishment, "I would have guessed Albert instead."

"Nah– Daniel's all about educating his minions," Whitt says with affection. In the face of seeing his dad, Whitt must realize Daniel isn't the monster he made him out to be. At least Daniel stuck around and showed up when he was needed. Annoying is the fact that he shows up when he isn't needed too.

"When he's missing Uncle Jack, Daniel has us all empty out into the drive in front of the house, then he rides shotgun as we drive up and down the driveway to the gate. Sometimes he lets the kids drive to Crestview's main gate."

"How old?" I ask, voice quivering with worry.

"Queen, really?" Whitt laughs at me, foot turning to lead on the accelerator pedal. Zipping past heavy traffic on the highway, a sense of wild abandon fills his features. "You forget I was driving this car at age six."

"Shit," I hiss with feeling, missing a time in my life I'll never get back, nor can I ever revisit. It was a time when I was innocent and everything felt electric. Raw with the power of freedom without responsibilities. Then I realize Whitt experienced it with me, because he was born with a purpose and has never been free of responsibility.

"Daniel knows we're married?" I tread lightly.

"Yes," is all Whitt gives me.

"He didn't find it bizarre? What was his reaction?"

"I know where you're going with this, Regina," Whitt warns. Uh-oh, he called me by my given name. "We're not getting an annulment simply because the cat's out of the bag. Daniel knows I know he's my grandfather and Grant is my father, and he knows we got married and I'm adopting the kids. I realized there was no way of getting around it."

"So if he knows…" I spread my hands, realizing Whitt can't see the gesture as he drives in the dark. "So why…"

Whitt's foot presses harder on the accelerator, proving Jackson's wild spirit is riding shotgun in this car. "I love you," he admits like it's not common knowledge. "I know what you're thinking and why you're thinking it."

Silence rings as Whitt drives far and fast, heading deeper into Upstate New York. The minutes trickle into more than an hour, and I split the time looking out the windshield and staring at the side of Whitt's face as his jaw clenches and releases. The sound of his harsh breathing and teeth grinding is almost deafening.

The landscape changes to woodland bordering fields, with fewer and fewer cars sharing the road with us. The Roadster slows to a crawl, then smoothly flows to a stop on the shoulder of the highway.

My breath catches in my throat as Whitt jerks his door open, flows out onto the road, then slams the door behind him. A few seconds later, my door is being wrenched open, with a hand unhooking my seatbelt while the other tears me from the car.

Visibly gasping for breath in the cold winter night, Whitt leans against the car, and I can tell he's counting backward to get control of his emotions. "I'm not mad at you," he says after a minute or so. "As I said, I know why you're thinking what you're thinking."

Knowing better than to push my luck, I wait patiently for Whitt to say what he needs to say. I focus on a dairy barn in the distance, looking at the golden glow escaping the windows of the nearby farmhouse. Is the family inside happy? We're all so caught up in our own lives, we don't realize every car and house we pass features another family trying to live theirs.

The air is so brisk, I can hear cars coming up the highway from more than a mile away, judging by how long it takes before the car drives past us. Some slow down because it's not every day you see a 1965 Shelby Cobra sitting on the side of the road.

"I have come to terms with the fact that there are things you cannot tell me," Whitt begins, and his words halt my breathing out of fear. "I trust you infallibly, Queen. With that trust, I know you're protecting me by not telling me the truth, and I know you'll tell me when the time comes."

"Yes," is a breath on the wind.

"So don't feel guilty." Whitt's fingers twitch, pinky hooking mine as they rest against the side of the car. "I know you'll forever be in love with my sire, no matter how much he disrespects and hurts you. I also know the rat-bastard is still in love with you." Voice turning wistful, "The way you two looked earlier… But I'm not jealous or afraid of that connection, because without it, I wouldn't know you."

Eyebrows scrunching together, confusion laces my voice. "What do you mean?"

"What you have with Grant, I want that someday, but in a healthy way." Head turning slightly, Whitt looks me in the eyes. "I love you."

Whispering the truth, "I fell in love with you a little bit the night I met you, as I was sitting on your bed reading you a story. I was in a bad place right then with my mother dying, and you were the only bright spot I could find. After I lost her and was forced to Misery Castle, I called you my sunshine because you literally filled a hole that was sucking my soul dry."

"Melodramatic, I like," Whitt teases me, squeezing my hand. "Hell, I think I loved you before you showed up. I was waiting for something, unsettled. Even at such a young age, I recognized it was you I was waiting for when you finally showed up."

"Yeah…" flows softly from my lips, filled with sadness and hope.

"I was thrilled how you and Grant had an instant connection." Whitt huffs a sharp laugh at his own expense, then he shoulder bumps me. "It meant I got to keep you."

"I still…" The brutal truth spilling between us creates an intimacy I can't ignore. "I'm still confused on whether or not what I felt for Grant was real– what he felt for me."

"I'm going to be a dick right now, because I refuse to help that bastard keep you by telling you the truth." Whitt looks away sharply, jaw working to grind his molars together. "It was just after you became pregnant with Niel that I became possessive of you, and jealous of my own goddamn father."

"I know." Now it's my turn to laugh at myself– the sound of my discomfort flutters in the air between us.

"Yes, there are a dozen reasons to why I wanted to marry you. Some are for survival. Some are out of selfishness. Most are for the right reasons. Yes, Daniel knows we're married, knows I know about *my* legacy, so it makes the whole scheme moot from that perspective. So I can understand why you would want to have an annulment, for the both of us."

"I want you to be able to marry the person who drives you fucking nuts." My mind lights on Grant, quickly passes over him, and then hovers over Marcus. "Hell, I want that for me too."

"Oh, I'm not blinding myself to the possibilities. I just don't think it's annulment-worthy for a person who isn't in my life yet. If and when I meet this person, if they love me, they'll be patient and wait for me. Same goes for you and whatever is happening between you and Marcus. Four years and a handful of months, then I promise I will not contest a divorce between us."

"Why?" I breathe, confusion causing my voice to warble.

"I trust you. Hell, I even trust Daniel not to change the bylaws for Whittenhower Enterprises. Daniel and I drove up to Albany for Kent's fundraiser last night– just the two of us, and we really talked the entire way. He was proud that I bested him, so I know my legacy will be waiting for me on my twenty-fourth birthday as long as I respect him."

"I…" Baffled. "Wow."

Whitt turns slightly, resting a hip on the side of the car. "Daniel sounded afraid, and I know it connects to what you refuse to tell me. Very afraid. He asked me if anyone pulls my strings, and I said no. Blackmail, he said. Then he asked if anyone pulls yours, and I told him I'd guess yes. The fact that Daniel gave me his blessing to adopt his grandchildren made me terrified as well. But I trust you, and I'm now learning to trust Daniel."

"I hear a *but* coming?"

"We can't do the annulment until after I'm the head of Whittenhower Enterprises. I have to adopt my heirs so no one else but me has any influence on their futures. History won't repeat itself like how Niel and I were conceived. Daniel is compromised– *you* are compromised. I don't need to know what's going on, because I know right from wrong, and I will protect the interests and happiness of my heirs."

Whitt pulls away, releasing my hand as he goes. Pacing the length of the car, he gazes out into the field like it holds the secrets of the universe. "I made Grant vow, knowing damn well if it fit his agenda, he'd go back on his word. How can I trust the vow of a man who will leave the woman he's obviously in love with and his three children? Grant left Daniel for fuck's sake, and Daniel needed him."

"Grant's leaving spoke more of who he is as a person, no matter who or what is influencing him. I don't wish to hear his excuses *yet*," I stress.

"All Grant has to do is reclaim his name, and we'd all be beholden to him– all of us. As long as he hides as James Atwater, as long as Niel and Ella are legally my heirs, our family will be safe. But since I don't trust my own father, I won't be able to truly sleep until I'm twenty-four and everything is mine."

"What about Daniel?" I offer as a suggestion, because I know Daniel doesn't want it all to himself. He was born and bred to partner with whomever ran Whittenhower Enterprises.

"Daniel is merely a placeholder for the resurrected Grant or for when the heir comes of age– our bylaws state that's at age twenty-four. Niel will have more influence at age eighteen than Daniel ever has."

"So if the cowardly bat ever leaves his belfry…" I trail off, not realizing until now how volatile this situation is. If MdJ tells Jamie to go back to being Grant, their power will grow exponentially, and we'll all be fucked. But as long as Whitt is legally in possession of all of Grant's heirs, MdJ can't access anyone but Daniel and me.

"Yeah, no annulment," I finally agree.

"I hate him," Whitt admits without shame. "I hate him so much I can hardly breathe. I know whatever you're protecting me from, whatever has Daniel utterly terrified, is the same bullshit that tore Grant from our lives. It's also the same thing that has him coming back. So I hate Grant for putting us all in danger, for yanking you around by your heart."

Shuddering in immense pain, my knees go weak.

"C'mon, let's get you back in the car with the heat on," Whitt purposefully misunderstands why I shuddered. Supporting me, he opens the car door and deposits me inside, reaching over me to buckle my seatbelt.

A few minutes into our car ride, with the heat going full-bore, Whitt yet again surprises me. "Promise me something, will you?"

"In my advanced age, I've learned to never make a vow on an open-ended subject," I murmur with wry amusement.

"I'm placing my trust in you, Regina." There isn't even a shade of amusement in Whitt's voice. "I need you to do the same with me. I won't dig into what's happening around me if you make me a promise in return."

"It's for your own good," I remind him. "I'd tell you if I felt it was the right thing to do."

"I know– so promise me," Whitt demands, hands gripping the steering wheel. "Promise me you won't go digging into what was brought up earlier, how identical Daniel and Grant looked during their hug."

"Why?" I mutter, completely baffled.

"No DNA tests– promise me."

"I'll promise if you explain why," I negotiate, beyond confused. "Considering your parentage was a total lie, I'd think you'd want to know whether or not Daniel is your grandfather or great-uncle."

"You can blame yourself for how I see Daniel in a different light." Whitt chuckles softly at my sharp intake of breath. "The shit you told me about him while we were at Denny's, I couldn't get it out of my head. So I started self-reflecting, and I came to many realizations."

"Like what?"

"Daniel's changed like you've changed, Regina." Whitt keeps calling me Regina, not Queen, so I know we're spiraling down into some hardcore shit. "You've hardened and Daniel's softened. I was too busy being angry to notice he was really trying to connect with me all these years." Sighing deeply, "We talked," is so quiet I barely heard it.

"Last night?" I ask, getting a quick jerk of his head as affirmation. "About what?" I know Daniel doesn't lie. If you ask, he'll most likely answer. If he doesn't want to answer, he'll just tell you it's none of your business and walk away.

"When Albert pulled up in the garage tonight, I feared Daniel knew about Grant all along, and it made me furious after how we connected last night. But then I saw Daniel's face, and it scared me."

"Scared you how?"

"The pain was back, Regina." Whitt concentrates on driving, barely voicing the words. "You can't imagine how Daniel changed. Last night, he explained some of it."

"Daniel is Grant's biological father, isn't he?"

"I don't know," Whitt's voice breaks. "Daniel doesn't know. Grandmother doesn't know. I doubt Jackson knew. But we're never going to find out the truth."

"Why?" My voice pitches high in confusion. "I don't understand what harm the truth would do."

"Jackson's dead and gone, Regina. The pain–"

"I was in the study," voice haunted, I remember it like it was a minute ago. "The death wail Daniel made, after Jackson's heart stopped for the very last time, it still rings in my ears."

"Yeah, well… I'll raise you the sound the man made when he found out his son was dead. What Daniel did and said to you afterward was mild by comparison. Then he had to mourn you after you didn't come back. It wasn't pleasant. The pain."

"Jesus Christ." A sob threatens to tear itself from my chest.

"So after you told me about how Daniel is asexual, and about how… about how you think maybe he was Jackson's partner in all ways, it got me to thinking, putting pieces of my life together until it made sense."

"What did you discover?"

"Jackson's death loomed over Daniel from the time he was a teenager, right? Daniel would do anything to find an anchor to Jackson, even if that meant pretending his own son wasn't his. So Grant was born, and he looked exactly like Daniel, and Jackson loved him unconditionally because of how much he loved Daniel. Then the girls were born, looking exactly like Daniel… then I was born, looking exactly like Daniel–"

Heart clenching, I finally get it. "Jackson wasn't long for this earth, so Daniel needed a piece of him to remain."

"Regina," Whitt's voice breaks. "I cannot imagine being as connected to another human being as Daniel and Jackson were to one another. I love Niel with every fiber of my being, but I know I could survive his loss. I know you understand."

"Yeah, I do," I whisper. "If it hadn't been for Ella, I don't know if I would've survived Grant's death, not after losing my parents and Jackson so close together. Then losing you and Niel at the same time. It was too much. But in order for Ella to live, I had to survive."

"I hate him so goddamn much," Whitt snarls underneath his breath. "Daniel needed his own Ella, ya know? Jack had died and was resuscitated, which is why my birth was so important to both Jack and Daniel, even if Grant was only fifteen when they started to stud him out."

Shuddering, "Just thinking about that makes me sick. Imagine in a year or two, if that happens to Niel."

"That's why we got married," Whitt reminds me. "Anyway, after I was born, I looked just like Daniel. So that was the wedge between us. Jackson loved me just as much as he loved Grant– I could feel it. But Daniel needed a sign that Grant was Jack's, and I proved otherwise."

"Shit, he admitted that last night, didn't he?"

"Yeah, he did," Whitt breathes like it's a confession. "Daniel is surprisingly candid when asked direct questions– questions I never should've asked." Whitt shudders in horror. "Everyone in Misery Castle felt Daniel's offishness toward me, which is when you came into our lives."

"Which is why I fell in love with you, because I couldn't imagine how anyone couldn't love you." I reach over to rest my hand on top of Whitt's as he grips the gear shift.

"So Niel was born with Jack's wild hair and stocky body," Whitt mutters, causing me to clear my throat. "I know– *I know*. I think Jack was stacking the deck by picking out a woman who had a few of his attributes. Attributes which would genetically overpower the recessive Whittenhower genes, lending Daniel comfort."

"You truly believe Daniel is Grant's biological father, don't you? Because that hair and stock body comes from me– from my father."

"Ninety percent positive," Whitt admits without hesitation. "But the kid is like a mini Jackson, whether it be traits handed down from grandfather to grandson or great-uncle to nephew remains to be seen. But I don't want to know, because Daniel needs Niel to be proof that Jackson still lives and breathes through Grant, me, Niel, and Ella. I will never take that away from him, Regina. Never."

"I'm so sorry, Sunshine. So fucking sorry that you've had to live like this. So sorry."

"No pity," Whitt barks. "Daniel is the one I worry about. After Jack's death, right around the time Grant started acting squirrelly and disappearing constantly, no doubt getting in deep with whatever bullshit is still plaguing us, Daniel latched onto him like a leech. I'd hide in the draperies, watching Grant rock Daniel while rubbing his back, because the man was catatonic with grief."

"I didn't know–"

"You had enough shit going on, Regina. We didn't want you to know." Whitt's thumb wraps around my pinky finger as we hold the gear shift together. "Plus, a man has to have some pride. Daniel resented me, then Niel was born, Jackson died, and Daniel got clingy. He started wanting to be around me, know everything about me, and I couldn't handle it. I said I was self-reflecting, and that was part of it. I pushed Daniel away when he was trying to connect with me, highlighting how Niel was the chosen one and I was the ignored one. Then Grant died, and it exacerbated it."

"Daniel doesn't understand that type of emotion. Everything's black and white, so he probably didn't know how to connect with you after that."

"We discussed that last night," Whitt mutters, sounding shy all of the sudden. "I loved how focused Daniel was about my studies, because it placed me at his desk, where he'd give me his undivided attention. But I kept telling myself I was Grant's replacement, like how I tried to lie to myself about how Niel was Jackson's. Which made me hate Grant all the more."

"But you're not Grant, and Niel isn't Jackson," I mutter more to myself than him. "And Daniel genuinely enjoyed your company."

Guilt and sadness war in Whitt's voice. "I was a kid– I didn't understand."

"You're only nineteen," I point out, laughing to myself. "You're still a kid."

“Not funny,” Whitt growls a warning, voice shifting to Master Daniel’s. “Don’t make me demonstrate how I’m a grown man again, Regina.”

A shudder works its way down my spine, and it’s not from the cold or fear.

“So… um… how are things between Daniel and Priscilla?”

Whitt’s sharp bark of laughter is answer enough. “Before last night– I would have told you about how they hug and kiss out in the open in front of us kids. How they cuddle on the sofa while they watch TV, but also how they do live very separate lives. Grandmother never has any men floating around, so I assume she’s satisfied. Diane is always underfoot, but it’s more of Daniel needing a partner-in-crime, not one in his bed.”

“But after last night?” I prompt, trying hard not to laugh at the puckered-sour expression riding Whitt’s face.

“Never ask Daniel a question if you’re not prepared to hear the answer. He’s not salacious, just very thorough.” Unable to help myself, the laughter flows, and Whitt joins me.

“Yeah, I got that very advice from your dad years and years ago,” I mutter with a chuckle.

“Curiosity killed the cat–”

“Oh, my God! You asked *that*!”

“I asked. Daniel answered. It was an uncomfortable education I didn’t want. Needless to say, being a Master of Restraint and buddies with the incestuous cousins helped to keep the car vomit-free.”

“Wow… yeah, I– I always figured they went there.”

“It was painful,” Whitt croaks out, and not in a humorous kind of way. “When I say Daniel’s pain, I mean that in a very tangible sort of way. Jackson was Daniel’s partner in life. Losing him was like losing half of himself.”

“I didn’t abandon Niel,” I finally admit to myself out loud. “I gave Niel to Daniel minutes after Jackson died, knowing we couldn’t survive losing both of them at once.”

“Daniel admitted he would’ve killed himself if Grant hadn’t been Jack’s son, with Niel proving it. He was being so open, I even asked him about being molested. If I didn’t already hate Grant, I’d hate him more for abandoning Daniel when he was in so much pain– Niel and I weren’t old enough to soothe him. The abandonment isn’t only mine I’m feeling– the pain is all of ours. So sitting in that meeting room, with Daniel’s joy flavoring the air, it killed me. Because that rat-bastard was hiding out across town while Daniel was dying inside, while you were clinging to Ella instead of harming yourself. We were all bleeding agony, and Grant got off on it."

Gut-wrenching sobs threaten to spill forth, the remembered pain as if it were yesterday. Wrapping my arms around myself, I try to give myself a comforting hug.

"He'll never deserve you, Regina," Whitt states unequivocally. "Maybe I'll understand it once I fall in love with a man. But right now, if you continue to cleave to Grant, a part of me will begin to hate you too– hate you for disrespecting yourself. Disrespecting all of us."

Sucking in a sharp breath, I release it as agony-filled words. "The truth sure does hurt with you, Sunshine. I'm so glad we don't tell each other pretty lies."

In the ringing silence, I notice Whitt's sitting in the car with his hands in his lap, like he's not sure what to do or say next. Looking around in confusion, I realize we're parked in The Edge Building's garage, right next to my car.

Turning slightly to the side, Whitt gains my undivided attention. "This is what we're going to do, okay? First, Ella's at Misery Castle, in case you're wondering."

"Good God, I'm a horrible mother," I mutter in horror, never once wondering where my daughter would end up when I fled.

"You're a mother with a lot of painful shit happening." Whitt stares at me for a second, debating whether or not to say something. "I know what Ella said to you when you told her about Grant still being alive. She was vicious in the car. I kept my mouth shut until she was done, but Niel kept lighting into her. I had to pull over because they were throwing down in this tiny car."

A huff of a laugh spills from my throat. "Real siblings beat the shit out of each other, didn't you know that?"

Now it's Whitt's turn to laugh. "I have no idea what you're talking about." Looking away, cheeks blushing, I know damn well Whitt has beat Niel's ass a handful of times. "So I'm going to go home and rescue the kids from Daniel– he's probably flying high and fighting with Grandmother for lying to him. Yeah, I blame her too."

"Will there ever be happiness at Whittenhower Estates?" I muse more to myself than Whitt.

"Sure," he mutters sarcastically. "We don't call it Misery Castle for nothing. Resentment and pain bleed from the mortar."

"Are you going to be okay? What are you going to do about Grant?"

"I'm taking control of my life, Queen, as should you. Grant doesn't factor into it whatsoever. He can contact us, but we should never go to him. If Ella and Niel want to see him, fine. They don't remember him like we do, so they didn't mourn like we did. They're happy right now, while it feels like a goddamn slap to the face for us."

"Yeah," is wrenched from my throat. "Exactly that."

"The bastard doesn't want Katie and Kent to know, so I have to look into Whitney and Prissy's eyes every fucking day and lie." Whitt's growl is deafening in the confines of the car. "But I guess if they know, that would mean James Atwater was reclaiming the Grant Whittenhower name, and I'd lose my legacy. So there is that."

"There is that," I mutter sardonically.

"So I'm going to go home and rescue the four kids. We'll camp out in my bedroom, watching movies and eating junk food until we fall into a coma, because I don't want to be alone tonight."

Reaching over to touch Whitt's forearm, "I–"

"You may be my wife…" Whitt looks at me, amusement riding his features. "But you're a one-man kind of woman. We're not like that, I get it. We will consummate our marriage, maybe a few times in the next four and a half years, but that's it. I know I'm not the man you want to marry."

Pain fills my voice, "Sunshine–"

"I know you love me." Whitt takes my hand off his arm, squeezing my fingers. "It's okay. I need to focus on those four little shits, because when they come of age, I'll be free to do whatever the fuck I want to do."

"You're gonna… you're going to do something else with your life?" Shock hits me straight in the chest.

"I have no idea what the future holds, so I'm leaving my options open. I do know I have many options, when a year or two ago, I felt like I was being strangled to death. I have hope now. So, yeah, Misery Castle can be filled with happiness. Eventually. Once the taint is cut away."

"I better get out of your car, then." Chuckling at myself, I unhook my seatbelt.

"If you go to Grant tonight, I will kill him the next time I see him."

"Don't look in the mirror, then," voice tight with fury. "You don't get to order me around and threaten me."

"You aren't thinking clearly, Regina," Whitt's voice is stiff with tension. "You need to take a step back. Marcus is waiting at home for you, because he *is* putting you first right now. No one is telling you to stop loving Grant. We want you to feel what you're feeling, instead of burying it."

Fingers curling into fists, I breathe through the need to lunge from the car and run as fast as I can. "I guess you missed where I hit Grant, didn't you? Because that's the emotion I'm feeling. Rage."

"Yeah, but I didn't miss how if we hadn't been in the room, you two would've been fucking on the table." Now it's Whitt's turn for his hands to turn to fists. "I can handle my wife bedding her lover, but I will not accept you touching my father. Anyone but him."

"I was channeling the rage into lust so I wouldn't murder a man in front of his children and father." Even to my ears, my admission rings as false.

"Sure," Whitt ain't buying my bullshit. "I don't care what you do with him– just not tonight. You need some distance. Not on the night he hurt us. Not on the night you and I connected. Not tonight. The bastard deserves nothing but being alone."

"I'm going home, and I will not contact Grant," I grit out, infuriated at Whitt now too. "I'm not staying away from him because you told me to. It's because I made a promise to myself as I sat in the hallway tonight. I'm not a stupid woman. I get that as soon as I'm in Grant's proximity, I lose my fucking mind."

Laughing, a mix of relief and irony, Whitt's face is alight with life. "I'm terrified of the day I meet someone who does that to me. Truly. I said I was going to be a dick, but I can't stop rooting for the cowardly bastard. Grant has the strongest self-control on the planet. It must have killed him to stay away from you, because he goes fucking nuts when he's around you too."

"Good." I open the car door. "I hope it hurt Grant just a fraction the separation caused me."

Arm lashing out, Whitt's palm wraps around the nape of my neck, tugging me down for a soft kiss goodbye. Pulling away, laughter frozen on his lips, Whitt's smile takes on a bloodthirsty edge. "I have the feeling it hurt him more than we can imagine, and he deserved every *agonizing* moment."

And with that, I crawled out of the car, got into my own, and made my way home, because I can only handle so much of Whitt's honesty.

Four years until the present

Restraint - Unleashed

Chapter Twenty-Eight

"For fuck's sake," I snarl down at my keyboard. "I'm not shady enough for this task." Pushing back from my desk, my chair rolls across the carpet until I can view all the monitors in my cave. Noises filter in, the sound of my girls decorating and cooking up a storm for Whitt's birthday celebration tonight.

These past five months, I've taken everyone's advice and concentrated on me and mine. Romance and lust aren't in the equation. Sure, Marcus stays over one night a week. But more often than not, it's intimacy and affection, not seduction. We commiserate, then sleep it off. We're too busy to focus on *us*.

Marcus is busy playing interference now that Katya Waters showed up earlier than expected. Whatever was holding her back from coming before the school year let out, she showed up at the end of April. I know Pennsylvania lets out earlier than New York State, but not *that* much earlier.

Ezra's both even-keeled and batshit fucking cray-cray, depending on Cortez. Ezra's keeping his distance from Katya, allowing her to get acclimated in Dominion. That caring and considerate part of Ezra, I admire and respect. But since Ezra won't allow Cortez access to Katya, Marcus has had to play mediator nonstop to avoid Armageddon between Ezra and Cortez. I knew in theory Cortez was a highly jealous and possessive person, but I'm witnessing it first-hand now.

Truthfully, Ezra and Cortez are driving me nuts, and I feel horrible I've left Marcus to deal with the fallout by himself.

With Marcus out of my hair, I've focused on my family and work, spending all of my nights at Restraint. I needed the sensation of control running Empowerment and Restraint gives me, especially with MdJ making demands on a weekly basis for my services.

Usually MdJ tells me to buy or sell specific stock, and donate to charities or campaign fundraisers. Once I was told to hire a person. Another time I was told to fire an employee. Last week, I was forced to transfer one of my employees over to

Whittenhower Enterprises– espionage at its finest. I'm sure Daniel was blackmailed at the same time.

"Shady bastards," I mutter, leaning forward to grab my wireless keyboard. "I have no idea how to do this shit."

"What shit?" Niel's soft voice has me jumping out of my skin. Looking over my shoulder, I catch the naughty smirk cross his lips before my son hides it. "Can I help?"

With a fingertip, all of the monitors in my cave go black. "I thought you were escorting the birthday boy here later tonight?" my upward inflection makes it a question.

Niel walks into my home office, giving me time to drink him in. At almost fourteen, my son has grown inches and many pounds of pure muscle, all of which I wouldn't have noticed had he not came back into my life. The loss would have been indescribable.

Running a hand through his wild hair, getting redder by the day as the blond of childhood darkens. "I just came for a visit." Niel rests his hip on the edge of my desk, almost in touching distance but not quite.

We don't have a mother/son relationship, and probably never will. Truthfully, sometimes my son terrifies me in the way I terrified my parents. He's a grown man in a grown man's body, with a mind that's petrifying, but the heart and age of a boy. Niel can be silly and playful, but then he can speak with wisdom and reason in the next breath.

The fact that Niel can grow a full beard isn't helping matters, either.

"How did you get here?" With the press of a fingertip, the security feed is brought up on the central monitor on my desk, showing Albert isn't standing by.

"ATV." Niel smirks at me– my lips, but that asshole expression is the Grant I know today.

Jamie still texts me every night at 1 a.m. There are nights I don't reply because I'm busy at Restraint. In the past two years since I met James Atwater, Jamie would ask about me, failing to give me details of his life. Our relationship was one-sided, something I needed more than air to breathe. But I realize now how tainted it was.

Since Jamie revealed himself, those texts have changed. Jamie's no longer trying to be supportive because I won't allow it. When I stopped giving him details of my daily life, he started giving me his. Now he texts heavy shit, and all I reply with is co-parenting bullshit about Ella. It kills me, because there will always be a part of me that is dying to connect with Grant via Jamie.

I loved Grant. I love Jamie. I loathe today's version of Grant.

LOATHE.

There is no face-to-face between us, because I know I'll lose my fucking head and either kill or fuck him. Neither of those options are acceptable.

"ATV?" My voice quivers, but I know better than to mother Niel. He won't allow it. I lean back in my chair, pretending to be relaxed, and my son sees straight through my bullshit.

Smiling a real smile, Niel relaxes, causing me to relax for real. "There's a logging road that runs from Misery Castle, around the wall surrounding The Gates, ending behind your housing development."

"Convenient," I murmur, wondering how the little shit found it in the first place.

"Very," is a purring sound rolling off Niel's tongue. The voice may sound like the Grant we all lost, but the devious intonation is all Jackson.

"And Albert just let you go?" Eyes narrowed, I find that hard to believe.

Wiggling his cellphone in my line of sight, Niel chuckles. "LoJack. I'm sure if he could swing it, Albert would put a chip in the back of my neck like a dang dog. But Dad won't allow it."

Eyes drifting shut at the sound of my son calling Grant Dad, I hate myself for the longing and hunger I experience. "Are you…" Fuck it. Maybe Niel takes after Daniel and will answer anything asked. "Have you met Whitt's mother yet?"

Disrespecting Gwen would show more about my personality than it would hers. Being the bigger person, and all that jazz. I've come to terms with the fact Gwen will be orbiting my life forever, just as Grant will be. Just as I will be orbiting their lives.

Chuckling a sound only men make when they find a woman being transparent. "Nice, Mom. Nice." Niel chuckles some more, the melodious sound eliciting a shiver to worm its way down my spine. "No, I haven't been to a founder's meeting. Dad says they're not ready for me yet."

"Ready for you?" Leaning forward, I rest my feet on the carpeting. "I assumed Grant kept you away until you were of age."

"Nah– Dad started going when he was twelve. He said every generation has a few key players. Alpha. Beta. Omega. Mother. Accountant. New blood. Enforcer. Master."

"Really?" Voice pitching high, my eagerness is beyond obvious, earning me a grin from my son. Niel gifts me with shit no one should ever know. "No need to tell me who the accountants are." My mind drifts to the Ponzi schemer's oldest children. Fate and Boyd.

"The current ruling generation." Niel looks me over, contemplating if he's telling me too much. Shifting slightly, his leg kicks out, toes connecting with my open door. Once we have privacy, he begins again.

"Dad said they aren't ready for me yet because I'm the alpha of my generation, like Ezra is right now. Everyone's terrified of Ezra, with Boyd as his beta. Dad's the Omega– the one they underestimate. Stanton's Dad's beta, but no one realizes it because he's this badass mobster. Gwen's the Mother. Ezra's woman– Kat something or other –she's the new blood, but Ezra said they'd have to kill him first before he involved her."

Shivering in horror, "Ezra would probably kill the entirety of the founding families if they involved Katya." He's been like a nuke waiting to go off lately.

"They call the position the Enforcer, but Dad says Executioner is more accurate. It's Levi Wilson, but Master is controlling and assumes that role too."

"Faith?" I hazard a guess.

"Yeah, but I've never met her." Niel slides from the edge of the desk to plunk his behind on the carpeting by my feet. "They're already filling the roles for my generation– that's what they do. Nonstop calculating, maneuvering– determining the future. Dad's not who I expected him to be."

"Did Grant tell you who the key players are in your generation?" Knowledge is power.

"Alpha," Niel points at his chest. "Most of it's up in the air until they see how we tick– they're already testing us. Names are thrown around, but I have no idea who these kids are because they don't go to Hillbrook for some reason.

"They're keeping you separated, because past generations were too connected– friends make better allies than enemies… freshmen orientation," I mutter to myself, understanding dawning. "You'll either meet them at a founders meeting or at orientation."

"Huh," Niel grunts, mulling that information over. "Some guy named Torian is either going to be the Beta or Omega– still testing him, I guess. They're torn between Ella and some girl named Spyder as the mother, which pissed me off. They're tight-lipped about the Enforcer, but I know it's a girl. They want Whitney as the accountant, but I told Dad if they involved her, I'd turn into Ezra on their asses."

"Something tells me Whitney can take care of herself." A flash of memory lights in my mind, the video of Whitney defending Prissy at the circus. MdJ will want Whitney, no matter what, especially with her father's political connections. "Which precious child is being raised to enforce and issue punishments?"

"Dad's not the fluffy guy I thought him to be. He's ruthless, underhanded, and calculating– silent, unassuming, and deadly." Niel's pride twists my guts. "Dad says he's the only one who knows she exists, but it'll start a war between the families when they find out. She's Dad's secret weapon against Ezra. Zane." Niel pauses, checking my reaction. "Zane's already dubbed Master-in-training. Younger than me and already attending meetings."

"Jesus Christ, help us all," I mutter, crossing myself for the first time since I graduated.

"Dad said Zane will be a benevolent presence instead of malevolent. The Master and Enforcer positions go hand-in-hand, a partnership. Dad says Zane will keep the Enforcer's bullet in her barrel. Dad wants Ezra to hurt but remain breathing." Shrugging, Niel shifts on the floor to get comfortable. "Dad seemed to really like Zane– said he wanted to castrate the kid's dad, though."

"I'm surprised you haven't figured out who Zane's dad is yet." A bitter bark of laughter is torn from my chest, confusing my son, which amuses me more. "Are they forcing you to do stuff already?"

"No." Niel laughs at something private playing out inside his own mind. "Dad said the first strike is telling me who to befriend, but since I'm not allowed around anyone, that can't happen yet. Besides, I've got a few irons in the fire."

"What?" I squawk.

"Mom." Niel puckers his lips, exasperated with me. "I'm not an idiot." Green eyes roll so high, I fear my son will never see again. "I know you're sitting in here, trying to figure out something they're blackmailing you to do. The instant Daniel and Diane go haywire, I stalk them to find out the blackmail demands. I love Dad, but he pisses me off too. So, yeah, I've got my own shit going on, and some ideas on how you and I can have some fun together."

"Excuse me–" leaning down, I get into my son's face. I'm proud that he doesn't flinch. "Explain."

"Justice. They have bled our souls dry. Don't you ever want to get some justice? Beat them at their own game because they don't realize you're playing their game and your own. I have all those journals, and everyone always plays by their rules. How about we play a parallel game to herd them in theirs."

"Wow," passes my lips as I lean back in my chair. The click of the door opening stops whatever else I was planning to say.

"Reg?" Fate peeks into the room. "Checking in to see if you needed a snack– oh! Hi, sweetie. When did you get here?"

Watching my son's expression change from that of a serious young man to a boy-like lackadaisical grin is beyond disturbing. Who the hell is my son when he's not acting?

Other than bending to MdJ's demands, the only offensive measure we've taken was Whitt pretending he and Daniel were still estranged. Whitt loathing Grant isn't put on whatsoever. I guess Whitt and I aren't the only ones with an offensive strategy.

"I just wanted to pop in and have a quick chat with Mom." Niel raises to his feet in a beautifully fluid motion that reminds me of his father. "I'll be back later." A green peeper winks at Fate, causing her to blush. "With our birthday boy."

"Nice, son," I murmur, more terrified than proud. "Nice."

Leaning down to give me a hug, lips flutter against my earlobe. "If you don't have the stomach to do whatever they're asking, call someone who does." And with that, my son walks past Fate and leaves as silently as he arrived.

"Niel looks so much like you." Fate is bursting with happiness now that my boy can come visit whenever he wishes. "I swear he's grown a couple inches this month. Amazing."

"I'm good," I answer Fate's earlier question about a snack. With a smile, she turns to leave, but my son's parting words finally register in with my brain. "Wait, Fate!" I grab for her wrist, thrusting my cellphone into her palm. "Give me your brother's number."

"Pretty sure you have it," Fate teases me, but I detect the leery note in her voice. "You married him."

"No, your other brother." My tone is demanding, brooking no room for argument. "I need Boyd's help this afternoon for a few minutes."

Hands shaking, Fate does as she's told, but I can tell she wishes I didn't ask this of her. "Don't worry. I'm obeying, not disobeying."

With lose fingers, Fate hands me my phone back. After releasing a shuddery breath, she leaves my office. Fate and I have had exactly one conversation about Maître du Jeu, and there will never be another.

Master Thief Extraordinaire, I need your expertise on an assignment.

After sending the text, I toss my phone onto my desk. Then I tap a few buttons on my keyboard to bring my many monitors to life. One of which features my missive from Ezra.

Kent's opposition is anti-LGBTQ. Hack his Twitter account and post no less than three tweets, scattered over the course of 24 hours. John Easton will be outed as a self-loathing, closeted gay man. Add something to make him look racist. A religious fanatic too. Add a fetish or two.

"Lord, help me," I mutter to myself just as my cellphone vibrates against the desk.

5 minutes– your house.

"Wow," I mutter to myself as I come to my feet. "We're getting a visitor!" I shout to my girls who are in domestic bliss in the kitchen. Three extroverts hosting a party– this introvert's worst nightmare. They don't hear me over the clatter of pots and pans, their nonstop chatter, or the music flowing from the surround sound.

Leaning against the back of the sofa, I spend my time between staring at the door and my cellphone to see the time. I'm curious to see if Boyd is as anal as he appears to be. After three minutes, I hear his car in my driveway. That's one benefit of living just outside Crestview's gated wall.

I'm reaching for the doorknob before the light knock sounds. "Thanks for coming–" Gobsmacked, I forget how to speak. Taking a few steps back into the living room, "Holy mother of God."

The boy offers me a polite smile, stepping into my house and to the side to allow his companions entrance. Tall and willowy, never will I call Ezra angelic, not after I've met his son.

Remembering how to speak, "You must be Zane– it's nice to meet you." I reach forward to shake the boy's hand, but it's intercepted.

"Hi!" a small hand wraps around mine, mocha skin baby soft. "It's nice to meet you, Mrs. Whittenhower."

Blinking a few times, I register what I'm seeing. Before me stands a tiny fellow who's grinning up at me, but it's the laser beam of blue-white eyes that has a lump forming in my throat.

"Torian?" I ask, eyes flicking up to Boyd's in question. Boyd's quintessentially what you think when you hear geek. But I would never doubt that Torian doesn't belong to Boyd, because I can see all of Gwen's kids shining from the features written across his warm skin. "Aren't you the prettiest thing I've ever seen?"

"I get that a lot." Torian grins, looking like a cuddly puppy wagging its tail. "Dad gets that same look you flashed him a lot, too. People can't believe I'm his kid– not because I'm black, either."

"Tori's all mine," Boyd deadpans, but then he reaches over to mess up his son's mass of curly hair. "Two sets of mediocre genetics created a charming menace."

Ezra warned me about his son's hair– pure white, tight ringlets frame Zane's pale, heart-shaped face. A head taller than his uncle and cousin, Zane is looking at me with his face tilted to the side, like he's listening to things none of us can hear. It's an odd dynamic. Torian jumped between us when I tried to touch Zane, yet Torian and Boyd keep touching each other, leaving Zane in a bubble of space no one dares to enter.

These are the boys Grant was warning Niel about.

Voice eager, eyes shining, lips grinning, "Is your son here?" Torian must be the spokesman for their group.

"No, Niel will be back later."

Torian's crestfallen expression lasts all of two seconds, then warps into anticipation. "Ella?" He flashes a look over his shoulder at Zane, snickering so softly I almost fail to hear it.

I look to Boyd for some help.

"Don't leave them alone together," Boyd warns. "Appearances are deceiving– Torian's twelve going on forty. A prepubescent nightmare. Zane's a few months younger than Ella."

“You’re only ten?” Mouth hanging open, I stare at the mature-looking boy in awe. “Ella’s helping Fate and Kristal in the kitchen if you want to meet her.”

That got a reaction out of Ezra’s odd child. “Will there be cookies?”

“C’mon–” Torian grabs for Zane’s hand, tugging him through my living room, nose scenting the direction of the kitchen. “We get to meet a girl. Aunt Fate’s told us all about Ella.”

As they go past me, Zane whispers in my direction. “Your mind is utter chaos.” Voice eerie, reminding me of how I used to get premonitions. Shuddering as if being near me is physically harming him, Zane curls into his cousin, then flees the room.

“Alrighty then,” I mutter to myself. “My office is this way.”

As soon as the door is shut at my back, Boyd tries to explain. “Two answers. First, the answer those without faith will understand. As an elementary school teacher, it was my wife’s duty to take Zane to be tested to see where he fell on the spectrum. As punishment, my sister took my son away from us.”

Pulling out a spare chair from the closet, I offer Boyd my seat. I say, “Zane is autistic?” but think, “*Your sister is a vicious cunt*.”

Proving the man is worthy to be called a genius, Boyd begins multitasking before his ass hits the seat. His eyes are reading the missive from Ezra, his fingers are keying up Twitter, and he continues to have a conversation with me.

“Autistic or gifted, it depends on perception. Zane is highly empathetic. Touch increases the strength of the emotions felt. The boy has no idea how he personally feels because everyone else’s emotions are battering him. Zane only allows Torian to touch him, because Tori doesn’t take no for an answer.”

“That poor child.” No pity leaks into my voice, all sympathy and compassion.

“The boys are homeschooled by a tutor, along with a few of Stanton’s teenage employees.” Boyd’s talking slowly while his fingers fly across my keyboard at a rapid pace. I don’t dare look to see what he’s up to– probably robbing me blind.

“That was what the ‘*we get to meet a girl*’ comment was about. Zane and Torian should be at Hillbrook, but Faith is controlling.” My snort has Boyd’s fingers pausing. “Why exactly do you need help with this?”

As punishment for showing my dislike of his sister, Boyd talks down to me like I'm in preschool. "I can hack the asshat's Twitter account in my sleep." I purse my lips, refusing to say what I really want to say, because it's rude to ask for help then treat the help like shit. "I couldn't think of what to tweet– nothing sounded damaging enough."

"Ezra's always obsessed with dick," Boyd growls, sounding like a bigot. "Don't look at me like that, Regina. I'm saying Ezra always has an agenda. You have no idea how many of these fucking sabotaging tweets I have created, all of them the same. If Ezra was comfortable being gay, why use it as a weapon against those who aren't?"

"Point taken," I begrudgingly concede.

"Ezra hasn't figured out the climate has changed, and he ought to have by now. Sure, John Easton's constituents might be put off by the gay allegations, but he'd pick up some sympathy votes from independents, and possibly steal some of Kent's followers who had been in the closet at one point in their lives. Ezra needs a new tactic."

"So do it," I say without hesitation. "Kent has to be reelected– not only is he a good person, he cares about his people. I'll take the blame for not tweeting what Ezra wanted. But what do we do instead?"

"Really?" Boyd looks shocked, as if it never occurred to him that he could do anything but obey. Beta. "Anarchist," he mutters with a smirk. "I like, as long as you take the blame."

"So what should our bad boy, John Easton, tweet about?" Leaning forward, I get a spike of adrenalin. Being naughty feels good.

Eyebrow popping high, Boyd proves he's the man you call when you don't have the balls to do what needs to be done, as long as he doesn't have to take the blame.

"Child molester?"

"Hardcore, Boyd– that's hardcore."

Chapter Twenty-Nine

Still feeling sick to my stomach after Boyd's visit, I'm having a hard time getting into the mood to celebrate. The party is in full swing, my house, the pool area, and the yard beyond are packed with well-wishers vying for Whitt's attention.

The sickness is due to two things. One, my gift to Whitt is consummating our marriage five months after the fact. Two, I don't like the person I've turned into, which also connects to what I have to do later on tonight.

Earlier, I left Boyd alone for all of two minutes so I could use the bathroom and check to see how the kids were getting along. When I returned, I found a very proud of himself Boyd. Boyd is like a weapon in an untrained hand. I pulled the trigger, expecting a squirt gun, but ended up with a rocket launcher instead.

Boyd's suggestion of releasing pervy tweets ended up with illegal pictures being remotely uploaded to John Easton's personal computer, a thread requesting underage fun in a chatroom, and a call to the FBI tip-line… Boyd did all of that in the time it took for me to take a piss and wash my hands.

It's no wonder Ezra puts his pet hacker on a leash, only allowing him to do as he was told. I unleashed the weapon, and I caused more destruction than I expected.

An hour ago, there was a breaking news story featuring Senator Kent Preston's opposition in the senatorial race for New York State. John Easton was charged with the solicitation of a minor and the distribution of child pornography. The news broadcast showed the FBI carrying Easton's laptop as evidence.

Swallowing down my panic, I remember how I made Boyd promise to make this all go away before Easton spent a single night in jail. Allegations are one thing, but I couldn't in good conscience allow an innocent man to go to prison and become some man's prison bitch.

Spotting me in my hiding space between the pantry and living room wall, "Hey, Regina!" Aaron shouts on his way by, with Kayla attached to his arm. "Great party!"

The guest list was impossible to nail down with so much bizarre shit going on in our lives, so Kris suggested we invite the Restraint crew, most of which are related to Pretty Boy Whittenhower somehow or another. Whitt's having an intimate gathering at Misery Castle tomorrow with the family. Grant can rot at the brownstone, because he's not invited to either.

I tried to force Ella on a playdate, fearing deviant behavior would be displayed in my home. My daughter refused to leave her big brother's party, so everyone is on their best behavior when Ella is in eye-shot and hearing range.

"Lesson learned," Marcus murmurs into my ear, finally catching me after I've avoided him for the better part of two hours. Marc and I have a deal where I don't tell him what I'm doing for Maître du Jeu if it's illegal. But this was just too much for me to bear alone. The asshole thought it was funny for half a second, just because of how crazy of a scenario it was. Then he panicked as badly as I did.

"I promise I'll never burden you with my disturbing fuck-ups ever again," I vow, accepting a comforting hug and a quick kiss. "I'll never play with Boyd for the rest of my life."

"Since your ethics are now dead," Marcus murmurs quickly and quietly, making sure no one nearby can hear us over the din of the party. "You need to help me do something that will add to our guilt, but make our lives exponentially easier to live in the near future."

Following the line of Marc's gaze, I spot the problem immediately. Ezra is animatedly chatting with the birthday boy, because he can't help but react to Whitt. Especially since Whitt is wearing a gigantic birthday hat, a sash across his bare chest, with party balloons tied to his belt loops. All the girls left lipstick kisses on Whitt's chest, and some of the guys donned lipstick and left marks on Whitt's cheeks.

The tube of lipstick is dangling from Whitt's neck like a pendant, with the sash advertising **Kiss the Birthday Boy**. Throwing the guy who's had a lifelong crush on him a bone, the red smudged mark on Whitt's pouty mouth was from Ezra.

The problem is Cortez openly glaring at Ezra like he's envisioning murderous fantasies. My buddy is shoveling a mountain of cake into his mouth, and it's not a pretty sight. The plastic fork is clutched in his fist, ready to impale Ezra's flesh instead of buttercream frosting.

"Cortez is horny and stressed out, and about to snap. Ezra's so fucking happy Katya's in Dominion, but he won't let Cortez near her… that fire is about to erupt." Marcus stares into my eyes, pleading. "I can't get hard for him anymore, Regina– I can't do it. Not with the amount of self-punishment he needs."

"I have an idea," I murmur out the side of my mouth. "But let me gauge Ezra's mental state first. I need to know he can handle what needs to be done."

The simple, "Thank you," is filled with an immense wealth of relief. "I'll let you get to it– I'll go shadow your daughter. Last I saw her, Kris was teaching Ella how to tend the open bar."

"Oh, bloody hell." I clutch at Marc's arm. "Put a stop to that immediately."

"As long as Ella doesn't drink any, I don't see the harm in it." Marc smirks, darting away before I can smack him. Calling over his shoulder as he blends into the crowd, "Want me to order you a drink from your baby girl?"

"I need some liquid courage," I mutter underneath my breath, but refuse to drink in front of my children. Niel's around here somewhere, no doubt plotting global domination. Last I saw my son, Niel and Roman had their heads together.

"Well, hello there, handsome." I pull on the lipstick tube, refusing to allow it to touch my mouth. Lord knows, with these party guests, those mouths were probably performing oral sex in my bathroom minutes before they kissed my husband's chest.

Whitt smirks at me, crystalline eyes glinting with pure pleasure. The guy is glowing, but he hasn't had a single drink. Whitt's getting a high off the attention and positive vibes.

Tugging harder on the lipstick, I draw Whitt's ear down to my mouth. "Go work your magic on Cort before he eats the entirety of your birthday cake."

"Are you whoring me out, Queen?" Whitt's words are slurred– amazing. Jumping in the air, balloons billowing around him, the birthday boy smacks his own ass. "Magic activated!"

"What the–" Ezra laughs in awe, and every eye follows Whitt as he stalks his prey. "That's a guy who knows he's getting laid tonight."

"Shut up," I snap, hitting Ezra in the chest.

Ezra and I watch Whitt work his magic. Cort's staring, confused, cake-filled fork forgotten half way to his mouth. Whitt takes the plate out of Cort's hand, plopping it on the buffet table, then moves in for the kill.

Stealing the fork, the bite of cake disappears into Whitt's mouth, returning shiny with his spit. "Everyone has to kiss the birthday boy." Whitt's voice takes on a pouting edge. "Didn't you want to congratulate me? I've gone to every single one of your birthday parties."

"I... um– what?" Cortez has a frosting soul-patch on his chin, and completely loses his train of thought as Whitt licks it off him.

"Mmm... yummy." Whitt smacks his lips. "Lipstick or frosting?" The options confuse Cortez as much as me, but the chuckling Ezra catches on immediately.

Eyes held wide, all I can do is stare as Whitt paints Cortez's mouth with frosting. "This is so disturbing."

"Hey, you put him up to it," Ezra reminds me.

"Yeah, but... this is not the Whitt I know," I mutter in shock.

"It's the Whitt who's chased my ass since he figured out what my ass was for." Ezra may sound smug, but the pride he feels for Whitt is louder.

"We need to get that boy laid by another boy," I promise as I watch a blushing Cortez reach up to give the birthday boy the kiss he demanded, leaving no traces of frosting behind.

"Tongue– nice," Ezra purrs, clapping, evidently not as possessive as I thought him to be.

Cortez's eyes flick quickly to Ezra, blush riding high on his tan cheeks. The guy underwent a transformation during that kiss, going from the man on the edge of turning serial killer, to the lusty marshmallow melting into the floor.

Whitt swaggers back over to me, huge grin on his face. Whispering so only Ezra and I can hear, "That guy is gayer than I am– someone fuck him already, or I will." Lasering in on Dalton, like he can see beneath the drab garb of his disguise, Whitt leaves us to go stand in companionable silence.

"How'd *Operation Affection* go with Cort last night?" I pick the safest topic, avoiding the fact that Ezra praised me the instant he stepped into my house over the whole John Easton debacle. Apparently I'd inadvertently managed to land on Maître du Jeu's top ten political assassination attempts list.

Marcus and I have been double-teaming the Ezes, with Marcus on defense and me on offense. Ezra and I have a pretty solid relationship at Restraint, sharing news about Katya and discussing Ezra's quest to woo Cortez.

Marc's job is to relieve Cortez's pressure release valve, but lately he hasn't been *up* for the task.

Cortez and I are having just as much trouble staying connected as friends. Sucking my boyfriend off constantly will put a wrench in any friendship. At this point, I'm ready to do just about anything to get Cort's lips off Marcus, as is Ezra and Marc. Obviously I've spun down the rabbit hole, considering what I did earlier today with Boyd.

"Your advice would work on anyone less stubborn than Cortez. That man fights me no matter what," Ezra murmurs out the side of his mouth, all the while watching his confused partner.

Cortez is gazing around, looking lost now that he no longer has cake to use as a distraction. We both breathe a sigh of relief when Roman intercepts Cortez. When my son joins them, my relief turns to suspicion.

"Every night for over five months, when I touch Cortez, he flings my hand away and storms off to his room."

"I hear a *but* coming," or maybe I'm hoping and praying there's a but coming.

"Last night I changed the procedure." Ezra's pale cheeks are enlivened by an intense blush. "I sat on the edge of Cortez's bed while he pretended to sleep. So I talked while he ignored me, but I knew he was listening. I tried to explain the steps to Katya's therapy, and why he can't see her until *she* is ready. Then I moved on to tell him every single detail I could think of about Katya. The air around us felt different, as Zane would say, so I touched Cort's hand, but he pushed me away. Then I waited for him to fall asleep and curled around him. When he was half-awake this morning, he cuddled back." Voice turning dreamy with remembrance, "I thought I'd died and gone to heaven when Cortez kissed me."

"Ah… that's so sweet." My heart breaks and mends for Ezra. Meanwhile, my mind is calculating how much more time and energy Marcus and I would have if we didn't have to deal with them on a daily basis.

"And then Cortez woke up." Master Ez's voice tries to break through, so I know what I'm about to hear is bad. Blinking rapidly, Ezra tells me the rest. "Cort kneed me in the balls, then shoved me out of the bed so hard I hit my head on the edge of the dresser. Checking on me, Cort leaned over me. I thought he was going to help me up, but he backhanded me instead. Then he locked himself in our bathroom."

"That stubborn asshole should just give in," I snarl, visions of alone time with Marcus evaporating.

Ezra beams at me, smile blinding. "It was fabulous."

"Huh?" Ezra's always delusional.

"Cortez may have been livid, but he was also horny as hell. I was curious, so I pulled up the live feed to our bathroom. Cort was jerking off like a maniac the second he closed the bathroom door. Then a second time in the shower. The entire time, Cortez kept touching his lips with his fingertips."

Ezra gazes at me with a dreamy expression and bedroom eyes.

"You are a sick and twisted individual." But then I remember the last time I saw Grant face-to-face, where we were both getting off on me hitting him.

"Your expressions are beyond transparent, Regina," Ezra reveals, terrifying me. "You have a few kinks trying to erupt that you're purposefully ignoring.

"Oh, my God." I groan, embarrassed. Then I try to erase it by running my hands over my face. "What am I going to do with you?" I grumble out from between my parted fingertips.

"At least I know Cortez wants me, when I was terrified he didn't anymore. Cortez wasn't fully awake, but he knew he was touching me. His inhibitions were down, and he took and gave what he wanted for about five minutes. When Cort was in the shower, he kept saying my name over and over again while touching where I'd kissed him."

"Stockholm syndrome is the only answer to how you've mind-fucked me so hard that I'm about to break my own moral and ethical code to get you what you want. Be prepared– Marcus and I are coming for you and Cortez. *Tonight*."

Ezra's, "Oh!" blends into the background noise of the party as I escape him, looking for another hiding place. Realizing there are people cramming into every square inch of my home, and Fate locked my bedroom and kept the key so I couldn't hide in there, I settle for cleaning up the kitchen.

I'm not a partier– I can't be happy on demand. It's too much pressure. It doesn't help that today is a day where I do a lot of things I'm uncomfortable doing, most of which feels like I'm selling my soul.

Under pressure.

"Shit!" I hiss with feeling, feet stalling.

Turning her face to disconnect from hungry lips, "So much for hiding in the kitchen, eh?" Kristal says knowingly, causing Roman to chuckle against her neck.

Kristal and I have been good, now that we don't have miles and miles of secrets and lies dividing our friendship. We both know where the other stands. Kris is more confident since she has me riding her ass at home and work. Then at Restraint, Whitt gives her nonstop sexual gratification. All of Kristal's needs are met between Whitt trying to show me he's a grown-ass man, and Roman being a good boyfriend. No more revolving door to Kristal's pussy– I mean guest house.

"Eww…" I tease, a genuine smile crossing my face, because Roman and Kristal truly are feeling each other. I wouldn't say love, but definite chemistry and friendship. "Get a room– no one wants to see that."

Pulling away to rest against the countertop, "Liar," Roman teases back– now our friendship, that's about as tenuous as it can get. Roman is Grant's creature first and foremost. Whereas Kristal is conflicted, because she longs to put me first, which I respect beyond measure.

After wiping her mouth, which still has a bit of Whitt's lipstick staining it, Kristal straightens her dress. Looking busy, she grabs a dishrag.

Karma.

What I'm about to do is to lessen the burden consummating my marriage will create. "I need your help," isn't a phrase Roman ever expected to hear me to say.

Stunned, Roman's sharp jaw lowers, leaving him speechless.

"I need help from the both of you," I direct to Kristal and Roman, refusing to look them in the eye. It's my turn to grab for a dishrag. "It's for Whitt."

"Anything," Roman immediately agrees, not knowing what I'm going to ask. I'm not surprised, since Grant's hand is shoved so far up Roman's ass, in a parody of a ventriloquist act, Grant's words flow out of Roman's mouth.

Kristal is a smart girl. She doesn't agree until she hears the terms.

“Whitt has a crush on Dalton,” I announce.

“Eww…” Kris hisses in disgust, shuddering.

Roman purrs, “Niiiiice.”

“Roman, I know you hang out with Dalton, so I need you to put him in situations where he has to deal with Whitt.”

“If this was high school, Regina would want them to work on group projects together,” Kristal teases me. “How is Roman gonna pull that feat off?”

“With your help,” I say pointedly to Kristal at the same time Roman is answering my earlier request.

“I can definitely do that.” Roman grins at me like we’re partners in crime, and I miss him so goddamn much it hurts. “Dalton’s a really fun guy once you get to know him, and he’s definitely feeling our Pretty Boy too.”

“What the hell are you talking about?” Kristal grimaces. “Dalton’s a total douchebag, and ugly as shit.”

“Check this out,” Roman pulls his phone out to show us a picture of Dalton tied up and blindfolded. The small, effeminate man is covered in tattoos with a gigantic cock jutting from between his legs.

Kristal eyes the picture covetously, while I whisper, “Dayum,” in awe.

“Oh, I’m down for anything you have in mind, Regina. I can most definitely conquer that beast.” Voice husky, Kristal can’t seem to wrench her eyes from Roman’s cellphone. Roman and I share a smirk, then he snaps the phone shut to break Kristal from her trance.

“Good,” I rumble with laughter. “Because I need you to pester Dalton– come on to him like crazy. Since Whitt is your master at Restraint, beg him to ask Dalton to join you both.”

“Ah– you want to see if Whitt’s control will snap and he’ll take his crush.” Kristal murmurs her approval.

“Yeah, that and give them each a bit of incentive while they fuck you into oblivion.”

“Niiiiice,” Roman repeats, awe lacing his tone.

“Well, Ezra's deviousness has finally worn off on me.” I release an evil chuckle. “Start flirting with Dalton tonight, Kristal. Whitt shouldn’t have to wait to get what he really wants.” *Instead of having me as his consolation prize* goes unvoiced.

Roman and Kristal take to their mission with gusto, bothering poor Dalton to death. Instead of watching what I created, I grab the dishrag and a garbage bag and wander around cleaning up after everyone.

The party flows flawlessly around me. Whitt's beaming like an idiot as everyone dotes on him. This group of people truly loves and cares for him. It just goes to show how bonds don't always involve blood ties. Being family doesn't create loyalty– it's the small moments that bind us all together.

After making sure everyone is having a good time, I go about another deviant mission. I locate Marcus holding up the hallway outside of my bedroom with a glower on his face.

"It's locked." Marcus jabs a finger at my doorknob, pouting. "I wanted to escape without leaving, but all the bedroom doors are locked."

"Same here, partner." I slump against the door next to him, rubbing our shoulders together. "Wanna shake Fate down for the key?"

Marcus smirks, no doubt envisioning just that. "I enjoy all of Whitt's guests–"

"Separately," I mutter with wry amusement.

"Exactly."

Pulling a bent bobby pin from my jeans pocket, I drop to my knees and get to work on my doorknob. "Just call me Reggie from the block– desperate times call for desperate measures." I answer Marc's unspoken question as I pick the lock to my own bedroom.

"If I'd known you could do that…" he trails off, avidly watching me.

"Alakazam!" I shout in victory, standing back up. With a quick kiss to Marc's stunned lips, I breathe, "It's go time, baby. You ready?"

"What's the plan, Stan?" Marcus teases me, because he's no one's baby.

"I need you to tell Cort his oral services are required in my room." I run right over Marcus as he tries and fails to speak. "Put a blindfold on Cortez, then lead him in there." I point behind me to my open bedroom door. "Make sure Cort sits on the edge of the bed."

"What the hell are you up to, Regina?" The awe in Marc's voice is getting thicker.

“My moral ethics are dead,” is my only answer. “Ezra and I will be in my bathroom waiting– gimme five minutes before you lure Cortez in here.”

I start to walk away, but Marcus grabs my wrist, pulling me back. “What are you up to, Regina?” Marcus intently stares at my transparent facial expressions, trying to get a read on my intentions. “I don’t want to undo all the work we’ve achieved, or harm either one of them.”

“Same here– just trust me and go with the flow.” Without as much as a backward glance, I hunt Dr. Lunatic down.

Ezra’s easily located at the edge of my dining room, leaning against one of the open French doors, gazing out at the pool beyond. I ignore the tiny person Ezra’s chatting with, because I do possess a sense of self-preservation. “Come with me,” I whisper in Ezra’s ear, causing him to jolt. Somehow Syn overheard me, and I receive a death glare that would drop a lesser woman dead.

Walking away, I don’t bother with social niceties. Syn and I have found a common ground these past few months, but I can still feel her animosity. I’m not sticking around, waiting for Ezra, while receiving her blisteringly judgmental glares.

I needn’t have worried, because Ezra’s hot on my heels. He doesn’t ask any questions, getting the gist of the mission. Silently ghosting a step behind me, Ezra follows me through my bedroom and straight into my bathroom.

Before I get the chance to explain, the sound of my bedroom door opening and closing has Ezra and me on high-alert. Smirking at each other, we move in tandem to press our ears against the closed door.

“Sit right there– don’t move.” Marcus orders Cortez in a deep voice I’ve never hear before.

With a deep breath, I push the lever down to soundlessly open the door. Leaning a bit, I peer out the crack, catching sight of Marcus positioning Cortez on the edge of the bed, just as I requested.

"We never–" Cortez begins to balk as Marcus materializes a scarf. “We don’t do it this way.”

“Close your eyes,” Marc murmurs softly, yet another tone in his voice I’ve never heard. This is truly master and submissive language– intimate in a way I can never give Marcus, a way he can never give me.

Stomach twisting in on itself, insecurities begin to get the best of me. Then I realize Marcus and I are not master and submissive– we are *partners*.

"Breathe," is whispered as Marcus covers Cortez's eyes, knotting the scarf behind his head.

Placing a finger against my lips in warning, I make sure Ezra knows to tread silently. Then I propel Ezra from of my bathroom. With a serene expression of devotion, Ezra gazes down at Cortez sitting on the edge of my bed.

Arms spread wide at his sides, silently expressing '*what are we doing here, Regina?*' Marc looks at me like I've lost my ever-loving mind, and maybe I have.

Trying to breathe heavily without making a sound is nearly impossible. At the same time, I have to move slowly so the displaced air doesn't alert Cortez that there's more people than just Marcus in the room with him. My heart is hammering against my ribcage, with anticipation and fear forcing endorphin-spiked blood through my veins.

With a silent, deep breath, dropping to my knees before Ezra elicits two very different reactions.

Marc's amber eyes blaze with rage, but he stops himself mid-movement. *Hurts, don't it?* I want to say to him, and I'm not even going to do what he thinks I'm going to do. Ezra and I have to live with Marcus and Cortez being intimate on a daily basis. Marcus can deal with me having to do what I have to do for the health and happiness of our futures.

Then there's Ezra, who starts to pant excitedly as I fumble with his zipper. I struggle to get his fly open because he's beyond aroused. Blushing, I shush my victory call when I succeed.

Cock popping out, shaft brushing against my cheek, I hold a hand over my mouth to stop the nervous giggles from flowing.

"What's wrong, Master?" Cortez calls out in reply to Marc's vicious growling. "What's taking so long?"

"Be patient," is a soothing flow of words, belying the snarl on Marc's face as he watches me silently chuckle like a lunatic with Ezra's cock a hairsbreadth from my cheek.

Thick, curved slightly upward, ribbed with heavy veins, pale with a rosy head– when a gorgeous cock is ripe for the picking, it's beyond difficult not to reach out to stroke it. The struggle is very real, but I overcome it.

Poor Ezra, he's trying to keep his shit together, but on the edge of failing. Laughing without sound, he's painfully aroused and dripping precum onto my carpeting.

I'm trying very hard not to touch Ezra anywhere inappropriately while Marcus is watching– seeing does make the difference. Ezra's offered to show me the security feed featuring the skull-fucking, but I always say no. I'll give Marcus the same consideration tonight. Besides, I haven't touched Ezra like that but the once all those many months ago. We're colleagues of a sort now, and I won't risk that for anything.

With my hands settled on Ezra's hips, I move him into position at the foot of the bed, situated between Cort's thighs. Playing marionette, I grab Ezra's wrist, forcing him to grip his own cock at the base, then I wiggle his arm up and down.

Biting back laughter, Ezra gets the gist, and begins tapping his cockhead on Cort's pouty bottom lip.

I arch an eyebrow in Marc's direction to prompt him, but he just looks back at me with confusion and concern. Evidently we're not in sync tonight, because our silent communication skills aren't functioning. Rolling my eyes, I open my mouth and make a lewd gesture with my hand.

Chuckling darkly aloud, Marcus finally gets it. "Cortez," is an order of attention. "Open up– don't suck my cock. Swallow. It."

Stunned, three people in my bedroom are instantly aroused by the tone and command Marcus uses. I'm embarrassed to admit I have to clench my thighs together to stop myself from moaning.

Recognizing how enthralled by his power we are, Marcus gives a lust-filled groan in response.

Leaning forward eagerly, Cortez immediately complies, with Ezra's cock disappearing between his parted lips. The reaction is instantaneous. Cortez jolts as if electrocuted when recognition hits, and I worry he'll bolt from the room.

"Ezra, don't!" Cortez growls around the invading, imposter cock, causing Ezra's spine to bow.

Moving quickly, I hop on the bed and fuse myself to Cort's back just as he starts to struggle. "Knock it off," I snarl when Cort nearly dislodges me. Surprising help arrives as Marc's hands join mine.

"Behave." Marc's master tone does nothing to get his submissive minion to relax. Cortez is struggling, making nonsensical words because there's a cock in his mouth, and

Ezra's shuddering in bliss… because how could he not when he's getting an unintentional epic blowjob.

"Listen up, fuckers." Queen's tone is so commanding, Cortez freezes instantaneously. "You will do this, and you will enjoy it. Your stubborn bullshit has gone on long enough. So get to sucking," I command breathlessly.

"Regina?" Cort's gasp is flavored with betrayal, but it comes out muffled around Ezra's engorged cock.

"Yeah– I'm so not going to apologize for this." My unresolved anger decides to make itself known. "Marcus and I have no time for each other right now, yet he has time for you every fucking night." Voice dipping lower and lower into the pits of hell. "Then I have to listen to Ezra bitch and moan, then Marcus bitch and moan. Then watch you sulk around."

"Regina!" Marcus barks, trying to get me to shut up.

"No," I snarl directly into Marc's face as we hold Cortez down on my bed. "This has to be said. There's a goddamn cock in your apartment that you want to suck, yet you're too fucking stubborn to suck it. You're fighting instead of dealing with your problems, and it's spilling over into my life, damn you!"

"I can't believe you're forcing me to do this," sounds like muffled nonsense until my mind makes sense of Cort's words.

"Yeah, this is borderline assault," I admit without a shred of guilt. "But since no one had any issue with Ezra literally raping me… Welcome to the club, Cortez," I taunt, voice thick with bitterness.

"I don't– I shouldn't." Ezra starts babbling, but I notice he doesn't pull his dick out of Cort's mouth.

"Fuck his face," is a commanding order Ezra can't disobey. At first I think Marcus said it, then I realize the words flowed from my throat.

Ezra's eyes go wide with lust, and Cortez begins to renew his struggles.

"Yeah, struggle," voice taking on a taunting edge as I curl around Cortez's back, whispering directly into his ear. "Ezra loves the thrill of the chase– there's no denying you want to be his prey."

Whimpering, Cortez's hands jerk out to hit everything and anyone but Ezra. He doesn't try to pull his mouth away, and he doesn't lash out at Ezra. I get a palm to my forehead, but I just clamp tighter around Cort's torso in retaliation.

"You're not going anywhere," I warn directly into Cort's ear, knowing it will make him feel safer to be restricted. "Look at the tent in your pants." Movement rough with suppressed violence, I yank the blindfold off Cortez's head. "Look!"

We all obey my order, collectively staring down at the evidence that Cortez is struggling out of emotional fear, not because he doesn't want Ezra. Cort's crotch is tented obscenely, an impression of his cockhead visible, with moisture seeping through the linen pants to form a damp circle.

"Suck," I demand breathlessly, and Cort obeys with a groan of pleasurable surrender.

Hiding my face in Cort's hair, I try with all my might to cover the high glowing from my eyes. Earlier Ezra said my kinks were showing… Nothing gets me off more than playing puppet master, orchestrating the things people secretly want but are too terrified to ask for.

Marc buries his face against the back of my neck, lips latching on to my nape. Teeth sink in, then he begins to suck. His hands are no longer holding Cort's shoulders because they're sneaking beneath my sweater to grip my tits.

Body falling lax, I don't dare let go of Cortez, knowing he'll try to get away for the simple fact he craves Ezra and it terrifies him.

"Marc," I hiss in a combination of shock, lust, and annoyance when his hand crams down the front of my jeans, fingers seeking entrance. "That's inappropriate," I chastise him, unable to swat him away.

"Yeah, and so is holding Cort down so Ezra can fuck his face." Marc's voice is rough with lust and fury. "There's a dick in my submissive's mouth, and it isn't mine. Later tonight, you're going to give the birthday boy his present. Neither of these things I have any control over, so excuse me for the next few minutes as I lose my shit."

The Marcus I first met is back in action, erasing the guy who makes love once and a while and sleeps the rest of the time we're together. Grunting in shock, I'm no longer holding Cortez down. I'm using him as an anchor to the bed as Marcus attacks my jeans, tugging them off my ass and partially down my thighs.

Holding Cort on the bed has put me into the perfect position to get violated. My ass is in the air with one arm around Cort's shoulder and the other around his torso. Marc gets behind me and swiftly enters me without any foreplay. His cock glides into me like butter since I don't think I've ever been so turned on in my entire life.

"Marcus," is a rolling moan from my throat. I ought to be furious, but this isn't even the hundredth time Cortez has been in the room while Marcus hammered me from behind. The only difference is it's been almost a year since the last time, as Marc and I playacted domesticated bliss and ignored our problems.

Fingernails biting into Cortez's belly to hold on, I'm on the verge of apologizing, but his grunts of pleasure stop me before the words flee my lips.

It's been too long since Marc's dick felt like it was too big to fit inside me, hurting me with every thrust. This version of Marcus never left us– he's just been riding below the surface of what Marcus thought I needed and wanted from him.

"This shouldn't feel so goddamn good." Shuddering, I'm already on the edge of orgasm. "Fuck," I breathe out in shock, thighs quivering as a trickle of moisture escapes.

Ezra leans down and kisses me for the very first time, and it almost shocks sense back into me. Firm lips coax mine open, then a hot tongue invades my mouth.

Cortez renews his struggle between us, causing Ezra to pull back with a bitter laugh.

"What?" Ezra turns on the innocent angel act as he stares down at his partner, cock still lodged deep between Cort's lips. "Don't you like seeing me kissing Regina?" He taunts, and a choking grumble sound emanates from Cortez's throat. "I take that as a no," Ezra purrs, tone smooth and deadly.

"Revenge is a dish best served cold, correct?" Ezra levels at both Cortez and Marcus. "Marcus wanted to murder me merely because my cock was near Regina. Now Cortez is having a fit because I kissed her. But day in and day out, you do those things to each other with total disregard to our feelings."

I watch in utter shock as Ezra pulls from his partner's mouth, cock slick and shiny with Cortez's spit. For a moment, we all freeze, almost terrified this signals this insanity is over, but also relieved it's over before we do something irreparable.

"This time, I'm going to kiss you," Ezra threatens. "And Regina's going to make sure you can't stop me." Leaning down slowly, Ezra gives Cortez a chance to react. "You *will* kiss me back, damn you."

I blank out for a long while, burying my face against the side of Cortez's neck as he kisses Ezra back with wild abandon. The four of us are so close, connected, Ezra's cheek is caressing mine as he kisses Cortez.

My nerves are on fire– even the wisp of air flowing over my skin is too much on my sensitive skin. The feel of Marc's cock gliding in my moisture. The way his fingers bite into my overstimulated tits. The way his teeth sink into my shoulder, drawing blood to bead.

Then there is Cortez quivering in front of me, so much emotion because of a long overdue, passionate kiss.

"Fuck me!" Cort begs over and over again in a raspy tone. "Fuck me!"

Ezra doesn't stop kissing Cortez, doesn't react whatsoever to the demands. We all know Cortez doesn't mean it– it's what he always does. Probably what he always will. I've witnessed Cortez begging Marcus and me just like this during my training sessions.

Marcus is barely thrusting in me now, holding me close as his wry amusement rumbles against my back. "How I love you, Regina," he whispers into my ear in a voice raw with emotion. "I can't believe you'd go to these lengths for my two idiots. But, not only that, you're enjoying it with me."

Shuddering to the soundtrack of Cortez whining, Ezra looks on the verge of coming. No doubt ready to shut Cortez up, Ezra pulls from their kiss.

"I'll fuck you, all right," Ezra warns, then shoves his cock down Cort's throat. Raising his head, eyes staring sightlessly at the ceiling, Ezra's scream of release is no doubt heard down the hallway where the party guests are celebrating.

"I guess I better get us off since the fun is about to end," Marcus whispers to me, then begins to thrust with abandon.

Shaking my head no, I firmly hold on to Cort's shoulder and belly. "Hold him down with me," I gasp to Marcus– he smiles against my shoulder when he figures out what I'm doing.

Ezra stumbles back in ecstasy, knees about to buckle, cock still hard and dripping all over my carpet. The smile on Ezra's face is one I've never seen him wear, as he gazes down at Cort with eyes filled with love and utter devotion.

"Let me up!" Cortez demands when he can't take the emotions Ezra is forcing him to feel. "NOW!" he shouts in a panic.

Manhandling Cortez, I yank him further up the bed until he's resting on his back. Then I drop all of my weight onto his chest so he can't get away as he struggles. Marcus grabs for Cortez's hands and holds on tight.

Trying to gain his attention, "Ezra?" I gasp breathlessly as I struggle to contain a bucking Cortez.

Ezra's eyes snap to mine, looking a question at me.

"Suck Cortez off," I command. "And you better do a good job, so he'll want a repeat later."

"Cortez has never–" Panic etches across Ezra's features. "He's never let me do it before."

"He's not letting you do it now either– *we are*," I stress, trying to hold Cortez down. "Show him how badly you want to do it, and maybe he'll understand he's part of the problem you two are having."

"Why are you doing this for me?" Ezra's eyes water and his voice warbles with intense emotions.

"Because you deserve to be happy, Ezra– you deserve to be happy with Cortez. Because Katya Waters deserves a better life than to be ambushed by two train wrecked men. Because being stubborn, spiteful, and prideful is a broken road leading to misery."

"Thank you," Ezra murmurs reverently, sounding genuine. Then he flashes an evil smirk, and I know something shitty is going to flow from his mouth next. "I love you too, Mom."

"Oh, good Lord– you're so fucking nuts."

Pleadingly so, Cortez looks up at me, shocked I'm going to force Ezra on him. I shake my head no, snuggling harder against him. "This is for your own good," I say with firm finality.

Ezra divests Cort of his trousers, shoes, and socks. He even unbuttons Cortez's dress shirt and pulls the undershirt up so he can look at Cort's perfectly tan body. Fingers clenching, I hold a thrashing Cort down as Ezra takes his sweet time licking, kissing, and sucking every inch of bare flesh. But Cort isn't struggling to get away any longer– not really.

Sometimes you have to push people to do what's best for them. Cortez is scared of Ezra– scared of his feelings for him. Cortez loves Ezra so much, he'd rather push him away out of fear than enjoy him. Cortez is stuck back in the time when Ezra was stolen from the night. The agony, pain, and anguish have never left Cort's nightmares. He pushes the love of his life away because he fears he'll fall deeper into love, knowing if he ever loses him, it will kill a large part of his soul.

I recognize this in Cortez because I've lived it. Cort knows this but won't accept it. Marcus knows it, but has always enabled Cortez to hide behind it. Ezra's the only one who doesn't understand, and it's killing him slowly as Cortez deliberately pulls away.

Moral ethics are dead– sometimes you have to do the wrong thing for the right reasons. Black and white doesn't fit situations like this one. Out of context, I look like a monster right now, but I know it's the right thing to do– the hardest to swallow.

I lie on top of Cortez's chest, holding him down as Ezra's mouth covers him for the very first time. The moans filling my ears are proof positive I'm not a monster in the making– not the woman who accidentally gets a guy arrested for child pornography, or forces a man to perform oral sex on someone other than the person he expects it to be, or holds a man down as another sucks him off. I'm not the woman who will take another's virginity tonight, even though she doesn't want to.

Yeah, all those things are me– at least they are for tonight.

I won't be that person tomorrow, because I don't like myself today.

Sensing my disquiet, Marcus curls behind me, no longer going balls to the wall with his possessive streak. Instead, he's slowly making love to me how we has been for the past few months.

Maybe Marcus isn't that man anymore either, like I'm not the person I used to be. Hopefully as we grow, we grow together rather than apart. Hopefully we like these new versions of each other. Hopefully we still like ourselves.

Marcus isn't watching the Ezes as I expected him to be. Instead, his face is buried against the side of my neck as he breathes words of devotion in my ear. I've never been told I love you as much in my lifetime as Marcus has told me in the past few minutes.

Marc's words to me are echoed from Cort's mouth as he spews adoration at Ezra. Cortez has never let Ezra touch him this way before, but now he's begging him for it. Cort even allows Ezra between his thighs to enjoy other places that he's long denied access.

Ezra's eyes mirror Cort's starvation– starvation to make love to one another. Yet Ezra denies them both the pleasure. Even half insane with want, Ezra's too cautious to take what's freely being offered by Cortez, because the man is high on lust.

Shifting on the mattress, I disentangle myself from Marcus. After a struggle to kick off my jeans, I tug Marcus from the bed to join me in the bathroom, wishing to give Cortez and Ezra the privacy they deserve.

Our time together is bittersweet, tainted with what else the night has to offer. All this time, half my heart ached thinking Marcus didn't understand my pain when he'd go to Cortez, even knowing the reasons behind it.

I was wrong. So very wrong.

First Marcus had to count down the days until my initiation, anger turning our interactions brutal. On the morning after my initiation, Marcus was left to count down the days until today, turning our interactions to intimate and connecting, because our relationship had to be strong enough to survive what must be done.

Sometimes you have to do the wrong thing for the right reason, but it doesn't make it hurt any less. It doesn't take away the shame or guilt. Doesn't make me feel less like a whore or mistress, even if it's a wrong act for the right reasons with my husband.

With tears in his eyes, Marcus wouldn't finish what we'd started. He's learned from past mistakes, no longer marking me roughly or leaving his cum behind as a way to claim me. Out of respect for me, out of respect for Whitt, out of self-respect, Marcus simply held me in the shower, helping to preemptively cleanse away my guilt and shame.

Marcus whispered a constant stream of comforting words–all lies to make us both feel better. Going as far as to give me permission, begging me to enjoy it. Telling me it's okay to love Whitt, maybe even be in love with him a little bit. To connect with Whitt by using that tiny thread of my being I refuse to give to another person, yet so easily gave it to my sunshine.

When we part, it's the hardest thing I've ever done, but it's hardest on Marcus.

Revenge is a dish best served cold, but it cuts both ways–deepest for the one serving it, because Marc's pain is compounded on top of my own, and my pain is compounded on top of his.

A part of me knows there's another person who is hurting far more than the rest of us combined. The Grant I lost would be dying inside. The Jamie I grew to love would turn introspective and use reason to work through the negative emotions.

The Grant I know today, I hate him because none of us would be hurting if he hadn't put this into motion.

The pain is agonizing, exorbitant yet ironic, because Marcus is the Trojan Horse for the evening, showing up at Jamie's front door, forcing him to witness the pain he's caused.

As I said, my pain is Marc's and his is mine–

Vengeance can't heal us, because the one we loathe is the one who has the capacity to hurt us the most.

If we cut Grant, Marcus and I bleed.

Chapter Thirty

Knowing there's a party going on around me when the last thing I want to do is see other people, I hide in my bathroom, scrubbing myself clean. The water is running cold, the body wash bottle is empty, and my poof has holes in the webbing, leaving my skin abraded.

At least I know Ezra and Cortez have moved on since Marcus was nice enough to knock on the bathroom door to signal I'd be blissfully alone for a while. I don't know if I can face Cortez again, at least not look him in the eye.

Hell, at this point, I can't look in the mirror without grimacing at the stranger starting back at me. Wet hair slicked back to my skull, my angular face is exposed– all sense of softness is gone.

Hard.

The look in my eyes is that of a person who's been in combat, survived to live another day, but is haunted by the very events that shaped them into who they've become.

Would Curtis and Ella Regal like the person their only daughter grew to be?

No.

But then Mom's voice whispers through my mind, sounding exactly as she did when she was alive, when I've long ago forgotten the subtle nuances of her voice. What should be a breathtaking moment turns sour, as I fear what Mom has to tell me will wound deeply.

I'm proud of you, baby.

Grunting, clearly I'm delusional. But then I remember Mom pushing me at Grant, knowing damn well what was really going on way before I did. After Dad died, before the sickness took hold, I know Mom did things no woman should ever have to do to feed her child, so maybe Mom would understand the woman I turned out to be.

Taking comfort from something that may be a lie, I cover my body in a layer of soothing lotion to take away the fiery bite of my cleansing ritual. Drying my hair, I let it do whatever the hell it wants.

I'd mulled over what to wear tonight for five months. I almost wish I would've been with Whitt on our wedding night, instead of spending it with Jamie and Marcus. The pressure would be gone. Five months of anticipation just about did me in.

Forgoing Queen's badass clothing, my usual sloppy '*I don't give a shit what I look like*' version of pajamas, I went the traditional route. Whitt's a twenty-year-old horny kid about to lose his virginity, but he's also a goddamn Whittenhower, and they are about as traditional as traditional gets.

No matter how angry I am at the Whittenhower family, I wouldn't taint this moment for Whitt. Pulling out the silk nightgown and robe set from its hiding spot behind the towels, I allow the virginal white fabric to slip between my fingertips.

No lace– I wore lace for Grant when I gave him my virginity.

Sighing, the fabric flows down my body as I slip it over my head. I haven't worn a nightgown like this since I turned jaded– seems apropos that I wear it while I jade another.

Perhaps I've never been innocent, because I know Whitt has never been.

Without looking at the scene of the crime, I stalk to my closet, in search of the sheets I bought for tonight. No way was I doing this on sheets ever used before, and never to be used again. I don't think I could force myself to incinerate them in a funeral pyre in the backyard like last time, but I'll never sleep on them again. Maybe hide them where I hide everything else I can't bear to part with but also can't bear to touch again.

"What the–" my fingers light on an empty shelf in my closet, the brand-new sheets are gone, along with every other piece of linen I own. In their place is a packaged set of lavender bedding. Grabbing to examine it, I see it includes a duvet, sheets, and a fuzzy blanket has been folded on top. The new bedding was hiding four new pillows.

Stepping backward out of my closet, my head hitches into my bedroom beyond, I take in the scene with surprise.

My bed has been stripped, with only Whitt's sheets and my old pillows on it. Everything that was on my bed when I ran to hide in my bathroom has poofed, including my favorite pair of jeans.

There's a handwritten note glowing from its home on the navy sheets– navy because it's Whitt's favorite color. Utilitarian, the note is written on a piece of paper scavenged from my printer. With trepidation, I pick it up. Relief slams into me the instant I recognize the slanted masculine handwriting.

Reggie,

Since I know how you operate, I thought I'd give you the lowdown. No way could you relax if you had other shit to worry about.

Kids first– Albert picked up Niel and Ella less than five minutes after you disappeared into your bedroom to do whatever you had to do. (Alright, I called him) Little Regina and Grant are tucked in their beds at home. Niel's probably playing video games and Ella's chatting Prissy's ear off. All's good with the tikes. Both were excited about the family party tomorrow, using those puppy dog eyes on me, wanting me to beg you to go home. I told them to knock it off and quit stressing you out. For some reason, I freak Niel out but Ella thinks I'm a big softie. Go figure. One kid is smart, the other is too sweet for her own good.

House– there's one consolation on having a party with all the guests being our Restraint natives. After the party was over, the submissives were more than pleased to serve their Queen by cleaning her house. It's sparkly clean with Fate making sure everything is how it should be. Don't freak out on me. I didn't allow anyone in your bedroom. Marc let me in, told me where to find the special sheets, and then disappeared with all of your bedding. By the time I was finished with your bed, Marc returned with that purple stuff. I'm supposed to tell you...

Anything touched by anyone other than Marcus has been disposed of. Your bed is Marcus-only after tonight. If you wish to be with Whitt again, Marc's agreeable as long as it's not in your shared bed. By agreeable, I mean he wouldn't look me in the eye.

Gotta tell ya, Reg. As long as Marc's cock gets sucked by Cort, you do whatever the hell you want, girl. No shame. But I agree– not in this bed. Not in this house. You'll never set foot in Shadow Haven's living room, just saying...

Restraint– Aaron ditched the party early to go make sure all of our employees were behaving. Obviously the dungeon was closed for the night, but the club was hopping like crazy. Roarke says there are no issues to report. With Aaron and Roarke not with Ezra, it's probably how you got the jump on him and did whatever you did in here. Your bedroom stunk like spunk.

Your ladies– Kris is with me, making my bedroom smell like spunk... did you grimace again, Reg? Fate is staying at her sister's apartment, getting laid. Yeah, your girl's been screwing someone off and on with regularity for years. That's my boon to you, but you'll have to deduce who yourself. I pretty much told you who it was if you use that big brain of yours.

Update on Operation Get Pretty Boy and Dalton Laid– I pulled Whitt into a conversation I was having with Dalton. My boy wanted to murder me. He couldn't not respond when I asked him direct questions. Whitt was pulling out all the stops to tease the piss outta Dalton, which had the opposite effect. Dalton left, looking like I betrayed him. Fail. I'm gonna get the cold shoulder for a long while now– you owe me. Kristal's got a better idea. We'll wait and see if it works out before we plot some more.

Your husband– Pretty Boy disappeared before the party ended, which is why it ended when we noticed. Took me ten seconds to find him. Ha! He's predicable. Said he needed a few minutes to compose himself. I'll let him explain what that means. Like moths to flame, the whole lot of you.

Your men– don't worry about them tonight, Reg. They've hurt you over and over again. I know it bothers you that they may be hurting, but they need to feel the pain to learn to treat you right. You deserve more. I give Marcus mad props for being a quick study. I know better than anyone, while Grant may evolve, he really doesn't change.

Since I know how you dither in your bathroom for hours, I'm no doubt lying in bed with Kristal riding my cock right now. Feels damn good too. So that means Marcus and his Jamie are being weirdos on the other side of my house.

Forget about them, you lucky bitch. Enjoy the twenty-year-old horny virgin. Make it memorable. No pressure, right?

Laughing as I write this...

Grant's hand is not up my ass– these are my words, sweetheart. I'm no ventriloquist's dummy.

–Roman.

Chuckling while ignoring how my hands are shaking, I fold the note into thirds, then store it in my safe. I store mementos like a demented squirrel. Grant returned all the letters he'd ever written to me, somehow retrieving them from Misery Castle– not that I'll ever read them again. My parents' wedding rings and our photo album now reside in the safe, along with copies of the pictures taken during my stay at Misery Castle. The only engagement ring I'll ever receive is doubly hidden in the safe to stop me from catching sight of it ever again. Whitt's self-portrait stares up at me with anticipation just as I shut the door.

Everyone wants something from me, taking pieces from my soul that I need to survive.

Drained, I'm at a total loss as to what I'm to do next. Waiting is the only option. The night is unseasonably warm, and I need fresh air, so I open the double French doors leading out to the back lawn. After pulling a chair from the corner of the bedroom, I sit inside my room with my feet resting on the patio beyond.

Instead of thinking, I breathe– I feel.

Thinking back to when I was resting against the side of Whitt's car, I realized inside every house, inside every car, there are people who have lives of their own, problems that feel inescapable. Every person on this planet is complex, with thoughts and dreams and wounds all their own. Mine are no more or less special than the next person.

The navy midnight sky twinkles overhead, proving nothing is impossible while making me feel smaller than I've ever felt before.

"Hi," Whitt whispers from behind me, entering my bedroom. Voice not sheepish, not confident or smug– just Whitt.

Looking over my shoulder, I watch as Whitt drags the mate to my chair over to the open doors. Out of respect, he sits near me, because to stand above me is to intimidate me– take dominion over a woman as a husband does.

Bordering on rudeness, I can't stop looking at Whitt. If Whitt is in my proximity, I have to look at him, same with Niel and Grant. That decade-long separation caused a starvation that will never be satisfied, even if I stare at them for a decade nonstop.

Whitt isn't the pretty boy right now, nor is he the birthday boy. The attention high has dissipated from his eyes, the lipstick necklace is gone, as is the sash. Whitt has showered, put on fresh clothing, and finger-combed his hair.

The man sitting next to me isn't Pretty Boy. He isn't my husband. He's the Whitt I know and love, and because of that I finally relax.

"I could be a dick–"

"Your version of honesty hurts as much as when you're being a dick," I mutter before I can stop myself, then I feel bad because of it. "I apologize."

Laughing sardonically, Whitt's fingers seek out his hair in a nervous gesture. "Damned if I do, damned if I don't with you, Queen."

"True."

Voice soft in the intimate darkness, every word is like a revelation. "I was going to be Master Daniel tonight because I thought it would help matters. Force it. Prove I was a man. Hold you down, make you submit so that tomorrow you wouldn't feel guilty because you didn't have a choice."

"Like last time?" I hitch my chin in the direction of my bed, where five months ago Whitt did the same thing to me, causing me to beg like a wanton whore. "Yeah, it helped with the guilt, but multiplied the shame."

"This is where I don't be a dick, but probably hurt you more in the process." Whitt reaches out, pinkie hooking mine. "Marcus treated me like shit for almost two years. He was furious, couldn't even look at me. I know why– you know why. It made me feel powerful, fed into the fury and pain I hide away."

"You and I, that black pit is made of the same shit, Sunshine." After squeezing Whitt's hand, I let him go. I'm too raw right now for physical touch. "Same people fed the fire."

"You were the only one who read my intentions right during your initiation. Do I feel like a dick? Yes, but I felt vindicated some. When you were hiding in the bathroom at Denny's, Marc's and my relationship shifted. Grown men on the same team, wanting the same thing."

"You've been selling me Marcus for the past few months while you tear your dad to shreds," I whisper, not having the foggiest where this is going. "It's obvious you're trying to hurt Grant, but you confuse the piss out of me sometimes."

"Marcus came to me today, didn't even pretend it was about my birthday. As a present, he brought me some tattoo ink that was being elusive, but then we started talking about you instead. He's worried tonight will destroy you, and I finally understand."

"We have to," I mutter softly, voice barely a breath of a sound. "As everyone has pointed out tonight, I'm too transparent. If asked if our marriage was consummated, should someone try to blackmail me, I wouldn't be able to lie."

"I know," Whitt breathes back. "I don't want this for the reasons spinning around in your head. It's not to hurt Grant. It's not because I'm possessive of you, trying to assert my dominance over Marcus." Looking away as I stare at him, "God, Regina. It's not for any negative, selfish reasons, because I'd never want to hurt you. But I can't do this– I can't force you."

"What was Marc's advice?" I can't examine what I'm feeling in this moment, so I change the subject to something I can understand.

"I got the same advice from both of them." No need to elaborate on who the other person was. "I woke up to Grant sitting on the edge of my bed this morning. The bastard was inside Misery Castle, inside my bedroom. He just sat there looking at me. He gave me a kiss, then left as silently as he came, leaving behind a journal with every entry written to me. The journal was started before I was even conceived. All hopes and dreams and pride."

"Jesus," I hiss, heart clenching. "As far as birthday presents go, that's impossible to top. Grant's a hard man to hate."

"And way too easy to love… I left in the middle of my birthday party to go to him." Ah– Roman's note makes so much more sense. *Like moths to flame*. "He was Grant." Whitt's voice quivers, then breaks. I realize why he's not looking at me– he's hiding his tears.

"He wasn't that bizarre fucker you call Jamie. He wasn't the cold-hearted guy we call Grant today. He was my dad–" Whitt's head whips around to stare me down, tears splattering his cheeks. "Do you want me to be a dick with what I say next, or not?"

"Erm… um– not."

"Devastated. Remorseful. The man looked like he was praying for a goddamn time machine. Grant was shaking like he was on something, but it was his emotions terrorizing him. I told him to remember how he felt in the moment, because it was his own fault."

"I've thought of nothing else all night. Grant and Marcus and you. A small part of me is feeling the vindication, but the rest just hurts. It reminds me of when Niel was little, and he'd want to do something dangerous, but I had to tell him no. He would scream his head off, making me feel horrible for denying him anything. But then he'd do it anyway and get hurt. Those were hard lessons learned, for the both of us. Niel caused the pain I felt. Niel caused his own pain–"

"The pain Grant is feeling tonight, he has to feel it to move on," Whitt finishes for me, having raised Niel more than I ever did. The young man has been a parent for as long as I have. "I'm so angry at Grant, I can barely breathe. But I don't want to hurt him."

"I'm sitting here because Grant won't be entering my bedroom tonight, not even in my thoughts. It's not fair to you or me. I'm trying very hard to shut my mind off and just feel."

"That was the advice they both gave me," Whitt comes back full circle. "There is nothing I can do but be me. No playing Master Daniel. No playing Pretty Boy. Just be me, and the rest is up to you. My only task is to make sure you lead with your heart, not your head."

"Yeah, because my head is filled with shame. It's reminding me how you were a little boy when I met you. How I'm the mother of your brother and sister. How I loved your father, and always will. It's reminding me how you're gay, and I feel like a predator."

"That's all in your head," Whitt tells me something I already know. "I am a grown man in all ways. When I look at you, I don't see the awkward teenager who showed up at Misery Castle's front steps. You're the woman I see now. You need to respect me enough to see me clearly."

"You're gay," I whisper like it's a painful secret. "You're worried about how I'll feel in bed tonight, while I'm worried about not being who you need."

Whitt's laughter is full of amusement, when I expected resentment instead. "I've always known I was gay. I was born that way. I've heard more times than I can count from Marcus how I somehow imprinted on you. That my jealousy and anger toward Grant erupted during my sexual development, so I wanted you for myself to hurt him."

Hands gripping the arms of my chair, my voice is rough with emotion. "Heard it. Thought it. Found it true." With a deep breath, I release the private thoughts I've never voiced. "Is it because I'm masculine? Is that how you can go through with it?"

"What?" Whitt barks a sharp laugh of astonishment. "Queen, you are the most feminine person I know. Femininity isn't about size. You're the mother of two– I've watched you breastfeed for shit's sake. You have no idea how your ass looks when you walk in front of me. You're the one who cut her hair off to fit some bullshit gender stereotype. You're a badass dominant because you're a badass dominant. It has nothing to do with being tall with shorn hair. My sister can kick my ass and yours, and she weighs ninety pounds. Dominance knows no gender."

"Dominance might not, but sexuality does," I point out how Whitt evaded the part where he's gay.

"I was born gay– there is no arguing the fact that no one effected my sexual development, and that includes you. Sexuality is a fluid thing, Queen. Daniel Whittenhower II is gay, so therefore he can never find a woman attractive," Whitt mocks in a funny voice.

"Stop it," I snarl, batting at his arm. "What's up with Ezra, then? I seem to attract all the gay men."

"How can you be attracted to my dad and Marcus?" Whitt's question has my head whipping to the side like I've been slapped. "That's not what I mean," Whitt tries to smooth my ruffled feathers.

"Explain," I bite out.

"If sexuality is solid, then it's no different than having a type. Grant is fair and Marcus is dark. Telling me I can't want you because I'm gay is the same as me telling you how you have to pick one over the other– if you like white guys, you're not allowed to like Middle Eastern men too."

"So you *do* want me?" Confused, my voice warps until I don't recognize it.

"For fuck's sake, Regina." Whitt's snort echoes into the night. "I can't say for sure if anyone is totally gay or straight– look at the people in our lives. I was comforted by owning the gay label, knowing people were out there like me. But a part of me sees it as stifling and restrictive."

"The fact that I run a BDSM club means the people I know are a bit more out there, so your hypothesis is flawed."

"Ha-ha," Whitt mock laughs. "What about Marcus? He doesn't fit in anywhere, not really. Then there's Ezra. I know every single person he's touched– love 'em all, actually. Other than using sex as a weapon, I'd say he's demisexual, where he has to be emotionally connected to a person. Only two people have been with Ezra more than one or two times, a guy and a girl. But on the spectrum, he leans more toward cock. But if he wants to call himself gay, he can."

After being raised by a blue collar Scotsman, it's all hard for me to understand. Marriage was one woman, one man, and there was no sleeping around or therapy oral sex sessions. "Just want who you want, and don't overanalyze it?"

"Thank you, sweet Jesus!" Whitt shouts, causing me to laugh. "That is the moral of tonight's lesson."

"But earlier you said Cortez is gay?" Confusion has my eyebrows knitting together in the center of my forehead.

"Cortez is a repressed gay man. I know what happened in this room tonight, Queen. Cort's problems run a lot deeper than Ezra hurting his feelings when they were teenagers. Hopefully he comes to terms with it before he's old and gray."

"I just want his mouth off Marc's dick," I grumble, annoyed.

"Maybe you ought to take that up with Marcus, ya think?" Whitt turns to me, one eyebrow raised high in challenge. "Cort isn't holding Marcus down and using his mouth as an instrument of rape."

"Fuck." Sucking in a pain-filled breath, I suffer through that axis-shifting sensation.

"Yeah, Grant and Marcus– both are assholes, and neither deserve you, but both are trying to be better. And I know you're telling yourself how you've fucked so and so, or have to touch me, so you have no room to be upset. But it doesn't work that way either, Regina. Feel what you feel– you have every right."

"How did you get so smart?"

"Because I've been watching these fools since I was born. I'm smart enough to learn from their mistakes." Coming to his feet, Whitt reaches out with his hand to take mine. "Have I proved I'm man enough for you yet, Regina?"

At an intersection in my life, I can either take the hand or I can destroy us all.

I take the hand.

But I don't allow Whitt to lead me to bed. I let go as soon as I'm standing. Gliding across the room, I slip my robe from my shoulders, then lay it across the foot of the bed. Without looking over my shoulder, I fold the sheet back, then slip inside, scooting over to my side of the bed.

I don't pull the sheet up to my chin like a virgin on her wedding night, but I think about it. Instead, I fold it at my waist, ignoring how the navy against the white of my nightgown accentuates the size of my breasts.

Unable to help myself, I try to let go of the shame as I avidly watch Whitt methodically take off his clothing. Judging by the private smile flirting with his lips, he can feel my gaze follow the movement of his fingertips as he unbuttons his shirt.

"I was surprised when you asked if I wanted you." Whitt laughs that masculine chuckle of a man who knows he's going to get laid. It flows over me like a sex-slickened body. "Because I've never doubted for a second that you want me."

Confidence. Not arrogance. No smugness. Whitt isn't trying to seduce me. He's just being real, and this helps me relax further.

"See, you have a type." That goddamn manly chuckle causes me to shiver. "You look at Daniel with female appreciation– the same way he looks at a piece of art. You look at Grant like you're a meth-head and he's your last hit."

"And I look at you like…" I trail off, curious, because I've never examined too closely how I look at Whitt.

Humming the same note a tattoo gun produces, Whitt removes his shirt, draping it over top my robe. Crystalline blue eyes flick up to meet mine. "You look at me like you love me."

The sound I produce is indescribable.

"Your eyes are always slitted, with green peering out at me through your lashes. You look at me like you want me, but you're ashamed to admit it– to yourself." Toeing off his shoes, Whitt proves his version of the truth always hurts. "You look satisfied, content in the way Daniel is when he gazes at art. But once in a while, when your heart overpowers your mind, that same covetous expression Daniel gets when wants to possess a piece crosses your face. The only difference, I always find the artwork hanging in Misery Castle."

"Because Daniel takes what he wants," I mutter, caught in Whitt's spell.

"And isn't ashamed to admit it," Whitt tacks on, hand hovering over the fly to his trousers. "Doesn't matter if the artwork is worthless, downright hideous, if it speaks to Daniel, he's proud to display it."

"You're priceless." My next words hold no meaning for Whitt, but they do for me. "Yet I hide you in my safe and refuse to look you in the eyes."

"Because they hold the truth." Whitt proves he has an uncanny capacity to understand me. "Now, this is how it's going to happen. I know you're conflicted, and I know who you love. I know this is a one-off, and that doesn't hurt my feelings."

"I call bullshit on that," I pipe in, because Whitt's tone of voice belies his words.

"I am a guy– I do have my pride." Whitt isn't humble enough to look sheepish as he slips his trousers off, eyes watching me look him over. "I'm hoping it's really good, for many selfish reasons and some selfless. But mostly, I hope maybe you'll let me touch you once in a great while, because I like connecting with you, Queen."

The insecurity in Whitt's voice has my eyes slipping shut. "I can't make any promises. I'm so drained dry, I don't know if I have anything left to give you."

Laughing that goddamn sexual man laugh, Whitt crawls into bed next to me. "I'm not asking anything of you– I'm here to give you what you've already given me."

"I don't– what?" I turn to the side, facing Whitt, confused out of my mind.

"Some of us are born to take care of others. In the process, they drain us dry. You call me a kid still, yet I figured out a long time ago how I have to put myself first. I won't be strong enough to take care of anyone else if I let them drain me dry."

Whitt reaches out to finger a lock of hair near my forehead. I've been letting it grow out again for some reason I hadn't examined. Staring intently into my eyes, his emotions are so potent, I'm compelled to flick the lamp off out of reflex, so I won't have to deal with it.

"This isn't about anyone else. This isn't about getting off. This isn't about consummating our marriage or losing my virginity." Whitt's words are spoken so rapidly, they blur together, yet get quieter and quieter the more he speaks. "I expect nothing from you, and will take nothing."

Fingers ghost from my forehead, slide down my cheek, curve along my jaw, and slowly make their way down to my arm, where they lace with my fingers.

"The only energy cost to connect with someone is love– let me love you, Regina. Let me show you how much I love you."

Soft lips purse, then slowly move in to pepper a kiss to my forehead, then my eyelids, then my cheeks. "Let me open up your heart and shut off your mind– forget the world with me for a few hours. Just you and me, where it's safe and no lies are ever told."

Mouths melding in the sweetest of kisses, I lose myself in the utopia Whitt promises. Light dims, the edges of my consciousness taking on a dreamlike quality, as if I'll suddenly wake up and find that none of this is real. Yet somehow my nerves are raw, every touch as sharp as a knife's blade.

My hand is raised, then pressed against Whitt's chest, with his fingers slipping free of mine. As we kiss, tongues laving against one another, I concentrate on the rapid beat reverberating beneath my palm.

Panting breathlessly into my mouth, Whitt is just as lost in the moment as I am. Skating smoothly along the silk nightgown, his palm encompasses my breast, finger sneaking beneath the fabric to touch bare skin.

Neck arching, gasping for breath, I realize my hands are now roaming Whitt's chest and arms– I'd moved first.

So far gone, neither of us has the breath left to kiss. Stuck in a state of erotic bliss, Whitt is feasting at my arched throat, making noises I never thought I'd hear.

Hands moving without thought, I glorify in the textures of Whitt's torso, his hips, the roundness of his ass. Every movement I make, he takes it as permission to touch me the same way.

"Meld with me, Queen," Whitt pants against my throat, fingers rucking up my nightgown near my hip. Shifting, he rotates into position between my thighs, and I help by spreading my legs for him.

"Christ!" is a groan from my throat, body arcing so violently my fingers seek the sheets, knuckles turning white as I try to restrain myself.

Proving this is his first time, Whitt tries to enter me without his hand guiding him, missing my hole but hitting my sweet spot. Chuckling at himself for being inept, it takes less than a second for Whitt to realize he found a reaction he wasn't looking for.

"Like this?" Whitt shifts his hips slightly, palming the back of my thigh, allowing his cock to rub slickly across my clit. "Yeah, you love that."

Unable to help myself, my hips rock back and forth in time with his, rubbing his cock against me faster and faster. Whitt palms the back of my thighs, spreading me farther open to him.

"I could make you come doing this, couldn't I?" Wonder wars with pleasure in his voice. Both of us are so far gone, our rocking motion turns to longer strokes. "Fuck!" is a shout as

Whitt slips inside me for the first time– inside anyone for the first time –joining us as husband and wife. “Oh! Oh, God!”

“Like this?” I tease playfully, mocking his earlier words. Counterthrusting, I show Whitt a good tempo where neither one of us will pop off too quickly, but it’ll feel amazing on the journey there. Every muscle in his body quivers against me, jumping to meet my questing fingertips. “Yeah, you love that.”

Laughter tickles my lips as Whitt moves in for a kiss, but the amusement only lasts long enough for lust to smother it. Writhing together, we can’t touch each other enough, get close enough.

Movement spastic, my nails dig into Whitt’s ass cheek, while the other leaves crescent moons on the nape of his neck. Knees pulled closer to my chest, I try to get as much of Whitt inside me as I possibly can.

We feel good together, warm and alive. Without taint– pure. No lies. No shame. All truth and loyalty and trust and survival and love.

Sometimes the brightest of loves consumes itself the quickest, because there’s a hotter, more violent, toxic love connected to your soul that nothing can ever sever. The communion is meant to cleanse the taint away.

Just for one night, I allow Whitt to open up my heart, to show me a utopian place where there’s nothing but trust and safety– a happy place where I can accept being loved.

Chapter Thirty-One

Free– like a heavy weight has been lifted off my shoulders, one that had been placed there for far longer than five months. Every single day, the dread of feeling shame was my passenger. Now, after the moment has come to pass, I feel lighter than I have in my entire adult life.

No matter what happens, I feel loved, even if it was just for a few stolen hours.

My house is clean and empty, with everyone safely where they need to be. I have no edicts from MdJ requiring my attention. It's Sunday, so both Empowerment and Restraint are closed for the day. Whitt's sheets have been folded, placed in a pretty bag, and hidden in the safe with the rest of my memories. The gifted set of bedding from Marcus is now gracing my bed.

I feel really good… good and bored. I don't know what to do with myself because I'm used to mainlining drama like it's oxygen. There's a devil on my shoulder, reminding me how this is my life, so the odds of bad shit happening soon are quite high, so I better enjoy this rare moment of freedom.

There are many triggers around my house, so I avoid places like the swimming pool, my bedroom and bathroom, even the dining room, kitchen, living room, and my home office. While the backyard holds a recent unpleasant memory, it was an empowering one. So I find myself lounging on a chaise I dragged from the pool area, naked as the day I was born, with the unseasonably warm May sun tanning my ruddy skin red.

There's a book in my hand that is neither a technical book, nor a James Atwater original. Chosen at random off Fate's stack on the coffee table, some train wreck of a teenage girl is trying to find her way through life, making so many mistakes she'll be wise beyond her years before the novel is through.

Bored, but I feel good.

Okay, so I'm beyond bored. My skin is burning, and the iced tea is too bitter. I'm trying really hard, yet failing with great dignity. The part of me that needs therapy is thrilled when I finally get my first text message of the day.

I was starting to think a dead zone opened up over my house.

Roman: *are you enjoying your day?*

–Fuck no. I'm bored outta my mind. What's up?

Roman: *Just watching a game.*

–You never text me. What's up?

Roman: *How to say this without saying too much...*

–Voldemort?

Roman: *YES! Thank you for making this easier on me. A gameplay maneuver.*

–You're going to make me earn this, aren't you?

Roman: *I'm trying very hard not to break the rules, okay?*

–20 ???

Roman: *You suck at this shit. The point is to ask a question, Reggie. Not name the game we're playing.*

–Fucker. Since you're pestering me, I assume this is about me, which explains the dead zone that has fallen over my house.

Roman: *Right, you are.*

–That's all you're giving me? Boyd inadvertently inserted the nuclear launch codes?

Roman: *an insane monster, who is so wounded everyone sympathizes with him, has struck.*

–Struck how? Struck who?

Roman: *My roommate hasn't moved from the whorehouse velvet settee in four hours. Our guest is just as mute as my roommate.*

–What the hell could Ezra have possible done to Grant and Marcus?

Roman: *For a genius, you're pretty fucking thick.*

Roman: *... ... did that get your attention, Reggie? THINK!*

Roman: *Ezra's known for one thing.*

–Rape?

Roman: *Good Lord, woman!*

–Stalking. Surveillance. Shit that should land him in federal prison.

Roman: *Bingo!*

"Christ!" Phone long forgotten, my feet are moving before my mind gets with the program. I fly through the French doors, grabbing up a chair without stopping. The chair is plopped in the doorway from my bedroom to the hallway, and I'm standing on the seat in a heartbeat. I know what I'm going to find long before my fingers connect with the cover to the smoke detector.

"How could I have been so stupid?" Staring deep into not one but two security cameras, it's like I'm looking directly into Ezra's eyes. "How could I have forgotten that you had to have proof Marcus was sleeping at night? Was that a lie, Ezra? Was it?" I scream, vocal cords warbling from the force.

Stalking to my closet, feet pounding hard, I grab a pair of shorts and a tank top. Not bothering with underthings, which is obscenely stupid with tits the size of mine, I tug the clothing on as quickly as possible. At a jog, I grab my cellphone from the yard and my keys from the hook by the front door. I run to my car, forgetting a pair of shoes in my haste.

Backing out of my driveway like a lunatic, *Sync* is already dialing Roman's number from my voice command. "No more twenty questions, just hit me with the damage."

"*The founders needed proof of the consummation.*"

"Are you shitting me?" Slamming on my horn, I demand a guy stop gawking at the geese that are always shitting all over the road. "Fucking Sunday drivers!" The closer to Crestview you are, the more ponds, tree-filled parks, and unnecessary curbs you encounter. Urban Planning is alive and well in Dominion, New York.

"*Divina was immediately taken to a gynecologist the instant she stepped off the plane from her honeymoon. Stanton was forced to witness Dalton and Bianca. It's worse for those in the council. Grant was ordered to watch Ezra and Faith because conception was required.*"

Eyes stinging, my hand flies up to chase away the tears so I don't end up wrecking as I merge into Dominion's downtown traffic. "Change has to come."

"*I believe you're supposed to be the catalyst of change, right?*"

"What actually happened?" I don't bother with a turning signal as I weave in and out of traffic. "I need details."

"*At approximately nine this morning, a mass email was sent to every member of... Voldemort, as was required. But Ezra was playing a side game, where he texted a link to Grant and Marcus, for his own personal revenge.*"

"It was dark in my room– only a lamp." Whipping into the parking garage entrance, I have to wait for the guy in the booth to put the security arm up. With a salute, I drive three times the posted speed limit. "The video quality had to be grainy as fuck."

"*Ezra went hi-tech with you, Reggie.*" *I hate the pity in Roman's voice.* "*Two camera angles. One pointed at your bed, the other at the French doors. Color and sound. Spliced together in a near HD quality performance.*"

"Motherfucker!" I slam the car in park.

"*You coming here? What's taking so long?*"

"I've got a pit-stop to make first," I snarl.

"*Where?*"

"None of your fucking business, asshole."

"*If I hadn't seen it with my own two eyes, I'd assume you're on the rag.*"

"You did not just go there– you did. Fuck off." Wrenching the key out of the ignition, I'm in the elevator before my mind registers my car door slamming shut. Shortest fucking ride ever– I don't even get two deep breaths taken before the elevator's spitting me out into the vestibule.

The Edge Building's security guard is shamelessly flirting with the lady manning the sign-in book. Both their eyes go wide, mouths forming a silent O when they see me approach.

"So what?" I flop my hands at my sides. "Haven't you seen a lady in a Pacman shirt, no bra, and a pair of boxers with happy frogs on them before?" I grab the pen out of the lady's upraised hand. "No shoes either. A sunburn." Tugging at my rat's nest, "This hair."

"Ma'am?" the security guard treads lightly.

"You know who I am." I drop the pen on the desk. "Gimme Ezra Zeitler and Cortez Hunter's apartment number, and I'll get out of your hair."

"Mrs. Whittenhower, the residents you're wishing to visit live on a restricted floor. You'll need a key to the elevator."

"So give me the key–" I can tell that ain't happening, not with me looking like a crazy lady. "How about you escort me to their apartment, hmm?"

"The Sirs have given instructions not to be disturbed for the duration of the weekend." Security guy's eyes go wide, and at first I think it's because of the murderous expression on my face. Then I feel a mountain-sized presence at my back.

"I'll escort her," Roarke's deep voice hits me at the same time he takes my elbow.

"Mr. Walden, Mr. Hunter said–"

"I'm allowed to have guests, am I not?" Roarke's words are polite, his facial expression frozen at concern, but I can read him pretty good after working with him for the past five months at Restraint.

Roarke is enjoying the hell out of my humiliation.

"Yes, but–" The security guard is conflicted, one hand on the phone to call Cortez, and the other wavering on the top of the desk.

"But what?" Roarke pulls me away. "The fact that I live across the hall from them?" Laughing evilly from his chest, the big man doesn't crack a smile until the elevator doors close.

"Pacman, eh?" is Roarke's version of '*how about those Cubs?*' as an uncomfortable segue.

"It was a gift," I mutter, watching Roarke shove a key in the elevator panel, twist it, then push the button to Ezra's floor. "One of my programmers gave it to me."

Leaning against the wall with his arms loosely crossing his massive chest, Roarke tries and fails to make small talk, when normally we have no problem conversing. "You play Farmville?"

"Fuck no," I gasp out. "Why?"

Shrugging, Roarke's pretending to look at my face, but his eyes are staring at Pacman. The slight blush he's wearing and the faint smile he's trying to hide screams he's watched my celebrity sex tape– many times.

Could this elevator ride get any longer?

"Work's gonna be fun tomorrow night," I deadpan.

Roarke's laughter is infectious, and he doesn't stop until his fist is rapping on Ezra's door, which I notice has no apartment number on it. Gray carpet. Gray walls. Nothing but a wall of spaced out doors on each side of the hallway, very few with apartment numbers.

Eye's flicking to the side, I wonder what would happen if I sidestepped Roarke and pounded on Katya Water's door. Hers has to be right next door. Ezra would want her shoved up his ass.

"Don't even," Roarke grumbles, reading me. "Kat's in the gym right now, anyway. Why do you think I was downstairs? I was making sure Kat arrived safely."

"I'm guessing she doesn't know you were stalking her," I mutter, wondering how long it's going to take before this goddamn door opens.

"Ha! You'd guess right." After another soft knock, "If you don't open this door, I'm going to unlock it and unleash Regina into your apartment." Another knock. "Quit being a coward."

"I was in the bathroom," Ezra's looking over his shoulder as he opens the door. "Why didn't you let Roarke in?" The man in question sidesteps, revealing me, and Ezra's face washes over in shock. "Oh, I see."

"I'll be in the gym, watching the woman walk on the treadmill. Fun stuff." Roarke walks away briskly before Ezra can call him back. "Don't kill each other."

For a suspended moment in time, all Ezra and I do is stare at one another. Months and months of friendship unravels before our eyes. Allies become foes.

"Please do come in, Regina." Ezra turns polite, no doubt due to Diane's upper-crust influence during his childrearing. "You're looking as lovely as ever on this fine Sunday afternoon."

"Cut the shit, Ezra," I growl, curving around him to squeeze between the door frame and his body. "We both know I look like death warmed over."

"You're delicious when you're angry," Ezra whispers in a creepy yet erotic voice as I slip past him into his apartment. Master Ez is riding shotgun today, ready to take the wheel should I overstep any boundaries.

Looking around, it's bizarre how I feel like I've already been here a billion times after seeing the security feeds running on Ezra's desk while we're at Restraint. Just past the small entrance way, I flow into the living room and stop dead in my tracks.

"Oh– that's what death warmed over looks like," I mutter, eyes taking in the train wreck.

With a soft pat to my back, Ezra walks around me, ignoring said train wreck. "Would you like a drink? You look like you could use one."

"Yeah– water. Unopened bottle," I request as a precaution, earning a devious chuckle from the kitchen.

Last I saw Cortez, he was begging Ezra to fuck him. Now he's glaring at me with betrayal in his eyes. Sitting in a chair facing the door, Cortez is eating an entire carton of ice cream, spoon jabbing it like he's fantasizing it's a knife parting my flesh.

A water bottle is thrust in my hand– the expensive kind. "Same shit, different day." Ezra doesn't bother to whisper as he talks about Cortez like he's not in the room. I just stand there, unsure what to do with myself now that I'm here.

"Have a seat." Ezra pats the cushion next to him. "This will be an interesting conversation, I suspect."

Cortez grunts loudly, evidently an epic grudge holder.

Sitting gingerly on Ezra's sofa, ass resting on the edge of the cushion, I've never felt more like low-rent trash. Especially as I unscrew the cap on a small bottle of water that cost as much as the five-gallon jug in my water cooler at home.

Eyes flicking around the space, I spot a painting worth more than my entire house– I remember when Adelaide commissioned it. Furious and despondent, Cortez is using a cashmere throw as a napkin.

Katya Waters is going to have a difficult time acclimating here.

Sighing heavily beside me, I've learned that's one of Ezra's ticks, along with blinking rapidly. Master Ez isn't fit for this conversation, so I ease into it instead.

"What's this about?" I wave my hand in a circle, encompassing the manic state Cortez is currently in. "I can't talk like he's not sitting right there, ya know?"

Cortez looks right at me, with my death in his eyes, then he pops a spoonful of ice cream into his mouth, like it's a challenge accepted.

Ezra covers his mouth with the back of his hand, chest rumbling audibly. After a few seconds, he composes himself. "He's so cute."

"Have you lost your ever-loving mind?" Awed, I stare open-mouthed at the side of Ezra's face, then I shake myself out of it. "Of course you have– you've already been diagnosed as clinically insane."

"You're going to kill him." Ezra does that silent laugh with his hand over his mouth routine again. "Regina, welcome to my world. This is what professionals call Post-Coital Tristesse, mixed with buyer's remorse, and a healthy dose of repressed emotions."

Tilting my head to the side, "Come again?"

"You tricked me," Cortez says around a spoonful of ice cream. "Forced me. Betrayed my trust."

"*You wanted it*," I growl, ignoring how my face flames redder.

"Doesn't matter." Cortez takes another spoonful.

"Finally someone else will experience this shit." Ezra leans forward to toss Cortez a box of tissues. "This is Cortez's version of sub-drop, only it's sexual in nature. Only happens with me– not with women, not with Marc. Only me."

"Oh," I huff, hurting for Ezra. I reach over to pat his arm, then I snatch it away before I make contact, remembering I'm supposed to be furious with him for the sex tape.

"Every time we touch, Cortez goes into this state-of-being, blaming me. Only this time–" Ezra smiles at Cortez as if he's the most beautiful sight he's ever seen. Bear in mind, Cortez has red-rimmed eyes, a splotchy nose, and chocolate sauce painting his chin. In other words, Cort looks like shit. Expensive shit, but shit nonetheless.

"Only this time?" I interrupt Ezra's mooning over Cortez.

"I'm not to blame." Now Ezra's looking at me like I'm his favorite person in the whole wide world. "Usually, this is where Cortez packs a bag and moves back to Shadow Haven. But he blames you and Marcus. Cort may hate me, but I'm the lesser of two evils right now, so he's staying put and allowing me to nurse him back to mental health."

"You and Marc broke my trust." The box of ice cream lands on the coffee table with a heavy thud, spoon clattering. "Marcus knew better."

Ezra just shrugs, looking sheepish. "Cortez will be right as rain by tomorrow. This isn't for attention. His brain released a bunch of chemicals and endorphins into his system, compounded with haywire emotions, and it takes a bit for everything to get straightened out. Truly, just like sub-drop."

"Like postpartum depression?"

"Very good, Regina." Ezra pats the top of my head–condescending fuck. "Similar in some aspects, yes."

"Well, now that we have the train wreck sorted out." I lean forward to place my bottle on the coffee table, seeing no coasters in sight. Men. "You know why I'm here."

"I respect you, Regina." Ezra turns on his psychiatrist voice, causing both mine and Cortez's eyes to flutter shut. False soothing. "I've been on my best behavior after our indiscretion."

Glaring at Ezra, my voice drips with scorn. "Is that what you're calling rape now?"

"Let's scroll back a few minutes, Reg." Cortez sniffles, pulling a tissue from his box. "I would've been on your side right now, but you just said to me, and I quote, *you wanted it*. Hypocrite."

Ezra ignores us both. "I swear that I only turn the cameras on at three in the morning, on the nights Marcus stays over, for no more than fifteen seconds. They're always off. I don't record any of it."

"Yeah… well…" I've got nothing but bitter laughter.

"Have you seen it yet?" Cortez's resentment toward me warps into something I cannot describe.

"Whoever contacted you most certainly told you why it was recorded. It was sent to those who needed to see it," Ezra hedges, which means half of everyone I come into direct contact with daily watched Whitt and me make love. "Including Grant, who was advised five minutes prior not to look at the incoming email."

Heart racing. "Did he?" Heart breaking.

"It was sent to him twice." Cortez gets sick satisfaction from telling me this. "Jamie opened it the second time, thinking it was a James Atwater book trailer."

Hands parted in a sign of good faith, "I. Did. Not. Send. It." Ezra sounds genuinely upset for me. "I wouldn't do that. I know how goddamn awful it feels to see your partner with someone else. I would never do that to Marcus, no matter how badly he deserves it. Grant and I may be adversaries, but some lines even we won't cross."

Cortez sits up, placing his feet on the floor, filthy cashmere throw landing in a pile. "You and Marcus betrayed me."

"You!" Lunging to my feet, I just gape at Cortez in utter shock, and he stares back at me all innocent. "I feel so *violated*." Voice breaking on the reality of what has happened, I have to hug myself to keep my heart from beating out of my chest.

"You were talking about me on the video!" Cortez picks the blanket up and hugs it to his chest like it's a talisman against his pain. "Everyone had to watch it this morning. Together– everyone but Jamie. We didn't know what was on it. You have no idea how demoralizing it was to see and hear you make light of my struggles. Everyone laughed at me. Marcus needed to hear it too."

"It was *private!*" My voice warbles from the strain, then breaks entirely. It's not without difficulty to force the words out. "Who gives a fuck about me– whatever. But what about Whitt? He's your friend, and you sent that to his goddamn father!"

"They were proud of Pretty Boy– so proud." Cortez covers his face with the blanket, hiding like a child. "We all were proud of him. He'll have no problems getting laid. We all thought you looked beautiful."

"Regina." Ezra takes me by the elbow, leading me back to the small foyer in his apartment. "This is me the psychiatrist talking to you right now. Many factors culminated, causing Cortez to send the video to Grant and Marcus. What we did last night. The Post-coital tristesse. Feeling betrayed and forced. Emotions he doesn't understand. Being bullied and mocked by a large grouping of his peers. Cortez broke down and did something he will regret– something he already regrets. I can tell, because he's trying to validate his reasoning with excuses right now."

"That doesn't change anything, though, does it?" Hanging my head in defeat, I can see Cortez out the corner of my eye, and I can sense he's crying underneath the blanket out of shame.

Gripping my upper arms in his palms, Ezra leans down to peer into my face, "I am so fucking sorry, Regina. So sorry. If Cortez hadn't sent it to Grant and Marcus, you would've never known about all of us having to watch it. Ask yourself which is worse: Marcus and Grant watching it, where you can look everyone in the eye with dignity and respect? Or everyone watching it behind your back, and you never knowing it?"

"I just can't–" swiping my hands inward and upward, I flick Ezra's hands off my arms, then bolt for the door. He tries and fails to reach for me again.

"I can't in good conscience allow you to be alone right now, Regina."

"I'm going…" Mind reeling, I don't know up from down anymore. "I'm going to *them*."

"Okay," Ezra calls softly as I yank the door open and flee to the hallway. I barely make out, "I'll notify Roman," as the door clicks shut at my back.

The walk through Edge, the ride down to the garage, and the drive to the brownstone meld into a blur, as if I never lived it. Like I teleported from Ezra's apartment and landed on the stoop outside of the red door with the cheery gargoyle knocker.

The door magically opens before I can raise my hand to knock, and a set of warm lips press against my forehead. As I'm tugged into the brownstone, the scent of home hits me where it hurts most. A sporting event of some kind is flowing in from the man cave, adding more of a homey feeling.

Roman doesn't speak to me– he just propels me into the front-most room on the left side of the house. It used to be a parlor in bygone years, but now it's the impact room. Marcus always gravitates in here, because his grandmother's velvet covered settee is butted up against the front windows.

They know I'm here– they don't ignore me, but they don't acknowledge me either. If poor Zane was in this house right now, the kid would be syphoning off so much chaos, he'd end up crazier than his father.

Marcus is sitting on the sofa, elbows on his knees, chin propped up in one hand, staring down at the coffee table. Grant is seated cross-legged on a hassock, bare feet visible. Between them on the coffee table is the Scrabble board.

Roman breathes softly into my ear, "Marcus hasn't spoken a single word since last night– go play." I'm pushed forward forcefully.

Stumbling over my feet, I reach for a pillow off the settee, then plunk it down opposite Marcus on the floor, with Grant to my left. I don't dare look at either one of them for a myriad of reasons. But Grant mostly, because I turn into a stupid fucking idiot around him, and I'm too raw to experience lust or rage right now.

No one objects when I grab a wooden tile rack from the box, then grab a handful of tiles from the baggie. Reaching forward, I snatch the pen, then scratch my name on the score sheet. I wait one round, then jump in after Grant takes his turn.

No one speaks. We play like this for hours. Roman pops in randomly, bringing us bottled beer and water. Roman answers the door, and the smell of delivery pizza flares our nostrils a minute or two before he plops two pizza boxes on the floor between Grant and me.

Hours later, the Scrabble board is full. Marcus reaches over and slides all the tiles into the box, then methodically places the tiles in the bag. I wait to see what comes next, but Grant takes a handful of tiles from the bag, sorting them on his rack, and we begin again.

Around the time Kristal shows up with Martha's Seven Layers of Sin chocolate cake, I realize we've been communicating with one another this entire time, subconsciously choosing our words in a conversation only the three of us could understand.

The levity I felt this morning returns, but with it comes peace.

Chapter Thirty-Two

Bluetooth earpiece squawking, I jolt upright. “Queen,” I murmur to whoever’s trying to gain my attention. Ezra’s been a no-show at Restraint all week, so his duties have fallen on my shoulders. I’m going over the payroll, and it’s boring me to tears.

“Reg, Fate’s in my stockroom,” Kristal growls into my ear, the seductive tone more smoky than angry. “Make her go home.”

“Ella’s at Misery Castle– Fate didn’t want to sit around the house all night alone.” Swearing underneath my breath, I go about the arduous task of removing yet another employee from QuickBooks. “We need to vet our employees better. I’m sick of adding and removing fuckers who only last half a week.”

“New guy already quit,” Aaron’s voice hits my ears. “I’m manning the front alone.” Major problem with having a private conversation on our Restraint-issued earpieces is that we’re all wired together. We pretend to give each other privacy.

“Of course he did.” I bring up the idiot’s details. “Ryan started last night.”

“He was too much of a pussy to be working security–”

“Hey!” Kris and I shout in unison. With me adding, “My pussy has bigger balls than your cock does, Mr. Farmville.”

Laughing at me, Roarke finishes what he started to say. “I’ll help with the hiring process.” No doubt the ex-cop has some interesting vetting practices.

“Don’t offer if you don’t mean it,” I warn.

“Shit!” Radio silence from Roarke.

“Can we get back to the fact Fate is in my domain.” Kristal’s voice cracks under the strain. “I have a system, and she’s fucking it up. You know how she is in the kitchen at home.”

“I’ll put her on payroll,” I purr sinisterly, fingers steepling.

“Oh, Fate will love that– I’ll go get her.”

“Just dumped an idiot out in the alley,” Roman joins us– he’s been playing bouncer lately, because Ezra isn’t around to intimidate the clientele, which means Cort isn’t around to charm them.

“Is The Boss ever coming back to work?” Ezra and Cortez are interchangeably called The Boss here at Restraint. But the employees defer to me as the actual boss.

“Going to monitor the dungeon now,” Roman tells us.

“Ezra’s on-site tonight.” Roarke’s voice is interrupted by static. “Walking him from the parking lot now.”

“Goodie.”

Leaning back in our shared chair– Ezra and I take turns in the office. If he’s here, I go man the dungeon, because two dominants trying to be in charge is a recipe for disaster –I stare at the monitor featuring the security feeds. Watching Ezra and Roarke move from section to section, I try to get a handle on Ezra’s mood.

Ezra’s been really good lately– like a normal human being. I haven’t seen him since I invaded his apartment because he was offering therapy to Cortez. But he’s been sending me about twenty to-do emails a day, none of which are MdJ related, so we’re good. No personal shit was discussed, just Restraint business.

As I watch them move into view of the security camera, Ezra and Roarke walk side-by-side, the cop on high-alert at all times. Ezra’s gait is smooth, smile genuine, so I assume it’s going to be a stress-free night with Master Ez tucked away in the back of Ezra’s psyche.

“Radio silence on my end,” I alert everyone. “Switching to channel three– only contact me if it’s important.”

“He’s in a good mood,” Aaron reassures me, but his word is not trustworthy when it comes to Ezra. “All issues flow to me until Queen is free,” Aaron gives as an order since his earpiece is the only one connected to that frequency besides mine.

“Later.” Leaning back in the chair, I plop my bare feet on the edge of the desk and cross my arms over my chest. I wait.

The door opens and Ezra appears in a designer three-piece business suit without a single strand of pale hair out of place. “Your dress code sucks,” is his version of hello before the door closes at his back. “The mongrels who work for you… now you’re infecting my establishment.”

“What?” Looking down at myself, I grin widely over my jeans and Restraint Security t-shirt. I passed the same t-shirts out at Empowerment– my employees loved them. The shirts looked good with their kitschy pajama pants and slippers. I gave them Restraint coffee mugs too. “Don’t like the new t-shirts?”

"Dexter's now wearing funny slogan t-shirts instead of wandering around in leather pants and little else. Aaron and Roarke are acceptable. But Roman and you need to dress more like Faith and Kristal."

"The last person I aspire to be more like is Syn… I'm the boss." I chuckle underneath my breath, because Ezra truly is an uptight elitist. Even his underwear and pajamas have designer labels. "So maybe I ought to wear a snazzy suit tomorrow night."

"You'll wear this." A black bag is thrust into my hand. Ezra's tight expression brooks no room for argument, because Master Ez is glaring at me from his eyes. "Tonight."

"No fair," I whine. "Aaron said you were in a good mood, and I thought you looked happy too." Sitting upright, my feet land on the floor with a bang. Voice mimicking Ezra's, "*It's good to see you, Regina. How have you been? Thank you for running my business for the past week without me*."

Face softening, Ezra leans his hip on the edge of the desk. "Katya is showing up this evening. I finally spoke with her face-to-face this afternoon. It did and didn't go so well."

"Ohhh," I drawl out, peeking into the bag. Black latex. "How'd that go?"

"Adelaide showed up," is muttered in an expressionless voice.

"Shit– forced fiancée collides with prospective wife."

I haven't seen my ex-best friend in months. No contact whatsoever. I miss her, but then I wonder how much of the woman I know was the real her anyway. Ade was using my kids as pawns, with my added jealousy over her having unlimited access to those I longed to hold, our friendship was decimated. Plus, she fancied herself in love with me, which frankly creeped my ass out.

"I *am* in a good mood." Ezra flashes me a cheeky grin. "But I can't have Katya coming here, expecting the BDSM experience with Doms and Dommes, and have her see Restraint being run by barefooted people in t-shirts."

Ezra points at the bag, raising an eyebrow in challenge. With a sigh, I yank off my t-shirt, then my jeans. After being forced to have sex with Ezra– twice –and the viewing of my infamous sex tape, I have no dignity left. Ezra's seen all I have to show.

"How's Cortez doing?" Grunting, I struggle into the latex catsuit. "Seriously, Ezra– this shit doesn't breathe. Sweat and latex don't mix."

"Then I guess you'll dress appropriately for a woman of your station next time, or you'll suffer with what I choose for you instead."

"Evil, evil man," I mutter with appreciation. "What about everyone else?"

"Dexter was told to lose the shirt," Ezra mutters wryly. "Roman is bitching up a storm right now, I suspect, but looking hot while doing it. Fate is turning herself into *Angel* in the stockroom."

"Lucky bitch got a breathable dress, didn't she?" With a harsh grunt, I tug the latex up my arm and hook it over my shoulder.

Ezra just smirks in answer, then reclaims the chair. "You look… *good* in black, Regina," Ezra's voice flows into a deep purr– Master Ez threatening to join us. "Intimidating. Powerful. Seductive. Frightening."

"So, you want me to scare the bejesus out of your woman?" I find a pair of ridiculous boots at the bottom of the bag. I own two types of footwear: slippers or flip-flops and functioning boots– warm and fuzzy for the cold, or snow-resistant with no-slip treads.

"First you force me to befriend Kat." The boots are a struggle too, zipping all the way up to my thighs. "Now you want me to intimidate her."

"Kimber and Queen can't occupy the same space," Ezra reminds me, knowing how fond I am of the woman. "You know as well as I do how much she needs the structure, power-exchange, and boundaries of BDSM. So Queen's going to give her that experience while Kimber plays the friend."

"I'm not used to having multiple personalities like you are." Reaching around Ezra, I grab my emergency toiletry bag from the file cabinet.

My private room is stocked with feminine products and contraceptives. But I keep a stash in here, since our office is across from the ladies room– I left a note near the mirror in there to knock on the office door for supplies. Once a night someone needs something.

"Cortez is doing better," Ezra finally answers my earlier question. I ignore how he's watching me primp in the small mirror by the door. "Thank you for asking. He's struggling right now. But at least he left the apartment today."

"Cort didn't leave the apartment in nearly a week?" Stunned, the eyeliner pencil is frozen in my hand.

"His adventure for the day was to go home to Shadow Haven." Ezra sighs deeply– a tick. "As I told you before, I gave him an ultimatum. Either he lets me in and accepts Katya, or we go our separate ways. I can't live like this anymore. I'm trying very hard to help Katya right now, and I can't be split between the two of them. Cortez has had me for a lifetime and not claimed me, and *we* broke her– that choice for me was easy to make. Cortez is fighting me every step of the way. He won't leave, but he's not truly staying either. No more eggshell walking and being tested."

"So what exactly is Cort's malfunction?" I switch out for a hairbrush, then look over my shoulder to Ezra.

"Old wounds. Insecurities. He has writer's block right now. He feels ashamed of himself and guilty as all hell." Ezra stands, walks over to me, then adjusts the back of my catsuit. "Cortez was so lost to his emotions, he allowed it to hurt those closest to him. I tried to explain how I feel like that all the time, hoping it will draw us together."

"Do I look okay?" I begrudgingly ask for Ezra's opinion, because I know how much Katya's first visit to Restraint means to him.

"You'll do," Ezra says in a voice with no inflection, then smirks at me a second later. "Cortez wants to apologize to you, Regina, but he doesn't know how. He's charming and charismatic, but it's just a disguise. Grant is Cortez's closest friend and writing partner. The connection he has to Marcus needs no explanation. Then there is you– Cortez loves and respects you. In a fit of insecurity, he pushed you all away to prove those insecurities positive."

"It's a good thing you're a psychiatrist who examines why people do what they do." I tuck my girly shit back into its bag, then stow it in the cabinet. "The rest of us idiots just get angry and freeze out the people who hurt us."

"I'm tired." Ezra returns to the chair, looking over what I was doing before he interrupted me. "So tired. Cortez is my heart, but the thought of ditching him and living a simple life with Katya sounds refreshing."

I snort at *simple life*. Katya is small-town. Ezra hasn't set foot into a Walmart in his entire life– probably never even seen one. Their incompatibility is going to become a wedge between them.

Expression intent, I can sense Ezra's queuing up the security feeds on his personal laptop– the laptop he locks in a safe when he isn't carrying it from place to place. What I wouldn't give to be in possession of it, all by my little lonesome.

"Are you sure Kat's coming tonight?" I sound like Ella and Kris on a road trip. *Are we there yet?*

"I promise Katya will be here tonight," Ezra murmurs to me absentmindedly, eyes glued to the laptop screen. "I baited her when we spoke today." Eyes flicking up to look at me, Ezra's lips curl into a satisfied smirk. "Don't you trust our efforts? She was leaving her apartment while you were primping."

"There are only four blocks between Edge and Restraint– switch over to the front door feed," I suggest.

"Katya isn't here yet," Ezra whines, pouting. It's annoying behavior until I notice how his fingertips are shaking.

Ezra has caused me to suffer Stockholm syndrome and PTSD. "Katya can't resist coming to Restraint. I've been drawing her in for weeks. Not only that, she won't be able to resist you."

"I love you too, Mom." Ezra snickers, giddy.

"Good Lord." I groan, wandering over to stand behind Ezra so I can get a good look. "There she is!" shouting, I hop and clap.

The orgasmic sound flowing between Ezra's lips creeps my ass out.

Leaning over the back of the chair, I whisper into Ezra's ear. "The spider has finally lured the fly into our lair."

Shuddering, Ezra's eyes flick over his shoulder to pin me. "Don't use that analogy again. You forget my adoptive sister's name is Spyder." Then he returns to gaze in wonder at the tiny square, showing black and white live video footage.

"You hooked my bedroom up with color and sound. We need to upgrade Restraint's security for our own entertainment."

Reaching up to pat my hand where it rests on his shoulder, "We make an excellent team, Regina. Try harder to keep your nose out of where it doesn't belong. I can only keep you safe if you're behaving."

"I've been being good!" I whisper in mock-outrage. "Doing as you told me to do."

"And so much more," Ezra murmurs with pride. Leaning forward to get closer to the screen, his eyes glow with anticipation as Aaron chats with Katya for the very first time. We both try to read their lips, but get nowhere.

Jolting, the Bluetooth in my ear sparks to life, and I can hear Aaron's gravelly voice speaking to Katya. Eyes held wide, for the first time ever, I hear my new friend's voice. Rich, not throaty or girly, with no accent. Kat has a no-nonsense voice– maybe Ezra and Kat will get along after all.

"You've got our girl," I mutter to Aaron, heart pounding out of my chest.

"Yeah, she has curly red hair. Short little gal. Says she's a switch, but by the look she just gave this guy out here–" Aaron's warm laughter fills my ears. "I wouldn't mess with her. I think she was imagining shoving his balls down his own throat."

"Get Kat in here," I order, impatient to finally see Kat face-to-face. Ezra's struggling to get close enough to me to hear my Bluetooth. "Entice her if you have to, but just do it."

"You make me proud," Ezra breathes nearly silent against my cheek.

"Katya Waters. Kat," flows into my ear when she answers Aaron's earlier question.

"Kat sounds pissed– impatient," I give a play-by-play as Aaron and Katya hold a conversation. Light-headed, I get the thrill of a high off the disturbing game we play. We're literally luring Katya to us through nefarious means.

Somewhere on this journey, my ethics and morality became skewed– the wrong things for the right reasons, by any means necessary.

Switching channels, I pop back on with the rest of Restraint's natives. "I need someone to escort Fate to my office. It's a go, people! It's a go. Katya Waters has landed."

Fate meets me in the hallway, pixie face twisted up in annoyance. She's holding a whip in one hand and a jeweled collar in the other. "Ezra!" I growl loud enough for him to hear me through the closed door. Sadistic laughter flows, skimming along my spine.

"I'll keep you safe," is a promised whisper. Fate may not want to sit home alone all the time, but she's also terrified at Restraint after a few incidences of groping on the floor. She usually hangs with Kristal behind the bar, or has Roman escort her between the office, my private room, or the stockroom. She's never alone.

Fate doesn't need to say she trusts me– I can see it flowing from her eyes. "Ludicrous." The whip is coiled around my arm by tiny, deft fingertips. "Ezra is making a mockery out of BDMS with this cliché bullshit." The collar is thrust into my hand. "Restrain me– oh, Master– my Queen," is a sarcastic flow of deference.

Biting my bottom lip in concentration, while trying very hard not to laugh, I fasten the jeweled collar around Fate's slim neck. Fate is not into the lifestyle whatsoever. She's what Hillbrook taught us was the Server Soul personality type, which does translate well as a submissive if they are into the BDSM culture.

Fate was born to help others, finding pleasure, pride, and contentment doing the tasks I ask of her at work and at home. This doesn't mean she isn't highly intelligent, crafty in the sneaky sense of the word, or knows what she wants out of life. She's going to be one hell of a mother and wife someday. Which will suck for me, because Fate and Kris combined are the wives in my household.

"I guess Ezra wants me to use you as a prop." We share an eye roll. "I'm the scary-assed Domme persona for the evening, rounding out an authentically clichéd experience for Katya Waters."

Pausing, Fate looks up at me with huge crystalline blue eyes, quivers her pouty lips, and knits her blonde eyebrows. "I've been a bad girl– punish me, Master."

"Oh, good Lord! You're priceless." I snicker as Fate wallows and pouts like a naughty submissive, her way of trying to get me to relax. "Someday you will look at a man like that, and he will die from gobsmackage."

"Only dominant men want me, so they can control me," she mumbles, showing insecurities I didn't think she had. "Or wounded men."

Roman let me in on a little secret about *my* Angel. Fate's been screwing someone on the down-low, and I have it narrowed down to a few suspects. There's a story behind that statement she made, no doubt. *Wounded?*

Fate needs a family man, someone kind and caring but also an alpha male. She won't find who she's looking for here at Restraint, because she's not into kink whatsoever. I always found it odd how MdJ didn't force Fate into a union, when she's the oldest. Why Faith and Ezra? It should've been Fate.

Thank God, it didn't go down that way– Ezra would have cannibalized Fate.

Weaving around the dance floor, not only do I hold Fate's leash, I hold her hand tightly too. She's no longer teasing me because she's terrified of being in the crowd. Looking at the crowd from behind the bar feels safe to her. Plus, Kristal would annihilate anyone who touches Fate. With me leading the way, the sea parts like I'm Moses.

"Oh, wow…" Fate's whisper reaches my ears before I notice what she's talking about. "That's her, huh? Not what I expected."

Our expected guest has paused to drink in her surroundings. Standing at the top of the stairs leading down to the dance floor, I can tell Katya's as overwhelmed as she is excited. Her expression mirrors a combination of mine and Fate's when we first set foot into Restraint.

Trying to hide my smile, I can almost read Katya's mind, thinking how Restraint is lame compared to what she expected it to be, and this is after I added upgrades in the past few months.

I like her. I like her a lot– her facial expressions are more transparent than mine.

"Kat truly does remind me of a cat." Fate holds onto my arm, resting her cheek against my shoulder. "It's the eyes."

"And the intelligence," I add. "Independence. Territorialism. Stubbornness. Dominance."

"Ezra's gonna love–" Fate's words are cut off, because Katya walks down the steps leading to the dance floor, then strides right by us, like she knows where she's going. The bar, no doubt.

Katya Waters is almost a foot shorter than me, but her presence makes her seem taller. Her creamy skin is set off by fiery red hair and green eyes as vibrant as laser beams. She's riding the fine line where she may be perceived as chubby by some or curvy by others. To all the non-assholes, Katya looks healthy.

Her blood-red hair is pulled up on top of her head, but I know from our conversations that it's a mass of unruly curls to her waist. She manages to make a pair of trousers from Target and a cheap vest look classy yet sexy.

Ezra's probably salivating all over his keyboard right now. Lord knows how many times he's whacked off while reading our chat logs. I've witnessed it first-hand while I played Kimber with him sitting next to me. Ezra's worse than a twelve-year-old boy who's finally discovered internet porn and hand lotion.

Erasing those uncomfortable thoughts, I go on high alert since Katya is on the premises. Our popularity has grown here at Restraint, and it's been getting out of control lately. We're having a hell of a time keeping the security guys we hire. The wage is good, with benefits, but they come and go within days, leaving few to do the job of many.

My eyes rove the club for people who need some sense knocked into their boundary-pushing heads. There's bound to be issues when you mix dom-wannabes, tourists, girls looking for trouble and boys up to no good, and copious amounts of alcohol. They try to stick out any way they can, hoping to catch the eye of one of the notorious Masters of Restraint and get a personal invitation to enter the BDSM dungeon.

Roman took care of several guys tonight, but he's on dungeon monitor duty right now. I spot Dexter and Syn near the steel door to the dungeon, no doubt coming out to catch a peek at Katya. We share our '*no problem children'* nod. It's better than the '*drag 'em out the backdoor and kick the living shit out of them in the alley'* chin tilt.

I've engaged in that activity a lot lately– ass kicking the badly behaving patrons. My fellow employees think it's hilarious how Roman and I tag-team the douche-canoes, saying it's the thug-life we left behind coming out in us. It helps relieve the sexual frustrations and man troubles I'm experiencing.

Marcus was already suffering from erectile dysfunction because of Cortez, which transferred over to us. I'm not sure the man has had an orgasm in months– all aborted attempts. After the sex tape, Marcus and I have had several long, intimate talks and one sleepover, but he still looks haunted. As for Grant, I'm not getting within ten yards of him. Last Sunday, Grant kissed me goodbye. If you can call violent sparing kissing. Marcus had to save me from myself, because I was on the edge of murderous lust. As it was, we were both left bleeding– I'd bit Grant's lip, so he bit my tongue.

Current Grant is not passive like Past Grant– too much Jamie in him.

I could use the dungeon to relieve some stress, but I have no playmates. No one tops Marcus, and James Atwater watches so he can write about it later, and neither frequents Restraint. That's okay– someone needs to be responsible enough to babysit the deviants while they engage in hedonistic activities, may as well be me.

"Reg," is a warning whisper to regain my attention because my thoughts were wandering. Fate tenses as eyes covetously drink her in. Fate truly is angelic in her flowy dress with the scent of prey wafting off her. Drawing Fate firmly to my side, I wrap her leash around my palm. Oddly enough, she relaxes at the sight of her leash in my hand. I guess she understands that they'd have to chop my hand off to detach her from me.

"Come along, my Angel," I purr, and Fate snorts in reply, nervous tension broken. "Let's go play with our new Kitty Kat."

"Looks feisty," Fate plays along. "Claws and fangs. Wonder if Ezra gets off on being hissed at?"

Shuddering, I say for Fate's own good, "Ezra's kinks are best left alone."

Katya's sitting at a barstool with a sarcastic smile flirting along her lips. Fate and I share a similar one as we approach her. "Welcoming committee– it's a go," I whisper, engaging my Bluetooth.

Chapter Thirty-Three

What a train wreck. Katya didn't trust me, as if she could sense there was something nefarious riding beneath the surface, which there was. I'll never doubt her intelligence and intuition, that's for damn sure. I really enjoyed the woman, as did Fate. But I fear once the truth is out there, any friendship Katya and I could've built will be dead. There will be too many secrets and lies between us. I know from first-hand experience how that destroys lifelong relationships, so our budding one won't stand a chance. Katya will never trust me again once she realizes I've been playacting Kimber for the past five months, so she'll never give *me* a chance.

Everything is Ezra's fault, but I'm to blame for going along with it. I take full responsibility for my actions and accept the consequences.

Katya is definitely more than she seemed, which is a relief. For a moment, I thought Ezra had sent that kid in there to grab Katya's tit as a test to see how she'd react. Somewhere Ezra had gotten ahold of a Bluetooth earpiece and was swearing bloody murder at me to kill the motherfucker. Proving herself worthy and ruthless enough to withstand Ezra, Katya showed her mettle when it came to the little punk.

Fate and I parted ways, with her going behind the bar to help Kristal. I was going to have her fix the errors in payroll, but Ezra's in the office. After an incident with Katya going to the bathroom, only to get trapped in our dark office with Ezra, I'm not trusting him with the safety of any of my people. It was bad enough when I was in there stripping out of my latex prison under his ever-watchful eye, and he knows better than to go there with me again. Ezra wouldn't wake up tomorrow if Master Ez tries for a repeat.

"I've done my duty for the night– Queen signing off," I alert my fellow employees as I stride down the hallway toward the club proper. "Aaron's in charge." The force of the music hits me first, with the scent of lust hitting me next– a potent cocktail firing a zing through my veins.

Too bad I won't be getting laid anytime soon. It took Marc's possessive urges over Cortez using his mouth on Ezra to get it up enough to pound me. I'm sure Whitt's birthday present had something to do with it. But that's not very flattering, now is it?

Yet another mistake made on my part. Cause and effect. Whitt's right– Cortez isn't holding Marcus hostage. Even if Ezra and Cortez end up living happily ever after with Katya, Marcus is the one skull-fucking Cortez. There's no excuse other than it's what Marcus and Cortez want. I could hold Cortez down and force Ezra on him for the rest of my life, but Marcus is still going to drift toward them.

Just like I can't blame the consummation of my marriage on why I had sex with Whitt. I did it because I wanted to. I did it because Whitt is the only person who loves me in the purest sense of the word, without demands and betrayals. I needed that once in my lifetime to reveal how I wasn't getting it from the one who should be giving it to me.

With that highlighted on the video, Marcus and I are beginning to fall apart– I can feel it resonating in every bone in my body. My intuition isn't being silent this time. It will never be Grant who tears Marcus and me apart. Only Ezra and Cortez have that ability.

"Pretty Boy's in the dungeon," Roman whispers through my ear as I skirt around the outer wall of the club, headed for the door to the dungeon. It's like Roman read my mind– I need a hit of sunshine to get through the night. "Dexter's playing with his new pet. It's gonna be a good show. Everyone stopped mid-scene to watch. He's drawing quite a crowd."

"Be right there." After plucking the earpiece out, I tuck it into the front pocket of my jeans. My ear is always sore afterward, so I spend a few orgasmic seconds sticking my finger in my ear and tugging on the lobe. My ridiculous groaning sounds have nearby patrons staring at me like I've lost my mind.

Without thought, the code on the door is punched in, and I'm stepping into the dungeon. My initial reaction every time I walk through the door is how I'd love to revamp the space. It's utilitarian, only serving its purpose, but it's not what I'd envision it to be.

Ezra may be perfectly fine with relinquishing control of Restraint over to me, as long as it involves the running of the place, but the atmosphere is solely his responsibility. Dreary bastard.

Dexter always chooses the spot in the far corner, because the man likes his privacy while he works. He's the only dominant I know who puts up sawhorses to keep spectators at bay. Then again, he's also the only one I've seen wield a bullwhip. If anyone got too close, they'd get injured on accident. Dexter may be a sadist, but he's the most responsible, cautious, compassionate sadist I've ever met. Granted, I only know two sadists, but still. He'll only cause pain to those who need it. Not harm, *pain*, and there is a distinct difference.

Standing back, I watch for a few minutes. Being one of the tallest people in the dungeon has its benefits, because there are more than twenty people crowded up against the barriers, trying to get a good view of the action. Roman is the only one wearing a Restraint Security t-shirt, which is a terrifying prospect. We need to vet a handful of responsible and reliable security personnel who will stay for the long haul. Either that, or Ezra has to get the non-members out of my dungeon.

I don't give a shit what Master Fontaine wants. Olivia is in Las Vegas, so she doesn't get a vote when the safety and security of my people are at risk. Maître du Jeu uses our BDSM community as a front for their nefarious activities– my guess is they blackmail their high-profile, anonymous BDSM clients. For some bizarre reason, Olivia demanded Ezra open our dungeon to the public. A handful in here right now are guests, but the rest had to ante up large sums of cash to enter– cash that lines Olivia's pockets.

If I ever come face-to-face with the woman…

Squeezing through the crowd, I come to stand next to Roman, noticing Whitt is next to him. Some eager bitch elbows me and snarls a string of profanity. One look into my eyes shuts her ass up– I'm not in the mood.

"Umm… not to state the obvious." I wave a hand toward Dexter's empty area. "Why are we all standing here if our sadist isn't in attendance?"

"Dex left to fetch his pet," Whitt answers for Roman. Flashing me a dimpled grin, he's glowing like the goddamn sun.

Leaning forward, pushing in front of Roman a bit to get closer to Whitt. "Did you get laid tonight already?" I'm not jealous– totally in awe. No one but those closest to us realize Whitt is my husband, and it will remain that way because of the bizarre relationship we have.

Chuckling, Roman fist-bumps a blushing Whitt. "Nah, just an epic blowjob."

"Heidi?" I guess, since Kristal's been working all night behind the bar.

"We'll have this conversation in private," Whitt whispers so only Roman and I can hear. "After the show starts."

"Fair enough," I concede.

I try to be in the moment, no woe-is-me while we wait for Dexter and his new pet. But something just feels off. I've been trying to live life, truly experience it, instead of going through the motions on autopilot. It hasn't been without difficulty, but emotionally I'm all over the place.

Standing next to my grinning, oversexed husband, with Roman chuckling and elbowing him all proud like, I feel hollow.

Empty.

Everyone around me is holding their breath, waiting for an exciting, heart-stopping show, and I'm just… *here*.

I feel lonely. Worse, I feel alone in the crowd.

I can work all I want, keep my mind off the truth. I can pretend my daughter and I have the same relationship we had before I told her Grant was still alive. She still irrationally blames me, and it hurts so fucking bad I can't sleep at night. I can fill my days so full, I can ignore the fact that my son is a stranger. I can concentrate on everyone else's drama, until I forget my own.

After working a billion hours today, I can't seem to shut off reality tonight. It's banging in my psyche, refusing to be ignored.

Syn's words. Roman's words. Whitt's words…

They mirrored the same thoughts. For five months, I've been working with Ezra to solidify his relationship with Cortez, for all their sakes. But it hasn't been altruistic. I wanted Marcus to myself… but if Marcus wanted me to himself, all he had to do was have me.

Because it was two guys, I hadn't realized how hypocritical I was being. I'm against women who blame the woman their husband cheats on them with, but never their husband. Here I am, placing the blame on Cortez. Placing the blame on Cortez and Ezra's fucked up relationship… when I should be blaming Marcus.

"It's not you, Regina. It's their dicks wanting in other people, because your pussy isn't made of gold and the sex is mediocre at best. They all either want to be deep inside or have

a dick deep inside their assholes, because women aren't good enough for them."

Since our reunion, five months ago, the only times Marcus and I have had sex successfully was the night Grant joined us, and the next night wasn't without a struggle.

Standing in the dungeon reminds me of my first time here, and it strengthens the hollowness I feel. For the few months leading up to my initiation, Marcus cut me out of his life. I wandered alone. Hours before my initiation, we reconnected stronger than ever. If I were to think back, it hasn't been right.

Ever.

This week of isolation, since the release of the sex-tape, has highlighted how my time with Marcus is in bursts. He ravaged me sexually, like a crazed, possessive beast. After my initiation, after my marriage, after my rape, the sex changed, then became nonexistent. Marcus opened up emotionally, but cut me off sexually. Months and months of aborted attempts– *let's go to sleep and hold one another*. When it did happen, it wasn't without a struggle and never to his completion.

I can't attest to how long this has been happening, because Marcus cut me out of his life before my initiation. So if I were to think back, it's riding up on close to a year with only a handful of sexual experiences that came to fruition.

Marcus is having erectile dysfunction from stress, but got it up when he was furious with me when I had Ezra suck Cortez off. He couldn't get off with me, no matter how hard he pounded, making excuses, and he hasn't attempted since.

The few hours I spent with Whitt highlighted how no one gives me their all. Sexually. Emotionally. One or the other, but never both. Whitt gave me both, but the type of love isn't the same.

After being around Ezra, there's no way I don't try to see it from the other person's point-of-view. I'm not narcissistic enough to think this is about me, yet I'm too insecure not to have it bother me. I want to be there for Marcus, but under the circumstances, there isn't a person on the planet who wouldn't internalize the situation we're in.

Partners from a far, yet we seem divided on the goal. Impatient, I want to get to the bottom of this, and the louder the crowd gets, the antsier I become.

"Toby!" a young woman's terrified shout ricochets

throughout the dungeon like a gunshot. We all freeze as the girl shoves her way to the barricade.

Dexter's walking out of the mouth of the hallway, headed in our direction, affect calm and confident. Dutifully following behind him is a naked boy, pink skin scrubbed raw. The new pet is the dumbshit who grabbed Katya's tit out on the dance floor. I'm glad to see him naked and cleansed of the taint he carried.

"Toby!" The girl pushes and shoves, having bigger balls than most. When a guy shoves back, she elbows him out of the way. "Don't do this!"

"Girlfriend?" Whitt whispers out the side of his mouth in my direction. "My gaydar sucks. Maybe this is his way of coming out, and we're about to see this chick go postal."

Roman snorts, and I shudder. Yeah, nothing like being surrounded by men who love cock, and only want pussy for the novelty of it– or when they want children. I don't know if it's sexist, misogynistic, or it's in the water. But I have a feeling Marcus is struggling with the same conflict of conscience we're all waiting for Cortez to work through– there's something there, and Syn was warning me.

"Niece," Roman answers. "The kid is straight, by the way."

"Niece?" Whitt and I mutter at the same time, voices being swallowed by the commotion. "She looks older than him. Is he even legal?"

"Eighteen," Roman replies, eyes lighting on the action.

"If you need this– if you're like Auggie –I'll take you to Robin." The girl's voice quivers with fear, tears streaking down her cheeks. "Let's go home."

"I hope they don't go home," Roman mutters, looking captivated. "We could use some fresh blood around here."

"Yeah," I grumble, pissed the fuck off at the vapid man display. "I'm sure it has nothing to do with the fact that she's a wounded looking natural blonde with huge tits and a gorgeous face. Young too– impressionable. You men fucking suck."

"We're getting the bitter feminist Regina tonight, I see." Roman rolls his eyes at Whitt, brushing off my comment as if it's not valid.

Rage always simmering beneath the surface, I concentrate on the action instead of beating Roman in the condescending face. Just on the other side of the barricade, Dexter has his hands full. The girl is tugging on her uncle, trying to yank him over a sawhorse, but he won't budge.

This Toby fella looked high out of his mind earlier, sickly. A few hours with Dexter has him calm and clear-eyed. "Tina." His small hands wrap around the girl's shoulders. "Go home. Go home and get help."

We all lean closer, feet glued to the floor, bodies arching like flowers finding the sun. Just another episode of Mistress & Master of Restraint playing out in the dungeon.

"Get help with me– what about seminary school?"

"Jesus H. Christ." Whitt bugs his eyes out. "Did I just hear that right?"

"Those kids should not be here," I hiss, furious, nails biting into Roman's arm.

"It's not my call– Dexter's." Roman flicks my hand away, then rubs the red marks I left behind.

"I can't." The boy turns his back on her, head bowing. "I can't go home. I want to stay here. I feel dirty inside and out– I can't get clean." Rubbing at his arms, the boy begins scratching deep furrows.

"Tobias." Dexter snaps the kid's mental leash, and he comes to heel instantly. I'd love to say that type of connection is fantasy, but we're witnessing it firsthand as Dexter soothes the kid with a singular word– the cadence of his voice speaking volumes.

This is a true melding. Not a dominant and submissive, but a master and slave.

"Roman," Dexter calls, deep in dominance-mode, expecting to be obeyed. "Please drive Miss Kline home. It's roughly three hours from here to her hometown in Massachusetts. The young lady will give you the address. Do not leave her with anyone but her father– I already called their family."

"I guess I'm getting no sleep tonight." Roman mouths to us, looking peeved.

"You wanted to spend more time with the pretty blonde lady." Whitt tries and fails to contain his laughter.

"Ha-ha, asshat." Roman slips through the crowd to join them. Evidently he was already introduced, as the kids don't seem startled by his presence.

Rapid-fire whispering, crying, and clutching seems to go on for minutes, with Dexter looking impatient. Reaching to the ground, he materializes a bullwhip. "I'd suggest you leave before you see something that will be traumatic for you."

With her gasping for air, Roman drags the girl down the

hallway and out the door to the parking lot.

"Please back up," Dexter orders. In thrall, no one moves. With the flick of his wrist, the crack of a whip hitting tile has everyone moving en masse several feet backward. "Spread out– stop clustering like this is a police barricade and you're ambulance chasers."

"Dexter doesn't like working in front of an audience," Whitt whispers into my ear, tugging us closer now that the crowd dispersed.

"I know." Taking a deep breath, I catalog the kid. Toby has marks on his body that aren't self-inflicted. "But he has to do this punishment in public for it to be taken seriously. I can guarantee more happened in Dexter's room than a thorough scrubbing."

"Gauged the kid's pain tolerance?" Whitt guesses.

"No." Tobias Kline and I lock eyes as Dexter swivels a St. Andrew's cross into position. "He was testing the boy's level of masochism." The boy looks exhausted by life, haunted by the truth, yet there is hope gazing out at me. Not the innocence of youth, but the blind faith that Dexter will help him– heal him. The kid wants to live.

I'm standing in the middle of a dungeon, about to witness an intimate act between a real sadist and masochist. No playacting. I feel no awe. No lust. Nothing physically, emotionally, or cerebrally stimulating.

I'm numb.

I want to feel alive too, but no sadist can help me. I refuse to be Apathetic Regina any longer, but not at the expense of unleashing Destructive Regina.

I just want to be Regina. I want to have hope, but I don't have the ability to have blind faith, nor is there someone willing to save me, help me– heal me.

All I've got is the truth.

I'm done not rocking the boat, done not going after what I want– I'm done suppressing who I am.

No more martyr Regina.

It's time the age of Empowered Regina began.

"Where are you going?" Whitt reaches for me as I stride away. Looking confused, he starts after me through the crowd.

A big part of me resents Whitt too– for causing me to love him, for using that love against me, for manipulating me into marrying him, into having sex with him. I resent my sunshine for illuminating the darkness in my relationships with others.

"No." I hold out my hand, freezing Whitt in place. "I want you to stay and watch. Then I want you to get another blowjob. I want you to go home and smirk at Daniel for staying up too late to watch Foxnews. Then peek in on your brother and sister. I want you to be happy and content as you close your eyes tonight."

"Queen?" Whitt reaches out for me, handsome face twisted up in fear– fear over me. "What about you?"

"What about me?" I mutter with a shrug, walking backward down the hallway toward the exit to the parking lot. "I won't be going to bed happy, but I will be going to bed free."

"What?" Whitt picks up the pace, jogging to catch up with me.

"Maybe I'm a bit too much like Ezra–"

"Batshit crazy?" No trace of humor rides Whitt's voice. "What's going on?"

Sighing, I stare at the ceiling, at the floor, at the doors lining the hallway, anywhere but at my husband. After I take a deep breath, I let it out in a rush of truth.

"Even when people hurt me, I can see it from their perspective and I can empathize. I take on their burdens, and mine just fester without being soothed or healed. Ignored. Forgotten. Not important as the next drama crops up. How freeing it must be for your sister, to be so narcissistic only her needs and wants and opinions matter. Squeaky wheel gets the grease syndrome. Well, I'm sick of greasing everyone while I'm left to be sucked dry."

Whitt just stares at me with his head cocked to the side, as if he's trying to yank what I'm thinking out of my mind.

"Grant may be silenced, but he has a voice stronger than ever." Walking backward, I stare at my husband, feeling just in my decision. "I think it's time I'm heard too."

Chapter Thirty-Four

Heart beating out of control, body shaking, I grip my steering wheel as I traverse through traffic, destination unknown. I had to get away from the way Restraint and all its occupants were syphoning off my energy– my will to live.

Without thought, Sync is dialing Ezra's cell number, and I'm amazed my voice doesn't quiver as I speak with him. "So tell me something, Ez–"

"Regina, why are you calling me?" Ezra's voice holds amusement. "Aren't you in the same building as I am? How's Dexter's show? I'm not one for displays of sadism."

"Now *that* is laughable," I murmur without humor. "I'm driving."

"Oh." All he has to say is *oh.*

"I'm glad Katya made your night," I say with all honesty. The dark intimacy of the car, of the night pressing inward from the outside, has me saying things I normally wouldn't. Being open and vulnerable with a person who has the capacity to annihilate my heart.

"I do care about her, Regina."

"I know you do… about the security feeds." Deep breath. "I don't want to see it, but I have a question that needs to be answered."

"Shoot." The clack of Ezra typing in the background lends me comfort and courage to go on.

"Do you watch them together every time they're together? Do Marcus and Cortez get off during their *therapy*?"

"Regina!" Ezra's bark of sharp laughter has me flinching, knuckles turning white as I grip the steering wheel. "What's the point if they didn't? And, yeah… I always watch, and they always get off. Even Cort climaxes just from the act itself. Why?"

Gasping for air, but having none to be found, I'm amazed I don't wreck my car. Idling at a red light probably saves my life.

"Regina?" Ezra calls out, the first trickle of unease filling his voice. "Are you there? Is the call breaking up?"

"I'm here," I force out, finding little relief as oxygen returns to my lungs. "Do you have eyes on Marcus? I need to talk to him about something," I mutter vaguely.

"Hmm…" Suspicion creeps into Ezra's tone, but he gives me the respect I deserve by not demanding answers to questions I refuse to hear. "About a half hour ago, Marc was visible on the outside cam of Dexter's house, headed up to Serenity Lake."

"Okay." Breathing deeply, I prepare to end the call.

"Regina," Ezra's voice flows in the darkness, the intimacy of not being face-to-face ratcheting up ten notches. "In everyone's life, there is always someone who *must* come first, no matter what."

"Who?" I know what he's getting at, and the implications terrify me.

"Yourself."

The call is disconnected without a directive from my mind– emotions unable to handle what was undoubtedly to come out of Ezra's mouth next. I need to be emotionally stable enough to drive, let alone drive through motherfucking Crestview, where all my demons dwell.

For Marcus, I make the twenty-minute drive, longing to turn off to my development before I make it to The Gates. The security guard opens the main gate, waving me through, knowing I belong in this haven of one-percenters. No matter how hard I ignore the fact, I'm still the mistress of Misery Castle, and I forever will be, in every definition of the word.

Too many hard truths are pounding at me. With single-minded focus, I drive down the singular street that is known as Crestview Drive, passing by houses hidden behind impenetrable gates– each one housing my enemies and allies.

Crestview is the hotbed of Maître du Jeu, cowards hiding behind their ten-foot walls and plots of land large enough to be at least a quarter mile each.

Fate and Faith Simpson's house is the first to my right, left empty since their father's death and their stepmother's suicide. Fate joined us at Misery Castle, while Faith ran to Stanton Green and transformed into Syn.

Then there is Gwen Meyers' home on my right, which I know is there but refuse to look at on principle. With the rage simmering in my blood, she'd be a convenient target.

Boyd Spencer's home is lighting up the night a quarter mile on the right from his sisters' mansion. Curiosity has me noting his gate is open and inviting to visitors, even at this late hour.

Another empty home, followed by another. They've been empty since I was eighteen and probably a generation before. My Dominion history teaches me these must belong to Stanton Green and Olivia Fontaine. Stan prefers to be in the heart of downtown Dominion– Lord knows, he's probably escaping nightmares of his father's past. Olivia fled to Sin City, where there was a larger population to torment.

I wish I could escape as Crestview drive branches into three. I'd rather be burned alive than enter any of these long drives.

To my left paves the way to Shadow Haven, where Marcus lives with Diane in a mansion I'll never visit, in a living room where he and Cortez are intimate. It's easy to ignore the fact that Marcus has a life outside of mine, outside of my bedroom and the brownstone. He has an entire life I'm not welcome to enter. A high-profile job, a campaign run for the judge's seat, political and charitable ties. A family and friends, while I'm relegated to the dark, unseen and ignored until needed. Denied and rejected when questioned, because it would be bad for business to be tied to a woman such as me.

If I look too closely, I'll recognize my relationship with Marcus Zeitler is more toxic to me than the one I had with Grant. At least the Whittenhowers treated me as if I was one of their own, giving me a home and a family… but they were wrenched away from me when Grant played dead.

To avoid a PTSD moment of epic proportions, I don't glance at the gate to my right. That path leads to Misery Castle, and my psyche is beating like an angry beast, trying to replay the first and second time I entered, and the very last time I fled.

Headed straight, relieved Dexter always leaves his gate ajar, I pass that whorehouse nightmare of a Victorian mansion, and precede to where the Zeitler home used to rise four-stories to the sky.

Serenity Lake.

Once, just after we first met, Marcus drove me down this same tree-lined tunnel at breakneck speeds. Now I go, sensing an ending, rather than a beginning is on the horizon.

As I park my car next to the Spyder, Marcus floods my vision.

I'd had an agenda this evening. To get my power back. To have a voice. But seeing Marcus slumped against a pylon on the dock, my intentions shift to ones of compassion and understanding.

I'm not broken, and I never will break, but Marcus is on the verge.

Stepping from the car, the sound of peepers and the hooting of owls fill the night. The grass is ankle-deep, sure to get thicker as spring shifts into summer. With the moonlight paving my way, I try not to stumble over hidden obstacles in the grass.

Marcus doesn't shift, doesn't speak, but I know he hears my feet tapping on the wooden planks. Flowing to sit down beside him, I war with myself. I'd rather dive head-first into the lake, swimming as far and fast from here as possible, than have the conversation that is sure to come.

"I've always gotten these premonitions," I admit to Marcus for the first time. He and I have a proactive partnership, where we take care of others, neither one of us truly voicing our emotions and needs and wants. "Whitt says he wishes for things and they come true. I met your grandson, and I understand Boyd's comment on faith versus science now. Is Zane an empath or autistic? Well, I sense things, and I don't want to be numbed out anymore to avoid it."

"I think Zane is both, or neither." Marcus is purposefully being obtuse to avoid what I'm trying to say. Gazing at the water lapping against the side of the dock, he ignores me, refusing to look me in the eye.

I don't need an extra sense to understand what that body language means.

"All night, this overpowering feeling of foreboding has been plaguing me–"

"I miss my house." Marcus interrupts me on purpose, ignoring our obvious problem. "I don't think I'll feel right until I live over there again." He points in the distance across the lake, voice weak and thready. "I think Dexter built that monstrosity at the base of the drive on purpose, leaving this for me, because he knows I need it."

"MdJ doesn't pull your strings, Marcus." Realist Regina will not be ignored. Not any more. It's time for the hard truths Whitt loves to spew. "At any time, you could divorce Diane, move out of Shadow Haven, and use your considerable money to rebuild Lake Serenity. You have your memories, your pictures, and the history to help you with your task."

"I could sit here all night."

Usually, Marcus can get me to back off, but not tonight. "I've been working on my problems for months, trying to rebuild my relationship with Ella and connect with Niel. Kris and I are in a good place. I go to therapy three times a week to deal with what Ezra unleashed in me, and he and I are generally in a good place now. I've focused on helping the Ezes. I'm doing as I'm told by MdJ. I've come to terms with my marriage and learned to see Whitt as an adult…"

Marcus looks away from me, gazing across the lake, purposefully ignoring me, but there is no way he's not hearing me. My words are sinking like a stone in the water.

"I've been busy, running Empowerment and Restraint, raising my children, and I've given you space. We see each other a few times a week, maybe twice. We don't talk every day, but I understand, I do. I thought we were both going headlong into the future to fix what is broken. But we're not, are we?"

While standing in the dungeon, watching a terrified young man show great courage and faith, I finally recognized what was going on around me, and I won't ignore it any longer.

"A part of you needs the chaos swirling around us, needs Cortez to need you, needs Ezra to be mentally unstable. You need an excuse to focus on their lives instead of your own. You could have that house. You could have your daughter. You could be with me if you wanted to be… but you don't."

"Regina." Marc's voice breaks, my name sounding torturous. "Don't go there– please."

"I'm not a monster. I can see you're struggling, and I'm not going to make it all about me. Talk to me Marcus." Reaching over, I try to comfort him, but my hand falls away as I take in his expression.

Staring at the sky, the gutted sound Marcus releases draws tears to my eyes. "I can't give you what you need. I can't be who you need me to be."

"I need you to be *you*," is the only way I can reply. "I want you to be happy and healthy, whether that's with me or not doesn't factor into it. You're miserable."

"It would be a lie if I didn't admit how much seeing you with Whitt hurt me– it hurt me more than it hurt Jamie, because it showed me reality."

"Reality?" Anger infuses my voice. "I came up here tonight knowing I'd have to be sympathetic and compassionate, while trying to have a voice. But that is insulting, and I'm not going to ignore it. From the get-go, I've done what you wanted. What everyone wanted me to do. Now you're shaming me for it. Is this why you don't want me anymore?"

"I didn't mean that how it sounded." Eyes flicking from the sky to meet mine, Marcus says with fierce conviction, "*I want you*, Regina."

"It's hard to tell, to be quite honest." Shifting on the dock, I refuse to keep quiet this time. "We've been together a little over two years now, and it's been a rocky journey. There's no consistency with you. You fucked me like a madman, because you feared Whitt– that's not about me or you. It's not flattering. It's not romantic."

"I just said I can't give you what you need," Marcus reminds me, voice strained.

"Don't interrupt me– *hear* me!" I grit out between clenched teeth. "You say you want me, but do you? Or do you want me because you're afraid someone else will take me? You fucked me, then you dumped me for three months without a word. Then you wanted me back again when Whitt tried to claim me, only to shift gears from passion to therapeutic cuddling in three days' time. Now we're back to that bullshit where we're too busy, putting everyone else first, but it's just an excuse."

"It's not an excuse– it's true." Marc's words have me on the verge of homicide, but the utter defeat in the way his shoulders curve inward has me going from rage to grief.

"Was it me blowing Dexter? The three-way with Ezra and Cort?" Voice warbling, I've never felt so vulnerable, and I hate it. "Was it me getting married to Whitt? I'd say it was because I consummated the marriage, but you've been cold for five months– eight if you forget having sex twice between the three-month ignore-fest and the five-month cuddling."

"It's not about you, okay?" Marcus snarls, rage leaking out.

"I could buy that. I can even empathize with you. I could even agree it's not my business, and not push, just like I always do. But, see… when someone says it's not about you, but they are only incapable of having sex with you… that pretty much means it is about you."

"It's nothing you did!" Marcus bellows, losing his false cool. Hands fisted in his lap, he shudders with the need to exact violence. "You're not to blame for any of this. At. All."

"But it affects me just the same, only you're angry I'm not

playing pretend by ignoring and sticking my head in the sand."

"Just let it go," Marc orders, but that tone of voice doesn't work on me anymore. I'm not that idiot woman who first met Marcus on the front steps of the brownstone.

"No." For once, I put me first, even if I look like a selfish cunt. "I'm in my sexual prime, as is my boyfriend, but we can't have sex. I know you've been getting off with Cortez– don't lie."

Stunned, Marcus quickly looks away from me, finding the dark water suddenly fascinating.

"Yeah, that's what I thought." Disgusted, I sneer, upper lip curling off my teeth. "In five months, we've had sex to completion twice. I keep thinking about those nights, going over them, trying to find where it went wrong."

"*You. Did. Nothing. Wrong.*"

Since Marcus isn't hearing me, keeps interrupting me, I bulldoze right back over him. "The night with Jamie… you were appalled at us both for having sex, thinking I should be broken after what Ezra did to me. In my mind, I don't know if I'm rewriting it, or finally seeing it clearly."

"Regina, don't–"

"The only reason you were able to get off with me is because Jamie was with us." The tears are no longer just warbling my voice– they're cascading down my face too. "The next night, you warned me how you had trouble keeping it up with Cortez. You didn't want to hurt my feelings, you said. We did fool around, but it was more about comfort, and that was the last time you got off with me."

"Don't–"

"That was all a bullshit lie, wasn't it?" I glare Marcus down, challenging him to tell me the truth. "You had absolutely *no* problem getting off with Cortez. Not that night, or any night since… or ever."

"Please, don't go there." Silent tears seems to be contagious, as it's now inflicting Marcus too.

"I came here for the truth," I remind Marcus. "I know this isn't a conventional relationship. I want a partnership, only truth between us. I don't want to feel as if the only thing binding us together is the fact we both love and want Jamie, but he doesn't want either one of us back."

Marc's palm lashes out to smoother my face, fingers splaying over my cheeks, but for once I will not be silenced.

Flinging his arm off me, I jump to my feet to tower over him on the dock.

"Which is it, Marcus?" I challenge defiantly. "Is the only thing between us Jamie, or is this real? We're both legally married to someone else. We don't go on dates. Now we don't even fuck. All we do is listen to your excuses on why we can't spend time together. I've worked so hard with Ezra to put his and Cort's relationship back together, but you're sabotaging it."

Eyes bulging from his skull, Marcus glares at me in open defiance. "It's not about you!"

"It's not about me, but it affects me, and I seem to be the catalyst." Heart breaking open to spill at our feet, I demand the truth. "Did. You. Get. Off. With. Cortez. That. Night?"

"YES!" Marcus screams up into my face, veins throbbing in his forehead. "Are you happy now?" is his reply to the fact that I'm suffocating on bitter rejection and torment.

In a flash, Marc is on his feet with his palm wrapped around my throat, immobilizing while silencing me with the constriction of his fingers.

"I'm so fucking sorry." Deep, wracking sobs flow between Marc's parted lips. "Ezra raping you broke *me*." Revelation shocking me, I lose the ability to stand on my own. Slowly lowering me to the ground, Marcus doesn't take his hand from my throat.

"Not because I was inches from you on the other side of the door while my *son* violated you– took your power away and rewrote who you are. Not because I'd already suffered through it myself, and knew him capable. Not because no matter how much help I got him, it didn't fix it. But because I *knew* something was off– I *could* feel it… and I didn't stop it."

Marcus lays me down on the dock, making sure my neck isn't wrenched. With his palm no longer strangling me, I take in deep gasps of air. Skin tight, no doubt wicked bruises are ringing my throat. But the rest of me… the rest of me is in shock.

Kneeling over me, Marc's tears land on my face. "I watched you walk out of that meeting room… I watched him follow you… and I knew before the door shut what was going to happen, and I didn't have time to stop it."

"I-I-I–"

"No, Regina." Shaking his head in disgust, Marcus looks on the verge of being sick. "Don't you dare say it's not my fault." Eyes flicking to the sky, to the water, then back to me. "I know how you felt in that moment, and that's what makes it worse. Terrified, confused, powerless and alone. "

Primal sounds of torment flow from Marc's chest, and I'm frozen in shock. "Ezra may as well have cut my dick off in that moment. It was a billion times worse than having it happen to me. Only I knew it was terrifying for you. I knew how you felt, and I was powerless to stop it. Powerless to save you."

Crumbling to the dock, Marcus covers his head with his upraised arms, sobbing hysterically while muttering retched things I wish I couldn't hear. Crawling to my knees, I curl over his back, trying to comfort him.

"*This!*" Marcus shouts, but I don't let go. "This is why I can't get it up with you. I should be comforting you. It *just* happened to you, but you're the one who's comforting me. Comforting me because I feel worthless for not saving you, when I should be comforting you for what Ezra did."

"Shh…" I try to soothe Marcus, but it only adds fuel to the fire.

"Talk about ignoring the issues… you won't talk about this. Ever. It's festering in me, worse by the day. It's not right– I feel emasculated. Skull-fucking Cortez is about fucking my demons. That's not how it is with you, and I can't… I just can't… That's not fair to you, and that's what I meant about not being able to give you what you need, no matter how goddamn badly I want you."

"It's not about the sex for me– I'm not an asshole. I just needed to know what this barrier was that you've erected between us. You've been so open about everything but what was wrong, so I was feeling rejected and confused."

"I'm trying," Marcus mutters from between his fingertips as he covers his face with his palms, scrubbing the pain away. "But I don't want this future for you."

"Future for me?"

Laughing without humor, Marcus sounds like he's dying. "The guilt makes it impossible for me to get it up with you, Regina. How disgusting is that? You're a victim, and I'm subconsciously punishing you for it. But seeing you brings back my past, and all I want to do is give and receive comfort."

Closing my eyes, I don't lessen or tighten my hold on Marcus. But inside, rage and despair are mixing into a toxic cocktail, and I'm terrified I'll release it to the world.

What I say next murders a part of my soul. "We don't have to have sex. There are different types of relationships, different types of love. We can be intimate emotionally without being intimate physically."

Choking on whatever he wants to say next, Marc's fingernails bite into my arm, piercing the skin and drawing blood. "So we turn into Daniel and Diane? Watch TV together at night and plot global domination by day?" Painful laughter fills the night. "That won't work, because being around you is torture. I want to touch you, but I can't. It's easier to not be near you."

Pulling away, "It's your call–"

"NO!" Marcus screams, tugging me back down to him. "That is *not* what I want. I'm talking to someone who is going through it too, but he's struggled for his entire adult life to touch his wife. It's been months for us, I cannot even imagine a lifetime. I won't do that to you– *to us*."

Treading carefully, doing the complete opposite of what I set out to do, I ignore my feelings because they don't matter. *They truly don't*. "It shouldn't be a struggle between us– it shouldn't. You need to get help. If you can't see me while getting that help, I will understand. If touching… if loving me is impossible now–"

"Regina, please don't," Marcus whines, leaving him sounding gutted.

"I've said it over and over again to Ezra how I never want to see you and Cortez together, doing *that*. Some things you can't unsee or unknow. I feared Whitt and I consummating our marriage would be a deal-breaker for you, even though it was nothing I could avoid. I couldn't avoid it, but I could've said no."

Settling on the planks to sit next to Marcus, but putting distance between us, I voice the sickening truth. "There's irony to the fact that the deal-breaker was actually the one thing where I had absolutely no say. Not an '*I had to do it*' excuse like all the other shit I made up to push off the consequences of my actions. But an actual inability to escape my circumstances is the one thing that had you falling out of love with me."

Scrambling to his knees, Marcus tries to stop me as I stand. "Please don't go." Hands outstretched, he can't reach me.

"I think– I think you and I need to figure our shit out." I nod my head in time with my speech. "We're both married to other people. We've always gone full-speed ahead into this relationship, then would shift into reverse. We need to grow up and finish what we've started elsewhere first. Be friends– don't make this what it's not."

"I love you." Reaching up, Marcus implores me.

"I love you too." My voice is filled with the potency of my emotions. "Grant loved me too, but it wasn't enough, was it?" Muttering, I look away from Marcus to stare up into the night sky. "Jamie is just resolute in our lives. I always said it would be Ezra and Cortez who broke us apart… Ezra raped me, and now you don't want me, can't even look at me or be around me… and I can't live a life with a man who has to skull-fuck Cortez. The common denominator is you– only *you* can change it."

Walking away, I refuse to allow the broken man crying out for me to influence how *I'm* feeling.

Tumblers click into place as I slide into the driver's seat, shutting the door on Marcus. "I can't help you." My words go unheard. "But I know who can."

Sync is placing the call before I have time to rethink my actions. I gaze out at Marcus slumped on the dock, as he stares at the location his ancestral home used to rest.

"Regina?" Syn's voice is hostile. "It's three in the morning."

"I don't want to talk to Syn– give me Faith back," I demand. "I *need* Faith right now, dammit."

"Jesus Christ, what happened?" The sound of rustling sheets fills the interior of my car from the sound system, then the soft murmur of a man's voice. "I know it's not Ezra– that sneaky fucker just snuck out of our apartment to wander across the street, just like every goddamn night."

"I know why you're in so much agony all the time." The sobs start, and I fear they will never end. Loud and pain-filled, one right after the other, not allowing me to take in a breath.

"Where are you? Is he there with you right now?" Faith's voice is filled with compassion instead of hostility for once.

"Get the address– I know what's going on." Faith's partner says. Levi Wilson. One of the puzzle pieces in this shit-tastic life we're living.

"What?" Faith asks both me and Levi, no doubt always in the dark when it comes to the man, no different than I am with Marcus.

"Serenity Lake," I say loud enough for both of them to hear. "I'm in my car, and Marcus is sitting on the dock. I just can't… I can't," I mutter in defeat. "I'm not who he needs, and I can't handle his pain on top of my own. It's too soon. Too raw. Too fresh. I feel like such a spineless coward."

The phone exchanges hands. "Regina," Levi speaks to me as if he knows me, and he probably does after stalking me. "I'll be there in less than twenty minutes. Don't leave. Just keep talking to Faith, please. She can help– I can help."

Palms covering my face, the sound of my agony filling the car, all I can do is suffer. Suffer in a way I never allowed myself before, even when I needed it to mourn.

"Oh, Regina." Faith's sigh is heartbreaking. "I don't know what's going on, and I know we'll never be close. I've been a cunt to you, and I can acknowledge that, but I was trying to stop you from feeling how I've felt for over a decade."

"I get it now, okay?" I stare at my onboard navigational screen, as if Faith can see me back, when all I'm doing is staring at her phone number. "Words you said, things Marcus has said… how do you deal with it?"

Syn doesn't have sex in the dungeon– the sadist causes pain rather than pleasure. Her hate-filled vitriol in the hallway at Restraint was directed inward, not at me. To be in love with a man who will never be normal. No son of Olivia Fontaine ever could be, mixed with what little Marcus has told me, then added to the contents of Nocturnal Silence.

Marcus fears he and I will have a relationship like Faith and Levi, where he fights his own nature. Wanting to be with me, but being unable as demons from the past plague him.

"If you love someone enough, it's worth it." Faith's words are hollow, vulnerable in a way I know the sadist never allows. Syn was born because she had to use pain instead of sex, because sex meant emotional pain. "Lying in bed next to him, wanting him, with him wanting you, but you can't go there. Affectionate touch but never sexual, in fear it will put more pressure on him. Ignoring how he goes off to fight his demons with men, telling yourself it's not cheating because he's not with other women. Knowing he only lets you into part of his life, part of his heart, part of his mind…"

"I can't live like that," I mutter with absolute certainty. "I won't."

"You shouldn't," Faith agrees, and I actually hear tears in the heart-hardened woman's voice. "Wil– I call Levi Wil. He only allows Levi from specific people and strangers. Marcus and Wil have gone through a lot together, but they aren't the same person, Regina. Marcus will overcome this, but Wil won't."

"I'm so goddamn sorry."

"Don't pity me," Faith snaps, turning back into Syn. "I refuse to give up hope. Grant's advice to me is that I stop worrying about pressuring Wil and actually do it. Don't let Marcus pull away– fuck him. Overpower him. Dominate him. Prove he's not broken, because he's not. It's a confidence issue with Marc– If he can get off with Cortez, he can get off with you. Wil can't– no matter who, no matter how, no matter what."

"I–"

"I said no pity," Syn warns. "An empowered woman isn't life's passenger. Either admit you're life's bitch, or be the creator of your own destiny."

Darkening the car, the screen goes blank– Syn hung up on me.

Unsure what to do next, but knowing I can't leave until Marcus is in capable hands, I stare at the dejected man in question, getting angrier and angrier with every heartbeat. Angier at myself.

Angrier at the world and all those in it.

Headlights cast on Marcus, showing him sitting on the dock with his feet in the water, staring forward as if in a world of all of his own. With his back to me, I can't get a read on his expression, but the curl of shoulders and the slope of neck are all I need to know.

Knuckles rasping on my window have me jumping out of my skin. Hitting the button, I'm in shock over Levi acknowledging my existence. I was fourteen when I moved across the street from Stanton Green's base of operation. I remember Caleb Green and Levi Wilson haunting the block before Caleb was shipped off to military school and Levi was probably dumped in Vegas.

It hurts to realize their absence marked the time of Marc's capture and torture.

In the past year, I've seen Levi ghosting around, but he's never spoken a word to me.

Window lowering, I roll my eyes up to glance at Levi from his waist to the top of his head. The innocuous man doesn't look like a cold-blooded killer, but that's the beauty of being who he is. The unexpected. Levi Wilson is MdJ's boogieman.

In my son's generation, MdJ is placing a girl in Levi's

position. What precious child will be forced to maim, bleed, and kill her peers? This has got to end.

"Do you want me to call you Levi or Wil?" is what respectfully pops out of my mouth.

Stunned at my question, the guy just gapes at me. Skin pale, hair shaved until it's impossible to judge its color or texture, the only remarkable feature are those laser beam white-blue eyes. Eyes I've seen before when I met Torian.

"You look nothing like I expected," I mutter in shock because he doesn't answer.

"That's the point." Words not teasing, voice playful. "My maternity is not common knowledge." But as he speaks, I do see their resemblance– Dalton and Levi. The facial structure. The Wilson bloodline overpowered the Fontaine, so the guy does look more like his nephew than his brother, skin color aside. "Are you doing okay?"

Levi's concern is baffling. "I'm more worried about Marcus."

"I'll take care of it." He looks over his shoulder, sighing as he sets sight on Marcus. "This is a change of pace. It's usually me he's talking down from the edge." Calloused yet nimble hands pat my hand– hands that have broken the necks of Ray's victims and then disposed of the bodies.

This is the man who will arrive at my doorstep should I step out of line and not do what Maître du Jeu dictates. He won't steal my money– he'll end my life.

"Are you okay to drive? You going right home?" Levi seems so normal, and it's utterly terrifying to realize I can't recognize the monsters from the humans anymore. But maybe it's because I know these monsters were bred and created, not born.

"Yes." My answer is a lie to both questions.

Those laser beams narrow at me, seeing through the lie. "Trust me."

"I do," is unexpectedly the truth.

"Go home then." Levi steps from the car but doesn't take his gaze off me.

I don't bother answering, because it would be a lie. I put the car in reverse, turning around, and then I drive away without looking back. I have my own demons to slay, especially while the gatekeeper isn't guarding the rat's nest.

Chapter Thirty-Five

With the key in the lock, I stare down the cheery gargoyle until it looks like he's staring back at me with silent judgment. I lie to myself, saying I need to see Grant face-to-face for the first time since his resurrection.

Grant, not Jamie.

I've texted with Jamie when I'm at my lowest, needing the connection, the comfort, and the warmth. I've texted with Grant, needing to co-parent. In my mind, I see them as two separate entities, but it's time Grant truly fused with Jamie.

Grant– I'm here to see Grant.

I'm here to just look him in the eye. I lie to myself, knowing it's a lie before it even manifests into a full thought.

These opportunities never reveal themselves. Kris is no doubt asleep in her bed, keeping Fate safe. I'm usually at home as well, so I'm not to be fussed over. Grant is *never* alone, which makes him untouchable. If Marcus isn't with his Jamie, then Marc's with me… but there's Roman. Roman's always either haunting my guest house when Marc's with Grant, or at home when Marc is with me, making one-on-one access to Grant impossible.

With Marcus sulking lakeside with Dominion's boogeyman keeping watch, Grant's gatekeeper is currently driving a young woman to Massachusetts, I can't help myself but to be drawn to Grant.

I need to send Tina Kline and Dexter a motherfucking thank you card for getting Roman out of my hair.

The predatory hunter is unleashed within me as I ascend the stairs with near-silent footfalls. The rage is driving me– rage over every-fucking-thing. I worried about wrenching an ankle with only the moonlight guiding me to the dock. But in a pitch-black house, my dominance is confidence personified. Surefooted, I'm in Grant's bedroom in less than ten seconds from the time I unlocked the front door.

Reading light switched on, Grant is staring me dead-to-rights as I enter his bedroom. Hands clasped over his bare chest, he looks as if he expected me and my arrival is late. Smug. He also looks smug.

Thwack!

The burning reverberates all the way to my elbow as Grant's head whips to the side, but the smugness cannot be smacked away.

Crystalline blue eyes gaze up at me in challenge, as my imposing form stands above Grant. At rest, hands lax, those goddamn scarred lips curl in silent invitation.

Smack!

The perfect side of Grant's face blooms red, but he looks at peace as my arm burns from the force I exacted. No screams of outrage, not from the mute's throat or my highly vocal one.

This will be a battle of wills fought in silence, save the reverberations of flesh meeting flesh.

Fist radiating pain, knuckles smeared with a crimson kiss, some unseen force propels me into a world of satisfying violence. Lunging to the bed, I learn a mature Grant is not passive. Grappling, fists flying and connecting, my head twists on my neck as artist hands become instruments of pain and clarity.

Startling, the pain clears the fog. "You fucker," I snarl, wiping blood from the corner of my mouth. "You *punched* me."

Blue eyes shine up at me wryly, smirk flirting with his goddamn lips in answer.

Elbow cocking back, pain blooms on my fist as I connect with Grant's skull. A mutual grunt is torn from our throats, and then the pounding begins.

"**IHateYou.**" Screaming bloody murder, we paint the sheets red.

Bodies flowing on the mattress like we're in a UFC cage, there are no rules. Riding Grant's back, I fishhook his mouth from behind, tugging his neck to the side. Ignoring the teeth gnawing on my finger, I lean down to whisper hatred into Grant's ear.

"I want to kill you so fucking bad– make the past decade a reality." Lost in the words flowing from my mouth, Grant catches me unawares. "I'm like a fucking addict, and I need my drug eradicated from this planet."

Fingers twist in my hair, getting a handle hold, and then I'm flipped over onto my back. Stronger than he looks, Grant wrestles for control. With age, he gained more than confidence. Power.

Grant sits astride my hips, smirking down at me with blood hiding the bruises blooming on his face.

Arching upward, "Fuck you," I snarl, as my head-butt connects with its target. "Ugh!" A sharp slap has me seeing stars, followed by a palm smashing into my forehead. Immobilized, all I can do is glare up at the mute bastard.

"*I love you*," Grant mouths down at me. Eyes held wide in horror, my heart ceases to beat. Darkness descends as a fist flies through the air. Held in place, agony spreads across my jaw as an uppercut hits home. Whimpering in more than physical pain, I blink and blink until Grant comes back into sharp focus. "*I hate you too, Mistress*," is mouthed down at me.

"You cowardly rat-bastard!" Snarling, the struggle renews. Wrenching my head to the side, Grant's palm slips off my forehead, at the same time I draw my knee up to connect with his thigh, just barely missing his junk.

Fists flying, blood splattering, time stills when it's probably only seconds of grappling. Our positions change many times. I'm in control. Grant's in control.

Neither of us are in control, not of ourselves or the situation.

Facedown with my cheek pressed into the mattress, a primal scream is released as Grant slams into me from behind, taking me like an animal. Dick stabbing me sharper than any knife, I have no recollection of how I lost my clothing– I'm losing time in the red haze of rage.

Ear-piercing agony flows from between my lips until I lose the ability to make sound. Grant fucks me through it, one hand wrenching my head back by the hair to open up my throat to release the pain.

Arms pull my back to his chest, until we're both upright on our knees with Grant seated deep inside me. Teeth set into the flesh of my shoulder, sinking in with the sharp clarity of pain. Shuddering, the scream cleanses me more than the tears washing the blood off my face.

"I missed you like a phantom limb, even when I was texting Jamie," is a whisper of sound as my hands skate over any of his flesh I can reach. Grant can't reply, but he doesn't have to. His body does all the talking, just as it did when I was eighteen. "The worst parts of you I compartmentalized as Grant, leaving the best to Jamie."

Refusing to be misunderstood or ignored, unrelenting hands

wrench me closer to his chest. A palm wraps around my throat, covering the marks Marc left behind earlier, while the other attacks my tits. Hips slamming upward, Grant forces me to acknowledge who he truly is.

"There is no Grant versus Jamie. You're wholly Grant," I admit out loud. "I hate you. I love you. I hate you. I love you." Over and over again I murmur the words, amazed over how alive I feel. Everything is vibrant after living in a world of numbness. "IhateyouIloveyouIhateyouIloveyou."

Fingertips tearing at my tits, Grant yanks me away from him, then shoves me to the mattress. Gentle hands return to flip me over onto my back. Gazing up in confusion, I try to get a read on Grant as he stares down at me.

Blue eyes heavily lidded, smirk smug, Grant is secure in the knowledge of the power he holds over me. It makes me hate him all the more that he knows he can hurt me and get away with it.

Hand flying out, a firm fist snares my wrist before I can make contact with his jaw. Smirking, Grant makes a *tsk-tsk* clucking with his scarred tongue while waggling his finger in front of my face.

Bloodied, bruised, and raw, with vicious scars bisecting his face, no one will ever be more gorgeous than Grant James Atwater Whittenhower, and that thought utterly terrifies me.

Humming from his chest, Grant looks at me with affection and lust as he taps the head of his dick on my slit. Wiggling slightly, he rubs directly over my clit, getting the reaction he was seeking.

"I should have torn your dick off," I grumble underneath my breath, earning haunting laughter as a response. Locking up my muscles, I pretend Grant rubbing his dick on my clit isn't getting me off, but the fucker knows anyway– he always does.

He always will.

With a sly glance, Grant slips into me, my arousal paving the way. Lost in the sensation, I'm too late to stop Grant from connecting with me emotionally as he does sexual. Settling on top of me, resting forehead to forehead, lips to lips, hips to hips, Grant stares into my eyes and communicates without words.

This.

This will kill me.

Rolling his hips, Grant makes love to me, and it's more than the sum of its parts. It's more intimate than consummating my marriage. It's sexier than being fucked senseless. Grant gives me all of himself, just like he always has, and it breaks my heart as much as it repairs it.

I hate him so goddamn much because I love him more, but not as much as he loves me.

Losing time again, from pleasure rather than bloodlust. Grant and I communicate and come to an understanding, knowing this isn't an ending nor a beginning. We'll be here again, many times over– beating our frustrations out of one another, having hate sex, followed by what can only be described as suffocating yet freeing love.

Chuckling a ghastly sound, Grant pulls from my body after we come down from the high. He reaches over to his nightstand to check his cellphone, no doubt wondering what time it is. Stepping from the bed, I can't help but watch him with female appreciation. Nothing is sexier than a sexually satisfied Grant, with his cock slickened with a combination of our cum, hanging loosely as he walks into the bathroom.

Groaning, I stare at the ceiling, silently bitching at myself in my head. *Jesus, Regina. What are you doing?*

It takes everything in me not to bat Grant's hand away as he runs a warm, damp washcloth over the worst of my war wounds. Humming a content sound, Grant is pleased I'm allowing him to take care of me. Things never change. From the outside looking in, Grant's need to be a caregiver may look like submissive behavior, but he's clearly displayed it's anything but in the past hour. It was a misconception I had when we were together before.

I know this mature version of Grant better than I ever knew the man who slept in the bed beside me every night and fathered my two children. No, they are not two separate identities for me anymore.

I love this Grant more.

As bizarre as it sounds, it makes me feel guilty, as if I'm dishonoring the memories Grant and I shared in the past. Even though we're the same people, we're not the same as we were back then. It's a discombobulating sensation.

I'll probably wake up hating his goddamn guts tomorrow, but I don't right now, so I ride it out. "Do you know why I'm here?" I finally ask as Grant rubs the corner of a washcloth over the abrasion near my right eye.

Folding his leg beneath him, Grant sits on the edge of the bed beside me. A slight nod of his chin is the way he answers.

"How? Who?"

Smirking slyly, Grant signs with his hands, knowing damned well scholarly Regina couldn't help herself but to learn ASL. This is the first time we've come face-to-face in five months, and it's the first time I get to apply my newly acquired skills.

Wil texted me on his way to meet you.

"You're friends with Wil?" I decide that's probably what most people call Levi Wilson. Grant's smug grin is answer enough. Of course the most harmless looking member of MdJ would be buddies with an equally harmless looking fellow who is actually the most terrifying motherfucker in Dominion.

Grant locates my bra, finds it shredded and tosses it into his bathroom– the same treatment for my underpants. Lifting me up, he helps me into my t-shirt, and I chuckle over how well Restraint's black security t-shirt hides bloodstains. My jeans are shredded in a few places, painted in crimson, but look like they were artfully done so on purpose.

"You kicking me out?" I mutter in awe as Grant redresses me after tending to my wounds… after he caused said wounds and fucked me into submission. "A walk-of-shame? Thoroughly fucked then shoved out of bed?"

Go home.

"Asshole," I snarl. "Same shit. Different day. When will I ever learn?" Struggling to get off the bed, I kick the sheets away as they try to wrap around my foot.

A hand flies out, fingertips catching my chin to hold me immobile. Grant waits a heartbeat, making sure I will stay still and silent, then the hand disappears so he can communicate with me.

Go home. Trust me.

"Fine. What do we do about Marcus?" Who better than Marc's *Jamie* to help fix this shit?

Grant's fingers fly, and I have a difficult time rewiring my brain to interpret what he's saying. *I will always be here waiting for when you need me. Always. Neither one of us is ready, nor is Marcus. When we are, I'll find you.*

"Great," I mutter begrudgingly, ignoring the jolt of emotion his words elicited in me. "But that doesn't help my current predicament."

Go home. Trust me.

"You already said that." I stare down at Grant as he gets comfortable in bed, cellphone already in his hands. "You're seriously texting someone while talking to me. Rat-bastard."

Grant rolls his eyes at me dramatically, finishing his text, then places his phone on his chest. *Be patient. Be compassionate. Be there for Marcus.*

"Thanks a fucking lot." Feeling childish, I stomp to the bedroom door, readying to slam it behind me. "Ugh! is a grunt as a book hits me in the back of the head, then lands on the floor with an audible thump. "Since when is your aim so true?"

Laughing that ghastly sound, Grant looks thrilled with our newfound acceptance of bloodsport in our relationship.

Here's a thought. Grant manages to inject sarcasm into words written with his hands. *Date. Go on dates. Get to know one another other than in bed or during damage-control.*

"What about us?" I sound like such a girl.

You know where to find me.

"What about your junkyard dog?"

I do take his leash off from time to time. Go home.

Grant's laughter follows me down the stairs and to the front door, which I almost left unlocked just to be a spiteful cunt.

I go home, and learn it wasn't the time Grant was originally checking on his cellphone…

"Hi," I mutter in surprise as I enter my bedroom, feeling like a shitheel. Marcus is waiting in my bed, covered in pajama pants and a white t-shirt, pretending to read a magazine.

I want to ask what he's doing here, or how he got here, because there's no Spyder in my driveway, but then I realize we're not teenagers. People fight. They argue. They disagree. They say things that hurt. But mature adults don't run away. Marcus isn't going anywhere, and that gives me hope.

The guilt from a lifetime of believing monogamy is the only way of life descends. I feel unfaithful, no matter what reindeer games Marcus may or may not have been up to tonight. I can only control my actions, and I was out of control tonight.

"Are you okay?" Marcus clears his throat, voice sounding dry, as his eyes track over the destruction Grant wrought. "Who did that to you?" The magazine is snapped shut, then tossed onto the nightstand.

Ah, so it wasn't Marcus Grant was texting.

Levi Wilson, I'd bet my considerable fortune on. Trust me, Wil said. Go home, Grant said. Conspirators, I say.

It says a lot that Marcus isn't freaking out about my

appearance. What have our lives boiled down to if no one bats an eyelash when a woman walks into her bedroom covered in bruises and blood?

I have two options: lie or tell the truth.

Without shame, I yank my t-shirt over my head, braless tits bouncing out like a promise. “Grant and I put a new spin on rage-sex.” I refuse to go into detail. I don’t want details of Marcus and Cortez– that’s between them. Even though it is affecting our relationship, the details are none of my business.

“Fight Club Sex?” Relaxing, Marcus turns wry, actually sounding relieved with the outlet I sought. “Does Jamie look better or worse?”

Jeans forgotten to the carpet, I crawl into bed, not giving a shit about the blood and semen speckling my flesh. “Smug. Grant looks smug.” I flick off the light, and then lie in my usual sleeping position.

Without hesitation, Marcus curls around me, rutting his nose to part my hair away from my neck. He finds the vicious bite mark Grant left as a souvenir. Instead of being jealous or furious, Marc finds it a comfort. After kissing the mark, he snuggles down to go to sleep.

We’re not playing pretend. We’re not going to ignore the problem. Grant took the numbness away– for how long, I don’t know. If it fades, we’ll beat each other again until it returns. It may take a decade to sort our shit out, but I’m patient enough to wait while not sticking my head in the sand.

Staring at the clock, I loathe yet am simultaneously comforted over Grant worming his way into my soul. Even in death, I’ll never be rid of him. But I fear and welcome the fact that I think Marcus has taken up residence beside Grant.

It’s not denying my feminism or relinquishing my self-respect that has both Grant and Marcus knowing they will always have a home with me, no matter how much they may harm me.

It’s unconditional love.

I get them– they get me and each other. I know the same applies to me. If I hurt them, I’m not going to be turned away. They may push me away out of emotional pain, the same as I do them. But when confronted, we’ll fight it out. I’ll deal with the fallout as it comes, because I need them to survive, and I think they need me too.

Chapter Thirty-Six

Life keeps on rolling, no matter what's going on in our lives. I sometimes feel like I'm the owner of a large daycare center filled with all the people in my life. I'm exhausted from running interference between everyone.

Maybe a daycare center isn't an accurate representation. An asylum, and I'm the helpful therapist they all want to fix their problems.

In the past few weeks, Marcus has spent every night with me, sharing meals when he wasn't needed in court. We're emotionally connected, touching with affection, and when we lie in bed together at night, Marcus is aroused. I tried once to take it a step farther, taking Syn's advice, and Marc flipped his shit. He's terrified, and I won't punish him because of it. I'm no sadist, and I'm also not a sex addict. We'll get through it. Eventually.

I thought I was strong before. The Regina I was at eighteen would've marveled at the one I was six months ago. The Regina who unflinchingly looked at me through the vanity mirror today would've frightened both the innocent and jaded versions of myself. I don't know if I entirely like who I am today, but I do know I don't recognize myself anymore.

Ezra and I have bizarrely grown closer. We're not exactly friends, but I understand him. We're slowly building trust. He speaks of his pain, and I want to take it away. He speaks of his past, and I understand how he turned into the man he has become. We're similar in the way we see why someone has hurt us, making it beyond impossible to hold a grudge. We've enjoyed meeting on a cerebral plane.

Katya is who Ezra and I bonded over, but it's another reason why Cortez and I have grown apart. We were friends for almost two years as we used the brownstone as a second home. But since my initiation, we've both pulled away, and for good reasons. Marc touches Cortez but not me. Cortez touches Marcus but not Ezra. Ezra and I are to blame for what happened in my bedroom on Whitt's birthday, even though we all played a part. I refuse to play the blame game anymore, so I ignore it when Cort gets bitchy toward me. Cort even had the audacity to get jealous, interrogating both Ezra and me about whether or not we were fucking.

Irony and hypocrisy.

I resent Cortez, and he resents me. We may not like the lengths we've both gone to, but we still like the other at the end of the day, but only once we let the hurt go. Now Katya is a wedge between us, because I do believe Ezra has her best interests at heart, but Cort does not. I love the man, but Cortez sees the world through possessive, jealous lenses, and it's my job to protect Katya from everyone.

The woman has been a source of amusement and one of my largest sources of frustration. I've watched from afar as Katya blossoms while Ezra and I play cat to her mouse. Her curiosity, tenacity, and inner-strength drive her. I'm awed as much as I am jealous. I see things in Katya that I wish I could be. I sometimes want to shake the shit out of her or slap her silly. Other times, as I watch her on the security feeds, I want to find her and hug her– comfort her. Allow us to comfort each other. She's gorgeous in that way that drives men mad because she doesn't see it. She's confident, tactful, and commanding. Katya knocks Ezra off his feet like a wrecking ball to the heart.

Yesterday, I watched as Katya played both Ezra and Cortez. It was the most frustratingly amusing twenty minutes of my life. It was worse than watching Kat stalk Kayla and take the young woman on the desk– Cort, Ezra, and I watched from Ezra's office. The boys nearly exploded, and it made my libido make itself known. It was so hot, it overrode the ego-deflation of Marc's no-sex drama. I had to leave the office, because the guys noticed my reaction, whether it was scent or body language. They stalked me to the door and nearly chased me down to the elevators.

The frustrating yet amusing play of yesterday was Katya pitting the Ezes against one another. As soon as Katya left her office yesterday afternoon, Cort demanded I sneak into her office and hack her treasure box. Her idea was ingenious, but it only took me fifteen seconds to open the box containing our chess board– and it is *our* chess board. This has been a long time coming, and a huge collaborated effort on all of our parts. Ezra, me, Cort, Aaron, Kayla, Roarke, Kris, Fate, and Marcus. We've all played a small part– in my case, a huge part. I just hope it isn't all a tragic mistake.

As I've watched our Katya blossom, she has ignored her online buddies. I miss her. I feel close to her because I watch her constantly. My life enables me to sit in my office and watch her night and day when I'm not at Restraint. When I monitor the dungeon, Aaron, Kayla, Cort, and Ezra take turns. Katya is never without an eye on her every moment– even embarrassing bathroom moments.

Dominion, New York has its own version of the Truman Show. *The Stalking of Katya Waters*.

The more embarrassing, private moments between Katya and Ezra, I've watched them in real-time. Ezra wouldn't allow anyone else to witness it besides me. He doesn't know that Cortez was at my side each and every time. Ezra doesn't realize this will only work if it's the three of them. Knowing how Cortez operates, I felt it better if he was included versus excluded.

All day, a niggling suspicion has tickled my brain. I wasn't able to watch Kat last night because the bullshit at Restraint is getting worse, our inability to keep outside employees. It was Cort's turn to watch Katya last night, because Ezra had to work beside me.

I no longer ignore the extra sense I call premonitions. This feeling has had me trying to contact Katya in every way possible all day long, and she's ignored my every attempt. Right now, I'm at my desk at Restraint, watching Katya sit at her desk four blocks away at Edge. She looks miserable and in pain, and I want to take it away. I want to soothe and comfort her. Most importantly, I want this niggling suspicion to go away.

I breathe a sigh of relief as I watch Katya log-on to a messenger app and type in Kimber's username. Lunatic. I quickly log-on and wait in anticipation. I'll finally figure out what's going on with Kat. It's amazing how attached you become when you have access to every facet of someone's life, and when they hold out on you, it's the worst kind of torture. It becomes an addiction.

Lunatic: *Kat? Do I need to put out a cyber APB on your behind? C'mon, girlfriend. I've missed you. Are you still here? Did the big, bad world swallow you whole?*

KitKat411: *I'm here. Sorry it's been so long. I've been busy with things, especially with work. I want to show my boss I was the right person for the job, probably biting off more than I can chew in the process. Plus, I have a minion who is a bit bitchy that I need to get in hand. So, enough about me. How's the virtual world been treating you?*

Lunatic: *KAT! You're alive! I've missed you!! I thought aliens abducted your ass. It's been* so long.

KitKat411: *I know. I know. I said I was sorry!*

Lunatic: *I'm just yanking your chain. Honest. There's nothing new with me, since nothing ever changes around here, you know that. I sit in my cave, writing new programs and creating and upgrading websites for clients. I make sure my ladies behave and bring me food when I'm hungry, lest I'd starve to death. I'm very proud of the growth of my company. I may have to hire a larger staff to handle the influx. The three of us are not enough anymore.*

With the groundwork Ezra laid for Kimber, I decided to warp the fake profile to feature events in my life from when I was the most lost. Those terrifying early years after I left Misery Castle.

KitKat411: *WOW! That is fantastic news. It seems like you've been busier than I have been.*

Lunatic: *The rest is just boring coding, which I won't bother going into. It would go right over your head, kind of like when you hit me with big words. So, how's your apartment? How's the job? Do they appreciate your Grammar Nazi ways? Your love of the English Language? How is your boss? Coworkers? Any new friends?*

Leaning forward over my keyboard, I try to get close to the monitor, curious to see if Katya enjoys my company– my real company. Smiling softly to herself, Katya strokes her throat as if it's ailing her, then she begins to type.

KitKat411: *Slow down, Kimber! LOL! I like my new place.*

It's comfortable, and suspiciously exactly as I want it. The job is great. I have three people who work directly for me. One is a pain in the ass, but we understand each other. If she didn't want my job, I think we could be friends. The others do as I ask, as soon as I ask, so the only issue I have is trying to do too much at once to prove myself. My boss… I'm pretty sure is the actual BOSS. Don't ask! I met a woman who I'd like to try to befriend, but that depends on whether or not I can trust her. Her name's Queen. I feel connected to her for some inexplicable reason.

Jesus Christ, guilt and happiness flow through my veins, warring with each other.

Lunatic: *Aww! I bet Queen feels connected to you, too. You're so easy to get along with.*

KitKat411: *Ego-stroker! You know damned well I can be a bit of a bitch, and that is online. Imagine how I am in person.*

Lunatic: *I know why you turn cranky, so it's all good. This Queen person would understand if you let her, I'm sure. So, you were really excited to hit the scene for real. Did ya ever gather the nerve? Dude, I'm too terrified to leave my cave, let alone venture into a BDSM club.*

KitKat411: *Brave, I am not. But I did finally branch out and visit the club. I'm confused. I don't know how I feel about it. It's exciting, and for the first time in a very long time, I feel alive. But I thought it would be filled with rules and structure. You know how much I need that sort of thing. How do you let go if you don't know where you'll land when you fall? I don't have that much faith in anyone without boundaries and structure.*

That right there is why Katya and I get along. I wish this stalking business wasn't between us, because I think we could be great friends otherwise. But I'm not delusional. The façade will crack, and Katya will never trust me enough to open up ever again.

Watching Katya rub at her throat, wincing as she swallows, has my mind thinking of ways to coax the information out of her.

Lunatic: *I'm always on my computer researching stuff. Why don't you tell me what you mean & I'll look it up for you.*

KitKat411: *All of James Atwater's books were filled with stringent rules. Do A, expect B. It was negotiated upon beforehand, and completely voluntary. Then there were safewords for when you were uncomfortable and needed to stop. I've found none of that at all. I have no choice, and it's confusing me, making me rethink whether or not I even want to be around that sort of thing.*

Katya just had to bring Grant up, didn't she? My laughter fills the office, but it gets abruptly cut off as her words filter into my mind.

Lunatic: *I'm confused, because I thought that was how it was as well. I mean, can't you say stop if you don't want to do something? Just get up and leave?*

KitKat411: *It felt like that to begin with. If I didn't obey my master's orders immediately, he would punish me, saying it was an education to teach me a lesson I needed to learn. For the most part, I agreed. I'm a bit of a bullhead, so I'll be stubborn just for the sake of being spiteful. But the reward and punishment system changed. I thought you got rewarded when you earned it, and punished when you misbehaved because you needed to be educated with a lesson. I found out that wasn't the case.*

Lunatic: *Um... Kat, what did you do? I always took you for a good girl.*

Heart beating out of control, I've never let Ezra out of my sight when he was with Katya. My mind goes backward, gauging Ezra's mental status, finding it better than it has been since I met him. When Katya is alone, Ezra is generally with me at Restraint.

What the fuck is she talking about? God! I can't stand not knowing after being privy to every shit, shave, and shower the woman has taken since she landed on Dominion soil.

I'd feel guilty, but this is the least of my crimes since MdJ has been pulling my strings. I don't even want to contemplate the felonies I've committed in the past month. As I said, I don't recognize the woman staring at me in the mirror, but I'll do anything to keep my people safe.

KitKat411: *I didn't do anything, honest! I also didn't think I did anything that garnered a reward, either. We're playing a game, and when you win a battle, you move these chess pieces on the board we have set up. I won, and moved the chess piece. I thought that was the end of it...*

Lunatic: *Oh! So you were rewarded. That's awesome. From what I've read, masters do stuff like that. They aren't supposed to punish you for no reason, because that would be confusing. But rewards are different. It makes them happy to give their submissives nice things and to do nice things for them. I believe that's what being a dominant is about. I'm not in the lifestyle, but I can assume it's the same as how I feel about my employees. They love waiting on my ass, and I love buying them an endless stream of packages from Amazon Prime.*

Bullshit is streaming from my fingertips, as the niggling sensation becomes a screeching siren in my mind. Added to that, Ezra is going to flip out when he sees the idiotic shit I just sent Katya. I've had to dumb down my speech pattern to fit the background Ezra created, and Kimber is supposed to be completely witless when it comes to BDSM.

KitKat411: *I wish it was something as simple as goodies from online shopping. The thing is, he said it was a reward. But it was HIS reward.*

Lunatic: *Don't you want to make him happy? My employees seem very content with waiting on me, doing little things for me, because they know it makes me happy.*

KitKat411: *I do. I really do want to make him happy. But his reward went against all I thought I knew about the rules, while breaking my own moral code of ethics. I thought we both were to get something out of it.*

Lunatic: *Everything I've read says that. So you gave him a reward and didn't get anything out of it? That's not too bad, Kat. I thought submissives were supposed to want to please their* *masters. I know you're not a submissive. But I assume a switch would have a similar connection to their master.*

Fist bashing on the edge of the desk, I snarl out loud. "What the fuck happened, Katya? Jesus Christ, spit it the fuck out!" Breathing heavily, I hate having to sound chipper, upbeat, and compassionate in our messages when I'm anything but at the moment. "I can't fix it unless you fucking tell me what's going on, girlfriend. Stubborn, she said– accurate self-reflection, Kat."

KitKat411: *It's not like that at all. It was out of the blue, and for no reason whatsoever. He said my reward was my master's pleasure. Yet his pleasure was my punishment. I know punishments aren't supposed to leave lasting damage, but in order for him to get his reward, I was hurt. It won't go away for a long while. It hurts in a multitude of ways. I feel violated: mentally, physically, and morally.*

Lunatic: *Katya! What did he do?*

Leaning forward, I direct all of my brainpower into the screen, commanding Katya to explain. The more she evades, the more my inner Queen gets pissed off. "Kat's a switch, but she sure does give submissives a run for their money."

Sighing heavily, I try to get myself under control. "It's my job to protect you, girlfriend. Stop tying my hands behind my back and making me feel powerless."

KitKat411: *No. I don't want to say. It's too embarrassing. Just know that I'm having second thoughts. Hell, third or fourth or millionth thoughts. I can't trust what happened. I can't even trust my own emotions and intuition anymore. I'm fucked– everything is going haywire and wonky on my ass. But I do know I don't want to do this anymore. There is no balance, and it was the promise of balance that drew me to BDSM in the first place. I don't think he is the right master for me, but I don't think he will just let me walk away, either. Just forget it. Forget I said anything...*

Which one did it? The rapist or the little puke? What did they do to this innocent woman? Seething, a red wash settles over my vision, more potent than when I engaged in rage-sex.

Lunatic: *I'm not forgetting shit, Katya! We're friends. I care about you and your wellbeing. Tell me what he did, so I can get off this computer and kick his fucking ass! I'll shove his nuts down his throat!*

KitKat411: *You don't even know who he is or where to find him. Plus, you don't leave the house. I appreciate it. & Kimber, you are my only real friend. I'm so glad I have you to confide in, and I'm sorry I've avoided you for the past few weeks. I just didn't want to admit to you what I didn't want to admit to myself. When I talk to you, more comes out than with Dr. Jeannine, and I avoid you to avoid therapy.*

Tears of powerlessness and guilt stream down my face. It's my job to protect Katya Waters, and someone harmed her on my watch. It's so bad she won't even tell an anonymous Kimber about it. I'm not above begging to get Kat to tell me the truth.

Lunatic: *Please tell me so I can fix it. I beg of you!*

KitKat411: *I will. When I'm comfortable, I'll tell you. It's just too raw right now. Okay? I would have done it for him regardless. If he would've only asked, I would have said yes. I wouldn't have been morally comfortable, but I would have done it just the same. I wanted to make my master proud. It was the brutality of the act. It felt vindictive or something. I don't know... But I'll be okay. I always am.*

"NO!" I cry out, a sob lodged in my throat. All the feelings I experienced during and after my assault flood my mind. "What monster would assault a survivor of violence?" I rethink my words, then remember my experiences with MdJ and Ezra and Cortez.

Lunatic: *Katya, please tell me exactly what happened. Everything.*

KitKat411: *Don't worry about me. I'm good. Tell me more about your company. It's called Empowerment, correct? You must be so proud to be adding more employees.*

I can't take it anymore. Katya isn't going to tell me, and I have a very good idea what would hurt her throat. Cort punished Kat to punish Ezra in the exact manner Marcus taught him.

That little puke– the saner Ezra behaves, the worse Cortez does. Outside of moments where my friend peeks out from beneath the animosity, Cortez has been a total asshole since the switcheroo in my bedroom.

Now I feel guilty by association. If I hadn't forced everyone's hand that night, would Cortez still have harmed Katya?

A sob of frustration breaks from my throat as I sprint four blocks to the Edge building. Running headlong, people jump out of the way of the crazy lady who's bawling her eyes out.

The humid air hitting me in the face, and the pound of my soles hitting the pavement, allows me to think. It allows the fury to take hold. It gives me the clarity to enact the proper punishment, when nothing can make up for what Katya has lost.

Katya Waters is as innocent as a kitten. Her only consensual sexual activity was with females. In my eyes, Katya is a virgin. I have no doubt that she has never given a man oral, and I'm sickened as I come to a conclusion about what happened to that poor woman.

Cort skull-fucked Katya for her first time giving head. Her virginity was stolen from her. This intimate act should have been special. It should have been coaxing, or with Katya in total control.

It should have been an empowering moment, not one that will leave permanent scars in her psyche, when it was already battered and bruised enough.

No one stops an enraged six-foot tall, hundred and eighty pound shemale with double-d tits. I'm not a man, but my presence is more frightening than one. I fling the centermost door to the Edge Building wide, knocking a man in a business suit almost off his feet.

The security guard dashes out from behind the front desk with his palm resting on his gun. With a double-take, "Mrs. Whittenhower?" flows from his stunned lips, as if he doesn't recognize who I've become.

"George," I mutter politely, slowing as to not take out any more business people as I cross the atrium. "Is Mr. Hunter in his apartment?"

"No, ma'am." Chest heaving, the security guard tries to

dampen the adrenaline my arrival had bursting through his veins. “Mr. Hunter is in a meeting with Dr. Zeitler, in Dr. Zeitler’s psychiatry office.”

“Thank you, George.” I pat the guy on the shoulder to calm him further. “You’ve been a big help.” This way I don’t have to search ten different locations in this ginormous eyesore of a building to find the puke. Added bonus– two birds, one stone – they’re together.

Stalking down the hallway, I allow the rage to fill me until I’m positively glowing with it. I’ve been to Ezra’s office before. I had a consultation with four of Ezra’s colleagues in there, as a way to choose who fit me best. Since, I’ve been going to Dr. Smythe’s office three times a week, like clockwork.

I’m going to need an extra appointment this week.

Startled, Aaron jumps from his desk as I charge into the waiting room, placing him directly in front of Ezra’s door. “Forgive me,” I mutter without shame as I shove my partner at Restraint out of the way. Frozen in shock, Aaron doesn’t stop me as I crash into Ezra’s office.

Chapter Thirty-Seven

A crack echoes around Ezra's office as my fist connects with Cort's jaw– Grant will be so proud. Enraged, my fingers tighten around his perfect neck, and I squeeze. Cortez's gray eyes are eclipsed by his black pupils. His mouth opens on a pant, but he can't get any air to flow past his lips– I won't allow it.

It was my job to protect Katya Waters.

"Regina!" Ezra demands, trying to pry my fingers from his partner's throat. I can hear the panic rising in his voice from the knowledge he can't control me anymore– physically, mentally, or through sheer will. Ezra respects me too much to put his hands on me, even to protect Cortez. He also trusts me enough to realize I wouldn't be doing this if it wasn't necessary.

"I see the guilt flashing in your eyes." Nose to nose, I rest my face against Cort's as I strangle the life out of him. "I see you understand why it's taking everything for me not to kill you right now."

"Regina!" is digitally shouted from the speaker phone. Its only effect is to pause me long enough to think. Ezra couldn't stop me, so he found someone he thought could.

"Marcus, stay out of this," I snarl, not even twitching a fingertip around Cortez's throat. Disgust twists my expression. "Of course you'd protect your cocksucker."

"Regina, please." Marcus pleads from the other end of the line. "Our problems are between us– don't bring Cortez into it. They're my fault."

Leaning closer to Cortez, I spit the words directly into his face. "How does it feel? Hmm… to not be able to breathe? To have someone do this to you without permission? To make you feel powerless?" Cocking my head to the side, I watch the horror etch across Cortez's reddened face. "It's not the same as it is with Marcus, is it? Imagine what Katya felt last night."

"What the fuck is going on, Regina?" Marc's voice is tinny, warbling as he shouts. "Ezra?"

Ezra's staring at Cortez with horror and me with respect. A

quick dip of his chin is all the permission I need to continue.

"I will punish you for this," is a promise as I release Cort's throat. Palming his forehead, I shove him back against the sofa cushions, then inspect the reddening fingertip marks. It will bruise– no doubt it will hurt for Cortez to swallow, just as it does Katya. "You'll live."

Cort gazes up at me with heavily-lidded eyes glazed in need, and his reaction gives me back a bit of the power I had lost. Unbidden, I lick the marks I placed on Cortez's throat, and he cries out while writhing on the sofa.

"What's Regina doing to Cortez to make him sound like that?" Marcus hisses from the speakerphone, jealousy ringing in his tone.

I'll never forget Marc's reaction during the switcheroo. The one question I don't dare voice has been plaguing me in the weeks since. Marcus and Cortez behave as a bonded dominant and submissive, not a pair of dominants exorcising demons. Even now, I recognize the possessive air in Marc's tone as I dominate the man he sees as his own.

"Just turn on the feed." Ezra sighs heavily as he collapses into his office chair, signaling the battle of the personalities warring inside his psyche. The tap of keys informs me Ezra's checking last night's recordings for the source of my fury.

"You're in your office– there isn't a camera in there." Marc's voice is pure frustration, and a part of me gets off on hurting him for once, after all the pain he's caused me. Sickening. Toxic. But nonetheless true.

As I pepper Cort's neck and jaw with kisses and tiny licks, his fingers clench in my shirt to draw me to straddle his lap. Scooting down until we're aligned, I'm not surprised to feel his *exquisiteness* is as hard as a baseball bat. Growling in disgust, I grind on the offensive flesh that hurt poor Katya's mouth and throat.

"You shouldn't harm innocent women." I chastise Cortez as my hand finds his erection. Squeezing him through his pants, I dig my fingernails into the fabric until I find purchase with his sensitive flesh.

"Regina!" Cortez screams in pain, arching beneath me.

"I sent you the link," Ezra tries to soothe a worried Marcus. "Regina has me wired more thoroughly than you could ever pull off. Never piss off a genius with trust issues." Ezra sighs heavily, sounding exhausted. "Be forewarned, Queen's with us right now, not Regina."

"What is she doing to him?" Now Marcus sounds worried for all of us, and it almost brings me back into my head.

"You know what she's doing with him. You know Cort's sounds better than I do."

"Not true," Marcus denies. "Christ!" he hisses, and I know he's watching us live, and probably simultaneously watching what Cort did last night too. "Look at them– he's letting her dominate him."

"Ezra, Marcus doesn't touch Cort back," I admonish. Secretly thrilled how pissed Marcus sounds that I'm punishing his submissive, I shove it back in his face how he doesn't give a single person on this planet all of himself. "And you know it– unless you've been lying to me all along."

"Trust issues, Queen– no lies between us anymore." Ezra's eyes are glued to his computer monitor.

The urge to feel Cortez's flesh give way beneath my fingernails has me unzipping his pants. With brutality, I squeeze his cock until the bulbous head turns dark purple and engorges with blood. A hiss of breath passes through Cort's clenched teeth as he tries to control the pain.

"Not a good idea to train with someone who may punish you in the future– I know all of your triggers." I taunt Cortez, gliding my hand smoothly up his shaft. Jerking him off, the calm before the storm.

Cortez reaches for the fly of my jeans, and I tsk-tsk him.

"No sex," I warn with a gentle squeeze, then add a pinch of my fingernails as punishment.

"Why not?" Cortez slurs in confusion, already flying high. For a trained dominant, this man doesn't have a single dominant trait.

"No sex," I repeat, squeezing harder. Cort unleashes a silent scream, cock pulsing rapidly in my fist.

"But you want to though, right?" Cort's voice dips into an insecure whine, thinking it will manipulate me into doing him. My training buddy is back. I missed him so much, the switch in my brain flips from violence to sex.

Tossing my head back, laughing, I'm so high right now I'm in heaven. But not high enough to forget Cort only wants to fuck me because he's riding high too. We'd both regret it immediately.

Leaning forward, I kiss the fresh bruises ringing Cortez's

throat. He whimpers and thrashes in pleasure. I add pain to the mix by squeezing him so brutally that I'm surprised he doesn't pop like over-ripened fruit. My nails sink into his flesh as he screams out my name.

Covering his mouth with the palm of my hand to silence him, I suck Cortez's neck while jerking him off with my other hand. As an apology, I allow him to come in my hand.

While waiting for Cortez to come down from his orgasm, I wipe my hand on his shirt. A pliant Cortez will be one who has the ability to listen to reason, versus the defensive, childish one I was strangling on arrival.

With a deep breath, I stand. "Tuck and zip up, big boy. Accept my apology for nearly killing you. Jerking you off obviously wasn't your punishment– that will commence in a few minutes. But first, we have to finish what we started."

Walking over to Ezra's desk isn't without a struggle, and Ezra rolls his eyes at the way my jelly legs barely support me. Rolling my eyes back, I get serious as I bring up a browser, then log onto the conversation I was having with Katya. It was far too long of a wait– she's probably terrified about what happened to Kimber.

Leaning against the back of Ezra's chair, I allow him to do the typing since I don't have all my faculties online yet after dominating Cortez. Shaking my head, I read mistake after mistake the deviant makes as he speaks to the woman.

KitKat411: *Kimber! Where did you go? Are you okay? You're scaring me.*

Lunatic: *Ah, Kitty Kat. I do understand. You can come to me for anything, anytime. Always! You realize this, don't you?*

KitKat411: *What, say again? What did you just say?*

Lunatic: *Katya, I typed it out, silly. You can just reread it. But I'll type it again just the same. You can come to me for anything, anytime... Always... I will be here for you!*

"You did that on purpose," I bitch at Ezra while swatting him upside the head. "Nice trashy exclamation points you added in there."

"Do we really want this game to take forever?" Face turning

slightly, Ezra murmurs in my direction. "Katya's doing well, but we aren't getting any younger… As for the classless, shouting punctuation, it sounded more your speed."

"Dick."

"You said we had to have honesty between us, Regina," Ezra teases me in a pretentious tone.

Lunatic: *KitKat? What's wrong?*

KitKat411: *White Rook sweeps Black Knight, motherfucker! How could you? Stalker or not, this breaks some kind of covenant. Worthless piece of shit!*

I watch in silent horror, with a heavy dose of mystification, as Ezra changes our username. "Holy Christ, this doesn't seem very therapeutic, Dr. Zeitler."

"Had to rip the bandage off at some point– may as well be now."

DR.Lunatic: *Katya, calm down. I told you we all censor ourselves to different individuals. This was the only way. My story was real, with the exception of the agoraphobia, even the attack. Everything said was true emotions. I mean it, Katya. I will always be here for you. & I know what you've been through better than anyone.*

"Bad move, Dr. Lunatic," I seethe into his ear.

Ezra shocks the hell out of me by twisting my engorged nipple between his index finger and thumb. Screaming sharply, tears bead in my eyes.

"You and I are going to have a disagreement, Regina. You're getting too big for your britches." Master Ez's voice manifests, while blinking uncontrollably as the personalities wrestle for control. "Don't fuck with me."

"Don't threaten me– I'm the only one who's been on your side. We both failed in protecting Katya. But it's Cort who was fucking Katya's throat like she's some two-dollar whore kneeling on the floor of the dungeon. Cortez assaulted Katya, not me. Cortez took her power away, not me. Cortez upset all the hard work with Katya's therapy we've been doing, not me."

Arm flashing out, I yank Ezra's pale hair. "Get a grip,

asshole." Tugging harder. "We need Ezra right now, so back the fuck off, Master Ez."

"Are you guys always like this?" Cort murmurs lazily from his position on the sofa.

"Yes," we hiss in unison. Ezra and I found a happy medium, a truce of sorts, because we don't put up with each other's shit. Immediately addressing the issue, unlike the eggshell walking, enabler approach everyone else uses on Ezra. Sometimes tears are involved. Many tears.

"I'm more frightened than before," Cortez replies, pinning me with a look of pure jealousy.

"Of what?" Ezra asks in shock. "What are you talking about? We have bigger issues right now than whatever malfunction you're experiencing."

"We were both worried they were fucking," Cortez speaks to Marcus. Ezra and I share a look, shocked that we forgot Marcus was on the phone and watching us from the live feed.

"They aren't," Marcus says with complete confidence. "Sooner rather than later, they're going to either kill each other or have an epic fuck."

"Regina and Ezra both look extremely frustrated." Cort finds it hilarious how neither of us are getting any from our partners, while they smear it right in front of our faces.

Ezra's last encounter was Cort's mouth, and mine was at the same time while Marc banged me without completion. Marc and Cort have enjoyed countless skull-fucks since.

"Behave," Marcus issues as a warning to Cortez. "Don't forget how Regina has found a new outlet. We don't want her teaching Ezra anything about Fight Club Sex."

"We'd need Wil to clean up that mess." Cortez shudders on the sofa, and Ezra and I mirror him.

"Nice to know you bastards gossip about us like old biddies," I mutter in disgust while capturing Ezra's gaze.

"It is amazing how the mute is a font of information." Cortez rolls to sit upright on the sofa, high finally fading.

"That should have been private!" I snarl, feeling betrayed. Then I realize Cortez is so jealous he's sabotaging my relationship with Grant. "He didn't tell you, you cocksucker"

"Shit," Marcus slurs over the phone line, causing a wave of red to descend over my vision.

"Never thought anyone would be more cowardly than the rat, and here you were going to let him take the fall for it." Ezra's laughter has me continuing to flay Marcus apart. "I'm glad to see I'm the topic of your pillow-talk." Now it's my turn to feel jealousy over Cortez. "Reminds me of how men will chat with their mistress about their wife's inadequacies. Rude, downright disrespectful. Disloyal. Too many people in this small bed."

"Regina–"

"Shut the fuck up!" Master Ez barks, Ezra disappearing as the stress level hits an all-time high. "Katya's headed our way."

Noticing Cortez trying to get a read on me, I purposely stride over to the sofa and sit next to him. Glaring, I don't play the blame game, I tell the truth. "This is all your fault, cocksucker."

"What's going on?" Marc asks even though he has a bird's eye view of the office. Some things are more obvious in person.

"Stay quiet, or she'll hear you," I warn Marcus. "Katya doesn't know you exist."

A soft knock draws all of our attention. "Enter," Ezra's voice warbles with hesitancy.

Kat slowly enters, glancing around at all of us. As she looks at me, I see betrayal cross her face, and it cuts me like a knife. I want to reassure Katya, tell her I know exactly how she feels, but this isn't about me. I bite the inside of my cheek hard, and the metallic copper flavor of blood floods my taste buds. My heart aches as I lose a friend I never truly had.

She stares at us, and the three of us gaze back in silence. No doubt Marcus is staring at all four of us via the security feed. I can see the wheels turn in Katya's head as thoughts and emotions fly across her face. She's trying to figure out which one of us played what part, and which one of us violated her last night.

Emotions rapidly flash over Katya's expression: Devastation. Agony. Heartbreak. Mourning. All these emotions are overshadowed by betrayal.

It takes everything in me not to stand and embrace Katya. But she doesn't know me as I know her. Cort is struggling with guilt and shame. Truce found, we grip each other's hand to hold us back from comforting the woman.

Ezra looks dead.

Katya steps forward, placing something on Ezra's desk. She moves slowly, trying not to get within arm's reach.

What feels like hours has only been a few passing second as we freeze in this toxic tableau. "Katya?" Ezra breaks the silence, voice always sounding different around her– smoother, softer, and filled with affection.

Katya just shakes her head while pointing at her offering.

Ezra picks up the Black Knight and raises his eyebrows in surprise. My mouth pops open wide as I realize it's the play from a few minutes ago. As Ezra slowly reads Katya's note, his gray eyes turn stormy, with his brows drawing together in the center of his forehead, creating an intimidating V above his nose.

I give Ezra mad props for keeping his personalities in check, all the while trying his damnedest not to frighten the woman as fury boils in his veins.

The second Katya leaves, I'm going to have to play referee as Ezra did earlier with me. I'm thankful Marc's still on the line, hoping together we can keep Ezra in check if the worse comes to worst.

Ezra looks at Katya, eyes inspecting every inch of her body, no doubt looking for injuries. Blinking rapidly, he can no longer contain his fury. Drawing in a breath, I prepare to intercept him.

Kat turns her back on us, causing Ezra to fist the note in his hand. With a violent movement, he smashes the note down on the coffee table in front of Cort and me, releasing a feral growl. Ezra's so enraged, he doesn't hear the click of the door closing as Katya flees the room.

Cort gingerly picks up the note, smoothing it out so we can read it, acting as if his actions were justified since Ezra wouldn't allow him to play reindeer games with Katya by himself.

Ezra leans over us like a furious dragon, breathing so hard I swear I see puffs of his breath riding the air. Thankfully it doesn't contain the fire Ezra wishes he could incinerate Cortez with.

~Master Ez~

Ezra & Cortez

I know there is no backing out of the game. It's in motion and will not come to a rest until the final move– until I learn all of the uncomfortable truths, I will wish for the rest of my life I never learned. I know the rules are ultimately up to you (both?). Rules you seem to make up as you go along.

I have a request. You always say it's not what I want, but what I need. Well, I need consistency. The Dom/sub relationship is built on consistency and trust. If I do A, then I expect B as a result. (You) broke those rules, and I believe there should be a consequence for that. Unless you feel trust only flows one way, as if it doesn't matter if I trust you as long as I obey you out of a sense of fear.

Kimber was outside the spectrum, a betrayal of the deepest order, and that broke my trust in a way I doubt I will ever forget, let alone forgive. Compounded upon that, my reward last night breached consistency. (You) harmed me for your own pleasure in the name of reward. For my reward is my master's pleasure. I suffer the consequences of such a reward. The gift of torture that keeps on giving.

I do not wish to associate with people who lie, breach trust, break promises, and harm me because they can. With what I've already suffered through, I believe I deserve better. I realize at this point, that my life as I know it is directly tied to Master Ez: my job, my home, my co-workers, and the tentative friendships I've tried to develop.

With that being said, I will play your game under one condition. If I win, I am released from under your control, where I will go back to my family and live my life in peace and tranquility, as I should have from the very beginning. No job is worth this. No truth is important enough to lose your sense of self. I also realize that a person(s) who has treated me as you have, may not stick to the word he has given. Call me naïve, but I'm hoping you will.

If I lose, I will stay under duress as I make your life a living nightmare.

Last night the game changed for me. It's no longer a journey of self-discovery. It's for my freedom.

~ Game on, Bastard Ezes~

Lunging for his partner, I have to swiftly intercept Ezra before there's bloodshed. "Ezra, calm down." I try to comfort and restrain him with my assertive voice. Ezra isn't a switch like Katya, but he does heel well.

Pinning me with a stormy stare, Ezra growls, not realizing his fingers are biting into my arm to the point I fear he'll fracture it. Only the widening of my eyes betrays the physical agony he's causing me. I don't bring attention to it, because this isn't about me.

"This is what we are going to do," I say forcefully, allowing Ezra to take his frustrations out on my forearm– anything to keep from unleashing Master Ez on Cortez. I suck air in between my lips, and release it out through my nose to control the pain, but it's not without difficulty.

"You're going to punish Cort," I talk Ezra down off the edge. "Not out of anger, but because he needs to release the guilt… you need to feel in control again," I tack on, gritting my teeth. "Then you're going to go down to Katya's office and take care of her. You'll make sure she's physically well, and then you'll comfort her. It will be a good bonding experience. You'll have to explain how Cortez didn't mean to hurt her–"

Cort's sharp bark of laughter cuts into my speech. I shake my head at him in disgust. "Do you have a death wish?" seriously on the verge of hating his guts. I'm allowing Ezra to break my arm to save his sorry ass, when I could just unleash Master Ez and there'd be no meddling cocksucker coming between Marcus and me any longer.

"No," Cortez mutters sheepishly. "That laugh was a kneejerk reaction to an uncomfortable situation. Sorry, I really *am* sorry I harmed Katya, but I can't deny that I loved every second of it."

"I have no doubt about that, Cort. What I meant is for Ezra to explain how you are too jealous and it makes you a fucking idiot. He needs to explain how he was blocking you from seeing Katya, so he feels guilty over not anticipating your reaction."

"It's not Ezra's fault." Cortez scoffs.

"This is more for Ezra than you, asshole." I think of how the guilt of not stopping Ezra, when Marcus sensed something was about to happen, has plagued Marcus– no doubt Ezra is experiencing a similar emotional response right now. "Ezra needs to take ownership of it. It isn't an excuse, and it doesn't take your culpability away. You're responsible for your actions, but Ezra knew what his actions would make you do, because you're highly predictable in your behavior and Ezra is a psychiatrist."

Cortez grimaces, looking sick with shame.

Waging battle inside his own head, Ezra squeezes my arm so brutally I'm sure I have a hairline fracture. I show no weakness, taking it because I'd rather Ezra harm me in anger than suffer with the knowledge he hurt the love of his life. Ezra's strong enough to deal with dishing me pain, but never Cort.

"Ezra," Marc's voice commands through the speakerphone. My eyes drift shut at the sound. "Release her arm. You're hurting Regina badly."

"No, I'm not," Ezra mutters in denial, but his grip does lessen some. It's still painful, but tolerable.

"Son, trust me." I squeeze my eyes shut in pain, but it's no longer from my hurt arm. The concern in Marc's voice is my undoing– a tear escapes the corner of my eye, and I swear underneath my breath.

"I'm sorry," Ezra mumbles, releasing my arm. The sudden rush of blood back to my appendage hurts worse than the pressure he was placing it under. Throbbing so painfully, I have to hold my breath to contain the scream that is building.

Ezra's finger catches my singular tear, and it terrifies me that he won't be able maintain control. Ezra reaches for me, wishing to rub my arm better, but I sidestep away.

"I'm fine. You've done no harm." I bite the inside of my cheek again to redirect the pain– mental and physical. Retreating to the back of the sofa, I rest my uninjured hand on Cort's shoulder, then safely tuck the other underneath my breasts against my belly.

"Did I hurt you?" Ezra's voice breaks and his eyes shine.

"No, I'm fine," I lie again. The integrated personality I know best is Ezra, but he has two part of his whole who will take over if need be– Master Ez and Ez. Katya should only know Ezra, and I'll do anything to protect the woman, especially after what Cortez did to her and with the truth of Kimber just having been revealed.

"We need the punishment to commence," I try to be the voice of reason. "Katya's injured, and in need of your comfort, Ezra. While you're with Kat, we'll discuss your punishment." I give Ezra a pointed look to distract him from my throbbing arm.

"Okay, what do you propose?" The mention of punishments and injuries has taken the heat out of Ezra's fury.

"An eye for an eye seems just. Cortez skull-fucked Katya to get back at you, and you will do the same to him." I tighten my grip on Cort's shoulder when he tenses at my suggestion. No doubt the little puke is preparing to run.

"I…" Ezra is rendered speechless.

"Do it!" I shout, unable to handle any more of their theatrics. The throbbing is getting worse. I need medical attention– medical attention I can't get until this is settled. I realize my priorities are skewed. Ezra hurt me, but I refuse to hurt him with the truth, not when his hold is so tenuous and he's fragile.

Ezra's eyes are huge, hand shaking as he lowers the zipper on his trousers. I know right then that nothing except for brotherly affection has happened between the partners recently.

No doubt the week of nursing Cortez back to mental health after our switcheroo is playing out in Ezra's head.

Cortez tenses to bolt from the room.

"Calm," I breathe into Cort's ear. "You do this for Marcus on a daily basis. Why do you fear this with Ezra, when he can't harm you as Marcus can?"

"It's not that– I know you're going to make Ezra suck me for his punishment." Cortez's voice quivers in an intoxicating mix of anticipation and fear.

"And you'd love every second," I tease to calm Cortez. Then I kiss the fingertip bruises running along his throat and the bruise from where my fist connected to his jaw. "You know I'm more creative than that, and I'd never use a repeat."

Ezra walks forward with his cock at half-mast. Eyes flicking to look at my arm cradled to my belly, guilt and shame bleed from the man. Ezra wants his cock in his partner's throat, but doesn't believe he deserves it. I can read Ezra better than the members of my own household.

Rubbing the hinge of Cort's jaw, I coax everyone to get this over with. "Open up and show Ezra how sorry you are. He'll even make sure Katya doesn't blame you if you show him how sorry you are."

Releasing a moan, Cortez opens his mouth wide. He even sticks his tongue out, trying to reach Ezra. Ezra lets out a moan of his own as his cock swells toward the wet embrace of Cort's eager mouth.

My eyes fall shut upon hearing their mingled moans, and the last thing I see is Ezra sliding deep down Cort's ecstatic throat. My groan joins theirs as I hug Cort's shoulders and rest my head against the side of his neck. Ezra's warm thigh brushes my cheek with every thrust.

I groan because my arm hurts like a sonofabitch, but also because I love the powerful feeling of directing people to do something they refuse, especially if it's for their own good. I moan because I miss the feeling of an engorged cock thrusting down my throat– the pressure, the beat, the precum that flows eagerly.

I miss satisfying my lover.

I concentrate on the mechanics of a blowjob to redirect my mind from my injury.

Hiding my face against Cort's neck, I cry silently, because it reminds me of the early morning they became my lovers– my initiation. I'd connected them so they'd come together as one. The emotions are the same for me this time. I cried then and I cry now. Both times Marcus looked on. I'd do anything for these assholes, and I've proven myself time and time again, and I hope this is the last test I endure.

"Cortez," Ezra hisses. One of Ezra's hands fists Cort's hair while the other affectionately pets mine. Cort's fingers tangle with mine on his shoulder. Both of them are including me in their punishment– their passion. It's so unlike the one and only time the three of us came together as one. This time it's because we're all friends and the test of time has bonded us.

A part of me understands the emotions they're feeling, and why they're feeling them, and that part smothers the judgmental, justice seeking part of myself, alleviating the rage and betrayal. Flashes of Hillbrook Freshman Orientation flash through my mind, seeing the qualities the young boys displayed in their adult versions. I'm helping them, even if it's hurting me to do so.

I watch their expressions as Ezra reaches his climax. It isn't lust or passion that's dominant– utter devotion screams from their eyes. They hold each other's gaze while Ezra cries out. I have to look away from the raw emotion that's expressed on both of their faces. I've never seen nor experienced anything that even comes close to that– maybe after the birth of my children as I gazed down at them as they suckled at my breast for the first time, but never have I ever experienced it with a lover. Never have I had another being gaze at me with such raw passion and utter devotion.

I'll do all that I can, because Cortez and Ezra will never be whole without the other half of their soul. I don't believe in soul mates as the ultimate lover. I believe there are people in this world who we need to be whole, whether it be a friend, partner, lover, child, or parent. They will be the light of your life. They chase the shadows away in the way that Whitt brings my sunshine.

I realize in this moment, that as I push Whitt away, I'm pushing myself away too. Whitt will never be my lover or partner, and I need him on a different level than I need my children and friends. Whitt is my conscience in a time when I've lost my moral and ethical code– he's the mirror I need to gauge right from wrong. I'd feared loving him too strongly after the fallout of making love to him. I needn't have feared– my love for

Whitt is pure.

Stepping away from the sofa, I surreptitiously wipe my eyes free of tears. We all look a little bit shell-shocked.

"Go to Katya, Ezra." I plead with my eyes and voice. "I need to speak privately with Cortez." I don't have the energy to argue and fight with him. The pain has lessened to a numb tingling, both in my arm and in my heart.

Eager to help Katya, Ezra doesn't argue or even speak. He kisses Cort gently on the forehead, then me on the lips. He whispers, "Thank you, and I'm sorry about your arm, Regina." Then he flees the room.

"Damn, I never thought Ezra would leave." I joke as I fall to the sofa next to Cort.

"That really wasn't a proper punishment," Cort teases me softly. "Ezra always pulls his hit, never actually skull-fucking me. That was just a good ol' regular blowjob."

"No shit, asswipe. That was the point." Grumbling, I wiggle around on the sofa to find a comfortable position. "I needed Ezra in a good headspace before he went to Katya. Actually skull-fucking you would be *his* punishment, since it freaks him out."

"How is your arm, really?" Cort turns his head to the side, looking me in the eyes. The buddy I trained with peers out at me, and I contemplate telling the truth. But I lie instead, because Cort and I are not in a place where I share my feelings anymore. Marcus is a wedge between us, but so is Ezra.

"It's fine," I say firmly without a trace of the lie betraying my voice. "How is it between you and Ezra?" I may not share my warm and fuzzies with Cortez any longer, but I'm hoping he will with me. I need them to be okay, for Katya's sake, but also so Marcus and I will have time on our hands. I could blame Marcus, but I know exactly how intoxicating it is to be needed by the Ezes, and time consuming.

As I've learned, only hearing one version of events is only half the story. To get the full picture, I need both Ezra and Cortez's perspective. My soft spot is to my detriment, making me empathize with the one venting while causing me to resent the other. Marcus must feel torn down the middle between them, every minute of every single day since he was seventeen.

"I resent the hell out of Ezra– the more he pushed me from Katya, the more it brought back the past. We share a bed at night in a platonic sort of way. Sometimes, when he thinks I'm asleep, he touches me differently. When I'm positive he's asleep, I do touch him differently. I can't help myself, but I don't have the balls to do it when he's awake. Lately, he's been too crazy about Katya, spending half of the night staring at me and the other half staring at her."

"Ezra sleeps with Katya," I admit the sweet yet creepy truth. "When Katya's fully asleep, Ezra joins her. Subconsciously Kat knows he's there, but she doesn't wake."

"That should make me jealous, but for some reason, I'm not," Cort confesses.

"I understand better than you can imagine," I mutter in a wistful tone, thinking of how sympathetic and understanding I've had to be as Marcus pushes me away sexually but keeps visiting the asshat sitting next to me on this sofa. But I understand Cortez when it comes to Katya and Ezra, because that's how it is for Marcus and me when it comes to Grant.

"Ah– kinda like watching your husband fuck one of your best friends on a nightly basis?" Whitt wanted to share his second venture into sex, by dragging me into the dungeon to watch him and Kristal. "Whitt's cock has been in more mouths than a cutlery set." Cortez snickers at his own joke, and I roll my eyes at him in response.

"That doesn't bother me at all actually," and it doesn't. "I watch Whitt's face, and he looks ecstatic and virile. It's all new experiences for him, and I can live vicariously since I forever ago lost any innocence I possessed." I can hear the smile in my voice, which causes me to actually smile.

"Yeah, but you get to experience it firsthand," he teases me and I don't have the heart to tell him that it was a onetime thing between Whitt and me, never to be revisited.

"I bet Whitt pretends it's your ruby-red lips wrapped around his cock when he shoots his load." I tease Cortez back, knowing it still rubs him wrong after hearing Whitt and me talk about him on the infamous sex-tape.

"How's Jamie's cock treating you?" Cort volleys back. "How do you keep all of your lovers straight?" His voice is filled with amused pride.

"Don't be a dick," I snarl, refusing to trade locker room stories like we're still best buddies. "I'm currently celibate, and you know it–"

"What are you talking about?" Cortez's eyebrows scrunch together in the center of his forehead, leading me to believe

Marcus doesn't share anything but an orgasm with the guy. It makes me feel a bit better that Marcus shares his emotions with me, even if he won't his body.

"Nothing," I grumble underneath my breath. "Grant and I are… battling, and it's not to be revisited."

"Just so ya know, so you won't get your panties in a twist." Cortez shifts on the sofa, looking uncomfortable. "I was being an assmunch earlier. No one told me about the Fight Club Sex. I showed up at the brownstone and eavesdropped on Marc and Jamie… and I saw the bruises."

"Oh…" I quickly change the subject so I can get the hell out of here. "I have a proper punishment for Ezra. It won't be painful, and it's solely for healing."

"This I have got to hear." Cortez releases a sadistic chuckle of anticipation.

"Your punishment was a skull-fuck for a skull-fuck–"

"Regina, Regina, Regina. That was not a skull-fuck. Someday I'll have to show you what one is."

Cortez interrupts me, so I ignore the little puke. "The issue started because Ezra was being territorial and possessive over Katya *and* you. As punishment, Ezra has to *share* the experiences. I know Ezra's crazy at night, and it causes none of you to sleep well. So tonight, both of you will share Katya's bed. She sleeps like the dead, but she'll know you're there. I want the three of you to cuddle up and sleep peacefully for the first time in your lives."

"Why?" Cort's voice cracks from shock and a bit of fear.

"Because I care about all three of you, and I want you to be happy. There's no Ezra and Katya without a Cortez. There's no Cortez and Ezra without a Katya. The three of you need each other to feel whole. We need Ezra to see this."

"You'd do that for me?" Cortez is misty-eyed and flushed from emotion. "After all the shit I've put you through?"

Moving to stand, I pin Cortez with my gaze. "Prove you appreciate it. Prove you're remorseful for releasing the recording of Whitt and me in bed. Prove you understand how much it bothers me what Marcus and you do to each other. Prove you get how much I care about you by doing whatever is in your power to fix your life."

"Regina–"

"*Prove it,*" is my parting shot as I flee the office, arm cradled to my chest. Sitting at his desk in the waiting room, Aaron looks up at me with sympathy as I shuffle by, but he remains silent.

Chapter Thirty-Eight

Staring at the tile as I enter the atrium, I feel foolish and lower than low after how I arrived. All those people saw me charge in here like a crazy person, knocking people off their feet. Everything went to shit– I wanted to avenge Katya Waters and remove the powerless feeling I was experiencing, but I ended up leaving broken instead of empowered.

Clutching my arm to my chest, I grit my teeth against the pain. Not looking up, I head for the front desk, wanting to apologize to the security guard. "George, I'm so sorry–" eyes registering what I'm seeing. Marcus is leaning against the front desk, chatting with the receptionist and the security guard. "Oh. Hi."

"Regina." Marcus fights a smile, but the dominant expression on his face is concern.

"Mrs. Whittenhower, don't fret." George pats my shoulder kindly. "We have fifteen psychiatrists and therapists offices in The Edge Building. We've seen our share of interesting arrivals."

"Yeah, that makes me feel so much better," I mutter underneath my breath, causing Marcus to laugh. "What are you doing here?"

Marcus points at the giant E in the center of the atrium as example, the one proclaiming Edge as a Holden and Zeitler property. "That's not what I meant." Fed up, I head toward the front doors.

Marcus hooks his arm around my shoulders, steering me. "I do have a space in this building, ya know? But I was across town at City Hall."

"Then what are you doing here right now? I thought you were on the speakerphone listening in while watching on a computer."

Marcus wiggles his cellphone in my line of sight, then draws me to the Spyder idling at the curb. Parking is insanity in Dominion, so being the owner of the building does have its privileges.

Once I'm all tucked in with my seatbelt buckled, which Marcus did for me, he slides into the driver's seat. "I already called ahead to get your arm checked out. It's a private clinic a few blocks from here, and they can see you immediately."

"Irony." I raise my arm, noticing the purple fingertip bruises are nearly black, with swelling bulging my arm until it's nearly unrecognizable. "This is the arm I used to jerk Cortez off."

Laughing without humor, Marc's eyes cut in my direction as he traverses through downtown traffic. "After you get checked out, I think we need to talk," he says ominously.

Silence descends, neither of us speaking until I check-in at the front desk at the clinic.

Ezra's strength is terrifying. After x-rays, Dr. Braddock said I have a hairline fracture in my radius. There's a reason Marcus took me to a private clinic– no questions were asked, even though I could have just said I tripped and landed on my arm wrong. Two hours later, I'm now sporting a cast from wrist to elbow, tucked away safely in an ugly as hell sling. I'll be right as rain in four-to-eight weeks.

Mind filled with clarity, I'm stepping away from Ezra and Cortez. I can't take it anymore.

"Where are we going?" Confused, I stare out the windshield as we pass the exit to The Gates, which is the same exit for my housing development. This is the first I've spoken since Marcus said we needed to talk. This late in the evening, traffic is lighter, only filled with people running errands or going out to dinner after work.

Turning off the main drive, we arrive at a restaurant popular with one-percenters. "You need to eat before you can take your meds." Marcus pulls up to the valet, waiting his turn.

"Marcus," I snarl, old insecurities cropping back up, from when I lived in my old neighborhood. "We've never been together in public before, and this is most certainly public."

"We're not hiding anything from anyone, Regina." Marcus looks at me with no emotional barriers between us. "Share a meal with me."

"Look at me, Marc!" I raise my arm as high as it will go in my sling. "I worked at Empowerment this morning, then Restraint for a few hours this afternoon. Then that bullshit with Cortez and Ezra. I'm wearing dirty jeans and a concert t-shirt, with a motherfucking cast on my arm. This place has a dress code."

"You're perfect." Marcus smiles at me, then winks as he exits the Spyder to pass the keys off to the valet.

Growling underneath my breath, I hate how mortified I feel right now. I've dreamed since I was eighteen that someone would be proud enough of me to show me off. Grant and I never went anywhere in public together, because I was his mistress and he was still married to Cora. Marcus and I have always just stayed at the brownstone or camped out in my bedroom.

I've never been on a date– with anyone.

I know this isn't a date, but this is a step in a new direction between Marcus and me. Had I known, I would have gone shopping with Kristal and Fate to pick out a new outfit. Then I would have had them fix my makeup and hair.

I may pretend I don't care, but I do have some pride left. "I don't want to embarrass you," I whisper to Marcus as he hooks my waist with his arm, herding me inside. "Or myself."

"I've lived my life trying to make good impressions, while dealing with people who are phony. Part of the reason I love you so much is because you're different. Real. Jamie escaped that life. Cortez spits in the face of it. I can't leave, so it's nice to be around people who don't live by society's standards."

Standing before the Maître D', "People will talk," I subtly remind Marcus of his campaign for judge and the fact that his current position as a district attorney is also a public office.

"These people know exactly who you are." At the height of the dinner hour, Marcus escorts me through the restaurant, with the waiter seating us in the centermost position, for optimal exposure.

Marcus brushes off the waiter when the guy pulls out my seat, waiting for me to sit. Relieved, I go to seat myself, but Marcus is there to help shove my chair in.

Preposterous.

Confused, refusing to look at my surroundings, I'm so out of my element. The eyes of every patron are boring into my back. I'm the injured, crazy looking woman who has the audacity to enter wearing jeans and a t-shirt, one who thinks she has a right to spend time with their golden goose. To the background soundtrack of Marcus ordering our beverages and entrees, I stare down at the fancy linen tablecloth in mortification.

Deciding to be honest, I go for broke. "I spent my youth at Transcend, then feeling out of place at Hillbrook as I learned the rules of polite society. Then I was hidden away at Misery Castle, not attending anything of importance. I spent my time at the university and in my office. Then I moved into my home and away from all the ridiculous social posturing. I've created a laidback work environment. The most high-class functions I've been to are IT conventions, where we get a commemorative t-shirt."

"Your point?" Marcus smirks at me in challenge, flicking his napkin sharply to unfold it, then he places the linen on his lap.

"Ezra's worse than you are," I muse, amused. "Katya is never going to fit into his social life."

"No, she won't," Marcus murmurs, looking nowhere but into my eyes. "But I'm hoping her rough edges will loosen Ezra up."

"I need to call Restraint, and I need to check in with Ella." Struggling to extract my cellphone with my non-dominant hand, Marcus stops me.

"I called Aaron while you were getting your arm fixed, so don't worry. Roman and Roarke will be tackling your duties tonight." Marc reaches for my hand, tugging it onto the tabletop, then he flutters his fingertips across the top of my hand in a soothing motion. "As for Ella, Fate is always home when she is."

"I'm a bad mother," I breathe silently, just as the waiter is placing an iced tea in front of me. Marcus ordered a beer, delivered in a fancy glass. Bread and dipping sauce are placed between us, as we wait to continue our conversation without an audience. Thank yous are given, and yet the silence stretches on after the waiter leaves.

"Here." Marcus retrieves my prescription from the inner pocket of his suit jacket. "Have some bread and take these with the tea."

"Yes, Master," I tease, feeling an odd warmth as Marcus takes care of me.

"You're the best mother I know," Marcus mutters conversationally as he tears off a piece of bread.

"The bar wasn't set very high for you, Marc." Chuckling underneath my breath, I take my pain meds. Nothing too strong, but better than over-the-counter. The doctor said it would also help with the swelling. "You never speak of your own mother, and the other one in your life is Diane. You don't speak of her either, but Ezra regales me with nonstop mommy issue venting."

"I was raised by my grandmother." Marcus never speaks of Rebekah Zeitler either, because it's bittersweet. "She was an incredible woman. Strong, dignified, and willing to sacrifice for Dexter's and my happiness and wellbeing. The other mother I was close to was Jamie's, and I've heard nothing but you singing Priscilla Whittenhower's praises."

"Fair enough." I pop a piece of bread into my mouth as an excuse to say little else. Emotions are battering me from every direction.

"I wanted to address something important." Marcus drops the bombshell I've been waiting to blow up my world, but he's interrupted as our salads arrive.

"Mmm… I'm impressed." No iceberg, but not frilly mixed greens that wilt on contact with dressing either. Closing my eyes, a homemade crouton melts on my tongue. "I've avoided fine dining since I left Misery Castle– ridiculous food."

Smirking, I remember Jackson whining about the food. A few times, he'd snatch me from my office to go hunting for artery-clogging tastiness.

"Girl, where can a guy find a real slice of pizza?" Jackson's haunting my open door, large palms curling around the jamb. "Not that thin crust horseshit. Sick of cracker pizza with caviar and shaved truffles. I want pepperoni."

"Let me jot down the address to Aniello's." Grabbing a piece of paper, I'm not about to order the beast of a man around. That's Priscilla's job.

"Catch," is a split-second warning before a set of keys is lobbed at my head. Hand flicking out, the keys land into my outstretched palm, saving my face from permanent scarring. "You drive– c'mon, girly. Let's get us a slice of happiness."

"You're letting me drive the Roadster?" Awed, I skirt the outside of my desk, nearly tripping myself in the process. "Are Grant and Whitt coming with us?"

"We've got a date with some pizza, girly." Arm wrapping around my shoulders, Jackson always makes me feel small in stature because he's larger than life. "No one appreciates real food like you do, and the boys will tattle on me."

"It's a date."

"What put that smile on your face?" Marcus gazes at me in wonder.

"Just thinking of Jackson," I admit, feeling odd speaking of the man since it's a painful subject. "He was the only one who would seek me out to take me in public. I don't know, sharing this meal with you reminded me of it. Except we always went to places your people would see as low-rent and trashy."

"We all need someone who has a finger on the heartbeat of reality to tie us to this earth." Marcus smiles wistfully, and I don't bother asking him to explain. In Dominion, people like Marcus are treated like princes. Ezra's so sheltered, he has no idea how ordinary people live their lives.

People like me are anchors holding helium balloons from floating into the sky. The people in this restaurant are obviously the balloons, filled with hot air, feet never touching the ground, with egos big enough they float.

I hope and pray Katya is Ezra's anchor, but I fear his weight will be too much for Katya to hold to the ground.

"Since our disagreement," Marcus begins, and my heart flutters wildly out of control, terrified of what's to come. "Cortez and I haven't engaged in our toxic behavior. I'm taking a break from all sexual activity."

"Oh." I shove food in my mouth as an excuse, because I have no reply to that, and I need to mull it over to figure out how I feel about it.

"I'm backing off from Ezra and Cortez as much as they will allow." Marcus isn't eating. He's staring at me as I stare down at my plate. "It's hard for me, Regina. It's always been us against the world since I was seventeen, with me running to Jamie for comfort. I know you've seen a glimpse that Cortez and I are not as we seem, in a codependency sort of way. But I need to let them live their own lives and work on my own."

"Yeah, I was thinking just that while I was having a cast molded to my broken arm," I mutter, refusing to meet Marc's gaze. "My ethics have deteriorated, and I can't handle it anymore. What we did to Katya, I understood why, but I know I've destroyed whatever friendship we could have built. But now that that's over, I can move on too."

"Instead of telling you, and not following through with it..." Marcus trails off, then begins to nosh on his salad. "I decided to show you. We're not perfect, and we never will be. But I'm not running away anymore."

“Are you getting help for your problem?” I haven’t brought it up since the dock, but I feel emboldened by all the eyes burning into my back in this restaurant.

“It isn’t about you, and it isn’t about you and me, even if it affects us.” Marcus places his fork on the side of his plate. “I need you to know this, Regina.”

“I get it–”

“But?” Marcus prompts.

“No matter how mature my thinking, I do have an ego. I do have pride.” Taking a deep breath, “Empowered woman or not, I do possess insecurities. It’s not so much that this all bothers me, it’s how it makes me feel inadequate, and I know that’s not fair to you.”

Chuckling lightly, Marcus takes another bite. “*That* I can understand.” The waiter is hovering nearby, no doubt gauging when he can bring out the entrees, so we move on to lighter subjects.

The meal moves smoothly, with a few people dropping by our table to introduce themselves under the guise of pledging their support to Marc’s campaign. It’s awkward as all hell, but then I remember who I am. I’m not some knobby-kneed girl living in squalor.

I’m Regina Regal, the creator and owner of Empowerment. My building rises high in the center of downtown Dominion, solely owned by me. I’m the Queen of Misery Castle, and I’ll wear jeans and rock my X Ambassadors t-shirt with pride.

Queen’s voice filters in through my mind as a smarmy older man and his fourth-upgraded-wife ask Marcus about Diane as an insult to me.

Wealth isn’t a gauge of your worth. It doesn’t matter if you’re Mrs. Whittenhower, or the poorer than dirt orphan from a drug wasteland. You’re a human being, and that’s the only empowerment you’ll ever need.

Chapter Thirty-Nine

Fighting tooth and nail, I tried with all my might to protect Katya. My lifelong edict from Maître du Jeu is to protect Katya Waters at all costs, including from Ezra. This isn't because MdJ is Kat's adoring fan-base. Ezra has been saner than he ever had been due to Katya returning to his life. If something were to happen to Katya, Ezra would burn Dominion to the ground, especially if he was the cause.

I fought with Ezra, with Marcus, with Cortez, even going directly to Syn, hoping my orders with MdJ would override this insanity, yet here I am standing in the middle of the dungeon for Katya's initiation.

We've never had an initiation that wasn't torturous for the initiate. While this is supposedly for the BDSM community of Maître du Jeu, I have a feeling it runs deeper than that. My enslavement started hours after my initiation, which is probably why Syn didn't put a stop to this insanity, even knowing Ezra will go off the rails if anyone has balls big enough to draw Katya into enslavement.

But the edict from MdJ is secondary to the rage warring with agony deeply rooted in my chest, nearly bringing me to my knees. The one I've been sworn to protect is currently being victimized while delivering a direct hit to my pride and heart.

It's not about you, Regina. It's not about us, Regina.

The past few months have been running smoothly as I strengthened my relationships with everyone in my life. I thought Marcus and I were solid, closer than ever, even without any sexual interactions. Marcus has been finding himself, leaving Ezra and Cortez alone with Katya, not taking his pleasure and demons out on Cortez's willing throat.

Smoke and mirrors.

Bullshit and lies.

Betrayal.

If it's not about me, then why does it only affect me?

I've never felt a rage so hot before, red washing over my vision, directed at Ezra, Marcus, and Katya, and no one steps in to stop it. Not even me.

Breathing deeply in sharp, jerky pants, I could melt the sun or burn Satan alive with the potency of my rage

Biting my bottom lip, then my tongue, and lastly the inside of my cheek, I stem the need to howl bloody murder at those who betray me.

Cortez grips my fingers, and I don't know if it's because my buddy is trying to restrain me from killing his partner, or Cortez wants me to make sure he doesn't kill Ezra. Either way, Ezra only has five more minutes of life in his veins.

I swore an oath to protect Katya Waters for Ezra's sake, even if it was to protect her from Ezra himself. But it's the promise to me Ezra broke that's tearing me apart.

No one breaks a promise to Queen.

We stand in the shadowed dungeon, wearing black cowls and night vision goggles. All very cloak and dagger, a repeat from my initiation. It's too bad the goggles bring everything into sharp focus. I long to close my eyes to block out the disgusting sight before me, but it would allow me to think, and we can't have that and survive.

The silence is deafening. I could hear a pin drop to the slate tile flooring, or in this case, breathing– Marcus and Katya's erotic breathing.

I enjoyed watching my wish-she-was-my-real-friend come out of her shell. Pride infused me as I watched Katya turn Monica into the ultimate submissive. I was impressed with Katya's natural skill, and Monica prospered from such a firm, confident hand.

Following, we all greeted Katya in turn, and I thought that would be the end of her initiation. I wanted to cry as Dalton humiliated her, knowing he had to do it, most likely also being blackmailed by MdJ. I felt for both Katya and Dalton as they struggled through the encounter. I wanted to throat-punch Syn for testing Kat so brutally, but something tells me that was more about jealousy over Ezra than anything else

But nothing could have ever prepared me for this.

No less than a billion times I've told Ezra I never wanted to witness Marcus– with Marcus and Cortez also instinctively knowing that's the case.

After months upon months of building trust, working side-by-side, and being Ezra's confidant, he trashes our budding friendship in an instant.

In this I blame both Marcus and Ezra, while trying my damnedest to see Katya as the innocent, injured party yet again.

Gutted, innumerable nights flash through my mind. Nights where Marcus and I cuddle in bed, with nothing between us other than platonic affection. I'd lay there, staring at the ceiling, wishing I could connect with my partner physically, feeling the unbridgeable divide widen between us.

Excuses.

It's not you.

Don't be insecure, Regina.

I'm working on myself. Please give me some space.

All we need is time.

In humiliation and mortification, I stand in a semi-circle with my fellow Masters of Restraint, all knowing exactly what this is doing to me. Sadists, the whole lot of them. No one puts a stop to it, knowing I'm unable without looking like a cunt

Tears fill the wells of my night-visions goggles– tears of betrayal.

Tears of agony.

Tears of inadequacy.

It *was* always about me.

Marcus sees his body as private, sacred, after growing up as a religious man, then experiencing the torture of having your autonomy taken away. Marcus doesn't share his body easily. No foreplay. Never a woman on top. Always fucking as quickly and violently as possible, attempting to get off before the demons of his past erupted.

Marcus always said it took a strong emotional connection for him to be aroused enough to perform. My connection to Grant is what made it possible for Marcus to bond with me in the first place.

All lies.

I'm done.

Maître du Jeu can do their worst– fuck 'em.

I'm not a hypocrite. I've always understood the bounds of our relationship. It's not that Marcus is seeking sexual gratification. It's because he's doing it in front of me. Most importantly, the act before me proves Marc's lies.

Demons plaguing him, to the point Marcus can't be with anyone anymore. How he grew up wishing to have a nuclear family. How he needs an emotional attachment to enjoy a sexual act. The worst is that he's doing something he's never truly allowed me.

Foreplay.

A blowjob.

A blowjob that isn't skull-fucking the demons away.

With another woman.

Gutted, my grip on Cort's hand cracks his knuckles. From across the circle, Syn's eyes are on me– the sadist getting off on the pain this is causing me. My fellow Masters of Restraint are torn between looking away out of respect as my partner betrays me, and utter fascination as they watch the ever-private Marcus perform a sex act for the first time, while enjoying the show our new blood offers.

My goggles fog up from bitter tears, muting the erotic sight of Marc's head thrown back in ecstasy as Katya kneels by his feet.

The woman I protected. The woman I did everything in my considerable power to join with both Ezra and Cortez. The woman I wished to be my friend… she's sucking her future father-in-law's cock, and she is none-the-wiser.

The levels of agony can never be fully explored. From Ezra to Marcus to Katya, layers and layers upon layers of betrayal bury me.

Heart-hardened, I can do nothing but watch Marcus shudder, eyes closing. I can do nothing but listen to his labored breathing and pleasurable sighs, with Katya making slurping sounds around his cock fading into the background.

Marcus becomes hyper-focused to my eye, and I lose myself to the pain.

The insecurities inundate me, grip me to never let go again.

The only sex I've had was rage-sex with a man who may as well have patronizingly patted my ass as he told me to go home. The very man who abandoned me, who left me because I wasn't good enough.

I'm strong enough to be a confidant to Marcus, but it's no different than the relationship I've built with Ezra over the past few months.

I'm the perfect listening ear, but little else.

Standing in a BDSM dungeon with the scent of sex permeating from the walls, I watch my partner seek release from another woman because he doesn't want it from me.

I've held my jealousy in check since I met Katya. Her long, curly auburn hair and vibrant green eyes are stunning. Her petite, curvy body is everything I could never be. She holds the affection of both Ezra and Cortez, and they love her freely. They would proudly shout it to the world.

Tall. Gawky. Ruddy skin and wiry hair. Masculine with mammoth tits. The only sex I've had since Grant abandoned me are fly-by-night encounters that are rarely repeated. Marcus has always been hot and cold, fucking me into submission, then playing hide-and-go-seek with my heart.

I wasn't deserving enough, beautiful enough, special enough to earn Marc's passion, but the gorgeous woman sucking his cock is.

Cortez releases my hand, unable to stand by and not join them. Another layer of betrayal settles on top of the growing pile as Cortez kneels beside Katya to give her pointers on how to suck my partner's cock.

No, not *my* partner's cock.

I hold no ownership over Marcus. If anyone can call that cock theirs, it's Cortez. Here he is sharing that piece of flesh with his new lover. Marcus doesn't do one-offs, so no doubt he's upgrading to a new piece of ass who will arouse and intrigue him.

I'm done. I always thought there was nothing Grant or Marcus could do to lose my unconditional love. Well, this is it.

Done!

Knees going weak, my heart breaks into a thousand shards of agony. Queen dies a painful death as I close my eyes to the sight of Marcus coming inside Katya's mouth, only it amplifies the erotic sounds pouring from his lips.

Eyes closed, I listen as Katya explodes over something baiting Cortez whispered into her ear. As I reopen my eyes, I watch as Cortez chases Katya down the hallway toward the Zeitler private room.

Taking a deep breath, I will all emotion from my body. I welcome Apathetic Regina back with open arms and a closed heart. We shared a decade together, and she's more familiar than the version of myself I've suffered with for the past two years. Apathetic Regina is the strong one– the one who could be Mom's caregiver without breaking down, bawling her eyes out, or puking her guts up as we watched cancer cannibalize Mom from the inside out.

Yanking the goggles off my face, I know a stranger is now gazing from my eyes.

I feel eyes on me– two sets –and I don't meet either. Instead, I lock eyes with my husband across the arc of Masters of Restraint. We silently communicate, Whitt telling me not to do anything stupid, with me telling him to shut the fuck up. I refuse to break eye contact with Whitt as everyone around me moves and chats.

Marc's rumbling voice turns my stomach as he accepts congratulations and words of astonishment.

Apparently having a death wish, Ezra tries to engage me by tapping on my shoulder.

When I don't respond, Ezra has the balls to actually speak to me. "Regina," he whispers in my ear. "I know you understand."

Still, I refuse to acknowledge him. I do to Ezra what Ade did to me– he's dead to me. Ade cut me out of her life after I married Whitt, but it solidified after MdJ forced me to be shoved up Ezra's ass. I've contacted Ade hundreds of times in the past three months, wishing to find a middle ground, and I'm always hung up on.

Adelaide's and my relationship was always flawed, but I wanted to fix it like I've been doing with everyone else. But Ezra came between us, just as he comes between me and everyone else.

No more Katya for me. No matter how innocent she is, no matter how understanding and empathetic I may be, there isn't a woman on the planet who could befriend a woman who just shattered her heart.

Refusing to be ignored, after repeated attempts, Ezra gives up on talking and stands in my line of sight instead. Whitt's anchoring eyes are blocked from mine– as the mirror to my conscience, that's not a good thing.

Ezra and I are identical in height, our eyes meet and I lock onto him. "That was a huge mistake." An animalistic growl emanates from between my taut lips.

"What was a mistake?" Ezra whispers, his hot breath caressing my lips.

"Whitt was grounding me from doing something stupid," I say so quietly Ezra has to lean forward to hear the words. "Now

I have no reason to hold back," I warn a split-second before I punch Ezra with the full force of my weight and height. I drop Ezra's ass to the ground, finding no satisfaction as he stares up at me in shock.

Everyone scrambles around me, shouts going up into the air. Someone grabs my upper arm as I prepare for another swing. "Let go," I seethe, prepared to take them out too.

"What are you doing, Regina?" Dexter's voice hitches on a gasp.

"None of your fucking business," I hiss menacingly. "Drop my arm before you lose a hand."

"Dexter," Whitt warns too, understanding me in a way no one else ever will.

All Dexter sees is a crazy woman who just hit his family member for no apparent reason. He doesn't realize Katya is my responsibility, or how what Ezra just put me through broke something vital inside of me.

I down stare at Ezra with utter hatred, and watch as Master Ez flows into the driver's seat– an expression promising mental and emotional pain crosses his blood-spattered face.

"Go ahead, Dr. Lunatic," I taunt, having absolutely nothing to lose now. "Give me your best shot."

"Out!" Marcus shouts in a panic, and the room clears in a rush of running bodies. Except for Dexter, because he's still holding my arm, and Whitt, as he tries to safely catch my gaze.

"Dexter, you too," Marc commands.

"What? Are you fucking nuts?" Dexter's fingers clench on my arm. "Ezra's death is shining from Regina's eyes."

"Doesn't matter," Marc commands. "Leave anyway."

My arm is released, and I know that I've lost any and all respect I'd earned from Dexter. He leaves the dungeon by going through the door to the club.

"Now that we're alone, I think it's time we cleared the air."

"The audacity!" I bellow into Marc's face, finding satisfaction as he flinches as if struck. "You've got to be shitting me, right?" Arms flapping at my sides, I'm struggling to breathe I'm so enraged. Yeah… why not? Let's do it!"

"I can't believe you're *this* pissed about Marcus getting his dick sucked by Katya." Ezra rubs his jaw to bait me. "Who here hasn't been inside you?"

"Yeah, I'm a regular ol' slut-bag," sarcastically flows from my mouth. "I fuck anything with a dick… I could count the amount of times I've had sex in the past year on one hand, and you fucking know that, you piece of shit!"

"Ah, were you still holding out hope that Marcus wants a future with you– you alone." Ezra says in mock pity. Whoever this nasty asshole is, I don't recognize him, so I can't give him a name.

"This is and isn't about Marcus." Huffing in, I spit in Ezra's face, saliva hitting him in the chin. "What's between Marc and me is between Marc and me. This is because of the promise you broke. You promised to always put Katya's welfare first, and what I just witnessed is disgusting."

This new personality of Ezra's refuses to hear me, and goes in for the kill. "If Marcus didn't want it, he could have said no." Shifting on the floor, Ezra makes a good show of wiping my spit off his chin, then he licks it off his fingertip.

"God," Ezra groans, lifting his lips salaciously. "Marcus loved the way Katya sucked his dick. Have you ever heard him come like that, Regina?"

"Shut up!" Reaching down, Marcus jerks Ezra backward.

Being tugged across the floor, putting distance between us, Ezra still doesn't shut up. "I know Marcus hasn't touched you since around the time of your initiation. Katya's a hot piece of ass, and I thought I'd share the wealth since Marc finds your dried-up pussy repulsive."

"Enough!" Marcus growls, foot flying out to kick Ezra in the ribs. "Shut the fuck up! Stop trying to destroy my life and your own at the same time, you destructive sociopath. You fucked up, so now you're lashing out because you know Regina will never forgive you."

Holding my breath, I stare at Ezra with complete and total horror, pretending his words hold no weight. Only those closest to us have the best ammo to harm our hearts.

"Ouch, Ezra, that really fucking hurt." I clench my chest dramatically, pretending the truth of it isn't killing me. "I'll say this so you have nothing to throw at me when I finally take your measure. My sexuality is nonexistent. I know I'm nothing. I know no one has ever truly wanted me. I'm Grant's throwaway, and that's what Marcus saw in me, now feeling the same way too."

"Let's not forget about Pretty Boy," Ezra reminds me, finger hitching in Whitt's direction. We all look as one, finding Whitt frozen in silent horror with agony written across his features. "He's gay– doesn't want ya either. Only did you because he had to– took one for the team."

"Yeah, my husband is gay. So what?" Shrugging, I really don't understand why Ezra thought this would be ammunition. "What's that have to do with me? Remember, we're born this way."

My shot hit its target, causing Ezra too look on the verge of being sick.

Still on the offensive. "I'm not a bad person because I'm not sexy. I know I'm the Whittenhower whore. But I also know it's none of your goddamn business."

"Oh, it's my business." Ezra has more to say, but only two of the four of us in this dungeon are actual members of MdJ. Enraged that he can't speak his mind, he tries a new tactic, smiling sadistically. "Do you want to know what Syn says about you?"

"I don't give a fuck," I snarl, but of course I do. "Does it make you feel better to know I can't stand the sight of myself when I walk past a mirror naked, or how I'm unable to touch myself because no one else can either."

Self-wounding words permeating, I watch as Ezra struggles to regain control. Blinking furiously, the man I befriended is trying to erupt because he wants to soothe me. No matter how much it hurts me, I continue, because it is the honest to God's truth.

"When we disagree, you love to throw it in my face how I'm being a bitch because I need to get laid. Hell, the last time I got off was while Grant and I beat each other bloody. Does knowing that make you feel better, Ezra?"

"Regina," three voices ring out in pity– Marc, Ezra, and Whitt.

"No, I'm going to get this out." I pin Marcus in my stare so he knows this is directed at him. "I've been nothing if not patient, compassionate, and understanding– empathetic. But what I witnessed proved it was all a lie."

"Regina." Marcus takes a few steps toward me, but the stranger peering out of my eyes freezes him in place.

"What happened to only touching those you have an emotional connection with? What happened to the fact that you've been avoiding sex because you're finding yourself? What happened to you saying you're not even doing Cortez? Why lie? Why throw us away on a quick blowjob in this dungeon?"

"It's not–"

"No." Hand held out, I ward Marcus off. "No need to explain… remember how you told me you were going to show me from now on? Well, that was pretty loud what you just did. From my point-of-view, you've lied about everything. I don't know you, but I wish you happiness and satisfaction now that you've found someone you truly want to take my place."

In a panic, face twisted in agony, Marcus tries to make his way toward me, but Whitt intercepts him. "Back off, Marc. I know I want to hear what Queen has to say."

"But it's not… it's not how it is." Marcus stammers, but Whitt pushes him back by a palm to his chest.

"You're always running off to Cort. Ezra's always suffering from Daddy issues. So my guess is Ezra is trying to entice you into their bed by using Katya." Shrugging, I'm not angry anymore. I'm not even sad. I'm resolute.

"Bye-bye!" Waving in Marc's direction, the smile on my face doesn't belong to me. "I always said they'd come between us, and *this* is the end of us."

"Back off." Marcus whips Whitt's hand off his chest. Charging forward, he gets into my space, but I don't back up. "I didn't realize this would affect you as it did– I wouldn't have done it if I realized."

"Oh, I'm not being an irrational, hypocritical little woman," I mock in the patronizing tone men take on with women when they mansplain things. "You didn't have to ask for my permission, but you could have at least told me what was going to happen." Voice twisting nastily, "What a surprise this was for me to see my partner getting blown by his new daughter-in-law. My emotions should matter, even if you think you have a right to do whatever the fuck you wish."

"Regina." Marcus lifts his hand to touch me, and I swat it away so hard the sound reverberates around the dungeon.

"But who gives a fuck about what I'm feeling anyway…" I mutter snidely, my tone taking on a hissing sound. "How about the fact that a rape victim was just shoved to the floor and ordered to blow a stranger she couldn't even see. Her power taken away.

When Katya learns who you are, she will be sickened by what happened. THAT. IS. MY. GODDAMN. MALFUNCTION.”

Breathing laboriously, my scream echoes in the resulting silence. Voice barely a whisper, “You and I know what it feels like to have our autonomy taken away, and yet you did it anyway. It’s not sexy. It has nothing to do with how I honestly do feel you just betrayed me. I had to stand by while being humiliated in front of my peers, forced to watch you get off on another while you won’t touch me, all the while my power to protect Katya was torn from me. THAT. IS. WHY.”

“Ezra, you promised me Regina understood and was fine with this.” Marcus turns on Ezra, chest rising and falling. “You said she understood how it was part of *your* therapy.”

A stranger looks at me, not a version of Ezra I recognize. “We didn’t need Regina’s permission.”

Crimson eclipses my vision. “You promised!” Lunging before anyone can stop me, I straddle Ezra’s hips. Smashing him in the face time and time again, my knuckles ache as I feel the tale-tell signs of a break.

Glowing with power, I’ve never felt so satisfied in my entire life. The sensation of Ezra’s flesh bursting beneath my fists is positively orgasmic. Beating Ezra, I wear a manic grin of delight. With ever strike of my fists, my moods shift, until nothing but my bitter truth is finally revealed.

Every word is accompanied with a strike. “You! Raped! Me!” Screaming until my voice cracks from the violent force. Covering his face with his upturned arms, Ezra gives me access to his chest and belly.

“You promised to never take your punishments out on Katya. You told me you only had her best interests at heart. I told you she was my responsibility, even if I had to protect her from you.”

The sound of flesh bursting flesh should cause a sickened reaction in me, but it just eggs me on. “You used Katya to atone for your own sins. Fuck your need for balance!” Lost in rage, another knuckle breaks on Ezra’s sharp jaw. “Katya will be devastated when she finds out that you had her suck her father-in-law in front of a crowd– when she learns why you did it… I’m so glad your conscience feels better, asshole. Now Katya and I get to shoulder the fucking agony!”

I sit on Ezra's thighs, weeping uncontrollably while Marcus and Whitt look at me in shock. Ezra's crying too, eyes red-rimmed and watering profusely, lips quivering with every sob.

The whole person– the one who is always being violated by facets of his own personality –Ezra tries to pull me down and embrace me. In response, I throw another punch to his jaw, screaming in agony as my broken knuckles protest.

"I'm sorry. I didn't think it through. It sounded right to Master Ez." Ezra grovels through his tears, begging me to understand. "I just wanted to make it right. Since I couldn't erase the past, I wanted to equalize it. It's all I could think to do. I raped you, and it broke Marcus, so I gave him Katya."

"Stop– just stop talking." Covering my face in my hands, I already knew the lunatic was going to say that. I want Ezra to shut up, because he's always cerebrally fucking me until I see his perspective and agree with him.

"I wanted to fix it. Fix Marcus. Fix it for both of you." Ezra tries to claw my hands away from my face, so I'll look at him. "I know I'm a horrible person, and you and Marcus have been hurt the worst by me. It's because I was comfortable enough to show you the real me."

"That's what makes it worse." Sobbing, I'm close to hyperventilating. "You betrayed me. I've passed your nonstop tests of loyalty, proving through my actions that you can trust me. You do these horrible things, and then play the martyr when we get pissed or hurt."

"Most of the time I don't realize how badly I'll hurt people until after the fact." I have no idea if Ezra's being real or playing me like an instrument.

"Make it easier on all of us. Just fucking stop this shit. Think it through first– ask Cort, Katya, or Marc if it's a good idea. You know I'll always be brutally honest with you, which is why you pretended that we discussed this– which means you knew this was beyond wrong before you did it."

"I did, because I knew you wouldn't understand. I felt it was just." Ezra tugs my hands away from my face, trying to get me to see it from his point of view. "I don't need your permission, but it wasn't fair that I lied to Marcus by saying I had it. I needed this, so I did it."

"*You needed this…*" Hiccupping on a sob, my sarcasm doesn't transfer. "I've given up a year of my life while I helped you chase your happily ever after… In thanks, you destroyed mine in the process."

Crawling off Ezra, I don't dare look Whitt in the eye, terrified what will be mirrored back at me. "I need to be alone." Gazing at the floor, I watch as my blood spatters in large plops on the slate tiles. "Everyone wants to give me a piece of their mind– to make excuses. If you care about me at all, you'll let me lick my wounds in peace."

Chapter Forty

Brain and emotions on lockdown, I quickly shower, hissing and wincing every time the cuts on my hands come in contact with the heavily chlorinated water. It's a lovely reminder that losing one's shit has painful consequences. Consequences that feel like shards of ice, fire, and brimstone are impaling my wounded flesh.

"Why have I turned into a bloodthirsty creature?" I ask the person lurking in the mirror, watching her lips move with mine.

"Because everyone uses you, knowing you'll stick around," she answers back.

"It's wrong," I tell the wounded woman looking at me.

She transforms, appearing stronger, until it's Queen looking back at me. "I know– it's not fair, but it's the truth. It feels amazing to show them how badly you're hurting on the inside."

"It does," I agree, happy someone gets me. "It's like… it's like we can see how much it hurts, because there's blood and bruises left behind."

"Exactly, because you hurt where no one can see it."

"What do I do?" Eyebrows rising, my voice is tinged with hope. Queen mirrors me, but she looks frustrated with me.

"Make them hear you. Beat them. Scream at them. Ignore them. Anything you have to do to force them to acknowledge the toll they've taken on you. Self-respect gains respect from everyone. It's not fair, and they need to pay."

"I don't want to hurt them."

"You're a doormat, Regina. They hurt you with premeditation, knowing it will hurt you and doing it anyway." Queen glares at me. Insulted, I feel myself glaring back at her. "Woman up. Make them earn it– make them deserve your friendship, your advice, your help, your comfort, your love. Make them earn the right to enter your body."

"Yeah, that ain't–"

"Shut up!" Queen points at me, and my finger jabs into the foggy mirror. "There's nothing wrong with being a woman– nothing wrong with your body. Back the hell up. Look at it."

Obeying myself, I stand in the middle of the bathroom in my private room at Restraint, having had to back up to the shower stall to see the entirety of my tall body. Squinting, I turn my face to the side.

Hands roaming the landscape of my body, I look at it with a critical eye. But the empowered part of me sees differently than the insecure part. My heavy breasts sag, with elongated nipples from feeding my children. My stomach is flat, with the declination of the muscles beneath, but it's zebra-striped with stretchmarks– as are my hips, the sides of my breasts, and behind my knees from my last growth spurt as a teenager.

"This is the body of a survivor," Queen reminds me. "Appreciate it. You've grown and birthed human beings, fed them from your body. This body is for your survival, not to please people who don't deserve you."

Queen isn't a different personality like Ezra experiences. But there are times I allow myself to use the dominant part of me as an excuse to act in a way men say women shouldn't. Women can't go two minutes without subtle chastisement, sometimes downright rude commentary about how we're not who someone else thinks we should be.

I'm tall like a man.

I'm too heavy to be a woman, but I'm too thin for my size.

I think like a man, but should silence my voice because I'm a woman.

My sex-drive is like a man's, but I shouldn't satisfy it because I'm a woman.

Everything in my bedroom is purple, and people laugh, expecting hues of neutral colors, because I'm not girly enough for such a feminine color.

In a career filled with geniuses, the men try to overpower the women, thinking themselves better at programming because they were born with a dick. As if the high-speed brain in our heads is altered by the excess of estrogen.

Your success is impressive for a woman.

You're not maternal enough to be a mother.

I'm sick of being handicapped to satisfy the egos of men. The misogyny is so subtle, we women don't even recognize when we fall into its trap and continually perpetuate it.

"You're Regina," I say to myself using Queen's tone. "It's not masculine or feminine– it's who you are. It's your personality, your view of the world, and doesn't have a goddamn thing to do with whether or not you have a cock or pussy. You love your pussy, don't you?"

"Yes," releasing on a sob, my hand skates down my belly to rest over my mound. I've gone months without touching myself outside of wiping or showering. "In their quest of all things cock, I started to despise it."

Green eyes heavily lidded, "It feels good," Queen reminds me in a coaxing tone. "It's yours. There's nothing wrong with it, just because they don't want it. There's nothing wrong with you just because they use your pussy to dominate you– to take your power away."

"I don't want my son to be this way," I tell my reflection in the mirror. "It terrifies me."

"Then you better show Niel how a man should treat a woman, by showing Niel how to treat *everyone* like a human being."

"I'm a bad mother."

"No one would ever call a man a bad father because he goes to work, puts his career first, knowing his children are happy and healthy and loved." Queen points out the hypocrisy.

"I'm not a good example. I'm scared it's too late– I'm scared I'm too dirty, too bad after the things I've done."

Queen and I hold our gaze in the mirror, satisfaction and shame warring. "People have to hurt to learn a lesson. If it's too easy with no consequences, why not do it again? And after they do it again, why not do something a step worse? There's a reason it's called punishment, it has to hurt. Don't forget your BDSM training, Regina– it's human nature training."

"What do I do?" I ask my reflection as I reach for my underwear.

"Teach them how to treat you. If they don't treat you right, then they can't be a part of your life."

"I'll miss them. I don't want to hurt them." I mutter rapidly as I tug on my bra.

"No, you fear they will forget you if you're not in their face," Queen pulls from the depths of my mind. "There is truth in the statement distance makes the heart grow fonder. It's called being taken for granted and ignored. If you're not always doing for them, they will miss you when they notice you're not there."

"What if they don't miss me?" I plead with my reflection. "Look at what happened between Grant and me."

"I don't give a fuck if they miss you or not, Regina. The only thing I care about is whether or not they respect you. Saying they love you is not the same as showing they love you. You deserve it simply because you exist– don't let anyone ever forget that."

"You're right." I pull on a Restraint-issued t-shirt. "Perfect is subjective."

"You. Are. Not. Getting. It." Queen points with every word, causing my finger to tap on the glass. "Your worth has nothing to do with your body. You treat people like human beings. You love. You care. You forgive. You understand. You empathize. You add value to people's lives. Eradicate that misogynistic bullshit narrative playing out in your mind. You matter simply because you exist. No one should be treated as you have been."

"I'm no victim." Yanking on my jeans, the numbness fades away, leaving behind a mix of grief and rage. "And I'll survive this too, no matter what happens." My voice melds with Queen's, until we no longer have to segment to fit into society.

Tugging a hoodie over my head, I step into my private room. "Uh!" I meep as my eyes pop out the collar of my sweatshirt. Marc is leaning against the door to the hallway, and Ezra is sitting on my sofa like a guilty storm cloud.

"What's going on?" I lean against my bathroom door, arms folded over my chest, making sure the entire expanse of the room is between Marcus and me, with Ezra sitting in between.

I hated Ezra a half an hour ago, but that doesn't mean I don't understand him. Actions have consequences. No matter how batshit crazy Ezra can be, he's predictable. If Marcus is culpable for my rape because he didn't step in when he noticed the signs, if Ezra was responsible for Cortez mouth-raping Katya because he knew his actions would force Cortez to do just that, then Marcus is responsible for what happened tonight.

Marcus should have reeled Ezra in. Marcus should have never trusted Ezra's word, because there is no way in hell I would have ever okayed what just went down in the dungeon. Marcus wanted that blowjob from Katya, using the misunderstanding and misdirection as an excuse to get away with it.

Perception.

From where I'm standing, I hate the whole pack of assholes.

Marcus stares back at me, expression warping as emotions scroll across my face, easier to read than a news tickertape.

"Punishment," Marcus announces, while holding my gaze in silent challenge. "We'll talk about you and me later, but first you need to get something out of your system."

"I'm not fucking Ezra," I growl, knowing both Marcus and Ezra enough to anticipate the direction of their thoughts.

"Why not?" Marcus has the audacity to ask me that.

"Are you shitting me?" Tightening my arms over my chest, I wince when the skin on my knuckles pulls. "I know exactly what you're up to. No more two wrongs make a right bullshit, in Ezra's Technicolor insanity dream ride fantasy world."

"You don't want me?" The whole Ezra is a mass of insecurities and issues, never feeling as if he's loved enough, with no friends, and always acting wounded. Well, I'm sick of feeling like I live in a fucking asylum.

"Not a cocksucking thing has to do with whether or not I want you." Ezra's words in the dungeon echo in my mind. "Why the hell would you want to fuck me?"

"Regina." Heat enters Ezra's eyes, and I'm pretty sure Master Ez is taking the wheel.

"Do you ever just listen to yourself, no matter who's driving the bus?" Slumping against the bathroom door, I just shake my head back and forth. "You're gay. You just got done ripping me a new asshole about how Whitt's gay and had to take one for the team. You actually said to me that Marcus was revolted by my dried-up pussy, and Katya was a hot piece of ass… go fuck your replacement pussy and leave me the hell out of it."

"You know I said those things to hurt you," Ezra tries to reason with me– manipulate me. "I know how you tick, so I plucked things out of your mind that would sting."

"Oh, and that so helps your cause." Chuckling without humor, I flash a look at Marcus. "My vagina is closed to people who harm me with intent. On second thought, my vagina is literally closed to everyone but me. I'm done with sex– it isn't worth it. I'll get myself off from now on."

"You understand my reasoning, don't you?" Ezra is utterly ridiculous.

"I'm not going to get back into any of this shit with you, or one of us may die this time," I warn, upper lip pulling off my teeth in a snarl. "Obviously I get *your* point-of-view, but I doubt you get mine."

"No more back and forth bullshit." Marcus stops Ezra before he babbles more insanity. "Punishment must be exacted, as is our way. Regina, you know damn well Ezra is a ball of guilt. I'm so furious after he played me, I need him to be punished so I can move on too… as do you."

"I'm not in the mood," I mutter curtly. "I want to go ice my hands and go to bed, thank you very much."

"These things must be taken care of immediately, Regina." Marc's voice pitches low with impatience. "You have a responsibility to finish what you started."

"Let's just call the beating Ezra's punishment, and be done with it."

"I can't go back to the Zeitler private room until punishment has been met." Ezra gazes at me beseechingly. "Cortez is just as angry with me as you are, and just as hurt for the same reasons. I can't go back until the need for punishment is satisfied."

"For nearly a year, every fucking day, what have I told you?"

"Mull over my decisions before I act on them." Shamefaced, Ezra looks away from me. "Sometimes parts of me do these things on purpose, even if I don't agree with them. You know that, so help me release the guilt they caused in me."

"That play had your signature written all over it, Dr. Lunatic. I'm not buying the bullshit you're selling."

"Regina." Marcus treads carefully, knowing better than to interrupt or leave his station at the door. "I have a proper punishment in mind. Not only will it equalize the imbalance and alleviate the guilt, it will also help both of you. You can take your power back, and Ezra can have something he's needed for a very long time."

"I'm not fucking Ezra in any capacity," I practically shriek, and a long-suffering sound of frustration bubbles up my throat.

"Your vagina will not be involved." Marc's voice breaks, and I can't decide if it's with pity or guilt. "You may keep all of your clothing on. It won't involve your mouth or hands either. However, it will be sexual in nature for Ezra."

"Of course it will be," I mutter sarcastically, feeling cornered, knowing I'm not getting out of this room until I do exactly what they both want. It just solidifies the changes I will be making in my life the instant I walk out into the hallway with my head held high and my shoulders back.

"What do you suggest?"

Sheepishly, Marcus points to a bag sitting next to Ezra on the sofa. "I'm not going to pretend I like this one bit, nor am I going to say I don't deserve feeling as I do right now. But I do believe in what's to come."

Ignoring the heartbreaking tone in Marc's voice, I eye the bag. "What's in there?"

"Pegging is a proper punishment." Marcus takes a deep breath, and a single tear escapes his amber eye. "A proper punishment for the event that started this all, Regina."

"When Ezra raped me?" I whisper, voice vibrating with emotion.

"Yes," Marcus breathes back just as softly. "We all need to move on from it."

"Fine– I'll do it because I understand the balance of this punishment, even if I'm not in the mood." Staring at the bag, back to Ezra, then over the Marcus, I enact my first empowered moment. "Marcus, you can go now. I don't want you to watch me playact a rape on your son."

"Ezra's not my birth child, Regina. We're practically the same age." Marcus teases to lighten the mood to a more sexual tone, trying to get me to engage him. But he ends up rubbing a hand through his hair out of frustration when I don't banter back. He's allowing his hair to grow out, and he's even more devastating for it.

"I don't want you here." It's not said in an unkind tone, merely the truth.

"It would help me too," Marcus stresses, but it rings of manipulation. "Both of us have been on the receiving end, and I can't in good conscience ever do this punishment myself. So I need to live vicariously through you."

"If Katya's willing to let you join them, then that's not my call. I don't get a say in anything you do, no matter what." Sighing, I try to force the pain out of my voice. "I don't want you to watch. Is that better? I was trying to be tactful and not hurt your feelings."

I ignore the hurt look in Marc's eyes, but I notice it. As sick as it sounds, I kind of enjoy it.

No lesson is ever learned without pain, and it doesn't necessarily mean physical. To be honest, the best lessons learned are when disappointment, guilt, or shame are felt. Who cares if I get off on the fact that he's hurt, as long as he learns from it? The lesson of the day is to not toy with my emotions, use me, and take for granted that I'll always be here. No matter what.

Reading the thoughts scrolling across my expression, "I'll be in the hall," Marcus mutters curtly, then leaves my private room.

"Good girl," Ezra praises me– the Ezra whose company I enjoy. "Marcus needs to get his head out of his ass. It's time you made him chase you."

"I'm not playing a game, Ezra." I growl as unzip the bag, revealing my new phallus. I wanted one as soon as I saw Katya bring it out of her bag of tricks and use it on Monica.

"Mmm-hmm…" Ezra murmurs. "Sure you aren't."

"I'm not," I defend as I tear into the fresh packaging. Why is plastic so hard to get into. What did Kat use, her kitten fangs?

"Game or not, make him work for it." Ezra says in support of me, suspiciously sounding like a disturbing combination of Syn and Queen.

"You're no longer my closest confidant." Yanking my sweatshirt off, I regret falling into Ezra's trap. He would lull me in, speaking of his own problems, then he would offer better advice than my own therapist. I always ended up saying too much, which is why Ezra was capable of wounding me so thoroughly out in the dungeon.

Cerebral fuckage.

"I always will be, Regina. You can tell me anything without judgment, because I've done so many bad things that I can never judge you back."

Snorting a sound of disgust, "Yeah, to me," I stress.

"After my punishment, I will be absolved, and we can both try to heal. But I will even do you one better– I heard every word you said as you pounded them into me. I understand how you feel toward all of us right now, your anger and betrayal, and I promise never to do it again."

"Make all facets of your personality vow that, Dr. Lunatic, then I'll buy it." Gazing into the bag, I don't even know how to use this contraption. "I believe this punishment appears to be for your enjoyment."

"Oh, it is," Ezra murmurs in a voice dripping with arrogance and lust. He's practically salivating, knowing I'm about to fuck his ass. "Cort told me how you mentioned using one on him while you trained together. Obviously you were teasing him, but we masturbated together while we talked about it."

“I’m glad I could be the catalyst for your bizarre bonding experience,” I deadpan.

Reading my confused expression accurately, Ezra pulls the harness from the bag. “Put this on first, and then we’ll work up to it.”

With one dong in my hand, another is revealed from beneath the harness. I stare at the two phalluses in confusion. One is larger than the other.

“Where is a lesbian when I need one?” Tossing the bag to the floor, I arrange the harness on the sofa cushion, placing two dongs next to it, confused as to what goes where and why. “This makes absolutely no sense.”

“We could call Ade. I’m sure my mother introduced her to one.” Ezra laughs as if there isn’t a bit of discomfort over the topic. Secondary is the fact that our budding friendship pushed Ade from my orbit.

“You love to keep it in the family, don’t ya?” I narrow my eyes at Ezra, grimacing in disgust for several reasons.

When the red of rage washes over my vision, there are three women who better never be in my vicinity. Gwen Meyers for molesting Grant, and then abandoning their son. Olivia Fontaine for holding Marcus captive. Diane Holden for warping Ezra and having the honor of being Marc’s wife.

“A few months ago, I fucked Ade because Master Ez had to, and Cortez and Katya saw.”

“Oh, that explains their odd behavior.” Snickering, I remember how off they were acting. I’ve stepped away from the security feeds. But sometimes I couldn’t help but be drawn back in, missing Dominion’s version of the Truman Show.

“I was going crazy with lust. Katya was off limits sexually until after she realized who I was from her past. Cortez wouldn’t touch me. You would’ve gutted me if I tried. It just happened to be the day my mom pissed me off by pestering me about marrying Ade. She wouldn’t listen about Katya, saying I was betraying our family. I knew damn well my mother wanted me to marry Ade so she could declare me unfit, and then take control of Shadow Haven and our fortune. Zane and Ava can’t come of age fast enough, effectively ending the committal threat.”

“Same threat Ade was spouting a few years ago– Christ, no more storytelling.” Shuddering in fear, I don’t like the look in Ezra’s eye, or the way he keeps blinking in remembrance. A few months ago, we learned Katya was keeping a major secret, one that was the cause of her not wishing to move to Dominion until school let out in Pennsylvania.

Ava.

The moment I heard of the precious child, I knew damn well Ava was the little girl destined to become Maître du Jeu's boogieman.

Lost in his own world, Ezra keeps speaking. "I knew Adelaide would come to me if I asked, and Master Ez had no problem making use of her. Then I sent Ade home to my cunt of a mother, smelling of my cum, and I won't apologize for it. My mother got the message to back off."

"Well, I guess since you've pissed off all the lesbians I know, you'll have to help me with this." I hold up the harness in one hand and its latex buddies in another.

"You geniuses can be so unimaginative." Ezra teases, while quickly assembling the strap-on.

"Um… Kat's wasn't like this one," I mumble, noticing how the smaller phallus is inside the seat of the harness, with the larger one protruding forward.

"It's supposed to be my punishment, but we both know that's bullshit. Marcus wanted you to thoroughly enjoy it too." Ezra clears his throat, pale skin blushing a pretty pink. "Um… maybe it's for later, and Marc's sending you a message."

"What?" I squawk, confused.

"This is yours to keep." Ezra hands me the assembled strap-on. "And you have a partner who has been having sexual difficulties– I promise Marcus has not been touching Cortez. That was part of the reason I had Katya do what she did. It's all fear-based. Maybe Marc's trying to tell you something– this strap-on appeared out of nowhere, so he must have had it ready and waiting, and not for my punishment."

My eyes go wide and my mouth forms a silent O.

"I…" stumbling over my words, my mouth goes dry as I contemplate the implications. I quickly change the subject. "What's this for though?"

Ezra laughs at me, calling me daft underneath his breath. Leaning forward on the sofa, Ezra tugs me to stand between his parted thighs. His fingers find the waistband of my jeans, then start to yank them down my hips.

"Hey," I protest, grabbing his hands. "Stop it!"

"We'll leave your panties on," Ezra teases me, rolling his eyes at how absurd I'm being. Floored by his expression, he uses it to his advantage. My jeans land on the floor a few feet behind the sofa.

Ezra sets the harness by my feet, then places my palm on his shoulder for support. Curious and a bit scared, but relaxed that I'm doing this with Ezra where it won't matter if I make a fool of myself, I step into the straps, still unsure how the contraption works.

"Ugh!" I grunt as Ezra's fingers enter me. Frozen in shock, I look at him in surprise, and he smirks back in answer.

"Like panties would ever stop me." Ezra releases a lusty chuckle. "Mmm… you're incredibly wet. I've missed your reaction to my invasions."

Checking in with my inner Queen, I decide to go with the flow. "Oh, that's nice," I purr as my ignored pussy finally gets some attention. Resting my head on Ezra's shoulder, I relax as he massages me from the inside.

"You like this, you'll love what comes next." Ezra murmurs against my cheek. Fingertips pull free from my body, then draw the harness up my thighs.

"Oh, God!" I cry out, jerking roughly in ecstasy.

I've never really played with toys before. I made Kristal use them during her punishment, but I've only used my hands. I can't believe, at my age, I'm still naïve. The smaller phallus was meant for me.

"Whoever designed this thing is a genius. I bow down to them." I moan as Ezra tightens the straps on my hips and waist, and makes sure everything is snug and where it needs to be.

"Don't come yet," Ezra teases. "It always makes you too relaxed and sleepy, and you have some work you need to do."

"What kind of work?" The added pressure of the toy resting inside me, with the base of the dong pressing down on my clit, has my breath wheezing out of me on a pant. I lick my suddenly dry lips and groan as I shift my hips.

Ezra shucks his pants and is lounging back on my sofa in seconds flat– he's an eager beaver. Thighs spread impossibly wide, his arousal extends from the thatch of white curls between his legs. The engorged, flushed head is beaded with precum, proving Ezra is incredibly excited by the sight of me with a phallus jutting from my pelvis. A pink tongue quickly dabs moisture to his lower lip, then disappears back into the depths of his mouth.

Our bitch and moan sessions have bonded us. The fear of powerlessness will never leave me, but I'm not afraid of Ezra anymore. There's a freedom I share with him, where there's no judgment. There's an odd chemistry that has been riding us, which is what Marcus and Cortez kept commenting on, as if our kinks feed into one another's.

The horrific things Ezra voiced about me in the dungeon were my words being echoed back to me. It was a therapeutic technique he used to show me how ludicrous I sounded, forcing me to voice the rest of the negative bullshit inside my head.

Ezra didn't think those things about me– *I did.*

Seeing the realization cross my face, "Suck me," Ezra orders.

Dropping to my knees without thought, I catch Ezra's gaze to make sure it's still Ezra driving the bus. Comforted by my friend gazing back at me with lust shining in his clear eyes, I flick my tongue out to swipe his cockhead free of moisture.

"You do know that your husband's favorite activity is getting his cock sucked? I realize Marcus is struggling right now, but that doesn't mean you have to deny yourself the pleasure."

"Whitt was a one-time deal," I murmur against his flesh. After dampening his cock with my saliva, I blow on it, causing Ezra to quiver on the sofa. Sexual confidence restored, I suck Ezra's entire dick down my throat.

"Regina!" Ezra screams, hand flying out to fist my hair, and I don't doubt the sound carried out into the hallway.

After thirty seconds, I come back up for air. "Whitt needs boy lips wrapped around his cock– maybe your lips," I tease, getting the expected reaction out of Ezra. Precum spurts out to flavor my tongue. "I've got three people working on the matchmaking, and they're both so stubborn."

"Ah– Dalton," Ezra grins down at me. "Whitt's noticed. He's just shy around guys, and Dalton won't give in because of his mission. Real lust is hard to deny."

"That's what I'm hoping." Enjoying my work, I hold Ezra's gaze while I draw him in and out of my mouth in a steady rhythm."

Voice breathy, Ezra struggles to speak. "Don't let anyone fool you– you give amazing head, Regina."

"You're just saying that to get me to suck your dick," I tease, licking him like a lollipop.

"Your cocksuckage skills rival Cort's," Ezra purrs in awe. "Once Marcus gets over his phobia, he'll have your mouth attached to his crotch incessantly."

"Until then, Marcus and I are going to have a different sort of relationship– one I can handle… I don't want to go there right now. Let me enjoy my work."

Nibbling Ezra from his knee to the inside of his thigh, I smile against his skin as his muscles constrict to halt his need to writhe. I ignore the arousal throbbing against my cheek, sucking at his thighs instead. I never get to explore a lover's body, not with Marcus or Grant.

Ezra becomes passive, and I know it's because no one takes the time to touch him either. Spreading his legs wide, I nip at the globes of his ass. The more attention I give him, the more desperate his pleas become. I pleasure Ezra's pucker with my tongue and fingers until he's wiggling and grunting uncontrollably.

Crawling up Ezra's body, I kiss him passionately for curiosity's sake. Sucking his tongue as if it's a cock, he groans directly into my mouth. My t-shirt dampens over my breasts, and I jerk my eyes downward to watch precum flow from his throbbing shaft.

Using the saliva I left behind, "Ah!" we moan together as I use my hand to slowly slide the phallus inside him. I have to pause, because every mental trigger snaps at once. I nearly come from the thought alone– I'm fucking a man instead of getting fucked.

We fight over who gets to control the kiss, battling with teeth and lips as I awkwardly thrust. Ezra doesn't seem to mind my novice attempts, since I've only had a cock for five minutes, not thirty years.

We stop kissing, and simply enjoy the sensation. I rest my head in the crook of his neck and moan constantly. Every thrust inside Ezra moves the dong deep inside of me, while simultaneously pressing the base against my clit. My eyes drift shut from the ecstasy of it, body tightening in anticipation of an epic orgasm. For some bizarre reason, I want us to go together– to erase the destruction of the last time we came together.

Reaching down, I stroke his slick cock in time with my thrusts. "Regina," Ezra hisses, and I know it will only be seconds before he fills my hand with his release.

Too late… I'm going now. I can't control my thrusts as my body twitches in the throes of release. Ezra saturates my hand and shirt as his animalistic grunts fill the air.

Ezra's hips buck upward, fucking himself on the dong, and I have no doubt he's missed this part of his relationship with Cortez. My needs are fed by fucking someone for the first time as his are fed by getting thoroughly fucked.

Kneeling on the carpet between his thighs, I rest my head against Ezra's chest and pant breathlessly. My heart is beating a rapid tattoo within my chest, my body keeps spasming and twitching in delight, and my mind floods my body with endorphins until I feel high.

"I'm a gay man trapped inside a woman's body." I giggle, sounding higher than a kite. "Just kidding– I'm all woman, one who loves men. But I'd be down to adding pegging to my repertoire."

"If you were a guy, I'd have to fight to the death for the chance to fuck you," Ezra admits breathlessly.

"If I were a guy, I'd be a total man-whore." I giggle again. "I'm high– I can't even feel my hands anymore," I slur in wonder.

"I get Marc's malfunction, and he'd understand if you took a lover. You're a highly moral person, which is part of your problem, because sex isn't amoral."

"I know that," I sputter, offended.

"Do you?" Ezra's voice pitches on an upward inflection. "One of these days, your bones won't fuse back together," Ezra warns, but laughs a second later. "Instead of being sexually frustrated and feeling down on yourself, go get fucked– fuck someone. You don't have to beat Grant to fuck him. Whitt would probably die and float to heaven if you'd suck his dick– maybe he'd let you peg him. You have options that will leave your conscience clear, Regina."

"But it's Marcus I want to make love to," I whisper inaudibly.

Ezra has bat-like hearing. "I know," he whispers, pity and wistfulness filling his tone.

"On that note… you better get back to your partners. I'm sure Cort is going to freeze you out for a long time after this newest stunt."

"It was worth it to have you peg me." Ezra groans as he pulls the dong out of his ass. "So worth it. Since Cortez refuses to touch me, maybe I could convince Katya to peg me. You think?"

"I think." Chuckling, I don't doubt the woman would love it. Ezra helps me with the buckles at my hips, then slowly lowers the harness. I grunt as the phallus leaves my body and a flood of moisture pools at my feet.

"Jesus, so much for my panties." I hiss, pulling the saturated fabric from my body. I pat myself dry with them, then pull my jeans back on.

"Katya rains too. Granted, not as easily as you." Ezra's delighted laughter is filled with pride. "I like that in a woman. It reminds me of a man ejaculating on me– I crave it."

"The older I get, the easier it is for me. I never did it for Grant when I was young. But my first time was with *Jamie* and Marcus," I admit with a blush.

"This I something I did not know… Tell me more."

"Another time," I murmur shyly, blushing deeper. "Ten bucks says Marc's sitting in the hallway."

"Not a bet I'm willing to take, since I'd lose." Laughter drying up, we both gaze at the closed door. "I'm going to use your shower. It seems wrong to get into bed with them after what we just did." A trickle of shame enters his voice.

"Fuck– I'm sorry."

"Totally my fault. I fucked us all with my actions. I'm the one who will have a ton of groveling to do. You better let Marcus in before he slits his wrists in the hallway," he sounds serious.

"Huh?"

"Just let him in– he probably thinks we killed each other by now."

I slowly crack the door and peer out into the hallway. Amber eyes pierce my soul. Marcus is holding up the hallway wall, sitting with his knees drawn up. A hand dangles over his knee and he's picking his cuticles. Black ringlets fall across his face to hide most of his stormy expression. His bronze skin is paler than usual.

Grant is the most beautiful man I've ever seen. Ezra is the most animalistic. Cort is the most charismatic. The man sitting on his ass, leaning against the hallway wall, is the perfect combination of all those things and more. My breath hitches in my throat because I want him that much– total devastation.

"We didn't kill each other." Feeling beyond awkward, I open the door all the way.

I step back in invitation for Marcus to enter. He flows fluidly to his feet, then strides into my private room. Eyes taking in everything, I bet Marc's looking for blood spatter. He walks to my bathroom door and puts his ear to the wood and listens. He hums deep in this throat when he finds everything satisfactory.

"Did Ezra hurt you again?" Marcus won't look at me, busying himself by tidying up the room.

"No, we didn't even argue– we did as we were told." Suddenly exhausted, I don't want to fight anymore. Not with anybody. "I'm pretty sure Katya will be using her new toys if Cort won't step up to the plate."

"I need to peek at Ezra to make sure he's okay." Marcus makes his way back over to the bathroom door. "Do you need me to make an emergency appointment at the clinic for your hands?"

"No." Flexing my fingers, I gaze down at my battered hands. "I think they're just bruised. The knuckles hurt, but I don't think they're broken."

"I'll take a look at them." Marcus slips into the bathroom, then juts his head back out, reading my mind. "Don't run away, Regina– I mean it. We need to talk in private."

Deciding to be an adult, instead of a spiteful, cowardly child, "Okay," flows from my lips.

Chapter Forty-One

"May we walk?" Marcus gestures to the hallway after he escapes the bathroom. "I need to be in motion. We can have someone drop your car off tomorrow morning."

"Okay– sure." Leading the way, I try for small talk. "I miss taking nightly walks with Ella through the neighborhoods. It gave me a chance to tell her about my parents and how I grew up."

Marcus is as silent as a ghost as he walks behind me down the hallway, but I know he's listening. Taking the exit to the parking lot, I just let my feet carry me where they may. As soon as the night air hits my face, I feel like I can finally breathe again.

"I'm going to let you talk, and just listen," I warn. "I pretty much said everything I needed to say back in the dungeon, except for the stuff I thought but it didn't flow out of my mouth."

"You were very articulate as you pounded Ezra." Marcus stills beneath a streetlamp, hand skating down the inside of my arm to capture my wrist, then he draws my hand into the light. "You were pulling your punches, I could tell. I was impressed with how careful you were, even while in the midst of bloodlust."

Prodding at my knuckles, I wince slightly. "It's not too bad– nothing's broken. Do you still have your prescription from when you broke your forearm?"

One of these days, your bones won't fuse back together.

Hearing Ezra's voice in my head, I end up chuckling at the most inopportune moment. "What?" Marcus questions as he checks out my other hand.

"Just replaying something Ezra said," I go for honesty. "Yeah, I have most of the pain pills left. They're mostly ibuprofen, so it'll take the swelling down."

"Good." Marcus tucks my arm in the crook of his, cradling my hand, then he begins to walk us down the street. "Maybe you should focus on your new-found violent streak with your therapist."

"You think?" I mutter sarcastically, because even though Marcus tried to sound serious, I picked up a faint hint of amusement. Turning serious, I whisper softly, "I already am."

In companionable silence, Marcus and I walk the streets, nodding at passersby and observing anything of interest. My mind focuses on two things: Katya's mouth working Marcus, and every facet of what that truly meant… and how much I don't want to lose him.

"I'm not a hypocrite– okay?" I speak to Marcus as if he can hear my private thoughts. "I get how wrong it sounds for me to throw a tantrum because Katya blew you, especially since we've never been exclusive."

"I get it," Marcus whispers in a soothing tone, sounding slightly leery of my reaction. "Those thoughts, you did voice them. Rather loudly, I might add. There isn't anything you need to repeat."

"Okay." Taking a deep breath, I try to be a mature adult. "I'll listen, if you're ever ready to tell me. Just don't leave me hanging. As I've told Grant, we're not star-crossed lovers in a tragic romance novel. I won't abide by miscommunication as a form of conflict. If it involves me, don't leave it to fester into apocalyptic proportions. If it doesn't, just tell me it's none of my business and you're working through some shit."

"But don't tell you it's not about you, or about you and me, and then have it affect you to the point you go postal on Ezra in the dungeon?" Marcus mutters wryly. "Yeah, I heard that too."

"I'm trying not to be a jealous, irrational female, Marcus. But I can only pretend so long that something doesn't bother me."

"I thought you understood," Marcus whispers. "But now I realize you didn't."

"In theory, sure. In practice, I've got to admit that telling me you can't perform, then getting off with your new daughter-in-law negates everything you said prior."

"While you were in your room with Ezra, I sat in the hallway trying to figure out how to voice this without sounding like a liar."

"Impress me," I tease, trying to lighten the heavy mood. We both step to the side to allow a frazzled man and his pooch to pass. "Poor fella is exhausted, but Fifi has to go potty."

"Yes, Ezra said you were okay with the plan. Yes, I should have immediately approached you. Not an excuse, but Ezra sprung it on me while Katya was performing with Monica. I didn't have the opportunity… and to protest once a vulnerable woman is at my feet, with a crowd watching on, would have been one of the highest forms of rejection."

Biting my tongue, I barely suppress a growl.

"I saw it as a triage situation, categorizing who would be hurt the most. Ezra was at the top of the list, and he was the one who wanted me to do it. To say I was upset about your rape would be an understatement. I won't reduce what you went through, but I've never met a stronger person than you, Regina… Ezra was suffering the most. So when he asked me, I didn't say yes because I wanted Katya. I said it to help Ezra."

"There is a part of Ezra that is fragile and innocent, and all we want to do is wrap him in bubble wrap and give him hugs. But he's learned to manipulate that, and I never allow it… not always, anyway. Sometimes he manages to sneak underneath my skin and get shit past me."

"Now we start at the beginning," Marcus announces ominously. "I've said this before. I'm a religious man who wanted a wife, children, and I wanted to live my life stress-free at Serenity Lake. But there is no more Serenity Lake, and that's not what life offered me. Every mistake I've made in my adult life, I'm trying to right, and it's going to take time. What Jamie had to say to us in his letter was accurate."

"I know," I whisper, finally admitting the truth. "We act and react like children, but we're more destructive."

"Right now, we're not in a place where we can drop everything and start over together, but that doesn't mean I don't want to so fucking badly, Regina." Slowing, Marcus wraps his arm around my shoulder, then brushes a kiss to my hair. "It all sounds so trivial, but I don't want to destroy what is good in my life as I try to erase the bad."

"What do you mean?"

"You and I want exactly the same things, and we have exactly the same barricades. Jamie calls you his echo, but sometimes I think you and I are walking parallel paths at the same time, going through the same shit, and neither one of us can jump from our track to join the other. I'd say it's us echoing each other, not Jamie. I just hope someday the tracks finally merge."

"Out of curiosity… what are these barricades?" I'm always either holding my thoughts, or screaming them in Marc's face, so I'm curious to see his take on it.

"I will hit on Ezra and Cortez last, but everything always connects to them. I'm in the middle of an election. If I were to divorce Diane, I would lose. This isn't career motivated. I want to be a judge who isn't corrupt, for the sake of Dominion's residents. I'm already losing, and this would be the final nail."

"You can thank Voldemort for your struggle."

"I know." Sighing deeply, Marcus releases it in the form of words. "Until Ezra is stable, I cannot divorce Diane. This is why I've stayed for so long. Pearl passed her considerable share to both Ezra and Divina. Divina passed hers to Cortez to give to Ezra. Diane has a small fortune, but for her, it's not enough. With it in Ezra's possession, Diane could snatch it away should he be found incompetent. It's part of the reason Diane pushed for Ezra to marry Adelaide, whom she's also in control."

"How does that effect your marriage?"

"I'm Ezra's adoptive father. Legal or not, in the courts, if I divorce Diane, I'll look like a lesser influence in Ezra's life. They will side with his biological mother in matters of competency. The threat of Wintercrest Asylum is not an empty threat. It was built for this sole purpose."

"A power grab," I mutter in disgust.

"We're billionaires, Regina– we're not talking living paycheck to paycheck. When we lose money, it's enough to support small countries. Tides turn with our influence. Once Ezra marries Katya, I won't have to worry about this. As husband and wife, Diane will have no say in Ezra's life anymore, nor will I."

"Which was why Diane wanted Ezra to marry Adelaide, and since he's not, she was also threatened with a stay in Wintercrest."

"Precisely." Marcus pulls me closer. "I'm sure Voldemort has a hand in it. For the foreseeable future, I must remain married to Diane. For the next three years and a handful of months, you must remain married to Whitt. So that leaves us at an impasse in our relationship, doesn't it?"

"That would be one of my major issues, yes."

Herding us into the wooded park closest to my development, Marcus draws us to a stop in the center of a copse of trees. Turning me, he places a palm on each of my shoulders, then stares deep in my eyes.

"I need to apologize, and this ties into the no sex edict I enacted, okay?"

"Apologize for what?" This could lead anywhere, since the list is endless.

"From the time we first interacted with one another, until your initiation, my behavior was appalling. I wasn't lying when I said I was working on myself. I've done a lot of soul searching, sought counsel with my rabbi, and have tried to connect with you in a more intimate manner."

Staring into Marc's eyes, I remain silent, hoping he'll continue to explain. After what I just witnessed in the dungeon, I need to hear it. Shaking fingertips squeeze my shoulders, and I realize Marcus needs to say it too.

"I was domineering, controlling, assaulting, forceful, possessive, and angry at the world at large. I took it all out on you, toying with your emotions, because misery loves company. You were so strong, with everything directed inward, and I wanted to test you to see what reactions I could get. I treated you subhuman– abusive. And for that, Regina, I can never repent. But I've been trying to show you how sorry I am that I destroyed our beginning."

"Wow…" is all I can say in the face of that admission. The sincerity and remorse in Marc's voice weakens my knees. But it's the glint of tears shining down at me that hurts my heart the most.

"Jamie was right–"

"Let me guess… you got the *date* lecture too?"

Chuckling mischievously, Marcus can't keep the grin off his face. "Jamie goes easy on you, Regina." Palms rise to cup my face, thumbs wiping tears away I hadn't realized were falling. "We've been best friends our whole lives, so the rules of common decency don't apply. Jamie can be rather ruthless with me. Besides, we're in competition with one another."

Scrunching my face up in confusion, I squawk, "What?"

"Jamie is never worried, but I always am. He assures me you'll be ninety years old, and one of us will be keeping you company." Smirking wryly, Marcus rocks my world. "We love each other, so we want the other to be happy. We don't outright sabotage the other, but we do erect a big wall between us and you, cutting off the flow of information that would have you running to one of us."

"What are you talking about?"

"Offense. Defense. As I said, we love each other and want nothing but happiness for the other. So if one of us is actively pursuing you, the other backs off. As you can see, I've refused to back off since your initiation. Sex or not, I'm not backing off."

"I'm trying to wrap my head around what you're saying."

"After what happened at the dock, I came right back to your house. That's my bedroom too now. Even if you scream in my face that you hated me after what I pulled tonight, I would still wander back to your room at the end of the day. If you tried to kick me out, I wouldn't leave. If you went somewhere else to sleep, I would just follow you and get right into bed beside you… long story short, Jamie backed off so we could connect."

"I gathered that from his note, and the way he kicked me out of the brownstone on the night of the dock incident," I mutter begrudgingly. I haven't seen Grant face-to-face since, because I'm ashamed of my behavior and never want a repeat.

"I've never been on a date, Regina." Marc's open honesty stutters my heartbeat. "I do have the added benefit of Jamie telling me how to fix what I've broken. I know you've never dated, either. I was settled into a married life with a woman who wanted my power at the age of seventeen… the rest is ancient history. That's why we've been going out to dinner, spending a lot of time with one another. It's one of the reasons why we don't have sex, because you and me and sex means the important shit gets pushed to the wayside."

Eyes narrowed, I can still see the way Marc's head was thrown back in ecstasy, with Katya sucking his mammoth dick between her lips. "You're not experiencing sexual dysfunction, are you?"

Marcus has the decency to look guilty. "Yes and no." Grabbing for my wrist, he's gentle because of my battered hands. Wrapping my palm around his bulge, Marcus forces me to cup his erection. "We sleep together with my cock hard against your ass every night, so stop with the insecurity horseshit. I do have several reasons why we're not having sex, but not wanting you isn't one of them."

"Stop with the evasion bullshit then." Fuming, I clench my fist around his flesh to the point we both hiss in pain. "There isn't a person on this planet who wouldn't see it as rejection. It's a kick in the pride, and it exacerbates my insecurities. Tonight I realized I've been loathing my own pussy because all the men around me want dick."

"Regina!" Abrupt and forceful, a hand is wrenched down the front of my jeans, fingers delving deep into my pussy. In shock, with my feet stumbling across the ground from the force of Marc's rutting, all I can do is stare wide-eyed as I get molested.

"Just because I love dick, doesn't mean I don't crave pussy." Fingers yanking back out of my jeans, he presents them to the moonlight. Tongue escaping his mouth, Marcus licks the shine I'd left behind on his fingers.

"That's just… I've got nothing," I grumble with a shudder, pussy awakening and then clenching in disappointment because nothing else will be happening.

Leaning forward, Marcus injects lust into his voice. "*I. Want. You. So. Fucking. Badly.*"

Eyes watering, flows out as a whine, "I didn't feel that way, Okay?"

"I get that *now*," Marc mutters wryly, while swishing his hips against mine to rub his erection on me. "I want to get to know you, Regina. I do have some heavy shit I'm dealing with– shit that will hurt your feelings. You'll get it in theory–"

"But not practice?" Arching a brow, I challenge him to explain.

"Precisely," Marcus banters back. "You are able to compartmentalize how you can love people in differing ways, with no less intensity, and it doesn't lessen the love you feel for each. But you struggle with loving both me and Jamie. I've been struggling too."

"But not about me and Grant?" I prompt, terrified over the direction this conversation is going. My axis tilts, giving me that sensation where the world drops from beneath my feet.

"Yes, my demons ride me, but not to the point I can't deal with life. I stopped having sex and skull-fucking so I could sort my feelings out, and compartmentalize like you do. Jamie is a fantasy *I know* will never be realized. I've let it go, and love him the way that works for us."

"I get that," I mutter, eyes dropping to gaze at the ground. I'm tempted to point out how a few leaves are scattered across the forest floor– autumn is coming early this year. Small talk, I'd rather engage in small talk.

I hate small talk.

"Regina?" Pity laces Marc's voice. "You don't get it. Jamie's not a fantasy for you, nor you for him. You're not a fantasy for me either. However–"

Heart pounding out of control, "Uh-oh! Here it comes."

Chuckling, Marcus gives me a shake, fingers curling back around my shoulders. "When Cortez and I started, it was about punishment. His and mine. We were miserable, vindictive, and filled with bitter self-loathing. This was the man you first met–*me*. But over time, our relationship shifted, and we didn't notice until it was too late."

"You're in love with Cortez," I say with little doubt. "I recognized it immediately in the way you interacted with one another. I even called Cortez out about it."

"No, Regina." Voice thick with tears, Marcus is crestfallen. "It's a different type of relationship, more possessive. It's one of a dominant and submissive. It's not without a struggle that I distance myself from Cortez for the sake of his happiness. I know from the bottom of my soul that Cortez and Ezra are meant to be together, that they balance one another perfectly. That one day, Cortez will come to terms with who he is, and Ezra will be forceful with Cortez for the first time, and their relationship will evolve."

"What of Katya?"

"I fear she is no different than I am in their relationship." Amber eyes close, eyelashes fluttering with emotion. "A distraction. A roadblock they're using out of fear. So I distanced myself, and it's a struggle, because I want my submissive back. I'm possessive of Cortez, so a part of me wants to tear him away from Ezra. One day, I fear the fallout of Ezra and Cortez truly finding their balance together."

"You mean the fallout for Katya?" Heart twisting, I look inward, terrified for many reasons. Katya's wellbeing is at the forefront, but so is the fact that if I don't keep Ezra and Katya together, MdJ is coming for me.

"And me– so I took myself out of the equation."

"Dating and the loss of your submissive is the reason for your no sex ruling?" Narrowing my eyes, I notice how sheepish and shifty Marcus is being. "I don't buy it. You were tormented on the dock. I've seen the haunted look in your eyes countless times since, sometimes you won't even look at me. No way is the no sex rule about Cort and me. No way– you're deflecting."

"UGH!" Marcus snarls, reaching up to tear at his ringlets. Stepping away from me, the man stares at the sky with his arms raised and hands frozen in his hair. "I kept saying it wasn't about you, or you and me, and you wouldn't listen… It's not about me and anyone. *It's all about me*."

Pulling a Grant, I decide silence is the answer. Waiting patiently, I never take my eyes off Marcus as he throws himself. Stomping, bitching and swearing, tearing at his hair, shouting nonsense at the sky to flow out into the universe. Dropping to his knees, I choke on a sob as I watch Marcus torture himself.

Knowing how a person being higher above a dominant feels like a challenge, causing us to pull inward and feel intimidated, I sit on the ground a few feet from where Marcus is kneeling. To occupy myself, I begin sorting the fallen leaves around me into piles of maple and ash, ignoring how the pine needles are poking me in the ass through me jeans.

Silence ringing, Marcus stares at me after about ten minutes of throwing himself, confused as to why I'm not joining him.

Patient and direct, "You done?" I am a mother, after all.

"I've never told a soul," is a hoarse whisper.

"Well, if you plan on being the one who's keeping me company when I'm ninety, then I suggest I'm the soul you tell."

Wearing an expression of torture, fear warbles Marc's voice. "If I tell you, I may not live two seconds after I speak."

"Marcus," I murmur softly, using my voice to comfort and soothe, unsure if my touch would be too much after such a display. After all, I had my own violent temper tantrum tonight. "I've been nothing but empathetic, compassionate, non-judgmental, and open and honest with you. If I can befriend Ezra after what he did to me, then I can listen to what's plaguing you without judging you."

"*It's bad*," Marcus admits, bleeding shame. "So very bad… and it does include you."

Pretending my heart isn't fluttering wildly in alarm, I put on a good front of indifference. "On a daily basis, I interact with hackers, rapists, child molesters, and a serial killer's clean-up man. I've destroyed lives to save my family. My moral code is skewed– I have no room to judge."

"I don't know how to say it," Marcus bites out, red-rimmed eyes challenging me to force him to say the words out loud. "It's *bad*."

"Did you murder someone?" I throw out there, knowing goddamn well he didn't.

"No, Regina." Marcus is properly horrified.

"Then it's not as bad as you think it is."

Laughing, Marcus scrubs his face with his palms. "If that's your moral measure, you're a different person than the one I first met." Flopping backward to lie on the ground, Marcus hides his eyes by resting his forearm over his face. "Something evil was unleashed in me while Ezra was hurting you."

"You mean raping me." I figure if I point it out enough, I'll become desensitized to it and someone else will finally acknowledge it.

"You're going to hate me," Marcus warns, voice wavering with shame. "So many thoughts were going through me. I felt so powerless to help you. I knew exactly what was going on. I was resting against the door, with my face pressed to the metal. I couldn't hear, but I could feel when you pounded on the door."

"Jesus," flows in a hissing sound from between my clenched teeth, as I relive the horrific moment as if it's happening in the now.

"Powerless. Terrified. Guilty. Ashamed."

"Why ashamed?" I can't seem to connect the pieces as to why Marcus is so distraught.

"I was imagining what was happening…" he whispers softly, every word harder to hear than the last. "I was aroused– I came."

"Were you reliving what happened to you?"

"No," he admits hesitantly. "I pretended I was involved."

"You mean in my place?" Marc's animalistic groan has me going in another direction. "Ezra in my place, and you in his?"

"No, Regina." Marcus sits up quickly, moving so fast he seems to blur to my tired eyes. "I envisioned it was me raping you… and I got off on it."

"Oh."

"Oh, she says oh," Marcus murmurs in disgust. "I sickened myself. While you were showering Ezra off your skin, I was puking my guts out in Dexter's room. When you came out of the bathroom to find me sitting on the sofa, I could smell you in the room and I was hard. That is why I refuse to have sex."

"As punishment?"

"I'm sick– I can't stop thinking about it." Marcus jumps to his feet, doing the tantrum routine again, tearing at hanks of his hair. "This isn't the first time I've fantasized about it, Regina."

"Fantasized about what?" I know what, but I need him to say it out loud.

Glaring down at me, Marc's chest rises and falls rapidly. "Overpowering someone and taking what I want while they struggle, and having both of us get off on it."

"Who first? Ezra?" I guess.

"No." Marcus closes his eyes, lashes damp from tears. "Never Ezra, no matter what he did to me." Pacing away with his back to me, he admits the truth. "Only two people– Jamie and you."

"Fantasy?" The slope of Marc's shoulders is answer enough. "There is a difference between fantasy and reality. Do you want to pick a random person out and violate them?"

"NO!" Marcus bellows a denial. "I'm not a monster. I-I-I– Jamie would frustrate me so much, I'd lie in bed, wondering how much he'd allow before he said no and pushed me away. I finally did one day, touched his cock, and it was a no. I did back off, but I kept wondering what would have happened if I hadn't. Would Jamie have given in?"

"I think…" I try to put this into words so I don't sound like I'm saying what Marcus needs to hear. "I think it's only natural to think that about an unrequited love."

"As soon as you moved into Misery Castle, I snuck into your room and watched you sleep." Marc's admission stuns me. "I wanted to take you away from Jamie. Later, when I was in the hallway and I saw you in the passageways, it took everything in me not to chase you through the passageways… and once I caught you."

"Oh," I repeat in a tone that belies the tumultuous emotions I'm experiencing. "That explains our first few times. The hard bang on the sofa, and the pseudo-rape on the hood of the Spyder."

"You think?" Marcus spits sarcastically, glaring down at me. "I'm sick. I… there's no fix for me. After your rape, it kept playing out in my head. You were at your most vulnerable, and a part of me knew I could exploit it. Sickened with myself, I couldn't touch you at all."

"Maybe you not touching me, maybe you being hyper-focused on the fantasy, it has strengthened the need."

Marcus flashes me a *get real* look. "I never want to hurt you– I love you. I want to care for you, hold you, and make you happy, so it makes these sick fantasies worse. When you found me on the dock… I had gone up there to jerk off while playing it out in my head, because it was private. You caught me at a raw moment."

"It's all fantasy, right?" Leery, I watch Marc's body language for cues.

"Give me some credit, Regina." Rage radiating off him, Marcus picks up a fallen branch, then pitches it through the trees. "The thought of doing that for real makes me sick to my stomach. I feel like a monster for these evil thoughts, because I know how traumatizing it is to be on the receiving end. *Never* could I do it in actuality."

"After… while Ezra was still inside me, he praised me." Taking a deep breath, I finally understand what Ezra had said. "Ezra said he unleashed a kink in me, and it complemented yours perfectly. Ezra said, and I quote, *you're perfect for him*."

Gazing down at me with confusion, Marcus is so lost in shame that he doesn't realize there is a healthy solution to *our* problem. This is about both of us.

Flowing to my feet, I yank my t-shirt back into place and tug my jeans up in the back. In preparation for what's to come, my heart is beating out of my chest in a combination of anticipation and fear.

With a deep breath, I take the first step, and then another, and another, moving faster and faster, using the moonlight to pave my way as I flow deeper into the woods. "If you can catch me, you can take me!" echoes off the trees.

Footfalls thudding in time with the pants of breath escaping my parted lips, I dodge fallen branches and upraised roots. Marcus is silent, but I can sense him stalking me.

In a primal dance of predator versus prey– the hunter and the hunted –I force Marcus to earn it. I force him to chase me, just as Syn and Ezra said I should. Words hold many meanings, and this is what they both meant.

Enlivened, eyes wide from the adrenaline rushing through me veins, I run faster and faster, leaving responsibilities and obligations far behind me. Morals. Ethics. Societal standards of normalcy. I leave the rules behind and make my own.

Marcus and I turn into the very core of our natures. Animals running on instinct. If a male needs to mate, he has to prove to the female he's the strongest, fastest, and most potently virile.

In the woods, there is no measure featuring height, weight, breast size, and facial beauty. The male doesn't decide the female is worthy based on vapidness. The female decides based on if the male is capable of taking care of her and their offspring.

Survival.

Dominants as strong as Marcus are closer to primal beings, running on instinct, but it's considered deviancy by polite society, and it's been filling him with shame.

A thick arm hooks my waist, but I sidestep, causing Marcus to careen into a tree. Laughing with delight, I hop over a root, with Marc's growl echoing through the woods.

Marcus isn't a rapist, any more than I'm a victim. We're unleashing our primal selves.

Ducking a split-second before I nearly decapitate myself on a pine bough, fear of maiming floods endorphins in my veins. "C'mon, old man– is that the best you got?"

Doubling back, tracks where Marcus slid in the wet leaves are highlighted in the moonlight. "City boy," I taunt, eyes flicking around in the silence. "Had enough, have ya?" Loping back in the direction of the park, I glance around unsurely, wondering where Marcus disappeared.

"Wha– ugh!" Falling face-first into a bush, a hand is wrapped around my ankle. Crawling from his hiding place, Marcus continues to tug me toward him. Leaves and pine needles embed in my hair and back as I fight his hold. After dragging me across the forest floor, Marcus crawls up my body, otherwise silent except for his breathless gasps.

Hovering over me, Marcus gazes down with victory glowing from his amber eyes.

Regina Regal is not easy prey.

Pausing a few heartbeats, warring with impatience, I wait for Marcus to believe I've surrendered. When a look of rapture etches across his features, I move quickly. Flipping from my back, wiggling out from beneath him, I lunge to my hands and knees, trying to get the leverage I need to leave the ground and take off in a run.

Hands grip my ankles, fingers wrapping in my jeans, to the background soundtrack of Marc's sadistic laughter. As my jeans slip off, the hands find stronger handle holds. T-shirt jerked from the back, the collar hooks across my neck, thankfully ripping before it strangles the life out of me.

Struggling, my heel kicks out to connect with Marc's sternum. Grip loosening, I use it to my advantage to crawl a few feet away. Regaining his strength, Marcus crawls up my body, hands grabbing whatever they can reach to still me.

A palm runs across my hair in a soothing motion, then fingers bite in to twist the strands. Wrenching my head backward, Marcus is riding my back, heavy weight pinning me to the ground. "I win," he murmurs with levity, breath brushing the shell of my ear.

"I'm cutting my hair again," I warn, hating how it's always used against me.

Yanking to this side of pain, Marcus releases a sadistic chuckle. "No, you're not. As long as you grow your hair, I'll grow mine."

"Fucker," I snarl, hating how he's got me between a rock and a hard place. "I love your hair when it's wild."

"I know," is murmured with arrogance into my ear. "I caught you– now I get to have you." With one hand controlling me by the hair, the other yanks my jeans down my hips in a rough, jerking motion.

I don't fight Marcus like I did Grant during rage-sex. For me, this is more play than anything. It's meant to be thrilling and fun, not wounding and emotionally painful. Panting, my pussy clenches in anticipation, longing to be filled by Marcus– to be taken by Marcus.

The metal-on-metal sound of a zipper lowering has every muscle in my body locking up. A moan spills from my lips, remembering how Marc's cock always has to fight to enter me. It's a pleasure edged in pain.

Slowing down and backing off, the Marcus who's erupted these past few months rears his sweet head, and now is not the time for a reluctant lover.

"Fuck me!" I shout. "Force that goddamn mammoth cock of yours into my pussy– make it hurt!" Clenching my fists around a wad of wet leaves, I draw in large gasps of air. "Take it. Take it. Take it. Take me. Take– AHHHH!"

Writhing, knees sliding on the ground from the force, Marcus shoves his dick in to the hilt, and I swear I can taste it on the back of my tongue. Blazing heat tears through my crotch, the pain instantaneously blooming into pleasure as my mind gets off on the force of the act.

Animalistic grunts fill the night sky, woodland creatures call back. Rough, Marcus takes me like an animal. On my hands and knees, his hips bruise my ass as he unleashes his raw potential.

Yanking my head backward by the hair, my neck arches as far as it can without injuring me. Marcus presses his lips beneath my ear, whispering menacingly. "He took you against the door– your fists and knees kept knocking, mirroring my movements. You kept sliding, struggling to stay upright… I pretended it was me taking you– it felt so real."

The more Marcus speaks, the harder his cock turns, throbbing a wicked tattoo inside my body. "I wanted to watch you fuck Ezra with the strap-on, because it was the only way my mind could handle me living vicariously through you. I can't even fantasize about taking back what he stole from me… but I know you didn't make it hurt, you didn't take your power back."

"I didn't want you to stay, because I didn't want you to feel as I did watching Katya suck you off," is torn from my throat before the words even register in with my mind. "Ezra and I played, not punished."

"I know," Marcus growls into my ear, sounding wicked pissed. "I fantasized about what I wished it had been as I sat in the hallway, listening to your moans flowing through the door." Teeth sink into my shoulder, biting deep enough to draw blood. Snarling, Marcus gnaws on my flesh.

The burn and sting of the wound coalesces with the uncomfortable fullness in my pussy, flipping a switch where pain is felt as pleasure. Pounded me from behind, the flesh on my knees and elbows is sloughed off.

"One day… we're going to do this for real when you least expect it," Marcus warns, hand releasing my hair. "I need your permission now– I need to know you understand, not just in theory but also in practice."

Lost in the sensation of Marc's hands roaming my breasts, I'm too far gone to answer, let alone contemplate what he's asking of me. "Harder," is a thready sound released from my throat. "Pound my pussy harder– prove you want it. Want me."

"AH!" A shrill scream fills the night, and it takes seconds of hearing the sound to realize it's emanating from me. *Thwack!* Marcus swats my pussy again, hand hitting harder than the first time, fingernail accidentally scratching my clit. “That’s not what I meant.”

“Answer the question, Regina.” Deep animalistic grunts reverberate against my back as the cock deeply rooted inside me jerks. “Hurry!”

“Yeah– whatever. You have my permission.” In a lust-fog, chasing the pleasure of release, I don’t realize what I’m committing to. “Oh, God. Marc, I’m gonna come…”

Writhing in a mass of arms and legs and body fluids, Marcus releases nearly a year’s worth of pent-up frustration and I syphon it off him.

Gasping for air, I collapse to the ground, with Marcus landing heavily on top of me. My tits are getting tore up from the ground, but I’m entirely too blissed out to give a shit. Flopping off me, Marcus has the ground moving beneath me. An arm returns, grabbing a hold of my hip, then I’m yanked onto my back. Now my bare ass is getting the pine needle treatment.

Sighing, I stare up at the stars twinkling overhead through the canopy of trees. “We should go camping.”

A second later, Marcus is laughing so freely, nocturnal birds take to the sky. Body quaking with laughter, I fear he’s losing his sanity.

“What?” I slur, feeling more than insulted. “You wouldn’t want to go camping with me? Too much of a city boy? I haven’t been since my parents were alive– I’ll just take my kids then.”

“It’s not–” Gasping, holding his side, Marcus thinks he’s a comedian. “You don’t realize… Oh, God. I have a stitch in my side… Camping–” high-pitched giggles erupt out of a grown-ass man, and I’m floored.

“There’s a tent in the woods surrounding Shadow Haven.” Marcus pauses to catch his breath. “And I pray to God you never see the inside of it.”

“You mean the one Faith had her sixteenth birthday party in?” Mind wandering backward in time, I vaguely remember it. It was the last time I saw the pink-cheeked Faith before she turned into the sadist known as Syn. “Whitt forced me to take him to Faith’s party so he could see Ezra. At the time, I thought nothing of it, but now I realize it was filled with Gwen Meyer’s spawn. Ezra has a group photo from that night in his office.”

“That tent. Ah–” Marcus sighs deeply, relaxed after his release and laughing fit. “That was Ezra and Cort’s love shack. They lost their virginity there.”

"Oh! Well, I meant like a campground. Or maybe we could pitch a tent at Serenity Lake, unless it's too painful for you."

"I'd like that." Too exhausted to move, Marc's pinky finger reaches out to hook mine, instead of just holding my hand.

"Was this…" I tread carefully, fearing the response. "Was this what you needed?"

"I– uh, I don't want to hurt you, Regina."

"Just tell me," I demand in a calm tone. "No pussyfooting around. No miscommunications. I need to know where we stand. I need to know if this was what you needed to get us back on track."

"Truth?" Marcus pauses, probably hoping I'll stop him. "This was fun, and I *loved* every deviant second of it, but only something a bit more realistic will feed the need."

"Are you going to be able to have normal sex– well, not normal, but you know what I mean." I wait for my heart to be broken.

"I have said it, and I've showed you countless times," Marcus warns. "So stop doubting me. I want you. I love you. I lust for you. I want to connect with you emotionally, mentally, spiritually, physically, and sexually. I plan on giving you my all. But we have roadblocks in the way, and until they're gone, it's going to be difficult."

Reading between the lines, I smother the need to go irrational female by screaming and crying in a fit agony and betrayal. "Not to be a hypocrite, but I cannot stand by and watch you with Katya. I can't, Marcus. That's a hard limit. I know it's ridiculous to give an ultimatum. If you touch another woman besides me, from this moment forth, we're done."

"I vow that will *never* be revisited. I more than heard you on that subject." Marcus rolls to the side, facing me, then rests his palm over my heart. "Jamie is a nonissue between us. I know Cortez is difficult for you to swallow."

"In practice, not in theory," I tease to lighten the mood, earning the resulting chuckle I was going for.

"If we've already been intimate with a person–"

"Besides Katya," I interject.

"Besides Katya," Marcus agrees. "If we've already been intimate with a person, it shouldn't be a betrayal, and we will revisit this conversation if it's too hard to handle in practice. However, I can't just let Cortez go. I am his master. He has come to depend on me. Until Ezra steps up to the plate and takes his partner in hand, I will always be there to catch Cortez should he fall. It's my duty. I would be a monster to release my submissive of over a decade when he so badly needs someone to guide him. This isn't some scene in a dungeon– this is reality, Regina."

"As long as I know you want me, that you'll support me, and give me your time, I can accept that." *For now*, I add silently. "To be revisited at a later date."

"Handshake?" Marcus puts out his hand, smirking slyly as he quotes me from long ago.

Moving quickly, I lick the seam of his lips, asking for permission to sneak inside. On a moan, our tongues mingle, the eroticism of the act slickened by saliva. "No, with body fluids," I quote him back.

The shrill cry of Marc's cellphone dissolves the warmth of our reunion. "It's Ezra," he murmurs hesitantly as I crawl off him.

"Answer it– it's probably an emergency." To the background noise of Ezra panicking about a media crisis, I try my best to get all the leaves and pine needles out of crevices they don't belong. After righting my clothing, I trek back to the park, listening to Marc forming a game plan along the way. Ezra finishes his fret session just as we enter my driveway.

"The daily edition of the paper was just delivered."

"At four in the morning?" I look at my doorstep, confused.

"No, to distributors." Marcus holds the front door open, allowing me to enter first. His voice changes pitch, lowering so he won't wake anyone in the house. "The local news is going to run the front-page story during their five a.m. newscast, which means it will go out to global media outlets."

"What could be so bad?" My t-shirt is stripped off my filthy body the instant my feet hit my bedroom carpet.

"Christ." Marc's tugging at his hair again, so I know we won't be sharing a nap or eating breakfast together with Ella. He's on calm Ezra and Cortez duty. "Well, the truth is out, spun to make Adelaide look like a victim."

"About their dissolved betrothal?" Head jerking, for the life of me, I can't figure out why that would make the newspaper.

"Spun to look like adultery, betrayal, hedonism, and hidden offspring… The real truth about Katya." Marcus slumps to the foot of my bed, head bowed, hands laying limply on his thighs in utter defeat. "Ade named the victims, which is illegal. The article points out Ava's paternity. Due to Ava's age, the timing proves Ezra is the one who raped Katya. With the names and relationships to their perpetrator released, it also proves Ezra and Cortez are first cousins."

"And Adelaide definitely said they were partners." Falling into a chair, I just stare at Marcus in silent horror. "This is the Ade I know, the one I avoid. I've tried to speak to her, to get her to see reason, but she's off the rails. Once I befriended Ezra, she cut me off."

"Regina," Marcus cries out. "It's like being victimized twice, but on a global scale. The victims' names are never released for a reason. It was public knowledge that Raymond Hunter kidnaped and sexually assaulted two minor children and two adults. Their names were released in Ade's article."

"This is not good." Exhausted in every way possible, I'm on the verge of passing out.

"Remember when I said it's different for us, because we aren't normal folks. Well, Ezra is a media darling, who was just outed for having a bisexual, triad relationship with his rape victim and first cousin, with their twelve-year-old daughter named as well."

"The fallout will reach every facet of our lives," I realize, horrified.

"Precisely." Marcus falls to his back on the mattress, talking up at the ceiling. "Well, there goes any chance of me sitting on the bench."

Feeling sick to my stomach with worry, I try to lighten the mood. "After the next judge is elected, Boyd and I could join forces and ruin his career. That would give you another chance."

"District attorney, remember?" Marcus points at his chest, but he's grinning. "Go ahead– just do it without my knowledge so I can plead ignorance."

Chapter Forty-Two

Fate and Kristal are haunting the guesthouse, getting their primp on, but I can tell they're avoiding me for some reason. Reaching down, I pluck the invitation to Kayla and Aaron's wedding off the dining room table. After fingering the expensive cardstock, I tap the corner to my lips, trying not to freak the hell out.

This event will be a test of my emotional fortitude. Not only have I never been to an event, been to an event as a Whittenhower, I've never set foot on Shadow Haven's property. As hypocritical as it sounds, especially when Marcus has had to watch Whitt and me, I'm terrified of watching Marcus with his wife.

I've struggled to voice my thoughts to my therapist without giving too many secrets away– which, let me tell you, it makes receiving actual therapy impossible.

I fear the moment I lay eyes on Diane Holden, the red wash of fury will descend. I'm doing better, but I've never met the woman who took Marcus when he was still considered a minor and twisted until he no longer recognized himself. Don't get me started on all the mommy issues Ezra has…

"Ah!" A soft chuckle has me jumping out of my skin. "So you are a woman after all– I had to ask Whitt and Dad just to be sure." My son comes to stand next to me, both of us staring at the invitation.

"How'd you get here?" Turning, my eyes drink in the sight of my not-so baby boy. "I thought we still had another twenty minutes." Smirking privately, my eyes cut down the hallway toward the bedrooms. "Your sister isn't ready yet."

"Albert dropped me off on his way to run an errand." Niel plucks the card from my hand, then it disappears in an inner pocket of his jacket. "He'll be back shortly."

"A woman?" I back the conversation up. "What does that mean?"

Tight-lipped as to not insult me, a few chuckles spill from Niel's mouth. "You're angsting. I thought people grew out of that, but you are… and you're wearing a pretty dress."

"You think I look pretty?" Blushing, I run my palms along my thighs, smoothing the violet silk. Groaning, I realize what I've done. When will my inner girl stop seeking validation from men?

"Wow, you look so handsome." Niel and I have firm boundaries, but he has no problem humoring me as I fiddle with the lapel of his jacket, then straighten his tie. "My baby boy is going to be fourteen soon– I can't believe it."

Eyes the same shade of green as my own roll in response, delighting me because it means Niel is still a boy, even with his adult mind. "Yeah, I look big now, but I just got some bad news from the doctor."

"What?" I gasp, heart beating out of control. "It was just a yearly physical– are you okay?"

"Shit! That came out wrong." Niel reaches up to pat my hands, then tugs them away from where I was wrinkling his jacket with my death-grip. "They did this X-ray thing on my hands to see how much I'll grow, something about how close the spaces are between my finger bones. Anyway, mine look like an adult's, so I won't grow more than an inch or two."

"Oh," I sigh in relief. "Hit puberty early, end up watching your peers bypass you. I get it."

"No, you don't." Niel smirks at me, tugging a chair away from the table to sit down. "It means I'll be looking up to my mother for all eternity."

"Now who's angsting," I tease, joining him. "That's not a bad thing. I am rather smart, and I give good advice."

"I meant it literally, not figuratively." The piss-pot grins at me, showcasing his Whittenhower dimples. "I'll be shorter than Dad."

"Well, you'll give good hugs." I try to find the bright side. "Hard to hug a person who is a head taller. I'd know– nothing like having everyone's face pressed into my boobs."

"You're my mom– your boobs don't exist for me." Blushing, Niel pauses, and he looks so much like Grant in this moment my heart mends then breaks. Niel looks exactly like me, but it's the mannerisms– the shyness Grant used to exhibit but died out as he aged. I hope Niel never loses it. "Ava is going to be as tall as Ezra, and he's the same height as you."

Muscles locking up, I've been waiting to have this conversation. I spend a lot of time walking on eggshells around my son. I may have grown him in my womb, birthed him, and fed him from my body, but for a formative decade of his life, we were apart. I give Niel respect by not butting in where it's none of my business. He's a grown man in my eyes, and I shouldn't meddle. But this is a conversation we have to have, and I'm glad my son is the one to open the line of communication.

"Ezra mentioned you were hanging out with his daughter." Ezra's spawn terrify me. I've seen Zane on three occasions– Torian too. Boyd loves to show his nephew and son how to torment the masses. We haven't spoken about it, but I know Ava will be groomed by MdJ for very bad things.

"Ava's interesting to be around– I like hearing about her hometown in Pennsylvania." Niel's innocent act is all Grant. But it is an act.

Deciding to smash those eggshells. "My question to you, son… is Ava a friend you wish to have, or one you were ordered to befriend? Is a goddamn betrothal already in the works?"

One corner of my son's mouth lifts, curling up as if he finds me cute– that patronizing horseshit must be written on a male's genetic code. But the confidence bleeds into embarrassment, causing Niel's face to bloom nearly as red as his hair.

Patient, I'm a mother– I wait my son out, refusing to drop my gaze.

"The latter," Niel mutters hesitantly, knowing the truth will gut me. "You know I can't discuss that with you, Mom. But I don't mind the girl. Ava gets along well with Ella and Prissy– Whitney *loathes* her."

"It's probably mutual, no doubt, if the girl takes after Ezra. I never wanted you to go through what your dad did, Niel." I tug a paper napkin from the holder on the table, and begin shredding it as an outlet for my emotions. My therapist taught me this coping skill. So much better than drawing blood to release the energy. "I want you to fall in love organically."

"I will. Ava's really young–"

"So are you–"

"Not by MdJ standards." My son takes after me evidently, loving to interrupt.

"Have you gone to a founders meeting yet? Shit!" My palm is covering my mouth before the words reach my ears. "Have you met Zane and Torian? Sorry. I shouldn't press."

"Mom." Niel sighs, sounding frustrated and exhausted by me. Moods shifting quickly, a naughty light shines from his eyes. "Those guys." Chuckles bubble up from his chest. "Are hilarious. There's a shortage of eligible girls, and they don't go to Hillbrook yet. So they say I'm hoarding Whitney, Ella, and Prissy… and now Ava. They say they're my harem."

"That Torian." Rolling my eyes, a montage of how many times that little charmer flirted with me while we ruined people's lives flashes through my mind. He always found a way to seek Ella, and flirt with her too. He even flirted with Fate, and she's his aunt. On the other hand, Zane seems to be obsessed with cookies, not girls. The boy is just as scary as Boyd when it comes to wreaking havoc, but he glows when Fate and Ella bake him cookies.

"It's admirable that you'd protect your family… so I take it you have been to meetings, then."

"Yes, I've been to several, but I can never discuss what happens at the meetings with you. Yes, a betrothal contract between Ava and me is being negotiated, but I understand why."

"Why?" jumps out of my mouth before I can stop it.

Chuckling, Niel looks and sounds older than he is. "It's a good thing Whitt is gay, because what a twisted family tree we have. I understand this, Mom. Sure, I'll fall for a girl someday. But it's best if we both aren't ignorant. Because if we were, we may end up committing a sin."

"I'd suggest you not date a girl by the size of her family's bank account, and you should be fine against matters of incest."

"That's not how it works." Our eyes hitch to the side at the squeak of Ella's door opening. "I was raised in this culture, and I will marry into it, and my children will be born into it. I don't want to marry a waitress and give her a Cinderella story. I'm not built like that– I love all the bullshit you hate."

My mind flits to Katya and her Ezes. She's a fish out of water, struggling to breathe. She's my priority. Ezra may issue me edicts from MdJ, but I have one tasks that never ends, one Syn gave to me via all members of MdJ– keep Katya with Ezra.

Ezra assures me Ava fits into their lifestyle flawlessly, but Katya doesn't. She's insecure, and doesn't feel as if she belongs. I can see Niel's point, which means I agree with MdJ. Wealth isn't about money– it's a culture. Someone outside of the culture would be eaten alive. If you love someone, you won't drop them in with the sharks circling.

The media storm has been torturous, and I've tried to speak with Katya numerous times. She doesn't trust me, and I don't blame her. Worse, she just found out she's pregnant with twins, not knowing if they belong to Ezra or Cortez. She's in so deep, she's drowning, and I'm terrified she'll run back to Pennsylvania, leaving me at the mercy of MdJ.

Now it's my turn to see if I can survive an event thrown by the one-percenters. I know I can survive it, but I'll never thrive in it. That's the distinction. I belong here, no matter how I was raised, but I don't want to belong here.

There is a difference between Katya Waters and me. I know the rules, but refuse to adhere to them. Katya doesn't. One of us will look brave for refusing to bend to their idiotic rules of polite society, while the other will look like a bumbling fool and will feel humiliated and bullied. I've been there, and do feel the stinging bit of insecurity, so I plan on sticking to Katya like a fly on fly paper today to help her traverse this landmine of a wedding.

As one, Niel and I rise from our seats as Ella wanders into the dining room– Niel, because that's what gentlemen do, and me, because I think it's rude how women are told to sit and be pretty. We share a side look and grin at the ridiculousness. No doubt, Whitt has told Niel all about how I used to bitch and moan when Whitt had to take etiquette classes as a boy.

Stepping around the table, I reach out for my daughter. "Ready for me to pull your hair up?" Ella's suffering from the same thing as Niel. Early puberty. Girls usually go through it before boys, so they're both too big for their ages. Ella won't get any taller either. But unlike Niel, Ella will be average height.

"You look lovely," Niel purrs in a rehearsed voice, but I know he's being genuine to his sister, because she does look beautiful in her frilly pink dress and kitten heels.

"Thanks." Preening underneath the praise, Ella glows like the sun. Rolling my eyes, I take the brush out of my daughter's hand– like mother, like daughter. Always feeling pride and happiness when people with a Y-chromosome find us worthy.

"Up on the stool," I order. I may not be girly, but my daughter is. Trying to be a good mother, and wishing to spend time doing things with Ella that she enjoys, I've learned I'm pretty good at knotting hair. Finding makeup and nails tedious, because I suck at it and end up making Ella look worse, I chose her hair instead.

Glowing with pride, I braid Ella's hair in an intricate design as she sits on a stool at the kitchen island. My daughter shivers every time my fingertips brush her neck, and winces when I pull a stray hair. All the while Niel watches on, and I am bloated with happiness by being surrounded by my children.

"You're really good at that, Mom," Niel praises me, but this time I don't get all swoony. Ashamed– I feel ashamed at the reason I'm so good at fixing Ella's hair.

"Saw a bunch of tutorials on my Facebook feed," I lie. I mean, I did, but that's not why I'm good at it. "Fate loves it when I braid her hair too."

"Uh-huh," Niel isn't buying the shit I'm selling, which means Whitt is too dang chatty and not being age-appropriate with my son.

My, "I like knots," has Niel choking on laughter, and Ella looking confused.

Okay, so I learned to braid hair after failing repeatedly at Kinbaku and Shibari. I'm Regina Regal, and I have to excel at everything. It may have taken me a billion hours to perfect it, because I'm not the most creative person on the planet, but I did. Now I'm fabulous at braiding hair into intricate designs.

A car door bangs out front. "Whitt's here!" Niel announces, walking toward the front door. "Are you guys almost ready?"

"I thought we were going with Kristal and Fate?" I mutter in confusion, sliding the last of the pins into Ella's hair. With a swat to her butt, I help her down from the stool.

"Kristal and Fate were leaving when I arrived." I can and can't read my son, but he is definitely looking like a sneaky snake.

"What's going on?" Too curious for our own good, Ella and I follow Niel out the front door, each having a different reaction to a stretch limo sitting in our driveway.

Ella sees the limo as Cinderella's carriage, whisking her away to a magical wedding celebration. For me, it feels like Charon the ferryman is ushering me onto a boat to transport me over the river Styx to the Gates of Tartarus, where Hades awaits.

Whitt flows out of the limo like a tuxedo-clad dream, and Ella flows inside with a girly squeal of delight.

With the impressionable ears safely tucked inside the confines of the car, I have no issue speaking like a sailor. "What the fuck is going on?" I demand of Whitt and Niel.

Hands outstretched, palms up, like he's talking down a jumper, Whitt tries to reason with me. "These events are high-profile, Queen. We have to arrive and attend as a family."

"I have the feeling that means something different in these circles," I mutter underneath my breath. "Why?"

Now it's Whitt's turn to look sheepish. "Aaron and Kayla's wedding is a big deal. Aaron was named with Ezra and Cortez, and you know how obsessed the media has become with Ezra. For fuck's sake, they did a 20/20 special on him last week, and the wedding was mentioned."

"Why do I get the sneaking suspicion that car is filled with a bunch of blue-eyed, blond-haired Whittenhowers?"

Shaking, I try to hide my nervousness with bravado. Since I was eighteen, they've tried to force me to join the family. It's getting harder and harder by the day not to give in and move back to Misery Castle. Grant keeps me firm in my resolve. I'm not moving back until he does– it only seems fair, and it keeps me in my own house.

I've avoided reconnecting with them, even though I so badly want to, because seeing them would weaken my resolve and I'd be drawn back in.

"Mom." Niel laughs at me, the one who has continually tried to maneuver me where he wants me. "Let's you and me add a bit of ginger to the vanilla." Then the boy swaggers to the car, disappearing inside.

"My son set me up," I mutter in defeat. Not a question, a resolute fact.

"Of course, he did." Whitt presses his palm to the small of my back, herding me toward the car as I drag my heels. "Niel was sent as a diversion while we loaded up the limo with girls who take way too fucking long to get prettied up."

"I'm scared," I admit, feeling vulnerable and weak. I know they're all in there– every single person with Whittenhower blood flowing in their veins is in that limo, except for Grant. He should be with me for this.

"I know." Whitt is truly sympathetic to my plight. "They miss you– you miss them. So let's rip off that Band-Aid, shall we?"

"We shall," I mimic Whitt's tone. "Since I have no say in it."

There is no elegant way for a woman as large as me to crawl into a limousine, especially while wearing a dress and heels. Lungs burning, I hold my breath to keep my voice from quivering, then I let it out in a rush.

"Hello, Whittenhowers and Prestons." Refusing to be a coward like Grant, I roll my eyes up to take them all in as I enter the car.

Elegant, dripping in wealth, two young ladies are flanked by two grown women, with Daniel sitting next to Niel… and Ade turned to the side, refusing to acknowledge my presence.

"Sit here, Mom." Niel slides down to make space for Whitt and me between him and Ella, like we're a nuclear family. Settled in, I gaze across the large car and hold my breath to keep the tears at bay.

If I ignore the hatred wafting from Ade, they all look so goddamn happy to see me, like it was only yesterday we saw each other last. Silent and in awe, but deliriously happy. The last time I saw Priscilla, Katie, and Whitney, we ate breakfast together as a family with Daniel, Grant, Whitt, and Niel. Then the horrific happened, and I never saw them again until now.

Then there's Ade, who's avoided me since Whitt brought Niel to my house the first time and we had it out. The few times I contacted her afterward, she ignored me. After Ade found out I helped Ezra with Katya, she vented how I betrayed her. She's since written me off, saying I was dead to her. No matter what, right or wrong we've done, I miss Ade.

They're waiting for me to say or do something, and the silence stretches on.

Eyes fusing to the one I've never met, I try to moderate my voice to hide my emotions. "You must be Prissy." I don't reach to shake her hand as Albert backs the limo out of my driveway.

"Wow!" The tiny pixie-like girl grins up at me, dimples on display. "Aunt Regina is just as everybody described."

Aunt Regina guts me, and there is no hiding a betraying tear from slipping down my cheek. Surreptitiously wiping it away, the ice has been broken.

"It's so good to see you, Regina." Swathed in a designer gown that probably cost more than my car, Katie leans across the space to give me a real hug. Not a fake pat with an air kiss. The curvy woman clutches me to her bosom and squeezes. "I've missed you so much," is whispered in my ear, and she means it.

Unable to speak, or else a sob will release, all I can do is hold the woman back who was supposed to become my sister-in-law… but I ended up married to her nephew instead. Knowing how upset I am, Katie doesn't make any demands. She holds me longer than what is polite, then pulls away with a huge grin on her face.

"Daughter," Priscilla draws out, moving in to take her own daughter's place. I'm enfolded in a mothering hug by the only woman other than my own who's held me with such affection and care.

Huffing in gulps of air, I try to keep my shit together as Priscilla leans back against the bench seat. I've been alone in this world since I was fourteen when my father died and my mother was diagnosed with cancer. My mother tried so hard to get me to see it from her perspective when Grant came nosing around. She wouldn't leave me alone in this world without a family, and finally let go once she thought I had one.

The Whittenhowers accepted me as I am, but both Grant's exit from the family and my own bullshit destroyed it. I tried to carve out a family of my own with Kristal and Fate, while pushing Ade away– I was in control and I didn't give them my heart and soul, so I could survive their losses someday.

It's too much, too soon after so long, and I don't know if I can emotionally handle it.

Moving down the line, I greet Whitney next. "You probably don't remember me–"

"I remember you, Aunt Regina." Whitney has a steel spine, I can sense it. No-nonsense demeanor, a stoic expression on her pixie face, and eyes seeing far too much. "We speak of you more than Uncle Grant."

We don't hug, because neither of us are that type of woman, and I do see Whitney as a grown woman, instead of a child. Needing to connect somehow, I shake her small hand, and she squeezes back instead.

"I've heard a lot about you." Most would assume it was from Ella, but my daughter doesn't enjoy being bossed around by her older cousin. "You're Niel's favorite subject." I earn an elbow to the ribs from my son for that.

"Since I have you trapped in a moving car," I issue as a warning. I lean forward to reach out to Ade, who's pretending she's not paying attention and as equally upset as I am. Refusing to be ignored, I grab her chin, relieved the bony woman isn't strong enough to break my hold.

Knowing it won't shock anyone in this car after living through the era of Jackson's affections, I kiss Ade on the lips, lingering because I've missed her that goddamn much.

Ade tries to snub me by shifting her eyes to the side, but my hold on her chin makes it so she can't hide the tears slipping down her cheeks. Drawing her into a hug, I whisper into her ear.

"Sometimes we have to do things we don't want to do, and it's seen as a betrayal," is my way of apologizing for hurting her feelings.

"Sometimes it doesn't matter when my future is on the line," Ade hisses back beneath her breath so no one else can hear.

"Or maybe," I suggest, holding Ade closer with my mouth pressed to her ear, "Or maybe someone is trying to drive a wedge between us, knowing we can't stop them."

I've often wondered if MdJ was blackmailing Ade in the way they do Diane and Daniel, with her not knowing of their existence. Just as it's my duty to keep Katya and Ezra together, Ade has been threatened with Wintercrest Asylum if she doesn't marry Ezra. MdJ is forcing me to hurt the only person I've ever seen as a sister in order to protect us all.

Watery blue eyes pop wide, staring at me in silent horror.

"Today is going to be difficult for both of us," I remind Ade, knowing she's not ignorant of my relationship with Marcus any more than I am of hers with Diane. "Our partners will be together as the Mistress and Master of Shadow Haven Estates, and we'll have to watch them from afar feeling like garbage."

"Truce." Ade smiles at me. "Just for the wedding, though."

"Deal." Smiling, I retake my seat, with everyone breathing a sigh of relief that Ade and I aren't spilling blood.

"Master Daniel," Albert calls from the driver's seat, causing two heads to turn in his direction, which amuses Niel to no end.

"Far too many Daniels in this car," Niel whispers out the side of his mouth in a teasing tone. "Albert has taken to calling me Prince Whittenhower to alleviate the confusion."

"Sure, that's why," I mouth back, earning myself a sadistic chuckle. "What does Albert call the mute?"

"Elder Whittenhower or simply Master." Niel leans forward, craning his neck to see what Albert and Daniel are discussing. Daniel's leaning halfway into the front through a small window.

The girls catch on first– Prissy and Ella are smooshing themselves to the window, with Whitney peeking out between them. "Niel," Whitney cautions, and my son reacts as if his leash has been pulled.

"What is it?" Niel squeezes in with the rest of the kids. "What's taking so long? Why are we stopped?"

Since the window behind me is unoccupied, I turn to see what's going on. "We're stopped in between the empty Green mansion and the gate to Shadow Haven," I muse.

Glued to his phone, Whitt answers all of our questions. "There are news vans and satellite trucks lining Crestview Drive." He points to the opposite side of the car where the kids are pressed up against the window. "There's a shit-ton of paparazzi trying to storm the gate to Shadow Haven as guests arrive. Paparazzi are climbing the wall and sneaking in through the woods, and there are helicopters with video and wide-angle lenses capturing everything."

"How the hell did they get past the security tower?" A feeling of ill-ease overpowers me. If The Gates can be infiltrated by the media outlets, there is no protection for our buildings downtown, Restraint, the brownstone, and especially my house resting unprotected just outside the wall.

"My guess," Albert answers me from the front. "When one of us entered, they crept in bumper-to-bumper so the guard couldn't stop them."

"This will have to go away at some point," I muse to myself. "Right? It can't be like this forever."

"These things come in waves," Katie answers, knowing better than anyone after being a politician's wife for fifteen years. "The next big news story will hit, and they will leave the Zeitlers and Holdens alone. But it's never really truly forgotten. If there is any more controversy in the future, it will be ten times worse than this."

What should have taken about five minutes has turned into nearly an hour of torturous small talk as we get stalked from the outside. We crawl at a snail's pace, enduring paparazzi taking photos through the tinted passenger windows, trying to see who's packed inside the car.

Albert comes to a rest at the front of Shadow Haven. The massive stone mansion looks miniscule compared to Misery

Castle, but it's meant to house a singular family. Not that the house is small– it's about fifteen of the size of mine put together.

A pair of medieval doors greet us, but I don't venture inside. Waiting for our family to exit the limo, I look around, ignoring the tightness wrapping around my heart.

This is the home Marcus shares with Diane.

I could ignore that fact if every surface wasn't dripping with white and pink floral arrangements and twinkling fairy lights screaming marital bliss.

Chapter Forty-Three

I growl at the night sky as the vultures circle overhead, "Jesus, I could never live with this." The loud *whomp* of rotor blades is deafening, added to the fact that the yard is enduring gale-force winds because of it. The extra staff employed for the event has spent most of their energy relocating chairs and decorations that zipped across the yard. Guests are being nice enough to place asses on seats to keep them from blowing away. All those pretty dresses and intricate hair styles are fucked.

Kayla took it in stride when her veil blew off her head and whipped Kat in the face– Katya was her maid of honor. The moment was humorous, but equally frustrating because it's not right to be invaded during your wedding ceremony.

"I hope we never have to experience this insanity." Daniel growls too, more frustrated than I am.

We all are equally terrified after experiencing the car ride from hell. I'm worried about a future that may never come to fruition, where my house is invaded. I have no large wall surrounding my community, a security guard at a gate, another wall surrounding my property, and another gate keeping everyone nice and safe. My house is a sitting duck. Empowerment isn't defensible with it rising high in the center of downtown Dominion.

Daniel's worried because he's higher profile, with more skeletons than Misery Castle has closets– and it has a lot of closets. The Whittenhowers would be decimated if they became a target of sensational news.

I stand on the back terrace, hiding while the reception takes place inside. The staff diligently removes all of the chairs from the ceremony space in the yard to set up for the dance floor. I stare up at the helicopter as it circles overhead and ignore Daniel. He won't let me out of his sight as the rest of the family enjoys themselves.

"Why haven't you gone inside?" Daniel smirks, revealing those same dimples all the Whittenhowers employ as weapons.

"It's a beautiful night," I reply pleasantly, refusing to go anywhere I may catch sight of Marcus and Diane together. Nothing is as horrific as watching Diane be escorted all over Shadow Haven on Marc's arm. They look like the ultimate power couple. Perfectly gorgeous in every single way, poised, wealthy, and powerful. The heiress and the politician hosting a wedding at their immaculate estate.

Now I *really* feel like a married man's mistress.

I could puke, hypocrite that I am. But then again, I'm not going around announcing I'm Whitt's wife. I hang onto my legal name of Regina Regal like a badge of honor, and only use Mrs. Whittenhower as an honorific.

Blond hair billowing around his sculpted face, "Ah, yes… the breeze is quite splendid this evening." Daniel's voice is dry with sarcasm as he straightens his tie.

Snorting, I almost choke. "You just made a joke– it was pretentious, but it was definitely a joke." We share a rare laugh.

"You do find yourself in the most precarious situation." Daniel answers his own question as to why I won't go inside. "Hiding from your partner's wife, I presume."

"I have no partner." Daniel and Diane are tighter than tight. I'm so not going there with him.

"You really have no reason to lie." Daniel is an instigator, but I guess the guy has to get his jollies off somehow. "Other than the fact that you'd create an apocalyptic scandal should your secrets ever be released." Daniel's words causes me to shudder, voicing the fears that have been hamster wheeling in my head all night.

"Don't you have someone else to bother? I know Niel wanted us to get along, but I doubt he meant as bosom buddies." The sarcastic tone flows nicely over the hurricane strength winds from the helicopter.

"I'm just waiting for someone," he pleasantly offers, as if he's babysitting me, which has warning alarms going off inside my mind.

"Wait for them elsewhere."

"Ah– finally! Here she is," Daniel announces grandly, causing my heart to drop to my feet. "Regina is most impossible to occupy, my dearest Diane." He kisses my nemesis on the cheeks, then disappears inside Shadow Haven's depths.

Breathing deeply, I close my eyes until I get a handle on my rampaging emotions. I know I'm the other woman, and I'm ashamed of that fact, even under our odd circumstances. The anger isn't due to jealousy, but rather Ezra's mommy issues and the way Marcus was captured and released to Olivia Fontaine by his own wife.

"Diane," my tone is tainted with hostility. The woman is spectacular, which has my insecurities blooming. *Why would Marcus want to be with me when he's married to Diane? Because he loves you, you idiot! Because Diane is a lesbian. No, you are not replacing a woman he can't have.*

Counting backward from twenty, I try to use techniques my therapist gave me to calm my rage. I once said, if I ever came face-to-face with Diane, I'd want to blow her head off with a shotgun. My fingers twitch in eager anticipation.

Marcus loved this woman when he married her. He truly did want to create a life with her– we've discussed how he was a traditional, religious man many times. Marcus proudly screamed to the world that Diane was his and he was hers. I can't compete with that…

The woman before me is in her late forties, yet she looks my age. Genetics, not surgical augmentation. Huge, alien-like gray eyes glitter with evilness. Silky white hair falls in a frothy wave around her shoulders and back. The hair is as unnatural as Diane's eyes, reminding me of spider webs or caterpillar silk. Her waiflike body is hidden by a pure white, gauzy dress. She looks ethereal, or like an angel, but pure evil radiates off her. I hate her because she is everything I am not, and everything Marcus ever wanted.

"The feeling is mutual, my dear," Diane's tinkling voice sings to me. It's the tone Ezra uses when he's pissed– glass grating on glass.

"I'm glad we can agree on something," I mutter snidely. Is this how teenage girls feel in high school? I never had a crush, or had to fight over a guy with other girls. It's so irrational, but I can't help this insane urge to annihilate Diane off the face of the planet.

Perfectly pouty lips curl up at the corners, as if Diane can read the thoughts scrolling in my mind. Adversaries, we stand on the woman's terrace overlooking her back lawn, eyes roving every inch of each other from toes to the top of our heads.

Evidently, neither one of us likes what we see, for varying reasons.

"Marcus was once in love with me, and Adelaide was once in love with you. So I'd say we're even, don't you agree?"

"Diane, I was hiding here for a reason," I remind her. "Out of respect for you, your home, and your family. I didn't want to rub myself in your face, so please extend the courtesy to me. Seeing you hurts me."

"How eloquently put, my dear." Yes, Diane is insulting me. "I only wished to speak to you where no ears could hear." Pausing for dramatic effect, the lady wants to see if I'll lose my shit. I'm positive word has gotten out about how quickly I can turn feral. "Thank you for trying to help my son."

"Even if it was to help Ezra catch and keep Katya?" Narrowing my eyes at the woman, "You confuse the piss out of me, Diane. I can barely stand the thought of Marcus touching you. Yet you would honestly be okay with your lover marrying your son?"

"It is a rather confusing notion, but not one I necessarily had any control over." Diane looks at me pointedly. "Daniel and are allies, and neither of us wishes for our children to be harmed in any way. Ezra does love Katya, but I did have my reasons for wanting to merge my family with the Whittenhowers."

"At the expense of Adelaide's happiness and mental health?" Deciding if there was one person on this planet who loves Ade more than me, it would have to be Diane. "Ade has avoided me to hide the changes in her personality. I just spent an hour trapped in a car with her, and she scares me. Ade is not in a good place."

Silver-dusted eyelids close and reopen so fast I almost think I imagined it. "I can say this with confidence, Regina, and I know you'll get the context. I believe there are several warring forces at play, and I'm powerless to stop it. You are correct in your estimation. Adelaide is not healthy, and I believe we both miss the young woman who was replaced with this unstable creature."

"Another thing we agree on," I mutter begrudgingly, not wanting to like the woman.

Diane gazes over my shoulder, expression turning wary. A split-second later, a possessive palm rests on the small of my back. With a sigh of relief, I lean back into Marc's comforting touch.

"The dancing is about to begin," Marcus announces, no doubt he had been eavesdropping and felt it time to intervene.

As if by Marc's command, the band begins to play, eclipsing the sound of the helicopter rotors swirling overhead.

“Thank you for asking, husband– I’d love to dance,” Diane says demurely, placing her hand on Marc’s forearm.

I’m not sure who Marcus was asking, but I find it a relief to get away from Diane. Guilt and shame are marvelous emotions. I spot Whitt near the entryway to the terrace, and make a beeline for him.

“Marcus. Diane.” I nod to each of them in turn, not meeting Marc’s gaze, then walk steadily to Whitt– I want to run, but it would be most undignified.

“Well, that wasn’t at all awkward,” I whisper in Whitt’s ear.

“There are at least ten awkward encounters occurring all over the incestuous Shadow Haven right this second.” Whitt and I share a chuckle at the ridiculousness our lives have turned into.

“Let’s hope the rest of the skeletons remain in our closets, or we’ll never be rid of that fucking flying wind machine.”

Undoubtedly having overheard our exchange, Daniel huffs a laugh underneath his breath as he walks by us with Priscilla on his arm.

“Shall we dance?” Whitt offers, not waiting for a reply. Then whisks me down the steps to the dais.

Swirling amongst the elite is similar to people-watching at Walmart, only on a grander scale. Classy versus trashy– shame shit, different location. They may be rich, but they have just as many problems as the common folks. The amount of infidelity, snide commentary, and dirty looks is better than watching Ella’s favorite reality programming.

Laughing it up, Whitt and I are having a better time than I imagined, as we point out deviant behavior by those who are above reproach– and here I find myself hypocritical.

“You should at least dance with Marcus once.” Whitt teases me after three songs.

“You should dance with Dalton,” I taunt, ignoring the fact that I can always sense where Marcus is located on the dance floor, purposefully turning before I catch sight of him. I will never forget Katya kneeling at his feet, and I will never put myself in a situation where I have to suffer with the memory.

“Queen.” Whitt sighs as if I exhaust him. “I may be out to the people who matter, but I cannot dance with a guy at an event filled with the press and a helicopter filming overhead. Besides, Dalton doesn’t want me that way.”

“The boy hasn’t taken his eyes off you since we entered the dance floor.” Squeezing slightly where my hand rests on Whitt’s shoulder, I try to lessen the dig that’s to come. “You know who you remind me of?”

“Who?” Whitt’s dimples appear, and I know he’s just making me say it out loud for my own benefit. He knows exactly who he’s acting like.

“Me– the disillusioned me who is in denial of her true feelings. You like Dalton, and he obviously likes you. Go for it!”

“I will negotiate terms.” The guy turns into a devious shit. It’s no wonder my son terrifies me when his biggest influences are Daniel and Whitt. “For the duration of your dance with Marcus, I will talk to Dalton.”

“Deal, but Marcus may not want to dance with me under the circumstances.” My voice quivers with a mix of nervousness and shame. Truth be told, I’m terrified of how I will feel being in Marc’s arms in such a public setting, and equally terrified at what will be mirrored in his eyes.

“Hmm… disillusioned is the perfect word to describe you.” Whitt teases, then catches someone’s eye over my shoulder.

Whitt gazes at me, smiling mischievously, then he leans in to bite my bottom lip. I’m sputtering a protest just as that possessive hand makes a reappearance at the small of my back. My eyes flutter shut with the touch, then snap back open when Whitt laughs.

“Laugh it up now, Whitt– you just wait and see how you feel when Dalton touches your naughty parts.” I taunt him and he laughs harder. “My eyelids going all droopy won’t be anything in comparison.”

“What is this I hear of naughty parts?” Marcus asks, smoothly drawing me into a dance that’s too close to be friendly. His hands traverse the landscape of my back and shoulders, with his nose skimming the column of my throat.

“I was trying to get Whitt to talk to Dalton.” Suddenly, I’m so nervous I can barely speak. Licking my dry lips, I find no relief from my cotton-mouth.

“They do like each other.” Marcus releases delighted laughter against my throat, not giving a shit that he’s touching me inappropriately for a happily married man– people are staring. “Look how shy they’re being.”

A smile flits along my lips as I watch Whitt and Dalton both shuffle from foot-to-foot while awkwardly trying to hold a conversation. The wallflower came with Roman, but hasn't found anyone else to interact with because he's hit every member of Restraint with his douchebaggery, except for Whitt and me.

The sensation of how right this feels to be in Marc's strong, supportive arms has my knees going weak. There's a subtle vibration on the small of my back where his palm is resting, and I take comfort in the fact that Marcus is feeling exactly as I am.

"Aww, that's a good boy," I murmur against Marc's cheek as I watch Whitt cross the floor to ask Katya for a dance. "Kat needs to feel welcome here. I know how it feels to be an outsider in a community of legacies."

"You belong here, Regina." Marcus pulls me tighter against his body, fitting us perfectly together. "In my arms." A nose glides down my cheek, then lips press beneath my ear. "You took my breath away when I saw you arrive. I so badly wanted to run down the front steps and stand by your side as your children exited the car."

"I'm being eaten alive with guilt and shame, Marcus," I warn, trying to put a few inches between us. "Don't make it worse."

"I know," Marcus breathes back to me like it's a secret, not allowing me to have any distance. "But I also know what's truly bothering you."

"Oh, yeah? What's that?" I challenge.

"Or rather, *who* is bothering you." Tugging me as close as humanly possible, I can feel the outline of every dip and groove in his body against mine. "The car ride here must have been a nightmare for you, with the one person who connects you all absent. It must have felt as if Jamie truly died."

"I don't– I can't…" Burying my face against the side of Marc's neck, I try to block out the world, even with the titters of gossip flowing around us from our obscene behavior.

"Regina," Marcus murmurs softly, causing me to glance up and find my pain mirrored in his eyes. "This has to be hurting Jamie–"

"Oh, no!" I cut Marcus off as I stare in horror at Ade. "This can't be good."

Weaving around party guests, Ade purposefully stalks through the crowded dance floor toward Katya, eyes wild with insanity and desperation. I don't bother stopping Ade– I run as fast as I can to the children. I grab for the tall, lithe towhead and yank her to my chest, covering her ears with my palms.

"Shh…" I murmur against the top of Ava's head. "Your mom's going to be okay– just don't listen, and don't believe anything you hear." Tears forming in my eyes, I feel for the precious child. Ava's had to deal with things no child should, with all the media coverage and the controversy over her conception.

I'm pleased my children have befriended her, as long as it's for friendship and not edicts passed down from on high. No little girl should see her mother humiliated in public, at her ancestral home no less.

"You have to fuck every person in this group– I think you add a whole new level to being a whore." Ade's voice rings out clearly above the din of the band. Seconds later, you could hear a pin drop as the band ceases to play.

I don't look back to see what's happening, because I yank Ella and Prissy into my arms, holding all three little girls to my chest. "Don't listen to Auntie Ade, sweeties." Catching movement out of the corner of my eye, I watch as Niel holds Whitney back from going to her aunt's defense.

"Adelaide, leave!" Katya's sharp voice cuts through the deafening silence.

"Are you trying to get back at me by screwing my baby brother? You're such a vicious cunt, no matter how dignified the media paints you."

Whitt and Katya's voices register to my ears, but I can't make out what they're saying.

"Everything is your fault, Katya– I had a good life. I was going to be a Zeitler wife and make Ezra lots of heirs. You're living my life as you fuck your way through the population. You begged Ray Hunter to rape you, hoping to snag Ezra– admit it. You're so sick and disgusting, I bet you have sex in front of that bastard daughter of yours."

A sharp snap cuts off Adelaide's tirade, and I know Katya just lost her shit and hit Ade. I ignore everything around me, as I war within myself: the need to protect Adelaide from herself, help Katya, and keep the children innocent, when it's impossible to do all three.

My son chases his furious cousin down, yanking her back to us as she struggles and hisses like a pissed off cat. Whitney is a right-fighter, and a protector of her family– she could give two shits about why this fight is happening, just that her aunt is involved.

I sense a scuffle behind me, then I hear the rapid murmurs of Whitt, Daniel, and Marcus, but my sole focus is directed at Ava. Ella and Prissy pull away from me, and immediately try to smooth Whitney's ruffled feathers.

"It's okay, sweetheart." For the very first time, I look into the eyes of a young girl who may someday become my daughter-in-law. "I'm sorry that we had to meet like this." I smooth Ava's silky hair back, trying to ignore the fact that she's an exact replica of Diane. I replace the image of Diane in my mind and cover it with Ezra. I convince myself Ava looks like Ezra, and she's sane like Katya.

"My name's Regina– I'm Niel and Ella's mom." Once Ava realizes who I am and that I'm safe, she relaxes in my arms.

"Hi," Ava murmurs shyly in the same tinkling voice of her grandmother's.

"You doing okay? You didn't hear that." I stare into Ava's eyes, willing her to forget what she just heard her father's ex-fiancée scream about her mother.

"That woman was being mean to my mom… Adelaide Whittenhower, she was my dad's ex-girlfriend, wasn't she?" Ava glares at no one in particular, lips curving into a sinister smirk Ezra often wears. "She won't be an issue now that she did that with all these people watching." Trilling a laugh that matches her smirk, "Mom won't have to worry about her stealing Dad from us anymore."

I look at my son, then close my eyes and pray. *Lord, please protect us from the unholy union of my child and Ezra's. If they were to procreate, it would surely be a bad seed. Please help them bring the goodness out of each other and not the evil. May God protect us all.*

Next, I promise myself I'll do anything to keep my son safe, no matter what edits Maître du Jeu passes down. Betrothing children is bullshit, when they haven't even developed full personalities yet. Imagine the nightmare if Ezra and Ade had actually married.

Coming up behind me, I sense Cortez before he touches me. "Thank you, Regina," Cort breathes in my ear while rubbing at my back.

"Dad!" Ava exclaims, running into Cort's arms.

"How's my monster?" Cortez murmurs affectionately, squeezing Ava tight while wearing an expression of terror and love.

Monster? How appropriate.

The band starts to play again, the party resuming as if nothing happened. Ella and Prissy grab Niel's hands and pull him into a three-way dance, with Whitney being comforted by her mom… and by comforted, I mean confronted as Katie gives Whitney a thorough tongue-lashing.

"Dance with me, Dad!" Ava chirps, causing Cortez to spill delighted laughter, thoroughly charming the man.

Sensing the erratic energy Ezra releases, "I'm scared," I whimper to the heat at my back.

"Me too," Ezra says, drawing to a stop to stand next to me on the edge of the dance floor.

Always on keep-Ezra-sane duty, I've learned the signs of when he's about to go off the rails. Like father, like daughter. "I know it's difficult to see it with Ava being so close to you, but you must recognize the signs."

"I do– Ava's only like that when someone threatens one of us. I feel like it will be a good thing, as she won't lash out in anger and vengeance. She's justice-minded. But, yes, I do see it."

Squeezing Ezra's hand slightly, I try to lend him comfort and sanity. "How's Katya? What happened to Ade?"

"Daniel and Whitt escorted Adelaide from the premises, and I just left Katya in Cortez's and my shared bedroom." This time Ezra squeezes my hand back. "I do recognize the signs. I did enjoy Adelaide's company and respected her as a person, but she has been acting erratically since Katya arrived."

"And I wonder why," I mutter sarcastically.

"No, Regina– not like that." Ezra leans down, trying to minimize people eavesdropping. "Stalking Katya. Sending threatening notes. Releasing our private history to the media. My birth father was released from prison– to say it's been difficult would be an understatement. I know Ade's put on a good front for everyone, but she is not well."

"I know," I cry out, hand flying up to cover my mouth. "Ade's had me so worried."

"I'm sorry, Regina. I overheard the Daniels talking when they came back from escorting Adelaide off the property. I honestly didn't think Daniel was going to commit Ade, or maybe

Whitt was influencing him not to, but her recent actions have given him no choice. Daniel already called in the injunction."

Crying silently, I try not to remember Ade as the twelve-year-old girl who befriended me on my first day of school at Hillbrook. Ferocious and brave, Ade went after everyone who insulted me. Then a montage of moments play out in my head, decades' worth. Ade was the grown woman who protected me and comforted me in Grant's absence, even if she was doing it with an agenda. Ade loves me and was *in* love with me.

Gutted, heart clenching so painfully in my chest I fear I'm having a heart attack, devastation settles over me like a welcoming coat on the coldest of nights. I'm so used to being miserable, it's no surprise bad things happen just when I feel a spark of happiness or contentment.

"I need to find my family," I murmur to no one and everyone, feeling lost.

Ezra places a hand on my shoulder, directing me. "They're inside– do you need me to show you the way?"

"I need a moment to myself." Taking a deep breath, Ezra and I share a moment of understanding. "I'll find them."

With tears streaming relentlessly down my face, I have so many worries swarming around in my head like angry bees, it barely even registers that I'm walking around Shadow Haven. This is where Ezra and Cortez grew up. After Serenity Lake burnt down to ground, this is the only place Marcus calls home. This is where the infamous living room resides, one in which I hope not to accidently enter for sanity's sake.

Speaking of sanity. Ade terrified me, between her behavior in the car, her shouting match with Katya, and what Ezra just told me. She was always so single-focused when it came to obtaining goals, I'm not surprised she's not handling Ezra breaking off their engagement well. But the biggest reason I agree with sending her to Wintercrest is the fact that she wouldn't be under Maître du Jeu's influence.

Adelaide would be safe, including safe from herself. Once she's better, she can come home. I've said over and over again, if Grant returns to Misery Castle, I will. But, for Ade, I would too. If she needs all of us together to feel whole again, I'd go for her. If she needs to move in here with Diane, I'd let her go. But she needs help first, because she has the tendency to become obsessed in an unhealthy manner, and everything else ceases to exist.

Randomly walking, fretting over sanity, I use my knowledge of Misery Castle to help pave my way. Where does one go to sign away your daughter's autonomy? It's Daniel Whittenhower I, so it's an easy guess to say a study or library.

Rooms are generally in similar locations in these mammoth houses, with the ebb and flow of daily life. In my mind, I remove several wings off Misery Castle, guessing there isn't a ballroom in this house, and quickly locate the study.

Daniel's panicked voice spills from a cracked doorway, catching my attention. "Whitt, I can't do anything else." Leaning against the hardwood jamb, I peek into what can only be Shadow Haven's library. Two-stories of mahogany filled with volumes of books– a reader and writer's dream.

With his palms resting on the top, Whitt's leaning over the desk, trying to intimidate Daniel as he sits behind it. "You promised, but I bet you were going to do it anyway."

"You saw Adelaide," Daniel's voice fractures under the strain. "I only threatened Wintercrest in the past because she wasn't going to go to college. Adelaide was inappropriate when Ezra was so young, and I needed her to go about life. I wasn't actually going to do it– Regina would have castrated me."

"Damned right Queen would have, and I'm going to help her do it now," Whitt seethes.

"I didn't make Adelaide behave as she did. She's been acting erratically for weeks, and it isn't safe for her, or any of us. Adelaide has to go to Wintercrest for her own welfare."

"I won't sign the paper that commits Ade." Whitt shakes his head left and right, sounding thoroughly disgusted. "I won't do it."

"This isn't about appearances," Daniel stresses, voice fracturing. "You have no idea how hard this decision is for me. Adelaide is a harm to herself and others. I worry that she'll hurt Katya Waters. If we don't help her, everything that happens next will be *our* fault."

"Goddamnit, Daniel!" Whitt snarls over the desk, leaning closer to intimidate his grandfather. Anger is rising with the stress level.

"Stop!" I call out as I slip between the double doors to the library. Both men look up at me in relief. One wary I'll argue with him too, and one seeing me as an ally– both couldn't be more wrong. "You can't put this on Whitt's shoulders, Daniel. He'll forever feel guilty."

"Regina, dammit! This needs to be done!" Daniel shouts at me, pounding the desk with the edge of his fist, just as I remember him doing all those years ago. Some habits you never break. "Adelaide is my daughter, but I have to protect everyone *from* her."

"What do you need?" I speak calmly to defuse Daniel's tantrum.

"What?" Muttering in shock, the fight bleeds right out of Daniel.

In a disturbing twist, I become the calm, rational one. "Why does Whitt need to sign the commitment paperwork?"

"I have power of attorney over Adelaide. But as a check and balance system, the judge put in a stipulation that I needed another family member to sign as a witness."

"I'll do it," I say without a shadow of a doubt. "Do I count as a member of the family?"

"Regina!" Whitt yells at me, appalled.

Reaching out, I try to soothe Whitt, but he flings my arm away.

"Whitt, Ade's not the same as she used to be. You have no idea the lengths she's gone to lately." Whitt and I share a look of total understanding as Daniel watches on. No matter how wise he may be, he's still a young man. This is a responsibility too large for Whitt to bear.

"We're not locking her up as punishment. Ade needs help, a place to get out of the middle of all this bullshit– sounds like heaven to me," I mutter sarcastically, hating how there is never a moment's peace. "I love Ade with all my heart– I always have and I always will."

"How can you do this?" Whitt's voice takes on a note of a child's, but I can't fault him for it.

"Ade is my *sister*– you can trust that I feel this is in her best interests, and has absolutely nothing to do with power or appearances. She needs help."

I'd love to sink to the floor, let it swallow me whole, and run away from my responsibilities. I'd love to pretend that tonight, and all the nights after, I won't be staring at the ceiling in indecision. I'd love to think that Adelaide won't blame me for life, and never speak to me again… but I'm not a liar, even if lying to myself would be a comfort.

"If someone has a broken arm, you take them to the emergency room. If someone is addicted, you take them to rehab. If someone is mentally hurt, you take them to a therapist. If they become a harm to themselves or others, you have to do what's right, even if it hurts."

A part of me is relieved Niel and all the female Whittenhowers are still enjoying the party, because Whitney would have been a bigger adversary than Whitt is being right now.

"What has Ade done that was bad enough to deserve this?" Whitt sounds utterly defeated. Abruptly, he pounds his chest like his grandfather had the desktop.

Sharing a glance with Daniel, he gives a slight tilt to his chin in invitation, knowing Whitt will believe me over him.

"Ade pulled away, wouldn't talk to me, or let me help her, because I would have seen the changes in her personality. She was hiding the truth from me… Ade helped to get a rapist out on parole so he could torment his victims. Ade sent Katya Waters threatening letters to frighten her, hoping she would run back to Pennsylvania. Ade released articles that were completely false, violated privacy laws, and is the reason we have the media swarming… How about the scene Ade just caused during a wedding reception. What more do you need? Do we wait for Ade to hurt someone or herself? If we wait, we'll be the ones to blame."

I stare Whitt down and try to get him to see it from my point of view. I worry that for once I'm on the same side as Diane and Daniel, but they both love Ade as much as I do. Whitt closes his eyes, chaotic thoughts flashing rapidly across his face.

Whitt slowly nods yes in heartbreaking defeat, then Daniel pushes the paperwork to me. His signature is as fresh as the tears in his eyes.

I see it now, from Daniel's perspective– it really was just a threat. Daniel never planned on ever committing Ade to Wintercrest. Adelaide used it against me, manipulated me into seeing Daniel as the villain in all things. All so I'd do her bidding, which was to get Ezra at any cost, even at the cost of his happiness.

With a scrawled *Regina Regal*, I sign away any hope of ever repairing my relationship with the woman I've called sister for eighteen years. Ade will hate me now, but I'd rather have her hate me, than have her hate herself for doing the unthinkable.

Squatting down to the floor, I can't contain a sob, as if signing the document made it more realistic. Even knowing I did the right thing, it doesn't make the agony and guilt any less.

"Thank you." Daniel mumbles, his voice cracking under the strain of emotion and stress. The look he levels at me is one filled with respect.

Glancing between his grandfather and me, indecision is marring Whitt's perfect features. "I hope this was the right decision–"

A high-pitched, blood-curdling scream pierces the air, and I'm running before I have time to think. Katya– it was Katya.

Following the resulting deafening silence in the aftermath of a primal scream, I try to focus on the sounds *inside* the house. Frustratingly so, all I hear is the band outside and the murmur of guests.

Intuition slows my feet as I walk down a hallway toward where the scream emanated. Whitt tries to pass me, but I grab his arm and turn to Daniel.

"I– please do this for me, Daniel," I plead, breath stuttering in my lungs. "I instinctively know that neither of you should see what's inside that room."

Blue eyes widen impossibly in fright, I watch as the emotions of the house settle over Daniel. He can feel it too. He closes his eyes, then slides his back down the hallway wall just outside of Ezra and Cortez's childhood bedroom.

"Whitt, Regina has to do this alone. Sit with me– I need you," Daniel pleads in a tone reminiscent of the past. That mournful sound will never leave me– it's the sound Daniel made when he told me Grant was dead. "I need you, son. I can't do this again."

The manliness leaches out of Whitt, and the child who experienced this eleven years prior is left standing in terror. Whitt folds his larger body into his grandfather's lap and stares up at me in shock.

Standing in the doorway, all thought escapes me. I can't think or speak. My eyes refuse to bring the scene before me into clarity. My mind protects me from the truth. I stare at the red walls, carpet, and bedding, and they blur into a crimson wash of violence. Blinking tears back to clear my vision, I regret it instantly.

Sound is loud and quiet at the same time, as if I'm cresting and sinking back under water. Time stills, then speeds up, only to still again. I know I'm surrounded by people, recognizing their presence, but my mind refuses to give me the information.

Slowly reality sharpens into clarity. Ezra, Marcus, and Cortez surround a man I don't know, but my mind supplies the name Raymond Hunter. All of them stare at me, and they may be calling my name, judging by the shape their mouths make, but I hear no sound.

In a panic, Whitt runs past me into the bedroom, and the men try to intervene but fail.

Vision sharpening, I spot Katya lying in the middle of a blood-soaked bed. She's semi-conscious, moaning as if she's still battling an adversary. Her arm is bent at a strange angle, and blood runs in rivulets from her forehead and a knife wound on her neck.

Katya was mine to protect.

The urge to scream at the men overpowers me, demanding to know why no one is helping Katya, but I've lost the ability to have a voice. A man's hand holds Katya's uninjured one, so I follow the hand and it leads me to Whitt.

Whitt's eyes are devoid of life as he stares downward and to the side at the floor. Just as I followed the hand, then the arm, to lead me to who was holding Katya's hand, I follow the direction of Whitt's gaze, and see nothing but red. Squinting, I try to make out what the lump is.

Red.

Red.

RED.

Red. Wet and dripping red.

Blood.

"Ahhh…" I cry out, covering my mouth with the back of my hand. "No…no… no… no." I repeat over and over again in horror as the yellow blonde color emerges from the sea of red. As soon as I recognize one part of the whole, it slowly coalesces into Adelaide.

I'm torn. My body wants to do two things at once, so I do neither. Under my protection or not, I want to strangle the life out of Katya with my bare hands for killing Ade.

There is no way my sister lives– nothing is recognizable on her body. There is too much blood. Too much blood everywhere. Painting the walls, soaking the floor, covering Adelaide's body until it's unrecognizable as a human being. The meaty scent wrinkles my nose, the smell of what should be *inside* of Ade's body.

Frozen in conflict, my mind wars between killing Katya and running to Ade.

A siren cuts through the air as someone runs into my back. Not a siren– Diane. Diane's scream. Our eyes meet, and we reach an agreement. We both want to kill Katya and tend to Ade. Diane blinks, and I know she's weighing the options– Katya, the love of her son's life, the mother of his children, a pregnant woman… or her lover?

The five seconds since I entered the room is a lifetime as Diane and I make our choice. We move as one and fall to our knees. Ade's life blood soaks the carpet and splatters up our thighs, hot and thick on bare skin.

Diane looks for Ade's hand as my hands hover in the air looking for a piece of flesh that is whole and blood-free. A symphony of mourning fills the air: Diane's high-pitched cry, my deep sobs, and Whitt's mournful moan. The tortured keening of a parent losing another child before their time floods from the hallway– the animalistic wail will forever haunt my nightmares.

I can't feel Ade anymore– inside me, that space where the souls of those I love reside. She's gone, and I refuse to let her leave me before we've gotten our happy endings.

On auto-pilot, I tear my dress from my body and wrap it around Ade's head, knotting the fabric tightly to staunch the bleeding, but it instantly soaks with blood. No air passes through Ade's lips or nostrils. Turning her head to the side, red flows from her mouth in a torrent. Tilting Ade's head back, I begin to breathe for her. Training from over a decade ago pushes me to try to resuscitate her.

"NO!" I yell at Ade as if she can hear me. "I won't lose you too. Why– why did you do this?" I screech, frustrated and terrified. "You just couldn't wait so we could help you!"

So involved with my struggles, I don't hear or see the paramedics until they're pulling me from Ade's lifeless body. No double-take as I realize it's Levi Wilson in uniform, with a ginger-haired partner. I don't care who works on Adelaide, as long as they keep her alive.

Syn's small hands hook underneath my armpits, dragging me across the carpet painted red with Ade's blood. Dropping me into the hallway, Syn goes back in pushing a gurney.

"Is she dead?" Diane whispers next to me, and I finally take stock of my surroundings. Diane and Daniel sit shoulder to shoulder, with me slumped against the wall next to Whitt. I'm even with the open bedroom doorway– a hysterical bubble of laughter flows from my throat as I witness MdJ's executioners in the act of their day job.

"Irony. Syn and Wil are paramedics?" flows off my numb tongue. "The fuck?"

The red-haired paramedic meets several more who are rushing in with a gurney. "No, the young woman isn't gone, but just barely." There's a haunted look in his eyes, and I can tell he's never seen anything so gruesome in his entire career.

Chapter Forty-Four

"How's Adelaide?" Marc's voice is rough as he flows into the seat next to me in the waiting room. Talk about divided loyalties– Marcus has been on the other side of the hospital with Katya, while I sit here with his wife.

I don't give a fuck about anything at this point. All I need is to hear Adelaide is going to survive.

"We've lost Ade four times, so far." Staring sightlessly at the door, nothing else matters but the men and women in uniform who keep coming and going, bringing updates. "I worry we won't get her back next time."

"She's strong," Marcus whispers, placing his warm palm between my shoulder blades, but I shrug him off me. "Have you gotten up and walked around? Had a drink? Gone to the bathroom?"

I don't give a shit about me, but it's nice someone cares. "They're going to run out of blood– Ade leaks more than they can put back in as they try to patch up her injuries. Too much internal bleeding. They think they've got it all, only to discover she's bleeding somewhere else."

Etiquette would dictate I ask about Katya at this point in the conversation, but I don't care one bit about Ade's murderess. I assume since the hospital is still standing, Kat and the babies are doing fine. Ezra hasn't bulldozed in here to kill us all… Ade may have attacked Katya, it may have been self-defense, but I don't give a fuck. I've sat here in stasis, fluctuating between grief and rage, for the past ten hours.

Kristal and Fate are in caregiver-mode. The girls are going back and forth between the waiting room for Adelaide and the one for Katya, bringing food and drinks, magazines, and clean clothing. I was so out of it, I sat here in a bloody slip for a good four hours before Kristal manhandled me into a pair of yoga pants and a t-shirt, right in the middle of the waiting room with Diane and Daniel watching. That's how much I don't give a fuck about anything but Ade right now.

Catatonic with the need for positive news, I didn't even fuss when Fate gave me a bath with wet wipes.

Tucking my knees to my chest to comfort myself, I don't have the energy for polite conversation. Directing all of my energy to the doorway, praying for a doctor to tell me Ade is going to be just fine.

"How's Whitt?" Marc moves to touch me again, and I shake my head no. Touch is distracting– I need to focus on sending positive vibes to Ade.

"Whitt's… not good," I trail off, only half-ass paying attention. I wish Diane or Daniel would give out the necessary information like they have when everyone else steps in here. But this is Marcus, whether he's married to Diane or not, they see him as my responsibility.

"Whitt's with all the kids at my house. Priscilla was placed in a room due to exhaustion and dehydration." I finally look at Marc, showing him what I think about that. "Grief is more like it– Katie's with her. Whitney's inconsolable." I don't share how Whitt had to wrangle the young woman out of the waiting room the last time the doctors came in to say they'd lost Ade on the table, only to bring her back. "Niel refuses to speak."

"I'm sorry, Regina." Marc flows from his seat to kneel before me, forcing me to look at him instead of at the doorway, like a dog awaiting its master's arrival.

"Katya will be fine." Marcus rests his palms on my upraised feet, honestly thinking I give a shit about Katya. I may be her sworn protector, but I'm taking the day off. "Kat has a few broken bones and a small cut on her throat that will scar."

Marcus smiles softly, and it rankles the hell out of me.

"A small scar?" I snort, sounding like a cunt, thinking of what Grant's face looks like. "That's good. I wouldn't want to hurt Katya's pretty face," I mutter in a snotty tone. "Ade looks like a Rorschach test– we would've needed dental x-rays to identify her body."

"Regina." With endless patience, Marcus is trying to connect with me, but I don't have anything to give him in return.

"I'm sorry, Marcus. I know it was Ade's fault, not Kat's. I get it– I just signed commitment papers to place Ade in Wintercrest. So cut me some slack. My sister's in an operating room, fighting for her life for the fifth time. I could give a shit less about Katya's tiny scar on her throat, when if Ade lives, we may not even recognize her face. Ade may be brain-dead from blood loss or the amount of time she spent *dead.*"

"Regina–"

"Say something like, '*Kat's going to be fine*' and leave it at that. Have some respect when you talk to Adelaide's father, lover, and sister for Christ's sake."

Closing my eyes, tears stream down my face. I hurt. I just hurt. My mind plays conversations from the past, where Cort, Ezra, and Marc called Ade a cunt…. cunt… cunt… I see Ade's face as she told me she loved me. I remember finger-combing Ade's hair while she bathed covered in cane marks– marks she earned protecting me. There is no right or wrong side– we're all wrong and right. It's just a matter of perception.

I look up to Marcus and unleash my emotions. My eyes mirror every thought, and he reads them clearly. Marc tries to hold me, but I don't allow it. *Can't allow it.*

"Go to Ezra and Cortez as they sit vigil by Katya's bedside." As I said, divided loyalties. It's been ten hours, and this is the *first* time I've seen Marcus. I know I'm being unreasonable, but I'm only human– I can't help what I feel or why I feel it.

"I'll call you if Ade makes it," I murmur hollowly. "I'm sure Kat will want to know if she needs to press charges. I'm sure it would be easier on your family if Ade died."

"Don't," Marcus cautions. Scowling, he grabs my hand. As I fight him, his grip tightens.

In my mind's eye, in the middle of my terror, I see Marcus in the corner of the dripping red room, discussing a cover-up with Ezra, Cortez, and Raymond Hunter, all the while Ade bled to death on the floor. None of them tried to resuscitate Ade, or stem the flow of blood from her skull. I don't know if I can ever get over that.

"Adelaide Whittenhower is a human being, with hopes and dreams. She was pushed to the brink with falsehoods and false promises, most of them from your son," I whisper the truth as I see it. "I don't care what Ade's done. She deserved better than bleeding out in the house she thought she'd live in one day. After she was rendered unconscious, Katya should have stopped. Yet Katya kept beating Ade's face in– *beating her to death.*"

It's all I see in my mind when I close my eyes. Ade bleeding out on the carpet, with no one moving to help her.

"I can't forgive that, Marcus," I release as a wretched whisper.

"I love you," is Marc's only reply to that.

"And I love you," I choke out on a sob. "I just can't be around you right now."

"This isn't about us, Regina," Marcus begs, squeezing my hands in his. "Don't let it affect us."

"It's not about us, but it does affect us– as you've proven through your actions, time and time again… protecting Ezra and Cortez comes first, even at the detriment to everyone else." Pointing at my companions who aren't even pretending not to listen. "Notice how Diane's in here with Daniel and me, not sitting with Ezra and Cortez? Because Ezra and Cortez have each other. It's pretty bad when you leave your wife and mistress, so you can sit with two capable men over a woman with some scratches. I've broken many bones with no vigils being had… Ade is *dying*, Marcus. DEAD."

"Regina–"

"I'm raw right now, okay?" flows from between my taut lips, nearly pleading. "I don't want to discuss anything. This isn't about you and me. If you're allowed to use that excuse, then so can I."

Sighing heavily, I slowly pull my hands from Marc's grip, only to cup his face in my palms a second later. "I love you. I need you. No matter what she's done, right now, I just need to put all of my focus and energy on positive thoughts for Ade. Everyone else is fine, battered and bruised physically and emotionally, but they are *alive*."

"I honestly didn't think you'd want me around, Regina." Marcus isn't getting it.

"I realize I pride myself on being a strong, independent woman–"

"Marcus," Diane interrupts, and I'm too tired to give a shit. "Young Daniel is with the Whittenhower youngsters, because their welfare is of the utmost importance. Katherine is sitting with Priscilla because her health and mental wellbeing matters. Foregoing their honeymoon, Aaron and Kayla are with Ava. Ezra and Cortez are with Katya, because her health does matter, most importantly because of the babies."

"I know all this." Marcus still isn't getting this.

"These people have rallied together for a singular purpose," Diane continues. "To make sure Adelaide's father, sister, and partner were here for her if she wakes. You, my dearest Marcus, ran off to soothe my son and his partner, who had one another, who were neither injured nor mentally or emotionally incapacitated, instead of being in here with your partner in the event Adelaide should die. Which Regina has suffered through four times already– that is the distinction."

Staring at Marc's gobsmacked expression, even the least emotional of our merry band of crazies gets it. "I'm not with my wife because Priscilla will be okay, and my daughter is keeping her comforted. My youngest daughter comes first right now. Strong and independent, a woman still needs a support system. Diane and I have one another– Regina should have had you for the past ten hours."

"I'm–"

Pressing my palm over Marc's mouth, I silence him. "No," I warn. "You being here wouldn't be about comfort anymore. It would be about you trying to ease your own guilt at abandoning me when I needed you the most– I don't have the energy for that right now. Ade is all I give a shit about, because I know everyone else is perfectly fine."

"What do you want me to do?" Marcus murmurs against my palm.

"Just be anywhere else but here, that's all." My words have an angry bent, but they're spoken in an emotionally exhausted tone. "I'll be fine– I always am, which is why you felt comfortable in leaving me to my own devices. I'm choosing to see that as a compliment from you… So thank you for respecting my wishes by backing off."

As Marcus rises to his feet to leave as I requested, the waiting room door opens. We all go on alert, waiting for any news, good or bad.

Gripping my chest as if I'm having a heart attack, I'm rendered speechless. With red-rimmed eyes and a look of defeat, Grant slowly makes his way toward us.

"If you hadn't come," Daniel says with force. "I wouldn't have only seen you as dead to me, I would have made you a corpse."

"That's why you had multiple children, dear." Diane cracks a dry joke to lighten the stress-filled pressure we're under. "You still have Katherine and your grandchildren. I'm stuck with only

Ezra– I don't have the luxury of killing my son when he disappoints me."

"Disappoints?" Daniel stares at his best friend. "For the past ten hours, I've experienced my son's death on repeat. I was sitting here, begging Grant to man-up and show up."

And here I am... Tear-filled eyes skip over Diane to land on me, with Grant's fingers speaking words. *Kids. Mom. Ade. Now I'm here. Not at Father's request.*

"I didn't think I'd ever see the day," Marcus slurs, eyes held wide with wonder. "You left your cave."

"How are the kids?" Pops out of my mouth to take the focus off of Grant. I know how uncomfortable being the center of attention makes him.

Grant takes his cellphone out of his pocket, then begins dialing. The tone plays over the speakerphone as we wait for someone to answer.

"Is Ade okay?" Roman's worried voice fills the waiting room.

Grant quickly signs an answer and Marcus translates. "Jamie has you on speakerphone in the waiting room. Regina, Diane, and Daniel are here with us. Jamie wants you to put us on speakerphone too."

The volume of noise emanating from my house has us all flinching after being in near silence for so long, then it fades out as Roman leaves my living room.

"Okay, I'm here… as you can tell, everyone is perfectly fine. Whitt helped me drag Fate's mattress into the living room. Niel's surrounded by a harem of girls. Ava's with us too, so Aaron and Kayla could take care of other matters. The kids are watching a cartoon movie that has way too much adult innuendo, which is why Whitt's enjoying it–"

"It's hilarious!" Whitt's voice hits my ears, coming closer as he speaks. "Stop calling me a little kid, Roman– I needed the distraction."

"Are you okay?" Speaking loudly, no one could miss the concern and sympathy in my voice.

"Yeah, I'm okay," Whitt talks so softly I can barely make out the words. "Being with the kids is helping. Grant is a sneaky snake coward, only entering the house through your bedroom to meet Roman for a powwow."

"Hey, now– I came and got you, didn't I?" Roman protests. "It was too many people in one small space for him. Don't be a puke."

"Trouble in paradise?" I direct at Grant, and his blush is answer enough. "We're just waiting on the doctor again. I'm scared with the amount of time Ade's been under anesthesia."

"Well, everyone keeps calling us, sending their positive thoughts–"

"Looking for gossip," Whitt cuts Roman off. I can tell by how far away the movie sounds, they must have relocated to the kitchen. "Fate and Kristal popped in about an hour ago and picked up some more of your things. They're having trouble getting into the hospital parking lot with the paparazzi camping at all the doors."

"Jesus," we all hiss in unison.

Marcus turns to Grant. "How'd you get in?"

The only reply is an eyebrow raise and a tiny smirk.

A shadow. A ghost. Grant can sneak anywhere. Doubtful anyone even saw him enter the hospital.

"The kids are gobbling ice cream and microwave popcorn, and Ella wants to make cupcakes next–"

"They're going to bed after the movie." This time Roman cuts Whitt off. "So are we. I'm calling dibs on the mattress on the floor– you can have the couch."

"Bachelors trying to watch three tween girls and two teenagers," I tease, smiling for the first time in ages.

"They live with me," Daniel deadpans, causing Diane to bark a sharp laugh. "Diane commiserates with me about Ezra's spawn. I wish you gentleman luck getting them to sleep tonight."

"Are they getting along okay?" Chest aching, I wish I was home to witness all of the children together in one place, being children.

"Whitney and Ava had a hair-pulling tantrum," Whitt mutters, sounding exhausted in every way imaginable. "*It's your mom's fault! No, it's your aunt's fault! Your mom's a whore! Well, at least I'm not the whore!*" Whitt mimics in a bitchy voice, then a tinkling tone. "You get the idea."

"Did they stop?" Marcus is trying hard not to laugh.

"Eventually," Roman and Whitt say in unison, then share a chuckle.

"How?" Diane is more maternal than I expected.

"I said we dragged a mattress into the living room…" Roman trails off. "I didn't say it was to lounge on."

"What?!" I shout.

"I could only take so much whining and bitching," Whitt's voice is so dry, it cracks. "I'm gay, and a girl's grating voice makes me want to tear my own balls off."

"We tossed a queen-sized mattress on the floor, then told them to knock themselves out." Roman sounds as if he's enjoying himself, and enjoying Whitt's company. "After two minutes of hair-pulling, and the most unoriginal name-calling, they started laughing."

"It evolved into a tickle-fight, with me being dragged to the mattress." I can hear the blush in Whitt's voice. "For half a movie, Ella and Prissy were fused to me."

"Aww– that's so sweet." My heart clenches. "I really wish I could have been there to see it."

"No one wanted to cuddle with me," Roman pouts to keep the levity going. Then his mood shifts to serious matters. "How is Ade?"

"We don't know yet, but you guys will be the first I call when I find out," I vow, and then we do pleasantries to end the conversation.

In silence, we go about our praying, positive thought directing, and worrying. Marcus didn't leave, and I knew damned well he wouldn't. Grant took the seat between me and Daniel, and Marcus flanked me on the end.

At some point, I realize we all joined hands, forming a solid wall of emotional support, whether it be good or bad news.

After the doctor came in to personally give us an update, explaining how it would be touch and go for the next few days. There are no guarantees on Ade's quality of life, what the long-term effects will be, or what damage the head injury will have on her mental state.

Adelaide will live.

Maybe it was the stress, or the relief, or the fear of what's to come, but I found myself in a weak and vulnerable position, in front of Daniel and Diane of all people. Sobbing uncontrollably, it took both Marcus and Grant to keep me from shattering apart.

Present
Dexter – Dalton

Chapter Forty-Five

Eyebrows arching, I'm a bit surprised someone is typing in the code to my front door at this hour, but it goes to show how the big, bad monsters under the bed don't affect me anymore. I just roll with it, especially since they know the code and it's only one in the afternoon. The boogeymen in our midst would most likely sneak up behind me and assassinate me like we're playing Halo.

My son's cheek is visible first, so I relax, but then become overwhelmingly embarrassed. "Well. Well. Well, what do we have here, Mom?" Niel teases me as he shuts the door, locking us in together.

Sitting on the sofa, with crafting items strewn all over the coffee table, floor, and cushions, the living room is a total disaster.

"Never thought I'd see the day," Niel comments, fingering a packet of cutesy stickers. "You're more of a digital photo frame and a thumb-drive kinda mommy." Creating a pile, he cleans himself off a seat next to me.

"Why aren't you at school?" I deflect, ignoring how ruddy my skin feels as it burns with mortification.

"This close to graduation…" Niel drawls out, which is exactly what has me turning crafty in the first place. "Does it really even matter? I could probably ace college degree level midterms at this point."

"I know you're Hillbrook's little prince, but you better not make a habit of skipping school. You only have a handful of months left, and you'll miss out."

Niel snorts, leaning forward to check out my progress. "Scrapbooks?"

"I… um… I missed out on a lot of time with you kids." And I feel like a shitty mom and aunt goes without saying. "You're seventeen–"

"Getting closer to eighteen every day, Mom." The kid is forever saying that when I try to turn maternal on him.

"Exactly." Heart aching, I stare down at an image of Ella and Ade– my daughter is missing both her front teeth and she has chocolate smeared on her chin, and Ade was whole and happy and free. I decide to explain the best I can to Niel. "A little bit torture, a little bit of a walk down memory lane, a whole helluva lot of bonding and never forgetting."

"I get it, Mom." Niel's heavy palm rubs at my back as I lean forward to work on the coffee table. "I'm guessing you want to do this with all the girls."

"Yeah, they're all coming here after school today– Ella made snacks last night." Smiling to myself, my heart suddenly feels warm. "She was excited."

"Of course she was," Niel murmurs, sounding indulgent rather than annoyed like most big brothers would feel over their fourteen-year-old girly sister and cousin. "Is Whitney coming too?"

"Whitney's driving the girls since Albert is busy." Most mothers would freak out about that, but Whitney is hilariously responsible. Niel and Whitney share a birthday, and with usual Whittenhower flare, they were given cars on their sixteenth. Niel received an Escalade to fill with the girls, and Whitney was ecstatic with her Volvo because of its safety rating. Irony, Whitney can drive the girls anywhere in that car, Niel isn't allowed– an edict passed down by every adult female in the family.

The boy has a lead foot, just like Jackson and Whitt.

"I'm so sad I wasn't invited." Niel turns snarky, not sad at all. "Don't you want to do special things with me?"

Rolling my eyes to the side, our silence lasts all of two seconds before we're chuckling. Niel and I will never have a mother/son relationship. I treat him as an adult and equal, and he treats me with the utmost respect– the affection and love is unconditional.

"I'm assuming since you showed up when you should be elsewhere, we have deviant business to attend to in hopes no one is the wiser?" That's how we bond, over the monsters hiding beneath the bed. "I swept the house for bugs earlier."

"Didn't want family bonding to be spied upon?" Niel teases, knowing I do it several times per day. There are no cameras in my house anymore, not even the security cameras I had to keep an eye on the entrances, because they could be hijacked for nefarious reasons. The cameras Ezra placed in my bedroom are long gone.

For Ezra's peace of mind, Marcus and I take a selfie before bed, then text it to the lunatic to keep him out of my bedroom. There have been times I wake at three a.m. to Ezra standing beside my bed, staring down at us with a worried expression. The selfies were for my sanity's sake.

Nothing changes. Marcus and I get one another completely, which means Ezra and Cortez are still a wedge between us. Grant and I have a co-parent relationship that turns too close when we text at night, but it's been platonic affection for years. I don't dare go there with Grant, because I fear the violence erupting in me again. After what happened to Ade, violence gives me nightmares. As for Marcus, I pretend the codependency between him and both the Ezes doesn't exist– I lie to myself a lot.

There's a timer clicking above our heads, winding down to Whitt's upcoming twenty-forth birthday. A lot of changes are coming. I want my life back. I want to be free of the very rules I abhorred when I lived in Misery Castle. I love Whitt, but I do look forward to the day the ink is dry on our divorce decree. I've been working double-time to get Whitt to give in and pursue Dalton, but our marriage keeps him from moving forward.

My children are closer to adults every day. MdJ backed off slightly after I proved my worth, giving me positive duties, like helping the founders instead of harming them. It's time I had my own life. I just fear Marcus will always have an excuse to stay in stasis.

"I wanted to talk to you about something…" Niel catches on quickly, organizing the photos by child and age. Bizarrely, he's concentrating on Whitney's and his pictures.

"Obviously," I murmur dramatically. "I know you so well."

"Better than anyone else," Niel agrees, since he's comfortable showing me his calculating side, only showing everyone else his boy-like innocence. "I haven't spoken to anyone else about this, but it's been bothering me.

My mother-radar leaps in excitement. My son needs me, needs my advice, and it makes me feel valuable.

I know it sounds stupid, but there are days I feel set adrift because no one needs me like they used to. Kristal and Fate are living their own lives. My daughter looks like a grown woman, with a vast intelligence and a need for traditional roles. Ella tries to be *my* caregiver, not letting me smother her anymore. Empowerment basically runs itself. Restraint is the only facet of my life that gives me a purpose. Grant's never needed me, which is part of the appeal. Marcus, all he needs is to be needed by Ezra and Cortez, with Ezra more concerned with Katya and their three children.

Lately, I just feel like I'm only *here*– not necessary. Which is why I'm looking forward to my own life, but the one I want to spend it with is too focused on the wrong things. Niel needing my help is an amazing change of pace.

"I want to train to be a Master of Restraint–"

"Oh," I mutter deflated. This is not mothering territory. I know I have to look at this from a perspective I don't want to use. I want to shake my son, then ground him, knowing that reaction would destroy the relationship we've built over the past four years.

"I don't have anyone else to talk to about this." Tone filled with shame, Niel stares down at a stack of pictures of himself. "I'm supposed to be so strong, you know? Like you. But sometimes I feel like Dad."

"Your father is not weak." A coward, yes. But I won't say that out loud. "We don't make fun of Ella because she finds fulfillment in taking care of us. I've tried to raise you kids to not think in gender roles."

"Tell that to Ella," Niel deadpans, earning a grin from me.

"That's her natural personality, and has nothing to do with being a girl. Ella is like a bulldozer when she wants something. So wanting to feed us and make sure we're comfortable is not a weak notion– it's who she is. Your father is one of the strongest, most self-restrained people I know. He doesn't have a submissive bone in his body. But you need to know that dominant doesn't equate strength and submissive doesn't equate weakness. Sometimes life doesn't mirror BDSM– there are nuances that go beyond dominant and submissive."

"A switch?" Niel's question makes me wonder how much Whitt has been telling my son.

"Let's just cut to the chase." I'm short with Niel, because fear has me needing to be at the heart of the issue. "What's going on in that terrifying head of yours?"

"Voldemort is honing me to be the alpha, like Ezra is for his generation. But Ava knows how to press my buttons, and I give in… and I *like* giving in. It's not so much that I want to be stronger, but just learn how to not let people like Ava steamroll over me."

"So you want the discipline? The rules and boundaries? The ethics?" I tread carefully, never once having a conversation on sex. Ava's fourteen now, and I have no idea if they're doing inappropriate things all teenagers do. I've left that up to Whitt, but he's not the best choice for that type of conversation either. Whitt's a man-whore at Restraint, and a virgin when it comes to his own sexual orientation.

"Yeah." Niel won't look at me. "There is no doubt I know what I'm doing, and I know what I want. But sometimes I enjoy it when Ava takes my choice away by telling me what to do."

"It's comforting," I murmur in understanding. "To not have to take responsibility for your own choices. This is human nature."

"BUT," Niel stresses. "When it comes to the founders, I have to learn not to bend because it's easy."

The kid does have a point, which is why I'm now helping members find jobs, keep their spouses, make their kids happy, instead of destroying lives, because I didn't bend.

"And you think training will help?" I coax, feeling like there is more to the story. Niel is always thinking ten steps ahead, and all decisions are double-edged. This is the truth, yet I know there is more. But it's Niel, so I know I'll only find out if he wishes me to know.

"Yeah, I do." He finally looks at me, while wearing a funny little grin Grant used to wear when he was getting one over on me. "I've thought about it a lot."

"You'll train with Marcus." Maybe that will keep Marc's head out of Cort's business. "You won't go to the dungeon when anything sexual in nature is being explored until after your eighteenth birthday. You will never see a relative engaged in a sexual act."

"That narrows that down to nothing," Niel grumbles, sounding exactly like a teenage boy. "Imagine if Whitt had that rule."

We share a demonic chuckle over that. Whitt can't walk two feet without running into a blood-relation. They've all come to terms with the fact that Whitt's dick will be lodged inside a throat. Whitt never sees them engaged, but they all know what his orgasm face looks like.

"Thank you, Mom." Niel reaches over to rub at my back again. "I'm not toying with you– I really do need this."

"Good." I try not to preen under his gratitude. "But how about you tell me what you really want?"

Green eyes connecting, we communicate on another level– pure understanding of how the other works. My parents didn't live through my teenage years. I couldn't imagine not being in Niel's life right now, but that doesn't mean I'll ever underestimate the boy. I lived through Jackson, Daniel, Grant, and even Marcus, Ezra, and Cortez. Just because Niel is a sweetheart doesn't mean he isn't a man.

All men do the bait and switch. They ask for help from a woman. Make her feel worthy and valuable, then hit her with their real request during the afterglow.

Smirking devilishly, one dimple popping in his right cheek, Niel proves my point flawlessly. "Well… I did have something else to talk about."

"Of course you did."

"Grandfather and Diane are being blackmailed by Olivia Fontaine something fierce, and they've began to hatch their own offensive strategy."

"Which is why you actually want to be at Restraint?" I hazard a guess.

"And you'd be right." Niel has the decency to look guilty. "I eavesdrop well, and their plan is a good one. They blame Master Fontaine for Aunt Ade–"

"Are they right?"

"Yes and no." Niel treads carefully, because what is said at a founders meeting doesn't leave the founders meeting. "Master Fontaine is now doing things outside of the rules– *I'd know*," Niel stresses pointedly. "Grandfather has been blackmailed to do things not passed down through us."

"Shit!" I hiss, frustrated. "These poor people, being torn apart nonstop. It's bad enough for me, and I barely know anything… I can't imagine not knowing anything at all– the terror your secrets will be revealed."

"That is why the system works, Mom." Niel rolls his eyes at me. "That was the point of it all. But the system breaks down when one of us goes rogue. I think it's amusing what Grandfather and Diane are doing. It proves them worthy adversaries."

"You are so fucking twisted, kid," I mutter in awe. "You're enjoying this, playing all the sides."

"It's a high like no other," Niel murmurs with a devious glint shining back at me. "Grandfather's plan got me thinking. What if we beat them at their own game?"

"It's *your* game," I stress, bugging my eyes out. "You're one of them."

"So?" Niel shrugs, not giving two shits that how he speaks to me is exactly what had his father silenced in the first place. "They deserve it and more."

"What do you want?" Niel always has a reason for everything.

"Knowing what Voldemort is up to has me at an advantage. Knowing what Olivia is doing to Grandfather and Diane puts me at an advantage. Knowing what Grandfather and Diane are doing in retaliation puts me at an advantage. Instead of quitting while I'm ahead, I think it's time I stir the hornets' nest."

"Lord, please save us all," I mutter dramatically, making the sign of the cross.

"You're proud of me, and you know it," my son taunts. "I thought I'd do something with the pawns of my generation. Only three of us know what's going on, and I'll leave Torian and Zane in the dark since they're on the opposing team."

Looking down at the pictures scattered around my living room… Niel learning to walk. Whitney taking first communion. Ella playing in the mud with leaves in her hair. Prissy standing on a balance beam before she could even count or read. Whitt in a tiny tux, with Jackson's hand ruffling up his hair.

"Kids?" my voice breaks in fear. "You want to bring these precious children into it."

"They won't know about… everything. Just what we're doing." Niel levels me with a potent look, the one that has our relationship between adults, not mother and son. He'll do it with or without my permission– the only choice I have is whether or not I'm involved. "My plan is actually in opposition of Grandfather and Diane. Imagine them learning their own grandchildren thwarted them."

"What's the plan?" With more self-restraint than I thought I possessed, I'm surprised my voice doesn't quiver.

"Grandfather and Diane are writing a little book in Aunt Ade's name, just to piss off Master Fontaine." Niel grins in the face of my disgust. "I thought it would be fun for us kids to make a newsletter and website filled with gossip. Why should the paparazzi have all the fun?"

"And the gossip is leveled at who?"

"Every-fucking-one," Niel states dramatically. "No hypocrites allowed, Mom. *None*. If some dirty laundry is aired, then it all gets hung out to dry. No one can hide. It takes everyone's power away when there's nothing left to blackmail.

"Checkmate." Eyes held wide with pride, I've never respected my son more, nor have I been more terrified of him

"Generation Next is our checkmate, Mom– it's time a new ruling generation takes over, one with an actual code of moral ethics."

"I'll help, but I'm a ghost on this," I demand. "No one but you will ever know of my involvement. Ever."

"Agreed," Niel vows.

For the next two hours, my son and I devise a plan for Generation Next. By the time our three girls arrive, our checkmate is already in motion. Niel does stay to bond with us, eating Ella's snacks while helping us all with our scrapbooks.

This is what it means to be a family, and I finally feel like I'm no longer walking this earth alone.

Chapter Forty-Six

Emotions taint the air, choking me– pure malevolence. An evil flows through Restraint tonight, calling out for me to flee. This energy riding the air has been doing so for so long I forgot what it felt like in its absence. None of us have time to enter the dungeon anymore. We spend our nights policing the patrons. Every Master of Restraint, our submissives, and membership are scattered around the club.

The more publicity the Zeitlers and Whittenhowers receive, the more popular Restraint becomes. Years ago, when Ezra broke off their engagement, Ade revealed the skewed truth as she saw it, even outing Restraint as one of Ezra's businesses. Recently, Diane and Daniel published a tell-all in Ade's name– The Mistress & Master of Restraint.

People flock in droves, even from states away, to get a peek at the infamous Masters of Restraint.

Blaming Olivia Fontaine for Ade's condition, Diane and Daniel hit Olivia in the pocketbook. The tell-all not only revealed all our secrets at Restraint, our entire membership, but also targeted Maître du Jeu, the BDSM branch that Olivia runs.

Our biggest tenet is trust. With the trust in our organization broken, members across the world are pulling their funding, terrified they will be targeted next. Diane and Daniel didn't anticipate the waves of consequences their actions brought forth.

The new clientele is dangerous. They didn't come here because of their interest in the lifestyle. No, they want fifteen minutes of fame, and they'd do anything to gain it. Alcohol flows like water, creating a volatile mix of sex and violence. The riot police have been called out four times in the past few weeks. I spend most of my time kicking the shit out of drunken douchebags out in the alley. I have a master's degree and own a billion dollar corporation, and here I am playing bouncer to the next generation of entitled rich kids and assholes.

I'll give Olivia, or Diane, or whoever the fuck they are credit– as a master of manipulation and coercion, somehow some unnamed person has managed to drive off our security force and employees. Every fucking time I hire a person, they leave as quickly as they came.

Same shit, different night. We'll have ten security personnel on the books, and by morning, it'll only be five. As for regular employees, they all up and quit after being hired. Tomorrow morning, Aaron and I will have to hire another batch, just as we've had to do for the past forty-five mornings.

I barely make time to brush my teeth anymore. I don't know the last time I ate or slept. The bags underneath my eyes say it's been a while, and my loose pants say I need a double-cheeseburger and a dozen donuts.

Kristal, Fate, and Heidi are our bartenders for the evening, because we can't keep the bar staffed either. Roman stands behind the bar with his arms crossed over his chest for the girls' protection. He looks like a pissed off Mayan God protecting the innocent sacrifices. Syn and I flank the bar, and it's still not enough. A hundred feet spans us– a hundred feet of drunken chaos.

"Get your hands off my girlfriend, dickwad!" is slurred from my half of the bar. Seeking Roman's eyes, I tilt my chin in our silent way of asking for assistance.

"Help!" a high-pitched squeal calls. "Get off me! Help!"

Running toward the scream, I find a huge male with his hands in someone else's cookie jar. The guy is the size of Aaron, with the boyfriend not much bigger than the woman he's trying to defend. The asshat's hand disappears underneath a girl's skirt, and her boyfriend can't do a damned thing about it.

Powerless, I know how the couple feels.

I close my eyes and do my duty, allowing the volatile rage simmering in my blood to rise to the surface on a wave of violence.

Hating how I spark to life, knowing I will be rendered into a pile of regret come bedtime, I don't speak as I crank my arm back to punch the fucktard in the kidneys. No one violates anyone, for any reason– not on my watch.

Crying out in pain, hand slipping free from the poor lady's panties, the asshole falls to his knees.

"Monica," I order into my Bluetooth. "Code yellow. They'll be waiting at the bar. Jersey girl and Bieber– both are crying. "

"Thirty seconds, Boss," flows intermittently with static.

Roman and I haul the trash out while Monica takes the couple's information. I don't allow crime in my club. This will be reported to the proper authorities.

We drop the frat boy, rapist-in-training on the ground, making sure he lands in the oil-slick puddle that's filled with drunken piss.

"I'm getting too old for this shit," I snarl, staring down at the asshole. Reaching forward, I dig my fingers into his back pocket, locating his wallet. "Chaz? Why am I not surprised? Your parents expected you to grow up to be an asshole with a name like that."

After taking his ID, I toss Chaz's wallet on his rumpled form. On the way out of the club, I may have accidently-on-purpose hit Chaz's head on the door jam, knocking his ass out cold.

"Jane!" I shout to the homeless lady who takes up residence in our alley. "If you watch him until the cops get here, you can keep all his cash." Counting the bills, I flash a smirk. "Three hundred and sixty-two bucks."

Jane makes more money in a night than most people make in a week. Our last homeless person, Frank, was able to return to the straight and narrow. Roman and I dump at least five guys out here a night. I always give the watcher all the cash. Jane fought another homeless person for the right to claim our alley as her territory. We have five more waiting to replace Jane.

It's wild kingdom inside Restraint, and Fight Club outside. I've tried to help the homeless by finding them places at Transcend, but the fuckers just wander back like stray puppies.

"I need a drink," Roman complains. With a hand on my arm, he drags me back inside the club.

"I could use a nap. My office is calling me," I mutter in exhaustion. "I can't keep this pace up for much longer."

"We need to hire fifty people, in the hope ten of them will remain in our employ, just so we can find the time to take a piss." Commiserating, we walk past my office door, staring at it with unveiled lust.

"Roman, I hire twenty people every damned morning. By ten p.m., I'm down to five, but not five new hires. Those same five guys have been with us since we opened. This city may be big, but the pool is getting shallow. I'm thinking about hiring people off the street and offering them a grand a night as long as they stay 'til closing."

"Jesus." I've learned to read people over the past four years. This is not MdJ's doing. The shock and fear in Roman's face speaks volumes. I grew huge motherfucking balls and outwardly pulled anyone I knew who was ruling in Maître du Jeu into one-on-one powwows. All swore up and down they didn't know who or how this is happening. They all had terror in their eyes, even Syn and Ezra.

I believe them, and that makes this all the more terrifying. We're being invaded. Have we pissed off another twisted organization, when we thought we were so goddamn special we were the only one in existence?

"You didn't hear this from me, but we're thinking of closing Restraint."

"What?!" Roman shouts, completely floored.

"Maybe permanently, or maybe until we get our shit together– doesn't matter to me either way." Leaning against the hallway wall leading to the mouth of the club, I keep watch, but I'm not ready to enter the fray.

"We don't need Restraint– I suggested we just find a secure location and make it an exclusive club. It would alleviate this bullshit. Ezra's being sentimental, but did you notice Ezra isn't here? *I'm a family man*," I mimic Dr. Lunatic. "I'm a wife and a mother of two, who also watches her nieces twice a week. I own a business, but I'm here running Ezra's business while he hides with his tail between his legs at Shadow Haven. Marcus too! If it's Diane, the entire family is cohabitating with the person raining shit on our parade."

"What do you expect them to do, sweetheart?" While empathetic, Roman looks defeated.

"Niel assures me it's not Daniel. If it's Olivia, sure our hands are tied. If it's Diane– fork her… spoon her… I don't give a fuck, just lock Diane in a room away from a telephone so I can keep our employees. What I don't expect them to do is hold a conversation with Diane while eating eggs benedict in the morning. Benedict is right– Benedict Arnold –the whole lot of them."

Shoving off the wall with my palms, I stalk away. As I enter the club proper, a wave of violence hits me in the face, causing me to back up several steps into Roman's chest.

"Fuck me up the ass with a Barbie doll," I mutter in awed horror as the melee before me sharpened into focus.

"What?" Roman snorts, and then his eyes turn as hard as diamonds. "Good luck, sweetheart– let's break some skulls." After sharing one last look, Roman and I move as a unit to enter the fray.

Charging off into the riot, I grab the first fist-wielding asshole I find, yanking the wiry guy off two girls who are screaming like cats. Nearby, Roman's grappling with two men who stopped fighting each other to fight Roman instead.

Violence spreading like an airborn disease, it's as if I can see it weaving its way from patron to patron. A person will be standing in shock, and once the violent wave touches them, they go off on their neighbor. Tourists and regulars start going at each other's throats, fists thrown and hair pulled. People are shoved to the ground, being trampled by those fleeing in a panic.

Furious that this is happening in my club, I don't even wince when I take an elbow to the cheek. With a backhanded slap, I knock some sense into two young woman tugging at each other's clothing while spilling years' worth of bitter resentment. They're using the riot as an excuse to let their shit out. One woman's tits are hanging out, as her ex-bestie calls her a whore for wearing a skimpy dress. Irony, she's the one who exposed the girl's tits in the first place.

"Walk it off," I warn them, holding a bottle blonde in each of my hands, keeping them an arm's length away from the other. "Discuss your issues elsewhere– get outta here." I drop their arms, amusement quirking my lips as they both fall to their asses.

"Dexter!" Syn's scream cuts through the air, pierces me until I'm rendered immobile. I've never heard that tone from Syn's throat– that woman isn't afraid of anything, but she is now.

Running toward the bar, I duck and weave through the crowd. Anyone who gets into my way gets elbowed, and I could give a shit less if I hurt them or not. Panicking, I hurdle another fight, not bothering to stop them– these assholes can take care of themselves. I'm here to protect my people from them.

A cry of alarm flees my throat as I take in Fate on the ground with two men riding her. One is ripping Fate's dress off and the other is going for her panties. Fingers trespass without invitation, causing me to turn feral like a wild animal.

The hundred-foot bar is too long, and it feels like an eternity as I fight my way from one side to the other. I curse under my breath as Syn tries to take on one of the guys who's violating her sister. Arm raised, the guy tosses the ninety-pound sadist, causing her to fly through the air. Crying out again, Syn's head hits the bar, jarring her neck at an odd angle.

The flash of Fate's bare flesh makes my skin run cold and red to cloud my vision. Jumping to the bar, feet pounding, glasses breaking under my steps, I traverse the length in a second instead of minutes while fighting the crowd. Jumping down, I land inches from Fate, managing to grab the asshole by the back of the neck a split-second before he rapes Fate.

Cock hanging out of his pants, Fate's bare body on display as she tries to crawl away to safety behind the bar, I distantly see Dexter taking care of the second man.

Enraged, all I know is the man beneath my fist. I feel no pain as my hand splits his skin like over-ripened fruit beneath the force of my punch. Nothing exists except for the primal need to protect.

"Syn!" Dexter screams and shakes her, but it's all just muted background noise to my ears. "Get Fate to her room and shower with her, comfort her. I have to get our girl off of that asshole before she commits homicide."

I know I'm *our girl*, but I don't care. I *need* to commit homicide to release this pressure building up inside me. I need to protect what's ours. At any cost. My partner's the fucking DA. If he can't save me from a life in prison, then he doesn't deserve me. I live my life doing exactly that for MdJ– they better return the favor.

Distantly, as my fists repeatedly pummel a rapist in the face, I watch as Syn picks up Fate, then carries her big sister away. I'd sigh in relief, but I'm not finished rearranging this guy's internal organs yet.

"Regina!" Dexter shouts, but I ignore him. A guttural moan draws my attention to the guy Dexter punished. Hopping off my prey, I mount the asshole Dexter took out.

"She was mine to protect!" I keen as my fists meet his face. *Fate*. Innocent and sweet, Fate. I didn't protect her. I didn't want Fate here any more than she wanted to be here, but we needed her since we couldn't keep our employees. Whoever is taking them away did this– they deserve to pay.

"Where's Kris? It'd be just my luck both of my girls are hurt." I moan. Praying for their safety, I take my frustrations out on the unconscious man beneath me.

"Shit!" Dexter hisses underneath his breath with worry. But I hear it, and it makes my blood run cold.

"Pretty Boy's got Kris, Heidi, and Kayla taken care of. Stop beating on him." Dexter tries to reason with me, but I'm beyond reason.

"No." Growling, I punch the fallen man in the nuts. I can't help the manic smile that slides across my face as he screams, a jolt of energy enlivening me. "No one should *ever* have their power taken away."

All around me, chaos ensues, but it's not as chaotic as my emotions. I've never felt closer to my nature as I do now, by letting my instincts run wild. My senses sharpen, and I wonder if this is how an animal feels when they're on the hunt and end up capturing their prey.

"Regina, I can't stop you." Dexter slumps to sit next to me as I methodically and premeditatedly go about murdering the man. "Go ahead and kill them, but you'll regret it later. I doubt you could live with yourself."

That gives me pause, but after a second, I don't give a fuck.

"Regina, knock it the fuck off!" Dexter commands, but I ignore him. He's not mentally strong enough to bend my will, nor physically strong enough to stop me.

"Fuck, you're going to get arrested for assault," Dexter mutters hopelessly, hand resting on my back, and I sense the violence ebbing as the police enter.

"Queen." Voice compassionate yet confident, Whitt squeezes the back of my neck, hitting the nerves that control the function of my arms. My hands fall worthlessly to my lap. I sob out of pure frustration– I wasn't finished. They're still breathing.

"Queen wasn't here. Queen didn't do this. No one saw anything," Whitt rapidly murmurs to Dexter as he lifts me into his arms.

"Queen?" Whitt commands me to look at him, but I can't. Instead, I gaze out at the destruction in the club. Bodies litter the floor, groaning and writhing in pain. People are milling around, looking for their friends and loved ones. Police officers are handcuffing those who are still trying to fight. EMTs arrive, trying to sort out where to begin.

Whitt steps into the dungeon, making sure the door latches and locks at our back. "I can't do this anymore! I can't. Fate is never stepping foot into this place again. You didn't see it." Howling my pain, I'm transported to years ago, back to a defenseless place I visited with Ezra. "They were violating her!"

I watch the innocence leach out of his beautiful eyes, and it kills me on a soul level.

"You can't imagine what it feels like to have someone force their body inside yours– to be violated. The sense of helplessness." Groaning in pain, I remember my time, not Fate's. "This is a threat that forever hangs over a woman, no matter what. In our homes, at our jobs, when we're out just trying to have fun and forget our responsibilities. Just walking home is an exercise in self-preservation."

"Queen." Whitt sounds gutted as he carries me across the dungeon floor, then enters the long hallway to our personal rooms.

"Fate's not strong like me, Whitt. Your sister was already afraid of being here. She's the sweetest, kindest person I know." Gripping his dress shirt in my fingertips, I press my mouth against the side of his neck, trying to silence the scream that is building.

Entering my private room, Whitt turns hesitant. "The girls are in the bathroom– after what happened, I don't want to disturb them. I'll fetch some more clothes and towels from my room, and be right back. I won't leave you but for a second. I promise."

Whitt sets me on my feet, making sure I can stand on my own, then quickly leaves my room in search of his own. Slowly, I turn the doorknob, fearing what I'll find on the other side.

Chapter Forty-Seven

In a mass of sobbing, hugging females, they're huddled up in the corner of my private bathroom. I don't know if I can do this– I cringe when it comes to upset ladies. I just want to give them anything they ask for to make the sound stop. It's why my daughter is a mini-diva. I love all these girls, but I'm too stressed out to listen to the weeping.

I understand why Whitt shoved me in here, knowing only another female would make them feel safe. I start with the closest. Tipping Heidi's chin up, I gaze into her hazel eyes. She sniffles, imploring me to help them all. I pull a few washcloths off the shelf, pressing one into Heidi's hand.

"Blow," I coax Heidi, waiting for her to obey. "Good girl," I praise, and she seems to relax now that someone she trusts is in control of this out-of-control situation.

Kristal is the next. No, my chica isn't weeping. Fury radiates off her as she holds Heidi and Kayla, acting as a mother lion would with her cubs. If I didn't already respect Kristal's protective side, the look in her eyes would do it.

"I'm proud of you." I try not to get choked up as I say the words, but my voice breaks. My fingers skim the shiner she's wearing. "I hope you punished the fucker who did this to you."

"I broke her arm– she got one hit in before I smashed her arm with a bottle of Jack." Kristal's voice is filled with badassery. "That made everyone else back off."

I smile, trying not to laugh as I examine Kayla. Her pretty pink skin is flawless. "How'd you manage to go unscathed," I muse as I run my hands along her voluptuous body.

"Taser." Kayla answers without hesitation, and I bark out a laugh.

"Your husband's one of my favorite people," I tease, but my mind is spinning over the possibilities of stashing several Tasers beneath the bar for our protection.

Monica stares up at me defiantly, but I know she's not angry with me. As I wipe blood off her face, I notice none of it is hers.

"You're a strong bitch," I murmur in appreciation. "You're perfect for Dexter."

Arching a brow in surprise, for the first time, I notice the lone male in the room. "Toby? I guess they pushed all the submissives into my bathroom."

The blond cutie opens his mouth to speak, then shuts it. Tobias is a studious fellow, religious too, but he needs what Dexter has to offer. My guess, Monica pulled him in here at Dexter's request. If a man is too worried about his family, he'll fail to protect others and himself.

Toby's covered in blood too, and he doesn't fuss as I clean it off. Wiping it away, looking for a wound, I realize it doesn't belong to him either.

"It's not ours." Monica answers my unspoken question. "We took down a few people before Alex shoved us in here." Roman goes by Master Alex at Restraint to protect his identity at Transcend. As Monica mutters Roman's nickname, her voice twists in anger.

Ah! Monica's pissed at Roman for ruining Toby's and her fun. Dexter's family is a bloodthirsty little lot– I like.

I dampen two cloths, then toss them in their laps. Retrieving them both, Toby washes his master's fiancée with great care and gentleness. Monica closes her eyes, sighing in pleasure, but it's the affection and comfort between family members, not of lovers.

A tiny gal is huddled between the wall and the shower stall. She's our newest submissive. Cassie is a girl from my old neighborhood, who I used to babysit for extra cash. She was sucked into the mentality of the neighborhood, and finally found her way to Transcend after her husband nearly beat her to death. Roman recommended the kind of therapy that only a seasoned dominant could provide.

"Cass, how are you doing, sweetie?" I pull her out of the corner, then check her over thoroughly. Smiling reassuringly, I can tell she's just frightened.

"I'm okay," Cassie mumbles. "I was bumped around in the crowd, but no worse for wear."

I decide the best place for Cassie is between Monica and Kristal, because they both look pissed off and fierce at the moment. Cassie is a true submissive in all ways, and the energy the girls are giving off will make her feel safe.

Sighing heavily, I come to my full height, then begin stripping out of my bloody Restraint Security t-shirt. I groan when I see the state my jeans are in– another pair of my favorites straight into the trashcan.

Holding back the urge to cry, I gaze at the two women huddled together on the shower floor. The sisters are so tiny that neither weighs a hundred pounds, and both are exactly five feet tall. In everyday life, Syn looks feral. But as she cradles her older sister in her arms, she looks like the little girl I used to know.

After stepping inside, I shut the door. My large body fills the space, but the girls are so small we all fit. Crouching down, I look into their faces. Two sets of identical, sad blue eyes gaze up at me. Fate's bottom lip quivers, because she knows how much I worry about her, and she never wants me to worry. Syn's eyes may look sad, but she still looks feral enough to lash out and murder anyone who is a threat to her sister.

"They were still breathing, but just barely." Then I issue a promise to the sadist. "They'll have lifelong ailments."

Syn tips her chin in my direction in thanks, and I fear what will happen to the men once the police let them go. Syn is MdJ's Judge, Jury, and Executioner. Her husband, Levi Wilson, he was the man who cleaned up Raymond Hunter's messes. Together, the paramedics are the most terrifying power couple I know.

"The one who touched you down there." My eyes flick to Fate's privates. "He'll never get another erection again. I crushed his balls in my fist until I felt them pop."

Fate's resulting smile is pure evil, looking exactly like Syn in this moment, and I praise, "That's my Angel."

A snippet of memory flashes through my mind– Syn being backhanded, flying through the air like a ragdoll, with her head connecting with the bar, neck angled wrong. Reaching out tentatively, I manipulate the back of Syn's head, looking for the spot that connected with the bar. The skin isn't broken, but she has a huge goose egg.

"Change is coming," I promise them both. "Fate will never step foot into Restraint again until I'm satisfied. This goes for all the submissives. If their masters want them here, then they cannot leave the dungeon– I don't even want them walking in the front doors and through the club. If we don't have enough manpower to run the club, then I want it to be shut down."

Syn's nodding in agreement the entire time I speak. She's always quiet, but I see the wheels spinning in her mind. She's coming up with a list of changes. No one cares for Fate's safety as much as Syn. I'd kill for her, but Syn would die for her, and that is a huge distinction.

My hands follow the path of my eyes as I take inventory of Fate's body. She has a few bruises and scratches on her perfect breasts, but it's the bite mark above her left nipple that has me growling.

"I saw his fingers touch you." Suffocating on the memory, I can barely get the words out. "Did he rape you?" My voice doesn't carry over the spray of the shower, so only the three of us will know the answer. This is private, and it's up to Fate to tell the rest of our people if she wants them to know. Far too often, the victim is made to repeat the events ad nauseam, purely so those asking can get off on it.

"I… no… he didn't rape me," Fate stumbles over her words.

Fate is my perfect submissive, because her only want in life is to make me happy. I can't trust Fate to tell me the truth right now. If the truth is rape, I won't be happy, so she'll lie. I tap her knee, and she complies, not seeing it as a violation because it's me doing the examination.

"Your thighs are tender." It's a statement, not a question, because her pale skin is scratched red and raw, with a few fingertip bruises dimpling her slender thighs.

Touching Fate gently, I slide two fingers inside her. Fate isn't one to have sex often, running off to another member of MdJ when both are in the mood. I know who, but we don't talk about it. Until she shares with me, I won't press.

Fate's very tight, and shows no signs of discomfort as I slip my fingers out of her. "Good girl," I murmur, pressing her thighs back together. "Are you going to be okay?" I look Fate in the eyes, trying to gauge her emotional climate.

A shout echoes from the confines of my room, reverberating against the bathroom door, but I concentrate on Fate instead.

"I was so scared," her voice quivers, then breaks on a sob. "You saved me– I knew you'd come. But I don't ever want to go into the club again."

"Done," I decree with finality.

"You better go out there." Syn pushes as Whitt's voice gets louder. "I'll take care of everyone. The dominants will be collecting their submissives soon. You better calm Whitt down before that happens."

Grabbing for a towel, I have nothing to change into, so I leave the bathroom after I wrap it around me securely.

Marcus is sitting crossed-legged on my sofa with a seething Whitt towering over him in fury. "Never again!" Whitt screams at Marcus.

I lean against the bathroom door to keep the submissives contained. Roman is opposite me, leaning on the door to the hallway, and I can guarantee every dominant in this building is waiting on the other side in the hallway right this minute.

"My sister!" Whitt bellows, veins in his forehead bulging. "My. Sister. Was. Almost. Raped. My other sister was bashed in the fucking skull. My wife almost killed two men. Shut this shithole down!"

Sighing heavily, Marcus closes his eyes in utter defeat, while resting his head on the back of the sofa as if his neck is too weak to support its weight. Marc's silent reaction pisses Whitt off even more.

"Queen almost killed a man!" Whitt tries to force the gravity of the situation on Marcus. "I'm making a decision for my entire family. I will not come back here until this is fixed. Kristal and Fate will not step foot in here. I'd love to say Queen and Syn won't either, but they can make their own decisions. But I will not be swayed. Those women won't be back! You're training Niel, Marcus You're training my goddamn brother. HERE!"

I step forward the instant Whitt's elbow flies back in preparation for a punch. Grabbing his arm, I still him. "Shh… calm yourself."

Glaring over his shoulder at me, "Don't you fucking take Marc's side on this," Whitt seethes in my direction. "I don't give a shit, Queen. NO!"

"I agree with every word you just said." I don't say it just to calm Whitt down– I mean it. "I just don't want you to hit the man you respect as a father, knowing you'll regret it when you calm down. Look at his face, Daniel," I coax, using Whitt's birth name to get his attention. "Marcus gets it. We need to calm down in order to find a solution."

"How come you're being so agreeable all of the sudden?" Whitt growls at me in his dominant voice. After witnessing me in the throes of murder, I can understand where he's coming from.

"Go look in the bathroom, and see if that doesn't fizzle you out." Sighing, I run both hands through my wet hair.

"I'm sorry." The fight bleeds out of Whitt. "I'm being rude and inconsiderate. I hated seeing you unhinged like that– it made me think of Ade." Shuddering in horror, "I can't get the image out of my head, you bent over that man as you tried to beat him to death… your voice as you explained what rape feels like. Oh, my God. I'm so sorry, Regina."

Whitt pulls me into a tight embrace, and I lose all coordination. Catching me, Whitt settles me next to Marcus on the sofa. Then Whitt helps me dress in a pair of sweats and a hoodie.

Marcus doesn't try to help, because there's some unspoken rule between the pair of them. If Whitt's acting as my husband, then Marcus isn't my partner, and vice versa. It's how we've lived through the past four years. It's not about sex, because I've only been with Whitt once. It's about support.

After the blowup in the hospital waiting room, Marcus learned that just because I'm strong and independent doesn't mean I don't need support. Dominant men think that supporting their mate is the biggest indicator of male worth. I'd realized I'd been emasculating them by refusing their help and by not seeking their comfort and guidance when I needed it. I thought dealing with it alone made me strong. But they taught me that the strong know when to ask for help. Going it alone doesn't make you stronger, it makes you an idiot. Marcus hasn't learned this lesson yet, but he's trying.

Yeah, it was Grant's texts that hammered all of this home for me.

"May I?" Marcus asks politely, and Whitt nods in assent.

Before I can ask what, I'm encapsulated by Marc's warm body. He wraps his arms around my back and his legs around my waist. Soft lips graze my neck, parting, his breath flutters the small hairs at the nape of my neck and tickles.

Reaching out, I grab Whitt's hand because I need both of them right now. A sob escapes my throat as I fall lax in their embrace.

"I'll give you privacy." Roman's voice is thick with emotion.

"No," I whisper softly from the crook of Marc's neck. "We need to have a meeting and get this figured out."

After pulling out of their arms, I sit opposite Marcus, and Whitt joins me. I can feel Whitt's need to hold me, need to erase what we just went through, but he doesn't give in. Only a handful of people know about our connection, mostly family. But the rest are in the dark, and they're going to stay there.

The timer on our marriage is slowly ticking down, causing Whitt to become clingier than ever. Our four-year anniversary was a few months ago, and we're quickly approaching Whitt's twenty-fourth birthday.

Katya is the first to come into the room. Must be the Zeitlers were notified about the latest riot. Either that, or Marcus knew it was time for a change.

The dominant female fluctuates between confidence and insecurity– Katya looks around, unsure where to sit without Ezra or Cortez nearby. Marcus puts her out of her misery by patting the seat next to him.

After the initiation blowjob, it took a long time before the jealousy didn't rear its ugly head when Marcus and Katya took up the same space. But it's hard to feel that way on a nonstop basis since they both live at Shadow Haven.

Understanding Marc's codependency with Ezra and Cortez, I've kept my mouth shut. But as I've watched from afar, I've noticed the connection between Katya and Marcus is familial in nature, if not a bit strained, as if Katya still doesn't feel as if this is her home and she can't trust those around her.

Ugly, baggy jeans come into my line of sight as I stare at the floor, and a rare smile curves my lips. I quickly grab the layers of shirts that cover Dalton's body, then yank him down between Whitt and me. Whitt's growl of protest is cut off as a smooth boy hand accidentally makes contact with his. Both guys stiffen for a moment before they fall lax from the relief of finally sitting next to each other.

Not that I'm trying to find my replacement or anything, but Whitt is a natural caregiver, which is why he's struggling to hang onto me just as it's time to let go. We both need Dalton in his life, and I think Dalton needs a support system, love and companionship. The boys are a good match, yet stubborn beyond belief.

Roman is last to enter my room because he was busy playing door keeper. After shutting us all in, he sits on the arm of the sofa next to me, hand settling between my shoulder blades. Roman and I share a look at how cute Whitt and Dalton are together– we've been playing matchmaker with Kristal's help for years.

Last night, Kristal finally got Dalton and Whitt together in a three-way. Whitt sparked to life and Dalton's asshattery turned to bashfulness. It must be true love.

Roman snorts just as a giggle slips past my lips– it has a manic quality, but it's a form of release.

"I have something to say," my voice is gravelly and cracks near the end of the sentence. I look around the room, noticing Dexter staring intently at the bathroom door with a pained expression etched across his face– his two favorite people are in there, and he's justifiably worried.

"Syn's in there with all the submissives," I say to ease their worries. "Everyone is accounted for– for the most part, they're just shook up. Dexter's Monica and Tobias are pissed they didn't get to inflict more damage." I chuckle underneath my breath, and I'm surprised Dexter doesn't look proud. If anything, Dexter looks even more worried.

"I get it better than anyone, how we let them all down. How we didn't protect them. It's our responsibility to take care of them, and we didn't– *couldn't.* Dexter, be happy that they're smart enough to take care of themselves. Hey, Aaron," I call out to my co-manager.

Aaron doesn't look worried at all. Pissed off is too mild of a word, because Restraint is his place too, and it was invaded with our people violated. "This won't happen again," he makes a promise he can't keep. Aaron and I spend a lot of time together, and we both said we'd do a walkout if they didn't fix the problems.

"Your wife looks soft and pretty, but Kayla works a mean Taser." Mulling it over, I still feel it's extreme, but necessary. "Maybe we should invest in several for the bar area. This shit shouldn't be happening, and we aren't going to live like this anymore. But in the event things erupt out of our control, our people would be safe."

Now Aaron looks proud, but it doesn't soften the furious resolve that lines his handsome face.

Finally locating the root of our problem, since he ghosted in here while I was playing matchmaker, I know I'm going to ruffle his feathers. "We have a problem." I pin Ezra with my unflinching stare, and he recoils.

Old rage erupts. I see Katya in my peripheral, and it angers me. Looking scared and compassionate, I want to drag Katya by the arm and toss her in with the submissives so Syn can come in here where she belongs. What gives Katya the right to wear that expression? She isn't here– Katya goes to work, then goes home to her family every night. Sometimes Katya works from home even. Ezra, Cort, Marcus, and Kat never come here except for Saturday nights to play around. We're all here working nonstop to save their goddamn business, and they pop in for fun visits. I'm so glad their family time is more important than mine. This is their fucking mess, and we're the ones with blood on our hands.

At the root of it all is Ezra. I rationally realize how I'm pushing the blame off onto Katya, because no one seems to blame Ezra for anything. But another big part of it is jealousy. I don't have the luxury of being a mother to my kids because I have obligations Katya's husband forces on me. Because Ezra is fucking scary when he's off his rocker, Katya is safe from the influence of MdJ.

"I want to be tactful, but I'm not Whitt." I talk to Ezra, when I really want to look at all four Zeitlers in accusation. Hell, I haven't seen Cortez inside this building in months.

Diane and Daniel wrote that book in defense of Ade. Ade who is in Wintercrest, a shell of her former self, all because Ezra married Katya instead of her. If it's Diane who's scaring my employees away, it's doubly the entire Zeitler-Holden household at fault… yet it's me cleaning up the mess.

Regina Regal, always relegated to a lesser position because I wasn't born into this bullshit legacy.

"This is your club, yet you're never in it. You leave us every night to fight in what constitutes as a warzone. I get it. You don't want this life anymore because of the kids. Well, I have kids waiting for me at home that I haven't seen in weeks. Why are your kids better than mine?"

"They're toddlers." Katya's excuse hits my ears like a nuclear strike.

"You chose to have them– we didn't." I remind Ezra and Katya. "I leave here at three a.m. bloodied and broken with my girls walking dead on their feet. I'm back here at eight a.m. every morning to vet new employees, only to be at my job an hour later. I get nothing out of this. I'm only here to protect us from your bad decisions. I'm sure Aaron would love to sleep in a bed with his wife, not teach her how to defend herself. All of our issues are your fault–"

"Regina!" Dexter's outraged voice bellows in my tiny room.

"Shut the fuck up!" I bark at Dexter, and he flinches. "Everyone defends Ezra and his piss-poor decisions." Glaring the smaller man down, "I don't give a shit what your opinion is on *my* schedule, especially since you show up at nine p.m. to patrol the club for a few hours at night. You have to work during the day." I throw my hands up in the air dramatically. "Well, I employ thousands of people, so your little audits can just go fuck themselves. Without me, Restraint won't run, and I want this place closed down."

A gasp, a heavy sigh, and a sharp intake of breath echoes throughout the room, yet I easily ignore everyone who resides in Shadow Haven.

Resting my head in my hands, I breathe deeply through the panic and anger. Two hands rub soothing circles on my back, one small and one large. No one speaks while I swallow down the rage that never truly leaves me.

Rage that seeped into my soul as I identified my father's remains. Rage that strengthened as my mother's body cannibalized itself. Rage that balled up after I was coerced into creating the Whittenhower heirs. Rage that laid dormant for nearly a decade while Grant played a ghost. Rage that was reborn after Ezra and Maître du Jeu took my power away. Rage that erupts so easily because of the injustice and imbalance I suffer beneath constantly.

"I apologize." I choke on it, because I'm not sorry. *At. All.* "The reason Restraint needs to close is because I can't keep it running as it is now– no one could. We used to have a rotation of ten bartenders. Kristal liked to manage the bar on the weekends because it was fun for her, and she got to meet new people and interact with them. Do you know how many bartenders we have employed now?"

Looking around the room, I notice everyone shakes their heads in reply.

"None," Aaron's gravelly voice answers. Hero-worship vanishing, Aaron places the blame where it's due, instead of calling me out like Dexter did.

"*None*," I reiterate. "Every morning, Aaron and hire new bartenders, and they last an hour at most. This is how it goes for every single employable position at Restraint."

Pausing in heavy silence, I wait for the information to sink in.

"Kristal, Fate, and Heidi run the bar six days a week. They have day jobs– important ones. Heidi is a nurse, mother and daughter. Kristal is my accountant and Fate is a financial advisor, and my shareholders count on them to keep Empowerment running. They are also a third of my household, as I like to joke– my wives."

After allowing a few snickers from people around the room, I continue. "A business can't run without employees. Everyone looks at us as if we should just do it, as if there isn't a major sacrifice involved. Our submissives and members are holding down employable positions, being treated disrespectfully and in a begrudging manner.

"Syn, Roman, and I try to protect the girls, but the bar is a hundred feet long, and we can't police it. We can't have a repeat of tonight. We won't. I promised Fate that she will never enter the club again. Kristal can make her own informed decision." Whitt growls wildly at that. We may be Kristal's dominants, but I afford her freewill.

"How many security personnel do we employ?" I ask the room.

"Five," Cort answers with a wince. He may not be around much, but he is highly observant.

"Yes, we only have five. Roarke spends all of his time hiring people too. Dane, Sam, Chris, and Brent have been here as long as I have, but no one else sticks past a quarter of a shift. I have suggestions set into place, but no one ever wants to hear them. It's unimaginable the amount of needless frustration and time-wasting Roarke, Aaron, and I have to deal with."

"How long has this been happening?" Dexter sounds so deluded, I want to ask about his powers of observation. "Why is it happening?"

"Forty-five days," Aaron and I answer in unison, but I continue on. "Why? Someone is mad as all hell at Ezra, or over Ade's book, or the BDSM community in general. I'm not here to figure out why. I'm here to put a stop to it."

"Maybe I should figure out why." Dexter challenges me, expecting me to be a bitch about it.

"Knock yourself out– go for it."

"What are your suggestions?" Marcus tries to sound reasonable, as this isn't news to him. We no longer share a bed because I'm never home. With Ezra, Cortez, Katya, Ava, and the twins all living in Shadow Haven, Marcus never seems to leave it. When we are together, or talk on the phone, we speak of little else.

"Repetition is a sign of insanity. We just had our fourth? No, fifth riot. At this rate, I need to be with Ade right now, since I've done the same thing every morning for almost two months and expected different results. I suggest we close Restraint while we get a real staff into place, one that won't be coerced into quitting, because this is no goddamn coincidence. While we're shut down, we should remodel the club to accommodate the large influx of people. Especially the bar area. I do the work, I know what's going on, yet no one heeds my advice as if they're the experts, so I'm officially done."

I stare at Marcus while trying to ignore Katya's green cat eyes staring at me, and the way her pink lips are quivering because I want to shut her playground down. I try to ignore the fact that Marcus is rubbing Katya's back to comfort her. Oh, right– I guess I don't ignore it. I like her as a person, but Katya's the only woman on this planet who makes me feel jealousy.

Diane. Begrudgingly companionable.

Olivia. I want to gut her for multiple reasons.

Gwen. I want to destroy her, but it's not because I'm jealous.

Katya Waters. I'm jealous. Full stop.

"I…I–" Ezra stutters, and Marcus continues where his son left off, "We have to have a solution that doesn't involve closing the club. It wasn't a solution I chose, mind you. Tomorrow evening, we have a meeting set up with Maître du Jeu–"

All us guilty fuckers share a loaded look, because we *are* MdJ, and we're sitting *right here*… then realization dawns. Olivia Fontaine is on a warpath, and she's headed our way. In the aftermath, I notice Dalton starts to shiver uncontrollably, enough so he doesn't seem to realize Whitt is rubbing his back.

Mommy dearest– poor Dalton.

Marcus continues speaking as if we weren't all having a silent conversation around him. "–Devlin Conrick will be joining us for the unforeseeable future. Let's see what he has to say before we make any permanent decisions."

"Who is this guy?" Dexter asks.

I don't need Marcus to answer. In this, Marcus and I have bared our souls. Devlin Conrick was the fella who made Marcus feel comfortable when he arrived in Las Vegas. Devlin was Marc's friend, then there was the bait and switch. To add insult to injury, the man has been raising Marc's daughter, Spyder. Judging by the way Dalton perked up at the sound of the man's name, Devlin raised him too.

If Devlin Conrick is coming to Dominion, then Olivia will be following in his wake.

I growl deep in my chest before I can stop myself, causing Marcus to give me an inquisitive look. "Um…" Marcus stammers as he tries to figure out what could've possibly put the murderous expression on my face.

"Devlin and I were brothers under the same master. He'll help us all he can, but it will be uncomfortable. When Devlin arrives, even though we own this building, he will take dominion over all of us."

"Let me get this straight…" I draw out for effect. "As long as Olivia Fontaine wants up and operational, we have to be? Is this correct?" I direct to Marcus.

"The black and white of it, yes," Marcus admits, not looking any happier about it than I am. "Imagine being overthrown by a foreign government, but you won't have to imagine for long, as they will be here tomorrow night."

"What will it take, Marcus– a death? Will you see reason when it's too late?" Furious, I glare at my partner. I know damned well the people in this room could put a stop to it, but they won't. MdJ wants to figure out who is thwarting them left and right, and in order to do that, they have to keep the point of origin open and running.

"Political maneuverings aren't worth the cost of life." Standing up abruptly, I walk over to the bathroom door. Pointing, "Aren't these people important enough?"

After opening the door, I fetch them to hand off to the people who are responsible for their health and wellbeing. Tobias and Monica to Dexter, Kayla and Heidi to Aaron, and Cassie to Roman. Syn walks out but refuses to let go of her sister, as does Kristal.

"Fate's going home with me tonight," Syn demands, and I nod in assent.

As Syn tries to leave my room, Fate releases a bleating animal protest as Kristal's hand slides from hers. "You go with them," I order Kris, the compromise pleasing all three of them. My eyes never leave my ladies until they disappear down the hallway.

"Whitt, you have somewhere you need to be." I remind him that the children are at Misery Castle, and one of us has to be there for them. I wish it was me, but that's not happening tonight.

"Yes, familial obligations. Queen, may I have a word." Whitt points to the bathroom, then enters, instinctively knowing I'll follow.

I keep my back to Whitt while I twist the taps on to cover our conversation. He hugs me from behind, and I melt into his chest.

"Is Marcus going to sleep over?" Whitt's arms squeeze me tighter, trying to support me in the only way I'll allow. "He's been sticking to Shadow Haven recently."

"I don't know…" I trail off, wondering if Marcus even thought about it.

"The house will be empty. I hate you sleeping alone, even when Kris and Fate sleep there, but now they're not."

"Maybe I can actually get some sleep for a change," I tease.

"What if you stayed at the brownstone?" Whitt offers as a suggestion, causing me to gasp in surprise. Whitt loathes Grant. *Loathes*. If he wants me to sleepover with his dad, then Whitt's truly worried about me being alone tonight.

I change the uncomfortable subject to something that makes Whitt uncomfortable. "Did it feel nice to have Dalton sit with you?"

Whitt's ears turn bright pink and I chuckle. Watching them last night, Dalton struggling against his nature, as Whitt egged him on, was the highlight of the past month. As they shared Kris for the first time, Whitt kept trying to look at Dalton and hold his hands. It was so freaking cute that I recorded it and watched it again later.

"I don't know what you're talking about," Whitt's voice cracks from nervousness, but then he decides it's time to be real instead of stubborn. "Sex with Kris is empty of emotion, same with the other girls who touch me. It felt different with Dalton. The thrill of trying to get him to look at me was exciting. I've never come so hard in my entire life."

Realizing what he said, Whitt has the common decency to look ashamed for admitting sex with me wasn't as explosive as just being near Dalton as he fucked Kristal. I try to catch Whitt's eyes to reassure him, but he looks away, worried he's offended me.

"I love you, Sunshine." Caressing Whitt's cheek, I try to show him the depth of emotion I feel for him. "Making love to you was special for me, because it was between us. But you're missing out on the animalistic passion of fucking out of pure lust. I saw the fire in your eyes last night with Dalton, and it made me so happy for you".

I shut the tap off, then pepper Whitt's face with butterfly kisses. "Give four kisses for me when you get to Misery Castle, would ya?"

I walk out of the bathroom and startle. Marcus is the only one left behind, and he's waiting for me.

"Well, tomorrow comes in a mere five hours," I mutter conversationally as I toe on my sneakers, ignoring how awkward I feel. "I'm going to hit the sack while I can. Night."

"Regina. Regina. Regina." Marcus sighs my name, following me down the hallway toward the exit door. "Always pretending it's my issues keeping us apart, but she runs from me when she needs me the most."

"Shut up," I bark, because Whitt's trailing behind us, laughing his ass off.

"Hmm… me thinks the truth hurts the lady," Whitt whispers into my ear, just barely evading my flying hand. "Yep, Queen gets punch-happy when she's emotionally uncomfortable. I'm gonna leave you two be."

"Night," Marcus and I call out in unison as Whitt slips into his Roadster.

Giving in, knowing I can be just as stubborn as Whitt and Dalton are, I don't put up a fuss as Marcus drives me home to my empty house, then sleeps with me for the first time in almost two months.

In the middle of the night, I crash. Whether it be fear, or memories, or nightmares, I turn into a bawling creature filled with rage, and Marcus holds me together until morning. Only giving, we don't even address the subject that Marc's nightmare from Las Vegas is entering Dominion's city limits tomorrow night.

Chapter Forty-Eight

In the middle of the dance floor, with police officers picking their way through patrons, I stand frozen in a state of shock. "Regina," Aaron whispers in exhaustion as his arms wrap around me in a hug. I hold the teddy bear of a man who just took down no less than ten men. I squeeze him, because I don't like the innocence lost or seeing hands that are so gentle bash in a skull. I sigh heavily as I run a fingertip along Aaron's lacerated eyebrow.

"No more, Aaron. I'm done," I vow. My voice cracks because Regina Regal never gives up.

Devlin Conrick arrived, changed shit up, and made it all worse at the behest of Olivia Fontaine. Every action taken was meant to incapacitate us, even dragging Bianca Green here to put Dalton into a spiraling tailspin. Just as we were making progress between Dalton and Whitt, Bianca shows up. Whitt was jealous enough of his *Toddler*, adding the fact that she's now the object of his affection's wife… this won't end well.

We were told we had to stay open, we had to allow non-vetted people into our dungeon, and our masters and their submissives had to train anew with Dexter. Everything bad everywhere was our fault.

Olivia Fontaine managed to gaslight an entire club full of dominants, and she's supposedly not even on Dominion soil, which I don't fucking believe for a nanosecond. No one on the planet, who creates such devastation, wouldn't want to sit back and watch it up-close and personal.

Meanwhile, we still can't keep any new employees, and those who were helping are now inside Dexter's private room for useless lessons, including my son. Devlin Conrick ordered Niel to join the festivities, and I was powerless to stop it. When I tried, Niel informed me I had no say in it, as Devlin was Olivia's enforcer in MdJ, and it was an edict he must follow.

There is literally no one but Aaron and me running Restraint, with a handful of people trying their damnedest to do the jobs of many.

Olivia Fontaine didn't want to help us. She wanted to destroy us after one of our own published The Mistress & Master of Restraint and ruined the bulk of her BDSM organization.

Aaron clenches me tightly, breath hitches. "Me too. Thank God, I wouldn't let any of our submissives in here." He expels a shuddering breath and tremors in my arms.

"My son is here for training tonight, in Dexter's room. What if it poured into the dungeon?" a sob builds and I choke in fear.

Aaron doesn't say anything. We stand in the middle of the dance floor in each other's embrace, completely silent and still. All around us EMTs tend to the wounded and push them out on stretchers. The riot police separated the instigators from their victims. I'm not tipping them this time. I need them to tell us to shut down. No more bribery.

Tonight was different– organized chaos. Every other riot has had a desperate quality. Tonight, I watched as four men did that chin tilt our security employs. I watched as they systematically created four separate riots around the club, and it meshed together into the hugest cluster-fuck I've ever seen. It was an epic bloodbath. I'm surprised no one died, a few came very close to the brink.

In the center of it all, I spotted people I never expected to see. Caleb Green. Gwendolyn Meyers. Levi Wilson.

Once I saw them, terror flowed through my veins, incapacitating me. It took an elbow to the chin before I realized they were helping us, not hindering us. Restraint has become a warzone, and Maître du Jeu had to run to our rescue. Either Olivia's gone rogue, or there are scarier forces at play. Perhaps, in our weakened state, we're being hit on all sides by different players who aren't working together.

Lord knows, Restraint seems to be the playground for Dominion's founders. If you strike here, you strike them all at once. With easier access than trying to get behind all those gates in Crestview Drive.

All I know is that Restraint's doors will not open tomorrow night, no matter what.

"What are we going to do?" Aaron's voice is deep with anguish.

"Marcus and I have to talk," I mutter ominously as I step away. We've talked it to death, but Marc's terror over his time in Las Vegas has clouded his judgment. He's eighteen years older.

Politically powerful. Has come into his own money. Dominion is his home field advantage.

Marcus is not the same innocent man he was, but fear has him bowing down to his oppressors, just as he did nearly two decades ago.

No more.

I need to see my son. I need to know everyone who was training in Dexter's room is safe and sound. This stupid-assed training took a huge chunk of my help away. I needed Dexter, Syn, Whitt, and Roman with me tonight. Plus, Tobias and Monica have proven to be a great help at extricating the baddies.

The training was a ruse, just as eliminating all of my bartenders and security. We're down to four on our security team now. We lost Chris to the bullshit. He left after the last riot– a broken wrist. It wouldn't be much of a surprise to learn we only have Roarke now.

A police officer pulls Aaron away from me, needing answers to questions we can't provide. Mind spinning wildly, I sneak into the dungeon, hoping the police don't follow. So far, we've been lucky, as the dungeon is considered a private space. But this is most certainly considered an active crime scene now, so it won't matter much longer.

"No one moves!" Dexter's voice hits me full force as the door clanks at my back. Blinking repeatedly to clear my vision, everything coalesces into a nightmare, and all I can do is stare in horror.

Dalton's trussed up on a rack, stretched taut and whimpering in misery. Spread out in an arc is a classroom full of Dexter's trainees, a bunch of people I don't recognize, and our trio of MdJ saviors.

Barking orders while untying Dalton, Dexter tries to get the situation under control. "Syn, peek out in the club and see if the riot's over, and if the men in blue have swarmed our asses for a sixth time. Then find out where our security went."

With one eye on the action, and the other on MdJ, I'm torn between helping Dalton and chasing down those responsible. Feet moving on their own volition, I don't realize until it's too late that I'm standing shoulder to shoulder with Caleb Green, Stanton Green's little brother. Why should I be surprised though? After all, Bianca Green arrived with Devlin. They seem to travel in packs.

"What are you doing here, Caleb?" I murmur out the side of my mouth as Dexter unties Dalton with Whitt's supervision. "Are you responsible for this?"

Unable to help himself, Levi Wilson creeps up to the action, hands held out as he tries to figure out how to help his baby brother. Their mutual maternity is not common knowledge, but who in their right mind would admit to being Olivia Fontaine's child? *Wil's* identity isn't common knowledge either, as no one here even knows he's Syn's husband.

Doing a double-take, Caleb flinches, but there is no way he doesn't recognize me. I haven't changed that much.

"*Gunner*," Caleb stresses, explaining the flinch was due to his birth name being used. "I'm Gunner, and that man over there is *Wil*."

Pointing at the petite blonde trying her damnedest to make the floor swallow her whole, my voice twists with sarcasm. "And she's the Whore of Babylon."

Jesus Christ, Gwen looks exactly as I imagined. An older version of all of her beautiful children. Dinky with curves, natural blonde and blue-eyed, and beautiful enough to turn everyone's head twice. But Grant was spot-on with how he described her demeanor– there's a hollowness to her expression that makes you want to protect her. She doesn't want to be here anymore than I want her to be. Maybe Gwen had to see firsthand what was going on inside her city.

"Regina," Caleb chastises me. "We have more important issues to deal with than your jealousy."

"Jealousy?" I spit, insulted. "Grown women having sex with fifteen-year-old boys isn't something one is envious over. You should agree with me, seeing as one of Gwen's victims is your own brother."

"Not now." Caleb squeezes my arm in warning. "We're already spread too thin in this dungeon. Dalton's hurt, Wil and Syn will need to take care of him as quickly as they can, because we'll need their help afterward. In the meantime, we need the dungeon cleared and those responsible questioned."

"When did you get home?" pops out before I can stop it, curiosity getting the better of me. "I thought you were on tour in the Middle East."

"IED and a stint in Landstuhl Regional Medical Center," Caleb mutters dryly. "No time to recuperate as I was dumped into this shit storm the instant I stepped on Dominion soil."

"So you're here to help?" Hope infuses me, because I've always trusted Stanton Green, the lord of Dominion's underworld, so I know I can trust his marine brother.

"Yes." Caleb looks at me, gauging how receptive I'll be to taking his orders. No doubt this man was an officer of some type in the Marines Corps. "I'd suggest you go with Dalton. He seems to not mind your company. I'll do my best to influence Dexter in a way where I won't say too much. Tomorrow, I'll be your new head of security."

"Roarke?" I coax for more information.

"Will agree," is all Caleb says. "You'll be safe from here on out, Regina."

"I want Restraint to be closed down," I seethe.

"It will be," he vows. "Now go with Dalton. Please."

Feet moving, I realize Caleb wants me out of here for a reason, but I do as I'm told, feeling relived someone else will be the responsible party for once.

Whitt picks up Dalton, cradling him to his chest, and the beaten man moans hollowly. Dalton didn't deserve this– no one does.

"I'll take him to my room and clean him up," Whitt says as he starts to walk away.

"No," Dalton moans in a panic, fingers curled into claws against Whitt's shirt.

"Put him down!" Wil demands, glacial eyes glowing with fury. "Now."

"Who the fuck are you?" Even with their bad blood, Dexter's feeling protective and possessive of Dalton. "That's an answer I want. *Right now*."

"I'm Gunner." Caleb steps forward to be the voice of reason. "And the guy checking out your young man is Wil. I'd suggest you let him do his job."

"Hey, buddy." Wil's entire badass demeanor changes to gentle examination. "Dalton, look at my eyes and relax. That's right, buddy. I've got you. Look at me."

If Levi Wilson is going to do that blue-white eye bullshit, maybe we better go fetch Devlin from wherever he's hiding and Torian too. All three of them possess the same eerie eyes, denoting a genetic connection. I have no idea why Dalton would be comforted by it.

Whitt's frozen in shock, holding a battered Dalton in his arms, while a man who looks about as innocent as a serial killer is stroking Dalton's beaten face. Not that Levi Wilson looks like a thug. That's the problem. He looks like an everyday Joe, but the intensity wafting off of him is terrifying.

Dalton's sharp intake of breath has all our hearts faltering. Then he's struggling to get away from Whitt, clutching at his big brother, trying to climb into his arms. "Shh… Buddy, you've got to go get patched up. I'm not going anywhere– I promise."

"I'll take him to my room," Whitt murmurs gently, trying to walk without jostling Dalton.

"Nooo…" the sound is long and mournful. "No."

"I'll go." Roman steps through the crowd, trying to take the struggling man from Whitt's arms.

"Just follow me. What's up with you?" Whitt accuses Roman as they walk away.

"Dalton doesn't like to be touched, is all. He trusts me, not you." Roman's voice fades as he follows behind Whitt. "You might hurt him on purpose."

"Cops are here!" Toby calls from the door as he's letting Syn back into the dungeon, and that's my cue to follow Dalton.

I have to have faith in the unexplainable, and trust there are people here who know what they're doing and can keep us safe. I'm just an MdJ underling. Not a pawn like most, and not a member of the council, but I know things I shouldn't. This is bullshit I'm not allowed to know, and it's difficult for me to walk away without answers. Dexter's in the dark more than I am, refusing to take his rightful seat on the council– it's about time he stepped up to the plate and did the job he was born to do. We need an ethical voice of reason.

Gliding next to Wil, I use the walk down the hallway to stabilize my control. I'm taken aback as we bypass the private rooms to enter a wide staircase that leads to the upper-floors.

Like a stalking panther awaiting its prey, Devlin Conrick is in Dalton's efficiency apartment. The man has to be closer to seven feet than six, corded with muscle, and has the contained power to harm instead of heal. Yet Devlin is gentle and caring as he touches Dalton, even while he takes over by barking out orders to Wil. After laying Dalton on his bed, working as a team, they strip the boy down, even going as far as to take his contacts out and pull the wig off his head.

Whitt and I stay in the doorway, rendered speechless and motionless as Roman performs small tasks around the apartment. He grabs medical supplies from the bathroom, washcloths dampened with warm water, and fetches chairs to be placed by the bed.

Gasping before I can stop myself, I stare wide-eyed as a beautiful creature is revealed beneath the drab clothing, muddy brown wig, and brown contacts. While his brother and pseudo-father take care of his wounds and wrap up his ribs, Roman slowly wipes the makeup off Dalton's face to reveal the real man beneath.

Dalton lies naked on his mattress, covered in intricate tattoos, completely unconscious and vulnerable. The intimacy of witnessing this is astounding, because there is something innocent, broken, and undeniably private about Dalton. The fact that the men would allow Whitt and me to be a part of this speaks volumes.

Roman flashes me a small smile, sliding his fingers through Dalton's hair in a familiar way. Leaning over the boy, whispering reassuring words, Roman displays their obvious friendship. Hair mingling until I can't tell where one man ends and the other begins, the glossy silk falls in perfect inky strands.

Backing up slightly to take in Dalton, Devlin looks exactly like the beast of a man from the show Spartacus. Doctore. Almost seven feet of midnight perfection that sucks all the air from the room, Devlin doesn't scare me, when he should. After seeing him take care of Dalton, I now find his presence a comfort instead. Those same eyes that shine from both Levi Wilson and Torian Spencer take on an alien vibe next to the darkness of his flesh, so pale that they glow white.

"How is he?" spills softly from my throat.

Not looking elsewhere but at the bed, I walk over to Dalton, then cup his small hand in mine. Dalton's always been nice to me while he ruined everything in his path.

"Dalton's mind is more injured than his body, completely shutting down from the fear. He's petrified of being bound." Devlin's voice holds equal softness. "Please keep this secret."

I meet Devlin's eyes to show him my sincerity. "I've always known who Dalton was," I say pointedly, causing his eerie eyes to widen in shock.

Through all of this, Whitt's eyes haven't left the sleeping man. Face glowing with awe, Whitt's mesmerized. He stares at Dalton in a mix of covetous lust and tender care. I watch his face, and I hear a powerful word echoing like a heartbeat… *mine... mine... mine*.

"Marcus gave me a picture of Dalton, but it didn't do him justice. He's such a beautifully exquisite creature." My voice doesn't sound like my own. Soft, like the expression on Whitt's face.

"Jesus," Whitt whimpers, completely starstruck. "Dalton's body is the perfect canvas."

"Do you like our gift," I tease the boy.

Eyes flick to me for a split-second in question, then return to Dalton's ruby-kissed lips. I watch as Whitt's throat convulses as he tries to swallow his need. I'm just waiting for his eyes to venture southward. I won't dishonor Dalton by staring, but saying the boy is hung, even flaccid and in pain, would be an understatement.

"What?" Whitt slurs, not bothering to look at me as he speaks.

"You can be so daft sometimes, Whitt." Chuckling underneath my breath, I touch Dalton's hair, allowing the silky strands to slide between my fingertips. "We've been shoving you at Dalton for over three years. So stubborn, the both of you."

"The only thing Regina ever wants to do is make you happy." Roman settles his hand on Dalton's chest, directly over his heart "Dalton will make you very happy, and you will make him happy."

"What's going on?" Devlin demands, stepping closer to Dalton, as if we're being inappropriate and disrespectful. We are, but we mean no harm.

"Dalton has a crush on Whitt," Roman admits. "Whitt has a crush on Dalton. Regina, Kristal, and I have been working our asses off, trying to get them to give into it."

"I'll take care of it," Devlin promises with hope glittering in his eerie eyes. He turns and addresses me out of respect.

"Is she as beautiful as Dalton?" I ask Devlin a very private question, one that only he would understand.

It was hard enough seeing Gwen tonight, but it isn't jealousy anymore– my resentment of Gwen runs deeper than that. I knew all of her children before I laid eyes on her, so their faces belong solely to the people I love and respect, not a reflection of their mother.

Grant isn't mine, so my reaction isn't based on jealousy. Gwen and Grant gave us all a gift by bringing Whitt into this world… but Olivia. To see Spyder in the flesh, a grown woman who I've never met, while Marcus and I are together, it would be impossible to deny the jealous rage that will inflict upon me.

If I have a hard time dealing with Ezra and Cortez, two men I've known since they were fourteen, men who were in Marc's life when I came into it, I can't imagine how I'll feel when I meet both Olivia and Spyder.

"Everyone pales to Dalton." Devlin murmurs as he gazes down at the beautiful boy, voice expressing that perhaps it's been Dalton's curse. "She looks like *him*," Devlin stresses him, and I know he means Marcus.

A smile creeps up on me out of nowhere, happiness because I want to see Marc's features carved on his daughter's face. I want to know Spyder like I know Whitt and my own children, but I feared my resentment over her mother bleeding into our interactions if they looked just alike.

"Good. I can't wait to meet her," I whisper, my voice filled with tears. "I need to be there when they meet." I look at Devlin, begging him to allow it.

"Soon," Devlin agrees, proving mother and daughter are indeed in Dominion right now. "Very soon."

They say those in a coma can hear what you say to them. Dalton's unconscious out of fear. It's not the same as a coma, but I hope the theory holds true. After brushing Dalton's hair away, I press my lips tightly to the shell of his ear. I don't want anyone to hear what I have to say.

"I'm so sorry, Dalton." Puzzle pieces connect, and I come to the realization that Olivia was targeting her own son for reasons we've yet to uncover. Dalton was sent here, told to hide himself behind a disguise, and treat us all with disrespect, baiting us to do awful things. Which is why the three scariest members of MdJ are here, ready to interrogate those who hurt Dalton, because it was the one person who should've protected him the most.

Dalton has an innocent soul, and when the truth is revealed, Olivia's gaslighting will break him.

As I murmur into Dalton's ear, Syn arrives. She's whispering loudly to both Devlin and her husband, enough so that my suspicions are proven correct. Leaving Roman, Whitt, and me to watch over Dalton as he rests in an emotional sleep, the three of them leave to do what most likely will leave a red stain on their hands.

"Don't blame yourself– your mother's evil, and I won't allow her to hurt you again." As I whisper into the boy's ear, I realize I've just made Dalton mine too. Not in the way Dalton will be to Whitt. Dalton is now one of my family, and I will do all I can to protect him and make sure he finds happiness.

Leaning into Dalton, I cry silently for the young man. What kind of monster tries to murder her own son? As a mother, who has fought for every second spent with my children, it wrecks me. I loved my children before they were conceived. Hell, a part of me loved the very idea of them, the second Grant came to me to request I carry his children.

Crying in earnest, I silently vow to protect Dalton and his sister. Marc loves my children as his own, just as I love the people he has claimed as his. Dalton and Spyder are no different. Spyder is Marc's only genetic child, and Dalton is her brother, and now they're mine to protect.

My arms ache to hold my neurotic son, my diva daughter, and my orphaned nieces. Parents are horrible monsters. Diane ruined her son's family with her tell-all book. Olivia tried to kill her youngest son. Even Katie left her children behind to help her husband's political career.

As I grow wiser, my perception changes. Watching from the shadows, making sure everyone is happy and healthy, Grant doesn't look as bad by comparison anymore.

Chapter Forty-Nine

Being pragmatic, Marcus, Grant, and I are hunkered down in my cave, sitting on the floor with lists all around us. Instead of sleep, we're in survival-mode. Marcus and I came back here last night to have an important discussion, only to have Grant walk in and take command.

Very bad things are happening if the bat was willing to leave the belfry.

Daniel and Diane's book bankrupted Olivia, causing her to lose her club in Las Vegas– Kink. They avenged Ade and destroyed their blackmailer, but they gave the insane woman a reason to go after all of us.

This isn't common knowledge, as we're feigning ignorance to draw the black widow from her web. The manipulative woman was able to hide her nefarious ploys of revenge as she targeted Restraint. When Olivia's father and husband died, she expected to receive the inheritance. However, it all was given to Dalton. After Dalton divorced Bianca, the boy was fair game again. If Dalton died, his small fortune would be given to his next of kin– his mother. But it couldn't look like she hired someone to take him out.

Grant repeatedly wrote on my whiteboard, in ginormous letters, how Olivia merely hijacked the riots, not that she was the cause. She only used the riots to take Dalton out. So now we're back to square one, not knowing who's targeting us in the first place, while we acknowledge Olivia's actions but not do a damned thing about them.

It helps that we each know different things. Grant's obviously the eyes and ears of Maître du Jeu. Via Niel, I have inside information to both Diane and Daniel's ploys with their book, and the children's use of Generation Next. Marcus knows the Las Vegas people better than any of us. Together, we try to find a plan of attack that will satisfy everyone and not cause aftershocks to ripple through Dominion.

“Just saying Restraint is closed for renovations is a fabulous idea,” I try to sell them on it. “We do need to revamp the place. In the interim, Roarke and Gunner could use their influence to bring in ex-police and retired military to act as our security force.”

“I think we need them in everyday life too, Regina.” Marc’s hand flies across the pages of his notebook, creating detailed lists that put mine to shame. “If Grant’s scared shitless, then it isn’t *our* boogeyman. Us pawn, both those who do and don’t realize they’re chess pieces, we’re sitting targets.”

Lips opening on a silent groan, Grant stretches on the carpet, foot hitting an empty can of energy drink. After sitting back up, he signs for both Marcus and me to see.

I agree. You need bodyguards.

“At least everyone we care about is tucked safely in Misery Castle and Shadow Haven.” I try to look at the bright side. When I came home last night, the air felt thick with promised violence. I didn’t even have to press to get Kristal to take both Fate and Ella to safety.

Roman stayed with Dalton, which is how Grant fled the brownstone, because his enforcers were doing other things and felt he was safer with Marcus and me.

“Even I will agree we need to be in The Gates.” Marcus has never pushed me to return to Misery Castle, when his home is at Shadow Haven. It would divide us yet again, as my home has always been a fantasy together as we forget reality for a few stolen moments.

“I can’t–” It bears no repeating how I won’t go back home until Grant does. “We’ll figure out a way to secure my home.”

“Regina.” Marcus shakes his head sadly, and I receive a swift kick to the shin from Grant. One thing about a mute, if you don’t look at them, they can’t communicate with you. When I’m feeling particularly pissy, I ignore Grant without a lick of guilt. But my poor shins bear the brunt of it.

My office door creaking open has all three of us jumping out of our skins. “I’m so sorry to spook you.” Roarke apologizes, hands held out to show he’s unarmed. “I let myself in.”

“Is there a giant keychain somewhere, with all of our house keys attached?” I turn sarcastic in the face of terror. “What’s going on? You’ve never shown up here voluntarily.”

Caleb Green brushes by Roarke to squeeze into my office–all business, no humor. A soldier. “This is an extraction.”

"What?" Marcus and I are too slow on the uptake, but Grant's ghosting through my house to look out the front windows. He's back before Marcus and I come to terms with what's happening.

"Pack a bag of essentials." It's Roarke's turn to talk down to the hysterical female. "I assume your daughter has duplicates of her belongings at Whittenhower Estates? Fate and Kristal will have to make due with whatever I fetch. Grab some clothing, your medications, your documentation, and your devices. Meet us in the living room."

"What the hell is going on?" Tugging Roarke back into my office, all I receive is a no-nonsense cop expression. Then he leaves my office in search of Fate's bedroom.

"Elder Whittenhower," Caleb says with deference. "The brownstone is not secure, but it will be shortly. However, you cannot be seen leaving this home. After we extract Marcus and Regina, the media will follow, and you'll be free to escape to safety."

Thank you, Enforcer Green.

Grant and Caleb's interactions reminds me of the few times I saw Albert and Jackson interact, and of the day Jackson passed, when Albert addressed Grant in a deferential way.

Grant turns to me, then squeezes my hand. *I'll pack your clothing and toiletries, you get your tech.*

"Someone explain?!" I shout my demand.

"Don't you fucking hear it?!" Marcus shouts back, voice breaking. "We are rats trapped in a goddamn defenseless maze. What about The Gates?"

Head quirked to the side, it finally registers. Helicopter rotors flying directly over my house. More than one.

Taking a deep breath, Caleb releases it in a torrent. "A second edition of the Mistress & Master of Restraint was released this morning, targeting those who were not included in the original publication, including children."

"That was not Diane and Daniel!" I protest, voice wavering.

"No, ma'am. We suspect it was Elder Fontaine, but we can't accuse her until we prove it."

"Oh–" Rolling my eyes dramatically, I flop my arms in the air. "God forbid, we accuse Olivia of something we know she's done."

"What do we do?" Marcus is more pragmatic than I am. "Where are we going?"

"The main gate to Crestview is…" Caleb fumbles for a word. "Essentially gone. There are so many media outlets camping along Crestview Drive, the gate cannot be shut. Even if it did, it would just trap them in there with us. The downtown buildings are a security risk, with news vans lining the streets. Whittenhower Estates' gate is impassable. To open it, to go in or out, means the media will flow in too. Dexter's house is exposed, as the gate is to the drive leading to Lake Serenity, not to his home."

"Shadow Haven?" Marcus holds his breath, waiting for news about his family. "Is Dexter secure?"

"Dexter's refusing to leave his home, and is currently on his front porch bitching at the press," Caleb mutters wryly, meaning Dexter's already going viral. "Ezra barricaded the main gate to Shadow Haven with vehicles. No one will be driving in or out. However, he has a car waiting for you at the bottom of the drive. If we're able to get you in from the logging roads crisscrossing the forest, you can enter through the south gate."

"South gate?" In shock, I'm barely registering this is happening. "Where are you taking me?"

"There's a gate in the south wall, big enough to walk through single-file and little else," Marcus rambles, mind obviously spinning. "We'll need an off-road vehicle to bypass Crestview Drive. I don't have to hazard a guess. Regina and I were targeted this time, as were our children."

"That would be why I'm here, sir." Caleb levels me a look. "We thought it best if you stayed at Shadow Haven until permanent arrangements can be made. Whittenhower Estates is impenetrable right now. The buildings aren't safe. Stanton's barely keeping The Green Building secure, and we have organized crime on our side. The brownstone's location wasn't released. However, it was mentioned. If you were seen coming and going, it would no longer be secure for Elder Whittenhower. Ezra has extended an invitation for you to stay at Shadow Haven."

"What about everyone else?" Powerless, mind spinning, my world is crashing at my feet.

"You and Marcus are our priority right now." Caleb's eyes cut toward Marcus, asking for some help. "Most skeletons were previously released. Adelaide Whittenhower's exposé kept the Whittenhowers, Zeitlers, and Holdens off the pages."

"Olivia?" Marcus gasps, looking ill. "This book was about Regina, Dexter, and me."

"Yes, and the children, including your own."

"That witch put her own daughter in the book?!" Outraged, I start pulling shit out of the draws in my desk to make a pile. "Why am I not surprised– she tried to murder her own son last night."

"That remains to be proven," Caleb points out.

"What skeletons?" Marc's hair is sticking up in every direction, must be he was pulling at it when I wasn't looking. "What could possibly garner *this* amount of exposure?"

"Regina, we have to hurry!" Roarke calls as he passes by my office door. A duffle bag hits me in the chest a second later. "Shut your trap, and fill the bag with your shit. The assholes at Dexter's will be coming here next. Let's get the fuck out of here before that happens."

Walking around my office like a zombie, I can barely stand on my jittery legs. The fireproof security box filled with all of our confidential stuff is tossed on my desk. I grab for the duffle, then begin filling it with my laptops, cellphones, and gadgets. Caleb collects the bag and safe, then leaves for the living room.

Running as if my life depends on it, there are things I can never leave behind. Coming to an abrupt stop, I gape in shock at Grant. He flashes me an apologetic quirk of his scarred lips, then continues to fill a tote with the contents of my bedroom wall safe.

Turning, Grant quickly signs. *I know you. These are your most important possessions. I'll take them with me, keep them safe, and deliver them to our home when it's time.*

"Grant–" the implications of what he's saying terrifies me. I won't be coming back here to live ever again. "We're going home?" I'm rendered utterly speechless.

You know when.

If I can ignore the mute by not looking at him, then he can ignore me by keeping his hands busy. Everything I hold dear to my heart is placed in a tote. My parents' wedding bands. The ancient photo album is the only thing I have left of my childhood. The letters Grant wrote me when I was only eighteen. The lacy nightgown I lost my virginity wearing. The engagement infinity ring Grant gave me on the night he died. The drawing Whitt did of himself so I'd recognize him. The nightgown worn and the sheets used when Whitt and I consummated our marriage and he lost his virginity.

Go! Grant orders, mouthing it too. *I'll get what you need. But you have to go now!*

Feet refusing to move, all I can do is stare in stunned silence at the remains of what I'm leaving behind. For over a decade, I built this home with my daughter and Fate and Kristal. We made memories here when I sometimes wasn't sure I could put one foot in front of the other.

Gnarled lips press against mine, getting through the fog that has descended. Grant grips the back of my neck, fingers biting in, lips attacking mine until I open up for his tongue. Panting heavily, I experience one of the most violently passionate kisses of my life.

Shoving me away abruptly, Grant mouths, "GO!" Then his hands propel me to the hallway.

Emotions centrifuging in my mind, snapping off to be experienced, I weave my way down the hallway. Lust and fear war with confusion over the kiss, then rage and guilt join the party.

Entering my living room, I find Caleb and Roarke loaded down with my bags. "I'm sorry," my voice quivers as I make my apology to Marcus. Believe it or not, I have absolutely no idea what I'm apologizing over. The fact that I just ruined Marc's life, or the emotions Grant just sparked in me.

"There's no way around this, Marcus." Eyes held wide in terror, I don't allow the tears to escape. "They'll find out about us."

"That was the point, Regina," Marcus replies matter-of-factly.

"Your campaign," I mutter in shame. "Not again." Four years ago, Marcus had to drop out of the race due to the controversy with Ezra and their family. This time around, that fueled positive recognition for Marcus, keeping him in the spotlight while his opponent failed to gain exposure.

A judge has to be above reproach, especially morally and ethically. Having a mistress isn't exactly moral or ethical.

"Doesn't matter. My campaign manager said I had no hope of winning the judge's seat with all the negative publicity centered on Restraint's riots. This will be the final nail in my political coffin. I won't be gainfully employed much longer."

"My fault." Covering my face with my palms, tears stream down between my fingertips. "If only I could have stopped what was going on at Restraint. If only everyone would have listened when I wanted to close it down. If only I would've never gotten involved with you–"

"Regina, dammit!" Marcus tears my hands from my face, then glares into my eyes. "Get your shit together before we walk out of this house."

"I ruined you!" I snap back, flinging his hands away.

"Bullshit!" Marcus snags my wrists, shaking me firmly. "Generation Next gave me the idea to be completely transparent to erase the risk of blackmailing and exposure. I was going to go public anyway, so I owe the demon a great debt of gratitude for forcing my hand sooner than I planned."

"I–"

"If you'd think for a second, you'd realize it's not just our mutual skeletons that have been revealed. Your marriage is now public. Your marriage, my marriage, added with our affair, equals disaster."

"What do we do?" Voice quivering, my entire body rolls in a violent shudder.

"We leave here as a united front. I make a statement, and then we make a wild dash for Gunner's Hummer. We'll find a way to get inside Shadow Haven. Then I'm taking a goddamn shower, having a meal, and sleeping for a week… but I'm not letting you out of my sight for a second."

"On a three-count," Roarke warns, then nods his head. One. Two. On three, he opens the door. The swarm parts to allow Roarke and Caleb access to the giant yellow hummer parked in my front lawn. As soon as the guys are at the vehicle, the media makes a beeline for my front door.

With a fortifying breath, I step out of my home for the last time– I won't be coming back. The horde descends, at least thirty people press my back into Marc's chest, with the rest scattered in the yard. Over the top of their heads, I can make out the news vans, satellite trucks, and cars lining the street in front of my home. No one is getting in or out of my neighborhood without a fight.

"Mrs. Whittenhower." A microphone is shoved into my face. Well, so much for that secret. I turn my face to the side to whisper in Marc's ear. "This seems like a lot of paparazzi?" I ask of the crowd of people who surround my property like a prison wall.

Aaron and Kayla's wedding had a helicopter– I have two.

Squeezing to get past us, Caleb enters my house to grab another armload, and Roarke answers. "Once everyone stopped scattering and found a fortification, these assholes ganged up together. You're the last on the move, and the most interesting."

Coming back out with my fireproof safe in his hands, Caleb gets to the root of it all. "You're no longer slumming it across the street from me. You seem to keep forgetting who you are, Regina." Pointing out at the sea, "They never do."

"You're higher profile than Marcus," Roarke reminds me on his way by. "And hella elusive."

"Mrs. Whittenhower, are you the brains behind Empowerment?" A small blonde with the personality of a pit bull screams up in my face.

Scowling, I have to get this in hand, or it's going to blow up in my face. "I will answer questions on one condition," I announce loudly, projecting to include the spectators. "Back away from my house. I'll answer from the head of the sidewalk."

Marcus and I stand at the top of the sidewalk, as close to the Hummer as we can get, with Caleb and Roarke taking up a defensive stance at our backs.

"Yes, I created Empowerment." I answer with the truth to get this insanity over with.

A thousand questions are fired in the next five seconds. Some reporters ask a dozen, spewing words like auctioneers. I point at the lady pit bull, and everyone shuts up.

"Are you money-hungry?" she asks rapidly, fearing someone will ask a question and I won't answer hers.

"Huh?" To clear up my confusion, I point behind me at my sprawling ranch house. It's modest in comparison to most of the homes in this neighborhood, and ridiculous compared to the mansions lining Crestview Drive. I could afford to buy the entire city– is this chick fucking nuts?

"A gold-digger? You started out as an orphan in the worst of our neighborhoods. We have proof that you're the biological mother to Daniel Whittenhower III and Ella Whittenhower. Four years ago, you married Daniel Whittenhower II, and now you're having an affair with Marcus Zeitler."

“Was that a question, or a statement?” Voice snide, I simply shrug, when inside I’m simmering with rage for having my accomplishments reduced to what’s between my legs.

“Everything I have, I earned. It was my knowledge and intelligence that built Empowerment into the global corporation it is today. My brainchild. I donate more money in a month than the lot of you combined earns in a year. To insinuate that my wealth was built inside my womb versus my brain is insulting to women across the planet.”

Biting back what else I have to say on that volatile subject, I turn to walk away. “If you don’t have any *actual* questions, then it’s time for me to say goodbye to my home of fourteen years. I need to thank you for taking my anonymity away and making my home unsafe.”

I start to walk away, but then the reporter speaks. “How long have you and district attorney Marcus Zeitler been having an affair?”

“Six years,” Marcus answers, voice ringing with pride, and I freeze in shock. A warm, reassuring hand slips into mine, and I envision a billion camera snaps going off to immortalize the connection.

“Regina Regal has only been married to Daniel Whittenhower II for four years.” The reporter states in confusion.

“Was that a question?” Marcus smoothly teases. He turns on the charm, but there is a cunning glint in his eyes. “Were you asking if we had an affair for two years prior to their union, and during?”

“I’ll take that as confirmation,” the reporter banters back. “Are you having an affair with your adopted son and his spouses?”

“Fallacy,” is Marc’s answer with no elaboration, and then he gives his infamous long-suffering sigh.

“Do you believe it’s ethical for someone of your pastime to hold an elected office that is built on honor and integrity?”

“My pastime is known as a lifestyle, and it’s built on stringent rules, and respect is the cornerstone. My relationship with Regina is not an affair. We’re not sneaking around on our spouses. You’d be surprised to know that the lifestyles of the rich and famous are quite scandalous.”

“Why don’t you surprise us by being honest?!” is shouted from the back of the crowd.

Marcus rolls with it, whereas I'm cringing inwardly.

"Regina is my partner, and our spouses have known from the very beginning. Marriages for people in our position are more like business contracts. What Regina and I do is more ethical than having affairs with your coworkers, or paying for prostitutes, and doing so without your significant other's knowledge, as the rest of our great nation resorts to. We negotiated terms, just as I do on a daily basis in my profession. Bear in mind, I don't need to work. I chose to do so for the greater good."

The reporter attempts to debate Marcus, but he holds a hand out to still her.

"I have an announcement– as of last night, our establishment of hedonistic delight." Marcus clears his throat as Roarke and Caleb's snickers die with a sharp cough. "Restraint will be closed until farther notice. We're doing an extensive renovation to accommodate our growing clientele. That is all."

Marc clasps my hand tighter, then tugs me to follow him to Caleb's Hummer. Camera flashes blind me as we walk. The helicopters hovering overhead broadcast us live to their news station affiliates. The sounds of the shutters clicking, screams of questions barraging us, and the whoop of the rotors is deafening.

Climbing in the car, I'm thankful to shut out the noise, the intense manmade wind, and the scrutinizing eyes.

Marcus pulls me into his arms, and I immediately bury my face into his chest. Flashes illuminate the interior as the paparazzi snap photo after photo through the windshield and windows of the car.

"Hold on tight," Caleb warns. "We won't be driving on any roads once we get out of your neighborhood."

As we depart, I leave the home I created in the Regal name, and I don't look back.

Never look back.

Chapter Fifty

In a way, I'm glad we arrived through the woods. Because I'm not sure I could have emotionally survived if I had to go through the main gate, up Crestview Drive, and voluntarily enter Shadow Haven's gate. Especially while driving through a gauntlet of media.

Eyeballs still jiggling in my skull, the Hummer comes to an abrupt stop inches from the massive wall surrounding Shadow Haven's grounds.

Groaning, I stretch out to my full height as soon as my feet hit the ground. "Yeah, ixnay on that camping excursion," I say to Marcus to break the sour mood that has fallen. "Unless it's in a cushy campground. No more off-roading for my ass."

"I'm about to pull a Jamie and become a goddamn hermit." Marcus slips out of the car, stretching out his own muscles.

"Laugh it up," Caleb grumbles as he comes to join us. "I have to drive back to The Green Building."

"Christ," Roarke hisses, hand rubbing at the back of his neck. "Never been so fucking happy I live here as much as I do now."

"That Hummer is only a few weeks old, and I'm going to have to take it in for a tune-up." Looking at the ivy-covered wall, Caleb tries to find the gate. "If I remember right…" he trails off.

"How do you know where it is?" pops out of Marc's mouth, and he sounds vaguely jealous that someone else knows where a hidden entrance is to his property.

"Ezra and I were buddies long before you showed up, Marcus," Caleb says in explanation. "Used to run these woods– pissed chubby, lazy Cortez off something fierce."

"I knew I liked you." Caleb and I share a grin. "How's Julio and your brother doing?"

"Good– real good." Caleb begins ripping down the foliage, finding no gate, only to move onto another section. Marcus joins in the search, with Roarke watching on in amusement. "Have you ever met a tiny ginger fella? Firefighter and paramedic? Runs with Syn and Wil?"

"Yeah, I'd never forget him." Closing my eyes tight, I try to forget the grisly scene, but nothing will erase the shadow of the Ade I know now. Once a week, Diane, Daniel, and I visit Wintercrest, and Ade never acknowledges our presence. "He helped when Ade and Katya were hurt. Why?"

"Cory is Julio's husband. He's Wil and Syn's chief, and they introduced him to Julio," Caleb says conversationally, palms still searching. "Yes!" is a victory cry. "Anyway, nice guy. I was happy to know everybody was good when I arrived home. This drama notwithstanding."

Marcus turns grumpy, not enjoying the sensation of being left out of the loop while we talk about people he doesn't know, but more so that Caleb found the hidden gate before he did.

"Hello," Aaron drawls, head peeking out to greet us. "Bit of a hike to the car," he warns. "So we need all hands on deck to get Regina's stuff to Ezra's SUV."

"We'll turn into pack mules, so Caleb can be on his way," I offer, reaching in to grab the bag Grant packed me. "Most of it has to find its way to Fate and Kristal."

"That has to go with you too," Caleb warns, piling bags on his shoulders. "Once I leave The Gates, there's no way in hell I'm getting back in. One of you will have an easier time getting this to Dexter at the foot of the hill, then have him get it past Whittenhower Estate's gate."

"Jesus," I mutter underneath my breath, disgusted. "Is this really our reality?"

"Afraid so." Aaron takes my fireproof safe. "If Caleb will help trek this to the SUV, we'll take it the rest of the way."

Grinning hugely, Roarke is practically dancing in place. "I could always take out the ATV. Go around Lake Serenity and up the mountain to Misery Castle."

"Really?" Aaron rolls his eyes. "That won't be necessary. We need you here to protect the place from that." Pointing upward, a helicopter buzzes overhead. "There's four of those cocksucking things randomly flying over Crestview."

Deflated, Roarke shoulders a few bags, then disappears onto the other side of the wall.

"I still don't get the big f'n deal." I squeeze through the gate, only to be surprised to enter a wooded area. Aaron wasn't lying when he said it was a trek to the driveway.

"Regina." Marcus stabilizes me when I almost upend over a fallen branch. "As you're well aware, Kent Preston was just announced as the vice presidential nominee for the republican ticket. Now, until well after the November election, this will be our reality."

"Yeah, but… what do *I* have to do with any of that?" Releasing a sigh of relief, I spot a clearing up ahead.

"You amaze me sometimes," Marcus mutters, and it doesn't sound complimentary. "You see yourself as an island. An orphan. Single. Living in your tiny house. Avoiding going to work in the giant building you own, like you're just a lowly programmer in her cave."

"What Marcus is trying to say," Aaron interrupts on purpose, probably to keep Marcus from angering me. Aaron knows me well. "You are a Whittenhower. Your children are Whittenhowers. Kent Preston's wife and children are Whittenhowers. You're connected to Marcus, who is connected to Ezra, with his incest partner, his father's victim as his wife, and the daughter conceived in the act of rape. Kent's opposition is going to have a field day with this shit."

"As you see," Marcus continues. "My political struggles mean squat when we're dealing with something of this magnitude."

"This is a big fucking deal," Aaron adds just as we hit pavement. "Now, drop your bags in the cargo area, and wave bye-bye to the nice marine."

"I'm not a child," Marcus and I grumble in unison.

"Then stop acting like one." Aaron hits beneath the belt. "We've got a mansion full of crazy who won't relax until his daddy crosses the threshold. So let's hurry this the fuck up."

After depositing the majority of the load, Caleb waves bye-bye to us, smirking the entire time. "This nice marine is going home. Have fun with Ezra."

"Jesus," I snarl as I swing into the backseat, the gravity of my situation finally sinking in. "I can't live like this."

"Too bad," Roarke rumbles from the driver's seat just as he turns the ignition over. "Short of dying, this is what it is. You've got to deal, Regina."

"Okay," I whisper as Aaron takes shotgun. "Having you both together at the same time isn't going to be fun." At Restraint, I worked with one or the other, because they have the tendency to steamroll over me when working as a team, which is why they are so efficient at micromanaging Ezra.

The silent drive is short, but I can't wrap my mind around the length of Shadow Haven's driveway. After growing up where I lived in walk-ups with parking on the street, even after living at Misery Castle, I still find it unfathomable to have a driveway miles long. My driveway is twenty feet from the curb to the front porch.

Maybe Marcus is right. I'm living in denial– a them versus me mentality. I see myself as I was for the first eighteen years of my life, when it's been exactly eighteen years since. I've lived this upscale life, trying to pretend I'm anything but, for the same amount of time I lived otherwise.

It's time to accept who I am, the power I wield, and take control of my own life.

The SUV rolls to a stop in the circular driveway in front of Shadow Haven. "Honey, we're home!" Roarke calls, hopping out of the driver's seat.

Proof that I'm still not like them, but I am. Aaron and Roarke each open a back passenger door, treating Marcus and me as something more than regular people. We're not asked to carry our bags this time. I even attempt to help– Marcus doesn't –but I'm playfully batted away.

I don't know if I'll ever grow out of this mentality, but I have a feeling it's one of the reasons Marcus loves me– I keep him grounded in reality, in a culture where the lines are easily blurred.

"Hey." Marcus spins me around with a hand on my shoulder. "Check that shit out."

"Holy Christ." Awed, my eyes are the size of saucers. Misery Castle overlooks Dominion as a whole. Whereas Shadow Haven lords over all of Crestview. Down in the valley, two lines of Mansions bracket a roadway. This far up the mountainside, I can't see individual vehicles, but the sun glints off mirrors and chrome. "It's like a warzone."

"Just be glad we're up here, and not down there," Marcus murmurs in sympathy.

Palm covering my heart, no matter how much they may piss me off, no one should have to live in that. "What about the people who live in those houses?"

"Everyone down there is related to Syn," Roarke reminds me, dropping a few bags on the front sidewalk. "They took off as soon as the helicopters showed up. They're hiding in The Green Building."

"Good," I murmur, amazed at how organized they were.

"C'mon, slowpokes." Aaron takes my arm. "Let's get you inside to meet the family."

Arching an eyebrow in question, Marcus puts me out of my misery. "Since Katya moved in, it's a different atmosphere." His hand slips into mine, thumb rubbing in soothing circles. "More laidback and filled with kids."

This is where the *us versus them* ends. Aaron and Roarke walk right in the front door ahead of us, calling out that we're home. Kayla rushes to greet them, and is sweet enough to check in on Marc's and my wellbeing. They disappear into the back of the house, leaving us to the family.

With the medieval doors at my back, surrounded by priceless works of art, there is no way I could ever feel at home in Shadow Haven. Marcus and I share a look, no doubt he's reading the transparent emotions scrolling across my face.

"Thank God!" The household crazy comes jogging from parts unknown, looking frazzled and out of sorts. "I was watching it live on the news, and I couldn't find you in the mad crush."

"We took the long way," I mutter wryly, causing Marcus to chuckle.

"Welcome, Regina." Ezra's personality shifts from anxious, to relieved, to the master of the house in mere seconds. "Mrs. Jessup will take your bags up to Marc's room, after we sort out whose is whose. Her grandson will take the rest over to Misery Castle."

"How?" Marcus and I mutter in unison. Just call us the Bobbsey Twins.

"Lucian will figure it out– don't worry." Ezra takes my elbow, always being slightly inappropriate with the touching. "You guys must be tired. Stressed out. In need of a drink."

"Ezra," Marcus stops Dr. Lunatic in his tracks. "You are well aware this is my house too. I can show Regina around. You don't need to be our tour guide."

"Sorry." Ezra runs his fingers through his cropped hair. "I'm stressing the fuck out."

"Oomph!" is forced from my chest as something soft yet solid rams into my thighs. "Oh, hello down there."

Gigantic eyes peer up at me, as if I'm the most fascinating thing ever. "Red hair."

"I see that you have red hair, sweetie." Since the girl is hugging my leg, I figure it's okay to touch her back. Running my fingers through her crimson locks, Azrael is the perfect melding of Katya and Cortez.

Chubby finger pointing upward, I get with the program. Crouching so the toddler can reach, I allow her to finger my strawberry blonde hair. "Have you met Niel?"

"Niel?" The little girl's eyes brighten like it's Christmas, looking around to see if he's here. Must be Azrael feels comfort and excitement in the familiarity, being surrounded by all this pale and shiny.

"I'm Niel's mommy." The more I speak, the clingier Azrael gets. "You're a cuddle monkey, aren't you?"

Marcus and Ezra just stand by, hiding their smirks, curious to see how I react.

Going with the flow, I just pick Azrael up, all the while she chatters nonsense in my ear. Her heavy weight in my arms blooms pure warmth in my heart. So cuddly and sweet. "Where's your other half?" Gazing around the opulent foyer, I know the boy twin must be lurking somewhere. Ezra tells me they travel in packs.

Katya and Ava appear out of nowhere, both looking uncertain with my arrival for different reasons. If MdJ gets their wish, Ava will be my daughter-in-law someday, so the girl finds me beyond intimidating.

Katya, the more I see her in this environment, the more *I* feel like I belong in it. After almost four years in this house, Katya still acts like a guest. The woman and I have a lot in common, but mistrust and a painful history keeps us from making a connection.

"Azrael's probably bothering you." Katya takes the cuddle monkey from my arms, all the while wearing an indulgent smile. I can tell she was comfortable with me holding her child, but she just didn't want me to feel pressured into it. Not all women are maternal, and Katya pegs me wrong.

"No problem– she's a sweetheart."

Katya laughs, a genuine laugh of pure pleasure. I begin to wonder if she's ever off her guard around anyone, because I've never heard her real laugh before. Judging by Ezra's instantaneous reaction, it doesn't happen often.

"As long as Az is fed, and not in need of a nap, she's a sweetheart," Katya mutters wryly. "If not, she becomes a demon."

"Did I hear my Kitty Kat laughing?" Cortez's voice announces his arrival before we catch sight of him. Swooping down behind Ava, "Oh, there you are," Cortez comes back up with a pale little boy who is the spirit and image of Zane.

"Oh, my God!" Palm covering my mouth, I'm in awe. "He looks just like–" Ezra shakes his head no rapidly and Marcus pinches the inside of my wrist. "Just like Ezra," I go with the flow.

No fucking wonder Katya doesn't feel comfortable around here. She must sense the goddamn secrets and lies. Mood shifting, I'm so pissed the hell off, I could flay them all alive. Who marries a woman, has three children with her, and doesn't tell her he has a fourteen-year-old son?

Only Ezra.

With narrowed eyes, I hold a vicious conversation with Ezra, while Cortez distracts everyone else with Marcus Zane.

The toddler's name is Marcus *Zane* for fuck's sake.

"Thank you for welcoming me into your home." I go for graciousness since we have three minors and an innocent present. "I'll only stay until I make arrangements elsewhere."

"Just move right in," Cortez teases me, looking more relaxed and happier than I've ever seen him before, all because his kids are swarming around him. Marcus Zane's hanging upside down in Cort's arms, with Ava tickling the little guy, and Azrael is struggling to get out of Katya's arms to join them.

Laughing at Cort's joke, "My kids might want me to be near them, and it's best not to put Ava and Niel in the same house."

"And on that note…" Marcus trails off, lacing his fingers with mine. "Regina and I need to crash."

It's bizarre because it somehow feels right. Marcus squeezes my hand, pulling me up the staircase, continually flicking his eyes to check out my expression. I can't get a real read on his emotions, but I'd say he's not acting as I expected. There's an almost giddy energy bubbling up from him, when I'd expect stressed and pissed.

"So…" Marcus hesitates, drawing me down a corridor I wish I'd never set foot into again. Being in this house is going to be a test of my resolve. I just hope to God it doesn't bring the nightmares back. "When I ask you something later, you have to promise to say yes."

"Surely you're joking," I mutter dryly to hide the fact that I'm teasing him. "Who in their right mind would ever enter an open-ended agreement with you?"

Growling softly, Marcus pulls me into a room I've never entered before. I'm so lost to curiosity, I agree to whatever the man wants. "Okay, sure– now let me check this place out."

Marcus lands in the center of his bed, chuckling maniacally as I investigate the rest of his room. In a wash of navy and bronze, he has the usual pieces of furniture. Most people wouldn't find it intriguing to notice he has a giant TV on top of his dresser, or the stack of books resting on his nightstand, or the fact that he has clothes laying in a messy pile in a chair.

Every interaction between us was on my turf, or at the brownstone– Grant's hidey-hole –but this is Marc's, and it makes it that much more intimate.

"Comfortable yet expensive," I murmur underneath my breath as I check out the view from his gigantic windows spanning an entire wall. "I was relieved when I looked out my bedroom window at Misery Castle, only to see the lawns and pond."

"Didn't want to feel as if you were lording over all of Dominion from the comfort of your bedroom?" The teasing quality in Marc's voice lessens the impact. "My first bedroom here overlooked the tennis court."

"First bedroom?" Leaning forward, as night descends, the lights from the camped out media sources lining Crestview Drive glow with intensity. The sheer volume surrounding Misery Castle's gate has my heart pounding out of my chest. I hope Grant made it back to the brownstone safely. I'll have to make a bunch of phone calls later.

"Yeah," Marcus whispers softly behind me. Arms slip around my belly, then pull my back to his chest. "Post-Vegas Marcus refused to sleep where Pre-Vegas Marcus laid his head." Quivering with unspoken emotion, he squeezes me tighter. "This room felt untouched– safer."

"Grant kissed me," blurts out of nowhere, mostly because the guilt was eating me alive. "I kissed him back."

A laugh loaded with sexual intensity vibrates the side of my neck, at the same time a bulge hardens against my ass. "I know,

Regina. I could tell when you walked back into your living room."

"You're not mad?" Needing something to anchor me, I rest my palm on the window, finding the coolness grounding. "I haven't touched anyone but you since the rage-sex years and years ago."

"Just remember how Jamie kissing you– and you kissing him back –doesn't lessen how you feel about me, every time you get nutty about Cortez."

"Not funny," I warn, wanting to pull away but I don't. "He's… he's going to go back home."

"I know." Marc's lips feather against my throat as he speaks. "So are you."

"Whitt's birthday." It's been unspoken between all of us, just a known fact. This new crisis made it so I didn't have any excuses not to do it. "What about us?" Gazing around this well-loved bedroom, the warmth in the house around us, I can't ask Marcus to follow me.

"Did you happen to notice Diane isn't present?" Marcus draws me from the windows, then pushes me onto his bed. In a move more reminiscent of Grant, he begins to undress me.

"Yeah, hard not to." My mind takes a mini-vacation as Marcus digs his fingertips into the soles of my feet. "Diane isn't a woman who can be ignored."

"You know, I've felt this timer ticking down above me too. I know we don't talk about it." More fingertip action, and I turn into a puddle of goo on the mattress. Leaning forward, Marc's expression changes to that of a demanding dominant male. "You *will* divorce Pretty Boy within three months of his twenty-fourth year."

"Last night, while we sat vigil with Dalton, something shifted in Whitt. I left him there with the boy. I plan on divorcing him for his own sake. Whitt needs to move on, and I want nothing more than his absolute happiness."

"Good." Marcus kisses the tip of my nose, then pulls away. "There have been things I've been concentrating on while you dealt with Restraint and all those Whittenhower heirs."

"Like what?" Curiosity has me reaching up to help Marcus undress too. Humming in the back of my throat, I unbutton his shirt, then slip my hands underneath to feel his warm skin. "Mmm…"

Releasing a sexual purr, "I love the way you look at me, Regina. Whoa–" Marcus finds himself upended, with me sitting on his hips.

"I love looking at all this gorgeous tan flesh." In a sea of my ruddy freckles, and the overpopulation of pink and pale skin in Dominion, Marc's darker skin is intoxicatingly exotic to my senses. "Kristal and Cortez always feel insecure because they're not ghosts like Ezra, and I just can't fathom why."

"Being different isn't always a comfort," Marcus reminds me. "It's why my granddaughter is so happy to meet a fellow gingy."

"What have you been concentrating on?" Rolling my palms up and down his chest, Marcus rises slightly to meet my touch. "Where is Diane?"

"My first order of business will upset you," Marcus treads carefully. After a lot of soul-searching, I've come to understand I'm not a reasonable woman.

Remaining fluid, when all I want to do is freeze stiff, I continue to give Marcus a massage. "Hit me."

Arching an eyebrow, "That saying takes on entirely different connotations when it comes to you and foreplay with Ezra and Jamie."

"Ha. Ha." I laugh without humor, rolling my eyes.

"Cortez has been going through something–" I can't help it, it's a kneejerk reaction. My hands freeze on Marc's chest. "That's why I needed you to remember how kissing Jamie back didn't change how intense your feelings are for me."

"Okay," I breathe, trying to dampen down my chaotic emotions.

"In my heart." Marcus presses a palm over mine on his chest. "In my head." He taps his temple. "And in my soul, I know Ezra and Cortez belong together. What's been going on with Cortez and me is just a leg in Cort's journey to Ezra."

The sadness in Marc's voice, and the sheen of tears in his eyes, has me forgetting my own insecurities. All I see is his pain, and it physically hurts me too. "You're in love with him."

"Maybe a little bit." Marcus shrugs beneath me. "But not how you think. Cortez is going through something, and I'm helping him. I don't feel used because he doesn't realize he's using me. But it will be okay– soon. I think he's getting ready."

"Ready for what?"

"To not hide anymore." Marcus flashes me a sad smile. "I know it frustrated you how Ezra, Cortez, and Katya haven't helped at Restraint, but they do have some heavy shit they're going through. Cortez has pulled away from them, causing Kat and Ezra to become stronger together."

"And Cortez is cleaving onto you," I say without a shadow of a doubt.

"Yeah, but not for the reasons you'd think." Marc's hands grip my hips, making sure I can't run away. "He's coming to the realization that maybe he only wants to be with guys."

Eyebrows scrunching in confusion, my heart is trying not to break. "Are you having sex?"

"No." Marcus grins up at me, swirling his pelvis beneath me. "Not so much skull-fucking anymore. We frot."

"Frot? What the hell is that?"

Continuing to smirk up at me, Marcus rolls his bulge against my crotch. "This is our definition of frotting. Dry-humping. With clothes. Always standing up. Never in a bed. With a ton of kissing, begging, and angst about wanting dick."

"So you're trying to say you're giving Cortez what he needs, but don't even try to deny how you're getting something out of it too."

"Don't pretend you haven't gotten something out of it when you touched everyone but me." Marcus waits a heartbeat for me to protest and get pissy, but I don't. "Sometimes this highlights how much you want the person you're not with, right?"

"You know me too well," grumbling underneath my breath, I can't look Marcus in the eye.

"Exactly," he murmurs knowingly. "I couldn't move on until I knew Cortez was safe and happy with Ezra. Committed to one another or not, it hasn't been a honeymoon for them. I worry about Katya when Cortez admits the truth… and I won't lie, at some point, Cortez and I will end up doing the deed, and it won't be about you. Okay?"

"I have no room to bitch." I hate it, but I keep my goddamn mouth shut.

"My uphill battle is worse than yours," Marcus teases me. "We all know Cortez and Ezra belong together. Just as everyone believes you and Jamie belong together. So I have to fight *that*."

"*You* have insecurities?" Shocked, all I can do is gape at Marcus. "I'm with you, aren't I?"

"Imagine me not feeling secure?" Marcus teases me, grinning. "I do fear you're running from Jamie by using me, in the same way you get all testy about Cortez. Then I realize life is too short, and I fight for what I want. The more I fight, the more Jamie leaves you alone."

"Fight, huh?" I purr, feathering my fingers through his chest hair. "You know how much I get off on passionate sex mixed with bloodshed."

"Never happening," he banters back. "But I'd be more than happy to chase you down and do whatever I please without your consent."

Heartbeat tattooing the inside of my chest, my mind plays a dozen encounters of predator versus prey. But it's never been realistic enough to feed Marc's need.

"My greatest fantasy is tying Jamie to a bed…" Marcus trails off, making sure I won't judge him for his perversions. This side of him intrigues me, so I just smirk. "Sometimes you fight me as I take Jamie. Sometimes you help."

"Help?" I gulp out, mouth suddenly dry.

"You hold Jamie down." The bulge underneath me pulses, getting harder by the second. "You prepare him for me. Toss a bit of bloodshed in there for your own perversions. Sucking his dick, eating his ass. Then you press me into him… as I ride him, you ride him too."

Marcus waits for the disgust to show on my face, but all he sees is how hot and bothered this is getting me. It's all fantasy, never to be reality. We won't cross that boundary. Marcus loves to test me, to see if I'll judge him for what gets him hot.

Pussy clenching on the bulge pressing against it, my hips begin swirling with no directive from my brain. Fingernails dig into my hips, stilling me.

"About the changes I've been making–"

"Ugh!" Palm pummeling Marc's chest, I growl in frustration. "You did that on purpose."

"Now, would I do that to you?" Sneaky hands lift my t-shirt, palms immediately seeking my breasts. "Diane–"

My raging libido goes from flame to glacier.

"–is most likely where you should be. We signed divorce papers yesterday. I gave her no choice, she understood, but she didn't like it. No doubt Diane was crying on Daniel's shoulder when the shit hit the fan. I suspect she will be living in Misery Castle for a while."

“Wow.” Then the implications of all Marcus said hit me out of nowhere. My body begins to shake convulsively.

“Shh… it’s okay, Regina.” Rubbing anything he can touch, Marcus tries to soothe me. “It was time. It was and wasn’t about you. I wanted my independence. I wanted to feel safe. I wanted my power back to make my own choices. I see Ezra’s family as my own, but this isn’t my house.”

“Where are you going to live? What are you going to do?”

“This isn’t said in a misogynistic bent– it’s just fact,” Marcus warns me that my feathers are about to get ruffled. “A man’s worth is tied to his home and the people in it. A woman’s is connected only to the people inside it.”

“I can see your point, I guess.” I just lost yet another home, but I’m more worried about my family than anything else. As long as I have them near me, I’ll survive.”

“Exactly. I’m a man without a home. Sometimes I go to Serenity Lake and just lie on the ground, and feel centered. Shadow Haven isn’t my home, so I’ll have no problem going with you back to yours.”

“You’re seriously thinking of going to Misery Castle when Grant and I go back?” Awed, confusion wars with worry.

“My marriage to Diane is being dissolved. Cortez will get over his issues and finally connect to Ezra in all ways. My daughter is now eighteen, and on Dominion soil, and I’m going to claim her. I want to build a home with you, Regina.”

“I-I-I–” totally rendered speechless.

“You promised to say yes,” Marcus warns me, voice breaking with worry. “You promised.”

“What are you talking about?”

“I don’t think I could live without you. I’ve lived without light in my life, and it was dark and depressive. But as long as I hold your hand, I’ll find my way through the darkness.”

“Oh, my God! Are you doing what I think you’re doing?”

“You made a promise to me earlier to say yes.” Marc’s serious tone doesn’t change.

“You tricked me into that open-ended promise,” I tease with a laugh, but his gaze doesn’t change to light-heartedness.

Leaning to the side, Marcus stretches out an arm to the nightstand, with his other hand pressing my palm over his heart. His hand is shaking as wildly as his heart is fluttering against my palm.

"What are you doing, Marcus?" My voice breaks, and then I see it.

My heart stops, my breath ceases, and my body betrays me. I fall back to the mattress with an *oomph.* My eyes glue to the object in his hand, and I begin to shake just as badly as he is.

"I've never done this before," Marcus murmurs with a self-deprecating grin. "You're the only person who makes me feel like a clumsy idiot, not the charismatic man that I am."

"What? Wow… Ungh–" nonsense words flow out of my mouth, mind taking a vacation, leaving only my emotions behind.

"I know you've done this twice before." Marc's voice now joins the quivering party. "The first time left a scar, and the second time was for all of our safety. I'm not trying to replace Grant–"

Marcus said Grant instead of Jamie. The man is being serious.

"It won't be tomorrow, or even two weeks from now, but I ask that you put me out of my misery in the next year or two. After all, I'm pushing forty." Marcus releases more self-deprecating laughter.

"Say yes," Marcus begs. "Promise or not, say yes and mean it."

Blinded by warring emotions, I stare down at Marc's hand and swallow audibly.

"Regina Regal, will you do me the honor of becoming my lover, best friend, ally, partner–" Marc's voice breaks, eyes closing. Then he slowly lifts his eyelashes, pinning me with his amber fire gaze. A gravelly sound emits from his throat. "My wife."

My breath hitches at the emotions that one word elicits. I stop shaking, and a nervous calm envelops me. Marcus publicly announced us this morning. He showed nothing but pride in being by my side. He's removing all obstacles in our path. Marcus means this– it's not a joke, or a ploy, or an edict passed down from Maître du Jeu.

Marcus wants to be my husband, and I want to be his wife.

"Grant asked me out of a fantasy. I'm not even sure he ever planned on going through with it. I love Whitt so fucking much." My voice tremors with the force of my statement. "I don't ever want to hurt him. He gives me confidence, like I could take on the world and win. He's the light to our dark. I call him my sunshine when no one but him is listening. But I don't need my way paved in light. You and I can walk through the dark as long as we're side by side, preferably holding hands."

Flashing Marcus a reassuring smile, he relaxes. Marcus honestly thought I'd say no.

"Give me time to finish my life with Whitt, and I'll gladly stand before our family and friends. Marcus, I'd be honored to be your wife, and even more honored to call you my husband."

"Oh, my God!" Marcus makes a girly noise. "I thought you'd say no, even after I made you promise."

Marcus slides a ring on my finger, and I do a double-take. It's an infinity ring, and it looks suspiciously like the first ring that was slid on my left ring finger.

"Um…" I arch a brow at him.

"I lied when I said the ring Jamie put on your finger was from me." Marcus has the common decency to look sheepish for his lies that tore me apart. "I went with Jamie when he was picking out a ring. We both picked out the same ring, and we both bought one."

"Jesus," I curse, mind spinning from the admission.

"Jamie and I have been stalking you since you were fourteen, Regina." Grabbing my hand, Marcus tilts it to the light to make the ring shine. "I can't believe you said yes. I can't believe you want to be with me."

"It's time I make my own decisions and take what I want." In awe, I stare down at the ring, feeling the rightness of it resting on my finger. "I'm taking my power back."

King

Mistress & Master of Restraint #8

The long-standing Mistress & Master of Restraint series is dark and mysterious, with a warped sense of morality. Erotic romance fans, would you prefer something just as twisted, but not as dark? Try the Blended Series, beginning with Good Girl. For a mix of both styles, try the Rusty Knob series.
To purchase any of Erica Chilson's titles, please visit her website (ericachilson.com) for details.

Acknowledgements

A lot of work goes into writing a novel, and it isn't just by the writer herself. **My parents:** for their unconditional support. **My readers**: thank you for reading my twisted words and spreading my books to the masses. For without you, no one would have ever heard of my stories. My readers are my lifeblood. A shout out to the members of the **M&M of Restraint Group on Facebook**: thanks for the endless entertainment and inspiration. Thank you to my street team: **Erica Chilson's Deviants!** You guys ROCK! **Wicked Reads**: (in all its incarnations) **Angela G**., thank you for taking over and making Wicked Reads better than I could have done by myself. & thank you for helping promote my work and the work of other authors. Angela? Have I told you lately how much I appreciate you? A huge thank you to the **Wicked Writer's Betas** for keeping me grounded and encouraging me to keep trudging along when I get frustrated. Your thoughts and observations are invaluable. ((Hugs)) Beta readers: **Kris** | **Suz** | **Darcy** | **Sandy** | **Di** | **Angela** | **Diane** | **Jacki** | **Linsey** | **Alexis** | **Billie Jo** | **Tassie** | **Caroline** | **Judith** | **Jodi Lynn** | **Jodi** | Someday, I'd love to meet you all in real life– it would be the experience of a lifetime.

About the Author

Erica Chilson does not write in the 3rd person, wanting her readers to *be* her characters. Therefore, writing a bio about herself, is uncomfortable in the extreme.

Born, raised, and here to stay, the Wicked Writer is a stump-jumper, a ridge-runner. Hailing from North Central Pennsylvania, directly on the New York State border; she loves the changes in seasons, the humid air, all the mountainous forest, and the gloomy atmosphere.

Introverted, but not socially awkward, Erica prides herself on thinking first and filtering her speech. There are days she doesn't speak at all. If it wasn't for the fact that she lives with her parents, giving her a sense of reality, she would be a hermit, where the delivery man finds her months after expiration.

Reading was an escape, a way to leave a not-so pleasant reality behind. Reading lent Erica the courage she gathered from the characters between the pages to long for a different life. Writing was an instrument of change, evolving Erica into the woman she is today– a better, more mature, more at peace thinker.

Erica has a wicked mind, one she pours out into her creations. Her filter doesn't allow all of it to erupt, much to her relief. Sarcastic, with a very dark, perverse sense of humor, Erica puts a bit of herself into every character she writes.

I love hearing from readers. If you would like more information on release dates, works in progress, teaser chapters, and random bits of madness, please visit my Facebook Fan Page:
https://www.facebook.com/thewickedwriter my website:
ericachilson.com or please contact me via email:
wickedwriter.ericachilson@gmail.com
DEVIANTS ONLY, if you'd like to join Erica Chilson's closed Facebook group, M&M of Restraint:
https://www.facebook.com/groups/MistressandMaster/

www.ingramcontent.com/pod-product-compliance
Lightning Source LLC
Chambersburg PA
CBHW070534030726
47505CB00001B/38

* 9 7 8 0 9 9 7 9 8 9 9 6 0 *